DARKNESS
Is Not
ETERNAL
by

Sidney L Jackson

™

El Cid's Books

Library of Congress Catalog No. 2019945140

ISBN: 979-8-218-03761-1

Published By:

ElCids Books
1833 Rangewood Ct.
Plainfield, New Jersey 07060

(http://Elcidsbooks.com)

<u>Other books by Sidney L Jackson (aka El Cid)</u>

The Big Lie - El Cid - Publish America - ISBN 978-1-4489-51376

Darkness Is Not Eternal - El Cid - Publish America - ISBN 978-1-63508-928-8

Darkness Is Not Eternal - Sidney L. Jackson (Digital Version) - HMG ePublishing - ASIN:BO7X13X4J9

Kingdom Planet (The Final Kingdom) - El Cid - Lighthouse Christian Publishing ISBN 978-1-52385-6886

Man's Law And Divine Justice - Sidney L Jackson - Lighthouse Christian Publishing - ISBN 9781643732497

The Liar's Gift - Sidney L. Jackson – Elcids Books – ISBN 978-0-578-88733-3

Table of Contents

Chapter 1 - My Keeper/My Brother 7

Chapter 2 – Transition 38

Chapter 3 - Eyes Have Seen 69

Chapter 4 - Change Time.. 101

Chapter 5 - Family 133

Chapter 6 - Due Change.. 165

Chapter 7 - Pride and Confrontation 195

Chapter 8 - Return and Prelude 224

Chapter 9 - New Horizons.. 247

Chapter 10 - Escalation and Depression...................................... 271

Chapter 11 - Daring Time.. 293

Chapter 12 - Desperation.. 316

Chapter 13 -The Return 338

Chapter 14 - Prophecy Fulfilled... 362

About the Author   391

To God Be the Glory for the Wonderful
Works He Has Done

In Him was life, and the life was the light of men,
And the light shines in the darkness,
and the darkness did not comprehend it. (John 1:4-5)

Chapter 1 - My Keeper/My Brother

It was just about twilight as the horse drawn wagon moved along the road toward the Sutter Plantation. The breeze rustling through the forest reminded the travelers that even though the calendar read April, spring had not yet sprung. Against the backdrop of the gorgeous Shenandoah trees lining the roadway the setting sun cast a long shadow on the wagon and its two occupants. They hardly spoke, but Byron and his son were keenly aware that the business they were about was going to take some tough negotiation. The buying and selling of another human being was no easy task.

As they neared the last few miles of the trip, an eerie feeling came over them that something was about to happen. There was no one else on the road and as the darkness approached; the task ahead seemed to possess each with a foreboding feeling. The creatures of the night were coming out of their roosts and the associated night music was coming alive. Sounds of the night owls and the Whippoorwills were rising in intensity as if keeping pace with the other woodland activities. Every so often a deer would spring from the woods and scamper across the road breaking the otherwise monotonous journey.

Jethro, Byron's son had never been with his father on one of these missions. Even though he was now approaching eighteen years of age, his life had been confined to the boundaries of the large tobacco plantation that his daddy had built up over several years. He and his father had often talked about what it was like, but he had never actually been a part of doing it. Inside he had mixed feelings about the whole business, but he was content to go along with whatever his daddy wanted him to do. His life on the grounds was somewhat pampered because he was an only son and had access to just about everything and everyone there.

It was Sunday, not a day that Byron would normally have chosen to take this kind of a trip. However, the urgency of making this transaction quickly prompted him to venture out. He knew that within the next few days he was going to need more help if he was going to meet the demands of sowing seed in his newly cultivated north forty acres. Mr. Sutter had already told him weeks before, when they met at an auction in Hampton, that he had a mind to sell some of his slaves. With this thought firmly embedded in his head, Byron was going to convince the old man that he should let him have at least two, maybe three of them. Sutter was not an easy man to talk to because he was getting older, nearing sixty or sixty-five as best they knew, and was extremely set in his ways. Even knowing this, Byron was determined to get what he needed and do it at his price.

They continued to move along at a kind of loping pace when suddenly a large buck darted out from the woods headed straight for the wagon. As it veered to avoid the collision and brushed hard against the steed, the horse was spooked. Its front legs stood up with a fury and when they came down took off galloping as if running for its life. Byron was holding on to the reins and pulling back with all his strength as the wagon pitched and bucked from side to side. The hard wooden wheels were starting to separate from the axle, but Byron regained control and the horse slowed finally coming to a stop. Byron wiping his brow turned to his son and asked if he was okay. Given assurance that he was shaken but otherwise in good condition, Byron got off to see what damage was done to the wagon. He walked all around it and after completing his inspection, got back on and they continued their way.

Byron couldn't help but wonder about the strange feelings he was having, and his mind somehow associated this recent brush with fate with the business ahead. Jethro, still shaking from the encounter, climbed off the front seat and stretched out in the back to regain his composure. His heart was racing, and he wondered too whether this had something to do with the day ahead. The rest of the journey was without another event and as the duo neared the final leg of their destination, they could see firelights emanating from the plantation. They got closer and could see the side path off the main road that led up to the big house. At the tee intersection, Byron guided the wagon onto the path, and they were just a short distance away from their final destination. As they moved along they heard singing coming from somewhere back in the woods just beyond the clearing of the path.

The sounds were enchanting as the voices rose and fell with a rhythm that made Byron feel as if he was being drawn toward them. He wasn't sure, but he figured that these were Mr. Sutter's slaves down at the river having their Sunday night religious gathering. He didn't allow this at his place, but he knew that some of the other owners went along with it. He wondered why Sutter did because he thought that they felt the same about this matter. It was not allowed at his place because in his eyes it was a waste of time. To him they should be spending this time resting and preparing for the next day's hard labor.

When they neared the circle that would take them right up to the mansion's front door, he heard a young voice cry out announcing their arrival.

"Massa, Massa, I sees de wagon coming down the road a piece," the youngster hollered as he ran up to the front door and banged on it.

"Alright boy, I hear you. Now you git on back out dere and guide`em in," came the voice from the old man inside.

The boy turned around and ran back to the rim of the circle with his lantern swinging and waited for the wagon to get closer. At just the right point, he grabbed the horse's harness and walked him up to the front of the house. Byron was impressed at how skillful this young boy handled the job. He looked to be no more than nine or maybe ten years old and Byron made a note in his mind that perhaps he could persuade Sutter to let him have this one too.

Byron and his son got off the wagon, grabbed their bags and walked up to the door behind their young escort. Arriving at the mansion front door, they hesitated to go in until they heard footsteps approaching from inside. Old man Sutter swung open the door and loudly greeted his guests.

"Come on in de house you ole pine toad," he said. "Come on in and set yourself down," he continued as he reached out and grabbed the hand of his friend. They shook hands vigorously for a few minutes and Byron was pleased to be acknowledged so enthusiastically. In the back of his mind he was thinking, this is a good start and I'm going to get all I can out of this old man before I leave here. Timothy Sutter was just glad to see him. They had met some time ago and shared a few good nights together telling wild and far-fetched stories in the town of Hampton. After the hardy handshake, Byron turned to his son and motioned him to step forward so he could introduce him.

"Tim, this ma boy Jethro an I'm gittin him ready to take ova when I'm done so I wanna git his feet wet startin here."

"Good lookin boy there Camp, good lookin boy. Look real strong and sturdy. You bringin him up right I s'pose."

"Yeah, well I do best I kin."

"How many mo you got?"

"Jest got him an a girl. The missus had a bad time wit the girl can't do no mo."

"Wellya got the boy, thas all you need. You teach him all ya know an he'll be fine. Bring him up right an teach 'em 'bout whas good and whas bad, an he'll be fine. I had four of 'em you know an I raise 'em all up to be good strong men with good sense. They all gone now an the place ain the same no more. I guess it's the way it s'pose to go, but sometime feel like ain no mo life in me since they lef. Ya know they mutha passed few years back 'fo the last boy lef an since then it's been jest me an my darkies here. Wasn' for dem I think I die too. Well 'nuff said 'bout me, let me git you some of my best hooch. Best corn likor this side of Richmond."

Mr. Sutter then turned to the young boy who was still standing in the room.

"Sonny boy go fetch Bessie May an tell her to fix up two plates for ma guests an set de table."

The youngster acknowledged the order turned and quick stepped toward the rear of the mansion to find the keeper of the house. The kitchen was in a separate part of the building almost completely detached. This was where all of the meals were prepared and brought into the dining room which was right off of the entranceway. Since Mr. Sutter didn't have a lot of guests and he didn't eat a lot himself, it took a little while for her to rustle up something worthy of serving. The slaves were not allowed to eat in the dining room except on some special occasions when old man Sutter was in a good mood and wanted to reward his charges with his good graces.

Mr. Sutter went into a smaller area off the living room and returned with a big jug that looked like a cider jar and some large cups. He set them down on the coffee table and commenced to pour. Looking at Byron he asked whether he should pour one for the boy and waited. Before Byron could answer, he said that helping him become a man by teaching him to handle his drinks is the best way to get him started. Byron looked back at him and hesitated for several minutes before agreeing half-heartedly. Mr. Sutter then poured a half-cup for the boy, and they all toasted the first round.

After about twenty minutes and two hefty drinks later and no announcement had been made about any food being ready, Mr. Sutter was getting angry. He hollered loudly toward the back of the house and commanded that somebody better be getting in here quick with some food. His sudden change of demeanor took Jethro by surprise, and he was startled at the behavior. Byron just laughed and patted his son on the shoulder saying that this was the true old man coming out now. The man he met at the door was just for show. Jethro wasn't quite sure what this all meant, but he went along with the joke and laughed with his father. The corn brew was taking its effect and personalities were changing.

Not long after Sutter's brief tirade, Bessie May called out from the dining room that the food was ready, and they could come and get it. By this time, Byron, Sutter and the boy were feeling pretty good, and the two old friends were again swapping tales about their life's adventures. As they all got up to head toward the food, Jethro stumbled drawing a hearty laugh from the elders who commented on his being introduced to his new state of mind. Byron grabbed hold of his son and walked him to the dining room table where they sat down before a full plate. Bessie May, the housekeeper, cook and general all-around handmaiden was good at what she did and had prepared a delicious meal of Virginia ham, greens, mashed potatoes and corn that was fit for the best of any genteel statesman.

Byron looked at his plate and commented on whether Sutter ate like this all the time. He responded by saying that this was hardly his daily bread and on some days he almost didn't eat at all except for some breakfast and maybe a light snack before going to bed. Byron, even in his inebriated state was observing closely, the manner of his host and he carefully noted in his mind that here was a lonely old man that was no longer really interested in the welfare of his plantation or his slaves. Tomorrow he thought he would really benefit from this knowledge and return to his farm a much wealthier man at the expense of his host. Jethro noted too that the old man seemed to be expressing his loneliness, but he was also seeing his father in a new light.

After the meal they returned to the living room and continued conversing. As the evening went on and the hour was getting late, Byron suggested that they all turn in and get an early start on the next day's activities. He mentioned to Sutter that he was anxious to get down to the quarters to look over what he had available. Mr. Sutter by this time was nodding and mumbling and hardly coherent with his speech. Bessie May, who had been sitting nearby but out of sight, was listening and well accustomed to knowing when the old man had reached his capacity. She eased her way in and gently helped Tim to his feet. Byron marveled at how this matronly figure of a woman who was rather hefty could walk so lightly as to not make hardly any sound at her entry. She was dressed in a rather atypical house servant attire with her burlap looking dress showing patches of repair and severe wear. Although Byron failed to note it, this should have alerted him to the fact that his host was not as well off as he once was. Her demeanor was very pleasant as she lifted the old man to his feet and then announced to his guests that she would return shortly to show them to their room. She still had her apron strung around her waist as she walked him out into the dimly lit corridor and disappeared.

Byron looked at his son who by this time was nodding heavily as he reclined on the couch. The room was comfortably lit with several kerosene lamps adorning the walls providing a warm glow. As Byron looked around he noticed that there were a number of pictures hung on the walls showing Tim's family at different stages of their growth.

He reflected on the fact that he didn't have many pictures of his family in the living room or anywhere else in the house. It occurred to him that this was something he needed to change because he had been devoting too much time over the last few years building his empire and not enough to the development of his family. While he was deep in reflecting, Bessie May appeared again at the entranceway and startled him when he saw her. She was just suddenly there as if coming out of nowhere. This triggered again an eerie feeling inside him that reminded him of that which he felt on the road in. She didn't look ghostly but the way that she moved was as light as any apparition that he ever recalled seeing.

Responding to her bidding he walked over to the couch and collected his son. Lifting him up and shouldering his arm he carried him to the hallway and up the stairs. At the top of the stairs a large, oversized portrait of Mr. Sutter, his wife and their four sons greeted him. He couldn't help but stare at the rendering because in the dimly lit passageway it seemed as if the figures were so lifelike, they were actually beckoning him. Bessie May turned to the right and showed them to the second doorway in the corridor. She opened the door walked inside and spent a few minutes lighting the lamps in the room before returning to the hallway. Then she motioned for them to come in and left. Byron helped his son over to one of the two large brass beds and deposited him on it. He thought of a question that he wanted to ask her and after laying his son down he quickly turned around and looked in the hallway. He was astonished that there was no sign of her in just that short period of time. . He looked up and down hard to see whether there was somewhere she could have ducked into, but then he thought if she went into one of the other rooms, he would have heard her open a door or something. Since he heard nothing, he again became a little uncomfortable at the eeriness of his new surroundings.

He walked back into the room undressed his son and placed him under the covers. Then he suspiciously checked around to see what else was there. Seeing nothing unusual and as the dizziness in his head grew, he looked under the bed to see if the night pan was there. Somewhat comforted at seeing it he undressed and got under the few covers on the bed leaving the lamps burning. It was not long before an uneasy sleep overtook him and he drifted off. As he slept the wind blew through the seams in the window casings adding to his uneasiness and he tossed and turned in his discomfort. The house was old and well-constructed for its day, but the lack of maintenance attention over the last few years had allowed it to deteriorate to its current state. When the last of the Sutter boys left, the old man had paid less and less attention to the mansion and even less to the state of his plantation business. It was because of this that he was starting to sell his property.

That same night down in the slave quarters on the row where there were ten cabins about a hundred yards behind the big house, Jobba shared his cabin with another family. There were at least two families in each cabin and the living space in all of them was cramped. Although Jobba's house was one of the larger ones having two rooms on the first level and a walk-up loft, there were a total of nine people squeezed into living quarters that were meant for only five. As the wind whistled through the cracks in the siding and whirled around under the tin roof he hoped for the signs of an early spring to show up. Between him, his wife and their two children there was not much in the way of what could be considered as creature comforts. The bed in the loft that he and Myanna, his wife, shared was an old wooden one that had been discarded by Mr. Sutter several months ago. It did very little, even with the thin mattress that came with it, to support the two of them. The children slept on pallets placed near the fireplace on the first level.

The family that shared their cabin had one more youngster then Jobba, but their sleeping facilities did not include a real bed for any of them. It was a challenge for all to live together under such conditions and to keep restrained from letting the stress of the day's labor boil over to warlike tensions at the blowing of the horn to end the day. They learned to survive by yielding to the fact that this was their state in life at this time and the hope that this was not a permanent condition of living. Each family contributed to making the living arrangements as comfortable as they could make it, and each member did his share to contribute. The days of labor were long and the work was hard but from the rising of the sun to the going down of the same it was given to them to be mindful that there was a spirit hovering above them that was greater than all of the hardships they suffered. There was always amongst them the feeling that even as they toiled like the slaves in days of old with hard bondage, their current slavery was not as one who suffered pains and agony without a Supreme Being who knew their suffering.

As Jobba lie behind Myanna with his arms wrapped tightly around her to keep warm, he whispered to her about the feelings he was having lately. He told her that he had seen in a dream some days ago that they were going to be sold and they would be moving. He couldn't remember what he saw the new place would be like and it wasn't clear in the images whether they would all be together. He was sure that the days ahead were not going to be any better than what they had now. Myanna, half awake, heard what he said and turned to face him.

"Was dis you talkin Jobba, you jest had bad dream thas all."

"No, no not jest de dream but seem like de Lawd talkin to Jobba tryna tell him somethin."

"What else de Lawd say to you? He tell you if'n he gonna help?"

"I didn' say I knowed it was him, jest feel like some'm gonna happen and soon."

"You was jest dreamin, now go to sleep," she said as she turned back over and closed her eyes.

Jobba wrapped his arms tightly around her again and tried to sleep, but he couldn't get the images of the dream from his mind. He lay there with his eyes wide open staring into the darkness and wondering whether the dream had been given to him as a warning. His breathing was heavy, and he could feel the tension building up preventing him from going to sleep. For several minutes he tried closing his eyes in the hope that the sleep he desired would overtake him, but without success. Finally, in desperation he looked at Myanna then eased his way out of the bed and felt his way along the wall to the stairs. He crept down the stairs quietly and eased his way across the room toward the door and went outside.

The night air was chilly and he immediately felt the cold as he left the cabin. He was aware that he should have put on his outer garment, but it seemed as if something was compelling him to move forward toward the big house and cold or not he had to go. His unshod feet moved stealthily up the path leading from slave row to a shed where the horses were kept. Except for the light of a full moon shining brightly down on the farm, he could hardly see a short distance in front of him. He continued walking slowly envisioning in his mind's eye how the path went which he had trodden so many times in daylight. As he neared the shed he could see there was a light burning in the big house. Where the light was coming from he knew that it was not where the master slept, and it heightened his anxiety about his dream. When he reached the shed he looked inside the window frame and could see a new wagon there along with a strange new horse.

Upon seeing this he was convinced that new arrivals had come in earlier and were now on the plantation. He tried hard to ease his mind by telling himself that maybe the slave owners from the farm nearby had come in as they did from time to time to sit with the old man. Somehow though this made no sense to him because he knew they had never come in the late evening hours before, so why come now. The chill of the night air was getting to him and his search for an answer about what was going on was not going to be gotten by him standing out here. He turned around and headed back to his cabin. Moving along at a faster pace this time it was just a few minutes before he opened the door and by the dim light of the glowing embers in the fireplace climbed the stairs. Not wanting to awaken Myanna, he eased his way back into bed and lay motionless staring up at the ceiling.

The thoughts running through his head were even more intense now than before he ventured out into the night. For what seemed like a long time he just lay there trying to put what he had seen into some kind of perspective. He wasn't sure just when he drifted off to sleep but his eyes finally closed, and the images began to reappear. This time it was not the same as before. This time he found himself drifting, as if on a cloud, back through time and floating along above the earth looking down on it. When he came down and awoke he found himself shackled to a chain along with several other men, some who looked like him and others who looked to be from a different race. He couldn't recognize the place and he was sure he hadn't been there, but it was a long room with many mats spread along the floor with the men sleeping on them. From a window high above the room opposite where he was he could see the night sky was giving over to the rising of the sun.

It was no longer cold, and he felt warmth that he thought was unusually hot for this time of year. The room was lit by torches placed along the walls; and he could see that at the end of the room on one side was an archway guarded by a heavy-set man in strange clothing who appeared to be guarding it. He felt very strange as if he had been transported not only through time but also through space to a land he didn't know. Not sensing any danger and considering there was nothing else he could do until he found out what was happening, he lay down and closed his eyes. What seemed like less than a minute later, the large man at the end of the hall was coming through the middle of the room snapping a whip summoning the men to get up. As they arose, each man stood at the foot of his mat and waited for the guard to lose his shackle. Jobba not knowing what this routine was all about just followed what the man beside him did.

When all of the men were free from their shackles they lined up marched toward the door and into the daylight. Jobba could see right away that he was in a strange land where all around him was nothing but sand and a few palm trees. The sun was moving higher in the sky and already the heat was rising. Without a word said the line of men moved toward a huge tent that was setup next to a building that looked like something he had heard the itinerant preachers who sometimes came by the plantation talking about in the land of Egypt. He couldn't believe that this was really happening to him and he was really here, until he looked off in the near distance and could see the beginnings of a pyramid that the preacher's talked about.

The line of men shuffled into the tent where they were given a bowl and marched through a serving line where they were fed a gruel-like substance with a cup of water. Jobba took his just as the other men did and followed to a bench where they sat down to eat. Jobba tasted the contents of the bowl and thought it wasn't so unlike the corn mush he had been given at home. He was surprised though that not enough time to really finish the meal was given before the big guard came through with his whip and snapped it. The men quickly stood to their feet and lined up. As if a silent command had been given they all turned and faced the rear of the tent and moved in unison out the exit. Like soldiers in a well-disciplined army they moved in ranks toward an area that contained many extremely large stones. Jobba had heard about this when he was young, but he couldn't believe what his eyes were seeing. The size of the stones was bigger than anything he could have ever imagined.

The men were marched over to the first stone, which was set upon a series of logs, and the group broke off into two lines. Each line was positioned in front of the stone where two long and very thick ropes were lying on the ground. In Jobba's mind he pictured what was about to take place, but he still couldn't bring himself to believe it. When the slaves were divided into two columns they were given a verbal command to bend down and pick up the rope nearest him. Jobba hesitated for a moment and that's when he heard the crack of the whip and felt the searing pain that shot down his back. He looked around to see who it was that was wielding the whip. The guard at the sleeping quarters had been joined by several others who looked to be less like the overseers he was used to but more like men who looked like him. This surprised him again, but it was not until the second lash struck with a deeper severity than the first blow that he realized that he was not in step with the others and if he wanted the beating to stop he better pick up the rope.

He grabbed the rope and since he was in the line on the left, along with the others placed it on his right shoulder. At another verbal command the line began to pull on the rope. With great stress the stone began to move forward and the line of about a hundred men straining under the pressure groaned and moaned from the task. After moving along under the hot sun for what seemed like an eternity his body was giving up. Jobba, who was used to hard labor, had never been exposed to this type of work and he felt an ache from muscles that cried out from recesses foreign to his nature. Inside he was praying that he could wake up from this dream, but it was so real that he wasn't sure this was a dream. With every muscle in his body now crying out from the pain of being overly used, he knew now what the hard bondage was that he had heard the preachers talking about in the Bible days. When it seemed like he couldn't walk another step, a voice was heard, and a command was given for the line to stop and the men sat down. By now the sun was high in the sky and the heat of midday was bringing out the sweat from his body in a steady stream.

As he sat on the ground reeling from this new experience and trying to figure out why he was here, a young girl came around with a water jug and gave him a drink. He poured the liquid down his parched throat and went to dip the cup for a second when the girl quickly grabbed the cup turned and moved on to the next man. His weary body already straining from lose of fluids was hard pressed to stand up again after the break, but he knew that if he didn't the lashing from the guard would begin again. He mustered up every ounce of strength he could and slowly stood on his feet. However, when the command was given to begin pulling the stone again his legs would not respond, and he fell limp to the ground. It was not long before the sound of the whip cracking and the sting of the blow was felt on his bare skin. He lay there in excruciating pain enduring each blow, when suddenly it stopped, and he was again lifted up into a cloud and transported through time and space.

This time when he landed he was in the middle of a village with huts made of wooden sticks and slanted grass thatched roofs all around him. The people there all looked like him and they were speaking a language that he was sure he had heard somewhere before but couldn't remember what the words meant. It was sometime after sunrise, but the sun had not yet risen high in the sky and the elders were instructing the men to form for the day's hunt for food. They were gathering together at the last hut in the village when they turned to see why he had not joined them. Lying beside Jobba was a spear and a shield of which he had no idea how to use. He looked closely at how the men were dressed and wondered if he was in what had been told to him many years ago was the mother land. He believed he was in the land of his true people. Although scantily clad, he could see that each man ready for the hunt had the body of a warrior and his physique was that of a well-conditioned human.

He gathered himself picked up the weapons beside him and made his way to the group. It was not as if the men didn't recognize him, but it was like he was supposed to be there. The leader of the hunt shouted a command and the group moved out into the nearby forest. The brush was tall and movement through the thick bushes was at first difficult but then they came to a clearing which on the other side they could see a herd of wild beasts which he could not make out. The pack leader gave another command and the men began to spread out in an attacking formation. Jobba felt a sense of excitement in all this and he raised his spear like the others and kept pace with the formation. As they moved closer to the prey, suddenly what sounded to him like a number of loud firecrackers that he had heard his master set off many times during fourth of July celebrations on the plantation, going off at the same time. When the first man fell to the ground and he heard noises like men trampling through the bush from just beyond where his group was, he knew that the noise was no firecracker. The other men turned to see why their leader had fallen but before they could assess the cause, many white men armed with guns came out of the bush with nets and ropes and started corralling his group.

He along with several others was caught in a net and like a trapped animal fell to the ground dropping his spear and the shield. A short time later his hunting group was marched along a path beyond the clearing tied together with ropes about their necks and arms. This time he could understand his captors and they were talking about the success of their hunt and how happy the ship's captain was going to be at the catch. What may have been a half hour or more later the march ended down by the sea and he could see a large wooden ship anchored in the bay. On the shore near the beachhead there were many large cages made of thick wooden sticks that already had in them, captured men who looked like him howling to get out.

The captors herded his group toward one of the empty cages and pushed them inside. All around them the noise of the captured was so loud that the captain came out of his tent and commanded that they be silent. Receiving no response, he raised his weapon and fired in no particular direction and directed his men to do the same. When the discharge of about thirty weapons all fired, the captive's noise suddenly stopped as the fear overtook the caged dwellers. Jobba had never been a part of this stage of becoming a slave, but he knew full well that this is how it started. He had been born on a plantation and was indoctrinated into the slave life right from birth.

Late in the afternoon men came around with large bowls of rice and placed one or two in each cage. It was up to each inmate to get his share as best he could and Jobba being one of the larger males had no problem in getting fed. However, when he looked around there was a smaller man who had been pushed aside when the food grabbing started, and he felt some compassion for him but was unable to help. After the brief meal, a tall slender man in a wide hat with a long gun instructed them to lie down.

When they did as told, moments later another man came along with a large bucket of water and threw it into the cage covering most of them. Shortly after, another bucket was thrown at them making sure that they all had gotten wet.

As the sun was beginning to make its descent into the horizon, several smaller boats from the ship came ashore with more men armed with guns. The cages were opened, and the captives were herded into the small craft. Each boat held about ten captives along with three crewmen. The water near the shore was very calm and Jobba felt an unseemly peace within himself as they moved toward the ship. He couldn't understand what was happening to him, but somewhere deep inside he believed that all of this was being shown to him for a good reason. In his thoughts his mind turned to Myanna and he wondered if this isn't a dream, then where is she? Was she being held like he was but somewhere else? If she was, how was he going to find her and get to her?

When the small craft arrived at the ship the captives were pushed up a rope-like ladder and onto the decks where they were reassembled into groups. The ship's captain gave the order and they were separated into groups of men and women. The women were then taken around one side and moved toward the stern while the men were prodded to move toward mid ship. They came to the center of the vessel where a large cargo hold was opened up and the men were escorted down the stairs into two lower decks that had been fitted with small compartments just large enough for each man to lie down in. The makeshift berths were narrow, confining and outfitted with a pole at the end that housed a ring for the containment chain to be inserted through. The captives were roughly pushed along the narrow isle and told to climb into the berths one to a slot. Jobba was looking to see whether the berths were all the same size, as he wanted to get the biggest one that he could. Before he could complete his observation the man with the gun pushed him into the next open slot.

He climbed in and was told to lie on his back with his head toward the wall. When all of the captives had filled the berths, a thick chain was slid through the loops on the end of the slots and through their ankle bracelets. Jobba wondered if the women got the same treatment since he couldn't see what happened to them. After the armed men left the hold and went up on deck, the clamoring started again and this time even louder than before. Jobba couldn't understand what they were saying, and it seemed like there were many languages spoken, but what he could recognize was that some were crying out the name Allah. He knew the name Allah was some kind of god that he had heard of before, but he also knew that his God didn't answer to that name and he wondered why they were not calling on his god. While he lay there, he pondered where his God was, and didn't He know about his situation. The noise seemed to grow louder as he tried to turn over on his side and cover his ears. This was not to be, because the chains would not permit it. After a while the clamor turned to crying and the crying turned to sobs and then finally the sobs stopped, and it was deafeningly quiet. They all went to sleep, except Jobba.

In the quietness below, Jobba listened intently trying to hear what was going on in the decks above him. He heard many voices talking and shouting things that seemed to him to make no sense. Then he looked around his confined area to see if there was a way for him to get out and noticed that the light that had been pouring through the portholes was now disappearing; the whole area was growing darker. He also noticed that the ship was beginning to rock as he swayed from side to side in his perch. The later it got the more severe the rocking became. In a short time, the rocking got so bad that he along with the others were tossed against the beams with such a slamming ferocity that he felt his skin being cut by the rough edges of the beams. He tried desperately to brace himself, but it was difficult because there was nothing to grab onto except for the beam that was assaulting him. Then he tried to anticipate the rhythm of the sway and move in the opposite direction from which the compelling force was moving him, but to no avail. After some time and the bruises rising on his body, the rolling and the rocking ceased, and he was able to lie in the center of his berth.

The room was now completely dark, and he couldn't see even his hand in front of him. His anxiety was mounting, and he was becoming fearful not knowing where he was going or what his destiny was going to be. Along with his tension another problem was surfacing. In all the excitement from the time that he started his hunt this morning through his capture until now he had not answered the call of nature. His loins were crying out to be relieved. He tried to hold on as long as he could hoping that maybe one of the captors would come down to check on them and he could voice his need. As the urgency grew and his hope diminished he finally let go and the needed relief came. He felt the warm liquid flow down his leg and there was an easiness that accompanied his release. Before long, as the stench rose and the smell permeated the room, it was apparent that he was not alone in his need to relieve himself. In the compartment, the confined space was filling up with an odor like nothing he had ever experienced before, and his stomach was reacting.

When it seemed that this was as much as he could stand before heaving up the little that he had in his stomach, light again started to pour through the portholes. After a short while the hatch was opened and one of the guards came down the stairs with a whip in his hand shouting for the men to wake up. Though he believed that he had not been to sleep, as he rubbed his eyes the condition suggested that he must have slept at least for a short time. The man, armed with a pistol in his belt, moved down the aisle cracking the whip with one hand while holding a large handkerchief to his nose with the other. He was shouting expletives in a loud voice cursing his cargo for doing what he knew they were going to do from the time they were confined.

While he was exhorting the captives to wake up, another man came down the stairs and started taking the chains out of the ankle bracelets allowing the men to get down from their perches. Once all were standing, they were motioned toward the stairs and directed to go up onto the deck. Coming out of the pitch darkness the brightness of the morning sun caused Jobba to squint and tear along with the rest of them. He covered his eyes and tried to adjust to see what he could see. It didn't take long, but when he was able to look around him, all he could see was water that really scared him. There was no shore, no land in sight at all. To him it was as if he had been taken from the earth that he knew and planted in the middle of a world that was all water.

Before he could fully adjust to this new state, the armed men shouted for others of the crew to douse the captives with buckets of water. The water thrown on them as it kept coming was in a way a welcome gesture because it washed away the smell that even they abhorred. After the washing a drum sounded from a crewman sitting on an upper deck and the man with the whip starting lashing at the feet of the captives shouting for them to jump up and dance to the beat. Although Jobba understood what they were saying, the others in his group he didn't believe did. The lashing was inflicting pain and the captives were just moving away as far as they could until prodded from the other side by crewmen. Jobba started to jump and dance to show the others what to do to stop the whip. They soon got the message after seeing Jobba get an approving laugh from the whip wielding man and joined him in the dance. The drumbeat moved faster and faster as the captives picked up on the rhythm and jumped to the beat. When they were all near exhaustion, the drum stopped, and the whip man motioned for them to sit down.

The group sat down exhausted almost falling to the deck. A few minutes later, a crewman handed each a bowl filled with rice and a piece of some type of fish. Jobba's hunger was great and he was glad to get this meal. With his bare hands he reached in the bowl and devoured its contents quickly, remembering his experience from the last time he was given food. As he was finishing his meal he heard a commotion and turned to see a line of the women being herded toward them. The man with the whip snapped it once again prompting Jobba's group to get up. Still looking at the women in wonderment, he was prodded to start moving toward the open hatch. He could see clearly that the women were no longer dressed as when they came on board. Most of them were naked from the waste up exposing a variety of breast shapes and sizes. Many of them were not walking comfortably but were striding slowly with their legs somewhat agape as if it was painful to move along. Looking at their faces and their movements it wasn't hard for him to imagine what had happened to them during the night.

The anger that surged inside him was building to its zenith and he fought hard to contain it. He knew that he was no match for the guns that his captors wielded but he also knew that he had to do something. The others in his group he could sense were having the same feelings, not by any verbal communication but through the look in their eyes, as he perceived that they had witnessed the same thing that he did. When the group got close to the hatch he noticed that the man with the whip standing just above the opening also wore the key to the lock that imprisoned them, around his waist. As his group moved he angled himself toward the man and feigned stumbling when he got close enough to fall on him easing the key from his belt and placing it inside his loincloth. The guard angered at the clumsiness of his charge was so intent on getting his whip in position to deliver a severe blow, took no notice that the key he possessed was no longer in his possession. He raised the whip and the blow came crashing down on Jobba cutting open a deep slit in his back that immediately drew blood. Jobba had turned his back to cover the presence of the stolen key and he painfully stepped quickly into the opening and down the stairs.

Once inside the captives were again directed into their berths and the containment chain slid through the anklets securing the bunch. Jobba, even though he had the key couldn't figure out how he was going to get to the end to open the lock. Not being able to communicate with his fellow captives he had no way of letting them know what his plan was. As he lay in his slot, he began to pray asking his God for some direction on how to make his plan work. He recalled hearing the itinerant preacher who used to come to the plantation from time to time saying that God was a very present help in trouble. If this was true, and he wasn't totally convinced that it was because he never really believed the preacher when he came, then he thought now is the time for him to test it. He prayed and cried, cried and prayed asking God for this deliverance and to be shown a way to do the thing that he desired.

Since nothing happened right away, and the clamor of the previous day was beginning again from the group, he just lay there wondering how long it would be before it was discovered that the key was missing and the man with the whip would be coming down the stairs to visit the group. In his anguish he was agonizing over the pain that he still felt from the last lashing and anticipating what it would be like when it was discovered that he had the key. While his mind was tormenting in agony over what had not yet happened an idea came to him. He thought that if he held up the key and let the others in the group see it while there was still light in the hold, maybe they would get the idea. He reached down and removed the key and touched his neighbor pointing to it. The man alongside him saw it and touched the man next to him. Before long all the men on that side of the aisle saw it. He motioned to his neighbor that he wanted to pass the key down the line so that the last man could reach the lock and open it. At first, Jobba thought this was like breaking in a new horse to the saddle and it was going to take some time but soon his neighbor got the idea and passed the key along. As the key moved down the line each man mumbled something in his native tongue and passed the key with both hands to the next man. At the end of the line, the last man was able to insert the key in the lock that was high and tight almost right next to him. With a quick turn, the lock fell open.

Even though the lock was open, because of the limited space in which the end man could maneuver it wasn't easy for him to get the chain to move away from the ring. He struggled to make it happen. Looking at the faces of the others in the group, the man with a renewed sense of strength pulled and pulled until finally it moved a little. Once it moved an inch the rest of the journey was not hard, and the chain fell away from the rings and onto the floor. Jobba was listening intently to hear if anybody from above was aware of what was happening below. While listening he also noticed again that the light was disappearing in the room. He knew that night must be coming, and the time would be right for the group to move. When the first man slid out from his slot, the second could hardly wait to taste the freedom. Each man in anticipation waited patiently for his turn and one by one they all hit the floor silently. Since Jobba was the one who got the key, they turned to him for directions. Even though there was no language communication, it was clear that he had been chosen as the leader and it was now his army.

As the room grew darker, Jobba slid by the line and moved to the front where the hatch was. He slowly climbed the stairs and lifted the hatch just enough to peek out. It was almost as dark above as it was in the hold, but he could see stars in the night sky and a dim light was given by a hazy full moon. Most of the captors in the immediate area were laid about the deck breathing heavily from the overindulgence of rum that had been passed around earlier. Jobba could see as he eased his way out that there were others on the upper deck entertaining themselves with some of the women and not likely to hear him moving. He motioned for the others to come up and eventually the whole group was on deck. They moved quietly among the crew disarming those that were nearby when suddenly a crewman came from around a corner and spotted what was happening. With a loud yell he drew his sword and lunged toward one of the captives. His cry woke up those nearby that were not beyond hearing and even those on the upper deck were alerted to the rebellion. The men on the upper deck disengaged from their activity and scrambled to put on pants. In a state of panic, they hollered for the captain who was in his cabin below.

The ensuing battle seemed to favor the captives at first due to the shear imbalance of the numbers. However, not knowing how to fire the pistols they possessed, the group started to wield the guns like a club and quickly lost their advantage. The gunshots from the crew felled many of the captives and the others seeing this panicked and started jumping into the water and many just sat down. Jobba's anger was not abated and he was not to be deterred as he rushed toward one of the crew who was armed with a pistol. Fearing for his life, the crewman raised it and fired hitting Jobba dead center in his chest. He felt an intense pain rush through his body, and he clutched at the wound with his body shaking violently.

"Jobba, Jobba wake up," Myanna yelled while shaking him hard. She shook him for several minutes trying to get him to respond. He was sweating profusely, and the old bed sheet was soaked.

"Help me, help me he said," as he tried to wake up. Finally, with a burst he sat up, opened his eyes and looked around the cabin wiping his head from the sweat. With blurred eyes he looked at Myanna and said "somthin bad gwine happen today. Somthin bad gwine happen to us."

Myanna not knowing what he was talking about tried to comfort him by telling him yet again that it was just a dream. Jobba refused to be comforted and went on ranting about what he saw in his dream.

"I know'd it jest a dream, but somthin gwine happen jest like I saw. When de mornin come we mus be careful and not let massa see we know."

"Jobba you talk crazy. Ain nuthin gwine happen lessn' you do it. Massa tol you jest de otha day he think you good man an he ain gwine sell nobody."

"Massa don know his self what he gwine do. You see the land done bin use up. Caint grow much tabacci on land das dead. He ain got no mo overseer `cause he caint pay him an he ain got no sons here no mor cause they lef'. We's all he got an he ain gwine keep us if'n dere ain no crops. An dere ain gwine be no crop' dis year cause de seeds didn't sprout. I see'd it in ma dream no good come from slavin for de white man. I even ask de Lord why dis be, an he ain said nuthin. Do you think he care?"

"Jobba you don say that. The preacher said we hafta have hope an everthing be alright. He say you mus believe in Him and truss `em."

"I been slavin for de man all my life an truss'n and hopin, an nuthin change yet."

As Jobba, still angry from his dream issued his last diatribe, the signs of morning began coming into the cabin. Through the windows the change from darkness was taking place and it was the beginning of a brand new day. The early sunlight slowly moved up the walls and outside you could hear the cock crowing. Others in the cabin also hearing the rooster crow were alerted to the arrival of another day and reluctantly started moving. Knowing that what this day held for them would hardly be any different than what yesterday offered, was not a great incentive to rush to get up. Especially now on this plantation where there was no more overseer and no more horn backing up the rooster call to get up.

Suliah and Linwood, Jobba's children were the first to get up. They both made their way up the stairs and over to where Jobba slept. Seeing him awake but sweating and not looking like he was in the best of moods, Suliah inquired about his health.

"Papa you don look so good. You okay?"

Jobba took a few minutes to respond and just looked at her for a minute.

"Yes bebe, I'se okay. Now you go on down an get washed up we be down soon."

Suliah looked at her father intently sensing that something was wrong, but she didn't pursue it. She grabbed her brother's hand and led him down the stairs to get the washbasin. Jobba then looked at Myanna waiting for her to say something he knew was going to come about his dream. She said nothing but just got up reached for her clothes and headed down. Jobba surprised at this didn't know what she was thinking so he gave up on the matter got his clothes and followed her down.

Back at the big house Byron also heard the rooster crow and was waiting expectantly on the sound of the horn before getting up. At his place this was the regimen that he followed as well as his overseers and his slaves. However, after many minutes went by and no horn sound was heard, he arose and set his feet on the cold floor. Reaching for his socks, he wondered just what happened to the wakeup call that as plantation tradition went the overseer would blow a horn calling the slaves to assemble and start the day. In his rush with his socks on and trying to pull up his pants he hopped over to the window to see what was going on outside. As he looked over the grounds he was impressed at how beautiful the landscape was, but he saw no activity, no signs of anyone moving. He was somewhat alarmed at this and thought maybe a mass runaway had occurred during the night. If this happened not only would his long trip have been for nothing, but he would still have the problem of getting the help he needed for his farm. Anxious to find out what was happening he turned to wake up Jethro who was still soundly asleep.

"Jethro, wake up boy it's time to get up, you been sleepin' too long."

He then turned to find the washbasin in the room so he could get cleaned up. But hearing no movement from that side of the room after several minutes passed, Byron stopped what he was doing and went over to the bed and shook the boy.

"Jethro now I dun tol you to get up. Now get up," he exclaimed loudly.

Jethro now realizing amidst his semi-conscious state that it was his father who was calling him made an attempt to respond. He was fighting the urge to continue with the dream that had taken him to a place that he wasn't quite ready to leave.

"I hear you daddy I hear you an I'm gittin up in a minute. Jest gimme a minute."

"One more minute is all you got an I want you washed up and downstairs right behind me" Byron said.

Byron finished dressing and scrambled out of the room making a dash down the stairs hoping to meet the housekeeper somewhere along the way. As he got closer to where he dined last night he could smell the aroma of breakfast being prepared somewhere in the back of the house but there was still no sign of Mr. Sutter or any other house slaves, not even the boy who led them in last night. His concern rising that something was amiss he started going through the house looking for the old man. Finally coming to a room just off the dining area he met Tim leisurely coming out of his room with a smile on his face. Tim greeted him with a hearty good morning and invited him to come back into the dining room where they could talk and wait on breakfast.

Byron was a bit reassured by the old man's composure as if there was nothing wrong, but he still wanted to ask him right away what happened to the wake-up horn call. He decided to wait and listened to what Tim had to say.

"I truss you slept well last night, did you enjoy the night air?" Mr. Sutter said.

"Well Tim, it was a little drafty in dere an those covers need a little help."

Both men laughed at this because Byron knew that Tim must be aware that the spaces between the window frames needed much attention and allowed the wind to enter at every opportunity.

"Yeah I bin meanin to get those windas fixed, but jest ain had the notion ta git it done. I'll git to it someday soon."

While they were still talking, in walked Jethro a little less bright eyed than when he arrived last night. Mr. Sutter sensing that he may be suffering from his first hangover offered to go get him a cup of coffee right away. Byron after looking at the boy good agreed with the old man's assessment and offered to go with him to get it. Mr. Sutter told him that there was no need he wanted to check on when the breakfast would be coming, and he would be right back. Byron's curiosity was getting the best of him about the old man's financial status and he really wanted to tour the house to see what state the rest of it was in. When Tim got up, Byron turned to Jethro.

"I know you didn't have no trouble sleepin las night. When I looked at you, you was out like a snuffed candle."

"No daddy, I slept kinda good. I was havin me a good dream when ya call me."

"Yeah I bet an you had a bunch of dem women all `round you treatin you like the king a England."

"No daddy twern't like dat, it was jest one gal, but she was treatn' me real good."

Byron just looked at him and smiled knowingly that given his son's age this was nothing unusual for a robust boy entering into manhood. Even though Jethro led a somewhat cloistered life his exposure to the activities of the farm amongst the slaves and the animals and his infrequent encounters with the daughters of other plantation owners when they came to the socials given by his father, he was well aware of the state of the birds and the bees.

"What we gonna do today daddy?" Jethro said.

"We gonna take cara the bizness we come here for an git what we need at de lowest price. Now you let me do all de talkin an you jest learn from me. If'n he ask you 'bout any of these niggahs, you just say I donno. If'n he ask you whether you like any of 'em, jest say no I don care for none of 'em. You got dat?"

"Yes, daddy I hear you."

Tim Sutter walked in the room carrying a pitcher of coffee and several cups. Right behind him was the boy that had guided the guests into the house last night. As the old man sat down, the boy began setting the table with place-mats, dishes, glasses and utensils. He appeared very efficient as if he had done this a thousand times and this was just another day. Again, Byron noticing the boys' skills at doing his tasks envisioned him in his own house greeting his guests. He wanted to say something to Tim right then, but he thought better of it since they had not begun any negotiations yet. They hadn't even talked about what Byron was looking for, although Tim had a pretty good idea.

Minutes later in walked Bessie May pushing a food cart. Sonny boy, the young house slave immediately came around picked up Byron's plate and walked it over to the cart as Bessie May filled it with breakfast. After returning it to Byron he then did the same for Jethro and lastly for Tim. Byron looked at his plate and it was all he could do to keep from commenting again on how well Mr. Sutter must have eaten regularly, but then he remembered what the old man told him last night about his eating habits, so he said nothing. The plate had eggs, bacon, grits and once again slices of Virginia ham that were sautéed in some kind of sauce that was foreign to his taste, but so delicious that he couldn't resist asking about it. Tim responded that it was Bessie May's secret recipe and nobody, but her children would ever get it. Byron looked at her when Tim said this and the expression on her face while she stood there waiting for Tim's next instructions never changed. Byron knew that she was listening, but whether she was paying attention to what he said he couldn't be sure. The whole time that he had been in the house, even when she showed them to their sleeping quarters, she had said hardly anything.

During breakfast, Byron was getting impatient to begin the talks about his intentions. He reminded Tim of the conversation that they had in Hampton during their last attendance at a slave auction and about what a good time they had together. Further he mentioned that Tim said he was ready to sell some of his. Tim taking the bait opened up the door for the talks.

"Now Byron, ole friend ya know that I got some of de bes niggahs in dis here whole county an I hates to part wit any of `em. But bein dat times gittin kinda bad `round here for plantin an bringin in good tabbacci, I do hafta let some go. But mind you I ain given away nothing. If I was ta take `em to the block, I know I could get a good price, but since you come all da way here we can work somethin out, if'n you got a mind ta bend."

Byron was taken back a bit by this statement, as he wasn't completely prepared to hear the alternative that the old man was suggesting. The idea of Sutter selling the slaves at auction as opposed to selling directly to him had never crossed his mind and he knew immediately that a new strategy in diplomacy was needed. He paused a minute before answering.

"Tim, ole friend, I'se heard good things `bout what you say is good stock, but I ain neva seen none of yours. I came prepared to make you a good offer, but I ain a rich man an you know I got limits. Now if we can go on down to the quarters an see what ya got, den we can talk `bout de payment. I needs ta ask ya somethn now though, if'n ya don mind?"

"Okay, what you need to know?"

"Why I ain heard no horns sound dis mornin for gettin up time in the quarters?"

"You ain heard no horns `cause we don do dat no more `round here. Ain no overseer here an dere ain no displin problems. I ain hadda whup nobody for weeks now. Dey all know what they gotta do an dey do it. I run dis place almos' by myself an we all git along. Dat answer yo question?"

Byron was a little startled by the abrupt response to his question and to the tone that Mr. Sutter took with his answer, but he politely said yes with the hope that he didn't damage his strategy.

"I'm jest `bout finished here what about you?" Byron said.

"Yeah, I'm `bout done too, you finished boy?"

"Yes I'm through eatin' suh, we goin now?"

"Okay les move on down the way an I'll show ya de bess in de land."

The group got up from the table as Bessie May along with Sonny boy standing there the whole time moved in to clear away the dishes and clean the table. Mr. Sutter opened the front door and the bright sunlight rushed in to greet them. Byron didn't think that they had been at breakfast that long, but it was now well past the ten o'clock hour and the sun was high in the sky. Although he was still skeptical about the low amount of activity that he saw coming from the field quarters, he said to himself the rest must already be in the field. He saw two men and a woman casually walking toward the big house carrying bags of what looked like kitchen supplies and he thought this was a little odd because it wasn't the way he did it at his place. Quickly it was becoming apparent to him, that because the way Sutter managed his property it was going to be a problem in retraining whatever he was able to get.

He was again surprised that instead of heading toward the slave cabins, Sutter led them to a very large cabin that had been set up as the communal slave kitchen and dining hall. It was in here that they were all still assembled just finishing breakfast. When the door was opened, Byron was shocked at the leisure pace which they casually ate. When Tim entered they hardly stirred, but some greeted him as if he was one of them. Byron was looking at this scene with an extreme sense of shock that the old man had allowed his charges to disrespect him like this. First he was still having trouble accepting that at this late hour, they were still eating breakfast and secondly that no one rose up to greet the master of the plantation. The expression on his face must have given his feelings away because when Tim looked at him he told him that this is the way he ran his place and that it works for him.

Moving toward one of the tables, Tim called out to the family that shared the cabin with Jobba. With some hesitation the family of five got up and came to the master. Tim pointed to the door and asked them to go outside. Following close behind them Byron and Jethro saw Mr. Sutter lead them to a small shed that was right off the path that led down to the cabins. The family was not aware of what was happening, but inside they also knew that the condition of the farm had gone down and something was going to change. Tim directed them to stand together over at the far side of the shack and he told them what the story was. He began by first saying to them how much he hated what he had to do, but because the crops weren't bringing in enough to keep them, he had to let them go and this man here was going to be their new owner.

Byron was so completely unaccustomed to this manner of talking to slaves and especially providing them with any kind of explanation about what was going to happen he just stared at Tim for some time before refocusing on the business at hand. Tim prompted him to take a closer look. Byron gathered himself and motioned to Jethro to step closer with him toward the family who had lined up just as sheep being led to a slaughter. Byron started with the father who stood about 5'10" when he stood up straight, with broad shoulders and muscular arms. But the amount of gray hair on his head prompted Byron to open his mouth and look at his teeth. What he saw immediately rejected this man as a prospect and he moved on. Next he came to the mother who stood about 5`5" who had a smooth brown complexion with comely features. Her legs were sturdy, and her body hardly showed the effects of producing three offspring. Byron, at first thought of perhaps adding her to his house cadre, but then quickly reminded himself that he needed field hands more than anything else.

Next he moved on to the children. The oldest was about the same age as his son, perhaps 18 or 19. He was a good looking boy with muscular arms and good teeth. Byron decided that he could certainly use this one and told him to step aside. He then moved on to the next boy who was just a little bit younger, maybe a year or two, but built sturdy like his brother and he passed muster also. Byron told him to join his brother. Last he came to the girl who was about thirteen with beautiful skin like her mother and the budding of a sturdy body was also like her. Byron wasn't sure what he would do with her, but since she was so young, he could probably train her to field work, so he told her to join her brothers.

When he finished his examination, Byron turned to Tim and said these will do just fine what will you take for them? Tim asked why he had separated the children from their parents. Byron responded that he didn't need the parents because he had no use for them. Tim quickly said that he wouldn't break up the family because it was bad luck to do so and that he had this family since the day they got married right here on this plantation. This was the first stumbling block for Byron, and he wasn't sure how to get over it. Inside he knew that in most cases a whole family would not be suited to what he really needed and to buy a whole family when he could only get a return in labor out one or two, wasn't exactly what he had in mind. He tried to convince Tim that this was not what he wanted, but the stubborn attitude of the old man was not yielding. Finally, after several attempts the negotiations failed on this matter and Byron asked Tim to show him what else he had.

They left the shed and met Jobba on the road coming from the tobacco shed where he had been tending to the seedling plants. Byron even at a distance could see that this tall dark African looking man who stood at least six feet or better whose carriage indicated a pride in his walk was worth a closer look. When near enough to greet, Byron asked Tim about this one. Tim reluctantly said that he was also available, but he had a family too. Because of the strong muscular features of this man, Byron was willing to take a chance on seeing what the rest of his family looks like. Tim told Jobba to go and get his family and bring them to the shed. Jobba knew immediately, that what he saw in his dream was now getting ready to happen and he walked very slowly to where his people were.

Byron, Jethro and Tim returned to the shed and waited for Jobba. In no small amount of time, Jobba opened the door and paraded his family in. Byron looking past the father this time immediately focused on his son who like his father was also of sturdy build and young enough to also have many other uses. When they were completely inside, Byron stepped closer and examined him nodding his head in approval and spinning him around and around. Next he moved to Myanna who overwhelmingly met his approval. Finally, he came to Suliah and wasn't sure what to think. Looking at the parents he was puzzled by her shoulder length silky black hair, the high cheekbones and the golden-brown complexion. Her comely features were reminiscent of the Powhattan tribe that in earlier years had occupied these lands. Byron could have never guessed the relationship that took place with Myanna's ancestors. Her eyes were hazel and though her body was still developing he could obviously see the potential for her breasts if they matured like her mother. He directed her to expose her legs and shyly she did as told to the delight of Byron's eyes. Byron was not alone when attracted by the beauty of this young girl; for when he turned around he saw that Jethro's eyes were locked on to her too.

Byron said to Tim "Okay these will do" trying to keep as business like a tone as he could manage after seeing the potential of this family.

"You sure you want dem, dey ain gonna be cheap now."

"Well Tim you said yoself dat times gittin hard for you, ya wanna sell `em or not."

"An I tol you, I wanna sell not give away. For this family you need $4,500 dollas."

Byron heard the quote and wanted to sit down immediately but didn't want Tim to know that he had struck the first deadly blow. Although he had the money with him in his saddle bag, he had no intention of spending that kind of money. If he did then he would feel that Tim won and he lost, and that was not his game. Byron went into his pre rehearsed pitch about his needs and their friendship and how spending that kind of money was going to put him at a severe disadvantage. He went on and on about how the prices for these people are not what they use to be here in this state and that Tim was trying to rob him. After several minutes of haggling while Jobba and his family were still standing there, Tim motioned to Jobba to take his family back to their cabin. Sometime later after they left, the final deal was struck with Mr. Sutter giving in to Mr. Candle's pleas and dropping his price down to a mere $3,000, which was an extreme bargain even for the day.

When Jobba walked out of the shack he wasn't sure how he felt. He didn't know whether what he heard from Mr. Sutter's reluctance to give in was a good sign and his family wasn't going anywhere or was the old man just trying to get the other master to meet his price. About an hour later Tim came down to the cabin and told Jobba that the deal had been done and they were all now the property of Mr. Byron Candle of Amherst County. He further said that they would be leaving here late this afternoon in Mr. Candle's wagon so they should pack up everything they wanted to take and be ready to go right after dinner. Having said this, he went outside and closed the door behind him.

Jobba after hearing these words looked at Myanna a long time and then sat down on the floor in disbelief. Myanna came and sat beside him and was soon joined by the children. They sat there for several minutes trying to console each other but as difficult as it was to understand how they could be uprooted from their home in just a matter of hours, it was more fearful not knowing what was going to happen to them. After a while they separated and started preparing to leave. There wasn't much they had to pack, as their meager belongings didn't amount to much except for some clothing and trinkets that Myanna had been given when the missus of the house was still alive. As for Jobba, he was a crafty man and had made some items for the house like weaved baskets and tables, but he didn't think that he would be allowed to take them. The children likewise had attained small gifts from the big house children who they had almost literally grown up with and were trying to stuff them into the few burlap bags they had.

The workday was over, and the other family came slowly into the cabin. They already knew what had happened as the word spread quickly around the farm. The man walked over to Jobba wrapped his arms around him and exclaimed his sorrow over his brother leaving. Jobba returned the feeling and they looked deeply into each other's eyes with the knowledge that they may never see each other again. Both families embraced over the new situation not knowing what was to become of any of them. They then sat around the one table in the cabin that they had shared for many months without so much as a squabble among them about whose turn it was to use it.

"Jobba my brother, I will miss you an yur family. For many days we shared this house an have known much pain. We have lived by de white man's laws an have stepped in de mud many times when he say so, but neva have I seen yur face to de ground. Yur spirit is strong within you an yu have de mind to do great things. Let dis change not weaken you for what will be, will be. As it has been foretold by the ancients our ancestors; one day all men will be free. May the gawd dat directs yur spirit be a lite to you so the path ahead will not be dark."

Jobba listened intently to his cabin mate and marveled at the wisdom that this man displayed. Though he was only about three or four years older, he had not been born a slave in this country but had come over on one of those ships that Jobba had dreamt about. He was just a boy in his early teens when he arrived here, but his memory of the old country and the ways of the villages and tribes were still vivid in his mind. Jobba having recently had the dream in which this man had actually lived the experience, regretted now that he had never asked him about where he came from. Jobba was determined to find out what spirit this man was talking about.

"Yu speak of my spirit brother. Do I control my spirit or does de white man who say I have none?"

"When I came to dis cuntry, for many days I rode on de waves of de water an dey threw me 'round like a small fish. The big boat had no room an we saw no signs of the great spirit dat my tribe elders talked 'bout. I saw my people go to the great beyond in that journey, an I was 'bout to join wit dem, when I heard my fatha say to me in my head – do not fear de unknown because yur ancesters watch ova yu an yur spirit is strong. I heard dat an I became strong believing dat de spirit was inside me. Dats how I made de trip an got here alive. So I say, yur spirit is yurs an nobody can control it, but yu."

Jobba heard these words and a new sense of courage came over him. Although he still wasn't completely clear on what the spirit was, he was a bit more accepting of what he heard the roving preachers say in their words. The two families continued telling stories about how they had survived the hardships of life on this plantation and about the strength they had gained from knowing one another. The hours passed by quickly and soon it was time for the dinner meal. Jobba got up first and went to check that Myanna had packed all that they needed and then Myanna went to check on the children. The other family, still not wanting to accept this new situation, remained at the table near tears.

While Jobba and the other family were still engaged in saying their farewell, at the big house Byron and Mr. Sutter were also having a discussion. The old man was having some second thoughts about letting his favorite family go and he wanted reassurance that Byron was going to keep them together.

"Byron, when you come here I tol' you dat my darkies almos like family to me an I treat dem good. When you leave here dey yours to do like ya want to, but I jest wanna hear ya say you gonna keep dem together. Deys all good hard workers, don give no trouble. Ain had ta whup dat man but two times since he bin here; de gal ain been whuped at all He got good sense an it ain like none of dem gona run no wheres. Now you let me hear ya say you gonna do dat."

"Now Tim ah really `preciate you lettn' me have dose folks, but I caint say now whut I will or won't do. I hafta see how dey works for me. You an me do things real different an I don let ma niggahs run free like ya do. I don let dem do much churchn an ain hardly no preachers comin in tellin me how dey needs ta live an all dat religis stuff. I think afta a few weeks an dey sees how I do things an dey `just to it, den maybe I kin tell ya how I'm gonna keep `em. You unner stan dat, don you?"

"Well yeah I guess ah do, but I jest think dere be somthin `bout dis whole thing of folks buying an sellin otha folks das wrong an we gonna hafta `count for it sometime."

"Old man I think you jest gettin too soft `cause you old. I ain worried `bout havin ta `count ta nobody `ceptin de auction man at harvest time."

The two men finished their conversation without Mr. Sutter getting any kind of commitment from Byron. The whole time they were talking, Jethro was sitting in the room, but hardly felt qualified to enter into the talks. He listened carefully and tried to understand the reasoning on both sides, but he was having a hard time seeing things the way that his father did. He knew that Byron was a hard driving man and that he had built up the plantation from a very small beginning to what was now one of the biggest tobacco farms in the county. What he could never understand was how his daddy could work the slaves so hard without really caring about what happens to them. Even though he didn't get much schooling about any religious stuff because it was forbidden, he felt deep inside just like Mr. Sutter did that the whole master/slave idea was wrong.

When it came time for them to walk over to the dining hall for their last meal together at this place, the whole farm had already been alerted to the upcoming change. The uncertainty about whether it was going to happen to any of them tomorrow or the next day or the day after that was in the forefront of their collective minds and each had to address it in his or her own way. Usually the evening meal was had with at the least some light conversation, depending on how bad the day was, but tonight there was hardly anyone talking. The quietness' of the hour was giving over to the feeling that in addition to the Thomas family leaving the plantation, something else was in the air that was bringing them a sense that this was just the beginning of a new era for them. There was something else they could feel was beginning with this night. This event would pave the way for someone to come and help in their plight. Someone to direct them in the desire to be their own person was on the way.

Though it couldn't be put in words, the feeling was pervasive and permeated the whole farm. From Bessie May and her helper in the big house to all of the field workers in each cabin they had been together for so long without any of them being sold off, this was now a major change in their culture. They had so many times gone down to the riverside where they would light the fires pray and sing songs about how free they were going to be in the sweet by and by. But now with the selling of the Thomas family it became painfully obvious that none of them may ever get to see that day.

In the big house Bessie May, as was her habit to always sit nearby but out of sight when Mr. Sutter had guests, overheard the men talking. She heard what Mr. Candle was saying and felt a deep pang in her heart because she sensed that he was not one to indulge the kind of man that Jobba was. But more importantly, knowing the kind of man Jobba was, she felt very strongly that this relationship was headed for serious trouble. With her gift of inner foresight, she could almost picture the dark days ahead for this family. In her mind's eye she envisioned Jobba becoming involved in an inner turmoil because he would not be able to defend his family the way he had been here. She couldn't see clearly how it would turn out, but her heightened sense of fear for him that had been sensitized by her exposure to such strong negative forces from this Mr. Candle, that she was almost ready to run down to the dining hall and warn Jobba. However, this was not to be, because Mr. Sutter would be very angry with her.

The time had now come and as the Thomas family got up to leave the hall, Mr. Sutter met them at the door along with Byron and Jethro. The day that had started out so brightly was now beginning to turn cloudy and the sun had difficulty making a steady appearance. Byron seeing the clouds forming was insisting that he wanted to get started quickly to avoid running into foul weather that may be up north. He then asked Tim to instruct the family to get moving. Tim turned to him and said: "They belong to you now, you tell `em."

"Okay listen ya'll we got a long journey ahead an I don want no trouble outta any a you. Git yo things an meet me at the stable house in five minutes an we gonna be outta here. I hope ya'll ain plannin ta try an bring a whole lotta stuff, `cause dere ain much room in da wagon. Grab only what ya really need an pack it good so don take up much room, an I'll try an fit it in. If'n it don fit, den ya got ta leave it here. Ya'll unner'stan whut I'm sayn?"

Jobba nodded his head and just looked intently at the man. Byron caught his glare and looked back at him intently.

Having said that, Mr. Sutter and Mr. Candle stepped aside and let Jobba lead the way back to the cabin to get the family belongings. Minutes later the Thomas family carrying what they could quick stepped up to the stable where the wagon was already prepared for the trip. When Byron came out of the big house and he saw the boy whom he had forgotten all about, tending to the horse and wagon, he immediately made an offer for him. Mr. Sutter just laughed and told him that he had already stolen his best family from him and now he wanted his only houseboy too, it wasn't going to happen today or any other day. With that said Byron walked over to the wagon and inspected it to make sure that everything was in order. He was thinking to himself, that normally he would chain his slaves to the wagon to insure against running, but looking at this family and how, although it was a tight fit into the small wagon, they huddled together peacefully there was no need.

Byron stepped up into the wagon and with Jethro by his side clicked the horse while snapping the reins. As the horse responded to the command and the wagon pulled away from the big house, Byron turned to wave farewell to his host as the journey began. Jobba, Myanna, Suliah, and Linwood all looked around as they slowly moved down the path leading to the main road, wondering if they would ever see this place again. The wagon bounced from side to side over the bumpy road and even the heavy weight of the combined goods and people didn't help to stabilize it. Jobba who sat opposite her was looking at Myanna trying to figure out whether she had finally come to acknowledge his dream about something happening to them today. She caught his stare but showed no sign one way or the other. Jobba then looked at his children and wondered what was to become of them. This especially bothered him since he was still in the shack when he heard his new owner talk about his lack of concern for keeping families together. The other thing that was in the back of his mind and really bothered him was how both the father and the son had looked at his daughter with such lustful eyes.

They came to the main road and turned into it. The partially blocked sun that had been peeking through the clouds was setting and darkness was approaching. Jobba couldn't understand why the new owner didn't wait until the morning light before taking this trip and he sensed that there was a great urgency for them to get back home. The conversation between Byron and Jethro was more active than when they were coming. Byron felt that he had accomplished his goal and he felt confident that he had taught his son a good lesson about how to negotiate and get what you wanted in the end. Jethro was just happy to be leaving that place and going back to his more comfortable surroundings. He couldn't restrain himself though and every so often he would turn around and steal a glance at the beautiful young girl who sat in the back of his wagon.

Byron looking far ahead even in the diminishing light saw what appeared to be storm clouds ahead started clicking the horse again demanding more speed. The horse responded and the pace picked up, but he knew that the weight of the wagon and the people placed a lot of stress on the powerful steed and he couldn't drive him at this pace long. The pace continued for some time and it seemed that they were making some good headway when the sounds of nightfall began again as when they were headed to the plantation. Jethro was reminded of the incident that happened with the deer on the way in and was cautioned by Byron to be alert.

Just as before, the sounds of the night creatures were starting up and the players in the symphony orchestra were warming to the task ahead. Jethro thought it a little strange that he never really paid attention to the amount of activity that went on in the forest at night until now. He listened closely and he could hear the Hoot Owls and Whippoorwills the crickets and bullfrogs entertaining each other with a rhythm that could only be divinely directed. He had never been exposed to much about religion, because his father didn't believe in it. What he learned he knew from things he had heard coming from the house slaves and from the itinerant preacher that Byron would allow to come in most infrequently just to keep the slaves from complaining. But now in the very presence of this vast open space in the middle of a road with no one else on it that led right through a wide forest, there was something very humbling about this experience and he fell silent.

Byron noticing that his boy had gone awfully quiet asked him if he was sick.

"You feelin okay son? The bumps gettin to ya?"

"No daddy I'm okay but I was jest wondrin about bein out here in da middle a nowhere listnin to all dem sounds comin out da forest what makes 'em all do dat. How come you neva listin to that preachin man dat come to the house sometime? You don believe in what he got to say?"

"No son, all dat man wanna do is come in dere an start up trouble. He be tellin these folks things dey ain spose ta hear. Like somethin in his bible 'bout some exodus to go to freedom. I heard him say that an I chase him off de land. These folks ain't meant to have no freedom, dey always meant to be slaves."

"Daddy you really believe dey an neva spose to have no freedom?"

"Yeah 'cause if dey spose to be free, why dey sittin in the back a my wagon. And 'cept for my good graces, dey be in chains. You think 'bout dat. Das the way the world is."

Jethro chuckled at this logic and reasoning, but for the first time couldn't fully bring himself to go along with his fathers' wisdom. They moved along at the faster pace for a good while when Byron realized that he had been really pushing the horse. He pulled back on the reins prompting the horse to slow down the pace and it was done. Now moving at a slower pace and getting nearer to where Byron thought that he had seen the cloud formation, he felt the first few drops hitting on his forehead. As they moved along the rain started to fall heavier and he pulled to a stop. Then he got off to find his tarpaulin tied under the center of the wagon. Releasing it from its halter he told Jethro to come around and help him tie it over the wagon. The tarpaulin was not meant to cover the whole wagon, so he just protected the front seat and a small portion of the back. Jobba realizing what was happening motioned to his children to change seats with him and get up under the covering. Suliah and Myanna were covered, but all of Jobba and Linwood's whole right side were outside the protection.

The rain started coming down heavier and soon torrents of the liquid moved through the sky with such force that the wagon was straining to keep moving. Soon after, the lightning started. The first crack lit up the sky with such brightness that it was for a few minutes as if daylight had happened all over again. Moments later the loud roar of thunder crackled across the heavens as if all the combined cymbals of the world had sounded at once. The noise shook the wagon and through it somewhat off course. Once again as had happened before Byron was hard pressed to hang on to the reins and maintain control of the horse which was reacting to the noise. The horse responding to the thunder was spooked like before and took off galloping headlong directly into the storm. This time Byron lost control and the wagon shifting from side to side ran off the main road and headed toward an area of the forest that seemed to have never been broached before.

Jobba hung on to his wife and children and tried to keep them from being thrown over the side as the wagon continued to buck up and down and pitch from side to side. Suddenly through a small clearing in the woods the horse for no fathomable reason headed in that direction and the wagon was catapulted through the bush at an alarming rate of speed. The wagon approached a hill and was headed down it toward the ravine as the wheels were beginning to separate from the axle. Byron who thought himself a master at hiding his fears, was now in the throes of yielding to the awesome power of something greater than him was at work. The wagon continued to roll faster and faster and as they sped toward the ravine Byron's eyes closed as he accepted his fate, but then something happened.

Chapter 2 - Transition

In the dimly lit kitchen of the big house sitting alone at her table, Bessie May was pondering the images going through her mind. The visionary gift that she had discovered as a child caused her to be silent most of the time for fear that if asked about her thoughts she would have to reveal the terrible things that she saw. Growing up on the plantation she had seen many visions of things that were about to happen, but they never seemed to happen exactly the way she saw it. This unstable state of the gift caused her to be withdrawn, but very sensitive to people close to her. Her relationship with Jobba and his family had become very close over many years even though because of her station in the big house and theirs in the field didn't permit daily interactions. When something needed repair in the house, it was Jobba that she called and relied on to fix it. Often he would make something for her that made life a little easier. In return she would often smuggle through Sonny boy, some extra food rations from the house down to the cabin and place them in a wooden box just outside. When Suliah and Linwood were born she was the doctor who delivered them. At Christmas and other special occasions when they were all allowed to assemble in the big house, it was easy to see how much they loved each other.

As the rain pounded on the tin roof and the wind whistled through the windows assaulting her lamp daring to snuff out her light, she was silently praying that the images she was seeing now were not signs of what must be, but rather could be. The link that she had with the Thomas family was a bond that time and distance couldn't separate and right now she was spiritually riding with them on their journey. What she was seeing clearly, as she stared vacantly through the window into the darkness, was the wagon speeding down the hill toward the ravine. In her mind's eye she pictured the crash and the bodies of both families flying from the wagon. She winced at the thought and pressed her hands to her forehead and cried out.

"Lawd, Lawd please let yur grace and yur mercy rule and yur will be done for dem dat dis not be dere las day."

Although no one could ever convince Byron that what happened next was anything but something attributable to his lucky day, when the right wheel came completely off the axle and the weight on that side of the wagon just grounded it to a halt, he opened his eyes and just said – "damn". Sitting on the hill, the right side of the wagon was sunk pretty deep into the soft grass, but everyone seemed to be okay. Byron got down from the front seat came around back and yelled at Jobba to get his tail down and go find the wheel. Then he told Myanna and the children to get down also. His next command was to Jethro for him to come help find something to prop up the wagon.

The rain was still coming down pretty hard, but Jobba responded to the command left the wagon and stumbled up the hill in search of the wheel. The night was fully accomplished, and the darkness prevented him from hardly seeing where he was going, much less the wheel. Byron realized this and after just a few minutes called him back to the wagon. In his frustration, he wasn't sure what to do next so he decided that they would just cover up and spend the night here. In Jobba's mind he was saying again, why did this man want to try this tonight anyway?

Byron got back on the wagon and got under the cover. Jethro joined him and they tried to make themselves comfortable preparing to go to sleep. The rain seemed to be lessening and the downpour was easing up. Byron turned around and looked back at his charges to make sure they were still there. Myanna and the children were huddled together and Jobba had gotten back in the wagon and wrapped his arms around them to provide comfort. Byron feeling assured that they were okay positioned himself to sleep and soon drifted off. Jethro followed into slumber land shortly thereafter. Jobba looked into the darkness to see if there was something or somewhere he could go to lead his family away from this situation but saw nothing, so he joined his family in sleep.

The rain stopped, and the hours of the night passed. Just before sunrise, Jobba woke up and again looked around and discovered that Byron and Jethro were still asleep. Taking advantage of this, Jobba reached for the wicker basket that Bessie May had Sonny boy hide in the back of the wagon. He opened it and to his delight saw that she had packed several pieces of fried chicken, some ears of corn and a large bowl of rice. In the early morning light, Jobba gently shook Myanna waking her and pointed to the basket. She became fully awake and also looked to see what the status of the Candles was. Assuring herself that they were still in another world, she gently woke her children and fed them.

All of them were able to finish eating and Jobba swiftly repacked the basket and concealed it again before Byron and Jethro woke up. When they did arise, Byron was in a foul mood and wanted to take out his frustration on somebody, so he turned on Jobba.

"Get down from there niggah, an go fine that wheel. We needa fix dis thing an get outta here. I ain got time ta be sittin here."

Jobba responded to the command got down from the wagon and once again started walking up the hill. This time with the assistance of the early light it was not hard for him to see that the wheel had rolled about ten yards from the spot where the wagon was mired. He pressed his way over to it and looked at its condition. It didn't appear that it was broken, so he picked it up and rolled it back to the wagon.

"Bring dat thing ova here boy an set it down," Byron barked.

After looking at the wheel himself Byron determined that it was okay, but the pin that held it to the axle was still missing so he hollered at Jobba to go back and find it. With all this early activity Byron's stomach reminded him that breakfast had not been put down there, so he stopped his hollering and got back in the wagon. Bessie May had also prepared a basket of food for him and Jethro so he got it out and opened it. It also contained the same thing that Jobba had but in addition his included slices of ham. He reached inside and handed Jethro two pieces of chicken and passed him the bowl of rice. He turned around to look at Jobba's family and was hesitating about giving them anything, but he relented and offered each one of them a single piece of ham. Jobba, who had stopped his search for the pin, accepted it graciously, but inside was laughing that if this was all he was going to get to eat from this man, he was glad he ate early.

Byron had a large canteen under the front seat that contained water. He shared the canteen cup with Jethro but wasn't sure how to let Jobba and his family drink. Certainly, he wasn't going to share his cup, but he knew that they would need water too. Finally, he decided that it would be just as good for them to make a cup out of their hands and he would pour some into it. As inefficient as this was, the amount of water that each of them was able to drink was good enough to help digest this recent piece of ham, but more so the earlier meal that they had. Byron somewhat contented with his meal and feeling better about the situation told Jethro to help him find something to lift the wagon up so he could put the wheel back on. He also commanded that Jobba do the same thing so all the men got out spread themselves in search of a fallen tree limb or something that could be used as a lever.

It didn't take long. The lightening from last night's storm had cut off several large limbs and they were strewn around the area. Jethro was the first to locate a long thick one that seemed ideal for the task. He tried to pick it up, but because of its length the weight was more than he could handle so he called to his father. Byron heard him and immediately instructed Jobba to go over and help. Together they dragged the log over to the wagon and then went in search for anything that could be used as a fulcrum to balance the log on. Again, this was not a problem for in the area were several large stones. When Jobba looked at them, he was reminded of the stones he had seen in his dream even though these were not nearly as big. Moving the medium sized boulder into place, Byron positioned the log under the wagon and then joined with Jetrho and Jobba on the far end. With all of their combined strength they pressed down on the lever and attempted to lift the wagon.

At first it seemed that their combined efforts were futile but after several attempts the wagon began to come up out of the mire. Byron's frustration level was rising again, and he was getting angrier at the amount of time that he was losing in getting home. Jobba again couldn't understand why it was so urgent that they get to his plantation, but he gave his best effort to get the wagon back on the road anyway.

"Put yo back into it boy, you ain doin nothin'. I know you kin do betta then dis. Come on boy, push down on it, push down on it" Byron yelled.

Finally, after several attempts, the wagon came completely up out of the mud and Byron ran around to the axle to put another rock under it to hold it up. Once it was fixed in place Byron hollered at Jobba to get the wheel and put it on the axle. Jobba did this and the wheel was in place, but there was no pin.

"Where's the pin boy, where's the pin? Didn't I tell you to fine the pin, now where is it?"

Byron had indeed told Jobba to find the pin, but when he decided that he wanted to eat he had also called him back before he found it to eat. Jobba tried to explain this to him but Byron was so upset at his own lack of foresight that he cursed Jobba and told him that if he had his whip with him that he would have gotten a whipping right there and then. Jobba was then instructed to go back in search of the pin and to do it quickly.

This was like looking for the old needle in a haystack adage. Jobba fanned out and searched the area, but he was getting a bit frustrated himself because this pin could have come out at any point during their downhill journey last night. There was no way for him to know just when the pin exited the wheel, much less to have an idea where it might have landed. Byron was not accepting of this and leaned on Jobba to perform the impossible and find the pin. He and Jethro also joined the search but finding something as small as the pin, didn't seem like it was going to happen, especially in light of the fact that the grounds were wet, and the pin could have sunken below the surface.

Jobba moved around the area with his eyes intently focused on the ground when something caught his eye. He wasn't sure at first that this was what he was looking for, but as he got closer it seemed to him that if this was not the original pin that came out of the wheel, it was close enough to the size and shape that he needed that it could work just as well. He came up to the object and bent down to pick it up. Sure enough, this was the pin that had come out of the wheel. He wasn't sure whether this was a stroke of luck or some divine intervention, but he quickly retrieved the pin and ran it back to the wagon. Byron was excited that the pin was found, but he didn't want to give Jobba too much credit for the find. As he sat there alongside the wagon when Jobba ran over holding up the pin in his hand, he just said, "good."

The pin was inserted, hammered in with a rock and the wheel locked on. Byron then watered the horse and they turned the wagon around. The effort needed to get the wagon back up the hill was not easy. Byron told everybody to get out and push to help the horse pull the wagon up. It really wasn't easy. Fortunately, the distance that the wagon had gone down the hill was not that far from the main road before the wheel came off. With a great amount of effort and sweat the wagon approached the main road and the horse finally was able to get it back where it needed to be. With the wagon back on the road, they all got back on and the journey began again. It was now a clear day and by this time the sun was full and almost at its height for the day. Byron clicked the horse and snapped the reins to start a moderate pace. Relieved that they were all again on their way, Byron looked at Jethro and asked him what he thought about all that happened. Jethro looked at his father questioningly not understanding why he was asking this question. Byron didn't bother to elaborate but continued on after that in silence.

The rest of the journey was without incident and hours later they finally neared the Candle Plantation. Not too far out they met a coffle coming in the opposite direction. As the train got closer they could see that there were three men on horseback with a number of slaves roped together. At the front was one man and then right behind him were about ten slaves including several women who were walking barefoot holding babies in their arms. Bringing up the rear were two men on horseback also. As they passed, Byron tipped his hat knowing that this was one of the slave traders that he had done business with before many times. Jobba and all of his family saw the line also and they just dropped their heads as they passed. They had never actually seen this kind of a parade because none of them had ever been off of the Sutter Plantation. For all they knew, whenever new slaves came there it was always by wagon and in the early evening hours or at night.

Before long Byron was turning off the main road and heading up the side path to his mansion. This side road was unlike Mr. Sutters because it wasn't as bumpy. Jobba's eyes were wide open now because he knew that this must be the place where they were going, and he motioned to his family to be alert. The road leading to the Candle mansion was a bit longer then at Mr. Sutter's place but because it was smoother, the ride didn't seem as long. The closer they got to the mansion the more Jobba was getting excited because from all he could see, this was a much better place. He could see fields of corn growing on one side of the road and on the other he saw wheat as tall as him. From a distance he could see many large cabins lined up in a row and they all appeared to be much bigger than the ones he had come from. Inside he was thinking this could be an improvement to his life.

When they arrived at the house front, Jobba's eyes widened to their max trying to take in the size of this colonial mansion. With four huge white columns standing tall along the front they supported three stories to the building. There were several young slaves waiting to greet them and attend to the wagon and each one had a task that he was assigned to do. In addition, there were two white ladies standing there also. The older one was dressed in a long flowing dolman that had a high collar and was button downed in front. Her light brown hair was turned up and held by an ornamental barrette that appeared to be made from ivory. Although her features were still attractive, life's experiences had clearly taken a toll on her former beauty.

The young girl standing beside her was in the prime of her youth and the glowing radiance of the young shone in her countenance. Her hair was darker and thicker than her mother's and her features were like those of her mother years ago. Her form was also most pleasing to the eye. Both ladies walked out ahead of the slaves to greet Byron and Jethro. Byron got down and quickstepped over to greet the older of the two ladies, first kissing her hand and then kissed her cheek. Next he did the same for the younger one. Right after, Jethro ran over and hugged the older lady first and then embraced the younger one. Jobba surmised that this must be the missus of the house and her daughter. After completing his greeting, Byron instructed his head slave to greet the new arrivals and see about getting them settled in their new quarters. Having given his instructions, he grabbed his saddlebags and went into the house along with his family. The slaves then as if on cue attended to the rest of the bags.

Clarence, the head slave stepped forward and looked Jobba and his family up and down before saying his own name and asking for Jobba's. With the quick greeting out of the way he turned and climbed up into the front seat of the wagon and guided it down the road toward the quarters. As they moved along Jobba's excitement grew when he saw all that this plantation held. The rich and dense forest all around the mansion was just a front for the beautiful mountains that sat in the background. Clarence turned the wagon left to go by the stable and the first cabin, which was the overseer's house. He made it a point to let Jobba know that this was where the headman lived. Jobba took note and planted it in his mind.

Moments later the wagon pulled up to a row of cabins well behind the mansion and stopped at number four which was the second one on the left as they came down the road. Clarence pointed to it and instructed Jobba that this is where he was going to live and to begin unloading his stuff. Jobba following instructions got down and went over to the door to open it, when suddenly it opened, and two children came running out laughing. Jobba jumped back because he thought it was empty and Clarence chuckled. Clarence now mentioned the cabin would be shared. The children's parents were in the fields, and they were not old enough yet to be put to work, so they just played around the house watched over by an elderly mammy. The elderly woman whose useful days in the field had long since ended was charged with watching over all the children in the quarters while their parents worked.

Jobba recomposed himself and went inside. It was indeed larger than his old place and had two complete stories. It was clear that the first floor belonged to the other family, because when he went upstairs it was totally vacant. He was pleased to see that there were three large beds with bedding already on them and he knew that Suliah and Linwood would be so happy to have real beds for the first time. As he went down the stairs he also noticed that in the far corner there was a wood-burning stove. He knew that this would please Myanna because she loved to cook but didn't get much of a chance to do so at the other place. With a smile on his face he went outside and told his family to get down and begin taking their goods inside and setting up their new home. Clarence who was still seated in the wagon didn't lend a hand to help but waited patiently until they finished before driving away headed back toward the big house. To Jobba, it seemed like this was going to be a good change.

Myanna and the children busied themselves putting their few things away and making their new surroundings comfortable. Jobba meanwhile went back outside and looked around the quarters to get familiar with the land. He looked up and down the road at some of the other children playing and then stared off in the distance at the verdant mountains. To him it all seemed like a most serene setting and the cloudless blue sky above just served to underscore the peace. Jobba turned around and went inside to help his family. Little could he have imagined at that moment, that in a very short time he would experience the beginning of his worst nightmare.

About an hour later as the sun was making its descent behind the mountains, Jobba heard a loud horn sound and he ran outside to see what was happening. The children all stopped playing and went inside their respective cabins. It soon became clear that this was the signal that ended the workday for the field hands, and they started returning to their cabins. Most of them sluggishly lumbered down the road and slowly went inside. Jobba was not unfamiliar with this sight because he had seen it many times over at his former home. These were the signs of an overworked body having been pressed into service to accomplish the mission for the day. It wasn't long before a man about his own age dragged up to Jobba's door and seeing him standing there asked who he was. Jobba explained that he had just arrived there, and this is where they put him. The man was too tired to complain so he told Jobba that his name was Penniman and his wife was coming up shortly behind him. Before Jobba could respond by telling him his name, the man walked by him opened the door and went inside. He never mentioned his wife's name, nor did he acknowledge whether he was glad to have a housemate or not. In a few more minutes a woman also came to the door and looked at Jobba who was still standing outside trying to understand what the routine for the little village was. She too asked him who he was, and he gave the same response. She never offered her name either but went by him straight inside and tended to her two children. At this point Jobba wasn't sure just what to think about his new surroundings and his new neighbors so he went inside to see if he could get them to talk just a little bit and help him understand what was supposed to happen now.

Penniman had gone and collapsed on his bed while his wife went to the stove and began preparing the evening meal. Jobba went upstairs to get his family to come down so they could all meet one another, but it didn't seem that either Penniman or his wife was interested at that point in doing this. Myanna went over to the stove said hello and offered her help but the woman just kept cooking. Myanna got the message and left the area returning to Jobba who was still standing by the stairs. Neither one of their housemates said anything. They didn't even talk to the kids who just sat at the table waiting to eat. Jobba motioned to Myanna to come up stairs with him and so they went.

Once upstairs he said to her quietly that there must be something wrong with these people and if they wanted to use that stove to prepare their own food and eat, they were going to have to figure out what it is. Myanna agreed but couldn't lend any insight as to what she thought might be the problem. While they were trying to figure out what the problem was and what to do about it, a loud knock was heard at the door. One of the children opened it and the boy outside said that massa Sammy wanted the new niggahs to come outside. Penniman's little girl ran up the stairs and delivered the message to Jobba. Jobba thinking that now he might find out what was going on motioned to his family to follow him down and out the door.

Outside there was a scruffy looking white man with rugged features, a scarred face and ruddy complexion who was sitting on a horse with a wide brim hat pulled down low over his forehead and a rifle on his shoulder. Looking up at the man Jobba estimated him to be maybe a little over five and half feet tall. He had strapped to his belt a long curled up whip.

"You gotta name boy?" he said with a snarl.

"Yassuh. I'se Jobba an dis here is Myanna an dis is Linwood an dis is Suliah" Jobba said as he looked up at the man.

"Don you eyeball me when you talkin boy. Yu look at de ground. Guess I gonna hafta teach you some manners right off. Ya'll ain gonna gimme no trouble here now is ya?"

"Nawsuh, we jest git here an needa fine out how ya do things thas all. We good at fittin in yu'll see. Jest needa know how."

Samuel Phelps, the overseer had been looking at Jobba, but when he heard his response he turned his attention to the rest of the family and looked them over. When his eyes came to Suliah they lit up and he asked her again her name. Suliah coyly responded and answered him. He told her to come closer to the horse so he could get a better look and she hesitated, looking at Jobba. Jobba kept his head down, but inside his rage was beginning to burn. Suliah sensing the situation moved a few steps closer to the horse, but not near enough so that he could touch her. He didn't try, but told her to turn all the way around, which she did. After devouring her with his eyes he motioned her back. Then he told Jobba that in the morning they would hear two horns early. The first one would be right after the rooster crows and that would tell everybody to get up. When the second one blew it meant they should be ready to work.

Having said this he turned the horse around and trotted up to his house that was right at the beginning of the quarters. Jobba hearing the horse moving away took his daughter's hand and pulled her inside. Myanna sensing that Jobba was about to do or say the wrong thing intervened and separated them looking at Jobba. He calmed down and started to go upstairs. But once inside, the other family was more hospitable and started talking. Penniman began by telling Jobba they knew that evil overseer would be coming there because he always did whenever somebody new came to the farm. They didn't want him to come inside so they avoided saying anything until he had come and gone. Penniman then reintroduced himself as Penniman Harper and his wife as Tralene.

Then he started in telling Jobba that this was a wicked place and massa Sam was the devil's helper. Pointing to a place in the direction of the stable, he went on to say that right behind there was the whipping post and the stocks that were used to punish them. As far as the use of the cabin Jobba was free to use whatever he needed. Penniman went on and explained that they were given food rations at the beginning of the week from the mansion which didn't usually last the week, but there was a river down at the end of the quarters that was full of good fish and on Sundays they could go there and catch all they could. As a final note, he capped his indoctrination lecture by saying that massa Byron didn't like no religious stuff so if he was a preaching or a praying man, don't let the massa hear or see him. To Jobba, what had started out when they arrived here as seemingly a good life change; now didn't seem so positive anymore and he reflected back on whether the dreams he had weren't some kind of warning.

Slowly he went upstairs with his family and sat on his bed with Myanna while Suliah and Linwood sat on the floor looking up at him.

"Now y`all dun heard what de man downstairs say an I dono if dis be a good thing for us. Tamarra we gwine see jest what it be like but do what dey tell you an don give dat massa Sam no truble. I guess we gits ar food den, but rat now I still got some a de stuff from Bessie May, so we kin eat dat. Y`all hungry?"

"Yeah, I wan somma dat chicken" Linwood said stretching out his hand.

"Yes papa I like me sum too" Suliah echoed.

Jobba got up and went over to where he had stashed the basket took out the remainder of the food and set it on the small table. There were two chairs at the table in the upstairs living area and Jobba told his kids to sit there. Myanna came over next to Jobba and looked in the basket to see what was left.

"You think de ole massa know dat Bessie May put dis food in de basket" she said.

"I dono, but I'se sho glad she did. Dis new massa wasn' gonna give us nuthin, but one piece a ham de whole way. Seem like he meaner den an ole rattle snake an I know dat ain good."

Myanna laughed and grabbed a piece for herself with an ear of corn and went back and sat on the bed. It was starting to get dark outside now and Jobba looked out the window. As the nightfall set in he was still somewhat apprehensive about what tomorrow was going to bring. He continued to go over in his mind the things that had happened during the trip on the way in and wondered about how strange it was that the wagon which seemed to be destined to shatter at the bottom of the hill suddenly lost its wheel and the rear axle just dug itself into the ground stopping the wagon. It was as if a giant hand had just reached out and took the wheel off letting the wagon grind to a halt.

Suliah and Linwood finished eating went over and put their arms around their father and for a few moments they just stared out the window at the stars in the night sky. A short time later the kids left and went to bed falling fast asleep, but Jobba stood there still gazing. Myanna sensing that there was something wrong called him over to the bed.

"You worried `bout dis place?" she said. "We here now an ain nuthin you kin do `bout it so why you don come on in de bed an sleep`till tamarra come an den we see."

Jobba heard the words took her advice and turned his gaze away from the window. Before turning off the lamp and getting into bed, he looked around his new home one more time and inside felt glad to have more room and his own stove, but was uncomfortable about what he may have to pay for it.

He then got undressed and crawled in behind her wrapping his arms around her as he usually did. The warmth of her body was comforting, and he started to relax. As he snuggled up against her smooth skin he began kissing her neck as he reached up and cupped his hand on her large breast. Myanna felt his need and responded to his touch. She turned over and wrapped her arms around him as he kissed her passionately. The deep kiss seemed to bring out the rage that was pent up inside of him and as he kissed his way down her neck he finally locked onto her breast and started to suckle her. She was moved by his extreme excitement, but when his lips wrapped around her nipple so tightly that it felt as if he was trying to draw out from her the life-giving substance that he knew as a child, she groaned. Hearing her, he relaxed and loosened his lock. Together they caressed passionately until he entered her and began the love strokes. The rage resurfaced and he was driving hard with an animal nature as if to pound away his fears and anxiety. Myanna felt at the same time both the tingle of an emotional release that she had not experienced in some time and the pain of such deep penetration that she was caught between the throes of joy and pain. The duration of his rage lasted for some time, but he finally collapsed with his last motion and sank into her chest breathing heavily. Though he couldn't see it in the darkness her tears rolled silently down her cheek. She felt all of his pain, but realized there was nothing more she could do.

The morning came the cock crowed and soon after a loud horn sounded. Remembering what the overseer had said about getting up, Jobba rolled over and got out of bed. As he got up he looked back at Myanna who stared back at him trying to see whether he was okay. He just said good morning with no particular reflection one way or the other with his tone. She heard him and made her way also out of the bed and put her clothes on. Jobba made his way over to the kids and made sure that they were getting up. From downstairs he could hear their neighbors were already up and the smell of breakfast wafted its way up through the rafters. Jobba wasn't sure whether he was going to get any of it,but was pleasantly surprised when he came down and found the Harper's, knowing that they hadn't gotten any rations yet, had set plates for Jobba and his family.

"Come on set down an eat" Penniman said. "I knows y`all ain got yo food yet so `till they git it to ya, you welcom to what we got. You mus a had a good night sleepin, `cause I heard yo ruckus `fore ya went off" he continued while smiling.

Jobba with a sheepish grin on his face scratched his neck looked at Myanna and they all laughed. Suliah and Linwood then came down and they all sat down and ate.

After breakfast Penniman told Jobba that the next horn would be blowing soon so they need to get out to the field. Both families walked out and up the road headed toward the field. Penniman wasn't sure whether massa Sam wanted him in the tobacco field or in the cornfield but knowing that this was planting time for the tobacco, he led him there. As they walked Jobba was still looking around to see what the whole place was like. They passed by the stable and he saw the wooden posts that Penniman talked about with ropes hanging off of them standing beside the stocks. Jobba had heard about these before, but had never actually seen them. Even the look to him was scary.

When they got to the field Jobba saw about twenty or twenty-five others already working. There were also two white men on horses moving slowly around the perimeter with guns on their shoulders. Penniman told Jobba to stand here and wait for massa Sam while he and Tralene went on into the field and started working. Jobba feeling kind of awkward standing there with his family doing nothing looked around to see if Sam was coming. He didn't have long to wait before Sam the main overseer came galloping up to him and stopped just in front of him.

"Did I tell you to come out chere boy?" he growled. "I bin down at yo house lookin for ya, an you up here."

"Nawsuh, sorry suh, but I jest thought here where you wan me ta be."

"`Round here boy you don think you jest do like I tell ya. Now git yoself up to de house, Mister Candle wanna talk to y`all. When you finish wit him, den come on back here an I'll see what you kin do. Dat go for all y`all."

"Yassuh, yassuh" Jobba answered as he took Myanna's hand and started leading her and the children toward the mansion.

When they got to the back door it was open, but the screen door in front of it was locked. He knocked on the wooden frame and said hello. Moments later Aunt Tee, the head house slave came. She was smartly dressed just like when they first arrived, and she unlocked the screen door.

"Massa Sammy say Massa Candle wanna see us," he said.

"Das right, now you go on in de kitchen an wait `till he come in," she said with a pleasant smile on her face.

After talking to her Jobba felt a little at ease thinking that he may have a friend here like Bessie May. A short time later Byron came in the kitchen and spoke to the Thomas family.

"Now I know Penniman mus have tol you `bout the way things git done `round here. But jest case he didn't I'm gonna tell ya jest one time. `cept for today, you git yo rashin's one time on Mondy mornin for de week. If'n you run outta food das yo fault `cause yo don git no mo. Dere's a big stream down dere behind yo house got plenny fish in it. On Sundays you kin go fishinan catch all yo want to keep for yoself. So don be comin ta me talkin `bout you ain got no food. You done already heard the horns dis mornin so ya know das time to git up an git ready to go ta work. I done brought y`all here `cause I need help in the tobacco field right away to help wit the plantin. Jobba das where you an yo boy gonna work along wit yo wife. The girl gonna work here in de house wit Aunt Tee."

When Jobba heard that he started to look at Byron hard, but thought better of it when Myanna grabbed his hand and squeezed it.

"Aunt Tee, - Aunt Tee come on in here woman," he hollered. "You movin slower than m`lasses in January evr'y day now. Fix dem up wit dey food for de rest of de week an den sen `em on back down to Sammy. The young gal, she gon work here in de house wit you."

Aunt Tee nodded her head but said nothing.

Aunt Tee, who was in her early forty's was about Myanna's height with a full build. She had a dark complexion with very smooth skin and beautiful pearly white teeth that she offered with her infectious smile on every occasion. Her eyes sparkled, but there was something behind them that Jobba picked up on but couldn't understand. He also felt there was something disarming about her smile, but he couldn't fathom that either.

"You got somethin to carry dis in?" she asked.

"Naw we ain got nothin here, but I kin go back to de house an fine somethin."

"No, das okay, I fine somethin here. Y`all kin jest sit on down while I put yo stuff together."

She then left the room and soon came back with a large wooden case and started filling it with what looked to Jobba like some fish, corn meal, bread, ham and some kind of vegetable that he couldn't tell what it was. She closed the lid and told him that this had to last him until next Monday morning when he would get his regular weekly ration. Jobba came over and lifted the box onto his shoulder and started to leave when she pulled on his shirt and whispered something to him that he really didn't understand. Myanna heard her also and looked as puzzled as Jobba.

"When de full moon come tonight yu be ready to do de dance," she said and ushered them out the door.

Jobba was having a hard time leaving Suliah in this house alone, but when Aunt Tee put her arms around the youngster and smiled he felt a bit reassured and walked out. As they walked back to the cabin Jobba asked Myanna whether she thought the woman was crazy. Myanna chuckled and said that she was just another strange housekeeper who been with them white folks and their crazy talk too long. Little did they know that she was neither crazy nor was it because of her association with the goings on in the house that she said these strange words. The Thomas's would soon find out what this all meant.

Once back at the cabin they stored the food in the large wooden icebox that had been brought to them by the houseboy. A few minutes later they left the cabin again headed back to the field. By now it was close to midday and the sun was high in the sky. It wasn't an especially warm day, but from the fast walking to the mansion then to the cabin and then back to the field, Jobba had worked up a sweat. When they arrived at the field, Sam the overseer saw them and rode over.

"Jobba I wanna see how you han'l dat plow so go ova dere an git behind it," and he pointed to it.

Jobba looked over to the far side of the field and he saw a young slave walking behind a large wooden plow being pulled by a mule. He had worked with a plow many times before, but he wasn't accustomed to working with any mules.

"Yassuh I sees it an I gwine rite ova."

"You two kin go help dem ova dere wit the plantin," and he pointed to another part of the field directing Myanna and Linwood to go to.

Jobba reached the spot where the plow was and told the working slave that he was going to take over. The young slave looked over at Sam for approval and once assured that it was okay turned the reins over to Jobba. At first Jobba felt a little uncomfortable at seeing how the mule's motions were different from the horses he was used to, but he soon made the adjustment. He was doing fine for a while and moving along in the furrow until the mule sensing that a change had been made in his handler, decided to sit down in the middle of the furrow. Jobba snapped the reins and hollered at the mule to get up, but without success. He snapped the reins again and again hollering at the animal until he caught the attention of Sam who had moved on again to the other side of the field. Sam, seeing what was happening galloped his horse over to Jobba and directed him to get that mule moving or he was going to pull the plow himself.

Jobba hearing this, dropped the reins and walked around to the front of the mule and started pulling on his harness. The mule just sat there making funny noises as if to tell Jobba that he was through working for the day and he wasn't budging. Jobba pulled and pulled on the harness with all his strength until finally he was about to kick the mule when he heard Sammy say:"Stan back boy, jest stan out da way, I knows how ta git him up." Seconds later the crack of the whip was heard, and the lash came down hard on the mules behind. The shocked mule jumped up and started running pulling the plow behind him in and out of the furrows. "Catch `em boy, go catch `em." Jobba took off running after the mule scampering across the field as fast as he could. At that point, all the work in the field stopped for that day because everyone out there was laughing uncontrollably, including Sammy the overseer.

Realizing that it was going to take some time before the workers would be ready to restart their tasks, Sam told them to break for ten minutes and everybody sat down except for Jobba. Jobba was so busy trying to calm the mule down after he caught him that he didn't realize that everyone else was taking a break. He patted his head then rubbed it and patted it again while talking to him so he could get him to pull the plow once more. The mule was standing, but not ready to pull the plow yet when Jobba decided that he would go around in back and snap the reins to simulate the crack of the whip. It was a good idea and the mule got the message as he started to run again, but Jobba pulled back on the reins and the mule started walking at a steady pace.

Sam was watching this and smiled to himself thinking that at least this one could think a little bit. When the mule started moving again, Sam declared that the break was over and for everyone to get back to cultivating and planting. Jobba was pleased with himself after he regained control of the animal and was hoping that Myanna had seen how he handled the situation. Myanna had indeed seen it all and couldn't wait to get home and tell him about how funny he looked chasing that mule all over the field. The rest of the day was hard work but there were no more incidents, either with the mule or with the overseer.

When the horn sounded to end the workday, Jobba believed that his first day on the job had been a good one. The sweat was pouring from his brow, but when he looked back at all the land that he alone had plowed, he felt like he had accomplished something. His bubble of pride was not to last long however, because Sam came over and told him that he did okay for the first day, but tomorrow he was going to have to do more.

Upon hearing this, Jobba was again tempted to look at this man's face, but remembered the words of warning and just said:"Yassuh, I do betta."

The field hands all started walking across the land headed back to their cabins. Jobba met up with Myanna and Linwood and they walked together joining in with some of the others. He could overhear some of them talking excitedly about something that was going to happen tonight. He couldn't quite make out what they were talking about so when he got to the cabin and Penniman and Tralene were already there, he asked them.

"Brother Penniman I hear de people talkin 'bout something gwine happin tonight. You knows what it be?"

"Yes an I'll tell ya. Tonight de moon be full an all a us goes up to de cave ta do de dance."

"Do what dance? I heard Aunt Tee talkin 'bout some dance, is dis what she talkin?

"Yes. 'round midnight when it be dark we all go up to de cave in de mountains. I ain gonna tell no more 'cause it be bad for me, but you an yo wife hafta come 'n see for yoself."

"You caint tell me no more den dat. What happen if'n we don go?

"Don say dat brother, you here now an you got ta go or it be bad for you too."

"How it be bad, tell me dat?

"I caint tell you no mo. Now you jest be ready to go at midnight an meet me down here."

Penniman stopped talking and went over to his bed to lie down. Jobba got the hint and went upstairs. Myanna had already gone up to lie down herself, so did Linwood. When Jobba came up he told her what Penniman had just explained to him and she was puzzled about why they had to go back out, because she was tired. When Jobba told her that Penniman said if they didn't go it would be bad for them she wasn't accepting that as a satisfactory explanation. She insisted on knowing why she had to drag herself back out to go to some cave unless she knew why. She was about to go downstairs and press Tralene for more information, but Jobba restrained her telling her that something strange was going on here and maybe the best way to find out is to go. After this rationalization she gave in, but said she was going downstairs anyway to help with the dinner meal. Jobba looked at her and knowing his wife, still suspected that she hadn't given up on her quest.

Myanna went into the cooking area and started to help Tralene without saying anything. They had worked it out that the meals would be prepared from the rations of each family alternately every other night. As they ate dinner that night, both families just sat there eating. Not much conversation was going on as if nobody wanted to be the first to talk about what the night was going to offer. Tralene's kids sensing the tension asked where Suliah was and Myanna told them that she was going to work in the mansion, but she should be coming here soon. Jobba wasn't so sure about that being the case and he wondered just what that massa Byron had on his mind for her. He didn't say anything, but Myanna knew exactly what he was thinking, and she tried hard to ease his mind.

After dinner Jobba went outside while Myanna and Linwood went back upstairs. There was hardly any activity in the cabin compound. The road up to the mansion was deserted. It seemed that everyone was inside waiting for the hour to go to the cave. The night air was calm and Jobba marveled at how bright the full moon was. He went back in upstairs and sat at his table talking to Myanna about whether they should go or not. Myanna reminded him that he was the one who said they had to go so don't ask her now if they should. They passed the time talking and finally the hour came. Jobba looked at his clock and it read 11:50 PM. He looked over to where Linwood was sleeping and at the vacant bed where Suliah should be. With a deep sigh he shook his head and then motioned to Myanna for them to go down.

At the bottom of the stairs Penniman and Tralene met them and together they all walked out. The deserted scene that Jobba had witnessed hours earlier was now replaced with a parade of slaves carrying lanterns moving up the road headed toward the mountains. They quietly walked past the backside of the mansion and passed the stables. About 100 yards further they came to a path that led up the side of the mountain through a dense forest. The brush overhanging the path clearing would have been an obstacle for anyone over six feet tall so Jobba was having some difficulty in keeping his head down as they moved up. The closer they got to the cave the parade that had the marchers moving along three and four abreast was now thinned down to a single line snaking through the brush.

The entrance to the cave was in sight and Jobba could look over the heads of those few ahead of him and see a yellow-orange glow coming out. When he and Myanna got there and looked inside they saw slaves, many who were already swaying back and forth raising their hands in the air around a huge campfire. The new arrivals hurriedly joined the circle and almost in a trance-like state echoed the movements. At the top of the circle was a figure of a woman with a long robe on with her back turned to the crowd facing the wall of the cave. In her right hand she had a long staff that she raised up to the figures that were drawn there. In her raised left hand, she held a long hunting knife that must have come from the kitchen. At the center of the figures on the wall was a pole with the skeletal head of a bull. Wrapped around the pole from the bottom were the remains of two long rattlesnakes with their mouths fixed in an open position and heads pinned to the top.

As the group continued swaying to the rhythm of drummers off to the side, a man also dressed in a long robe with a painted face cast something into the fire that gave off a strange aroma. The substance hitting the fire crackled loudly and the fire turned a bright orange for several minutes. The crowd reacting to the aroma from the fire became more like zombies and Jobba couldn't resist whatever it was. Both he and Myanna were totally entranced and found themselves drawn into the flow of the night movements. As the drums started to beat faster the rhythm caused the group to move more quickly and the motions became more violent with each increase. At the height of the dance the robed leader in the front began chanting to the beat and the people joined in. Jobba and Myanna could feel themselves speaking in a language that they didn't know, and the movements of their bodies were in step with the others.

Suddenly the drums stopped, the leader turned around and everyone fell to their knees except Jobba and Myanna. Fearing that they were going to be harmed Jobba started to kneel with Myanna when the leader pointed to the man who had the incense and motioned for him to bring the couple forward. He approached the couple and as they came closer to the front, Jobba could see now that the leader was Aunt Tee with her face painted with markings that Jobba had seen on the faces of the tribal men in his dream. Her eyes no longer had the sparkle he saw when they first met, but were now intense and almost vacant as she commanded the incense man to make them kneel before her.

From the crowd someone came to the front with a live chicken in his hand that he handed to Aunt Tee. She grabbed the chicken turned around to the pole and lifted it up while chanting some foreign words that Jobba did not know. When she finished chanting, she spread the chicken out on a table with a hole in the top that was placed near the pole. With the knife in her hand she cut the chicken's neck allowing the blood to drip through the hole into a pail below. She removed the pail and turned around to face the couple. Looking at them with a hard stare she mumbled something that seemed like the mumblings Jobba heard on the slave ship in his dream. The one or two words that he thought he understood seemed to be saying that she was dedicating these new worshippers to the spirit that dwelled in the cave. He tried to get up and escape, but his legs would not respond and even his hands couldn't move. Myanna was in the same state.

Aunt Tee then dipped a brush in the pail of blood and marked a small x on the forehead and a large x on the chest of each of them. Then she put her hand on each of their shoulders and chanted again. This time when she finished, she called the incense man back and he escorted the couple back to the group. Once they were back in line, the drums started again, and movements resumed at a fast pace. All of them were now focused intently on the back wall where the drawings were, as if waiting for something to happen. Dancing to the rhythm of the beat the whole group moving with violent motions waited for the spirit of the cave to appear. It was not long before the wall seemed to come alive and from it sprang something that appeared to be half man and half animal. The beast then took the chicken ate it and waved its hands over the crowd as if pleased with the offering. Its eyes like balls of fire glared at Jobba and Myanna as if sensing that the new arrivals were not acceptable turned toward Aunt Tee and raised its hands. Aunt Tee immediately fell on her knees and appealed to it. Apparently, she was able to convince it that they would be okay because it lowered its hands and melted back into the wall.

The dance continued for some time until the first signs of the morning light began to touch the entrance of the cave then they stopped. Quickly the whole group came to their senses left the cave scampered down the mountain and ran to their cabins. Strange as it would seem, no one in the mansion was ever aware of this nighttime activity, even though it had been going on for months. The loss of sleep from the overnight party never seemed to affect the slaves. It couldn't be determined whether their renewed strength came from the periodic release of their pent-up tensions or whether this cave spirit really had the power of regeneration.

Jobba and Myanna went upstairs and washed off the blood. Unlike the others they were feeling exhausted and wondering just exactly what was done to them.

" I don like dat dance," he said. "I think dey gwine make us do bad things."

"Why dey do dat to us? You think de massa know dey doin dese things?" Myanna asked.

"I dono, but we mus fine out how we kin keep from gwine back dere. I gwin talk wit Penniman an see what we needa do. I know de thing dat come from de wall caint be God."

As soon as he said God, a pain came across his chest and he doubled over. Myanna saw him grab his chest and asked him what was wrong.

"Pain come ova me here, bad pain. I'se okay now. I gwine lie down 'till de horn sound."

Jobba went to the bed and eased his tired body onto it. Just as he was getting somewhat relaxed, the rooster crowed and shortly thereafter the horn sounded. He thought about not getting up, but when Myanna reminded him about what Sam had told them, he dragged himself off the bed and went down. Penniman upon seeing him looked at him hard to see if there were any signs of something wrong. Jobba sat at the table and looked back at Penniman. Then he asked him what had happened.

"You one a us now, how you feel?"

"What you mean one a us?"

"You bin 'sorbed into the spirit an now you mus go wheneva de moon is full or half full an do de dance. If'n you don go den yo own spirit be taken away."

"How kin dat thing take my spirit?"

"Dono how it be don, but de firs time I seen it happen I knowd I don wann it to git me."

"What did you see?"

"Man come here jest like you an say he don wanna do de dance. He go to de cave one time like you an den don go back. Nex day dey fines him in his bed turn all white an he ded. Aunt Tee say he loss his spirit. Das what kin happen if'n you don keep goin."

Jobba stared at Penniman in disbelief at his story, but wasn't sure now what to think. He thought about the pain he felt when he said God and wondered if some kind of spell had been put on him. Myanna came down and joined them for breakfast. Moments later they heard the second horn sound and knew that they were going to be late getting to the field. When they got there, none of the overseers had arrived so they just went in and started working where they left off yesterday. Jobba was still thinking about the pain and decided to test his theory. When he got to a place in the far side of the field, he fell down on his knees and said:"God is you dere?" The immediate pain that shot through his whole body was a quick answer to his question and he ran to find Myanna.

Meanwhile at the mansion Byron had called all of his overseers to a meeting to let them know that he was going to be throwing a big house party this Saturday. He wanted them to make sure that all of the planting that he needed to have done would be finished before then because he was going to need some of the slaves to help in the house. Sam told him that it would be done, and all of the rest assured him that his orders would be carried out. Byron continued by telling them that he was going to be trying to get some of the other landowners to give up some of their land, especially the owners that were nearby. He explained that he was trying to have the biggest and richest plantation in all of Virginia and they could be a part of it if they helped him. They all just looked at him and nodded their heads. They knew that Byron was greedy and determined to get everything he could no matter what or who he had to step on to get it.

While they were meeting, Charlotte, Byron's wife, came in the room and wanted to know just exactly what that new gal was supposed to be doing. Byron upon hearing her dismissed the crew and told them to get down to the fields and get started. He sensed that something was wrong, so he asked her what she meant.

"Dat new gal you bring in dis house she ain good for nuthin, but bein pretty. She caint cook an she caint sew what do I need her for?"

"Common Charlotte she's a pretty gal an I knows she mus be able to help you do somethin. I want her 'round here when Satidy come so's I kin show her off to de otha geneman."

"I know what you keepin her for, an I don wanna see it. You hear me. Don let me see you messin 'round wit dat gal in my house. I'm gonna have her tend to Anna Lee, maybe she kin do somethin good for her.

Now you `member what I say `bout dat gal in dis house. Don let me catch you foolin wit her."

Charlotte turned around without waiting for any response and walked out of the room while Byron, somewhat embarrassed that she had seen through his scheme just sat down in his favorite chair and smiled. He wasn't sure just how he was going to carry out his lustful plan for Suliah and maintain the peace with Charlotte, but he was a determined man. He then turned his thoughts to the upcoming party and just as he had prepared a plan to fleece his friend Tim out of his precious property, so he began to formulate his new strategy on how to acquire more land. The land immediately adjacent to his property; was owned by a wealthy tobacco farmer whose personality was just the opposite of Byron's. Byron firmly believed that his new scheme would easily work on this man.

The overseers arrived at the fields and quickly surveyed the situation. Everyone seemed to be accounted for except Jobba was not where he was supposed to be. Sam galloped his horse around the perimeter trying to locate him and finally found him pleading with Myanna in the patch of land where the women were. He rode up close to them and hollered at Jobba.

"Boy, what chu doin ova here? Don you know where you s'posed ta be workin?"

"Yassuh I knows, but I needed ta tell the missus somethin `portant."

"Well I hope ya tol her now git on back down where you s'pose to be an git de rest of dat field plowed. If'n dat whole patch ain done end of today, I'm gonna whip you boy. You unnerstan me?"

"Yessuh massa, yessuh."

Jobba took off jogging across the field back to the spot where he had left off plowing yesterday. He had just started telling Myanna about his most recent experience and didn't get the chance to finish when Sam interrupted him, so he was angry. He was most concerned that she might do and say the same thing he did and get the same result and he didn't want that to happen to her. He wanted to warn her and to let her know that something had indeed happened to them last night that was not right. He wanted to tell her about his conversation with Penniman this morning and his story about the stolen spirit. He wanted to concentrate on his task at hand, but he just couldn't get it out of his mind that something had been done to him he couldn't control. Feeling helpless, he was determined to learn what he needed to do to erase the spell from him and Myanna.

The hours seemed to go by quickly and the horn sounded to let the workers know that the workday ended. Sam who had been busy most of the day in another area of the farm came over to where Jobba was and looked at how much was done. Thoroughly disappointed at how much area Jobba had completed and remembering what Mr. Candle had said this morning at the meeting about getting it done, Sam went into a rage.

"Boy didn't I tell you dat this whole patch needa be done today? Didn' I tell you dat? Seem like you jest don listn' so's I'm gonna hafta help yo hearin. Now you go on ova dere to de stable an wait for me."

Jobba could feel from the rage in Sam's voice that something bad was about to happen, but he had no idea how bad it was going to be. Sam called some of the other slaves over and told them to go to the stables while he went and got some of the other overseers. When they got to the stables Sam directed two of the overseers to grab Jobba and tie his hands up to the whipping post. They did so and pulled Jobba's shirt down over his hips. The next thing he knew Jobba heard the crack of the whip and felt the lash on his bare back. The first stroke sent a searing pain down his spine and he felt like the skin was being torn from him. His mind jumped back to the dream he had in which he lived the same experience, but this time he knew it was real.

"You gonna do what I tell you boy?" Sam yelled as he reloaded for the next stroke.

"Yassuh, yassuh," Jobba moaned.

"I don believe you hear me yet boy, you need some more to clean out yo ears."

The next stroke came down even harder and Jobba braced as he anticipated the next one. The lashes just kept on coming until Jobba was completely numb and he just hung his head. Finally, the vicious assault stopped, and the overseers cut the ropes holding him up and let him fall to the ground. The other slaves who had been summoned to witness the action were told to pick him up and carry him to his cabin. They gently lifted him up and put his arms around their shoulders while they walked him home. When they got to his cabin and went inside Myanna was downstairs wondering what had happened to him when he didn't meet her to walk home together. She saw him and screamed looking at the blood rolling down his back. Penniman immediately came over and helped her to sit down while he went and got some salve. While Jobba lay prostrate on the floor Penniman gently rubbed the compound on the stripes and told Myanna that this would help to close the wounds and help him heal.

Myanna still sobbing bitterly was totally distraught, but she tried to ask Jobba what had happened. He attempted to respond, but was only able to lift his head and no words came out. Penniman helped him up the stairs and placed him face down on his bed as Myanna noticed Linwood looking on and wanted to comfort him from seeing his father like this. She didn't know what to say. Linwood slowly walked over to the bed looked at the condition of his father's back and asked his mother why. She had no answer to give him, so she just sat on the bed rocking back and forth beside Jobba. Linwood sat on the other side looking deeply into the wounds as the anger inside of him began to rise in his young psyche. Jobba could hear them talking, but he was unable to move. His mind was rehashing the events of last night and now the actions of today and he just wanted to sleep. When he finally drifted off, he just saw darkness and it was darker than ever hovering over him.

The morning came quickly and the routine to begin the day was getting started. Jobba, still reeling from the pain inflicted on him found it difficult getting up from the bed, but he knew that if he didn't, there could be more of the same. He wasn't sure how he was going to walk behind that plow today because he could hardly lift his arms, but he knew he had to try. Myanna helped him downstairs and he gingerly walked to the table and ate. They finished eating and along with Tralene and Penniman walked to the fields well in time to beat the second horn. When Jobba got to the unfinished patch, he immediately got behind the mule that had already been brought there by one of the other workers and snapped the reins to get him started. By this time after several days together, the mule had developed a feel for Jobba's voice and unlike the first encounter moved with a rhythm comfortable for both. Jobba felt pain in keeping his arms up but he was determined to work through it.

A short time later Sam came over and looked at Jobba working and said: "Now I knows you gonna git it done today, ain't you boy?"

Jobba upon hearing his voice felt the rage rising up in him, but stifled his feelings and answered:"Yassuh massa Sam, yassuh".

Sam rode away and Jobba looked at the back of his head wanting to throw down the reins run behind Sam and knock him off that horse. Realizing he couldn't do this he continued driving the mule determined to finish the patch that he had been mandated to complete. Other slaves came around him to offer support, but they were very careful not to anger the other overseers. It was a comfort to Jobba to know that they felt his pain and wanted to be there with and for him. By noonday his arms were so tired that he just wanted to stop and sit down, but he kept on driving until he heard someone call his name from afar off. It was Mr. Candle calling him from the edge of the field. He was waving for him to come over. Jobba really didn't want to stop because he knew that he needed to finish the patch, but this was the real headman calling him, so what could he do. He dropped the reins and quickly walked over to the man.

"Heard you had a bit a trouble yestidy boy, what you do dat for?" Byron said.

"Dono massa, jest dono."

"Well guess ya lerned something an you ain gonna be stupid again. Dat ain why I come down here. I'm givin' a big party in de house Satidy an yo girl tol me you knows somethin `bout how to serve genemen when dey come ta dinner. Is dat right?"

"Yassuh I used ta do it for de ole massa in his house, but I ain got dose clothes no mo."

"Don worry `bout no clothes, you go on up to de house an tell Aunt Tee to fix you up wit something dat'l make you look right. Okay now go on up dere."

"But massa Byron, massa Sam say I got to finish dis here patch 'fore we stop work today."

"Don worry 'bout dat, now you go on up to de house like I tell ya an see Aunt Tee. I'll talk to Sam an git somebody else ta do dat."

Jobba felt relieved that he was getting the break because he wasn't sure how much longer he could continue, even knowing what the penalty might be. He took off walking with a purpose toward the mansion and looking back over his shoulder every few steps to see whether Sam had seen him leave. Mr. Candle was riding off in the opposite direction of where Sam was, so he wondered just when he was going to talk to him. Arriving at the back door he once again knocked on the door frame. Aunt Tee came almost immediately this time looking like the woman he had seen the first time. Her eyes were again sparkling, and that warm friendly smile was back in place. Jobba was a little unsure just what he should say to this woman because he hadn't figured out yet just what she was. He was still wondering how she could switch personalities like she did back and forth from night into day.

"Massa Byron say ta see you 'bout gittin some clothes for de party on Satidy."

"Okay come on in de house an leme git yo measure. Go wait in de kitchen"

Jobba walked into the kitchen and waited just like before. Moments later she came in with a measuring tape an took his measurements.

"You come back tomarra 'bout dis time an I hav somethin for ya. 'Fore you go, you know dat pretty young'n of yours stirrin' dis place up good wit her looks. De missus don know what ta do wit her 'cause she so pretty. She 'fraid Mr. Candle dun take a likn' ta her an he gonna be foolin 'round. Mr. Candle's boy, he be lookin at her too, but he 'fraid to say nuthn 'cause a his daddy. Jest thought I tell you so's you know whas goin on here."

This was the last thing that Jobba wanted to hear because it just served to confirm his suspicions about what he thought was happening. He couldn't wait to get to Myanna to tell her so they could figure out together something to get Suliah out of that house. Jobba went back to the field and over to where he had left off plowing. Mr. Candle must have gotten to Sam somewhere because in Jobba's place was another hand who was doing the plowing. Sam was nowhere in sight so Jobba walked up to the man and offered to take over. The other field hand told Jobba that he was told to finish the patch and Jobba was to go to the stable. Jobba had trouble digesting this because the last time he went to the stable it wasn't a good outcome. The man insisted that this was what Jobba was supposed to do so he took his word and started walking slowly.

When he got to the stable he looked inside and there was Sam and Mr. Candle talking. Jobba hesitated, but Byron saw him at the door and motioned for him to come in.

"Jobba I know's you might be a bit sore from yo lashin an I want you to be okay for Satidy. So I want you to work in here wit de horses 'til you heel up good. Sam gonna show you what ta do."

Inside Jobba felt a great relief and his body relaxed. He knew he couldn't take another one of those whippings, especially when he didn't know what it would be for. Byron turned and walked out of the stable leaving Sam and Jobba alone.

"Look like you gonna get it easy 'till afta Satidy, but don you go thinkin' dat you ain goin back to de fields. Come on ova here an lemme shows ya how to clean out de stalls an take care of des horses."

Jobba walked over to Sam and watched him clean out the stalls and then wash down the horses that were still in the barn. The task didn't look too hard except for the fact that he would have to lift his arms repeatedly. After Sam did a few other tasks he turned to Jobba and told him to take over and then he walked out. There was no one else in there so Jobba first looked to see whether Sam was really gone, then he sat down to rest his arms before beginning his chores. He spent the rest of the workday slowly performing his chores and making sure that the movements he made did not aggravate his arms or his sore back.

While he was working he reflected on what Aunt Tee had just told him and wondered whether she said something because she was an ally, or did she have some other reason on her mind. After last night and what she did to him and Myanna he had a hard time believing she would do anything to help him. No matter what her reason was, now that he knew for sure what was going on, the only thing he wanted to do was get Suliah out of the mansion and back into his house. The rest of the day passed, and the horn sounded to stop working. Jobba looked out toward the fields to see if he could see Myanna coming in, but was unable to locate her. Since he couldn't see her he decided to start toward the cabin anyway and maybe meet her along the way. He put down his pitchfork and patted down the horses then headed home.

As he walked toward the cabin joining in with the others coming out of the field, Myanna spotted him and moved up behind him.

"How you do ta day? You work okay?"

"Massa Byron move me out de field an tol me ta work in de stable 'til I heel up. I'se gonna help in de mansion Satidy 'cause he havin a party. Somethin else mo m'portant den 'bout me I got ta tell ya when we gits home."

Myanna looked at him strange and wondered just what he could be talking about. If he was going to be working in the mansion her first thought was what he would tell her going to be about Suliah. They continued walking until they got to the cabin and then rushed inside and upstairs. She could hardly wait for him to start talking so she prompted him.

"What you got to tell me, it 'bout Suliah?"

"Yeah. That Aunt Tee tol' me dat massa Byron got his eye on Suliah an he might be thinkin 'bout doin somethin'. I don truss her, but ya know I caint let nuthin like dat happen."

"Jobba, ya know she be turnin' seventeen nex' month an she fillin' out real good. Dat man can see it plain as day. How you gwine stop him from doin what all de massa's do?"

"I tol you he wan me to serve in de mansion Satidy at his party. I gwine git to her an take her outta dere. I dono yet how, but I mus do it. One mo thing I got to tell you. Las' night when we go to de mountain dat Aunt Tee dun put some kinda spell on us. You 'member when we firs' come back an I said dat thing in de wall cain't be G–," he stopped short from finishing the sentence." You know what happen nex'. Well I tes' it out again dis mornin' ta see what happn an shonuf when I said it, dat pain came back bad as b'fore. We caint even say his name. You ain tried ta say it is you?"

"No Jobba I ain tried, but we dun wash off de blood what mo kin we do? I dono what we kin do 'bout dat now, but I know dey don beat you good one time. If'n you try to steal Suliah out dat house, dey gwine kill you daid. How you think you gwine git her out a dere?"

"We got to figger somethin out 'cause I ain gwine let dat be. You kin think a something wit me caint you?"

Myanna was at a loss to help him come up with anything that seemed like it could work. She and Jobba spent the rest of the night plotting but to no avail. Finally, they agreed that it was out of their control and whatever was going to happen would happen. Jobba agreed, but was not convinced that there wouldn't be some kind of intervention from a source that he still believed in, but wasn't sure what to call it. The more he thought about it the more he felt some comfort in knowing that what happened on the way coming to this plantation wasn't just by luck. He felt assured that even if he couldn't do something on his own to rescue Suliah, there would be another way that the rescue would be done.

The next day at the appointed time Jobba went back to the mansion and met with Aunt Tee. She handed him his outfit and told him to try it on. The ruffled silk shirt that she had tailored from one of Byron's old ones and the knicker pants fit him perfectly. She also handed him a jacket and long white socks that completed the set. Jobba didn't know what to think of his new clothes because they were more elegant than what he had at Mr. Sutter's place. He thanked Aunt Tee and told her he would do the best job that he could. While he was talking, Suliah walked in carrying a bucket and some towels over her arm. She was surprised to see her father and didn't know whether it was okay to run to him or not so she waited to see what Aunt Tee would say. Jobba still dressed in his new outfit didn't wait for Aunt Tee's okay and ran to hug his daughter. Aunt Tee just stood aside and said nothing.

"Papa, papa I didn' know you's here." she said.

"Yes, Bebe I come ta git me new clothes. I'se gwine be here Satidy at de party wit you."

He was so glad to see her that he failed to notice that she was wearing lipstick and makeup just like Anna Lee and also wearing her old clothes. Aunt Tee stood there wondering just how long it would take him to see that, but he never did. He just looked into her eyes. Aunt Tee gave him a few more minutes and then separated the two telling her to put the bucket down and go back to where she was. Jobba watched her walk away and planted the picture of this maturing young woman in his mind so he could give a vivid description to Myanna when he got home. Aunt Tee quickly brought his mind back to the matter at hand and told him to take off his new clothes put back on his old ones and go on back to his work. He heard her and did just as she instructed, but not before asking her again about Mr. Candle's intentions. She refused to say any more about it except that he should be more concerned about Mrs. Candle than Byron. When she said this Jobba searched her face looking for some kind of sign that would tell him whether she was for him or against him. None was given.

Jobba with his new wardrobe wrapped in the bag that Aunt Tee had given him made his way to the stable and began his work. There was still no one there and he wondered whether this was because Mr. Candle wanted him left alone or was Sam just waiting for another opportunity to burst in on him and see him doing nothing and then find a way to string him up again. The whole day went by and Sam never came by nor did Mr. Candle. Jobba was free to do whatever he wanted. When the day was completed, he grabbed his package and hurried to the cabin to show Myanna. She was already there and upstairs lying down when he arrived, so he rushed over to shake her awake.

"Myanna wake up, wake up see what I got."

She turned over and sat up on the bed while he unwrapped his package.

"Was dis, you gonna look like de massa. You gwine run de house?"

Jobba laughed and told her that if he ran it the first thing he would do is run him off and send Suliah home. Then he launched in telling her that he saw their daughter and how grown up she looked, and she seemed to be okay. He then told her the new thing that Aunt Tee said about Mrs. Candle. Myanna responded that she thought about her when Byron first said that Suliah would be working at the mansion. She also brought to Jobba's attention the fact that the young Mr. Candle was only a little bit older than Suliah and that was something else to think about. Jobba's smile left his face and he sat on the bed looking at Myanna. After several minutes of silence following that last statement, they both made their way downstairs and got ready for dinner. Linwood who had made some new friends among their neighbors was just coming in and went straight to the table.

During dinner that night Jobba was still trying to get more information out of Penniman about the lost spirit story. He wanted Myanna to hear it from him the way that he had told it before. Penniman, even though Tralene tried to stop him retold the story and Myanna wouldn't believe him. Penniman insisted that it was true and if they didn't want the same thing to happen to them, then they would continue to go to the cave when they were supposed to. Myanna then asked him whether he believed that they had some kind of spell on them, and they could never break it. Penniman responded by saying that all of them had become part of that cave spirit and there was no way to get free. Myanna told him that she believed that there was a different spirit and she knew could break any spell and her G--, she didn't say the word because Jobba quickly grabbed her arm just as she was about to. When Penniman started to get angry hearing her talk, Jobba cut the conversation off and said they were going upstairs, and they did.

The air at work in the fields and in the mansion on Friday was filled with excitement about what was going to take place on the plantation tomorrow. In the fields the hands performed their respective tasks, but it was not with the same urgency as it was during the rest of the week. In the mansion everybody was doing something to help decorate the house for the big ball. Aunt Tee was directing the activities and things were starting to look like the palace that Byron wanted it to appear to be. Jobba in the stable was still enjoying his new leisurely assignment and more so taking advantage of his time away from being bothered by Sam. On the plantations in the surrounding area the notices had been received and the owners were also excited about going to the Candle place for a good time. This was not the first time that Byron had thrown a big bash, but it seemed that in his invitation this time he had hinted at wanting to do something special with them. The mystery he created made them all the more anxious to attend.

Work finished on Friday and it was understood by all the slaves that there would be nothing going on that Saturday morning except for what would be done in the mansion. Although on most weekends there was always a short day in the fields on Saturday, this time Saturday morning would be theirs to enjoy unencumbered. That Friday night the lights in the cabins were not doused at the usual time and it seemed that they were going to enjoy their own parties in a pre-celebration to the big event. Even some of them went down to the river to fish that was not usually done until Sunday.

Jobba realizing that he was expected to spend the whole day at the mansion helping out with last minute details told Myanna that he was going to try and get to see all of the house so he could come up with a plan to get Suliah out of there. Myanna cautioned him one more time as she rubbed his back and reminded him about what the consequence could be if he got caught doing something bad, especially on tomorrow. He grunted and went outside to look at the stars and some of the other men headed down to the river.

Saturday morning came and before the sun was fully up, activity in the mansion was already underway. Charlotte and Byron were still in bed, but Anna Lee had already gotten Suliah up from her perch on the first level and they were busy beginning to plan what she was going to wear. Anna Lee, about a year older than Suliah, had become very fond of her and treated her more like her sister than a handmaiden. Charlotte totally disliked this relationship and whenever she saw them together she would find a way to make Suliah do something to remind her of her station in this house. Aunt Tee too was already up and directing the preparation of breakfast. The other slaves who had been summoned to duty in the mansion for today were busy with the last-minute preparations of scrubbing the floors, washing the windows, cleaning the curtains and otherwise making sure that everything was in order. Jethro was just getting out of bed when he heard Anna Lee and Suliah running up and down the hall acting like two giddy little schoolgirls. He opened his door and literally bumped into them knocking both to the floor. He saw the pair dressed in petticoats and hardly anything else, not thinking that anyone would see them this early in the morning, lying there. His eyes were immediately drawn to Suliah who he had imagined before in his mind what her form was like, but her pose now just served to reinforce his image and stimulate his attention. Anna Lee quickly took Suliah's hand as they got up and scampered down the hall back into Anna Lee's room. Jethro still caught up in the moment couldn't get the image out of his mind and slowly proceeded downstairs to see what else was going on with all the noise.

Byron and Charlotte had finally gotten up and come downstairs. Charlotte was tense and very nervous. With all the hustle and bustle of last-minute activities, Byron was trying to convince Charlotte that she should try to relax and enjoy the day and not be overly concerned about what was going on. She was not in favor of this party from the time that Byron first mentioned it and now that she had become aware of his underlying motive for doing it, she was not at all pleased. Although she was happy with the increase of fortune that he had accumulated over the years, she was not in favor of his methods of getting it. Byron, sensing her reluctance thought he had the answer so he told one of the servants to get her a toddy and see to it that she should be catered to at all times tonight. Even though it was very early, she accepted the drink and went into another area of the house and disappeared.

As the day went on all preparations were completed and the mansion was ready, Jobba decided that with the lull waiting for the guests to arrive, he would try to stroll casually through the mansion and check it out. After he had put on his servant attire for the evening's gala and was sitting in the kitchen talking with Aunt Tee, she was called by Byron to attend to something he wanted done. Jobba saw this as his perfect opportunity to get up and see what he could see. He left the kitchen and walked down the hall to the long winding stairway and started to go up, when Jethro came out of his room and started to come down. Seeing Jobba he wasn't sure whether Jobba was supposed to be coming up for some reason or was it something else. Jobba looked at him with a stunned expression and didn't know what to do which gave away his idea of a stealth tour. Jethro picked up on this immediately and asked Jobba where he was going. Jobba didn't know what to say so he just shrugged his shoulders turned around and quickly walked back to the kitchen. Jethro thought about it for a second or two, but didn't follow him and went the other way into the living room to meet with his father.

The sun moved lower in the sky and evening approached. Guests started arriving in an assortment of wagons and carriages. Byron's cadre of slaves who knew their assignments acquitted themselves well as they attended to the arrivals. As the guests stepped down from their horse drawn conveyances each was greeted with a hearty" howdy ma'am or howdy suh" as they were directed toward the mansion's stately porch. The horses and wagons were then quickly whisked away to be refreshed in the stables. Among the attendees there were some old men, middle-aged men with their teenage sons, wives and daughters and several kids Included. At the door Byron and Charlotte stood waiting with open arms greeting their guests and directing them to the huge living room and parlor. As they moved passed their hosts, Jobba along with the other serving slaves met them and made sure that the first drinks of the night were taken. Byron had prepared a large quantity of his special nectar that consisted of fruit juices; lemon slices and a more than sufficient amount of his unique blend of corn liquor. The servers had been instructed to make doubly sure that especially the gentlemen were encouraged to partake of the beverage. Even the ladies, although to a lesser degree were encouraged and plied with the same potion.

The party moved into high gear swiftly and everyone seemed to be having a good time. Aunt Tee's special delicacies were served early and later the main courses were thoroughly enjoyed. About midway through the evening Byron was getting concerned about his supply. The guests were whirling and dancing about in the living room to the music of the musicians and Byron had already started making his overtures individually to the other owners that he had targeted for his private mission. At a timely hour into the night as the guests were deeply involved with the food and drink, Anna Lee made her entrance followed almost immediately by Suliah. The entrance was not without fanfare as Byron saw her come in and directed the guests to acknowledge her. He made sure that all the attendees who had not seen her before knew that this was his daughter and he rushed over to take her hand and escort her into the ballroom. She was dressed elegantly in a dress that highlighted her features in a most positive way and her mother seeing her from across the room was pleased. However, the spotlight on her lost much of its luminosity when Suliah entered shortly behind.

When Suliah entered, though she was dressed in a significantly lesser quality dress, one that had been discarded by Anna Lee some time ago, her ample assets could not be disguised, and all eyes turned from the supposed main attraction and focused on her. She demurely eased her way into the room stepping carefully behind Anna Lee, but there was no way for her to stop the gazes of the men and most of the women on her radiance and beauty. Anna Lee, who was very confident in her own appearance, was not upset at this and continued to move into the crowd and greet the guests. Across the room however, the expression on Charlotte's face changed dramatically and she was livid. She quickly made her way to where Suliah was and in spite of being in full view of the guests grabbed her arm and rushed her out of the room. Byron somewhat embarrassed by her action in front of the men that he was trying to persuade, casually but swiftly left the room and caught Charlotte in a nearby hallway. He admonished her and told her that Suliah's presence in the room would help him convince his gentlemen friends regarding his mission. Charlotte, not wanting to engage Byron's wrath which she well knew could be overbearing when he was provoked, acceded to his wishes and allowed Suliah to return to the ballroom. Though she submitted to his command, in her mind her ire had not been abated.

The evening was moving along just as Byron had planned and he had already convinced two of his biggest landowner neighbors that it could be in their best interest to let him have a portion of their land. His goal to become the wealthiest and most powerful plantation owner in the county, even in the state appeared to be taking shape and he was feeling good. Still seething from seeing how the guests, especially the young men, were more interested in looking at Suliah then talking to Anna Lee, Charlotte concocted a plan. She first went over to Byron and explained to him that she needed to have Suliah leave the room to get something from the guest room that she needed. Byron, having no idea what she was up to agreed. Charlotte then went over to Suliah who was standing by Anna Lee and attending to her every request, told Suliah that she needed for her to go up to a guest bedroom and retrieve a trinket that she wanted to show off to her friends. After telling her which bedroom and where exactly she thought it was, Charlotte sent Suliah off to get it.

Soon after she left the room, Charlotte went over to where two of the young men who had been admiring Suliah most intently were standing. She whispered something into their ears and almost immediately both of them left the room also. They walked quickly through the halls to the back of the house where there was a second stairway that was used mostly by the servants and made their way upstairs. Having been directed by Charlotte to the location of the guest bedroom where Suliah would be, they hopped up the stairs two at a time to the top and looked around. Seeing no one else there they found the room with its door open and saw Suliah searching around for the item she had been sent for. They moved in slammed the door shut startling Suliah who almost fell as she spun around quickly. Both young men lurched toward her and she sensing their intent backed up to the far side of the large bed. Her heart began to pound as she could see no way pass them. She moved around the bed hoping that when they came around to this side she might be able to scramble across and run out the door. However, the men separated and there was one on this side and one on the other. She started to scream but before she could open her mouth one of the men grabbed her and placed his hand over her mouth. The next thing she knew she was thrown on the bed and one was holding her arms down while the other started to undress her.

Fear ran through her whole body and a sense of the inevitable was overwhelming. As she closed her eyes, her mind ran through all the things that she had learned from her father about the possibility of this day coming to pass, but she could think of nothing that would comfort her. She struggled as much as she could but the weight of the man pressing down on her was more than her strength could move. The other man holding her arms was just anticipating his time to assume that position. Tears began to run down her face, and she was sobbing bitterly, but they elicited no sympathy from the two men who were now sensing total conquest. Just as she was about to give up and concede that this was to be her fate, she heard a loud noise, and suddenly the door sprang open.

Chapter 3 - Eyes Have Seen

The two fiddlers and the banjo player were performing at their peak and the music had the crowd high stepping to every note. Everyone seemed to be enjoying the Candle hospitality and the food and drink were far from running out. No one seemed to notice that two of the guests were missing for some time and Byron was still busy selling his land grabbing idea to his wealthy neighbors. Charlotte perhaps was the only one who was aware of what might be going on in another part of the house, but it was highly unlikely that she was telling anybody. It wasn't until Anna Lee sought her companion's service that she noticed that Suliah was not in the room. She excused herself from the young man she was entertaining and sought Jethro who was nearby talking to his friends.

"Jethro, have you seen Suliah?"

"No, not for a while. The last time I seen her mama sent her upstairs to get somethin from a guest room. She been gone now for a good while."

"Would you go up dere for me an see if she need help in findin that thing?"

"Okay sister dear, I'll be yo slave for de minute," Jethro quipped.

He left the ballroom and walked quickly up the stairs to the guest bedroom. When he got to the door he heard sounds like someone scuffling and thinking that someone might be having a problem he burst in. His quick entry caught the two young men by surprise and they immediately stopped what they were doing. Suliah reacted quickly when she saw Jethro and jumped off the bed pulling her dress up around her. The villains started stuttering as they tried to explain their actions. Jethro ignored them for the moment and looked at Suliah wondering just how far they had gotten. When he saw that only the top of her dress had been pulled down exposing her undergarments he surmised that he arrived just in time.

Then he turned his attention back to the young men and in an angry tone asked them just what they thought they were doing. One of them gathered himself enough to put a smile on his face and said: "She ain nuthin but a niggah so we jest thought we have some fun wit her. When he said that Jethro lunged at him crashing his fist into his face with all of his might knocking him to the floor. Then Jethro jumped on him pummeling him until the other man pulled him off. He got up and started in on the other man, but they both were able to escape and ran out of the room and down the stairs. Jethro put his arm around Suliah who sat on the bed shaking and asked her if she was okay. Then he told her to wait here, he was going to get Anna Lee to help her. Suliah nodded her head, but said nothing.

Jethro ran out of the room and downstairs to find Anna Lee. He located her still in the ballroom and whispered in her ear telling her everything. Anna Lee with a stunned expression exited the room quickly and headed up to the guest room. Jethro then turned to go and find his father. He searched the ballroom, but no Byron. Next he went into the parlor where he saw him talking to one of his prospects. At first he hesitated to interrupt the conversation because he knew what his father was about, but when he thought about how much Byron prized Suliah he decided to take a chance.

"Daddy, I don wanna interrupt you 'cause I knows you busy wit important stuff, but I gotta tell yasomethin."

Byron stopped his conversation and looked at Jethro. He knew that Jethro would not break into a conversation he was having with a guest unless it had to be something really mportant.

"Alright son, you got my 'tention now whas wrong wit you?"

Jethro motioned for his father to step away from his guest, which he did and then he told him what had happened. Byron in disbelief asked Jethro who the men were and wanted him to point them out. When Jethro explained who they were, the shock on Byron's face was enough to end the party right then and there if he had acted on his first thoughts. It seems that the young men were both sons of one of Byron's main targets he was pursuing for the evening. Byron told Jethro to say nothing to anybody else because he would handle it. Jethro then left the parlor and headed back upstairs to the guest bedroom.

Byron wasn't sure just how he wanted to handle this because he was weighing the idea of whether this situation could be profitable for him or not. He started thinking that if he confronted the father of these boys and told him what they did perhaps it would persuade him to severely drop the land purchase price that they had previously agreed upon. Then on the other hand if the father brought up the fact that they were just boys doing what boys do and Suliah was just a niggah, how strongly would he want to argue against that defense. Byron looked around for the young men who had melted back into the crowd in the ballroom as though nothing had happened. He decided he was going to gamble and press the father for a lower price, banking on the idea that he would want to protect his good reputation and the reputation of his sons. Byron would tell him that it would all be forgotten if they could restructure their deal.

Byron entered the ballroom and looked around for the father. There he was in one of the corners enjoying himself with one of the women and toasting heartily with a glass of Byron's special nectar. Casually Byron walked over to him and joined him in a toast while slapping him on the back. Then he asked if he could steal him away from the ladies for just a minute because he needed to talk to him about what they had discussed earlier. The man a little surprised by this move, looked at Byron and then agreed to go with him. Byron steered the man out of the main room and directed him to a smaller one just off of the parlor. Once inside, Byron stopped smiling and told the man about what his sons had done to one of his property just a little while ago.

Upon hearing this, the man stopped smiling also and wanted to know if Byron was joking because if he was it was in very bad taste. Byron assured him that he was not and this could be a serious matter. The man insisted that he wanted to talk to his boys before he went any further and hear their side of the story. Byron responded that he was a gentleman and certainly would grant him the opportunity to question his sons before going any further. Byron then suggested that he call the boys into this room and Byron would leave them alone to settle it. The man quickly exited the little room and went to find his sons. In just a few minutes he had both of them in tow and brought them into the room. Byron kept his word and left them alone, but stayed just outside within earshot.

"Boys, I jest heard some bad news `bout something ar host say you done. Now I know you boys like ta have fun wit the women, but I want the truth now. Did y`all do somethin to one of Mr. Candle's gals upstairs?"

Both the young men, who were afraid of their father, were panic stricken when they heard him ask the question. They weren't sure just what to tell him.

"Da, Da, daddy we was jest gonna have some fun wit her an den let her go. Didn't mean no harm an we didn't git nuthin done to her anyway," the older boy said.

Just as he finished his statement, the father's backhand came across his face and he hit the floor. His brother cowered waiting for the same treatment, but it didn't come. The father just hollered at both of them and told them that when they got home they could expect some real punishment for fouling the reputation of his good name. He then told the boys to get out of his sight and don't let him see them again until it was time to go. The sons exited the room hastily and disappeared. Byron, who was still standing nearby, saw them leave and went back into the room.

"Mr. Candle suh, I do apologize for my son's b'havior, but you know dat boys will be boys sometimes. Now how kin we work dis thing out so it don hafta go no furtha. Dey tell me dat nuthin bad happin to the gal anyway, so what is it you askin?"

Byron feeling the power tried to be cordial and sympathetic in his appearance, but inside he was reveling at what he was about to propose and unscrupulously possess this man's land. He told the father that he would be willing to forget the matter if they could redo their agreement and fix the price at this number – and he wrote down a figure. The man looked at him astonished at the figure, but after a long hesitation agreed to the deal. Byron patted him on the back and told him that the papers would be drawn up on Monday morning and be ready for his signature. The man nodded and with his head down humbly walked out of the room, apparently no longer in a party mood.

Upstairs Anna Lee was trying to console Suliah and calm her down. Jethro had re-entered the room and was looking at both of them without knowing what he could offer. Finally, he said to Anna Lee: "Maybe she oughtn't to stay down dere in dat hallway no mo. Why cain't she take one of those empty rooms upstairs?"

Anna Lee agreed with him and they lifted Suliah up and walked her up to the third level where there were three rooms that hadn't been used in months. Anna Lee opened the door to one of them and even though it was somewhat dusty it was still relatively clean. There was a bed there, an old dresser with a mirror and a large rocking chair. Anna Lee went over to the dresser and opened one of the drawers looking for some bedding. Sure, enough folded neatly were some sheets, pillowcases and blankets that had not been used in many days. She made up the bed and placed Suliah in it. Then she turned to Jethro and said: "Now you don tell mama nuthin `bout dis `till I kin talk with her, ya hear?"

"What `bout daddy, don ya think he oughta know?" He didn't mention that he had already told him.

"I'll talk to him too you jest let me do it, okay?"

"Yeah das okay."

"Alright now les get back to the party an see whas goin on."

They looked back to see Suliah close her eyes and go to sleep then they closed the door and went downstairs.

The hour was getting late and the party drawing to a close. Guests were starting to leave Byron and Charlotte stood at the door saying goodnight and seeing them out. Jobba, who had been watching the whole night observing all of the goings on with the people, was still trying to plan how to get Suliah out of there. While he was watching them, Aunt Tee was also watching him. He could sense he was being watched, but thought it might be Mrs. Candle, so he was careful to do the right thing all the time he was with the guests.

When the last family departed, the house was in disarray. Byron saw this, but he was feeling quite good. Not only was he happy about another successful entertainment extravaganza, but he was now soaring from the effects of his own nectar. He went into the parlor and took out the scraps of paper he had stashed after he concluded each proposal and sat down in his chair gloating over his prowess. His review revealed that he had annexed, at least potentially, another eighteen acres of land to his already vast property. The next thought on his mind was that he was going to need more help immediately to work the new land. This meant getting more slaves and he immediately thought about the coffle he saw on his way back from the Sutter Plantation. Making a mental note he decided to contact that trader and work a deal with him on Monday.

Charlotte, exhausted from the affair, went upstairs to go to bed. She stopped by Anna Lee's room first to see how she was, but the room was empty. Wary of doing a search, she just resigned herself to the possibility that her daughter was probably still downstairs somewhere. Though she knew what her plan for Suliah had been tonight, Charlotte was not made aware of what really happened nor did she want to know. Having imbibed of the Byron nectar herself to no small degree, as soon as her head hit the pillow her cares lie elsewhere. Byron entered the room a short time later, after giving instructions to Aunt Tee that he wanted everything cleaned up tonight so that when he awoke in the morning it would be back to normal. As he disrobed, he looked at Charlotte sleeping in the bed with a smile on her face and wondered just what she might be dreaming about. He thought certainly it wasn't about him.

Jethro and Anna Lee still downstairs after all of the guests left, were sitting in the ballroom talking about what had happened. They were unaware that within hearing distance Jobba was cleaning the little room off the parlor. When Jethro finished telling his version to Anna Lee about what he saw when he entered the guest bedroom, Jobba took it all in and froze in the middle of what he was doing. Anna Lee reacted to Jethro's version by telling him that Suliah was so shocked from the assault that she couldn't really remember all that happened. Jobba was now seething in place and wanted to run upstairs, find his baby and run out of there with her, but the words of Myanna popped into his head and he was reminded that she told him not to do anything that would get him killed. Unable to think clearly at that moment, he sat down in the same chair that Byron had just used to gloat and mourned the fate of his beloved daughter.

Aunt Tee called all of the slaves to the kitchen to relay the master's instructions and let them know that it had to be done tonight before they quit. When all the rest of them left to do their chores, she caught Jobba's arm and turned him around. He was startled and when he looked in her eyes, again the sparkle was gone and the same intense look that she had the night in the cave came over her.

"De spirit in de cave tol me dat you rebel an do not believe. You tried to tes him an you still don know. Dis be a warnin to you an yo wife, do not tes de spirit or me an you will live."

When she finished speaking and turned his arm loose, the sparkle in her eyes returned along wth that great smile on her face She then asked him what he was waiting for and why he hadn't started doing what he was told. He looked at her with a puzzled expression and said he was on his way to do his chores. Inside he was more confused now about her than before, but he was even more dedicated to getting Suliah out of this house. Quickly he exited the kitchen looking all around to see if there was any evidence that could lead him to where she was. Seeing nothing, he went on about doing his assigned tasks.

For another hour or two the slaves worked industriously getting the mansion back in order. When all of the chores were done and the house returned to its former appearance, Aunt Tee after her final inspection told them to return to their cabins. Jobba still looking at her suspiciously saw no signs of the personality she displayed in the kitchen earlier. She was as pleasant as he had ever seen her. Now he wondered whether the others were treated the same way he was, but there was nothing to indicate that, so he joined the throng and walked home. Outside it was pitch dark and the path leading to the quarters was obscure except for the light of the moon and the stars. None of them had a lantern so they eased along the path making their way from memory.

Jobba reached his cabin slung open the door and ran up the stairs to tell Myanna what he had heard. He reached the bed and saw that she was already awake having heard the door thrown open. She sat up and looked at him waiting for the explanation.

"Myna, Myna we gotta do somethin, gotta do somethin now," he blurted out as he grabbed her shoulders.

Myanna not knowing what he was so hyper about tried to calm him down so he could tell her the whole story.

"Jobba you make no sense. Now set down here an tell me what you talkin," she responded as she pulled him down to sit on the bed beside her.

He plopped down on the bed hard and tried to gather himself, but his words still came rushing out in spurts.

"Dey dun try to hurt her. Dun try to spoil her."

"Who, Jobba who try to do dis?"

"Som o dem boys who come to de mansion wit dey family. I heard de massa's children talkin sayin dem boys try ta jump on her. I couldn't fine her ta see fo me, but dey say she okay. We gotta git her outta dere an I'm gonna do it."

"Jobba I know you hurt now, but you caint act crazy. We hafta fine a way to see her an know dat she okay den maybe we kin work it out. Maybe Aunt Tee kin help you see an talk wit her."

"Aunt Tee - Aunt Tee, dat woman jest as crazy as de res o dem in dat house. She go into dat spell again tonight an she tell me dat de spirit in de cave dun talk ta her. She say de spirit tol her for us not ta tes him or her. She say if'n we want ta keep on livin, not ta tes de spirit. You think woman crazy like dat gwine help me?"

"What else kin we do? How you fixin ta git Suliah away? You think Penniman kin help you?"

"Naw he ain gwine help us. He don even wanna help hisself. I don think he even know what be gwine on in dat house an top o dat, he 'fraid of de cave spirit. Tomorra I fine a way to git back to dat house an see Suliah fo maself."

Jobba finished talking lay his head down and stretched out on the bed. There was nothing more that Myanna could add so she went to sleep.

Sunday morning came and in the quarters life was back to normal. The festivities that took place in the mansion last night, except for those who had to work the party, didn't affect actions in the cabins. For most it was a leisure morning and they were grateful for not having to respond to the loud horn and rush to get out of bed. Smoke from some of the cabins had already started to escape through the chimneys as breakfasts were being prepared, but for the most part inactivity was the activity for the morning. As for Jobba, his eyes opened well before the sun rose and he was busy staring at the ceiling contemplating how he was going to get into the mansion today to see his little girl. Myanna had also awakened early, but still could offer no solution to the problem. They both lie there reflecting, but not speaking until Linwood's getting out of bed broke the mood. He came over to his parents and asked if they were going to have breakfast. Myanna told him that she was getting up in a minute and then all of them could eat.

Linwood noticed that his father, who usually was the first one out of bed on Sunday or any day, was not making any attempt to get up asked him if anything was wrong. Jobba hesitated answering wondering whether he should tell him about Suliah's ordeal or wait until he had come up with some kind of solution to the problem. Linwood and Suliah were close and Jobba knowing this didn't want to lay this emotional burden on him prematurely. He chose to protect his son's feelings and said that he was just tired from working the party at the mansion last night well into the morning. This made sense to Linwood and he returned to his bed waiting for the call from Myanna to come down and eat.

Downstairs Penniman, Tralene and their kids had already eaten and gone out of the house to enjoy this beautiful Sunday. The stove and table were Myanna's all to herself, so she began preparing breakfast. While she was busy doing her task, she happened to look out the window and saw Sam along with one of the other overseers riding through the quarters. He seemed to be looking for something and was asking questions of all of the slaves that happened to be outside. She also noticed that Penniman was one of those who got asked the question, so she decided to inquire of him when he came back in. After several minutes the overseers continued on through the quarters and went down to the river and then disappeared around the other side. Myanna seeing them move on, relaxed and finished what she was doing. She thought for a moment that they might have been coming to her cabin because of what Jobba told her happened at the mansion last night. She completed breakfast and then hollered upstairs to her guys to come down.

Jobba and Linwood hurried downstairs and sat at the table. By now both of them were hungry and wasted no time digging in. While they were eating Myanna told Jobba what she saw outside this morning and she asked him if he thought it could have anything to do with last night. Jobba responded that he didn't think so because what happened in the mansion

Mr. Candle wouldn't be telling the overseers about it. After hearing what she said he was now anxious to question Penniman about what he was asked. He didn't have to wait long before they finished eating; Penniman and Tralene came back in. They all said good morning and exchanged pleasantries for a minute before Jobba broached the question to Penniman.

"What massa Sam talk wit you dis mornin `bout?"

"He jest askin ev'ry body if'n dey seen some niggah slaves dat run way from de place ova yonder. Dey think som a `em mighta come here."

"Why he think dey come here?'

"`Cause all de slaves `round here an yonder knows `bout de spirit in de cave an what he kin do for `em. Dey think de spirit kin set dem free."

"You think dat too. You think dat spirit up dere kin do dat?"

"I ain saying I `grees wit dem, but I know dat spirit up dere is mighty pow'rful an I don be askin fo nuthin less'n I kin give `em somethin back. An since I ain got nothin ta give, I don ask fo nothin."

Jobba continued to press Penniman about all he thought the cave spirit could do while hoping without saying it that Penniman might reveal something he thought could be helpful for his Suliah plan. Penniman was reluctant to keep on talking about the spirit, but he did say that there were a few who went up there some nights, even before they had to do the dance, and would take a sacrifice to lay before the spirit. They then would receive the thing that they asked for. He also told him it must be that none of them had ever asked to be set free, because none of them had ever left this place alive. When he used the word alive, Jobba's ears perked up and he relentlessly pursued that issue.

"What you mean dey ain neva lef here alive?"

"I mean jest dat. Some of dem who go dere an give de saca'fice b'fo de dance come, dey gits what dey ask fo, but not long afta, dey be founded somewheres out dere in de fields an don nobody know what happen to `em. You needa listn ta what I be tellin ya, an jest do what I do an y`all be okay."

Jobba listened to Penniman intently, but didn't hear anything that was going to help him with his mission. He thanked the man for his words of wisdom and got up from the table. Myanna had heard all that was said too, but she waited until she and Jobba got back upstairs before saying anything. Linwood also heard the tales, but since he didn't have to go to the dance ritual had no idea about what the man was talking about, so it didn't bother him what he said.

"Jobba you think he tellin' de truf?"

"I think he think he doin so. But half a what he said don make no sense. If'n anybody kin go up dere to de cave wit out Aunt Tee, den dat mean she don needa be dere when de spirit come out."

"You ain thinkin `bout gwine up dere by yoself is you?"

"I dono. I caint think a nuthin else ta do. If'n I goes up dere an do like he say an put down my saco'fice maybe I kin git dat spirit ta get her out dat house."

"Jobba you dono what you be messn' wit. You tol me yoself dat you dun already had pains from getting dat blood put on you. What you think kin happen when you go back dere an do wrong like Penniman say?"

"I dono but kin you think a somethin' else ta do?"

When he said this Myanna had no answer for him so she stopped talking, but in her heart she feared that he had made the wrong decision.

In the mansion that morning Byron was just getting out of bed. He casually walked over to his window and looked out to see it was a beautiful day in the making. Then his eyes moved on to the quarters to see what was happening down there. The overseers were still there when he arose, and he became concerned as to why they were roving the area. It was not usual for them to bother the slaves on a Sunday morning or at any other time on that day. Quickly he turned away and started getting dressed when he heard Charlotte moving like she was coming to life and getting up. He finished dressing ran down the stairs and outside hoping to catch Sam before he went away. He was anxious to find out what was going on. However, by the time he got outside Sam had made his way through the quarters and moved on to the other side of the plantation out of Byron's sight. He turned around and went back in the house.

Inside Aunt Tee met him and asked whether he wanted to eat now. He responded saying yes then went into his parlor. When he got there, it occurred to him that he didn't see Suliah who usually slept on a pallet in the hallway near the kitchen. He didn't see her or the pallet, so he went in the kitchen and asked where she was. Aunt Tee who didn't know herself was embarrassed to be getting caught off guard not knowing something about what was happening in the house. She offered that she thought Suliah might be up already and helping Miss Anna Lee. She made no mention about the pallet, but her answer was satisfactory to Byron, so he went back into his parlor. Aunt Tee now aware that something was out of order sought one of the other slaves to finish making breakfast and she went upstairs to Anna Lee's room. Carefully knocking on the door, she announced that it was she and then went inside.

"Miss Anna Lee, I'se sorry ta wake you, but I thought dat Suliah might be in here."

"Come on in Aunt Tee I must tell you something."

Aunt Tee walked further into the room and stood by the bed. Anna Lee started getting up while she talked, and she explained that Suliah had been moved to a room on the third floor. Aunt Tee looked surprised and wondered why that was done, but she didn't ask. Anna Lee volunteered the information anyway and told her about all that happened last night. Aunt Tee took it in, but the expression on her face didn't change nor did she say anything. She didn't appear to be surprised and didn't show any concern about the incident, but just asked Anna Lee if she was coming down to breakfast now.

Anna Lee a little surprised herself at the lack of concern about Suliah being attacked just answered Aunt Tee saying yes she would be down shortly. In her mind, Anna Lee wondered whether Aunt Tee may have known something about the attack before it happened. Her mind then turned to her mother and wondered if perhaps she knew something. She got dressed and made her way downstairs and met her father in the dining room eating breakfast.

"Good mornin daddy how are you?" she said smiling and putting on her best happy face. She moved around the table wrapped her arms around him and kissed his forehead.

" Good mornin' - you lookin mighty happy. Did you sleep well?"

"I slept wonderful and had the most pleasant dream."

"You wasn't dreamin `bout one of dem boys was ya?" Byron asked with a smile on his face.

"No daddy, I was dreamin' I was in Richmond city goin shoppinan and had money ta buy everythin I wanted. Wasn't that a good dream?"

Byron thinking that this could be leading up to something that was going to cost him some money, tried to steer away from this conversation by changing the subject.

"Did ya meet anybody here last night dat you might take a likin too?"

"Aw daddy the same boys come last night that always come. Wasn't nobody new here, so why you think I might like any of dem," she answered as she took her seat. Her breakfast was brought in and she started to eat.

"Daddy did you know that somehin happen here las night that shouldn't oughta happen?"

Byron surprised that she knew about it stopped eating and looked directly at her.

"Ya don say. Tell me what you think happen."

"I know that our gal Suliah got hurt by two a dem boys you want me ta like an she ain feelin good. I moved her up to a third-floor bedroom an put her in a bed there. I hope you don mind."

Byron pretended to be surprised by what she was telling him and asked whether she had talked with Suliah this morning. He was really most concerned about whether his prized prospect had been spoiled. Even though the young men told him that they didn't get far with their intended action, Byron couldn't be absolutely sure.

"I ain seen her yet this mornin', but las night she was all upset an shaking bad. That's why I put her up there. You gonna let her stay there ain you?"

Byron now thinking that this might be an ideal situation for him in the future responded saying: "Yes baby das fine. Das good dat ya put her up dere an git her up offa dat cold floor. Does mama know what happen?"

"I dono, I ain seen her yet this mornin'. Was she gona come down an eat?"

"I thought she might be right b'hind me, but guess she went back ta sleep. Leme go on up dere an see `bout her.

Byron excused himself and got up from the table headed upstairs. On the way up he met Jethro who was just getting up. They exchanged greetings and continued each on his way. When Jethro walked into the dining room, Anna Lee was still there. He greeted her and asked whether she had told Byron about what they did. Anna Lee explained that she did, and he had no problem with it. Jethro then asked her if she told mama. She said no because she hadn't seen her yet, but she would tell as soon as she came down.

It was really late that morning when Charlotte decided to go down. Aunt Tee was waiting around trying to keep the breakfast items heated and wondering whether Mrs. Candle would even want to eat now at all. When she walked into the dining room Aunt Tee met her and asked what she would like to have. Charlotte, who was still feeling the effects of Byron's special nectar told her that she would just like one egg, some biscuits and some of Aunt Tee's strong coffee. Aunt Tee nodded her head and went back into the kitchen to make it happen. Moments later she was back with Mrs. Candle's order and placed it on the table before her. Anna Lee who had gone outside to view the beautiful day came back in and saw her mother in the dining room. She walked over to her and said good morning then sat down.

"Mama you not feelin good. You look kinda tired?"

"I'm okay my dear, I jest shouldn'a drunk so much of yo daddy's punch."

Anna Lee laughed and said there were probably a whole lot of people who were feeling like she was this morning. Then as she watched her mother eat she casually mentioned what she told her father earlier. Charlotte acted just as surprised as Byron and stopped eating.

"What time did all this happen?" she said.

"I dono `xactly, but Jethro told me he went to look for Suliah not long afta you sent her up to look for somethin for you. And that's when he caught them. You remember what time that was?"

"Wellleme see, it musta been `bout 11:00 or 11:30 `cause I was talkin ta that Emmyjoe tellin her I wanna show her my bracelet that yo fatha bought me. Couldn'a bin no later than dat. Where is Suliah now, she okay?"

"Yes mama she be fine, but I moved her up to a room on the third floor so she kin get well. She was mighty scared last night afta it happened."

"That's okay for now, but don't you go gittin too attached to that gal 'cause I ain't gona have her 'round. here too long. She's gonna be trouble, I just know it. When she gets better, you send her on back down to the hallway where she b'longs."

"Okay mama but I don think she be any trouble, you'll see."

The conversation ended and Anna Lee got up to go upstairs and see about Suliah.

When she got to the room the door was still closed so she slowly opened it and peeked inside. Suliah was sitting on the edge of the bed looking out the window. She turned when she saw Anna Lee and got up. Anna Lee motioned for her to sit back down and walked over to her.

"How you feelin?" she said.

"I'm still scared, why dey do dat ta me?"

"I dono but they won't do it again. I told daddy what happened an I think he'll take care of dem. You kin stay up here for awhile 'till you calm down, but mama said she don want you to stay here all the time. Daddy might say different though, we jest hafta see."

"You bin good ta me an I thanks you. Yo bruther he bin good too, an I wanna thank him. If'n it weren't fo him, somethin bad mighta really happin an I dono what I would do."

"That's okay, now if you can - I think you need to see Aunt Tee 'cause she didn't even know what happened an I'm sure she's looking for you."

"Okay I gwine ta go down dere now an see her."

Suliah got up and left the room in search of Aunt Tee. Anna Lee followed her to the second floor and then went to her room

Byron was still wondering what the overseers were looking for, so he decided to walk down to Sam's cabin and ask him. When he got there Sam and the other overseers had just returned from circling the plantation and were sitting at his table. Byron knocked on the door and then entered. Sam saw him and stood up. He was unaccustomed to Byron coming into his cabin, so he was a bit startled to see him there.

"Mr. Candle what kin I do for ya?"

"I looked out my window dis morning an I saw you ridin down the quarters. What you do that for?"

"Suh I was gonna tell ya later or even tomorra if'n I didn' see ya today, but I got word las night when I went down the road to the nex plantation that sev'ral niggahs from ova dere dun run off an they could be hidn' somewhere 'round here. I went out this mornin' to check an see if'n they be 'round here."

"Did ya find any o dem?"

"No suh, there wasn't hide nor hare of any of dem to be found. It maybe that they crossed de river an went up into those mountains. I hear tell they kin live up there for many days b'fo they hafta come down. We'll keep a look out tho just case they might wanna come down here sometime at night."

"Good work Sam das good work. You do that an let me know if ya catch any."

"Yessuh we kin do that right away. Was there anything else yu need?

"No Sam I was jest wonderin why you was ridin in the quarters this mornin. I'm gonna head on back to the house now an maybe I'll see ya later."

"Yes suh, maybe later I'll come on up there for a toddy if thas okay."

"Why sure Sam you do dat."

Byron left the cabin and looked down the way toward the quarters. The slaves were out and milling around as they usually did on Sunday and everything seemed to be as normal. However, inside one of the cabins, cabin number 4, Jobba was still contemplating whether he was going to act on what Penniman told him about the sacrifice gesture that could perhaps give him what he wanted. Myanna continued to talk to him about the danger of what he was planning, but it seemed like he had already made up his mind and he was going to try it. He told her to find something he could use to present as the gift, but she refused to help him. In a huff he stormed down the stairs and went outside in search of something maybe down by the river that he could use.

At the riverside he saw many of his neighbors there fishing. He went and stood beside one of them and asked if there was anything in this river that might be good besides the fish. The man looked at him with a puzzled expression and asked him what else he would be looking for. Jobba thought about what he had asked and was embarrassed to answer the question. He moved away from the man and went further down the bank while still looking into the water. The moving water was quite clear, and he could see to the bottom in many areas. Finally, he got to a spot where he saw something glittering from a shallow place not too far off from the shore. He waded out to it and reached down to pick it up. It was a necklace of some kind that had probably been left there from the days when the Powhattan Indian tribe occupied the land. Carefully picking it up and looking it over he noticed it was very shiny and had markings on it he didn't understand. Content that he now had something he could use as the required offering, he made his way back to his cabin and gingerly walked upstairs to show it to Myanna.

He presented it to her, and she hesitated at first to even look at it, but when she did she reached out and took it. Then she told him how beautiful she thought it was and it looked like something that could have belonged to the indians that were there before them. Coninuing she went on to tell him it may have belonged to a maiden and it shouldn't be used for what he was intending to do with it. He laughed and ignored her admonition then went about developing his plan to carry out the mission tonight. There was nothing more she could say to him, so she went downstairs and sat at the table. Both Penniman and Tralene were still down at the river fishing. Jobba continued making his preparation for what he was about to do. In his mind were the notions of just how he was going to do it - what he was going to say and just how he was going to make his pitch to get the spirit to grant him his request.

Myanna sat there for a long time not knowing what else to do. Finally, she went out and down to the river to find Penniman. Not too far from the last cabin on the row, she found him sitting on the bank with his fishing line in the water. Quickly she walked up to him and told what Jobba was planning and asked what she should do. Penniman hardly moved and his expression didn't even change when he answered her.

"Woman yo man is a fool. I dun tol him `bout what happin to de othas dat do what he thinkin. If'n he wanna go, ain nuthin you kin do, but know dis, when he come back, he won be de same. You say he gonna offa sum jew'ry fo de saco'fice, I tell you dat won do no good. De cave spirit don wan no trinkets, what it wants mus have blood in it. Now you go tell yo man dat, b'fo he make it worse den it gonna be"

Myanna heard his words, but was far from comforted by his advice. She got up and ran back to the cabin hoping to make one last minute plea for Jobba to change his mind and to tell him about his sacrifice. When she got there, he was gone so she ran back out to find him. Up and down the quarters she looked, but there was no sign of him. It wasn't dark yet, so she didn't believe he had gone up to the cave. Next she started asking around if anyone had seen him. There was no positive response and she didn't know what to do now, so she turned and slowly walked back to the cabin. Her thoughts were running wild and she sought Linwood to help her find him. Linwood was nowhere to be found either, so she went back inside and sat on her bed.

In the mansion Suliah had come downstairs and now was at the entrance to the kitchen. Before going in she looked and saw Aunt Tee sitting at the table peeling potatoes for the dinner meal. Not sure what kind of reception she was going to get she just stood there. Aunt Tee continuing with her task, looked at her without saying a word for a few minutes. Finally, she motioned to Suliah to come in and sit down opposite her.

For what seemed to her like an hour nothing was said and Suliah was getting anxious about what the woman might be contemplating. In reality it was only minutes before the wizened elder spoke.

"When I was a young gal like you long b'fo I come here I was at a place wit jest a few gals dere. `Round yo age maybe a lil young'r one night de massa come to de cabin an drag me out. He took me to de barn an pull offa my clothes an den he jump on me. De firs time I holler `cause it hurt so bad, but nobody come an stop `em. When he finish he jest lef me dere wit my blood on de ground. I go back to de cabin an my mama she jest shake her head an hol me `cause she caint do nuthin. He come back two three mo times de next week an do de same thing. De las time he come, I say he ain gwin do dat no mo to me an I go to de healin man in de village. De healin man tol me dat if'n I wan him to help me an make de massa stop, den I hafta give him somethin. He didn't wan me he say he wan my inner mind, my soul. I didn' know what dat mean, but it seem good jest ta keep de massa offa me so I say okay. He cut off some o my hair an put it in a cup an den he pour somethin in it an start sayin many funny words. Den he made a fire an pour de cup out in de fire an he keep on sayin de words. B`fo long I feel somethin touch me while he stan'n on the otha side o de fire. I jumped `cause de hand was cold, but I didn't see nuthin. When de healin man finish talking, he tol me I was healed an de massa wouldn' botha me no mo. Den he gave me dis an say wear it alla time an I be safe."

Suliah sat there mesmerized by the story as she looked at the amulet that Aunt Tee wore around her neck under her dress. She wondered to herself just why she was being told all this, but it didn't take long before the answer was given to her when Aunt Tee continued.

"De next time dat man come for me I go to de barn wit him good, but when we git dere b'fo he jump on me, I show him dis an he start chokin an holdin his neck den fall to de ground. I jest stan dere lookin at him turn'n blue den I lef him like he lef me de firs time. He don die, but he neva botha me no mo an then later he sell me way from my mama. You was lucky dis time `cause de young massa come save you. But hear me good now, you a real pretty gal an when de ole massa come fo you, ain nothin the young one be able to do. You listn ta me an I kin help you keep de massa's ole an young offa you. How old are you?"

Suliah answered her and said that she was going to be turning seventeen next month. Aunt Tee then told her that it was the right age for her to become part of the spirits of the cave. Suliah asked what that meant, but Aunt Tee just told her that when she joined this group it would keep her safe. She went on to say that after Suliah's next birthday she would tell her more about how to join. This all seemed a bit scary to Suliah, but then she remembered what happened last night and if what Aunt Tee was telling her would keep that from happening again maybe worse, then she was all for it. She said to Aunt Tee that she wanted to join, but she would have to talk to her father first. Aunt Tee laughed and told her not to worry about that.

Aunt Tee finished talking and asked Suliah whether she was hungry. Suliah said yes and was fixed a plate from the breakfast leftovers. After she finished Aunt Tee told her to go see about Anna Lee who was back in her room. Aunt Tee also told her that this girl was the only one in the house that was really her friend, but to never let her see all of her. Again, Suliah had no idea what Aunt Tee was trying to tell her, but she filed the message in the back of her mind. She got up from the table and made her way back upstairs toward Anna Lee's room. On the way out she met Byron who stopped her and asked how she was doing. She wasn't sure how much he knew about what happened, but she assumed that he knew everything because that's what Anna Lee had said before. She wanted to ask him what happened to the men that attacked her, but thought better of it. Byron looked her over carefully as if inspecting a newly arrived package trying to determine from a visual perusal whether any internal damage had occurred. Satisfied that his prize was still worthy of the top shelf he allowed her to continue on her way.

At Anna Lee's door that was closed, she knocked and waited. There was no immediate response, so she eased the door opened and peeked inside. Anna Lee lying on the bed had gone back to sleep so Suliah turned around and was going to go back downstairs to talk with Aunt Tee some more and maybe even go outside. She could see through Anna Lee's window that the sun was still out even though it had already begun its descent for the day. Aunt Tee was still cooking when she came back so she asked her if there was something that she could help her with. Aunt Tee told that she didn't need help right now, but maybe later she could check back and see. She then asked if it would be okay if she walked down to the cabins to see her father. Aunt Tee hesitated thinking to herself whether Mr. Candle would want her going back to her father knowing that her father didn't approve of her working in the house. She said she thought it would be okay, but for her not to stay too long down there and then come right back before Mr. Candle might notice she was gone.

Suliah made her way outside and into the beautiful sunlight. She was happy to see so many of the cabin dwellers outside and enjoying the day. It didn't take her long before she arrived at her cabin and she wondered whether she should knock since she had lived there. Deciding that knocking wouldn't be necessary because everybody there knew who she was, she opened the door and went inside. There was no one on the first level and she thought maybe everybody was down at the river. However, she heard someone upstairs stirring and she headed to the stairs. Quietly she walked up wanting to surprise whoever it was that was there. When she got to the top of the stairs it was she who got the surprise. She saw Myanna sitting on the bed rocking back forth as if in pain. When she got close, Myanna looked up and reached out and grabbed her. Suliah could see that she had been crying and immediately asked where her father was. Myanna then launched into telling the whole story about what they had learned from Penniman and about the ritual they went through.

Suliah was shocked because she had just heard from Aunt Tee how beneficial it would be if she was part of this cave spirit. When she heard her mother's side of the story it seemed to be just the opposite. She asked when Myanna had last seen her father and where was Linwood. Myanna told her that she didn't know where Linwood was, and she hadn't seen Jobba since early afternoon. It was now about 4:00 p.m. and Suliah told her mother that she couldn't stay here long before they would be looking for her back at the mansion. Myanna told her that her father would be so glad to see her if she could stay just a little while longer. Suliah reminded her that if she didn't know where he was how she could know if he was coming back here before going to the cave. Myanna agreed and said for her to do what she had to. Suliah feeling badly that she didn't get to do what she came to do, and that was to see her whole family, especially her father, was standing at the fork in the road and not sure which path to follow.

With tears in her own eyes she told her mother that she would try to come again tonight if she could slip out of the mansion. Her mother cautioned her about doing anything that would make it bad for her and that she and her father would be okay. Myanna said that she was sure Jobba would come to his senses before going up to that cave because Penniman had told him all the bad that could happen if he did. Suliah said goodbye walked downstairs and out the door. Before starting toward the mansion, she looked around the quarters one more time to see if she could spot her father perhaps milling around with one of the neighbors. She didn't see him or Linwood and now she felt an urgency to make it her mission to sneak out tonight and return. After hearing the story that Aunt Tee told her and then another side to the same story, she wondered if she should confide in her for help in getting out tonight. Her final conclusion was that it was not a good idea and she would be on her own.

As she walked up the path to the mansion, she reviewed in her mind all the places that her mother told that she had looked. Then it occurred to her when she turned her head in that direction that Jobba had been working in the stables of late and could possibly be in there..She was tempted to go there and see, but that would mean she'd have to go by Sam's cabin and she sure didn't want him to see her by herself. Giving up on that idea, she kept walking toward the mansion. Still looking all around her as she walked, the closer she got to the back door the more she felt that something was very wrong with this whole situation here on this farm. Her innermost feelings were rising making her think that there was something even in the air that swirled around this place that was not in keeping with the things that she had heard from the old iterant preacher. He used to come to the old plantation. She was remembering his words even though the last time she saw him she was much younger. But the words that stuck in her mind, even now, were those that said believe in Me and I will deliver you from all your troubles. Somehow now these words kept resonating in her mind, and she wasn't sure why.

Arriving at the door she opened it and walked in. Nobody was in the living room, the parlor or anywhere else in that area so she stopped by the kitchen to see if Aunt Tee was there. To her surprise, she wasn't there either. Suliah began to wonder just where everybody had gone so she went to the front door and looked outside to see if maybe they were out there. Seeing no one there either she went upstairs to the third floor and into her new room. She sat on the bed thinking how she was going to get out tonight and make her way back down the quarters to her father's house. She knew that when the family finished eating on Sundays they all sat around in the parlor for a long while talking and drinking after dinner teas and cordials. They would do this well into the evening hours before anyone would retire from there. She thought there was no way she could get out while they were still in there because one of them could call for her or even see her going out. If she waited until after they retired then it would be dark outside, and she didn't want to be seen with a lantern leaving the house. This was a dilemma that she had no answer for at this point, so she fell back on the bed and took a nap.

As the sun was going down on what had been a gorgeous day, the fishermen at the river started stringing their catch and heading home. Linwood, who had been with his newfound friends all day down at the farthest end of the river, was starting to make his way back to the cabin. They weren't fishing but having a good time enjoying themselves on this day away from their daily toils..Linwood was unaware that Myanna had been looking for him and definitely didn't know that his father was hidden away from the group contemplating something that would affect all of them if he went through with it. Myanna looked out her window and saw that the sun was setting so she got up and went outside hoping to at least see her son. Not long after she got outside she saw him coming with his friends up from the river. She started waving frantically to get his attention and then motioned for him to hurry. Linwood seeing her urgent wave sensed that something wasn't right, so he picked up his pace. He left his friends and quickly got to his mother who hurried him inside. She started telling him all that happened today since he left this morning and even that his sister had been there. He was very disappointed that he missed her, but was now more concerned about where his father was. His mind reflected on the results of a beating that he had seen his father take not too long ago and his first thoughts went to him being under that kind of siege somewhere again.

He asked Myanna when she saw him last and where. She told him, but also said that she looked in all those places and even went up close to the mansion. Linwood was hard pressed to come up with any place new that she hadn't already looked in, but then it came to him as it did to Suliah that there was one place that she hadn't explored. He said to her he might be in the stable where he had been working. As if a unique revelation had been given to her, her face lit up and she conceded that this was a good possibility. They both agreed that the next step was to get to the stable without passing Sam's cabin. While there was still daylight this would not be an easy task because in order to get to the stable from the back way one had to go right by the overseer's place. The only other way was to go around the front of the mansion and come to the stables from the other side. Going this way would be more hazardous in getting spotted and questioned then the back way. It was decided that Linwood would take a chance on the first method and try to sneak past Sam's place without being seen.

He then waited a little while longer to let the sun descend lower and then ventured out and up the path leading toward the mansion. It was twilight time and there was still enough light so that he could see clearly where he was going, but it was also just dark enough that he was able to not stand out. He kept low as he made his way to the stable even almost crawling when he got near Sam's cabin. Once he got by Sam's place he stood up and ran the rest of the way to the far side and crouched under the window. Rising up slowly he got a good look at the whole area. The horses were lined up in the stalls and two of the carriages were parked inside. He let his eyes scan up and down then east and west over the whole building, but there was no sign of Jobba. Disappointed that he had come all this way risking getting caught by the man he knew had inflicted the stripes on his father, he sat down on the ground shrugged his shoulders and sighed. As he was about to get up and quickly make his way back home he heard a noise coming from the other side of the building. He fell back down on the ground and tried to hide behind the few shrubs that were there. His hope was that darkness would suddenly fall and cover him, but inside he knew this wasn't going to happen. He lay there preparing for his consequences and suspected that he was going to be caught by Sam. Suddenly a figure came around to his side. Unable to see him clearly, but he could tell the size of the man was larger than Sam, so he knew it wasn't him. Linwood leaned a little further out from the bush to get a better look when it dawned on him that this was the object of his search.

Before he stood up though, he wanted to be absolutely sure, so he called out in a little more than a whisper.

"Papa, papa is dat you?"

The man quickly moved forward and reached out for Linwood.

"Son dat you?"

"Yes daddy I come lookin for you. Mama say you dun hid somewhere an you gwine up de mountain."

"Yeah I was 'bout ta do dat, but come here firs ta do some thinkin'. Now I gwine back home ain gwine up der. You go on 'head a me an tell yo mama I be dere soon. Firs I gotta do somethin else."

"What you gwine do?"

"Don worry 'bout it, I be fine. Now you go on an I see ya back at de cabin soon. You be careful now an don let massa Sam see you."

"Okay papa."

Linwood again crouching as he moved past Sam's house made his way back to the path leading down to the quarters. He looked back to see where his father was going, but Jobba had already taken off. Darkness was setting in so going back was a bit easier then coming. As he got closer to his cabin he was still wondering what his father was going to do and also whether he should tell his mother. When he got to the house he decided to tell her only what Jobba told him and that was that he would be home soon.

With darkness setting in Jobba headed toward the mansion. He had it on his mind that he was going to see his daughter one way or the other and was determined to do it. He had changed his mind about going to the cave and making his offering because while sitting in the stable something troubled him there and his senses told him not to do it. With that something in his head driving him he was tempted to call on the name of God one more time to see if his condition was still the same, but when he also thought about what Aunt Tee said about testing the cave spirit he dropped the idea. As he got closer to the back door of the mansion he could see there was someone sitting on the porch. Although still too far away to clearly make out who it was, he slowed his pace not wanting to expose himself before he was ready.

Within a few yards of the house, he ducked behind some bushes and peeked through them to get a better look. Slowly he inched closer. When he was close enough to see clearly he could tell that it was Clarence the head slave who had come outside to dump the garbage. Deciding to take a chance Jobba moved close enough for the man to see him and he waved. Clarence looked at him and then looked all around to see if anyone else saw them. Jobba motioned for him to come over, but the man just stood there not moving. Jobba decided then that if he wasn't coming down to him, then he was going up. The man stood there seemingly paralyzed as Jobba got closer.

"You know who I be?"

"Yeah I know, I see'd you when ya firs come here. You dat pretty gal's papa dat be workin in here. What you want here?"

"I jest wanna see her. Kin you git her ta come out chere?"

"I ain gittin in no truble ova you. Why you want her anyway?"

"You got any chilren?"

"Yeah, but not here."

"Don you think `bout dem sometime?

"I thinks `bout dem alla time, but ain nuthin I kin do `bout it."

"Well my gal is here an I kin do somethin `bout it, but I need fo you to git her so I kin tell her. Now kin you do dat fo me?

Clarence looked at Jobba hard, but seemed to be relenting. He was considering what could happen to him if he got caught bringing her out here. In the end he relented and told Jobba he would deliver his message. A short time later Suliah was at the door and Jobba ran to her and hugged her. She was happy to see him, but quickly walked him back down the stairs and over near the bushes. In a soft voice, almost whispering, she told him that she had been at his cabin today and heard from Myanna what he was planning on doing. When she finished telling him what Myanna told her with tears in her eyes, Jobba was sorry. Suliah asked him if he was still going to do it and he answered no. When he said that a smile lit up her face then she told him that she couldn't stay out here long. She told him to look for her at the cabin again next Sunday afternoon. Before she turned away, Jobba reached in his pocket and pulled out the Indian necklace he found in the river and gave it to her. He had shined it up as best he could, believing that it would make a good sacrificial offering. He could see she really liked it and was glad. She kissed him and thanked him then turned away and ran back into the house. Jobba feeling much better now that he had seen her and talked to her by herself, carefully made his way back to the path leading to the cabins.

When he entered, Penniman, Tralene and his kids were seated at the table eating dinner. They just looked at him and said nothing. He said nothing either, but made his way upstairs and ran over to Myanna and Linwood and hugged them. For several minutes they all embraced, but said nothing. Then Jobba started to explain about what happened with him in the stable and the things that came into his head. Myanna told him that she was glad he returned to his senses and then she told him what Penniman said to her about the blood offering. Jobba laughed and said the only blood he was bringing in there was his own and that wasn't part of the offering. They all laughed at that and then went down to join Penniman and his family.

Monday morning came, and Byron was up and out of bed before the horn sounded. He was excited to get his proposals into a legal format and confirm his commitments so he could increase his empire. His feeling of conquest was enforcing his belief that there was nothing he couldn't do by using his conniving methods and powers of persuasion. Once in his parlor he gathered the slips of paper and rushed over to his desk to transfer the contents of the slips to real legal documents. Breakfast hadn't crossed his mind, but when he heard Aunt Tee busy in the kitchen he called out to her to bring him a cup of coffee right away. Responding to his call she sent one of the other house slaves to bring it to him.

He looked at the slips and estimated that he would be in possession of eighteen acres of additional land that would extend from his place all the way to the edge of the county. His hand couldn't write fast enough for him to get all the required information on the deed transfers. When he finished the transfers, he got up and quickstepped down to the stable to get a stable hand to prepare a wagon for a trip to the county registration office. Having made his orders clear he went back in the house, feeling more relaxed that things were under way. He went straight to the dining room and sat there waiting for his breakfast to be served. Once Aunt Tee realized he was back in the house she sent his meal down by Suliah who had been helping her in the kitchen.

When Suliah brought his meal in and set it before him he greeted her warmly and asked her how she was feeling. She smiled and told him that she was much better and feeling fine. He asked her if she liked the room she had and if she needed anything else in there. This caught her by surprise that he should be asking her that and she didn't know what to say. The words that Aunt Tee had said just a few days ago about his interests in her sprung to her mind and she coyly answered him saying she was fine and had all she needed. After she put the plate down and answered his probing questions she quickly exited the room and went back to the kitchen.

Soon Anna Lee, Jethro and Charlotte all came down and the house was abuzz with its normal Monday morning activities. Even Sam had come by to see if there were any special things that Mr. Candle would need for him to do today. Byron finished his breakfast and met Sam at the door as he was going out. He told Sam that the biggest thing was for him to make sure that the planting was finished on all of the cultivated acres. Sam tipped his hat got back on his horse and trotted down to the tobacco fields. Byron went to the stable and saw that Jobba was still working in there. He asked Jobba how he was and when the answer came back that he was okay, he asked Jobba if he wanted to go with him to town and drive the wagon. Jobba was completely surprised and was afraid to say no thinking this was more of an order than a question to which he really had a choice. Byron told him to get on and take the reins. Jobba got up in the wagon and took his seat right in front with Byron. He was totally uncomfortable because he had never sat beside a white man before in the front of a wagon. Then again he thought to himself he had never been a driver before either.

Byron said he was ready to go so Jobba clicked the horse snapped the reins and they started their journey. As they passed the fields all the others could see that Jobba was driving the wagon and when Myanna saw it also she wasn't as pleased as them because she wasn't convinced that this was a good thing. Once they left the side path to the mansion and got on the main road Byron told Jobba that it would be about an hour to get to the county seat so get ready for a good ride. Jobba just nodded his head and they went on. About a half hour into the trip, coming down the road on the other side was another coffle being driven by the same trader that they saw when Jobba came in. This time Byron told Jobba to pull over and stop while he waved down the trader.

The trader tipped his hat and stopped his train when Byron got down and approached him. Byron went up to him and they talked for some time with Byron waving his arms around and pointing to all the land around them. The trader was nodding his head as if in agreement with everything Byron said. When the talking was finished, they shook hands and Byron came back to the wagon. The trader signaled to his helpers and the coffle began moving again. Byron got back in the wagon and he and Jobba resumed their journey. Before long they were at the outskirts of the town where the county office was. As they rode in they passed the general merchandise store, a bank, a tobacco store and several other small stores. There were also many houses lined up along the main street. At the very end of the street was the courthouse where the county seat was. Byron directed Jobba to pull up to the front of the building let him off and then go around to the back and wait for him. He told him also that he would send someone around there to take care of the horse and for Jobba to make sure that the horse was watered and fed. Jobba heeded the command and after Byron dismounted rode the wagon around back.

Byron walked in the building and asked an attendant where the registration office was. He was promptly directed to the second floor and he went up feeling a surge of excitement. When he arrived at the office he opened the door and went in. Seated in the waiting area were the men that he had struck the deals with. He greeted them politely and then went over to the woman at the desk and told her he was there to transfer some deeds along with these gentlemen. The woman got up went in the back office and returned shortly with a rather portly man who must have been in his mid to late forties with balding hair and a long handle bar type mustache. He greeted Byron and the other men and pointed to a room next to his office then directed them to go there and wait for him. The men went in the room and took seats around a long table. None of the men except for Byron looked too happy about being there. Minutes later the county clerk came in the room and asked for the deeds to be transferred. Byron took out his papers and gave them to the man.

Over an hour later the deals were completed and Byron walked out feeling empowered. The other men left also, but no one said a word, not to Byron and not to each other. Byron with the signed papers tucked tightly under his arm went around back to see what the status was on Jobba and the horse. Jobba was there with a hat on that he found in the back of the wagon pulled down low over his head. Byron assumed that he was sleeping, and he was right. He stepped lightly to the wagon and clapped his hands with a loud clap and Jobba almost jumped out of the wagon. Byron who was in an exceptionally good mood now anyway laughed with a deep belly laugh and got up into the wagon. He asked Jobba if he was ready to go home. Jobba nodded yes turned the wagon around and headed back down the main street out of town. On the way Byron directed Jobba to stop at the general store so he could pick up some things for his family.

The trip back seemed shorter than the one going and Jobba was happy when they arrived at the turn off to the mansion path. He turned the wagon onto the path and drove up to the house. Byron got off and told Jobba he did a good job and for him to take the wagon back to the stable. Jobba was having difficulty understanding what had come over this man and why he seemed to be nice to him. He got to the stable un-harnessed the horse and bedded him down then headed to his cabin. It was now only about four-thirty and he knew that Myanna and Linwood would not be at the cabin yet, but he wanted to go and lie down before they got there. When he arrived and went inside Tralene met him at the door. He was surprised to see her, so he asked why she was there. Tralene told him that she had been feeling poorly the last few days and Sam said it would be okay if she went home early. Jobba looked at her to see if he could tell what was wrong, but nothing stood out to him. He told her he was sorry to hear about her condition and hoped she would get better, then made his way up to his bed.

Myanna and Linwood came in sometime later and when they saw Jobba he told them how Mr. Candle had taken him into town and about all that he saw. Myanna told him she saw him leaving and wondered what that was all about. After he explained to her what happened she felt relaxed and began to think that Jobba may have found favor with the headman. She would have been shocked if she could have just spent ten minutes looking inside the headman's mind to see just what schemes were being plotted, many of them included the fate of Jobba and her.

The next day about mid-morning, the trader that Byron had spoken to yesterday, was coming up the road with several slaves walking behind him. Jobba who was still working in the stable, much to Sam's dislike, saw them coming up the road and walked out to the front of the mansion to tend the trader's horse. He was joined by some of the house slaves who had been sent out to greet the trader. Byron, who was alerted that the man was here, came walking out and directed the trader to keep on going taking the coffle down to the tobacco barn across from the stable. The trader heeded the direction and guided his charges that were roped together to follow him. Jobba saw them roped together at the neck and felt deep compassion for them. He followed along behind them to the barn as Byron directed him also.

At the barn, Byron told the trader to free them from the rope and line them up over by the wall. The trader did so. There were four men and one woman. All of the men looked to be in very good condition, all about the age of twenty-five to thirty. The woman was a little overweight for her height, but looked to be strong and healthy and perhaps in her mid-thirty's. Byron went over to the wall and began his inspection. As he stood before each man he told him to open his mouth and he looked at his teeth. Then he felt his arms and his legs and told all of the men to take off their shirts and let him see their backs. He was looking for whipping scars. When he got to the woman he looked in her mouth also and told her to remove her shirt and turn around too. She did so exposing massive breasts that had long ago lost their muscle tone and appeared to have fallen from suckling. He asked her how many children she had, and she said five. Byron turned to the trader and asked him where they were, and the trader said he didn't know. He turned back to the woman and asked the same question; she didn't know either. Byron told them to put their shirts back on and go wait outside while he talked to the trader. Jobba who was still standing there during the inspection saw something strange. As Byron moved down the line examining each man, when he came to the third one, Jobba saw what appeared to be a glow surrounding the man and his demeanor, even while Byron prodded and squeezed him as if checking the produce of his fields for quality, was very calm and serene. The peaceful look on his face gave Jobba the perception that this man was much different than the others.

Jobba paid close attention listening to the bargaining conversation. Byron was haggling with the man attempting to bring the price down, as was his usual buying strategy. This time the trader was resistant and not budging on price. After a long debate it was Byron who finally conceded and paid the full amount.

Byron then turned to Jobba and told him to find Sam and tell him to come to the barn. Jobba shuddered at this command because the last thing he wanted to do was have anything to do with Sam. However, responding to the order he left the barn in search of Sam. He didn't have to go far because Sam had seen the trader coming in also and he knew he would be called soon, so he was already making his way up to the barn. When he saw Jobba he almost ran over him with his horse, but Jobba jumped out of the way falling to the ground. Sam turned around and laughed and kept on going to the barn. Jobba got up and brushed himself off thinking to himself that one day he was going to deal with that man. The trader was coming outside when Sam got to the barn door. The slaves were standing by the barn. Sam got down from his horse and walked inside where Byron was waiting. Byron told him to take these new arrivals to the quarters and get them settled in and then come up to the house because he had to tell him about all the new land that they now owned.

Sam went over to the line and started in hollering at all of them, as he usually did, to put the fear of him in them right away. He went through his explanation about what the routine was for the place, how they would be fed and about the horns. Jobba was nearby and looked at them as they stood passively listening to his words. The trader put the rope around them again, so they were yoked together as before. Then Sam on his horse took the rope and trotted along while they were running behind him down to the quarters. Jobba noted this also and added it to his retribution list. Before they got to the cabins one of the men fell and was being dragged along. Jobba saw that it was the same man who had the strange glow, but it didn't seem to help him. Sam feeling the pull on the rope turned around saw the man on the ground and stopped. The last thing he wanted was for Byron to see him damaging slaves that were just bought. They arrived at the last cabin on the left just before the river and Sam told the men this was where they would live. He took the woman to another cabin where two families already were living and told them while laughing that they had a new house-guest.

When the horn sounded to end the workday Jobba as he usually did looked over to the fields to see if he could see Myanna and Linwood coming. He saw Myanna walking with Penniman and Tralene, but no Linwood. Linwood had lately been spending a lot of time with some of the boys from one of the other cabins, so Jobba was not overly concerned. He went out to meet them at the head of the path to the quarters just in front of Sam's cabin and told them about the new arrivals. Penniman said to Jobba that he hoped they would be able to go to the mansion in time to get their instructions from Aunt Tee. Jobba asked him what he was talking about and Penniman reminded him that tomorrow there would be another full moon and it would be time to do the dance again. Myanna picked up on the conversation and looked at Jobba wondering if he was going to participate in the ritual again. He looked back at her and then excused himself from the group saying that he was going down to the new arrival's cabin to welcome them. Penniman tried to restrain him by telling him not to talk to them before Aunt Tee did, but Jobba wouldn't heed the warning.

Jobba didn't go directly up to the door, but circled around the cabin to see if there was anything strange about it since they arrived. Seeing nothing that looked out of the ordinary, he went up to the door and started to knock when he heard voices coming from inside. These voices weren't just talking, but it seemed that something else was going on. He knocked lightly on the door and after a few minutes when there was no response he quietly pushed it open. The door was opened wide enough for him to see the men kneeling in a semi-circle on the floor while the man with the glow was in the center with his arms lifted in the air. In front of them was a wooden cross about twelve inches long that had been tacked to the wall. As Jobba moved closer he heard the man say: "Thank God A'mighty in Jesus name we pray. Amen!"

Jobba hadn't heard these words in quite some time and as he moved in closer almost right up to the circle the pain that he had felt before returned and he stopped and clutched his chest. The leader of the circle sensed his presence and arose and turned around. He looked at Jobba in his discomfort and stretched his arms out to him. Jobba tried to recover and properly greet the man, but the more he attempted to get close to him the greater the pain became. The man sensing something was wrong lowered his arms and said: "I am Daniel, the preacher man and these are my friends. Why have you come here?. Jobba still holding his chest tried to speak, but it was not until he had stepped away and moved back several paces that he was able to get any words out.

"I am Jobba I come ta talk ta you `bout dis place an all dat go on here. If'n you ain met wit de head woman in de mansion den lem'e tell you ta watch out fo her. She gwine try an git y'all ta come to de cave in de mountain an do de dance. I see y`all ain got yo food yet so I guess ya ain bin dere. She dun put a spell on me an my wife an dis why I got dis pain here."

"Thank you Jobba for your words. We know what goes on here and we have been sent to see how bad it is. Now hear my words to you, when you see me away from this house, you must not let them know that I am a preacher until such time that I say to you it is well. Call me Daniel. The pain that you feel will be healed, but not right now. You must not continue to serve one who is not worthy. Now go back to your wife and let her know what you have seen and for her not to fear."

When Jobba heard these words and the way that they were spoken, he was sure now that there was definitely something different about this man. Although he could not get any closer now than before, the pain he felt was subsiding. He wasn't sure it was because of what the man said or because of the fact that he had moved further away from him. Whatever it was, he knew that the spell on him was real and it had everything to do with what happened to him and Myanna at the last dance. While still looking at Daniel and his friends he eased backward toward the door and stepped outside. On the other side of the door he turned and quickly moved toward his own cabin.

Once inside he bypassed Penniman and Tralene who were seated at the table and went upstairs. Myanna and Linwood were there, and he called them over to the small table and told them to sit down while he told about his visit to the new arrivals. The words were coming out in such a torrent that Myanna had to tell him to slow down so they could understand him. He took a deep breath and started again. When he explained what he felt when he got close to this man and how he seemed to glow when he first saw him in the barn, Myanna didn't know what to think. Linwood thought it was funny. Myanna then asked Jobba whether the man said anything about going to the dance tomorrow. Jobba responded that the man said that they shouldn't serve one that was not worthy of being served. Myanna then reminded Jobba about what Penniman said concerning those who defied Aunt Tee's warnings. Jobba said to her that he saw something in this man and heard something in his voice that made him feel like he was the one that he should listen to – not Aunt Tee. Myanna who had not experienced any of the pains that Jobba did because she had not tried to test the cave spirit was tempted to do something just to see and she told Jobba this. He persuaded her not to and she didn't.

The next morning after the horn sounded it was Clarence who came to the cabin of the new arrivals to escort them to the mansion to get their rations. When he got to the door he knocked and before getting a response went inside. The four men were seated at the table as if they were just waiting for him to come. He told them that he was there to take them to get their food for the rest of the week and they should bring something to carry it in if they had anything. Daniel responded for the group and said that they had bags that could be used. Clarence also noticed something different about this man and he was cautious about getting too close to him. Although he was not stricken with pain when near the man, he did feel a strange sense of loss of power. The men got up followed Clarence out the door and got into the wagon headed to the mansion.

Clarence pulled up to the back of the mansion and told the men to go up to the door knock and wait until Aunt Tee came to answer. The four men did as told and dismounted with their bags in hand. At the door that was closed they knocked and waited. There was no response for some time and Clarence who was still sitting in the wagon wondered what was wrong. He started to get down go up to the door and go inside when it opened. Aunt Tee had been busy attending to Byron's needs and was held up. She got to the door and the three men were in front of Daniel, so she invited them in. However, when Daniel stepped inside the house and passed by her she felt a shudder run down her spine and she turned to take a closer look at him. Not being able to see anything that was outstanding or different about him she just cast off the feeling as perhaps being caught in a draft when the back door was opened. As was her custom she told the men to wait in the kitchen while she prepared their rations and left the room.

When she returned she started filling each of their bags with the specified quantity of goods. The first three men held their bags open and she loaded the rations in with no problem, but when she came to Daniel as he held out his bag she accidentally touched his hand and a strong shock ran through her body. She jumped and looked directly into his eyes. For a moment they were both locked in a confrontational stare, but the episode quickly passed. Aunt Tee knew then that this was no ordinary man and she had to quickly convert him or there would be trouble. She finished filling their bags. Then as they were getting ready to leave Aunt Tee's smile disappeared and the cave spirit took over.

"On tonight at midnight when de moon is full you mus come an do de dance at de cave."

Daniel and his friends heard what she said and as they looked at her each of them just nodded and walked out.

The four men walked back to the cabin with their bags slung over their shoulders. Jobba could see them from the stable when they left the mansion. He wanted to run out to them and find out what happened when they met Aunt Tee, but he saw Sam fast approaching the group, so he quickly changed his mind. Sam galloped his horse right up to the first man and stopped short just in front of him. He told him and the rest of them that as soon as they put their rations away they were to come back here and he would show them where they were to work. The first man stopped his pace and looked up at Sam staring directly into his eyes. Sam was furious and launched into his tirade about no slave could eyeball him. He reached for his whip and unfurled it getting ready to strike. After he shook it out to its full length he raised his arm getting ready to bring it down again hard across the man's chest, Daniel raised his arms and it was as if an unseen hand reached out and pulled Sam from his saddle throwing him on the ground. Sam was so stunned at what just happened he didn't know what to do next, so he just lay there looking at the men. Without hesitation they turned away from the fallen body and continued on their way down the quarters.

Jobba witnessed the incident and couldn't believe what he was seeing. What kind of men are these that could make someone fall off a horse without even touching him he thought? If it happened any other way, seeing Sam get back some of what he deserved Jobba would have laughed, but this was no ordinary act of retribution by an ordinary man. Sam recovered from his initial shock stood up brushed himself off and while still looking at the men walking down the quarters lane thought hard about what just happened. He couldn't decide whether to get on his horse and pursue them with the intent of inflicting the punishment he had in mind or go back to the fields and take it out on some other poor slave. He chose to do the latter.

The rest of the day in the fields was extremely hard for the workers because Sam's ire had been aroused and for no other reason than he could do what he wanted, he wielded his whip as the means to pacify his anger and the brunt of the punishment fell on all who came within striking distance. Even Linwood, who happened to be in an area that was under scrutiny because it seemed that the crops were beginning to fail, caught one or two strokes from the lash. He recoiled from the lashing and fell prostrate to the ground. Myanna who was nearby saw him go down and ran over to shield him from the next onslaught. Sam saw her cover Linwood up and started to exact the same on her, but for some reason he relented and moved away. Myanna held Linwood up and examined him. The blows were apparently less severe than how they looked from a distance. Linwood was more shocked than hurt. He stood up and went back to work. Myanna went back to her area.

No horn sounded at the usual time because Sam was still in a foul mood and wanted to prolong the day. But when it finally did the slaves who all knew that tonight was their special night and they had to be ready moved at a quick pace from the fields and into their cabins. Jobba who had tried to wait for Myanna was not obedient to the horn sound and left the stable when he thought it was time and went home. Myanna and Linwood along with the other cabin family arrived sometime later. Jobba was upstairs lying down when they came in. Myanna rushed upstairs to tell Jobba what happened with Linwood. Upon hearing the story Jobba jumped up from the bed and went to exam his son. Satisfied that there was no extensive harm done he went back to Myanna who was sitting on the bed and told her what he saw with the new arrivals. He then told her that they weren't going to the cave tonight. Myanna was a little confused about how she really felt. On one side she was afraid for them not to go, but then after what Jobba just told her about these new men she felt comfort in his decision.

Nightfall came quickly and just as before the seemingly abandoned road, at an earlier hour at midnight once again became the path for the parade. The slaves lined up and with their lanterns casting off an eerie collective illumination began to make their way in a slow procession up to the mountain. This time for the first time they were joined by the four new arrivals. The four men came out of their cabin with no lanterns and joined the throng. They fell in at the end of the line and moved along with them. Anyone who turned around to see them would wonder how they were negotiating the darkness. Were they able to follow along by the dim light from those ahead of them or were they able to see clearly by means of a different light?

Inside Jobba's cabin Penniman and Tralene were pleading with Jobba not to do what he was planning. They spent more time than they should in the effort and when finally convinced that he had really made up his mind not to go, they walked out the door to see the procession had moved quite a ways ahead of them. Both of them jogged briskly to catch up with their lanterns swinging beside them. Jobba peeked out the door behind them and saw the lights from the lanterns disappearing as they moved away from the quarters. He went back inside held Myanna and said to her that they would know before morning what would be. Linwood while all this was going on had gone to sleep because he was exhausted and still somewhat shocked from the result of Sam's outrage.

As the procession moved closer to the opening of the cave, again the orange glow from inside illuminated the approach. Penniman and Tralene had caught up with the group, but were behind the new arrivals. When they entered the new arrivals stopped at the opening and positioned themselves around the perimeter. Penniman and Tralene thought that because they were new they were just waiting to see how things went. They moved past the men and took their places in the circle swaying to the rhythm of the drums. At the front of the circle again Aunt Tee was into her chanting raising her arms to the images on the back of the wall and praising the pole. The rhythm started moving faster and again the robed man with the incense threw some in the fire that sent it soaring higher than ever. The crackling from the flames sent the worshipers into a fury and with their violent movements arms were flailing and legs stepping. Suddenly just as before, the drums stopped, and the group fell to their knees except the four men.

The robed man came before them and escorted each up to the front of the circle. They willingly were led and took their place at the front of the cave standing before Aunt Tee. The men were directed to kneel, but when they refused she motioned the robed man away and was going to carry out the ritual anyway. She took her brush and dipped it into the chicken's blood, but when she drew it out it was not saturated with blood, but was wet with plain water. Suddenly the wall again came alive and the beast of the cave issued forth with fury and hurled itself toward the men. Aunt Tee dived aside and watched from the ground as Daniel lifted his arms and called on the name of the Lord. The flash that took place at that moment was so bright that all who saw it were temporarily blinded. When the brightness returned to just the light of the fire and the lanterns the beast was gone and the four men stood before the crowd. Aunt Tee stared at the wall wondering what had happened to her protector. The pole had toppled on its side and the snakes that were on it were just embers.

"You have just seen the power of the one true God and yet you do not understand. You have come here to sacrifice before an idol that does not care about you one who takes from you yet does not give back. Hear my words and be admonished, do not continue in idol worship and praise one who is not worthy. All of you who want to be released from the curse that you are under, meet with us down by the riverside tomorrow night and you shall be dipped in the water and be cleansed."

When Daniel finished speaking he and the other three men casually walked to the rear of the cave and exited. Again, without the need for any lantern they made their way confidently down the mountain and back to their cabin. Inside the cave the worshipers were in awe at the spectacle and were looking to Aunt Tee for guidance. She got up from the ground and turned to the wall for guidance herself. Nothing happened. She dismissed the group by saying that she was going to pray to the cave spirit after they left, and she would let everyone know tomorrow what the outcome was and what they should do. The group slowly broke up and exited the cave. On the way down many of them began to itch uncontrollably and in the midst of scratching to gain relief they threw themselves down on the ground rolling over and over. Penniman and Tralene were spared from this episode, but they were fearful that they would not see tomorrow.

The crowd, some moving slowly and scratching, others running wildly in an effort to outrun the agony made their way back to their cabins. There was none among them who understood exactly what was happening, but they all remembered the words that the four men spoke before they left. If this was going to be the result of not going to the river and being dipped, then they couldn't wait for tomorrow night to come so they could get cleaned. Even in their agony there were some who relied on Aunt Tee and were going to wait to hear from her before doing anything with Daniel at the river.

In the wee hours of the morning Jobba and Myanna were still awake wondering what was going on in the cave. He kept feeling a strange sensation coming over him at different intervals and he asked if she felt the same thing. This time she said that she did and asked him if he thought that what Penniman had said to them was beginning to come true. Jobba answered her and said that after he saw what that man Daniel could do, he believed more in the new arrivals than in anything Penniman had to offer. They held each other awhile longer, but then their fight against the inevitable was lost and they lay on the bed fully clothed and went to sleep.

The morning came the horn sounded and the call went out across the plantation for all to start a new day. Penniman awoke and looked at Tralene to see if there was anything different about her. He examined himself also and except for the remains of the grease paint they had used for the ritual it appeared that everything was normal. He got up and went to look at the kids to make sure they were okay also. Satisfied that all appeared to be right with them he said to Tralene: "Do dis mean de spell be broken?"

Tralene sat up and just looked at him having no answer to give.

Moments later as Penniman was getting himself cleaned up and ready to start his day, Linwood came running down the stairs.

"Mista Penniman, mista Penniman come see come see."

He grabbed hold of Penniman's arm and started dragging him to the stairs. Penniman moved as best he could to keep up with the youth as he was being pulled. Tralene hearing the commotion quickly got out of bed and ran behind them. Linwood ran halfway up the stairs then turned around reached back and again grabbed Pennimon's arm. When they got to top of the stairs Pennimon, although he had talked about it many times was not prepared for what he was about to see. He cautiously negotiated the last step and finally stood on the second level gazing over into the far corner. His eyes beheld it, Tralene saw it too, but neither was ready to believe it.

Chapter 4 - Change Time

Well into the wee hours of the morning Aunt Tee remained in the cave kneeling before the images on the back wall trying to entice the beast to appear again. She drifted in and out of her trance-like state chanting with all of her deepest emotions imploring the return of her idol. Sunlight began to appear at the cave entrance and she saw it but refused to leave until some response was granted. She took the amulet that was around her neck and raised it up begging the idol, which she believed had been her protector since childhood, to remember the promise made to her by the healing man. Pausing for a minute she looked over at the pole that had fallen to the ground and wondered whether the beast's failure to reappear was because of this. She got up quickly and drove the pole into the ground once again between the wall images, then continued chanting. She knew time was running out for her not to be in the mansion before she would be missed so in one last desperate effort she called on the name Beelzebub.

Suddenly the cave went completely dark as if a solid door at the entrance had closed off all access to light. There was a loud roar a clap of thunder and the beast emerged. The impact of the roar caught her by surprise and she fell backward on the ground. Looking up at the beast that was staring down at her with eyes blazing and arms outstretched in anger, she tried to recover and assume a kneeling position before it. Unable to move regain her balance and get up she rolled over and lie prostrate on the ground. With her face to the ground she heard the beast lambaste her for being an ineffective servant and not being able to successfully confront her nemesis. She lay cowering taking the abuse and asking for forgiveness. The beast continued in an angry voice and told her that if she wanted to redeem herself and keep her status she had to confront the one called Daniel. She was further told that to reinforce her position as a leader she must take advantage of what he had done to the ones that failed to appear at the ritual last night.

Aunt Tee wasn't quite sure what he was referring to, but when she got up and looked at the wall the beast showed her the reflections of the bodies of Jobba and Myanna lying on their beds in the cabin. She knew then that she could reclaim her people and again get them to fear the cave spirit by telling them what happened to Jobba and Myanna. She would emphasize that their plight was because of their disobedience. After she was shown this, the idol melted back into the wall and once again light flowed into the cave. Aunt Tee realizing that she had overstayed her time exited quickly and ran down the mountain trying to beat the sound of the horn and get to her room. She moved through the brush and made her way to the mansion back door hoping that no one had gotten up yet. Pausing at the door she looked around. It was apparent that inside the activity for the day had not begun so she opened the door and quietly moved to the back and into her room.

Once she was in the room that was shared with Clarence she looked over at him in his bed to see whether he was okay. Last night Clarence, who was the robed man with the incense, was one of those who suffered from the itching episode as they ran down the mountainside. He appeared to be back to normal. Her curiosity was getting the best of her about the couple. She wanted to run back outside and down to the quarters to see for herself the condition that the cave spirit had left the Thomas's in. Feeling re-empowered by the evil spirit she was even anxious to meet this Daniel man again. However, knowing that going back out right now wouldn't be the wisest thing for her to do before she had taken care of what was expected of her in the house, she eased over to Clarence and gently shook him awake. After explaining to him what the spirit told her she exhorted him to get up now go to the cabin and witness the punishment. Clarence upon hearing these words got excited knowing that his idol had not disappeared, but was indeed exacting revenge for the interruption of its ceremony. Aunt Tee assured that he was going to do what she asked changed her clothes and went in the kitchen to start preparing breakfast.

The first morning horn sounded almost simultaneously with the crow of the cock and the plantation activity for the day was begun. In cabin number ten where the four new arrivals were housed Daniel along with the others was up and getting ready to face the day. Before going out they knelt before the cross and offered up their exaltation and the sacrifice of praise. During this brief communion it was given to Daniel to know that on this day he would be challenged to make believers out of all those who were willing and to baptize them with the power of the Holy Spirit. He was further advised that a situation near him needed his attention. It was unclear to Daniel just what this meant, but he knew from many past experiences that he would be led accordingly. The four finished praying got up and went out.

When they were outside no more than a few steps up the road headed toward the fields they saw Clarence stepping quickly coming in the opposite direction. They paused to see what his urgency might be and to give Daniel a chance to allow his spirit to direct him. Clarence arrived at cabin number 4 without knocking burst in the door. Seeing only the children on the first level he rushed to the stairs where he saw Tralene, Penniman and Linwood standing in awe looking back toward the far end of the room. He scampered up the stairs and moved them aside and then he saw it too.

At the end of the room where the bed was, sprawled out over it were the bodies of Jobba and Myanna. Their appearance was as if all the blood had been drained from them and their ashen faces failed to reflect any signs of life. Their eyes were wide open, but there was no light in them. Their arms were folded across the body as if placed there by the gravedigger and they lay side by side. Clarence felt a sense of delight being assured that what Aunt Tee said about this punishment was true, but he wanted to make sure so he moved closer to get a better look. As he stood over the couple his joy lost some of its elation. Even though they lay motionless, he could see from the slight movement of the chests of both of them that life was yet still inside. Clarence wanted to touch them to see if their hearts were in fact still beating, but he was afraid. Not sure just what to do next he turned around and ran past the onlookers down the stairs and out the door. He couldn't wait to tell his discovery to Aunt Tee.

Daniel and the others seeing Clarence fleeing back toward the mansion, walked to the cabin that he came out of. The door was still open, as Clarence left it, so they went inside. It was then that Daniel felt a strong and moving urge that this was the situation to which his attention should be given. The four men saw the children still sitting at the table but from their appearance they knew that this was not the issue. They then moved over to the stairs and looked up. The group just as before was still standing looking at the couple without knowing just what to do for them. Daniel made his way up and parted the group so he could see what they were looking at. When he saw it was Jobba, the man who had visited him upon his arrival and warned him about the plantation, he felt compassion.

Daniel walked over to the bed and invited his associates to come and form a circle around the couple shielding them from the view of the onlookers. The men joined hands one to the other and with one free hand Daniel placed his on Jobba and the end man placed his on Myanna. Daniel looked up and started to pray. He prayed fervently joined by the others chiming in for several minutes. Penniman, Tralene and even Linwood heard the words of the preacher and felt a tingling sensation inside. It was a moving feeling that was foreign to them, but so warm and comforting they didn't want for it to end. Daniel's eyes still focused on the heavens felt a surge of power move through his body and he knew that his prayers were again being answered. When he looked down at the couple a change began to take over.

Where color had been absent a rich brown hue was present, where the eyes had been vacant a sparkle moved in, where their chests rose and fell slightly from shallow breathing, they now inhaled and exhaled with the fervor of the cry of a new born child. The signs of life were no longer in question and as they returned to their normal health states, both of them blinked three times. Daniel gave thanks in closing and the group disengaged from the link. Jobba and Myanna sat up and looked around. Jobba's first question was what happened? Daniel said nothing, but turned and led his group down the stairs and out the door. Penniman and Tralene continued to stand there still unsure themselves about what just happened but Linwood ran over and wrapped his arms around his parents with tears in his eyes.

While they were all still bewildered by the events that just occurred, the second horn sounded and the thought that they weren't where they were supposed to be popped in their heads. Jobba still reeling from his experience got up from the bed and walked downstairs. Myanna disoriented as well was helped up by Linwood and followed behind him. Penniman and Tralene came down moments later. There was no sense of urgency in their movements and no one ran to exit the cabin to get to the fields. The feeling that seemed to be inside all was that after what they just went through and saw, there was nothing that Sam could do that would harm them. Even so, they got themselves together and went to the fields.

Sam and the other overseers saw the group coming, but for some reason paid no attention as they took their places and started working. Jobba was no longer working in the stable after his trip with Mr. Candle and he was again relegated to the hard labor of the fields just like the rest. He was puzzled though as was the rest of his cabin family about why nothing was said or done to them for being late for work, but just as he was going over it in his mind he saw in the far distance standing on the top of a hill that Daniel was watching over the fields.

In the mansion kitchen Clarence had come running in and blurted out what he saw at Jobba's cabin. He told Aunt Tee that indeed the couple had been stricken with what seemed like a paralyzing punishment, they were not dead but just lay there. He went on to say that although they appeared to be all but dead they were still breathing. Aunt Tee went on with her task as she listened to his words and she finally responded.

"De cave spirit dun tol me dat dey be punish, didn' say dey be dead. When all de people see dat deycaint move no mo, den dey know it was him who did it. Den dey come back to de cave an do de dance agin. Now you go on 'bout yo work. When de massa see dat dey ain good fo nothin he gwine hafta ta sen 'em away an ev'rybody know why."

Clarence left the kitchen and went on about his chores. By this time Byron and the rest of the Candles had all come downstairs and were in the dining room waiting on breakfast. Anna Lee asked her father about the new slaves he bought and whether any of them were going to be coming to the house. He quickly answered no while looking at Charlotte. He then explained to his young daughter that he had recently acquired some more land and that all of these new ones would be used to work those fields. Byron was curious about why she asked because she had never taken such an interest in new arrivals before. She told her father that when she saw them walking up the road behind the trader, there seemed to be something different about one of them. He asked her what she meant, but she couldn't explain it any further. Byron made a mental note of this and dropped the subject.

After breakfast Byron decided he would go and check on his crops and then ride out to the new lands and see just what had to be done. He stopped by the field where Jobba was working and could see that the tobacco plants there weren't doing at this point as well as he thought they should be. He saw Sam and motioned him to come over. Acknowledging the call Sam started toward him. When Sam got there Byron asked what was happening to the crops. Sam responded that they weren't doing so great because it hadn't rained for awhile, but he didn't think this short drought was anything to worry about yet. Byron took his word and moved along. He rode on to the newly acquired acreage and went up the hill to where Daniel and his companions were working. All four of these men were working close together and Byron thought this was a little unusual so he called one of the other overseers over and asked him about it.

"Why dese niggahs workin' so close tageth'r? Dey kin git more done if they be spread out caint they?"

"Yas suh boss, but when dey gits too far `part seem like dey caint work at'all."

"What you talkin' `about man, you soun crazy?"

"Yeah I know suh, but leme show ya what I mean."

He rode closer to the group and while Byron was watching, instructed them to separate and move farther apart. He told one to move over here another to move over there and so forth. They heeded his instructions and went to where he directed them, but the farther they were separated from each other it seems that their strength was drained and they began to droop. Byron saw this in disbelief and hollered at the overseer.

"You know what they need so git to it. I don believe I paid good money fo no good fa nuthin niggahs. Now you make `em work no matta where dey be or you gonna be outta here, you hear me?"

"Yas suh boss," the man replied as he unfurled his whip and headed toward one of the group. When he got close enough he struck the first one with a sharp motion and the man simply stood there and looked at him. There was no reaction to the blow and this infuriated the overseer who knew that Byron was watching. He drew back his arm and struck again with an even sharper blow, but again the impact seemed to have no effect. He rode around to the back side of the man and again struck, with the same result. On top of the lashes having no affect, the man continued to stare right into the eyes of the overseer and said nothing nor did he fall to the ground. Totally frustrated, the overseer got down from his horse and ran up to the man with the intention of striking him with his fists. When he got close to the man and looked directly in his eyes his forward motion was curtailed and his strength left him. He stumbled forward trying to maintain his balance, but when he got to the man all he could do was fall on him grabbing his shoulders to hold on. The man held him up and gently pushed him back away from his body.

The overseer felt a sharp pain surge through his body so he turned got back on his horse and rode up to Byron. Byron saw all that happened and again in disbelief took his anger out on the overseer telling him he was through here and to pack up his belongings and get off of his land. The overseer wasted no time in getting out of the area because he sensed that something unnatural was going on here. Byron just stared at the field worker and his mind went back to what his daughter said at breakfast. The group drifted back together and continued to work at what they were doing. Byron, not knowing what else to do at that point, galloped back to where Sam was and told him what happened. Sam, remembering what happened to him just the other day, was reluctant to get involved again with that group, but fearing for his job told Byron that he would look into it when he finished here. Byron satisfied that Sam could handle the situation left the area and went back to the house.

Around the plantation all the workers were talking about what happened last night both in the cave and at Jobba's house. The communications grapevine was swift and there was hardly anyone on the grounds that didn't know all that went on. The challenge that had been offered by Daniel in the cave about coming to the river tonight to be cleansed was resonating with many of them and they were anticipating going. However, there were those who had gotten Aunt Tee's message about the cave spirit punishing Jobba, so they were leaning toward sticking with her. By late afternoon there was a distinct division between the factions. Those that sided with Aunt Tee had no intention of going to the river. Those that were with Daniel could hardly wait.

Just before the horn was to sound ending the workday, Sam rode up the hill as he had promised Byron and came near to the group. They were still working in close proximity and doing their chores at a leisurely pace. Sam observed that none of them seemed to be putting much effort into what they were doing and his first mind told him to step in and encourage them to pick up the pace. His second thought was that of being cautious responding to what Mr. Candle had said a short time earlier. He was about to ignore his second mind and charge in toward the group when the horn sounded long and hard. Instead of charging toward the group he turned the horse and galloped down the hill.

It was a strange day for Jobba and Myanna. Although they felt completely recovered from whatever it was that they had gone through, and they still weren't sure what that was, as they toiled in the fields they didn't feel at all tired when they knew they should be exhausted. When they heard the horn sound Jobba looked to see where Myanna and Linwood were and then he met them at the top of the quarters road to go home. On the way walking down to the cabins Jobba turned around to see whether the preacher man and his group were following them. There was no sign of any of them. Not only had they seemed to disappear from the fields, but Jobba had a strange feeling inside that they were never actually there at all. Every few paces he turned around to see whether his instinct would be confirmed. Myanna noticed what he was doing and asked about it. He told her about his feeling and she said that she felt strangely about them also, but didn't believe they were not really there.

At dinner that night the conversation centered around who was going to the river and who wasn't. Penniman was not yet convinced even though he saw the recovery of Jobba and Myanna first hand this morning. He was still more afraid of Aunt Tee and the cave spirit than he was in awe of the power of the preacher man. Jobba was wholly convinced that if the preacher man was still here he and Myanna were going to the river and be baptized. Just as Penniman pleaded before with Jobba not to go to the cave before time, Jobba was now imploring Penniman and Tralene to come to the river at the proper time.

The more Penniman resisted and gave his reasons Jobba felt compelled to get them to go and he gave his rebuttals. The rest of the early evening was spent in the back and forth argument and defense of why and why not should they do this thing. The children from both families heard all the talking, but were confused about the whole thing so they said nothing.

Later that night when the sun was completely down and it was dark, Jobba and Myanna who had finished with Penniman and gone upstairs looked at each other. It was time for them to go and a certain excitement was coming over both. Jobba who was sitting at the table motioned to Myanna who was sitting on the bed to join him and go down. Before they left, Jobba asked Myanna whether she thought that Linwood should go also, but she said let us find out first what it is like and then do for him what is called for. Jobba agreed and they descended the stairs. Penniman was waiting at the bottom still not thoroughly convinced that he should go, but he told Jobba he wanted to see what it was all about. Tralene elected not to go, but decided to wait until her mate returned and learn from him what would be best for her. Jobba and Penniman picked up lanterns lit them and went out followed by Myanna.

As they moved toward the river they could see smoke from the fire and wondered if it could be seen from the mansion. The closer they got they could hear the sound of someone singing. Once inside the perimeter they could see the blazing fire and many of their neighbors sitting around in a semi circle. At the semi circle opening Daniel stood with a book in his hand while one of his associates sang a hymn. At first the associate sang alone, but after he had sung the first verse he motioned for the assembly to join with him in the next. Most of the slaves there had never heard this song before, but through the process of call and response the associate was able to teach them. Within a brief period all the patrons were singing along as if they always knew the words.

Wade in the water,
Wade in the water children
Wade in the water,
God's gonna trouble the water
If you don't believe I've been redeemed
God's gonna trouble the water
I want you to follow him on down to Jordan's stream
(I said) My God's gonna trouble the water
You know chilly water is dark and cold
(I know my) God's gonna trouble the water
You know it chills my body but not my soul
(I said) my God's gonna trouble the water

They sang with such feeling that the emotions stimulated by the words of the song were already preparing them for what was to come next. The heat of the fire was cool compared to the fever that was building up within the souls of all who sat around it. When the singing finished, Daniel rose up and started preaching in the night air.

"My brethren where can you run that God will not see you. Where can you hide that He shall not find you. If you were to flee to the furthermost parts of the earth, He Would find you there. He knows your rising up in the morning and your lying down at night. He knows your suffering and He knows about your toil. Though your toiling may be hard and your days may be long, there are better days ahead. As He did for the children of Israel when He led them out of Bondage in the land of Egypt, so shall He do for you at the proper time.

He has given you a savior who has come on your behalf and His name is Jesus. To become free even while a slave you must become one of His own. Join with Him now and be set free - `he who believes and is baptized will be saved, but he who does not believe will be condemned.'" (Mt. 16:16)

When Daniel finished preaching and invited the throng to join him in the water and be baptized there was such a rush to the water that it was hard for the four to control the onslaught. Jobba looked at Myanna and felt the urge to get in the water also and she was right by his side. One by one, they stepped up to Daniel and his associates and were dipped in the water and immersed completely. When they came up many exclaimed the words I'm free and many said Hallelujah recalling days long ago when the last itinerant preacher was allowed on the grounds. Jobba and Myanna were both baptized and the spell that had been cast on them was completely broken and washed away.

Baptizing went on well into the night until all who had come to the river were dipped in the chilly waters. When all had completed the act and confessed their belief and commitment to the Lord, Daniel's associate led them in a final hymn and then they departed for their cabins. This new feeling that possessed both Jobba and Myanna was so overwhelming that each of them wanted to run, not walk, back to the cabin to tell Linwood. Jobba even wanted to run right up to the mansion in the middle of this night break open the doors and tell Suliah and everybody in there how he felt. He was saved and he wanted the world to know.

Several weeks went by after the initial gathering at the river. Daniel continued to hold his meetings twice a week, but with the exception of Linwood there were no new converts. Jobba and Myanna had convinced Linwood to become a believer, but Suliah remained outside of the covenant circle. Tension between the factions was growing and throughout the plantation there was a sense of an imminent confrontation. Although none of them would allow their differences to cause neither the overseers nor the headman to be aware, even so, interactions with each other was strained. Aunt Tee and Clarence continued with their rituals and those that were dedicated to that end followed them. The division between the groups had separated them into almost equal amounts with a little more than half continuing to follow Aunt Tee.

Outside the mansion tensions among the slaves was prominent to those who could recognize it. Inside however, other things were happening that were not tense at all. Jethro could no longer hide his infatuation with Suliah since the time that he first saw her. From the time that she first started working in the house, in his own subtle way, he made extensive overtures to her to gain her affections. Whenever they were near each other he would find a way to say or do something that he thought would please her. He knew that it was within his power to demand her attention, but the way he felt about her precluded him from exercising that authority. Day after day he would find more excuses to come to Anna Lee's room when he knew that Suliah was in there. Anna Lee, not oblivious to what she suspected was happening, neither endorsed nor denied any possibilities. It was Charlotte who was also tuned into what could be happening that although she said little was waiting to see just what would play out.

Byron never abandoned his goal of completely possessing his prize, but when he had gone to the fields weeks earlier and saw that his crops were not doing well, his attentions were focused almost entirely on that issue. He became driven with the thought that those new arrivals had something to do with the lack of rain. He also started focusing his attention again on Jobba whom he thought was a little too close to those four and must have something also to do with the drought. Almost daily he would find something wrong that Jobba did and make an example of it. Jobba wasn't getting whipped that much because Byron knew that this would diminish his value should he want to sell him, but he was spending more time in the stocks now without much food, then any other slave on the plantation. Jobba couldn't understand why Mr. Candle had singled him out as the brunt of his anger, but he was even more confused at why God was allowing this to happen to him. He thought that once he got baptized everything was supposed to be alright.

At breakfast this morning the entire Candle family was assembled at the table and Byron was talking about how if it doesn't rain soon then they were going to have some real trouble.

"Ain seen it like dis for sometme. Rain ain comin like it 'spos to an my crops gettin mighty sick. Y`all know what kin happen if we don't git a good crop in the fall, don't ya?"

He was really asking a rhetorical question, but Anna Lee took it upon herself to respond.

"Now daddy you know we ain neva had no problem wit the crops eva. The rains they gonna come soon, I know it."

"Thank you chile, I'm glad one a y`all thinks we gonna be okay."

At that point Jethro jumped in.

"Daddy you knows I think that too, but we caint run the rain. Its gonna come when it come. But sister is right we ain neva had no truble before. Why you think its gonna be bad now?"

"'Cause of dem four new niggahs I jest got. I think one of 'em kin run the rain. Anna Lee you said yo self you thought one of 'em was strange didn't ya?"

"Daddy I said that a long time ago. I ain seen nothin more since then that make me think that way. I don't even know if I was right even then."

"Well I bin watchin 'em, an they sho ain like the othas. They caint even work less'n they be almos side by side. What y`all think about that?"

"Aw daddy, you don't know what you sayin. They prably jest don't wanna be too far away from each other`cause they use to bein close. I don't think anything strange about that."

"Chile you don't know what I seen out there in the fields. Jest ain right, I know somethin jest an right."

After he said that, Byron started to get up from the table when Charlotte broke in.

"What we gonna do about that Suliah gal still livin' here in the house?"

Byron paused then sat back down.

"What you mean what we gonna do? I thought she be helpin out Anna Lee ain that right girl?"

"Yes daddy she's doin fine."

"That ain't what I'm talkin about. You got eyes an you caint even see what's happenin."

Both Anna Lee and Jethro looked at their mother and then at Byron to see his response.

"Woman what you talkin about?"

"If' you don't know then I caint tell ya," Charlotte said her piece then got up from the table and walked out of the room. When she left Byron sat there looking at his kids as if they were going to explain their mother's actions. They sat there looking puzzled just like he was for a few minutes so he decided to let it go. He shrugged his shoulders got up and left the house.

After Byron walked out, Jethro looked at Anna Lee and asked her what she thought mother was talking about. Anna Lee smiled back at him and said: "I think you know."

Jethro was a little embarrassed because he didn't think his actions had been that obvious. He looked at Anna Lee and grinned at her.

"You know I really like her don't you?"

"Yeah I know that, but you betta not let daddy see you doin anything to her 'cause you know he likes her too. She's a real pretty gal, but she's the wrong color for you and you know you caint really do nothin legal."

"I know that, but I can't help it. You eva think about why things be the way they are?"

"Sometimes I do, but then I don let it botha me, an you shouldn't either."

After she said that she got up from the table and went up to her room. Jethro sat there a little while longer pondering his dilemma and thinking about what he could possibly do about it.

Byron was on his way to the tobacco fields, but he made it a point to stop by the stocks where Jobba was still being punished for the last infraction. He walked up to him while Jobba's head was still down and grabbed his head.

"What you dreamin 'bout boy?"

"I'se not sleepin suh, jest caint hol ma head up no mo."

"Why you an dose otha boys won't let it rain on ma crops now? You thinkin if there ain't no crops this year you gonna git outta here?

"Nawsuh we knows we ain gwine nowhere, but we ain got nothn ta do wit de rain. It rain when God say it rain."

"Don't be talkin to me 'bout no god less'n you kin git him to make it rain. Kin ya do that boy?"

"Naw suh, like I say it rain when He say it rain an not b'fo."

Byron dropped his head and continued on to the field.

Sam saw him coming and rode out to meet him.

"How things lookin today Sam?"

"Suh we doin de bes we kin tryna keep all dese here crops goin, but lessn we gits some water on 'em ain no way dey kin grow."

"I got all that water down there in the river an caint get none up here to dese crops. Ain't that somethin?"

"Well suh we might kin do somethin 'bout dat if we kin fine 'nough buckets. We kin fill 'em down dere an put 'em in de wagon den bring 'em on down here an dump 'em on de plants."

"You think that's gonna work?"

"We ain got no mo choices suh?"

"Aw right round up all the buckets you kin fine an git it done. Take some of them rain barrels back a the house too, I think they got some water left in `em from the last time it rain."

"Yas suh we git right to it."

Sam left Byron and headed over to the stable to get one of the wagons. While he was there he saw Jobba still in the stocks and couldn't resist the temptation to go over and chastise him. But just as he was about to grab his head like Byron did he heard Byron call his name and tell him that he aint got time to fool with Jobba. He needed to get on with getting the crops watered. Sam somewhat disappointed turned around went inside the stable and led one of the horses out. He harnessed it and hooked up the wagon then looked around to see if there were any buckets lying around. There were two large ones just outside the stable so he checked them for holes then tossed them in the back. Next he drove the wagon up to the house and checked the rain barrels. Sure enough both barrels were still full so he made a mental note of it then continued looking around for more buckets. After he finished his search twelve large buckets were loaded on the wagon. He knew he was going to need help so he rode back down to the field to get it.

On the way it occurred to him that this was a chore that would be good for the defiant four as he thought of them. They would be close together and they didn't have to rush to get the job done. These were characteristics that were perfectly suited for them in his mind. He passed the first field and headed up the hill to where they were working. As usual they were all within ten yards of each other and leisurely performing their tasks as though they didn't have a care in the world. He stopped his horse at the edge of the field and observed them for a few minutes before calling out to Daniel who he had come to know was their pack leader. Daniel looked up and acknowledged him then slowly started to make his way over.

"Tell yo brothas I want dem ta git in de wagon `cause y`all gonna hep me fill dese here buckets down at de river."

Daniel turned around and waved to the others to come to him and they did. Once in the wagon they all rode down through the quarters to the river. At the riverside he instructed them to start filling the buckets so they got down and began the task. Again Sam had to laugh, to himself, at how leisurely they moved with no sense of urgency. Since the last time he had tried to whip one of them and the results were not good for him, he decided that as long as they did what he told them, even if it took longer than it should, he would just go along with it. The men started filling the buckets and loading them in the wagon until all twelve were full. Sam, who had not lent a hand at any time to help them sat in the wagon and watched them work. When they finished they all looked at him then got back in the wagon. It still bothered Sam that they were the only ones he allowed to make eye contact with him, but he had no other choice since he couldn't whip them. He knew too that Byron would not allow them to be placed in the stocks just for that reason.

They arrived back at the first tobacco field and Sam called some of the others over to take the buckets and start watering the crops. The chain they set up at his command was working and for as much of the field as they had buckets to water, the dry earth quickly absorbed it crying out for more. Sam observed this and saw that it was practically a useless effort because it would take hundreds of buckets meaning many more trips to the river. This task was more than he wanted to supervise to get enough water on the ground to make any kind of significant difference. After the first and second loads were emptied he sent the slaves back to their stations and decided to go tell Byron the bad news. He wasn't sure just how to break the news to him, especially when he didn't have an alternative solution. No matter what the consequence, he had to tell him before Byron's expectations rose too high and he came back out to the fields and saw that the bucket idea had no effect.

Byron was inside the house in his parlor going over some scenarios concerning his financial situation. He was projecting what his yield would be based on a full complement of all of his tobacco crops at the current rates. Then he did the same projection based on half of the complement. Finally he thought to himself, suppose he had a total crop failure and looked back at scenario number one. This would be disastrous not only for the building of his future empire, but there were some outstanding obligations that he had right now that would be in jeopardy. Looking at these possibilities, Byron's frame of mind was not ready for what Sam was about to tell him.

Sam got to the door and hesitated before knocking. He was going over in his mind what he was going to say and got prepared for what he envisioned the reaction would be. Gathering his courage he knocked. Clarence opened the door and directed him to the parlor where Byron was still sitting pondering his fate.

"Mr. Candle, suh we dun bin to the river three, four times and emptied the buckets on the land. We even refilled the rain barrels and dump dem too. Don seem like dey do no good, `cause the ground still dry. Onlys't thing dat gonna wet the land enough is a good rain. Maybe need one or two, day's steady."

Byron heard what Sam said and sat there stunned with a blank expression on his face. Sam braced himself for the rebuke and waited. Surprisingly, after a few minutes instead of displaying his ire, Byron asked Sam what else he thought could be done to save the crops. Sam relieved at not being chastised had a thought come into his head that he wondered why he didn't think of before.

"Dere's one thing we might try an I ain sure it gonna work, but dere's an ole indian medicine man from dat Shawnee tribe used ta be `round here, that live up on the Arbrister farm. People say he kin make it rain up dere when dey need it. Some say dey seen him do it. Maybe we kin git Mr. Arbrister to let us have him fer a day or two."

Byron heard the name Arbrister and cringed thinking that if this was his only way out, then he had a problem. It was Charlie Arbrister's sons that had assaulted Suliah and caused him to strike an unfair compromise deal with Byron. Byron knew he had taken advantage of the situation and now he was going to be at the mercy of a man he had swindled. He pressed Sam hard to see if there was another way out.

"Sam ya think dis man kin do what you say he kin?"

"I dono suh, but seem like we got no otha choice. I caint think a no way else 'cept ta jest wait for the rain an we don know when dat gonna be."

Byron got up from his chair walked across the room and looked out the window. He was trying to decide whether to humble himself and ask Charlie for his help, but his pride wasn't letting him make a quick decision. However, when he reviewed in his mind the last scenario on his projection's list he decided that if he wanted to save his crops then he was going to have to take this only option. His big concern was that if he had to pay Charlie the money that his land was really worth and this Indian medicine man was a fraud and no rains came, what then could he do? Without having anything point to what he was used to having, like an unfair edge, he was very uncomfortable. He told Sam that he needed some time to think it over and he would call him in a little while and let him know. Sam left the house and went back to the fields.

As he started toward the first field he looked at the stocks again and saw that Jobba's head was not just down, but it looked like he wasn't moving or breathing. He rode over closer to him and Jobba didn't even try to raise his head. Sam got down from his horse and walked up to him. He grabbed his head and raised it. Jobba's eyes were blank and it looked like he was near death. Sam went over to the horse trough and found a cup hanging on the side. There was still water in it so he dipped the cup took it over to Jobba and poured the first one over his head and then went back and refilled it. The second cup he raised Jobba's head and let him drink. Jobba gulped down the water and looked at Sam in disbelief that this man was helping him. But before what seemed like a genuine act of mercy was completed Sam took the cup away and slammed Jobba's head back down.

"I don want you dyin on me yet niggah, I still got plans fo ya." Sam said.

Then he got back on his horse and went back to the mansion to let Mr. Candle know about Jobba's condition. Byron with all that he had on his mind about the drought and the crops had completely forgotten about Jobba still being punished. He told Sam to go back and let him loose and send him back to his cabin for the rest of the day. After Sam left, the idea came to him about how he could settle up with Charlie and get rid of what was becoming a real headache for him. He could give him Jobba in exchange for the services of the medicine man for a week. When this idea popped in his head a big smile crossed his face and he knew he had the perfect solution.

He almost ran out of the house in search of Sam so he could tell him. First he went to the stocks to see whether Sam might still be there, but Jobba had already been freed. Then he walked over to the quarters' road to see if Sam was there, but there was no sign of him. Not wanting to walk all the way down to Jobba's cabin, Byron decided to wait at the edge of the field and wait for Sam. While he was there he looked over the crops again and observed the feeble attempts of the workers trying to preserve them. Without some serious rain coming, he knew each day would bring him closer to having a total crop failure. He hung his head.

A short time later Sam, who had been checking on the other fields, came riding to where Byron was standing. He picked up his pace and came up to him. Byron explained what his idea was and he wanted Sam to ride over to the Arbrister Plantation and speak to Charlie about the deal. Sam didn't show it, but he wasn't in favor of exchanging Jobba as part of the deal because he wasn't finished with him. He nodded his head in agreement with Byron and said that he would go over there first thing in the morning. Byron said okay and walked back to the house while Sam rode the perimeter of the field watching over his charges.

Inside Jobba's cabin Sam had left him on the floor of the first level. Jobba realizing that he was loose used all of his remaining strength to crawl over to where the water bucket was and take a long drink. Gulping down the water, he finished and lay on the floor for several minutes before even attempting to walk upstairs and collapse on his bed. When he finally did make it to the bed he plopped down on it and slept for some time. There was no one in the cabin because Myanna, Linwood and the Harper family were all still in the fields. Harper's kids were with the mammy.

Byron, feeling much better about his idea, especially since it would keep him from having to give up any of his real money, walked in the house smiling. Charlotte met him almost at the door when he came in and informed him that she wanted to take one of the wagons and go into town. He asked her why and she responded that she needed to get some things for her and Anna Lee at the general store for the social coming up. This was not an unreasonable request so Byron said okay. Charlotte then informed him that Jethro and Suliah also would be going with her besides Anna Lee. The fact that she was taking Suliah, caused Byron to wonder why, but what could he say he had already given his permission. He did ask whether she was taking Clarence to drive them and she said she would.

Anna Lee was in her room with Suliah deciding what they were going to wear for this trip to town. Suliah was excited because she had never been anywhere off the plantation and in her attempts to help Anna Lee get dressed she dropped several things. Anna Lee tried to calm her down by telling her that it was okay. Jethro kept popping in and out as he usually did trying to catch Suliah in some state of undress. Anna Lee, very aware of what he was doing didn't object, but when she and Jethro were alone she let him know that she knew. He always just smiled sheepishly. Charlotte also was observant of what was going on and she was caught between telling Byron to open his eyes and telling Jethro that he was bordering on uncharted territory and it could be dangerous.

The good carriage was prepared and brought up to the house by Clarence. Charlotte, Anna Lee and Suliah sat in the back while Jethro hopped up in front with Clarence. Suliah sat next to Anna Lee opposite Charlotte and during the whole trip Charlotte stared at her making her very uncomfortable. Anna Lee tried to break the tension by saying some funny things, but Charlotte wasn't laughing and Suliah was afraid to. Finally Charlotte spoke and said to Suliah that she knew what she was doing and it wasn't going to continue. Suliah hardly knowing what she was referring to started to ask her, but thought better of it. Charlotte continued by telling her that she wanted her to get out of that room and return to sleeping in the hallway by the kitchen. Suliah heard her words and was very disappointed because she had become used to having a room of her own. She answered Charlotte and said she would do that as soon as they got back. Anna Lee tried to intervene by asking her mother why she had to do that, but Charlotte hushed her.

When they arrived at the general store, Charlotte told Clarence to take the carriage around back and tend to the horse. Suliah wasn't sure whether she was to go inside or wait with Clarence in the carriage. Anna Lee spoke up as they were getting out and told her to come with them. Charlotte looked at Anna Lee and told her that Suliah was not going inside with them what would the people think. Anna Lee looked back at Suliah and told her gently that maybe she ought to stay with Clarence. Charlotte and Anna Lee started walking in the store, but Jethro came around to Suliah and told her that he was going to buy her something and he didn't care what his mother said. Then he followed them into the store. Before Clarence got back up into the driver's seat he looked inside at Suliah and told her that she needed to be very careful because of what was developing in that house and with this family. Suliah, who was smiling after what Jethro said to her, dropped her smile and heeded the words of caution from Clarence.

For over an hour the Candles roamed around the store examining this and touching that. Jethro separated from the group for awhile to find something for Suliah that he thought she might like. He tried to give the impression that he was off looking for something for himself, but when he headed toward an area that had nothing to do with men's goods, eagle eyed Charlotte noticed. He saw a silver bracelet that in his eyes would be perfect on her and he cleverly strolled around trying not to draw attention until a clerk came over. He looked around to see if anyone was watching then told the salesman that he would like to have this gift, wrapped. The salesman picked up the bracelet and headed to the back to accommodate his customer. Jethro eased away from the area while he waited and pretended to go to the men's wear department. He kept looking over at where Anna Lee and Charlotte were busy looking at dresses and felt confident that they were so absorbed in what they were examining that they couldn't be paying any attention to him and what he was doing. The salesman returned from the back and sought out Jethro. Jethro saw him and hurriedly moved over to where he was and completed the transaction then hid the gift in his jacket pocket.

They finished shopping at the general store then went to some smaller specialty stores. When they returned to the carriage they saw a group of white men gathered around it who had spotted Suliah and were trying to talk her into getting out. Clarence had tried to object, but was told to mind his manners or they would have him whipped so he just sat there. Charlotte seeing what was happening from a short distance away moved faster and approached the men. When she told them whom this slave belonged to, the men immediately backed away apologizing profusely. They removed their hats, bowed, quickly turned around and left the area disappearing behind one of the stores. Charlotte looked at Suliah and said: "Causing trouble again, huh." Suliah lowered her head and said nothing. Jethro looked at her and then at Anna Lee, but neither said anything got back in the carriage and they started for home.

The horn sounded ending another workday and Myanna and Linwood joined the others walking home. When they got close enough to the stables to see the stocks Myanna, as she had done for the last three days looked over to see how Jobba might be doing. She saw the empty wooden posts and immediately thought that he might be in the cabin. Grabbing Linwood's hand she left the group and hurried home. Inside she rushed up the stairs and saw Jobba sleeping on the bed. She ran over to him and hugged him and when he woke up and turned over she kissed him. Jobba still feeling weak and somewhat groggy tried to respond appropriately, but it was going to take some time. Linwood then came over and hugged his father too. Myanna asked him if he was hungry and he told her he was starving. With that said she made her way downstairs again and began preparing something for him. Penniman and Tralene entered a short time later with their kids in tow and saw Myanna already busy making dinner. A little surprised that she was starting so early they asked her why. When Myanna told them that Jobba was upstairs, Penniman was glad to hear it and went upstairs to see him.

Since the first gathering at the river when Daniel baptized almost half of the slaves, Penniman even though he went with Jobba that night was not convinced and remained a follower of Aunt Tee along with Tralene. It was difficult for both families to coexist in the same cabin feeling strongly in two opposite directions about their faith. Penniman went upstairs to see Jobba, but he was very reserved with his greeting and just asked how he was doing. He told Jobba that if he had not become so close to that Daniel man, he wouldn't be going through all this stuff because he would still be under the protection of Aunt Tee. Jobba was sitting up and even though still feeling weak, told Penniman that he was wrong it was him who needed God's protection, even from Aunt Tee. Penniman heard that got up and went back downstairs.

Jobba was able to walk down shortly after him to eat and while both families dined together not much was said. They just ate and ever so often something was said that was very bland and non-directive purposely staying away from anything that could be even remotely associated with their religious beliefs. After they finished, Jobba felt strong enough to go outside and look at the stars. Spring had definitely arrived and the night air was beginning to warm as he breathed it in like he never did before. Spending time awkwardly positioned in the stocks had severely humbled him and during his incarceration he often wondered why this was happening to him. The thought crossed his mind often that all the things that Daniel said about God and this Jesus that walked the earth many years ago, if they are really true then when would he be set free. When would he know the joys that Daniel talked about. As he looked up at the stars he felt like he was alone, but then he remembered something that Daniel said:

"Be strong and of good courage, do not fear nor be afraid of them for the Lord your God He is the One who goes with you. He will not leave nor forsake you." (Deu. 31:6)

Feeling a sense of calm reflecting on these words Jobba turned around and made his way back upstairs to Myanna who was lying on the bed. Linwood had already gone to sleep when Jobba looked over in that direction. He went over to the bed put his arms around her kissed her and hugged her tightly. She looked at him for a moment to see whether he was really ready to do what she was thinking he wanted to do. Jobba looked into her eyes and realized that his strength had not fully returned so he released her and lay down beside her. She layback holding him close and with a deep sense of understanding they both went to sleep.

In the mansion Byron met his family as they walked in loaded with boxes and bags of different things. He commented to Charlotte that he hoped she left something in the store for other people. She didn't think it was funny and went into one of the bags and pulled out some cigars for him to divert his attention from all that she had. Being a cigar lover, for the moment he was pacified and didn't inquire any further into what she had bought. Charlotte moved on by him and headed upstairs with her things. Anna Lee and Suliah followed her, but at the top of the stairs Charlotte caught Suliah's arm and reminded her about what she was supposed to do. Suliah nodded her head and Charlotte went into her room. Before Suliah started to go up to the third floor, Anna Lee told her to come with her to her room and wait. She was going to talk to her father about her moving. Suliah walked with Anna Lee to her room and dropped the things on the bed. Then Anna Lee turned around and went back downstairs to look for Byron. He was still in his parlor going over how he wanted Sam to pitch his appeal to Charlie so he could tell him in the morning. As usual he was trying to come up with a scheme that would keep Mr. Arbrister from gaining any sought of advantage while Byron got what he wanted.

"There you are daddy, I was lookin for you. I thought you went back outside, its such a beautiful night."

Byron was immediately on guard. When Anna Lee came to him with this type of approach she usually had something in mind that she wanted from him, and she usually got it.

"Yes chile now you foun me what kin I help ya with?"

"Oh I was jest thinkin 'bout how you said yoself you didn' think it was right for Suliah to be sleepin down here on the cold floor. Well mama don told her she gotta move out that room an go back to sleepin down here. You don't want that now do you daddy?"

Byron paused for a minute knowing he was being set up, but after he thought it over and considered what his ultimate objective was he said that he would speak to Charlotte.

Anna Lee then asked him what she should tell Suliah to do in the meantime since mama told her to move now. Byron responded saying let her stay where she is. Anna Lee smiled and wrapped her arms around her father hugging him. Byron returned the hug, but wasn't so sure that he did the right thing knowing that when he told Charlotte about this conversation, he was going to be in for a long night.

Anna Lee ran back up the stairs and into her room. She could hardly wait to tell Suliah the good news. Suliah was more elated to hear the news than Anna Lee had joy in delivering it. The two of them started unpacking her things when as usual the door opened and Jethro popped in.

"Don't you know about knocking on a lady's door before you come rushin in?" Anna Lee said.

Jethro stopped right at the open door and knocked on it.

"May I come in?"

Both girls laughed because he was already half way in with the door behind him.

"Well come on you already half in."

Jethro walked over to where they were and told Suliah that he had something for her. Suliah looked at Anna Lee and wasn't sure what to do. Anna Lee looked at Jethro and she wasn't sure either whether this was a good thing to do knowing how daddy felt about Suliah. Jethro didn't wait for her approval when he reached in his pocket and pulled out the bracelet and gave it to her. Anna Lee looked at the nicely wrapped box and wondered to herself what it could be. Suliah looked again at Anna Lee and when she nodded her head shyly accepted the box. She started to unwrap it and her hands were shaking she was so excited. When she finally got the wrapping off and opened the box she couldn't believe that this was for her. Anna Lee saw the bracelet and was a little surprised at the beauty of it and wondered how much he spent for it. As Suliah put it on, Anna Lee cautioned her about wearing it around the house when Charlotte could see it and ask her where she got it. Suliah was so busy admiring it and holding her wrist up in the air that she almost didn't hear what Anna Lee was saying. Anna Lee repeated what she said to make sure that Suliah got the message.

Suliah told Jethro thank you, but wasn't sure whether she should do anything more. Jethro told her she was welcome and that it looked real good on her. Anna Lee looked at her brother who was smiling and staring at Suliah. She shook him and told him that it was time for him to go so she could talk to Suliah alone. He got the message stood up and left. Once they were alone again Anna Lee told Suliah to sit on the bed by her and then she started talking to her.

"You know he's very fond of you, but I don't think its a good idea for y`all to git too close.

Ya know mama don't like you and she wants to get you outta this house soon as she can figure a way ta do it. You have to be very careful when your around her especially if Jethro is there too. Don't let mama see you wearin that bracelet eva or she's gonna take it from you. You hear me?"

Suliah nodded her head.

"Now you go on upstairs and put that some place where nobody's gonna find it. I'll see you in the mornin."

Suliah nodded again then got up from the bed and went upstairs to her room.

Charlotte came downstairs looking around the kitchen area to see if Suliah's pallet had been put back down. Aunt Tee was in the kitchen putting away dishes from the dinner meal. Charlotte walked in and asked where Suliah's pallet was. Aunt Tee had no idea that Charlotte told her to move back downstairs so she said that the pallet was in the back of the house where it was being stored. Charlotte told Aunt Tee that she wanted that pallet put back down here immediately because Suliah was going to be sleeping on it again. She emphasized that it was to be done now so Aunt Tee left the kitchen to find Clarence and have him move the pallet back to the hallway. Having made her demands known Charlotte left the kitchen and walked toward the parlor.

Byron was still there finishing up the final details for Sam's presentation. Charlotte walked in and sat in a chair opposite his desk. His head was still down when she came in, but he stopped what he was doing to acknowledge her. She started in telling him about what happened while they were shopping in the general store. The way that she framed the story it came out sounding like it was Suliah's fault that the men came up to the carriage. She kept saying that Suliah would be nothing but trouble as long as she is in the house. Byron heard what she said but he still wasn't quite ready to make any changes so he tried to pacify Charlotte.

"Now darlin I know you don care for dat gal, but she's bin a real help to Anna Lee an I don't see how she's gittin in yo way. Mos time she keeps out da way an she be in Anna Lee's room or in the kitchen. Why don't you like her?"

Charlotte was stung by his question and she really didn't have a good answer except that Suliah was so much prettier than her daughter, but she certainly wasn't going to say that to Byron.

"It ain't that I don't like her, its jest that she caint do nothing 'round here. 'cept for helping Anna Lee. She's worthless. We caint even go ta town lessn' one of us stays with her all the time."

"Have you talked wit Anna Lee 'bout what you wanna do?"

"Well no, thought I'd talk to you first. I'll talk with her if you say she's gotta leave here."

"Now I ain't said dat, I think she's good for Anna Lee an I don wanna see Anna Lee hurt 'cause the gal gotta go out from here. You kin work out what eva ya need ta do to keep her out yo way, but she's stayin."

Charlotte knew that Byron had made up his mind and there wouldn't be any changing it so in a huff she got up and left the room. Byron just looked at her as she left and shook his head. He then put the final touches on his scheme.

The next morning Byron was up earlier than usual and on his way to Sam's cabin. He had written down all the things he wanted Sam to say to Charlie to accept his deal. Once inside Sam's place he went over the plan several times to make sure that it was understood. Sam said he understood and was ready to go. Byron then reminded him that he was not to let Charlie see the sheet and Sam laughed thinking - does this man really think I'm stupid? When they finished talking Byron told Sam to go down and get Jobba so he could take him with him and let Charlie see what a good physical specimen he was getting. Sam readily agreed.

Byron left Sam's cabin and went back to his house while Sam went to the stable and got the horse and wagon ready for the trip. At Jobba's cabin both families were up and getting ready to start their day. Jobba was still feeling a little weak, but he made up his mind that he was going to do whatever he had to do to keep on the good side of Mr. Candle and Sam. At breakfast Myanna reminded Jobba that in two days it would be Suliah's seventeenth birthday. Jobba asked her just what they could do to celebrate. She looked at Tralene and asked if she had anything they could make a cake with. Tralene responded that she didn't, but she could ask Aunt Tee if she would help her when she told her it was Suliah's birthday. That was settled and Tralene was going to get the ingredients. While they were talking the door burst open and Sam stood at the entrance.

"Alright boy you goin wit me," he said pointing to Jobba.

Jobba and the rest of them were surprised because he had just come off of being punished. Myanna was thinking the worst that he was about to be taken away from her for good and she dared to ask Sam where he was going. Sam was as surprised as she was courageous and looked at her in disbelief that she had enough nerve to ask him something. He responded with a smile on his face knowing that this would taunt her endlessly.

"I'm taken him wit me ova to de Arbrister place an he ain comin back."

The shock of hearing this sent Myanna falling back from her chair and if Jobba had not been able to grab her before she hit the floor she certainly would have fallen.

"Why you do dis, why you do dis?" she said. "He ain don nothin wrong. Why you do dis?"

"Neva you mind. Come on boy git yo things an come on wit me."

Jobba went upstairs got a jacket and another pair of pants then came down ready to go. Sam pushed him out the door and told him to get in the wagon. Inside Myanna started crying and neither Penniman nor Tralene could console her. Linwood heard her and came running to see what was wrong. When she told him he ran out the door, but by this time the wagon was at the top of the road. Linwood went back inside to try and help his mother cope. Penniman held her up and told her that even though Jobba was gone she still had to go to the fields. Myanna picked her head up realizing what Penniman was saying was right, and with his and Linwood's help she walked out.

The trip to Mr. Arbrister's farm didn't take that long and a little over an hour later the wagon was headed up the road into the hills to his mansion. Once at his front door, Sam was met by two house slaves who came out to attend the horse. Sam yelled at Jobba to get down and they both walked up to the door. A brief rap on the door brought Charlie's man servant out to open it. He greeted Sam politely and told him that Jobba would have to wait outside. Jobba was glad to hear it because he was still a little weak from his last ordeal and the bumpy ride up the hill didn't make him feel any better. Sam walked in and was directed to a room off the living room where he was told to wait and Mr. Arbrister would come to him shortly. Sam took a seat and quietly eased his instruction paper out and reviewed it. He wanted to be absolutely sure that he remembered every thing that Byron told him to say.

Charlie Arbrister walked in the room and Sam immediately stood up. After hearing who Sam was Charlie told him to sit back down and asked him what he could do for him. Sam took a deep breath and launched into his prepared speech. Not being the most eloquent spokesman in the room, Sam stammered on several occasions, but got his point across. Charlie was a little surprised that Byron would have the nerve to come to him making any requests after how he swindled him out of his land. Charlie chuckled and then repeated the bottom line of the request to make sure that he understood what Byron's man was asking.

"You tellin me that he wants me to let my rainmaker Indian Joe go with you to make it rain on the land that he stole from me? Is that right?"

"Yas suh that's 'xactly what he would like. He also gonna give you de man outside for yo farm ta do what you want wit."

"I don need another darkie 'roun here an I don't lend Indian Joe out for no rain makin service. But I'll tell you what I kin do, if he really wants to make up for what he did to me, then he kin pay the rest of the money he owes me for the land jest like we first agreed. Ta show you jest how fair a man I am, I'm gonna send Joe back with you for a week, but at the end of the week I want him back along with the money Mr. Candle owes me. You okay with that? You kin even take that boy ya brought with you back ta him."

Sam thinking that all Byron wanted was to get the Indian man to the plantation and make it rain never considered the part of the deal that said there was a major financial string attached. He was also elated at not having to give up Jobba since he wasn't through with him.

"Okay, I think I kin git him ta do dat. What you wan me ta do now?"

"You jest wait here while I go an let Indian Joe know he's goin on a trip for me."

Charlie got up and left the room. As Sam sat there one of Charlie's son's came by and poked his head in to greet Sam. However, when he found out who Sam was the greeting was abruptly ended and the son left the room. Sam decided to step out for a minute and check on Jobba. Jobba had taken a seat on the swing that was on the porch and Sam got upset that he wasn't sitting on the ground.

"Git offa dat thing it ain fo yo kine. Sit on de ground if'n ya gotta sit."

Jobba quickly got off the swing and sat on the porch right in front of it. Sam started to shout again, but he heard Mr. Arbrister coming back and he turned and went back inside.

"This is Indian Joe, the best rain maker in this here county," Charlie said.

Sam looked at the elderly Indian who had long gray hair and a rugged tanned face and hardened hands. He wondered whether he should shake his hand or not, but before he could decide Charlie directed them out the door and bid them to get started. As they walked to the wagon, Sam hollered at Jobba to get up and get back in the wagon because he was going home. When Sam hollered, Indian Joe looked at him strangely. Although he knew that other plantation owners treated their slaves harshly, at the Arbrister place he was not accustomed to it. The three men mounted the wagon and started down the hill. On the way Indian Joe kept looking at Jobba with a curious look. He was trying to determine whether Jobba was just tired or was there something wrong with him because every few miles Jobba would drop his head and almost keel over in the wagon. Indian Joe who was sitting in front with Sam started to ask whether Jobba needed some water, but he thought better of it. The trip back was quicker than the one coming because it was mostly downhill and the group arrived at the mansion in less than an hour.

After allowing the slaves who usually greeted new arrivals to tend to the horse and wagon, Sam told Jobba to go down to the fields while he took Indian Joe inside. Byron heard them coming and was a little surprised to see Jobba get down and head back toward the fields. He rushed out to ask Sam what happened, but when he saw Indian Joe standing there Jobba became less important. Sam introduced Joe and Byron grabbed his hand, put his arm around his shoulder and walked him into the house.

"Glad ta see ya, glad ta git ya here," Byron exclaimed. "I sho hope ya kin do somethin ta git the rains ta start comin agin. Come on an set down for a spell an I'll tell ya all what we need. Kin I git ya somethin ta drink?"

Indian Joe nodded his head no to the drink offer and sat down. Byron then started telling all about how long they've been without a good rain and that his crops were failing because of it. Indian Joe said nothing, but took it all in. When Byron finished his story he waited for Joe to say something, but the man just got up and walked out the front door. Byron puzzled by this action got up and followed him out. Outside, Joe asked him which of the fields needed the most rain. Byron thought this was a strange question because they all needed rain, but he pointed to the closest tobacco field. Joe then said that tomorrow morning before sunrise he would go out to appeal to the rain god. Byron didn't get a real comfortable feeling by the way he said this so cavalierly, and wondered if this was even going to work.

They went back inside and Byron called Clarence to show Indian Joe where he would sleep. On the way, they passed by the kitchen where Aunt Tee was busy as usual. When Joe saw her he stopped short and grabbed his chest as if something had touched him. He stared at her for a few minutes then quickly walked away and followed Clarence to the third floor. Once alone inside his room he shut the door took out his charms and prayed to his gods for protection from the evil spirit that he had just encountered. He said to himself right then that he definitely would not be staying in this place for a whole week. He was going to do what he had to do tomorrow and maybe one day more, but that would be it. If it rained fine, if it didn't then he would have to explain to Mr. Candle it was because of other spirits on his land.

Jobba was walking to the fields when it occurred to him that Sam didn't say which field he was to go to, so he decided to find where Myanna was working and go there. When he neared the edge someone saw him and alerted Myanna who was over on the other side. She stood up and froze for a moment trying to reassure herself that it was really him then she threw down her hoe and started running across the field. He saw her also and met her halfway at the center of the field. They hugged as he picked her up and whirled around to the dismay of the overseer who being unaware of Jobba's plight, was puzzled. He hollered at the two and demanded that they stop that and get back to work. The couple still smiling at the reunion separated and went to work again. Not seeing his son in the area, Jobba asked where he was. Myanna assured him that he was okay just working in another field.

After Indian Joe left to go upstairs, Byron continued his conversation with Sam wanting to know all that happened at the Arbrister Plantation.

"What all went on down dere an why is Jobba back here?"

"Well, Mr. Candle I dun what ya tol me an I said evr'y thin ya tol me ta say, but dat Mr. Arbrister he say he don need no mo darkies at his place. Den he say dat he ain happy 'bout the way you took his land an he want his money. He loan you dat Indian man 'cause he say he a fair man, but he want him back in a week wit the money."

"What? You fool! You told him I was gonna give him money. Why you think I sent Jobba ova there. That was in place of any money."

Byron went on raging for about ten more minutes while Sam sat there absorbing the blows. After he finished venting Byron realized that what happened was already done and he just had to deal with it.

"I guess I caint change nothin now, but that rain man betta make somethin happen 'round here or I'm gonna send him back wit out no money an I jest might sen you with him. Now you git on outta here an go down to them fields an help out, I don't wanna see you no more today."

Sam scrambled to the door trying to get out of Byron's way as quickly as possible. After he left, Byron sat back down for a minute, but then got up went and found his special nectar and poured himself a tall glass. Finishing the first one minutes later he got up and fixed himself another, and another until sometime later he was feeling very relaxed. He nodded and slept in his chair until the horn sounded calling an end to another workday. When the horn sounded he woke up and realized he was out for much longer than he planned so he got up and walked outside to get some fresh air. Just in time to see the slaves coming in from the fields Jobba was spotted walking with Myanna and Linwood. Byron's relaxed mind became uneasy again at the thought of having this man, who he believed was the source of his troubles, back on his land. Feeling now very disconcerted, he turned around went back in the house and upstairs to lie down.

At dinner that night in the cabin the Harper and Thomas families were eating their evening meal with very little conversation. Since the first baptism down at the river and the separation into two groups of believers, interaction between them was minimal. Though they had to work and live together daily it made life much more difficult especially after Aunt Tee conducted her dances and Daniel his church meetings. Although they hardly talked, when Jobba asked Tralene whether she had heard anything back from Aunt Tee about getting the ingredients for a birthday cake for Suliah, since tomorrow was her birthday, Tralene responded and said that she had. Then she told him that Aunt Tee, who had taken a liking to Suliah, would be making the cake and they would have a little celebration there in the mansion. Jobba got very upset at this because he still didn't trust Aunt Tee with anything she had to do with. Feeling frustrated he got up from the table and went outside. Myanna followed shortly after and talked with him. She was able to calm him down by telling him that there was nothing they could do and at least Suliah would have some kind of celebration on her birthday even if it wasn't the one they would like.

The next morning as he promised, Indian Joe was up before sunrise and out at the edge of the main tobacco field that Byron had pointed out. Byron who meant to be out there with him missed his opportunity to get up early because he was responding to the effects of a hangover from his nectar indulgence. When the rooster crowed and Byron realized the sun was already up, he jumped up out of bed and hurriedly got himself together. Running out the front door and down to the field he saw Indian Joe dancing around and waving some necklaces in one hand and a dry tobacco plant in the other. As he danced he chanted and looked up and down many times at the sky to see if there was any change. Byron stopped at the edge of the field and observed him. He also got caught up in the drama and looked up at the sky to see whether anything was happening. The dance went on for about a half hour before the medicine man stopped and sat down to drink from a container that he had beside him.

Byron couldn't decide whether to go over to him and get his sense of what was happening, or stay where he was until Joe finished. Finally, he decided to sit still and wait to see what happens. While sitting there, Sam saw him and rode over dismounted and sat down beside him.

"Look like anything happenin yet?" Sam asked.

"Naw, not yet, but I guess he gonna need some time to do what he gotta do."

"Yeah I reckon so suh. He gotta big job ta do."

Byron and Sam sat there looking at Indian Joe for several minutes before Joe got up and resumed his ritual. He continued and as time passed the fervency of his movements became increasingly passionate even to the point where he appeared to be almost exhausted and about to fall on the ground. Recovering each time he went on until finally at the end of over an hour he stopped. Giving a final look into the heavens he raised his hands and said one final chant, then paused and folded his arms. At this point, Byron thinking that he was through eased his way over to where Joe was standing. For a moment he stood beside him silently, looking up at the sky also before he said anything.

"You think that dancin gonna make it rain?" he said.

"Must wait an see, need time for spirits to hear prayer an decide. No one kin rush the spirits. Nobody make'em do what dey don wanna do, jest make prayer an ask."

These words were definitely not reassuring to Byron in the least and he started to let Indian Joe know how he felt. However, he held back and decided to give it one more day and hope for some signs of rain before confronting the medicine man. As Joe packed up his things, Byron walked ahead of him back to the house and directed Sam to the fields. Indian Joe followed Byron up to the house and when they were inside Byron asked him how many times he had done this before. Joe responded by saying that he had done it many times. Byron's next question was how often did he get rain? Indian Joe hesitated before answering suspecting that Byron was now looking for some kind of guarantee of success. When he spoke, the words surprised Byron.

"Many spirits walk this land in conflict. Spirits in heaven dat control the rain not happy 'bout it. Long as conflict stay here rain may not come. I kin only pray to the master spirit to see fit to ova rule an give rain."

Byron heard these words and went and sat in his favorite chair to reflect on them. He knew that there was something going on around his plantation, but had no idea really what it was all about. He also knew that not long after the new arrivals, including the preacher man, things seemed to change among his workers. He couldn't put his finger on any one thing, but he knew something was different. Although he had never actually heard any of the church meetings going on and was still unaware of the cave meetings, he was sure something was different. Conceeding he wasn't going to get anything more from Joe today, he got up from his chair leaving Joe alone in the parlor, and went outside.

It was almost noon and Aunt Tee was finishing Suliah's birthday cake when Anna Lee walked in. She saw the cake right away and asked whom it was for. Aunt Tee told her it was for Suliah and Anna Lee asked her how she knew. When Aunt Tee explained the whole story Anna Lee got excited and wanted to have a big celebration right away. Aunt Tee brought her back down quickly by reminding her of what her mother might think of that. Anna Lee then said: "Let's do something in my room later and surprise her, okay?" Aunt Tee agreed thinking it was a good idea. She also thought it would be a chance to plant a seed in Suliah's mind about coming to the next moonlight special of hers. They both agreed to go to Anna Lee's room about 3:00 O'clock and invite Clarence and Jethro to help celebrate.

For the rest of the early afternoon, Anna Lee kept Suliah busy by doing things around the house that kept her far away from the kitchen. Suliah thought it was a little strange because she usually by this time was sent into the kitchen to help Aunt Tee. The time passed quickly and just before the appointed hour, Anna Lee went by the kitchen to see if Aunt Tee and Clarence were ready. Getting the go ahead nod she told them to get Jethro and go to her room and she would bring Suliah in right away. The group made their way to the room without being seen and all was in readiness. When Anna Lee entered with Suliah right behind her they shouted happy birthday and Suliah was very surprised. It seems that she had forgotten her own birthday. They all sat down at Anna Lee's small table and ate the cake while Anna Lee promised her that she was going to get a gift for her the next time they went into town. Jethro felt the gift he had given her recently was sufficient and told her it was his birthday gift. Suliah was very happy and the group enjoyed each other for a little while until Charlotte was heard out in the hallway calling for Aunt Tee. She got up immediately and stepped into the hallway responding to the call. Rushing down the stairs she stood before Charlotte.

"Where've you been, I looked in the kitchen an all ova for you?"

"Maam, I was in Miss Anna Lee's room."

"Oh! What were you doing in there?"

Aunt Tee hesitated before answering not sure whether to tell her about the party or not. Deciding not to exacerbate an already tense situation she just said that she was helping her with some sewing. Charlotte easily accepted this explanation thinking that the good for nothing handmaiden was not up to any task like that anyway. Charlotte didn't want anything real important, but just needed to have Aunt Tee adjust some of the new clothing she was planning to wear this weekend at the other plantation's party. The task could really be done at any time since it was only the middle of the week. When Aunt Tee heard the reason why she had been called out of the party, she was internally upset because she didn't get a chance to talk to Suliah about becoming a convert. She wasn't giving up, but had to figure out another way.

Back in the room Anna Lee, Jethro and Clarence were still laughing and eating cake when another call rang out in the hallway. This time it was Byron for Clarence and he immediately left the room. After that Anna Lee thought that it was time for them to get back on their regular schedules and broke up the party. Before leaving Jethro made sure that he planted a big kiss on Suliah's cheek not missing her mouth by much.

Anna Lee saw this and wondered to herself did he intend to kiss her mouth, but because she was there changed directions. No matter, they all left the room and returned to the day's task as they usually did them.

Clarence got downstairs and Byron wanted to know where he had been also. Clarence not being as astute as Aunt Tee about the family relationship with Suliah blurted out that he had been celebrating Suliah's birthday in Anna Lee's room. When Byron heard this he almost forgot why he called Clarence thinking that this may be a perfect opportunity to do something for Suliah himself. His need for Clarence however, came back to him quickly and he told him that he wanted for him to take Indian Joe down to the cabins and let him walk around outside there. He wanted Indian Joe to let him know if he felt any bad spirits coming from anywhere down there and if he did from which cabin. He was really trying to confirm that Jobba was indeed the cause of his troubles. Clarence responded it would be done right away and took off in search of Joe. When he left, Byron's thinking reverted back to Suliah.

Clarence and the medicine man strolled down the quarters to the cabin area and as they passed by each cabin Joe just grunted until he came to the last one on the left. Outside the door he paused and turned to look inside. Without going in he said to Clarence: "Strong spirits occupy this place. Mighty spirits for battle or for peace. Can do either or both." That's all he said as they turned around and headed back to the house. When Clarence got back he separated from Indian Joe and reported to Byron telling him exactly what the medicine man said to him. Byron disappointed at hearing what he did was trying to figure out who stayed in that last cabin. It finally dawned on him that this was assigned to the new arrivals and his anxiety shifted to a new level. "Could this really be the source of his troubles?" he thought.

The next morning Byron made sure he didn't miss getting up before sunrise to catch Indian Joe going out the door. He met the medicine man just as he was about to walk out and followed him. Though neither one said anything to the other there was a sense of urgency in the air that could be felt between the two as they walked toward the field. Joe moved a few steps ahead of Byron and began putting on his ornaments. At the edge of the field he stopped and looked up at the sky for a long time without saying anything. Then he kneeled and opened his bag from which he took the necklaces and the plant. Rising very slowly he raised his arms and chanted something which to Byron was nothing but mumbling. Then he started to move and sway and dance slowly at first but stepping up his rhythm with each passing moment until he was at a furious pace. He kept this up for some time until he collapsed on the ground and lay very still. Byron observing this thought he had keeled over and died, but after a few minutes when he started to move and got up again, Byron knew he was okay.

For a second time Indian Joe went through the same ritual and received the same result. This time he lay there for a longer period. Three times he went through this routine receiving the same result each time until finally on the last time when he got up, he looked to the heavens and chanted then removed his ornaments. Over an hour had been spent but when Byron looked up at the sky there was absolutely no change. As a matter of fact the sun was shining so bright in the cloudless blue sky it appeared as if the chanting had chased whatever clouds were forming, away. Indian Joe packed up his gear and began to walk back toward the house. He passed by Byron without saying a word and Byron trailed close behind him wondering what to do. Indian Joe got to the house and went inside when Byron caught up with him wondering what was happening and asked him.

"So what happened?" he said.

"You have many evil spirits all around this place. Nobody make rain until master spirit say so" was Joe's reply.

Byron not wanting to hear this got extremely upset and told Joe what he thought of him. Joe didn't respond to his tirade, but calmly walked up to his room and got the rest of his things and came back. He told Byron that there was nothing more he could do here and wanted to go back home. He continued by saying that if rain was to come, then he would have to cleanse the land of the evil spirits. Byron was still very upset, but decided to let the man leave and not give him a dime to give to Charlie. He stormed outside found Sam and told him to hitch up the wagon because he was taking that useless medicine man back home. Sam got the wagon ready promptly and in a matter of minutes he and Indian Joe were headed down the path to the main road. Before leaving though, Sam asked Byron what he should tell Mr. Arbrister. Byron in an angry voice responded by saying don't tell him nothing except that his man is useless.

It was still early in the day, but Byron was feeling like it was very dark in his life. He walked back down to the fields and one by one inspected each to determine how long his crops could hold out without some much needed water. He saw all of his charges doing everything they could to protect the plants from the direct sunlight, but he knew that without water there would be nothing more they could do for much longer. While he was inspecting the last field he looked over and saw the new arrivals still working together in their usual close proximity and reflected on the words that Clarence told him about the spirits emanating from their cabin. He was tempted to call them over and test them by asking that they call on the heavens for rain. The more he looked at them work, the more he refused to believe that these men could have any power to do anything. He hung his head at his situation and rode back to the house.

That evening at dinner in the mansion he was in a somber mood and he translated that to the rest of the family. Though they tried to cheer him up their efforts seem to be going nowhere. Charlotte purposely was making attempts to lighten up the mood by reminding Byron about the plantation party that was coming up this weekend where he usually had a good time. She also seemed to be in an unusually jovial mood, for no reason. Byron for a minute thought about that and was a bit cheerful, but it was short-lived. He kept thinking about his crops and his financial outlook for the year and no matter what was said he couldn't get that off of his mind. Anna Lee and Jethro made their attempts at being lighthearted, but nothing seemed to be effective for Byron. At the end of dinner the family went into the living room as usual and sat around having light cordials and talking. Byron excused himself and went into his parlor where he took out his special nectar and began to imbibe.

Around the usual time the family broke up and each said goodnight and went to their rooms. Byron did not return to the living room to join them, but remained in his parlor continuing to avail himself of the liquid stress reliever. After some time he was again feeling somewhat lighthearted and decidedt he had enough to sustain him through the night. Although a little unsteady he got up and walked outside one final time for the evening and looked up at the heavens hoping he might see some kind of sign that Indian Joe's efforts had been successful. Something, anything indicating clouds were beginning to form he thought would be a good sign. However, the stars were bright just as the moon was and there was no sign of a single cloud forming. Exasperated he sighed, shrugged his shoulders and made his way up the stairs.

When he was just outside the room he paused before opening the door to see whether he could hear whether Charlotte was still up. Not hearing anything he eased open the door and went in. The lantern was turned down low and the dim luminosity showed Charlotte in the bed with the top portion of her nightgown pulled open. Normally, Byron would have just undressed and got in the bed after a day like today, but when he saw the plump breasts almost completely exposed he was aroused. He finished undressing and quietly moved over to the bed and got in. Half awake and feeling him get in the bed Charlotte turned her back to him. Byron wrapped his arms around her and starting kissing her neck. He continued for several minutes and then let his hands wander over her body groping her and feeling his way around. He thought she was being responsive and was about to turn over when she grabbed his hands and pushed them away from her. He started to try again, but then he heard her say sleepily: "No not tonight, not tonight maybe tomorra," and she went to sleep.

Byron had gotten himself worked up and was not prepared for this rejection, not tonight. He lay there looking up at the ceiling wondering whether he should pursue the matter anyway. The longer he lay there the more he wanted to do something. Then it occurred to him that he had someone up on the next level that had just turned seventeen and was not in a position to reject him. He had been relishing this prize from the time he made his purchase and waiting for the right time. Now that he was sure Charlotte was out for the evening and should have no way of finding out, what could be a better time than this for him to reintroduce himself in this fashion and launch a new relationship in the Candle house. He eased his way out of bed and into the hallway, looked around to make sure that no one else was up then crept up the stairs.

Outside of Suliah's room he paused to hear if anything was stirring. When he heard sounds he was a little surprised, but was glad because thinking she might be up doing something it would make things easier. Then he quietly opened the door and by the light of the moon pouring through her window he could see in the bed over by the far wall something moving in rhythm.

Chapter 5 - Family

Suliah's birthday came and went and nobody down in the quarters knew how it was celebrated. Ever since she was a little girl Myanna had made sure that no matter how adverse the circumstances were Suliah would have some kind of celebration. On the Sutter Plantation, even though he was a stern master, he respected weddings and birthdays and allowed his charges to do something special for each other on those days. Whenever Suliah or Linwood had a birthday it was Bessie May that made the cake and made sure that it got to the children in time for whatever celebration. Since coming to the Candle farm Myanna and Jobba quickly realized that things were much different here and observances for slaves like weddings and birthdays were not going to take place in any special or recognized fashion. Myanna's attempt to make sure that Suliah had some celebration, even though she and Jobba couldn't be there, was successful in ways that she would never have imagined.

From the time that she arrived in the mansion, Jethro had been pursuing her in subtle ways that became more pronounced and overt as each week passed. At times when they were close or just near enough to brush one another he would allow his touch to linger longer than the situation required. As a young slave girl in a place where the missus of the house was sensitive to everything she did Suliah was afraid most of the time to even look like she was doing anything wrong. So when he started getting closer to her and more often, she was afraid to repulse him or to even say anything to Aunt Tee. After awhile however, especially after the night that she was assaulted he became her hero. She began to look at him in a different light and was more receptive to his touches.

He would continuously make overtures to her and whenever possible steal a kiss in the shadows when no one else was around. It didn't take too long before her resistance was gone and she became enamored of him and looked forward to being near him. The shadowy brushes and secret encounters went on for some time until finally on the night of her birthday after the big celebration in Anna Lee's room he quietly eased his way up to the third floor and entered her room. It wasn't that late and she was still up sitting on the bed when she saw the door open. At first she was surprised because nobody usually came up to that level this late, but when she saw that it was him her whole demeanor changed from surprise to gladness. When he approached her she was no longer afraid, but receptive to his advances. Being it was a first time for her in this type situation she wasn't quite sure what to do, but she allowed him to take command. He moved slowly across the room never taking his eyes from her and sat on the bed beside her.

With very little conversation he moved from talking to kissing and embracing and then making the big surge. She offered very little resistance as her body became ready for the final act. Jethro was not the expert that he thought he was in these matters and it took some time before he was able to complete the mission that his soldier was undertaking. Afterward, they both lay back in one another's arms enjoying their new relationship, but also afraid of the new boundaries they had crossed. They lay together embracing off and on for most of the night until just before the early light when he got up and crept back down to his room. Before leaving though, he promised that he would return tomorrow and they would do it again. She readily agreed.

After dinner the day after her birthday the family went into the living room as they usually did and drank their teas and cordials and talked for hours. Aunt Tee and Suliah were not in the room, but were nearby also as usual to be available for any special requests. This night, Byron did not join them, but was in his parlor having some of his special nectar to release his stress of the day. When the time came for the family to retire, Jethro was the first one to get up and leave the room. He hurried to where he knew Suliah would be waiting and whispered to her out of Aunt Tee's sight that she should go to her room and he would be there shortly. Suliah checked with Aunt Tee to see if she would need her for anything more and then went upstairs. The rest of the family each went to their own room and went to bed, even Byron although somewhat later.

Jethro allowed sufficient time for when he believed they were all asleep and then made his way up to the third floor as he had done last night. Suliah was in bed anticipating his arrival and when he got there little time was squandered in preliminaries. He undressed throwing his clothes over the rocking chair near the door and turned down the lantern until it was almost out then eased into the bed. The kissing began instantly; mild at first but grew more passionate as each second passed. For her it was more comfortable than before and even though she felt some lingering soreness from her first encounter it soon dissipated from the heat of this current intromission. They were well into the rhythm of passion and writhing joyfully when the door opened. Too far down the road of no return they continued.

Byron entered the room and saw in the dim light the rising and falling of something in the far corner. He moved closer to the bed and it became painfully clear to him what was going on. In a fit of rage, he ran over and grabbed the man and threw him to the floor. Thinking that it was Clarence he rolled the man over and raised his fist to smash his face. As the figure turned into the light of the moon coming through the window the face became clear. When Byron saw it, his arm dropped to his side like a soaked dishrag and he fell backward on the floor in a state of shock. Jethro, although more shocked than Byron, was able to get up grab his clothes and run from the room down the stairs.

Byron continued to sit there in disbelief not wanting to accept what he had just witnessed. He turned his head to Suliah who was sitting up in the bed paralyzed with fear revealing all of her beautiful nakedness. Close enough to behold the magnificent view with clarity the image became etched indelibly in his mind, but what he had come for no longer mattered. He slowly got up and left the room not knowing what his next move would be. Still wrestling with the thought that it was his own son that defiled what he had set up in his mind as his prize possession, he wished that he could relive the whole day. He now wished that he had listened to what Charlotte was trying to tell him and been more observant of Jethro. Still groggy from the shock he staggered into his bedroom and got in the bed. By this time Charlotte neither acknowledged his entry nor did she move, but continued with the smooth rhythm of her breathing.

After Byron left her room Suliah calmed down enough to lie back and pull the cover up over her. Her mind was reeling from the thoughts of what tomorrow might bring. Her perception of what might happen to her now took into account all the acts that she had seen happen to slaves since the time that she was able to understand that their fate was not in their control. She lay there looking up at the ceiling in the darkness no longer able to cry, but unable to laugh either. The things that happened to her since the time she came here began to resurface in her mind like she was watching her life relived in slow motion. Unable to stop the images and feeling like she had brought all of this on herself, she turned over and tried to go to sleep.

Over 30 miles away someone else was feeling her pain also. From the time that Byron entered the room, shudders ran up and down the spine of Bessimay as she spiritually connected with her godchild Suliah and felt the danger right down to the possible outcome of the last minute. With all her heart and deepest emotions she sent to Suliah the thoughts of something she had said to her when Suliah was just seven years old.

She taught her to think these words whenever she found herself to be troubled.

Have mercy on me O God According to Your loving kindness;
According to the multitude of Your tender mercies
Blot out my transgressions
Wash me thoroughoy from my iniquity
And cleanse me from my sin (Psalm 51:1-2)

Confused and unsettled about her future her mind was all but devastated by what she had just experienced, when the Bessimay connection kicked in. Just as if the night had suddenly turned to day and the moon became the sun so were the negative thoughts extinguished by the link. She felt herself smiling feeling the power of the link and knowing that the connection was to someone she loved dearly. The words that popped into her head at that moment were just as she recalled having learned them and made her feel as though her sin was not unforgivable. She closed her eyes and went to sleep.

The sun came up as usual, the cock crowed as usual, the horn blew as usua,l but in the mansion the next day there was nothing usual about the morning. Byron dragged himself out of bed early and went down to the kitchen. Aunt Tee who was usually there preparing breakfast was not present. Byron walked back to her room to inquire whether she was okay, but she was not there either. Then he looked all over the first level trying to determine if she was anywhere in the house. Having no success looking inside he opened the door and looked outside. There was no sign of her anywhere and this was puzzling. He came down early so that he might eat before the rest arrived and be able to make a decision about what he was going to do about Suliah and Jethro. So far his plan was failing and his recollection of last night's event was weighing heavy on his mind.

Since he couldn't find Aunt Tee he decided he would make his own cup of coffee and go into his parlor to think. While he was attending to the task in walked Clarence and announced that Aunt Tee had gotten up real early and left the house. Byron asked him what that was all about, but all Clarence could tell him was that he didn't think she left alone. This started Byron thinking and wondering whether Suliah had come down early too and left with Aunt Tee. He left his coffee on the table and skipped up the stairs to the third floor. At her door he didn't hesitate, but threw it open to see the empty bed. Now he was really angry, not so much because she had beat him to making a decision about her welfare, but the fact that he wasn't the one to make the decision. He felt as if his power had been usurped or at the least diminished. Next he went down to Jethro's room to see if they could have left together, but when he opened that door there was his son sleeping as if nothing had happened. He didn't try to wake him, but quietly closed the door and went back downstairs to the kitchen to question Clarence some more.

The next battery of inquiries required that Clarence pinpoint a time when she left and also how was she dressed. On these issues Clarence wasn't much help because he said that he was still half asleep and only caught a glimpse of her when she was leaving, but it seemed like someone was waiting for her in the hallway. Byron started to add up the numbers and concluded that the two would equal Aunt Tee and Suliah but the destination had no solution. As he was still pondering his dilemma, the second horn sounded and the slaves started making their way out to the fields. Byron ran to the back door to see if perhaps he could see Jobba and Myanna coming so he could ask them whether they knew where the girl was. After giving this idea some further thought he backed off because he certainly didn't want them to know that Suliah was missing unless he sold her.

Not knowing what else to do he went in his parlor to carry out his original plan. However, all the pieces that he was going to work with in making his decision were no longer available to complete his scenario. This made him even angrier so he just sat there thinking. It wasn't long before he heard voices in the hallway and one of them sounded like Aunt Tee so he jumped up from his chair and went to see. It was she just coming back in.

"Where were you, I bin lookin all ova for ya this mornin?"

"Now massa Byron ya needs ta set down so's I kin tell ya all dat's happin."

Byron heard her words lowered his anger level a bit and sat down at the kitchen table. None of the other family members had come down yet and it was just the three of them, Byron, Clarence and Aunt Tee.

"Suliah dun tol me all dat happin here las night an she say ta tell ya she real sorry. Massa Byron she real scared an came ta me fer help so I hid her in de mountains `til you calm down."

After hearing this Byron flew off the handle again and told Aunt Tee she had no business doing anything with her because the matter wasn't any of her business. He then threatened to have her whipped, but when he said that and she stared him right in his eyes he immediately dropped that threat. He did go on to tell her that he wanted Suliah back in the house right away and he would decide what would happen to her. Aunt Tee held her ground and told him that she would stay in the mountains until he promised not to whip her. Byron was arguing with her as if she was an equal because he knew that the whole operation of his house was dependent on the knowledge of this woman. While they were going back and forth down came Anna Lee and Charlotte. Overhearing the noise Charlotte poked her head in the kitchen and asked what was going on. Byron stopped talking to Aunt Tee and told Charlotte to meet him in the dining room.

Anna Lee was already there seated and waiting to be served, but when Byron walked in with Charlotte she knew something was wrong. Byron waited for Charlotte to sit then he pulled up his chair and started right in telling the whole story about what he saw last night. Anna Lee was embarrassed, but Charlotte took the I told you so attitude and then wanted to know now what he was going to do about Suliah. Not having a ready answer for her he then went on to say that Aunt Tee had hid her up in the mountains somewhere so he didn't know right now what he was going to do. Charlotte told him that he was losing control of his own house and if he didn't discipline Aunt Tee then he would be the slave not the master. Byron heard this and really didn't know what to do now so he skipped breakfast and left the house.

In the fields that morning the slave network had already spread the news about what went on in the mansion last night. How information like that got to those who rarely got into the house was beyond knowing, but the news was seldom wrong. When Jobba got it, he was ready to throw down his tools head up there and get his daughter come hell or high water. Myanna, the cooler head once again prevailed and kept him out of the stocks or maybe worse. She told him they needed to learn more about the situation before they could do anything. He agreed. They both decided then that they were going to approach Daniel and see what he says to do about it.

The news circling around the plantation was that Jethro had become Suliah's lover and that he was going to take her away with him. It further said that Mr. Candle didn't approve of the relationship and he was going to disown his son and make him leave by himself. For the first time, the information spreading wasn't completely accurate, but contained enough truth to make it real enough for Jobba to be concerned about the fate of his daughter. The more he thought about how she must have been pressured into doing whatever she had to do, the more he felt that he had let her down by not being there for her. No matter how much Myanna reminded him that there was nothing he could do, he would not be consoled by his lack of power.

He was determined to get Daniel to intervene on his behalf to not only get her away from that house, but to also make a way for him to take his whole family away and be free. How it was to be done he had no idea. But the more he listened to the words that Daniel preached on Sunday evenings down by the river, the more he was convinced that the new day he said was coming was already here and he just needed for him to tell him how to take advantage of it. When Daniel spoke of how the slaves of Egypt were given a leader that took them away from bondage and servitude by the hand of God, Jobba was wondering why he couldn't be the leader for all these people here who certainly needed to be led away from this bondage. He wanted to know why his daughter, his baby had to go through what he suspected she did before she could be free and choose for herself who she would be given to. His questions about the unfairness of his life as compared to those who lived in that mansion kept on bringing up for him, does God approve of this? Tonight he was going to go down to Daniel's place and get some direct answers.

Charlotte and Anna Lee were still in the dining room when Jethro finally came down. He walked in not knowing that they had already been made aware of what he did so he sat down in his favorite seat as usual. At first they just stared at him saying nothing, not even acknowledging his good morning, until he sensed that something wasn't right. He looked first at his mother and then at Anna Lee and asked what the matter was. It was Charlotte who responded.

"I told you some time back when first I saw you lookin cockeyed at that gal that you betta keep your hands off of her. Now you dun did it and your father is fit to be tied. How could ya do that boy, right here in his own house?"

Jethro was shocked that his father had told and he dropped his glass on the table.

"But mama I love her. I guess I have since the time she got here. What happin last night bin comin for a long time, it jest had to happin that way."

"You caint love her, she's a niggah an we ain't gonna have no mess like that around here. Now I don't know what your daddy's thinkin about doing, but she will not be here much longer."

When Jethro heard that he left his breakfast jumped up from the table and ran out of the house in search of his father. Byron was down at the fields still trying to figure out how he was going to salvage his crops when he saw Jethro coming. He wasn't sure whether he was still mad at him for spoiling his plans or whether he was mad at himself for not seeing it coming. When Jethro got close to him he told him to stop right there.

"Daddy, daddy I'm sorry 'bout las night, but you gotta unerstan that I love that gal an I wanna be with her."

"You must be crazy boy. I thought I raise you better'n that. Seem like you ain't got the sense of that mule over yonda. You caint be with her, its agin the law and you'all caint do nothin about that."

"But daddy you know we kin go way somewhere. Maybe go way up north. They say up there we kin be together always."

"You talkin crazy son an I'm gonna haf to help you git strait. I'm gonna sell that gal way from here so's you kin come to ya senses."

"No daddy please don't do that. Please don't do that."

"Its gonna be done soon as I kin, now you git on away from me, you hear?"

Jethro knew that once his father made up his mind about something there was no changing it so he hung his head turned around and walked back to the house. When he got there he ran up to the third floor looking for Suliah. He didn't find her there and came running back down to the kitchen. Not seeing her there either he called to Aunt Tee who was in the dining room cleaning up the breakfast dishes.

"Aunt Tee you know where Suliah is?"

"Yes, I know. She's somewhere where you caint git to her. What you did las night yo father didn't want ta happin an I think you knowed it. He powerful mad at you, but I guess ya already knows dat too."

"But Aunt Tee I love that gal. I really love her an I wanna be with her. Where is she?"

"I caint tell you dat 'til yo father decide what he gonna do wit her."

Jethro was trying to figure out where she could be when it dawned on him that she might be back in the cabin with her family. He left the kitchen and ran down to her cabin slung open the door and searched all over. There was no one in the house at all. His last resort was to go back to the field and search there, but he knew that his father would not have sent her to work in no field so he gave up on that idea. With no other place that he could think of he wandered back to the house and went to his room. The rest of the morning was spent trying to figure out what he could do to find her. It finally occurred to him late in the afternoon that the only one who might know something was Clarence. He got up from his bed and went down to find him. Clarence was out on the back porch peeling potatoes.

"Clarence have you seen Suliah?"

"No massa not since yestidy."

"You don't have no idea where she might be?"

"No massa like I say, I ain seen her since yestidy."

"You wouldn't keep nothing from me like that would you?"

"No, no massa I jest don knows where she be."

Having exhausted his last resource his depression was growing and he had no other source to tap. Back to the room he went and stayed until dinnertime.

Byron spent the rest of the day roaming around his fields not really paying attention to the state of the crops, but his mind was more on where Suliah was and whether he was really going to sell her. It crossed his mind that where ever Aunt Tee has stashed her she was going to have to bring her food at some point. He decided he was going to follow her tonight and see exactly where that was. After coming to this resolution he left the fields and went back to the house and into his parlor until dinnertime.

Dinner was a silent occasion where they ate, but nobody talked. Byron kept looking at Jethro off and on and Charlotte looked at Byron the same amount. Jethro kept his head down afraid to return his father's glances. Anna Lee looked at her plate. They spent the whole meal in silence and when Byron finished eating he excused himself and went and sat on the back porch to wait and see if Aunt Tee was going to come out that way. The after dinner tea and cordials was called off for the night and each member went their own separate way. This gave Aunt Tee a good opportunity to pack some food and take it to Suliah. When Byron heard someone coming toward the back door he went and hid under the porch to see who came out. It was indeed Aunt Tee with a basket of what he believed was the food being delivered to Suliah.

He maintained his crouch long enough until she had a sufficient head start. Then he followed keeping enough distance between them so that she would not suspect. When he saw where she was going up the mountain it never occurred to him that the path they were following would lead to a cave. As they neared the cave he was surprised to see that the ground was well worn as if the trail had been used many times. Once he saw her enter the cave he knew that must be where Suliah was so he moved in closer and stepped inside. Not only did he see Suliah there, but also when he stepped inside what happened to him he was totally unprepared for.

Suliah was sitting on a rock with her arms folded as if she was in some kind of a trance. The light of the fire was not bright enough for him to see clearly all of the markings on the wall, but it was enough for him to know that this was more than just a cave that the Indians may have used in the past. As Aunt Tee moved closer to Suliah and placed the basket down in front of her a loud noise was heard as if thunder had come out from beyond the back of the cave. He felt the tremor and the shock knocked him to the ground. It was then that Aunt Tee became aware that she had been followed and her eyes went vacant and her smile disappeared. She turned to Byron and beckoned him to come forward. Byron no longer recognized the woman that he knew as Aunt Tee, but the person that stood before him seemed possessed. He was almost afraid to get closer, but something was compelling him to do so. When he got within a few steps of her he saw something emerge from the wall that he couldn't believe was happening. He tried to turn and run, but control of his body had left him and he was at the mercy of the wall creature.

Aunt Tee turned and kneeled before this thing and it touched her and communicated something. Although Byron was aware of all that was going on he couldn't move or say anything. Suliah got up came over to him and put her hand on his forehead. When she touched him her hand was cold and a shiver ran down his spine. Nothing was said, but he felt something inside him telling him that he would not do anything to harm this girl ever. He wasn't sure how long he remained in the cave, but sometime later he woke up and he was in his parlor sitting in his favorite chair. He wasn't sure if he just had a bad dream, especially with all that happened in the last few days or whether he really had been in the mountains in some kind of cave. When he looked at his shoes to see if there was any indication that he really might have been, there was no trace of evidence. He resigned himself to letting it be a bad dream.

That night after they finished dinner, Jobba told Myanna he was going to Daniel's to try and get some answers. Myanna asked if he wanted her to go with him and he said no he wanted to talk to him alone. Myanna reminded him that she didn't believe Suliah's fate was up to Daniel, but if he had an idea about how they could get her back home please let them know. Jobba agreed he would ask and left.

He stepped out the door and the warm air of the approaching summer season greeted him. Up and down the lane several of his neighbors had come out also to avail themselves of a beautiful late spring evening. He nodded to a few who were close by and continued making his way to the last cabin on the left just before the river. At the door once again he hesitated and listened before knocking. No sound. He wondered whether the four had retired early or were they down at the river. Often the word had circulated among the slaves that the four men could be seen on occasions other than the usual church meeting nights going down to the river. No one had ever followed them so there was no verification about what they did there. Jobba knocked again a little harder this time and waited. Soon the door opened and one of the associates greeted him and invited him in. He was directed to sit at the table in the dining area while his host went to get Daniel.

"Peace be unto you my brother, is all well?" Daniel spoke in a soft tone.

"Yes my brother, uh, well I really mean no. All's not well. I needs ta talk wit you `bout my little girl up dere in dat house. Dey ain treatin her good an yestidy I heared dat de boy up dere dun spoil her now. I caint do nuthin `bout it, but I believes you kin. Tell me how ta git her outta dere."

"Jobba, Jobba, how small is your faith. Why do you come to me believing it is I who can help you? When you were dipped in the water and became baptized did you not believe in what you were doing? Did you not understand the covenant circle that you entered? My brother you must know deep within that when your faith is small then that which you desire lies captive in the darkness. All that you hope for will not be attainable until you believe.

Now faith is the substance of things hoped for, the evidence of things not seen. By faith we understand that the worlds were framed by the word of God so that the things which are seen were not made of things which are visible (Heb: 11:1, 3)

Upon hearing these words Jobba, though still unsure what it all meant, felt a new sense of calm as if he was floating along the river being peacefully carried by the rocking motion of gentle ripples. He looked into Daniel's eyes and the serenity that he saw there compelled him to breathe easy and release the tension that had overtaken him. Daniel continued to talk and with each passing moment Jobba felt a new resurgence of strength. It was not until Daniel revealed to him that something else had happened to Suliah greater than her introduction into womanhood, that Jobba's peace was shaken once again. Daniel went on to explain that just as he and Myanna were exposed to the spirits that lived in the cave, but walked the plantation, Suliah had become one with them. He told Jobba that except for a powerful force that hovered over her coming from some distance away, she would have been totally consumed.

Jobba heard what the preacher man said, but couldn't imagine what force he was referring to until Daniel continued. He referred to something that happened on another plantation far away perhaps when she was a child. Immediately Jobba's thoughts leaped back to Bessimay and her protective but strange ways. He knew that she was close to the children, but until now had no idea how much of an influence she had nor did he realize that she was as spiritual as the preacher man was indicating. Jobba couldn't recall ever seeing her once at any of the meetings that the itinerant preacher who came to the Sutter place held. It didn't much matter now because if she was the influence, the force that was holding Suliah in check, then he was thankful. He asked Daniel what he should do now.

Daniel called to the others to join him and with Jobba they held hands and kneeled before the cross while Daniel prayed.

"Father in heaven, my Lord and my God, once again I come before your throne of grace and into your presence. With a bowed head and humble heart I come first to thank you for what you've already done for this family in leading them along the way. Your grace and your mercy is sufficient for them and I pray that you will open the eyes of this your new convert so that he may see with spiritual eyes and not those of the flesh. Let him know that the battle is not his to fight, but it is Yours. There is one of his flock that still sits outside the covenant circle and he needs your guidance on the matter. Grant unto him your wisdom and your courage so that he may move and act according to your will. Let it be done for him and the one that he seeks as you will it to be so. We ask for the guidance and the blessing in the precious name of your son Jesus, and it is in his name that we pray. Amen!"

When Daniel finished and they arose Jobba again felt the calm that he knew before. He left the house almost running to get home anxious to get back so that he could tell Myanna just what happened. He was excited to know that there was a protective spirit that watched over Suliah and he wanted Myanna to share in his good feeling. He was sure that she would know where the protection was coming from since he believed that she knew Bessie May better than he did. He pushed open the door to the cabin went inside past the Harpers sitting around the table and ran upstairs. Myanna was sitting at their table mending Linwood's pants when Jobba came bounding up.

"Myna she gwine be alright, gwine be alright," he blurted out.

"What you talkin?"

"De preacher man say she gotta good spirit dat be's wit her alla time. He say de spirit come to her when she a little girl. Ya know I think dat Bessie May got somethin ta do wit it."

"Why was he talkin `bout her havin dis good spirit, what else he say?"

"Well he say dat she bin taken to de cave an put under dat spell we got."

When Myanna heard that she dropped her needle and stared at Jobba.

"You mean she put under dat spell fer good?"

"Preacher man say dat she ain completely under their `fluence `cause she got dat good spirit ova her, but she ain one a us completely either. He say dat we gotta have faith an believe dat God gonna fight her battle. I believe he gwine do dat, but I still think I needs ta hep Him."

"You heard what the preacher man say an ya still gonna do it yo way, huh?"

"Well I reckon I gwine give him a little time, den yeah I'se doin it my way."

"Jobba I dono what gits into you sometime, but you gonna git yoself killed yet tryna do things yo way."

It was after midnight when Aunt Tee and Clarence sneaked their way up the mountain to the cave. This was not a night that a dance was scheduled, but Aunt Tee wanted to make sure that her newest tribal member was okay. She felt something odd happening during Suliah's conversion. It was not like any of the others, but seemed that even though she appeared to fall under the spell a part of her was resistant to the change. Aunt Tee especially wanted her because she felt Suliah would be pleasing to her idol. When they arrived at the cave the fire was burning very low and Suliah just sat on the rock not doing anything. She was staring at the wall as if she was in some communication with the thing, but when Aunt Tee touched her she turned her head without being startled and looked at the couple. Aunt Tee told her that she was taking her back to the house because Byron had been warned and he wouldn't be doing anything to her.

Clarence helped her up off the rock and they all slowly made their way down the mountain to the house. They went in the back door and in the quietness of the early morning hours led her up to her room. Suliah was glad to get back in her room and into the comfort of her own bed. Aunt Tee and Clarence gave her one final look and left. It didn't take Suliah no time at all before she was sleeping.

Byron had trouble sleeping that night. His subconscious wrestled with the images that he saw earlier in what he supposed was a dream and he had trouble trying to reconcile whether it really was a dream or was there something happening on his plantation. He tossed and turned in bed so much that Charlotte had to shake him more than once to try and get him to calm down. It was a fitful night that went on well into the wee hours of the morning when he finally was able to enter into a short period of REM. Charlotte woke up early like he did and as he started to get up questioned him about what was on his mind. He told her that the lack of rain and all that was happening with the crops and the notion that his son has about a slave in his house was enough to drive any man crazy and he just had to work it out. She understood his concern about the crops and there was no control for him over when it would rain, but she told him that he had total control of the fate of Suliah. She said also that if that gal was gone then after maybe a couple more social gatherings with some new young girls coming here, then Jethro would forget all about her. As Byron sat on the side of the bed listening to Charlotte, what she was saying made some sense, but he was still conflicted in his mind about what to do with his diminished prize.

He got up made his way over to the washbasin and got cleaned up. The horn for the start of the new day had not sounded yet and after putting on his clothes he moved over to the window to see what was wrong. The rooster had already made his announcement and what should have followed shortly thereafter was out of synch. Quickly he made his way downstairs and out the door to see if anything was wrong. He looked over at Sam's cabin and he could see the lantern light still on and his horse tied up at the post out in front. Wondering whether Sam may be ill he walked at a brisk pace to the door and knocked on it. When there was no answer after several minutes he pushed it open and looked inside. There was no sign of Sam and Byron got concerned. He went back outside and started to look around when he spotted one of the other overseers and called him over.

"Where's Sammie?" he asked.

"Dono suh, ain seen him since yestidy. I was jest comin by to git him myself when he ain blowed the horn an ain nobody gittin up."

"Well you go on an blow that horn an git them folks out here workin."

"Yas suh right away."

The overseer went in Sam's place found the horn came outside and blew it. The workers who were already up came moving up the path wondering what had happened. Byron met them at the edge of the first field and asked the first bunch if anyone had seen Sam. The response was negative which just added to the mystery and Byron was getting very concerned. He decided he would go back in the house and get some breakfast and then come back and search for his head overseer.

Inside only Anna Lee had come down this early to eat so he took a chance and asked her whether she had seen him. Anna Lee replied that she hadn't seen him in a couple of days, but the last time she remembered seeing him was with that Indian man that was here. It then occurred to Byron that he had not seen him either since he sent him back to the Arbrister Plantation to take Indian Joe back home. There was no reason for Sam to be detained there for any length of time and certainly not overnight unless Charlie was up to something. With the message that Byron sent back with Sam he now wondered if he had angered his neighbor to the point of taking it out on Sam. He couldn't imagine that Mr. Arbrister was that kind of a man that would do something like that, but when he thought about how much Sam said he was angry over being swindled maybe he was holding him hostage.

Byron thought about going up to Charlie's place himself, but then he thought what if I'm wrong and Sam is not even there and he would be standing in front of Charlie face to face. He didn't want that. He continued eating and thinking trying to figure out where else Sam could be. Before he finished breakfast a knock was heard at the door and Clarence went to open it. It didn't take long until Byron identified the voice of his chief subordinate and he hurriedly got up from the table to walk out and see where he had been.

The two met in the hallway and Byron questioned him about why the horn didn't blow this morning. Sam apologized, but then explained that late last night he saw what looked like a fire on the other side of the river and he wanted to get up there and check it out. He reminded Byron about what he told him before that he got news of some runaways living up there and now he heard lately that there was a new movement of many more slaves rebelling against their masters. He went on to say that he couldn't see anything last night because by the time he got to where he thought it was the fire was out. Before sunrise this morning he went back up to see if he could catch somebody. Even though he didn't actually see anybody there was lots of evidence that someone had been cooking there and left their scraps all over. He was real convinced that the runaways were there.

Byron thanked him for his vigilance and said keep watching out for them. Inside Byron was thinking that this was all he needed now was for some runaways to be roaming his property and maybe talking to his slaves at night about coming up to the mountains and be free. He told Sam to go on down to the fields and he would join him there shortly to see what the status was of the crops and maybe figure out what else they could possibly do to save them. Sam left and Byron went back in the dining room. By this time Jethro had come down and was sitting there eating.

"Daddy has you made up your mind for real yet 'bout Suliah?"

"Don't botha me now with that son I got other things on ma mind this mornin more important then that gal. You know you should be payin more attention to what's goin on at this here farm and then you wouldn't be so worried about her. We got a real bad crop situation and all's you thinkin about is that pretty face. You oughta be shamed."

"I know you said we got some trouble with the crops, but it's gonna rain soon I jest know it an then everything be fine, you'll see. But she ain't got nothin to do with the land so please don't let that be why you punish her."

Byron heard what Jethro said and started to lash out at him, but restrained himself. He just said he was still thinking on the matter and would let him know when the time was right. Jethro looked at his father and there was nothing more to say so he got up from the table and went outside. While Byron continued to sit in the dining room he heard a voice coming from the kitchen that sounded very familiar. He got up and moved closer to listen more intently. Sure enough it was Suliah talking to Aunt Tee. Byron stepped into the kitchen and stared directly at Suliah without saying anything. It was Aunt Tee who spoke first and told Byron that

Suliah was back, but he would have to treat her differently. Byron felt an urge to discipline Aunt Tee right then and tell her that she was forgetting her station in the house, but something came over him that restrained his actions and he couldn't understand why he was unable to carry out his threat.

He opened his mouth, but what came out was almost a plea to Suliah to behave herself while she lived in this house. Suliah was so surprised by his tone and his words that she almost laughed, but caught herself. Byron was so embarrassed at his lack of punishing authority in his voice that he turned suddenly and exited the room. Both Aunt Tee and Suliah burst out laughing.

When Jethro found out that Suliah was back in the house he wasted no time in trying to get her alone so he could talk to her. This was not to be for Aunt Tee had her so busy with various chores that she had little more than a minute to herself. When Aunt Tee didn't have her busy doing something, then it was Anna Lee who demanded her assistance. Jethro was growing more depressed each time he would pass by her and not be able to touch her the way he wanted to. The tension was building up to the point that he felt if he didn't get close to her at least one more time then he would lose his mind. He decided that tonight he was going to try and make one of his midnight excursions, no matter what the cost.

The evening came and the routine was as usual. After the teas and cordials were enjoyed in what appeared to be a return to some sense of normalcy in the house, the family broke up and each retired to his room. One change had been made. Although Suliah was not ordered to give up her room and return to sleeping in the hallway, to Charlotte's displeasure, Clarence was ordered to give up sharing his room with Aunt Tee and sleep just outside of Suliah's door on a bed taken from one of the other rooms on the third floor. Jethro knew this, but he also knew that when Clarence went to sleep he was one who slept so deeply that only the sound of the horn and the morning light pouring through his window would awaken him. Jethro planned his maneuver well so he thought. He would ease his way up the stairs long after he knew that his parents and sister were fast asleep, then he would camp at the top until he could assess the breathing pattern of Clarence who he also knew had a habit of snoring.

His plan was working and things were unfolding per his scheme. He was now planted at the top of the stairs with Clarence in plain view. Suliah's door wasn't directly behind Clarence's bed, but off to the side of it, which gave Jethro ample space to pass by a thoroughly sleep committed guardian. When he heard the snoring sounds he was looking for and the breathing rhythm indicated that only Clarence's body was in the hallway, Jethro started making his move. With feline grace he eased his way over to the door and turned the knob. Slowly he pushed it open and poked his head inside to see whether she was possibly still up. The light inside was dim and since there was no moon tonight he had a difficult time trying to see in the dark what her status might be. He tiptoed across the room until he came to the bed and looked closely to see if she was there. He was hoping his eyes would adjust to the dark quickly and help him discover what he wanted to see. This didn't happen. Not seeing clearly what he wanted he knelt down beside the bed and ran his hand across it hoping to feel the object of his desire. To his great surprise he felt along the bed from the foot to the head, but all he touched was the covers and the pillow. Suliah was not there. Frustrated and disappointed he returned to his room.

Once inside he was bewildered at where she might be. The thought never crossed his mind that he was not the only one who was aware of Clarence's sleeping patterns. No one knew better than Aunt Tee just how soundly he slept once the snoring started. It was Aunt Tee who, with her wizened instincts, suspected that a midnight move by Jethro might be imminent and invited Suliah to take Clarence's bed for awhile. All the time Jethro was plotting his moves Aunt Tee was one step ahead and provided an infallible defense. Jethro couldn't sleep from wondering what his next move would be. Suliah slept peacefully enjoying the false protection of her mentor. Jethro's mind was filled with confusion about whether Byron was really going to carry out his threat. Suliah slept peacefully enjoying the false protection of her mentor. Jethro was having great difficulty accepting the conditions of living between the races. Suliah slept peacefully enjoying the false protection of her mentor.

In the hills high above the Candle mansion there was a lot of activity going on. Sam was absolutely right about what he suspected concerning runaways. At least ten maybe twelve of them had fled from two plantations near Byron's and they were making their way trying to get to Aunt Tee to seek her protection. It was known by most of the slaves on all the plantations in the area that there was a chance if one could get to become one of Aunt Tee's followers then they would be able to find freedom. Never had it been confirmed that there was any truth to this, but most sought freedom with such determination that they were willing to believe anything was possible. Running from pursuing slave chasers and ducking the elements of the forest became a way of life for them for many weeks at a time. Sam was able to find only limited traces of their whereabouts because they would never spend more than one night in any given spot. At night covered by darkness and even during the day hidden behind the trees, they observed the goings on of the Candle Plantation for some time and were able to get a message down to a few of his slaves that they wanted to attend the next ritual ceremony.

When the word got to Aunt Tee that they were up there and wanted to attend the next affair, she was delighted at the prospect of new converts. It would only be a couple of days before the appearance of the next full moon and she was anxious to get word back to them on how to come.

She was having a hard time trying to figure out who would be the best candidate to be able to sneak up there into the mountains without drawing suspicion. She considered sending Clarence, but at night she knew he would be missed if not available for any length of time. Next she considered another slave who was familiar with those mountains, but after giving it extended thought she realized that this slave was not reliable and may or may not get up there in time to deliver her message. Finally she came to Penniman who she knew was a devoted follower and bore the fear of her that she foisted on her true believers. So it was decided that he would be the messenger to the runaways.

Clarence was given the task of getting to Penniman while he was working in the field and tell him what Aunt Tee's instructions are. It was no problem for Clarence to get out of the house when he wanted to, but his appearance in the fields was not usual and he was taking a chance by venturing out there without a specific reason. He was able to get around this by going to Byron early in the morning and telling him that he needed to talk with one of the field hands, who he didn't name, about his rations. Byron thought this a little out of the ordinary and asked Clarence what the problem was. Clarence responded by saying that he believed that with the last distribution, this hand got more than he was supposed to and the difference would be made up in the next one. Byron didn't think this was any major issue so he had no problem with Clarence going out to speak with Penniman. After attending to the breakfast dishes and dining room clean up, Clarence made his way out to the field where Penniman was working.

Penniman had no idea what was happening when he saw Clarence coming toward him in the field. It was so rare that Clarence was seen with any field hand during the day that Penniman immediately suspected that it had to be something to do with the needs of Aunt Tee. Penniman looked around to see whether Clarence walking toward him was okay with the overseer in the area and when nothing was said he thought it must be alright. The overseer just observed the interaction. Clarence got close to Penniman and explained all that Aunt Tee had conveyed to him. Penniman surprised that he had been selected to deliver the word felt a little uncomfortable about the choice. Although he was as much a follower as anyone on the grounds, he had witnessed so much with Jobba, Myanna and the Daniel believers that he was ambivalent about being the one picked from the crowd to do her bidding. He listened intently to what Clarence told him and committed it to memory word for word. The instructions said that the message must be delivered tonight so that the mountain dwellers would know to come down to the last cabin on the right meet with an Aunt Tee designee and be led up to the cave. Penniman told Clarence he would carry out the command and Clarence returned to the house.

Jobba and Myanna, who happened to be working this day in the same area, saw what was happening with Penniman and wondered what was going on. During the morning break, Jobba tried to angle his way over to Penniman and ask what Clarence wanted, but the overseer saw Jobba leaving his area and restrained him. All day long, attempts were made to find out early what the conversation was about, but all efforts were not successful. Penniman didn't communicate with Jobba or any other field hand for the rest of the day and concentrated on keeping the words that he was given clearly imbedded in his mind. It wasn't that the message was complicated, but there were some things that Aunt Tee wanted made clear to the prospects which was that they were to bring certain things that could only be found up in those mountains, to the ritual. Penniman had no desire to forget what they were and incur Aunt Tee's displeasure.

All day long there was a buzz around the plantation about who was watching them up in the mountains. As the news spread quickly and the knowledge that these slaves had been able to leave their plantations and exist in the mountains for some time without being caught was encouraging. Many of the field hands were anxious to meet these new prospects and find out how they did it and what were the chances that they could do the same thing. It was kind of an exciting time because they looked forward with anticipation that the news coming down from the mountains might be their way out. No one at this point could have possibly known that there were things developing on some other plantation that would affect their lives and every other slave in the state of Virginia. Not only were things developing in this state that would affect their lives, but developments in the national political arena were also beginning to take shape.

When the workday was over, Jobba made a dash to get to Penniman before he got to the house, but Penniman eluded him. He seemed to just disappear when he left the field. Jobba walked in the house expecting to see him on his bed, but he wasn't there either. Tralene was there so he asked her if she had seen him come home and she replied that she hadn't. Then he asked her if she knew anything about why Clarence came out to the field today and again she replied in the negative. This lack of knowledge about something that was coming down from the mansion was beginning to peak Jobba's curiosity and he was getting antsy to find out. He wanted to know anything and everything that took place in that house because it might concern the welfare of his child. Not getting any answers here he went upstairs to see if Myanna had heard anything, but she didn't have any idea either. Linwood was there so he asked him. Linwood told him that he had heard from one of his friends that somebody from down here had to take a message up to the people in the mountains and tell them about the dance tomorrow. He believed that Penniman was the person given the assignment.

Jobba heard this and immediately agreed that the conversation today in the field was probably Clarence giving Aunt Tee's message to Penniman. He quickly went back down the stairs and out the door headed to the river to see if he could see whether Penniman was waiting there until nightfall. He didn't think Penniman would cross the river before nightfall because one of the overseers might see him and think he was trying to run. There were two boats usually kept tied up at the river dock and Jobba moved to where he could see them. They were both still there so he knew that the trip had not been made yet. He looked around the area to see if he could spot him, but saw nothing. There were some other slaves walking around by the river enjoying the warm air so he went over to them and asked the same question of each. Nobody had seen Penniman since the fields and it made Jobba wonder how a man could disappear like that. Then he remembered that he was able to do this same thing when he went and hid in the stable for most of the afternoon. He thought to himself could Penniman be hiding in there until dark? His conclusion was that it was not likely. Jobba was able to do it without causing any suspicion because he had been working in there and anyone watching would just think that he was just doing his job. Penniman had never worked in the stable, as far as he knew, and there would be no reason for him to be in there now. He dismissed this idea and decided to walk up toward the mansion thinking that Penniman may have gone up to try and see Clarence one more time to reassure himself he had the message correct. Jobba got to the start of the quarters road and saw no one. Now he had exhausted all of his possibilities and himself, so he turned around and went home.

When he walked in the door Myanna had come down and was with Tralene preparing the evening meal. The kids were seated at the table and everyone was accounted for except Penniman. Jobba asked Tralene one more time where she thought he might be, but she had no idea and was starting to get a little worried herself. Myanna asked her if he had said anything to her about the rumor that there were runaways up in the mountains beyond the river. She said that they had discussed it because everyone here had heard the talk, but no one had seen any of them. Jobba then said if they were trying to get to Aunt Tee how would they know how to do it? Tralene replied that someone would have to tell them. Then she looked at Jobba.

"You think he de one ta tell `em?"

" I dono but Aunt Tee like him an don she truss him?"

" I reckon so but I dono if she would ask him ta do nothin like dat. He ain neva bin asked ta do nothn b`fo. But if she ask him, I know he would do it. You think dat where he gone?"

"I look all ova for him while ago an caint fine no sign of `em so he mus be hid'n somewhere `till dark so's he kin cross de river. If'n I hadda go up dere das what I'd do."

"You think he gwine stay up dere all night?"

"Naw, I think when he fine `em he tell `em what he got to an den come on home. He know those mountains good don he?"

"Yes. He bin up dere many times an he know his way `round."

"So you ain got ta worry none, he be fine. Prably be back early mornin."

That ended the conversation, but neither of them was comfortable about whether what they said was really what was going on, because none of them really knew.

The sun had fully receded behind the mountains and the moon replaced it in the sky. Twilight time was ended and now it was dark. The door to the last cabin on the right before the river opened and Penniman emerged. He stepped outside carrying a lantern that was set on a very low flame, looked all around then walked to the dock. The boats were swaying in the water as the movement of the current shifted them. Penniman loosed the one nearest him and got inside. Positioning himself on the bench with the oars he grabbed hold of them and began to row over to the other side. The excursion was brief, but the rowing was difficult as he fought to maintain his course against the river current trying to push him downstream. On the other side he found the place where the river was at its lowest point and he pulled up to the shore. Pulling the boat onto the ground he made sure that it was well grounded before leaving to find his party.

His instructions included directions to where the runaways would be waiting and the landmarks given were very familiar to him. As he traversed the forest and found the familiar trail that had been cut through many years ago he looked for the signs that would lead him right to the group. Markings on the trees made by the refugees were difficult to see clearly, but he was able to distinguish what he needed to see that would point him specifically to the clearing where they were. A small fire was burning in the clearing and when he got closer he could hear voices speaking just above whispers. He entered the clearing and was greeted warmly by men who looked much like him. They embraced enthusiastically one by one for several minutes and then Penniman sat down before the fire and they talked. The runaways were anxious to tell him all about their flight and their plight and how they sought to gain their permanent freedom with the help of Aunt Tee.

Penniman was impressed with their ingenuity and skill in avoiding capture, but he was quick to remind them that he had never heard of anyone escaping to freedom because of what she did. They were not to be deterred because of what they had heard about her and now believed, so he backed off attempting to dissuade them from their pursuit. He went on to deliver her message almost verbatim as he remembered it and was sure to tell them that there was a root in the forest near the river that only grew on this side that they must bring an ample amount to the ceremony.

Penniman didn't have to explain much about this root because the pack leader of the group seemed to know all about the fabled hidden powers of this plant. He agreed to find a good supply in the morning and bring it when they came. For over an hour they continued to converse and exchange stories about their mutual experiences during enslavement. Time passed and the hour was growing late. Penniman said he had to be getting back because even his wife didn't know where he was and the group acknowledged his reason for leaving. The group leader grabbed his hand and wished him a safe journey back across the river and vowed that they would be together again on the next night. Penniman left the setting made his way back to the river and navigated to the other side.

It was about 2:00 AM when Penniman opened the door to his cabin and walked inside. Tralene was sitting at the table with her head down on it and when she heard him enter she got up and ran over to meet him.

"Where you bin?" she said with an anxious tone in her voice.

"I bin to de mountains an couldn't tell ya `bout it `til now `cause I had a lot on ma mind to `member. I saw dem runaways. Dey really up dere. Whole bunch of `em an dey comin down tomorra to join wit Aunt Tee."

"You saw dem. How dey look?"

"Dey look jest like us an ain none of `em seem ta be hurt or nothin."

"Is you hungry, I kin fix ya somethin right quick?"

"Naw, dey even had food dere. I ate fish wit dem an some kind of veg'tible I ain knowed what it was, but it was good."

They talked for a little while longer at the table and then retired to bed.

The next evening came and all was in readiness for the dance ritual All that day around the mansion, Aunt Tee was in an unusually good mood in anticipation. She and Suliah were doing their chores with a new zeal and it transpired to Byron thinking that he had done something that pleased her. Charlotte was still fuming at the fact that Suliah had not been banished from the house or at least subjected to sleeping in the hallway again. Anna Lee was doing her best to console her father who she knew was going through some tough times and also keeping Suliah away from him as much as she could. Jethro was having some real heartache with the object of his affections so close yet so far unapproachable. He was dealing with it as best he could. The relationship between him and Byron had sunk to its lowest level ever and he was considering running away just like a slave.

As nightfall closed in Penniman and Tralene were getting excited as they had begun to do more in recent weeks. Penniman had not revealed to Jobba just what he saw on the other side of the river, but Jobba got the story from Linwood who got it from one of his friends. So Jobba was aware that there really were some slaves able to live up there in the hills and survive. He made a mental note of this for future reference. Penniman went out about a half hour before midnight and headed down to cabin number eleven where the runaways were supposed to meet. He stayed in the house for awhile, but as the hour drew near he walked outside to see if he could see them coming across the river. He was not disappointed. Like an apparition at first appearing in the middle of the water as they got closer he could see that they were all crowded in the small boat huddling in the middle and clinging to the sides to maintain balance. When they got to the dock he ran over to help them and looked to see if they brought what they were supposed to bring. The leader carried a large bag of what Penniman assumed must be it.

The group went inside the cabin first and met with the residents. Shortly thereafter they walked out and joined the procession moving up the quarters road toward the cave. For weeks now the Jesus believers watched the parade as best they could in the moonlight from their windows as the Aunt Tee followers made their way with lanterns swinging. Over this period of time, the tension between the factions had lessened only because their mutual hardships from their toil and labor had increased as Byron saw fit to punish them. So they endeavored to cling together for their mutual survival. The entrance to the cave was already glowing from the orange light coming from it. On the faces of the refugees you could see the excitement grow as they neared the opening. Once inside and they witnessed the ceremony in progress they couldn't wait to join in. The robed man saw when they entered and moved toward them to retrieve the bag. Sure enough as Penniman suspected, the robed man, Clarence, took from the bag three large plants and moved toward the back of the cave. Aunt Tee, whose back was to them facing the wall, sensed that the robed man was behind her turned and looked at the plants. She paused from her chanting reached for them then hoisted them up and chanted again. When she finished she gave them back to Clarence who walked over to the fire and cast them in.

The roar and crackle from the shooting flames was not bright orange this time, but the light gave off an extremely bright red luminosity that reached the top of the cave. At that point the runaways were taken by the hand and led up to Aunt Tee. Instructed to kneel, they happily assumed the position and Aunt Tee went through that portion of the rites that went along with this point of the ceremony. Once they were marked they were led back to the others and were engaged in the dance for the rest of the night. At the end of the ceremony, the refugee leader curious with the ending, asked one of the others when they would be able to go free now that they had joined. The strange look that he got without an answer caused him some concern He accepted that this person may not know the answer so he tried to make his way to the front and speak to the robed man, but he was prevented as the crowd was beginning to move out of the cave back down the mountain.

Back on the trail down the mountain the refugee leader caught up with Penniman and while they were walking briskly to beat the morning sunrise he asked him the question.

"Is we free now? Is the pateroller thru lookin fer us?"

Penniman looked at him curiously and tried to explain.

"You one a us now an you gits de protection of Aunt Tee, but she ain neva said an I ain neva tol you dat you be free once you join up. B`sides you free now ain't ya, y`all ain got no chains on."

This was not the answer the man wanted to hear and his misconception about what had just happened for him and his group bothered him so he asked the next question.

"What be de protection that we gits from her?"

Penniman was getting a little annoyed at this point because he was trying to get to his cabin and sleep for possibly a half hour before the horn blew, but he felt such earnest sincerity in this inquiry that he had to respond.

"Y`all runnin `round up dere in de mountains an dono who gonna fine you. Ya dono from day ta day what you kin eat or where ya gonna sleep next. Now dat ya one a us, you kin call on Aunt Tee no matta where ya be an she protects ya - all y`all. Dat ain ta say de pateroller dun stop lookin fer ya, but it say dat ya be okay while ya runnin."

After he said that he distanced himself from the leader made his way to his cabin and went inside. The pact leader continued on with his group down to the dock, got in the boat and headed back across the river. All of them were totally confused about what they had gotten into because they were just as mired in slavery with an untenable future with no hope as they were before. Once on the other side the leader tried to reassure the group by telling them what Penniman told him about Aunt Tee's protective services, but somehow it didn't provide any with the comforting feeling they desired. They moved deeper into the forest and resumed their lifestyle while waiting for the sunrise so they could continue looking over their shoulders for the patrols.

For all that was going on around him, Byron was oblivious to it. His concern for his crops was overwhelming him and almost daily he was looking for somebody to blame for his situation. His primary target remained the new arrivals and especially Jobba who he equated as their leader. The more the crops seemed to be at their last stage of survival the more he would take it out on Jobba and put him in the stocks for a day or two. Though he had no evidence to associate Jobba with the cause he didn't care and kept leaning on Jobba to get those four that seemed to have some strange powers to make it rain. Jobba was to the point that whenever Byron came around him he would cower at the very thought he might be incarcerated again on a whim. He tried to do everything he could to please the massa, but to no avail. Even Sam who never liked him since the day he arrived on the plantation was having a good time chastising him at every opportunity. Myanna and Linwood were distraught at seeing him go through all that he was, but they were powerless to help him.

Day by day the tensions increased among the Candle family, the slaves and anyone who came to the house could sense that there was something very wrong. Byron was at the point where the slightest thing gone wrong would elevate his charges against the four and Jobba. He began to imbibe more frequently in his special nectar and often he would try to get to Suliah who was now sleeping in her room on the third floor again. Byron had dismissed Clarence from his guardian post and he was now in his room also. Every time Byron went up to her room late at night he could get to the door, even inside the room but something that he couldn't understand restrained him from laying his hands on her. With each attempt he grew more frustrated and finally resigned himself to believing that she too was strange like the new arrivals. Charlotte knew about his midnight walks and withdrew into herself all but shutting him out completely. Anna Lee grew more devoted to Suliah if for no other reason than to have someone to be with in the midst of the family craziness. Jethro, like his father was at the brink of loosing his sanity and everyday presented a special challenge for him.

Aunt Tee observed all that was happening and while she was able to keep Byron at bay from doing anything that would affect her control of the house or prevent her from continuing her performances in the cave, she sensed that a major change was coming to the plantation. She couldn't quite see clearly in her spirit just what the change was going to be,but she knew that there was a clash brewing between her people and Daniel's. It was not often that she had occasion to go to the fields, but whenever she did and came close or even within the vicinity of Daniel and his associates, there arose in her such a loathing and desire to strike out at them, that it was difficult to control. Although neither Daniel nor any of his associates ever confronted her directly it was evident that the opposing spirits were at war even if it couldn't be seen.

On any given day over the last several weeks as the internal strife escalated, it was hard for Aunt Tee to maintain order in the house. Byron would go out early in the morning looking for clouds forming in the sky, but he never saw any and his frustration would set the tone for the day. Jobba and his family and the rest of the slaves were doing the best they could to try and maintain a tobacco crop that hardly lived, but it wasn't hard to see that the effort was all but hopeless. Byron would badger his overseers and threaten them to get better results. The overseers would in turn holler, scream and even whip some threatening more severe punishment if they didn't come up with a way to make the plants grow. Jobba often went to Daniel at day's end and asked why was this happening to them and since they suffered too why didn't he stop it. Daniel never answered his question directly, but he would just smile in the midst of it all and say:

"For I consider that the sufferings of this present time are not worthy to be compared with the glory which shall be revealed in us." (Rom. 8:18)

Jobba didn't really understand what this meant, but when Daniel said it the relaxed feeling and the calm that came over him thwarted all his sense of trepidation.

Summer came and Byron's tobacco plants were at less than half the height they should be at this time of the year. With fewer than three months before harvest time
Byron had all but given up on having a full complement to take to market. No matter how many times he worked and reworked his profit scenarios the results always indicated that his financial empire was going to crumble unless he could figure out another way to at least get money enough to pay his creditors for this season. Of course there was always his thought that if sufficient rains came, even now, he would be able to salvage his entire acreage and not only be able to pay his bills, but pocket a sizeable profit. The more he dwelled on the latter possibility, the more he encouraged himself to find a way to get those four who he was certain had the power to make it rain. Putting Jobba in the stocks repeatedly didn't seem to be working so he had to come up with another strategy.
One night while he was sitting in his parlor nursing his nectar and contemplating his future, the thought came to him that since punishing Jobba wasn't working perhaps diverting his attention to his family might be more effective. It had been some time since his last attempt at getting to Suliah failed so he decided if he couldn't make that happen then she might be more useful to him in coercing her father to get the defiant four to cooperate. His first thought was to go to her and tell her what he wanted so she could talk to her father, but when he considered what he would do if she said no, it wasn't such a good idea. He knew, after many attempts, that he could no longer punish her because when he tried he couldn't do it. The only alternative left was the one that he had been considering for a long time, but never really decided to do it, was to sell her and make sure that Jobba knew it. Not only would he sell her, but to emphasize to Jobba how strongly he wanted the four to make it rain, he would take Linwood and sell him too. When he finished plotting out this scenario in his head he smiled. To him this was the perfect answer to his problems. So convinced was he that the defiant four had the power to make it rain he was ready to resort to anything that could convince them to do it.
While he was still in the parlor Charlotte came in from the usual family after dinner session of tea and cordials. He was surprised to see her because lately she had hardly been even talking to him. She sat down in the chair near his desk and wanted to know what he was going to do about that girl. She reminded him that long ago she told him she would be trouble and directed his attention to what was happening to this family. Byron acknowledged that she had told him, but he stopped short of admitting that he had ulterior motives for keeping her around. He started to tell her right then what he had just been thinking, but not wanting to

give her the satisfaction of thinking she won that battle, he told her he was still considering it. Charlotte who was now getting very concerned about what was happening with Jethro wasn't about to let it go with that answer.

"Byron, have you taken a good look at your son lately? He's little more than flesh and bone. He don't eat and I don't think he sleeps good. You know why that is?"

"No, but I know ya `bout ta tell me."

"`cause of that gal, that's why. The longer she be in this house the worse he gonna git. An you know who gonna be ta blame?"

"Yes darlin I know who you wanna blame. That boy ain't got good sense ta git all mushy ova that gal. I tried ta tell him that, but I think she got some kind a spell on him."

"It's not a spell Byron, why can't ya see that. Her pretty face and the rest of her dun got him all outta sorts so's he can't think strait no more. Every time I look around he trying to figure out how to git close to her. If Aunt Tee didn't keep her out the way, then he be all up in her face. If you wasn't so busy worry'n `bout them crops, you would a seen it comin. Now I want you to give real thought to sellin her or puttin her in the field and lettn her live with her family in the cabins."

Charlotte finished her appeal got up and left the room. Byron leaned back in his chair and reviewed all she said. He knew she was right in everything, but what she failed to see and recognize was that her future was dependent on a good crop just as well as his. As far as Jethro was concerned he had little compassion for the boy. He chalked Jethro's dilemma up to him going through a puppy love phase and he would get over it. Byron refused to see his son as the young man he was becoming, but still viewed him as the little boy that he always wanted to follow in his shadow. The relationship that they once shared as father and son from the time that Jethro could understand that his father was the master of the house had deteriorated so much that Jethro no longer cared. Jethro's focus was solely on figuring a way to leave the house and somehow take Suliah with him. However, without any substantial means of his own and no connections that could afford him the opportunity to do so, he was at a loss.

By the end of the night before retiring to bed, Byron had made up his mind. It was time to put his plan into action. Tomorrow he would instruct Sam to get the message to Jobba that his daughter and son would be sent to the auction block before the next weekend if the defiant four didn't make something happen with the rain. He would tell Sam to make sure that he presented it in such a way that it would seem like this was the worst fate that could happen to his family. Feeling some perverse satisfaction at the power of his plan to not only gain his desired results, but to inflict some further punishment on Jobba, Byron was ready to go to bed and have a good night's sleep.

When he entered the bedroom Charlotte was still up with the lanterns up to their max setting, sitting at her sewing table pretending to sew. She was really waiting for him to come in so she could pursue her earlier conversation.

"Well did ya decide what you gonna do?" she said.

Byron was caught a little off guard because he thought that she was through with her speeches when she left the parlor. The fact that she was still dressed in her clothes and not her nightgown told him that this was going to be a long evening unless he told her something to pacify her right now.

"Yes darlin, I heard all dat ya said and I think I'm gonna have to let her go. I'm gonna have to git word to the trader and have him come up here an see what we kin git fer her."

Charlotte heard his words and was happy at her triumph, but she knew Byron well and was not about to leave it to him to schedule the event. She knew that even though he said he was going to do it, since he didn't say when it could be weeks from now before it happened.

"Good my dear that's a good decision. Now when you gonna git the trader here?"

Byron had to smile at this point because he knew that she knew him so well, she wasn't going to allow him to prolong this decision even though she was not aware of his previous plan. He marveled at how well she picked up on his delaying tactic.

He started undressing getting ready for bed feeling comfortable that he had the answer she wanted to hear.

"Tomorra I'm gonna send word by Clarence down to town and git that trader here soon as he kin. That good `nuff fer ya?"

"Yes. The sooner we get her outta here then this family kin get back to normal."

She stopped her pretend sewing got up from the table and started getting ready for bed. Byron watched her as she undressed and wondered if this would be a good time. Charlotte knew he was watching and took a longer amount of time in her routine than she normally would, allowing him to take in the view as she slowly changed. When she did get in bed, Byron hesitated wondering if that act she just performed was just to tantalize him or was it really an invitation to proceed. He decided to test the waters and found them to be warm. It was a good night for both for a change.

Byron got up the next morning feeling refreshed. He could hardly wait to dispatch Clarence to town to set that part of his plan in motion. Even better than that he was ready to run down to Sam's and tell him the other part of the plan. Quickly going through his morning routine he was dressed and out the door even before his wake up cup of coffee was downed. He got to Sam's right after the horn sounded and Sam was still standing at his door with the instrument in his hand. Sam was surprised to see him trotting down the road as if something was wrong so he started to meet him half way. When they neared each other Byron grabbed Sam's shoulder and blurted out that he had the solution to the problem. Sam anxious to hear what solution he had come up with embraced Byron and asked him what it was.

"Sam, you ain't gonna believe this, but I got it all worked out now. I ain't been leanin on Jobba the right way to git him talkin to those new arrivals good. I been punishin him, but I needs to work on his family. You git what I'm talkin 'bout?"

"No suh I ain sure what you sayin. What you mean?"

"I mean instead of puttin him in the stocks or whippin him some more, I'm gonna tell him that his family gonna be sold if'n he don't git them new arrivals to make it rain. When he hears his family gonna be broke up I know he don't want that so he gonna talk real good to dem fellas."

"Mr. Candle why you so sure dey kin make it rain when the Indian man couldn't do it?"

"I dono I jest got a good feelin about it. Every time I see them boys together look like somethin else strange happin. I knows they got some kind a power and I'm gonna make it work for me. Now here's what I want you ta do. Today when ya git Jobba workin real good in the field you go on up ta him an ya tell 'em what I just told you. Tell him that unless he gits them boys to do somethin about the rain then his children gonna be sold away from here. I'm thinkin 'bout doin it anyway, but you don't tell him that."

"Okay suh, I'll tell him dis mornin."

Byron left Sam and with a big smile on his face headed back to the house to find Clarence. That didn't take long because Clarence was setting the table in the dining room for breakfast. Byron strolled in the room and told Clarence all about the task he needed for him to perform today. Clarence listened carefully and acknowledged that he understood the urgency of conveying the proper message. None of the rest of the family had come down to breakfast yet so it gave Byron plenty of time to detail his plans.

Aunt Tee heard Byron talking with Clarence and came in to bring him his morning coffee. She saw the smile on Byron's face and wondered about it since she had not seen him smiling in quite some time. Casually she asked him if he had a good night's sleep and he replied that he slept better last night than he had in quite some time. Aunt Tee wasn't quite sure from his tone whether what she was thinking and what he was saying were based on the same idea. She didn't pursue it, but rather went on back in the kitchen to finish making breakfast thinking that the rest of family would be coming down soon. Byron didn't wait for his breakfast, but finished his coffee and went back outside. He wanted to catch Clarence before he left because there was one more thing that he wanted to tell him.

Clarence had hitched up the horse and the wagon was just coming up from the stable when Byron caught him.

"Clarence when ya talk with trader Bob make sure you tell him that I got a real pretty young gal that he gonna be takin a look at along with a good strong healthy young buck. So tell him he needs ta bring plenty a money with him 'cause they ain'y gonna be cheap. Git him to come on Friday if he kin "

"Yassuh massa I tell him jest what you say."

Byron let Clarence go and then he walked down to the fields to see if he could see where Jobba was working. He saw Sam's horse so he figured that Jobba must be somewhere in that field. He got closer to the edge and spotted Sam out there about the middle of the lot talking to Jobba. From the expression on Jobba's face apparently Sam had not gotten to the good part yet because Jobba was still grinning in Sam's face. Byron continued to look on and then what he was waiting for happened. Jobba's grin turned to a frown and the frown turned to a scowl as Byron witnessed the anger mounting up in the man. His fists were clenched as he dropped his tool and Byron could see that he was having great difficulty controlling his temper. He couldn't be sure what else Sam was saying to him, but with each passing minute it looked more like Jobba was going to explode. Finally when it got to the point that it looked like Jobba was going to raise his hands to Sam, another overseer came over and stood by Sam with his rifle on his shoulder and stared directly at Jobba as if daring him to act.

With a parting verbal shot Sam told Jobba that he needed to go to the defiant four right now and start begging them to get it to rain. As he turned away to get back on his horse Sam burst out laughing which elevated Jobba's tension even more, but he was helpless. Slowly Jobba walked to the next field to find Daniel and his associates. When he got there they were all together as usual working at their leisurely pace unchallenged. Jobba approached Daniel and told him the story that Sam conveyed to him. Daniel's reaction was not a surprise to Jobba because whenever he had gone to him before he never seemed to get excited about anything. Daniel listened to the whole story and then told Jobba not to worry, but go on back to his field and the "matter would be taken care of." Jobba, after hearing this felt a sense of relief that Daniel himself was on top of the issue, so he went back to where he was working before and continued to do so.

When the workday ended Jobba couldn't wait to catch up with Myanna who was working in another area so he could tell her what happened. As they walked to the cabin Jobba was rushing the information out with such excitement that she had to slow him down so she could understand fully what he was trying to tell her. When Jobba finished and Myanna was able to understand all that he was saying she had a problem maintaining her composure just like he did. By this time they were at their cabin door and went inside. Penniman and Tralene were already there and both were lying on the bed resting. Jobba wanted to tell them his story, but he wasn't sure whether this was the right thing to do. Penniman had never given up on telling Jobba that he made the wrong choice when he let Daniel baptize him. So by telling him that Linwood and Suliah could possibly be sold, he suspected that Penniman would say that the protection of Aunt Tee would be the only thing that could keep that from happening. Jobba definitely wasn't ready to hear that, especially in light of what Daniel said.

Linwood came in and Jobba rushed to tell him all that was happening. Linwood was as startled and surprised at the news as any of them because none of the overseers had ever said anything to him. He wondered too just what it would be like to be sold away from his family. Jobba and Myanna spent most of that night after dinner discussing whether Daniel and his associates really had the power to make it rain. Myanna raised the question that even if they had the power would they use it to satisfy a threat made by someone who treated them the way they did. Jobba wanted to believe that if they could they would because they knew that the unity of his family would be in peril if they didn't. He also reminded Myanna that Daniel said not to worry because "the matter would be taken care of." Myanna asked Jobba if he really knew what that meant. When he thought about it more he wasn't so sure about his answer and his assured feeling became tentative.

The next day was Wednesday and both Jobba and Byron were up early before sunrise gazing at the sky to see if any clouds were forming. Byron in anticipation of his threat being successful and the defiant four working their magic to get the rain started; Jobba in the hope that whatever power Daniel wielded would be used to protect his family. In either case nothing in the sky at this time indicated any change from the previous day. From all indicators today would be the same as yesterday; clear, blue sky and hot.

When they got to the field Jobba was hoping that he would be assigned a station near the defiant four so he could get some reassurance from Daniel as to when he was going to take care of the matter. He saw Daniel and his associates, but he was not near enough to him to go talk to and he didn't want to ask permission to stray from his post. Byron, who had come out, also was observing the four to see if they were going to do anything like what Indian Joe did. He was always angry about how these four men would almost huddle together when they worked and cover as little area as they could. But that didn't matter to him now if what they were going to do would make it rain. There was no apparent change in their methods and this set Byron wondering if Jobba had been persuasive in his talk with them. As the day progressed and nothing seemed to be changing in the weather pattern both Jobba and Byron were now getting more concerned. Each time Jobba looked over to where the four were it seemed as if the situation he discussed had not made any difference to them. Byron spent most of the day between observing them and looking at the sky and becoming more frustrated with each passing hour.

Thursday came and the routine for both men was almost a repeat of Wednesday. Even the weather pattern seemed to reprise the day before to the displeasure of both. Now it was at the point where Byron was so disgruntled and disappointed at the inactivity or ineffectiveness of the four that he was ready to carry out his threat regarding Linwood and Suliah in earnest. Although he didn't say or have Sam say anything more to Jobba, it was clear to Jobba that time was running out before something was going to happen to his children. His growing anxiety about the future was causing him to do exactly what Daniel said not to do and that was to worry. In his frustration he was ready to run over to Daniel and ask when it was going to rain, but just as he was about to lay down his tools and make his move, the overseer looked at him daring him to do what he was thinking. Caught between a desire to know just what the saying "the matter would be taken care of" really meant and not seeing anything happening Jobba was at his wits end.

Each night before Byron went to bed he would examine the skies to see if even a small indicator of rain was present. When he saw none, the sleep that he desired would not come easily and he spent most of the night fitfully tossing and turning. Down in the cabin Jobba's anxiety grew and he also was examining the skies for the same reason. Jobba was also growing more fearful that the thing that he dreaded the most was about to happen and he was powerless to do anything to stop it. Myanna shared his anxiety and the two of them were restless as they suffered through the night. Myanna wanted so badly to be able to at least see Suliah before what seemed like was going to happen, happened. Jobba told her that tomorrow he would make an attempt to get up to the house like he did before and ask Clarence to let him see her. He didn't think that Myanna would be able to do the same thing, but he assured her that if he got to see Suliah he would relay to her all that she said. Before they went to sleep Jobba looked over at Linwood to get a firm picture in his mind just in case this might be the last time that he would see him. The picture that was to be impressed in his mind was Linwood still sleeping with the black teddy bear that was given to him by one of the Sutter boys when he was only three.

Friday morning came. No rain and no sign of rain. Byron was now prepared to carry out his threat. He didn't go down to the fields, but he did search the skies desperately for any sign of growing cloudiness or even an overcast sky. His countenance had sunk to a new low and his belief in the powers of the defiant four was muddled in his mind because he couldn't determine whether they were being more defiant because he had threatened Jobba or maybe they really didn't have any power at all. Either way his situation had not changed and he was headed toward suffering a financial disaster before year's end. He wanted to just go out and punish everybody on the plantation because he felt that they now were collectively the cause of his woes. He had never experienced a drought like this and had never had such an obstacle placed in his path on the way to his empire building. As he moaned and groaned about his plight he wondered if there was a solution for his problem and what would it take for him to find it. The more he pondered the question the more he felt that the solution was eluding him for a reason.

The sun was now high in the sky on another bright day. As he stood outside on his porch looking down on his fields, he turned his head to see dust kicking up on the road to the mansion. As the traveler got closer he could now make out that it was Trader Bob.

Chapter 6 - Due Change

On other plantations in the area surrounding the Candles, life at this time presented a wide variety of experiences. Depending on how one's lot had been cast in the human spectrum it could be the best of times or the worst of times. If it was fortune that your lot was cast with the elite of the genteel society then you enjoyed all of the finer things available. However, if the opposite was your fate and the slave community was your society then at best it was difficult to enjoy life. On most plantations whether you fell into one category or the other determined just how much enjoyment you could derive from living.

The Candle Plantation was different. It had become a paradox on what would be considered the normal expectations of southern class assignment. Over the last few months it was Byron that precipitated the anomaly. What had been the happy order of joy in his household because of the lofty position he held in the community was now the epitome of disorder and dysfunction due to his perceived view of his future. Where the family had thoroughly relished being the hosts to which other plantation owners would rearrange calendars to make sure they were able to attend a Candle social, now they were not only reluctant to give a party, but hesitant to attend one. Word had spread quickly after the last affair about how he had mistreated other owners by conniving to steal their land. Lately whenever they went to town, in hushed tones the townsfolk would whisper and point to how the mighty have fallen.

Even though nothing had actually happened yet, it was the appearance of imminent disaster that caused Byron to react by letting his sanity turn to foolishness. His belief that slaves under his charge were able to control the weather and one in particular was able to lead them drove him to the point that his rational decision making, was questionable at best. Jobba had become such a focal point of his ire that Byron's zeal to inflict pain on one who had done nothing to him but be in his presence, caused him to extend his punishing ways to all his slaves. The plight of slaves on most other plantations was not enviable by any rational thinker, but now on the Candle land it had become so much worse that running away was being considered worth the risk of being caught. Byron had brought down the quality of life not only for them, but also for those who he claimed to love, inside his own house.

Looking at the man in the mirror this morning brought no comfort for Byron. When he faced that reflection and looked deeply in the eyes, he could only see negative possibilities and crumbling destiny for the empire he envisioned not long before as within his grasp. His decision to break up the family of a man he believed was the base cause of his problems was now in progress. He recalled as he continued to stare at the reflection, that ole man Sutter had warned him a long time ago that separating the family would cause bad consequences. Although he dismissed the idea at that time and put it behind him, now he was torn between the real possibility of what Sutter warned him about as being true and his stubborn desire to cling to his ways.

Now as he stood on his front porch and saw the dust on the road being kicked up by an approaching traveler to the mansion, he knew that his plan was about to be put into action because the rider was trader Bob. The closer he got the more Byron became ambivalent about his decision. On one side of the equation he was convinced that selling the Thomas children would elicit the desired response from the defiant four, on the other side he was fearful that Sutter's admonition might come true and exacerbate his troubles. Too late to change his mind when trader Bob arrived and dismounted; he greeted him with a smile and a hearty handshake.

"How ya doin? Ya got my message I see."

"Yeah Byron ya know I always come when ya call me."

"Glad to see ya could make it. I got something good I want ya to see. Hope ya brought lots a money."

"Well let see what ya got den we kin talk `bout the money."

"You wanna come in the house first and have a little swalla `for we talk?"

"Naw Byron you knows I don mix ma biness wit ma pleasure so let's go on an git right down to it. Where ya got `em at?"

"Gimme a minute I gotta go set it up."

Byron walked away headed down to the field. He got near the edge and spotted Sam riding on the other side. Waving his arms furiously he got Sam's attention and motioned for him to come over. Sam nodded his head and started riding in his direction. When he got there Byron told him to go get Linwood and bring him here. Jobba who was working in the lot where Sam was patrolling saw Byron and then watched as Sam went over to him. Suspecting that something might be about to happen he slowed down his work effort and paid attention to the matter. Sam went off to find Linwood and returned with the boy in tow moments later. Jobba saw this and his heart started racing, but he maintained his position.

After Linwood came over to Byron, he was instructed to go down to the stable and wait there. Byron then turned and went back to the house. When he walked in the door Charlotte met him and asked who that was that she saw coming up the road. Byron explained to her who it was and a big smile came across her face because she knew now that he had actually done what he promised her he was going to do. He moved past her and then his first stop was in the kitchen where he thought Suliah would be helping Aunt Tee. He got there and to his surprise saw no one. Next he peeked out the back door to see if they might be on the porch. No one was there either. Now he started to get a little anxious as he remembered the last time he had to go looking for Suliah, Aunt Tee had hidden her away in the mountains. Then he thought to himself, since he didn't tell Aunt Tee what was going on today why would she have taken her away. It didn't occur to him that Aunt Tee and Clarence shared a room and there wasn't much that he knew about that she didn't get to know.

He made one final search of the lower level then headed upstairs to Anna Lee's room. Before entering he paused at the door and listened to see if he could hear them inside. First he heard giggling and then outright laughter, as the girls seemed to be having some kind of party going on. Sure now that he had located Suliah he opened the door and entered. Anna Lee was surprised to see him and asked him the occasion for his visit that he had not done for her in some time. He casually said that he needed Suliah's services for a while and she needed to come with him. Anna Lee suspicious at his request asked him what for. He chided her for being so possessive of Suliah and said that what he needed her for would not take long. Anna Lee had no idea what he was referring to said to Suliah that when she finished with him to come right back there and they would finish what they were doing. Byron grabbed Suliah's hand and led her down the stairs.

When they got to the back door and Suliah saw that she was being led in the direction of the stable she questioned why. Byron ignored her inquiry and as she started to resist he pulled her down the back stairs. At the stable door Sam was waiting with trader Bob and Linwood. Byron motioned to all that they should go inside. Jobba who was able to see this going on had reached his patience limit and threw down his tools. He looked around to see where the overseer was and since Sam was at the stable the other overseer was way over on the other far edge of the field. Jobba made his way carefully in the shortest line to the edge and left the field. Right outside the stable he paused and looked through the window to see Linwood and Suliah lined up against the wall. Trader Bob was about to begin his inspection and Sam was standing at the door as if on guard.

Trader Bob started with Linwood and turned him around and around looking him up and down. Then he asked him to bend over and touch his toes. Next he opened his mouth and examined his teeth. Finally he told him to take off his shirt and he examined his muscles. Pleased with the results of his examination he turned to Byron and said that this one should fetch a good price on the block. Next he turned to Suliah and turned her around also. She hesitated to react to his command at first until Byron told her that he would whip her father if she didn't do what she was told. Reluctantly she turned around. When he told her to open her blouse and pull up her skirt she refused. Trader Bob didn't know what to do and he looked at Byron who said nothing more. Then the trader asked her to pull up her skirt just a little so he could see her legs. Again she hesitated at first, but then decided to comply reflecting on what was said regarding her father. She raised her skirt just above her knee and Trader Bob was delighted at this major sale prospect.

Jobba was fighting with all he had to control himself while witnessing this and he sat down on the ground with his back to the stable wall. Inside, trader Bob finished his inspection and was about to discuss figures, when Byron told Linwood and Suliah to go wait outside with Sam. The stable door opened and Sam was leading them outside when he ran into Jobba who came down across Sam's head with a piece of wood that he had found lying around. Sam fell to the ground and raised his arms to prevent the next blow that Jobba was about to deliver when the door opened again and out came trader Bob and Byron. Bob had his pistol drawn and fired a shot at Jobba, but missed. Jobba stood up straight and dropped the wood. Sam got up took the whip off his belt and started to unfurl it when Byron told him to stop. Jobba stared at his children with such a pitiful look that Suliah came over to him and whispered in his ear. He hung his head. Suliah then took off the necklace he had given her and put it around his neck.

Byron told Sam to take Jobba put him in the stocks again and then go tend to his wound, his business here was finished. Sam almost defiant in his look punched Jobba's stomach then grabbed his arm and pushed him toward the stocks. Once he had locked him in he struck him hard across the face then went to nurse his injury.. Byron turned to Bob and explained to him that this was the father of these two. Bob laughed and said: "He's a feisty one ain't he." Byron responded and said: "You don know the half of it."

The business of the sale had been concluded and now Suliah and Linwood were the property of trader Bob. Byron went back in the house and sought Clarence who was not hard to find. He told Clarence that he had just sold Suliah and he wanted him to escort her back in the house just to get her things, but don't let Anna Lee see them. He told him also to hurry down to the cabin and let Linwood do the same thing, but don't let anybody see them. Clarence complied with the order and went outside. First he walked with Suliah who was not defiant, but was accepting her fate believing she was still under the protection of both Aunt Tee and Bessimay not realizing that these were two conflicting spirits. They walked in the house and he escorted her up to the third floor where she packed the things that she wanted. Because of Anna Lee she had a lot more now than when she first came there, but she knew that this new master wasn't going to allow her to take all. She finished and Clarence quickly walked her back down stairs and out to the stable. Nobody in the house saw them leave.

Clarence took her back to trader Bob and grabbed hold of Linwood to go to the cabins. It didn't take long for Linwood to get what he needed, but in his rush to take enough clothes he left his teddy bear on the bed. Once back at the stable, Bob roped the two together and was getting ready to make them walk behind his horse when something came over Byron and he offered to loan Bob his wagon. At first Bob didn't want to be beholden to Byron for anything, but when he thought about how far they had to travel and it might diminish the value especially of Suliah, he accepted the offer. Byron motioned to Clarence to get the wagon ready and he did. Suliah and Linwood looked at each other sadly without talking. To them it was hard to believe they were going to be separated from their parents for the first time. Little did they know that not only were they being separated from parents, but would soon be from each other also.

The wagon came around and Linwood and Suliah got in. Byron stood there watching them as the cart pulled away and headed down the road. He felt no remorse, but his mind was filled with mixed feelings about whether this was really the solution to his problems. Suliah and Linwood offered no resistance as they looked around the plantation. They looked especially toward the fields to see if they could glimpse their mother and then at the stocks to view their father one last time. It was kind of a strange day because for the first time in months the sky became overcast, but Byron didn't even notice. For a long time after the wagon had pulled away he continued to stand there looking at the empty road until finally he turned and went inside.

The first one to meet him when he entered was Anna Lee who was curious about why Suliah wasn't with him. No longer could he expect to continue with his ruse so he just came right out and told her Suliah had been sold.

"Sold! Daddy you sold Suliah my best friend. You sold her without tellin me. Daddy how could you?"

"Ya know chile your mother bin wantin ta do it for a long time an I jest couldn't wait no more. B`sides you know its good for your brother too."

Anna Lee couldn't look at him anymore so she ran to her room and started crying. Jethro heard the noise of her running through the hallway and he came in the room and saw her.

"What's the matter?"

"Suliah, sh, she bin sold. Daddy sent her away."

"What! Sold Suliah. Are you sure?"

"Go see for yourself. See if you kin find her."

Jethro rushed out of the room and ran straight to the kitchen expecting to find her there. The only one present was Aunt Tee so he asked her where Suliah was. Aunt Tee responded that she didn't know, but she thought that she was up in Anna Lee's room. When Jethro explained that he just left there and told her what Anna Lee said, Aunt Tee's usual smile disappeared. Not from any transformation she was undergoing, but from shear surprise that Byron had actually carried out the threat he had been posing for some time. Aunt Tee put down the pot she was holding and told Jethro to go and look in the back of the house while she went to the parlor to talk to Byron.

Aunt Tee looked in the parlor, but he wasn't there. Then she went to the living room, but didn't see him there either. Next she went upstairs and knocked on the bedroom door. Only Charlotte was there sewing. Charlotte asked whom it was and when Aunt Tee responded she told her to come in.

"What's the matter Aunt Tee you look outta sorts?"

"Maam has ya seen Suliah, I bin lookin fer her?"

"No, I haven't seen her since early this mornin. Is there somthing wrong?"

"No maam I don think so, I jest needa fine her."

Aunt Tee left the room and went back downstairs to find Byron but he was nowhere in the house. It had finally dawned on Byron that the skies were overcast and he went down to the fields to see if the defiant four were doing anything to cause it to rain. When he found them they were doing the same things that they had done since their arrival. Not really surprised at what he saw, but feeling a surge of hope in the possibility that rain was coming. He thought now his move this morning had worked and the solution to his problem was being applied.

On his way back to the house he stopped by the stocks and spoke to Jobba.

"I guess ya happy now ain't ya niggah? You ain't got no more family an ya try to beat on one a my men. I oughta hang ya but that would be throw'n away money. Lookin like it gonna rain even without yo help anyway, so you jest stay there 'til I'm good an ready to send ya home."

He snarled then walked away. Jobba heard all that he said, but couldn't manage to raise his head to even try to look the man in his eye the way he desperately wanted to do. Inside he was feeling such a high level of frustration, not so much because his children had been sold, but because Daniel had said to him not to worry "the matter would be taken care of." When Myanna had asked him before if he understood what this really meant he wasn't sure, but he trusted the man. Now that his children were gone, doubts rose in him about the power of Daniel and his god. The questions coming into his head extended beyond just Daniel and the associates and he now considered whether his baptism was of any merit at all. His thoughts also swerved to what Penniman had been preaching to him about Aunt Tee's protection and he thirsted for more than just water.

When Aunt Tee finally caught up with Byron she asked him directly whether he had sold Suliah. He looked at her with a stern look and said that he had and if she wasn't careful she would be next. Aunt Tee was tempted to test her mettle right then, but the look in his eyes told her that he was not one to be confronted at this time and she backed off. He savored the small victory and went into his parlor. She let this battle be his, but avowed that the great war had only just begun and went in the kitchen. Meanwhile Charlotte had come down and was looking for Byron. She went in the parlor and found him at his desk.

"Aunt Tee tells me that you finally got rid a that gal, that true?"

Byron looked at her without saying anything for a minute knowing that she wanted to gloat over her victory, but he didn't want to give her that satisfaction just yet.

"Yes darlin, she's gone. That make you happy?"

"Byron you know it wasn't just for me, but your son needed to have her gone too. I don't know why you couldn't see that. Now that she's gone we all kin get back to some kind of normal 'round here."

She finished her statement and left the room. Byron shook his head and looked at her walk away and wondered whether she was right about his son. Would this change bring the family back into some kind of accord? He wanted to believe that getting rid of Linwood and Suliah and locking Jobba up on the same day would cause those four to acknowledge his authority and finally move the overcast sky to become more than just cloudy.

That evening when the horn blew to end the workday, Myanna looked around for Linwood as she usually did and couldn't find him. She walked to the head of the quarters road and waited a few more minutes to see if he was coming amongst the stragglers. When the last few had passed by her and he wasn't with them she started wondering where he might be. Then she thought maybe he had gotten permission to leave early if he wasn't feeling well and she quickly made her way to the cabin. Once inside she didn't stop to chat with Penniman who was sitting at the table but immediately went upstairs. At the top of the landing she looked over to his bed, but he wasn't there. This caused her to get more excited concerning his whereabouts and then she focused on the fact that Jobba wasn't there either. When she thought more about it she hadn't seen Jobba in the field since early this morning and she didn't see him coming down the road. Her instincts were running wild telling her that something was wrong so she rushed back down stairs and over to Penniman.

"Penniman has you seen Linwood or Jobba?"

"I ain seen Linwood since de early mornin, but I did see Jobba gwine ova to de stable."

"What time ya see him go dere?"

"Oh it mus a bin 'round 'leven or little later 'cause we ain had no break yet."

"Did ya see him come back?"

"Naw, now dat ya talkin'bout it I don recall seein him come back a'tall. I reckon he might be in dem stocks agin, but I don know what he did. I ain seen nothin go wrong."

When Myanna heard that, she wasted no time in leaving the cabin and headed up to the stable. She passed by several of the neighbors who were enjoying the warm breezes and nodded at them, but kept on going. As she got close to the stable she could see that Jobba was once again locked up in the posts with his head hung down. She looked around to see if anyone was watching then ran over to him. As he heard someone approaching he tried to lift his head but couldn't. Myanna got closer and lifted his head up enough so that he could see her. It was clear he needed some water so she found the cup by the trough filled it and brought it to him. Holding his head while he drank she cautioned him to go slow as he gulped it down.

After a drink or two Jobba struggled a bit then launched into telling her what happened to her children today. Myanna staggered backward and almost fell on the ground when she heard the news. Then she put her hand to her head to try and calm the dizziness that was overtaking her. Jobba's head had fallen back down so he couldn't see her almost feint, but he sensed it. Speaking now in a muddled voice because of his position he tried to console her as best he could, but she was beyond being comforted by words. She sat on the ground in front of him so he could see her and asked him what they were going to do. Jobba struggled to speak again, but was able to make her understand that when he got out of the posts this time he was going to run. When she heard that; she wasn't sure whether this was good news or not. At this point she couldn't decide whether running away was the best solution or was staying there and hoping for help a better option. What she didn't understand then was that Jobba said he was running, not they were.

For a few more minutes she stayed with him then got up and slowly went back to the cabin. Penniman and his family were still at the table having dinner when she walked in. The look on her face told them that something was very wrong so they asked her what it was. When she told them, Penniman's I told you so attitude was irritating, but she let it pass and asked him what they could do without going to Aunt Tee for help. Penniman was quick to reiterate the need for getting under Aunt Tee's protection again. Myanna ignored his admonition and slowly made her way upstairs where she collapsed on the bed.

Myanna arose the next morning after a fitful night's sleep determined to get to Daniel and ask him exactly what he meant when he told Jobba that "the matter would be taken care of." Especially now since her children had been sold it seemed for certain that the matter was not taken care of nor was it likely to be. She was out of the cabin well before anyone else hoping that she might catch him prior to getting to the fields. She looked all over for any of the four, but it was hopeless, there was no sign of any of them. Before going to work she walked by the stocks to see if Jobba was okay. Although his head was still in the same position as when she left last night, it appeared that he was breathing regularly and alive. As she turned to enter into the lot that she had been assigned to work today, she saw Daniel and his associates coming. She marveled at how they appeared and disappeared like lightening in a storm and wondered to herself just how they were able to do it. Walking slowly as was their custom they didn't seem to be bothered by any of the antics that Byron had been putting all of the slaves through.

She started making her way over to him when the overseer saw her leaving the field and hollered at her to turn back. The thought crossed her mind that she should ignore him and at least get close enough to Daniel to ask her question even if she couldn't stay with him long enough to hear the answer. When the overseer started riding his horse toward her it no longer seemed like a good move to try and do what she was thinking. She decided she would go against the slave protocol and go to Daniel's cabin after work. Getting the right answer from him now was more important to her than any mores established by the culture of the village. The overseer stopped coming at her when he saw her going in to work, but he kept looking at her for several minutes after to make sure she was going to stay there.

A little while later Byron was seen at the edge of the field where the defiant four were working, talking to the overseers. He was waving his arms and ranting just as he had been doing lately almost every day. Pointing to the sky and then down to the ground it wasn't hard for anyone witnessing the drama to see what the plot was all about. Finally when he had finished with them one of the overseers went over to Daniel and told him the master wanted to talk with him. Daniel put down his hoe and started toward Byron. The other three did the same and started after him. The overseer hollered at them that the master only wanted to talk to Daniel, but they ignored him and kept walking. When Byron saw what was happening, before allowing the overseer to get into a confrontation with them he held up his hand indicating that it was okay for them to come too. The overseer backed off.

Standing there looking up at Byron on his horse Daniel said nothing but waited for him to speak. The three associates stood behind Daniel without appearing to be defiant, but neither did they humble themselves before him.

"Dan'l I dun tried ta be good to y`all and all I ask is that you let it rain some so these crops can live. Why you hold'n up the water?"

Daniel without so much as smiling at the absurdity of what Byron was saying turned around and looked at his associates before answering. It seemed like they communicated with each other although not a word was spoken, then he turned back to Byron and said:

"O ruler of this land and oppressor of the poor, you who have taken, but do not give, it is not I who commands the rain, but it is God who thunders marvelously with His voice. He does great things that we cannot comprehend. For He says to the snow fall on the earth and likewise to the rain, shower and be a mighty downpour.

Byron was stunned by what Daniel was saying and he felt a tingle run down his spine, but his stubborn resistance to the words would not permit him to allow this man standing before him to convince him that he was not some kind of magic man. Even the speech of this man bewildered Byron and he was perplexed at his unusual behavior that was so much different than the others.

"Don't talk that god stuff to me it ain't nuthin but a lotta noise. Now is ya gonna make it rain or do I have to get harder on you and your people here?"

"It is within your power to do as you see fit here,but remember these words that I say to you.

Do not be deceived, God is not mocked: for whatever a man sows, that he will also reap. (Gal. 6:7)

Frustrated at not getting the desired response he wanted, Byron moved his horse closer to the four and then turned and rode away. He was furious because his demands were not being met and he felt powerless to do anything about it. But he knew he had made another threat and he was determined to carry it out. First he stopped by the stocks and released Jobba and told him to go directly to the fields and report to the overseer where Daniel was. Knowing that Jobba could hardly even walk the task of toiling in the dirt now would either kill him or convince Daniel to do what he was told. Next he went and found Sam and told him that there was to be no more breaks during the day and the horn in the evening would blow an hour later than normal.

Jobba stumbled when first set free from the posts and maintaining his balance was very difficult. Byron watched him stumbling and laughed before he rode away. Beforee going to far he hollered back that he would be coming by the field to check on him and he better be there. Step by step, unable to walk in a straight line Jobba moved slowly toward the lot he had been directed to. Sam saw him coming and walked his horse up to him.

"Was a matta boy you hav'n trouble walkin?" he said as he rode along side of him.

Jobba who could hardly keep his head up continued to trudge along the path to the field. When he arrived at the edge one of the other slaves came to help him, but the overseer yelled and motioned him back. Sam got down from his horse and pushed Jobba toward the middle of the field where Daniel was. In front of Daniel Sam threw him down so he lay prostrate at his feet until he was picked up by one of the other three. Sam started to push away the associate who picked Jobba up, but when Daniel stared directly into Sam's eyes he felt a chill and stepped back. Sam started to walk away and when he turned around to see how Jobba was faring, he couldn't believe his eyes. Jobba was standing tall in the arms of Daniel and appearing as if his strength had been renewed. His face showed no signs of the thirst that he had just exhibited moments ago and when Daniel released him he picked up a tool and started working.

Overwhelmed and frightened by this sight Sam was thoroughly persuaded that these men were more than slaves, in fact he felt they were more than human. He left them and at a far distance away he sat on his horse and just observed. The four surrounded Jobba as they continued to work and it was as if he had been admitted into their protective circle of mutual protection. Sam had no idea what to do next to chastise Jobba further as Byron had instructed him to do and he certainly had no inclination to confront the defiant four any longer. He was concerned for himself now and what he was going to tell Byron when he came back to the field and saw Jobba working as if he had never been punished.

The rest of the day went by and the sun that had come out bright and hot in the sky was beginning to set. Byron didn't return to the field but spent the time since he confronted the four, in his parlor searching for ways to bring about a solution to his problems. He was beginning to realize that his threats to further punish the slaves were not getting the results that he sought and he was running out of ways to make the situation worse for them. His assaults on Jobba, even the selling of his children, was not working and those four that he now loathed was driving him to even consider what Daniel had said about his God. He relished this thought for but a moment and dismissed it as hog wash which he had done so many times before.

When the time came for the horn to sound, all in the fields wondered why it was not happening. The overseers kept a sharp eye out for anyone trying to leave and made sure they continued to work. It was not until over an hour later than usual that the sound was heard and the slaves, feeling more tired were permitted to lay down their implements. Jobba made his way walking with the four to the quarters road and looked for Myanna. Though he did not converse with them he felt a strange feeling of calm while he was in their presence. Just before they reached the head of the road Jobba saw Myanna coming up with Penniman and Tralene on the other side. He paused and waited for her while the four kept on going. Myanna saw him also and left her group to move faster to him. She looked at Jobba very closely and wondered about how rejuvenated he looked after what she knew he had just gone through, so she asked him how. He explained to her all that happened and when he got to the circle of the four how they were able to strengthen him.

Myanna heard this and she was even more determined now to go and find out what the meaning of "the matter would be taken care of" is. She told Jobba what she had decided to do and he offered very little resistance at her going to see Daniel. He told her that he didn't think the village would mind her going by herself since Daniel was the preacher and not just some ordinary man. It was agreed then that after dinner she would go and pose the question directly. Jobba then discussed with her his plan to make contact with the runaways in the mountains and find out how they managed to survive. Myanna was still thinking that he was talking about the two of them running but when she voiced her concern about how they would do it, he made it clear to her that he was referring to himself only and that once he got settled he would come back for her. This idea did not sit well with her and she stopped talking. Jobba sensed her withdrawal and searched for the right words that would make it better for her, but he found none. As a consolation Jobba took from his pocket the necklace that Suliah returned to him just before leaving and placed it around her neck. She gently put her hands around it closed her eyes and lowered her head.

Later that night when the time was right Myanna left the cabin and went to see Daniel. Though she knew the question that was uppermost on her mind she wasn't sure how to put it to the man without seeming to be challenging. She longed to know that the fate of her children was with the God that Daniel professed but she had doubts now since they were sold. When she got to the door it was already open as if she was expected, but she knocked anyway. The voice from inside told her to come in. There was only one lamp burning and it was low. The figure seated at the table from what she could see did not appear to be Daniel or any of the other three. The voice sounded different also, but it was so assuring that she felt no fear.

"Come sit down my child and be comforted" the voice continued.

"Daniel is that you?" she asked.

"I am not the Daniel you know, but one who has been sent to tell you that your children are safe. You have come here because you are troubled by what Daniel said about "the matter will be taken care of." Let me put your mind at ease. The matter that he referred to does not apply to your children only, but to all who are oppressed in this place. The time is coming when justice that is not from man shall be apportioned to all who believe and trust in God. This is how it will be taken care of and according to His schedule. Your children shall not be free from trials that will test them severely, but know this, though the fire of tribulation shall be hot it shall in no way destroy either of them."

The voice stopped, the words ended, the lamp went out and it became completely dark in the room for several minutes. When the lamp came on again at a high level Myanna saw Daniel by the lamp and the others were seated around the table with her. She didn't hear them come in nor did she detect them taking seats at the table; they were just suddenly there. No one said anything for some time but just looked at each other in wonderment. Finally, Daniel came to the table and sat down with the others. He gently took her hand and told her that there were many things she will not understand that will happen shortly and it will be very hard for her. In due time however, she will come to know a peace that surpasses all human understanding. Myanna heard these words and felt such a release of tension that it felt like every burden that she had ever carried in life had been removed.

She left the cabin with her feet on the ground but she was walking on air. The warmth of the night air surrounding her was as embracing as the mother she remembered being held by many years ago. At her cabin she entered and the whole adult household was still sitting around the table even though the hour was late. It was not hard to see by any of them the glow that emanated from her body and the joy shown in her countenance. Penniman was the first to comment.

"Leenee look at her, look at her she shine'n."

Jobba got up from the table and went over to her to see if she was alright. When he got close to her and took her hands he looked in her eyes and was amazed. Not only was her face all-aglow but also he could see a radiance within her. He led her over to the table and sat her down.

"Why she shine'n like dat, she sick?" Penniman asked.

"Maybe she got de fever" Tralene added.

"Naw, she ain sick an she ain got no fever" Jobba responded. "Y`all caint even tell she bin wit de man a God can ya?"

"You talkin `bout dat Daniel preachin man down de road, he ain no man a god he jest fillin y`all wit all kind a nonsense. Ya betta fa-git him an come on back ta Aunt Tee `fo it too late."

Jobba shook his head and looked at Penniman. Myanna told him that she wanted to go upstairs so he helped her up from the table and went with her. Penniman and Tralene looked at each other as the Thomas's exited but said nothing more. All night long in that cabin though the house was divided there was a new unity on one of the floors.

Aunt Tee and Clarence had finished cleaning up after the family's tea and cordial after dinner routine and were in their room talking. She was telling him about how the master had talked to her and threatened to sell her if she didn't mind her station. Clarence listened carefully without offering any input other than a random uh-huh and um-hum when she finished a key point, because he knew that she was in the process of planning something to retaliate against the man. Over the number of years that he had known her, Clarence had come to understand, even before she rose to the position of spiritual leader for the cave, that she was not one to accept a threat from anybody. She had not been born a slave on this plantation and when she arrived here and took over the duties in the house it took some getting used to, to learn how Byron managed his affairs. In the beginning, though Clarence was already here when she came he didn't take to her easily because she, like Byron, had her own way of wanting things done. In a short period of time Byron realized how capable she was and he backed off more and more from trying to micromanage the house operation.

The room that they shared now was originally Clarence's as the head slave in the house, but when Byron told him that he would have to share it with her he was excited at first about the possibilities of the woman living in his room. It didn't take long before she made it very clear that what he envisioned and had on his mind was not going to happen and she meant it. Clarence couldn't understand what was wrong with her in the early period but after awhile when he got to know her better she told him about the experiences she had before coming here and how it ruined her. He wasn't sure just what all that meant but he resigned himself to the fact that if he was going to take care of what he needed he'd have to look elsewhere. They grew closer over time and when she became the spiritual leader he was one of her first converts.

As she continued with her tirade against Byron, Clarence was falling asleep in between his grunts, but he was conscious enough to hear her talking about how much the master wanted it to rain and that she was going to see to it that so much rain came at once that he wouldn't know how to deal with it. The last thing he heard before waking up the next morning was that after the next ritual dance she was going to call on the cave god to break open the skies and pour down a drenching rain. Aunt Tee knew that Clarence was not much of a talker but a good listener so she assumed that he was still with her when she made her final comments, but when she looked over at his bed he had leaned back, his eyes were closed and he had entered into the other world. She walked over covered him up and then went to bed herself.

In the morning she was the first to arise as usual even before the cock crowed. She got out of bed and did her morning routine then went into the kitchen to start preparation for the day. Clarence was still in bed but he heard her get up and wondered how much longer she had continued to talk before she went to sleep. He rolled over and went back to sleep until the familiar sounds of the call to get up were heard coming from down Sam's way. He strained to get out of the bed because he realized now that they had talked for hours well into the night or early morning. The rejuvenation that he usually received from the cave spirit after a long night didn't come because they had not had a session. Feeling thoroughly sleep deprived he had to force his body to comply with his mind's demands and move forward. After getting dressed he made his way to the kitchen also and sat down with her for his start up coffee. She had already set up his breakfast plate and coffee so he could eat and be ready when the rest of the family came down.

Byron was the first to arrive in the dining room and he sat waiting for his coffee. Aunt Tee heard him come down and she sent it to him by the hand of Clarence. They exchanged good morning greetings and Byron asked Clarence if he missed Suliah. Clarence hesitated to reply wondering if the master was being facetious or was he serious. He looked in his face for a moment and determined that it was a sincere question so he answered in the affirmative. It was not that he missed Suliah personally so much as he wanted to have her there because of the plans that Aunt Tee had been making for her. There was no one on the plantation that Aunt Tee wanted to pass along her skills as much as she desired to groom Suliah for the position. Clarence knew this and as Aunt Tee's second in command he wanted to preserve the order.

Not long after Byron sat down in walked Anna Lee who barely spoke to her father. Since the sale and departure of Suliah Anna Lee's interaction with Byron was severely strained and they spoke only when the situation required conversation. Byron tried often to make amends for his action, but there was nothing he could do to appease her. He even went so far as promising her that he would get another handmaiden to replace Suliah, but this didn't satisfy her. At a loss for knowing what to do next he abandoned trying and decided to just let the drama play out. Jethro strolled in next and the greeting was almost a replay of what Anna Lee offered. Jethro however, did ask his father when they would be having their next social. Byron's head perked up at this because he reflected back on what Charlotte said about Jethro getting over Suliah just as soon as there were some new girls in his life. He answered Jethro by telling him that they would be hosting another one just as soon as there was some rain to restore the vitality of his crops.

Finally Charlotte came in and the family ate breakfast together for the first time in quite awhile. She was the only one who came in smiling and greeted Byron with a kiss on his forehead. Both Anna Lee and Jethro greeted her with a pleasant good morning but wondered why she was so happy. It didn't take long for her to apprise them of the reason for her elated state. She told them that now that the gal who had been causing all the tension in the house was gone it was time for them to get back together as a family. She wanted to start out by having another party and do it this weekend. When Byron heard this he looked up from his plate and looked first at his children then at Charlotte. He knew Jethro supported her idea but he wasn't so sure about Anna Lee. Just as he had told Jethro before she came in Byron said the same thing to her. She was disappointed but understood his concern about his precious crops and said she would be patient and wait for the rain. There was no more discussion regarding the matter and Byron refocused his attention on what was uppermost on his mind, the weather.

He had already looked out his window when he got up this morning so he knew that it was going to be another bright and sunny day. Each day the drought continued, his attitude was to lean harder on the slaves because it was their fault and he was determined to make those four responsible, especially Jobba. When he left the house he walked directly to the field where he knew Jobba would be and set right in on making his life miserable. He no longer allowed him to be part of the defiant four gang but he kept him as far away from them as he could because Sam had relayed to him what had happened the last time he was thrown among them. Byron chastised unmercifully and everything the man did was wrong. Jobba, who was coming off of a rejuvenating night sharing the experience that Myanna had with the visitor to Daniel's cabin, was doing all that he could to bear the weight of the burden. He worked harder, kept his mouth shut and bowed as low as he could to try and appease the master but to no avail. No matter what he did it was wrong. By noon and the sun was high in the sky he had as much as he could take.

His temper flared and he threw down his tools running out of the field. The nearest overseer rode his horse at him and attempted to run him down. With a quick move he was able to get around the overseer and grab him from behind unseating him from the horse. When the overseer hit the ground Jobba kicked him in the head knocking him out and then mounted the horse and took off. Sam who was on the other side of the field heard the commotion and then saw Byron waving his arms desperately for him to come over. Sam galloped his horse over to Byron who pointed to Jobba racing away down the road. Sam took off after him and the pursuit was on. It wasn't long before both horses were out of sight and Byron took out his frustration on everybody else in the area including the overseers. He hollered and screamed that it was all their fault for his troubles so loud that it made the slaves wonder if he had lost his mind. He continued on like this for some time until he got tired and went back in the house.

It wasn't until late in the afternoon that Sam returned to the plantation leading the horse that Jobba had taken off on. Jobba wasn't on it. He went inside and explained to Byron that when they got off the plantation property Jobba was able to outrun him to the spot where the river ran under the bridge and he got off the horse and ran into the woods. Byron was furious that Sam didn't catch him and told him to go right back and immediately get hold of the patrollers who were in a nearby outpost. Sam quickly ran out the door and got back on his horse headed down the road. Byron was so angry that he took out his special nectar this early in the day and sat down and poured himself a tall glass. Clarence came in after he heard the yelling to see if Byron was okay, but was told to leave him alone, which Clarence did immediately. He then went out to the back porch where Aunt Tee was and told her all that was happening. She calmly responded to him saying that it was time for her to do her thing.

Myanna had seen all that went on because she was working in the field where Jobba was but not close to him. There wasn't anything she could do because the overseers were watching all of them more closely now thinking that some might get the idea to run also. She said to herself this was all Jobba needed to set him off in carrying out his plan to leave the plantation unauthorized. Inside she knew that he wasn't coming back, but she was afraid for what might happen if the patrollers caught him. She decided that whenever they finished today she was going to talk to the contact for the mountain runaways and do whatever she had to do to get a message to them to find him. She believed it was Penniman, but since the last time she and Jobba had talked about the runaways he seemed not to know anything or at least want to talk about it. The word that had spread around for weeks now was that they were still up there and the patrols were still trying to find them, but having little success. She figured if Jobba could join up with them at least he would be able to survive until he could plan a way for him to come back and get her. There was no doubt in her mind that Jobba could do what he said he would do if he was given the chance.

Sam drove his horse hard galloping down the road away from the mansion. He got to the point at the bridge where he found the horse that Jobba had taken and slowed to look for any signs that he might still be in the area. Seeing none he prompted the horse to pick up the pace again and rode off to the patrol shack. He knew that the more time Jobba had ahead of them the more likely he would be able to find those other runaways and blend into the dense forest. At the patrol shack Sam quickly dismounted and ran inside. Usually there were ten or more slave hunters in the place but now only three were sitting around and when Sam asked where all the men were he was told that they had been dispatched to quell an uprising at one of the other plantations. Sam had heard about such unrest so he was interested in hearing more about it. The hunters went on to tell him that a bunch of slaves had heard a story about somebody named Nat Turner who was able to rise up and get some freedom for awhile, and they were trying to do the same thing. More of them were getting together than before and running off the farms or just killing their owners outright.

When Sam heard these words he shuddered thinking that if someone like Jobba could get slaves together then he could build a pretty good army. He let the hunter telling the story finish then he hastened to tell them the urgency of catching the one that he is looking for. Pointing out the place where he had lost Jobba, Sam wanted them to agree with him that the time lost between then and now was to the runner's advantage. They sided with Sam without hesitation and got up to get the dogs. Outside, to Sam's surprise, there were only two dogs running lose in a fenced yard. One of the hunters entered the yard and quieted the barking animals that seemed more anxious than the hunters to start the run. He tied both to a single leash and brought them out. The other two mounted their horses and said to Sam lead the way to where he lost his runaway. Sam quickly pointed out that the runaway belonged to Mr. Candle, not him. The hunters upon hearing this elevated their attention to the matter.

The group rode off in a big hurry and arrived at the designated spot Sam showed them.

They all got down and started the search on foot with the dogs leading the way. These dogs had been meticulously trained to detect the distinct body aroma of the slave population and were chomping at the bit to find one. Straining to keep up with the dogs the hunter wielding the leash hollered back to the others to spread out, but keep in sight. Running through the trees it was difficult to keep eye contact as they weaved in and out. The fact that the dogs were running in a specific direction gave Sam the feeling that they were onto Jobba's scent and would be on him soon. However, when the dogs came to a spot and they pulled up in front of a dead raccoon covered with the shirt of a runaway, Sam's hopes were dashed. The dogs continued barking at the dead coon until the disappointed hunter cracked his whip and told them to shut up. He pulled them away from the animal and tried to get them to pick up a scent in another direction, but to no avail. The dogs just ran around in a circle barking at each other and the hunters.

By this time Jobba was well into the woods and panting for breath. He dared not sit down too long, but he knew he couldn't keep up the pace he set for himself. Stumbling over a fallen branch he put his arms forward to break his fall as he hit the ground and slid forward. He rolled over onto his back and looked up at the sky hoping to see some sign of mercy. He saw nothing but a beautiful clear blue sky. Lying there for what seemed like an eternity he questioned where he was going and what he was going to do when he got there. He really had no answer to either question. The mountain slaves were out here somewhere he knew that much, but exactly where they were at this time he had no idea. While still on his back he looked around at the trees to see if there might be a sign that they had been in this area and noticed that an arrow had been marked on one of them pointing in the direction that he had been running. He raised himself up and moved closer to the tree. Sure enough it was a sign that had been carved in the tree recently and he hurriedly moved in the direction of the arrow.

Not far from the first arrow he came to another one that indicated that whoever was reading the sign should turn left here and look for another. Jobba thought to himself that this wasn't too smart if it really was left by the mountaineers because if he saw it what would stop the hunters from seeing it also. However, when he came to the next indicators there were two arrows crisscrossing each other and one leading back in the direction he just came from. At this point he had to laugh heartily and the temporary release of tension felt good. Now he had to make a decision. If he continued to follow the arrow that led in another direction there was no guarantee that this was the right move, but he knew that following the other arrow would only lead back. For no good reason he happened to look down at the base of the tree and there was his answer. A rock formation had been arranged in the ground partially hidden by some brush but clear enough to see that the rocks were pointing in a direction that neither of the arrows indicated.

Jobba picked up on this and had the feeling that this must be the one to follow so he did. About a hundred yards from that tree was a clearing where there were many signs that the mountaineers had been there recently. He looked around to see if there might be an indicator to let him know where they were heading, but saw none. Disappointed he moved away from the clearing and sat down under a tall tree and rested. Feeling safe for the moment, his thoughts ran back to the events of the day and to Myanna who he felt would be the one to feel his absence the most. Though he felt a deep sense of longing to be back with her he knew that what he did would have come sooner or later and he was glad that it happened now because it let him get started on what he planned to do soon anyway. His eyelids were getting heavy and he wanted to lie down and sleep, but he knew that this was not the place for that.

Elsewhere in the forest the same mountaineers that had come down to the Candle Plantation and attended Aunt Tee's party heard the sound of the dogs and were on alert. They had become used to this noise from the almost constant pursuit of other patrols and it no longer frightened them, but made them all the more sensitive to the fact that they were not free. Had Jobba known how close they were to him he would have gotten up right then and ran to them. If the hunters knew also how close they were it would have been a short-term search to find them. However, with the dogs being scentless just out of the range of smell, the hunters were growing more frustrated and intolerant of each other not having a clue as to the whereabouts of this recent runaway. Sam was just as hyper as any of the others and maybe even more so because if they didn't find Jobba, he was the one who would have to go back and tell Mr. Candle. Having little success in their search thus far they decided to sit down and rest a minute and decide in which direction they should travel next.

One said to the other that the dogs were useless and the other defending the dogs responded that he was just as useless. The squabble was escalating due to the level of frustration and the fact that they were so limited in the number of men available that they knew it was quite possible that their target was well on his way up north. They were also aware that amidst all the talk about slave uprisings and rebellions that there was talk of some kind of train called the Underground Railroad that was making a way for the runaways to even get out of the state all together. Shifting from one foot to the other, the man with the leash challenged his cohorts to get up and continue the hunt. He reminded them whom this slave had run away from and how much could be at stake in payment if they found him. Sam was not ready to attest to the size of payment, knowing that Byron had not given him any authorization to quote an amount, but the men just assumed from the reputation and size of the plantation that Byron would be generous.

They got up and struck out in a direction randomly selected by the man with the leash on the dogs. The dogs were no longer running, but walking fast pulling at the leash and sniffing the ground with no sense of urgency. After a couple of hours and feeling exhausted the hunters felt the desperation in their search and were ready to cease looking for the day because the sun was going down. There didn't seem to be any assigned leader of this group, but when Sam asked them what they were doing, the one with the leash told him that they had done as much as they were going to do today and they were turning around. There was no disagreement from the rest and the dogs were rerouted and headed back to the main road. Sam could offer no good reason to continue so he joined them. The thoughts going through his mind were telling him he'd better stay with the patrol and not go back to the mansion without Jobba and face the wrath of Byron, but then on the other hand he knew that Byron would be expecting him to come and update him on the status of his property. Electing to follow his second mind he went back to the patrol shack to make sure they were going to start out again early the next morning, then he turned and went home.

Jobba could see that the sun was going down and he started to look for a safe place where he could spend the night and not be discovered. He went back to the clearing and continued to look for signs that could help find the people he was looking for. He searched the grounds thoroughly and all he found were the things they had discarded which were of no use to him. He left the clearing and walked around trying to get a bearing on where he was with regard to the plantation. It couldn't be that far he concluded because he had not ridden that long when he came to the bridge and he hadn't run that long in trying to elude the hunters. His desire if he couldn't find the mountaineers was to get close enough to the river to see if he could see one of the slaves on the other side and get their attention. Maybe they would help him stay in the mountains by getting food to him at night. Then he could have time to figure a way to come for Myanna. He kept walking and looking for signs when he heard noises that sounded like others were doing the same thing.

He stopped and crouched low to the ground to get a better position to hear. It was true there was something moving on the other side of the trees that were just ahead of him. He started to crawl toward the noise when he heard what seemed like voices. At first it sounded like animals, but as he got closer he was sure that it was men talking. Afraid to make much noise himself he stood up quietly and pushed his way through the trees until he came to the place where he heard the noise. There they were six of them making a clearing for their night's stay. When he was discovered the first man started to attack him, but relented when he saw who it was. Instead of an assault the man embraced him and asked where he was from. After telling him he was from the plantation down below the man opened his shirt and showed him the mark of Aunt Tee and claimed to be his brother. Jobba saw the mark, but didn't acknowledge the brotherhood. He just asked if he could stay with them for the night.

The man, glad to see him, beckoned him to follow as he was led to where the others were nearby preparing for the night. They had a fresh catch of fish and plenty of vegetables. Jobba was glad to see them also, but wondered if all had taken the oath to Aunt Tee. It didn't much matter now because he needed their help and he was willing to do what he needed to help them also. They invited him to pitch in and help make the clearing that he willingly did and in a short time they had made their home for the night with a circle ready for the evening fire. As they finished with the homemaking task several of them came over to Jobba and asked how it was that he was in the mountains. When he told him what had driven him to run, they were all the more ready to welcome him into the fold. The leader however, asked him about the protection of Aunt Tee and he said that he didn't feel the freedom they were supposed to get when they joined up with her. Jobba hesitated in trying to answer him now because he didn't know how much influence they received from her about the freedom thing. He did choose to tell him that he had been one of her followers, but he was no longer and he went on to relate the story about his near death experience.

After the leader heard his story and continued to press Jobba asking how he was going to get free. Jobba responded that he did not know yet, but he would only go back down there to get his wife and then he would be headed wherever he had to, to find his children and then north. He continued telling the leader what he had heard about the Underground Railroad stories and about freedom being for them up north. The leader confirmed his story about the railroad because he had heard the same thing from others who had come away with them at first, but then moved on to find it. The leader also said that this group was not a permanent one, but it was just a way to keep away from the hunters until they could move further along. Around the fire that night they traded stories about their adventures and tribulations well into the late hours until the fire went out and they huddled together for protection and slept.

Myanna spent most of the night trying to get Penniman to reveal to her how she could make contact with the runaways in the mountains. He was resistant to telling her anything since she was no longer a member of the Aunt Tee followers. He did offer however to let her know that even though she had been baptized it was not too late to come back and then he would get a message to the mountaineers for her. The push and shove conversation went on for some time, but Myanna refused to be enticed by Penniman into doing something that she knew was wrong.

Realizing that she was not going to get the help she sought from him she gave up and walked out the door. Into the night she looked up and down the quarters to see if there was anyone else who might be able to get a message across the river for her. Of the Aunt Tee followers none would offer help to one outside of their covenant and for the Daniel believers there were none who knew.

She considered going back to Daniel, but feared that he would tell her not to get involved with those hiding in the forest. In desperation she walked down to the last cabin on the right which was where she knew the runaways had come on the plantation before going to the cave. Although she had seen the residents of that cabin before she didn't know them well enough to be asking them for help. She thought they might be part of Aunt Tee's group, but she had never seen them associate with any of the rest of that crowd so she took the chance. At the door she knocked gently and waited for a response. The old man who came to the door was a stranger to her. She had no recall of ever seeing him on the plantation before - not in the fields or any place else. His appearance was a little strange with his completely white hair and his long white flowing beard. He also had on a long robe and sandals that none of the other slaves she had ever seen wear. In a soft voice he asked her what it is she needed and Myanna was almost speechless. She asked if he was the one that had always been living here and where the rest of the people were. He told her that they were all down at the river and he did not live there, but came by from time to time.

Myanna got extremely curious when he said that and wondered how it was that he was able to come and go at will as he seemed to be indicating. The man saw the puzzled look on her face and told her it was not for her to know his business, but if she needed his help just ask for it. Uncomfortable in not knowing who or what this man was she was afraid to let him know what it was she was seeking and told him that she would go down to the river and try and find one of the other residents. He responded to her to do as she wished, but then he said she should be careful in whom she placed her trust. After he said that he closed the door. This made her feel even more uneasy because she reflected back to her night at Daniel's and the strange voice that talked to her in the dim light. Although she couldn't plainly see who the voice belonged to somehow the voice then and the voice she just heard were eerily similar. Once the door closed she turned away and headed down to the river. There she looked for anyone that she recognized as being a resident of that cabin, but nobody stood out. Extremely disappointed she thought about going back to cabin eleven and trying again, but decided against it and went home. Inside her cabin she felt very much alone. There was no Linwood and now no Jobba who she could at least have someone to talk with. She lay across her bed thinking about what it was she might try next, but before a plan came to mind she went to sleep.

In the mansion during those same hours Byron had joined his family in their usual after dinner treats. Even though he had been sampling his own private stock earlier he wanted to get his family's input on what he had been hearing about the uprisings and the fact that Jobba had run. It was not without notice that the family recognized he was in pretty good spirits from something other than the cordials, but they were willing to indulge him because he had not been with them in this manner for some time.

"Anna Lee my chile you're the smart one, what you hear about these slave attacks?"

Anna Lee was caught somewhat off guard by the question, but managed to respond.

"Why daddy whatever are you talking about?"

"Come on chile I know you dun heard somethin aout these niggahs down the road and around the area tryin to get free by takin over their farms. Tell me what you hear."

"Daddy I ain't heard nothing like that `cause I ain't been nowhere to hear it."

Byron turned to Jethro and asked him the same question and received a similar answer. When he put the question to Charlotte and got almost the same response he got a little annoyed and stormed out of the room. They all turned and looked at him then at each other and laughed in very low tones acknowledging that his cups were getting the best of him and he was headed to bed. They spent a little while longer with each other and then followed in his path upstairs.

Aunt Tee and Clarence were waiting around in the area until the family finished their cordials then they went in to clean up. Clarence said to Aunt Tee that he thought Jobba's running away had more of an effect on the master than even he wanted to admit. Aunt Tee said back to him that if he thought Jobba's running away has affected him wait until she finished with what she was going to do to him for the way he treated her. She reminded Clarence that tomorrow there would be another full moon and the time would be right for her to petition the spirit to grant her request. Surely for what she had done for the cave spirit lately in that she had converted many new faces into their realm how could they deny her this simple request. Clarence started smiling in agreement with her and they went on cleaning in silence.

All through the next day, ritual day, Aunt Tee and Clarence were walking around as if one of the Candle's famous social gatherings was about to take place. The Candles were at a loss regarding their jubilation, but attributed it to perhaps them having a good night together. They had absolutely no idea what kind of bedroom relationship existed between the two. Clarence was moving through his chores with such zeal that Charlotte questioned him at one point about why he didn't approach his tasks like this every day. He smiled and responded that today he was just feeling something special and wanted to let everybody know it. Charlotte commended him for it and left him alone. Jethro noticed also the unusually bright spirits of the two house chiefs and commented that he thought there was some conspiracy afoot and he wanted to know what it was all about. He was hearkening back to what his father had brought up last night during the happy hour about the slave uprisings and wondered if there wasn't something going on right here. Clarence assured him there was nothing like that going on here, so Jethro dropped the discussion. Anna Lee who lately had drifted into her own world since the departure of her handmaiden and friend never even noticed the character change.

Byron who had left the house too early to notice the couple's exuberance was down at Sam's house trying to find out what the status was on Jobba. Sam who had returned from the patrol station too late yesterday to go to the mansion and report decided to wait until morning to update Byron. When Byron knocked on his door Sam opened it quickly and invited him in. Dispensing with the morning greeting Byron launched into the question of where is he. Sam composed himself before speaking and managed to get the words out that the patrol had lost the scent late evening and decided to pick up the hunt again early this morning. Byron, though not happy at the report asked Sam why he was still there and not down at the station joining in the hunt. Sam grabbed his hat and scrambled out the door to his horse. Byron left the house right after him and walked down to the fields.

When he looked around at the workers and even though he knew he had been driving them harder than usual lately he noticed that some of them seemed to be more excited than usual and this bothered him. He called one of the overseers over and asked him what they had to be so happy about. The overseer had no idea and tried to be funny when he said maybe they just liked to be whipped. Byron didn't think the comment was funny and was not in the mood for humor anyway so he flew into a rage and told the overseer that if he thought this situation here was funny then he better start looking for another job. The overseer became instantly contrite and apologized begging forgiveness. Byron just looked at him and rode away.

Byron left the tobacco fields and went over to where his wheat and corn were growing. Although they were faring better, it didn't seem that he was having any luck with none of his crops and he made sure that all of the workers no matter in what field they labored knew about his displeasure. He hollered and screamed at everybody out there threatening to whip them all if something didn't change. No one raised a head to acknowledge him because by this time they had become accustomed to his bazaar behavior and they felt things couldn't get any worse. The split in the factions was growing more intense as each month passed and the inevitable showdown was increasing in speed. Today as one side was dejected and reacting to the harsh treatment by the master the other was high in anticipation of an evening to remember. The word had already circulated through the magnificent slave network that Aunt Tee had a special ceremony planned for tonight and all who attended would be completely satisfied when they left. For many the workday would not end fast enough so they could return to their cabins and prepare for the evening. The network notice of complete satisfaction included reference to a change in the way they were being treated via a change in the master. No one on the plantation really knew what this meant, but like the fabled fish story the more it was told the larger it grew with each teller.

Myanna was watching how the interaction between the factions was going and wondered how it was that the overseers were unable to tell what was going on. Either they really didn't see what was happening because they couldn't recognize the difference or they were afraid to get too involved because Byron had come down on them a lot just like the slaves. They allowed a lot to happen just as long as it looked like the collective slave effort was focused on the crops. The fact that it was now the summer months and the crops were all but failing everyone who spent time under the hot sun knew that tensions rose due to the heat, but the rise in these tensions the overseers should have been able to see were not heat related.

No major incidents occurred between the groups when the horn finally blew to end the workday, but it was clear that one side was ready to celebrate while the other just wanted to go lie down. Myanna was still unable to get someone to accommodate her request for getting a message to the ones across the river and was giving serious consideration about going to the meeting tonight knowing full well what could happen. Feeling a sense of desperation and knowing that she had recovered once from under the spell and could do it again if it became necessary, she was tempted to try. As she was walking alone back to her cabin it seemed like Daniel suddenly popped up from out of nowhere and whispered in her ear.

"It is written again, You shall not tempt the Lord your God." (Mt. 4:7)

He said the words and kept on going never even turning to look back at her. But the timeliness of the words planted in her mind made her wonder how he knew what she was considering. The uncanny occurrence of this and the many other acts she had witnessed performed by this man made her all the more convinced that he was more than just a preacher. She gave up on the idea of going to the cave, but she still felt the need to find someone to get her message sent. It would not be until after the cave celebration ended that it would come to her in a dream, Jobba was already with the mountaineers.

In the cabin Penniman and Tralene were in exceptionally good spirits as they joined in with the feelings of the others in their group. Tralene was already preparing the dinner meal when Myanna walked in. Even though they were on opposite sides of the religious divide the families had managed to maintain a good relationship and stayed away from discussions that would force them to take sides in the house. Myanna greeted them when she entered then said she was extremely tired and was going to skip eating tonight and go upstairs to lie down. Tralene nodded her head in acknowledgment and went on with her cooking. Penniman said nothing and kept on smiling. The evening hours passed and it was time for the parade up to the cave to begin. Myanna was still awake and heard her housemates preparing to join the procession. She had no inclination to look out the window as she usually did when Jobba was there, but this time she walked downstairs and opened the door. She stepped outside to get a full view of all who were going and noticed that the line had grown longer than what she remembered. She wondered had more runaways come down from the mountains to join in or had some of her people decided to switch sides. She strained her eyes to see if she recognized any of her people, but they were moving along at a pretty good pace and even in the light of a bright full moon it wasn't easy to see. Not being able to solve the riddle she went back inside and went to bed.

At the cave the procession ended and the crowd moved inside taking their place around the circle of fire. Aunt Tee was already into her chanting facing the wall and the drummers were in rhythm. The robed man was moving around the edge of the circle throwing the spices into the fire that sent off an aroma that excited everybody. Space was becoming more of a premium as the crowd grew. Myanna's observation was correct. The reputation of Aunt Tee had spread throughout the plantations in the area and the cry for freedom was more intense. The belief that if they joined up with her then they would somehow be set free motivated many to take the risk and walk off their lands late at night and make their way to the Candle place. The cave was now filled with bodies swaying back and forth to the rhythm and Aunt Tee in a more excited fashion than ever before was imploring the spirit to grant her petition. At the highest point in the ceremony she offered up a whole goat as the sacrifice and the cave spirit emerged to devour it and returned to the wall.

In the midst of the high point Aunt Tee pointed to an effigy of Byron on a pole and she lifted it up and turned to her followers. Holding the symbol high above her head she said to them this was the promise. This man would have his attention diverted away from them for a time because the rain he has been seeking was going to come, but not the way he wants. She assured the people that the god of the cave had accepted her offering and agreed to grant her request and as a show of acceptance fire would come from the wall and consume the effigy. As the people continued to sway and raise their arms the rhythm increased to an exhausting level then suddenly a loud bang was heard coming from the wall and everything stopped. With all eyes focused on the wall image suddenly a flash of fire came out and consumed the effigy including the pole so that there was nothing but ashes left on the ground. After seeing this they all fell to the ground and lay for several minutes before being able to recover and stand back up.

The dancing and chanting continued as usual well into the night, but this time there was a new sense of rejuvenation. The feeling that the heavy load they all bore was being lifted had come over all of them. When they left the cave on this night it was with a deep sense of renewed commitment to their leader and to the spirit of the cave. Down in the quarters at this time a shudder ran up and down the spine of Daniel and his associates causing each of them to genuflect and call for renewed power themselves. Even in the Thomas cabin it was given to Myanna at this moment to see in a dream Jobba seated around a fire high in the mountains talking with the mountaineers. She saw further that even though he was seated with them, he was attended by an angel watching over him who was his protection, even from them.

The hike down from the cave was more boisterous than ever, first because of the additional number of new attendees and second because the excitement of tonight's promise had left the crowd still feeling a sense of invulnerability. As they walked, Aunt Tee became concerned that someone in the mansion might see them as they passed by the back of the house. She rushed to the head of the procession and raised her arms indicating to the marchers that they should restrain themselves and quiet down. As in the cave her command was instantly obeyed and a hush came over the parade. The Candle land marchers completed their procession and each follower was able to go back to his cabin undiscovered while the visitors continued down the road to go home.

In the mountains today Jobba got his first full day experience in roaming with the runaways. From the time that they arose early in the morning and started cleaning away the evidence that they had been there, until now which was about eleven-thirty in the day, they moved among the trees in no particular direction. Jobba wondered about this seemingly aimless trek and asked the leader where it was they were trying to go. His answer surprised him and he knew right then that he had to disassociate himself from this group. The leader with his reply said that after a night was spent in one place they would move on to find the next secure sight for the evening. He went on to say that they would do this until a sign was given that they should head one way or another. When Jobba asked about what kind of a sign was he expecting, the answer was that he didn't know, but he was sure it would be clear to him when it came. Jobba was grateful for them finding him, but this plan was not acceptable to him.

All during the day they moved carefully listening out for the hunters and the dogs. At one point they did hear the dogs and the sound didn't seem to be that far away so they moved deeper into the woods and closer to foliage they knew would camouflage any scents that they might give off. Jobba marveled at this and filed the knowledge away in his mind for future reference. When night came, word had gotten to them that it was time to attend the next ritual that Aunt Tee was hosting. Jobba heard the men talking about it and asked the leader whether he was going to go. He also asked how they knew where they were with respect to the river and the leader told him how they had marked the trees since they got up here. Wherever they moved they left indicators for how to get back to the river. Again Jobba filed this information away for the future. The answer to the question about going to the dance was answered in the affirmative and they invited Jobba to go along. When Jobba reiterated the story about his first encounter with Aunt Tee, the leader said to him he didn't want to go through that withdrawal experience nor did he want any of his people to either. What Jobba did want to do was to go with them as far as the river so he could see how to get there alone and it was agreed. The runaways from the mountains were part of the increased numbers that Myanna saw.

Early the next morning the lightning flashed across the sky followed by a loud clap of thunder shaking Byron from the bed. He jumped up and ran to the window. There was no rain, but the skies were very dark and threatening. With a great sense of excitement like a child witnessing his first snowfall he rushed putting on his clothes and running down the stairs. For the first time in a period that he couldn't remember how long he was up before Aunt Tee and Clarence. He ran outside and looked up at the sky. Everything was very dark and there was no sign that the sun was about to make an appearance at all. As he looked up, another flash shot across the sky followed by another thunder roll and his anticipation elevated accordingly. He was waiting patiently for the clouds to open up and deliver their content, but nothing happened. Staring for some time he stood watching until a break in the clouds showed a glimmer of sunlight about to burst through. His disappointment was obvious and he started rocking back and forth in frustration. When no rain came for about fifteen minutes from the time that he first went out there, and the sun seemed to be winning the appearance battle he gave up and went back inside the house.

Thoroughly exasperated from this taunt by the weather he went in the dining room and sat down. The expression on his face was not hard for anyone to see his frustration.

"Massa you okay?" Clarence asked as he poured his coffee.

Byron said nothing, but just stared at the cup before he picked it up. Clarence repeated his question this time with a little more emphasis.

"Massa, massa you feelin aright?"

"Yes Clarence. I'm alright. I was jest hopin that the rain I been lookin for was about to come."

"Well massa I know ya bin lookin an I' ses it `bout ta come. I feels it in de air."

Behind Byron's back Clarence was smiling and shaking his head with a knowing smile that it was certainly going to rain.

"Is you gwine out to da field ta day massa?"

"I dono Clarence if it don't rain, look like I get tired of watchin them crops just give up. Maybe I'll just stay inside today an see what happens."

"Massa you shouldn be feelin like dat. Ya gotta keep yo head up an think it gonna come."

"Yes, yes Clarence I know your right and I think that's what I'll do. Where's the rest of my family they all sleep`n in today?"

"Oh it's still real early massa. They be down soon."

Byron finished his breakfast by himself and went into his parlor. He kept looking out the window to see if anything was changing.

In the cabins Myanna was up early too after she heard the loud thunder roar. She too went to the window to see if any rain was coming down. Like Byron she wondered about whether this was the breakthrough he had been desperately looking for. When she saw the break in the clouds and the sun trying to come through she almost felt a pang of sympathy for him, but it only lasted a moment. It was early yet, but she decided to get washed up and go downstairs. It was still taking her some time to get used to not seeing Linwood in his bed or having to sleep by herself but she was managing. She then reflected on the dream she had last night and felt some comfort in what had been revealed to her. Though she was still having some difficulty in accepting the whole concept of an angel watching over him, she reviewed in her mind all of the things that she had seen and felt better that it could be true. When she got downstairs she was surprised to see that neither Penniman nor Tralene or any of the kids were up, but all sleeping soundly. Then she remembered that last night was their ritual night, but then she thought this never bothered them from getting up early the next day before. She wondered if anything had gone wrong.

Though it was a little late, the horn sounded and the day's activities started. As the slaves made their way out to the fields, the sun kept playing peek-a-boo with the clouds and everyone was wondering as Myanna did earlier was this the day. For those who attended the ritual last night, it wasn't so much a hunch as it was an expectation as to what was going to happen. For all others, including the overseers, it was for them a hope as much as a whatever feeling. When they entered the field all eyes were searching for the appearance of Byron so they could get a handle on what kind of a day it was going to be by how much he yelled at the day's start. For the first half hour there was no sign of him and things seemed to be moving along okay. However, when they saw Sam come out from the house they couldn't be sure whether he would be right behind him or not. Sam came in to the tobacco field area and just rode around the perimeter. Byron was still nowhere in sight.

Along about midday the sun began to lose the battle and the clouds were getting closer together. It was almost as if an eclipse had taken place because the darkness had changed what little daylight there was into a severe overcast. Byron who had been constantly looking out his parlor window, again was getting his hopes up. He got up from his chair and walked outside. Slowly walking down to the field he kept his eyes focused on the skies. He was right on the edge of the main tobacco field when the next big flash of lightening struck and the thunder the loudest of the morning came close after. He jumped from the noise, but picked up his pace as he neared the center of the field. It seemed that some of the workers had already thrown down their tools in anticipation of a heavy rain, but he wasn't so convinced yet and was about to chastise them for doing so. He looked around to see the horses that the overseers were on were reacting to the loud thunder and they were having a difficult time controlling them.

He turned his attention away from the workers and started to walk back to the edge of the field when another flash and another clap of thunder roared so loud that everyone out there believed that something besides rain was about to fall out of the sky. The horses were all rearing up and the overseers had to get them back to the stable before they would be completely useless. Byron looked all around and some of the workers were falling down to the ground looking up and cowering. Others were looking up and smiling. Byron wasn't sure how he, felt now but when he looked up again he saw something extremely odd.

Chapter 7 - Pride and Confrontation

Compared to the Candle mansion it was little more than a pauper's abode, but it was a nice house. Trader Bob, his brother and a few townsfolk had built the place almost fifteen years ago and except for the additions required for his growing business it had remained the same. Bob had not grown up in the flesh peddling trade, but when he was a young man his friend took him to a slave auction in Richmond and he became so enthralled at how lucrative the business could be, not to mention all of the side benefits, he had to get into it. At first he had difficulty in getting himself established because the other traders didn't trust him and were wary of any newcomers. However, over the years through his pleasant outgoing demeanor and his willingness to compromise he was able to get a foothold and had become known as a dealer by the name of Trader in high quality merchandise. His enterprise had grown so much that the small barn where he originally kept his chattel was now replaced by a large bunkhouse that could accommodate up to twenty bodies.

When they left the Candle Plantation just three days ago, Suliah and Linwood had resigned themselves to the fact that they would probably never see their parents again and now it was just the two of them. Though the distance from one location to the other was only about twenty miles and took about an hour, to Suliah it seemed that they were traveling for a considerably longer time. All through the journey she was looking around to see if she would recognize any landmarks that she could remember and maybe find her way back if she got the chance. Along the way there was nothing but forest and except for an occasional house scattered about and set way back from the road the scene was all the same. She did notice one outstanding feature that distinguished itself from the scenic monotony and that was the patrol station that was right off the road and prominent with its big sign out front. It was hard to miss and she made a mental note of it so if she did come back this way unauthorized, she would be sure to bypass it.

At Trader Bob's she and Linwood were placed in the bunkhouse along with three others, two men and a woman. They learned from overhearing Bob's men talking around them, that they were being held there until the next major auction was ready in Richmond in two days. Then they would be packaged together and carted down there to be shown as featured items. Living in the bunkhouse was not unusually harsh and but for the few times that one of Bob's men had more than a notion to visit with Suliah late at night, it was endurable. When they arrived and were being escorted to their temporary living quarters, the one man in Bob's employ whose eyes betrayed his desire for Suliah was already plotting how he was going to enjoy her company as often as he could. His few attempts at carrying out his plan however were thwarted when Bob, had noticed his keen interest in her and took precautions to isolate her from the group under his close surveillance.

In preparing to package his presentation and set minimum prices for his goods Bob noticed that in the paper work he got from Byron the proper signature had not been rendered. Since he was well aware of the recent crack down on the slave trade regulations and how the laws were being amended to get tougher, he knew that he had to make a trip back to the Candle place and straighten it out. The trip to Richmond was just two days away and he had everything ready except for this so he made plans to see Byron first thing in the morning. It was on his mind to take Suliah with him rather than chance leaving her in the bunkhouse unprotected, but he had to sleep on it.

When the morning came Bob decided rather than take Suliah with him and possibly cause seller's remorse, he would demand that his subordinate ride with him. The dark skies overhead made it look like an ominous trip as he prepared to go. He stopped by the bunkhouse to make sure that all was in order then he and his man set out for the Candle Plantation. As they moved further and further along the road the skies were becoming more threatening and every mile presented a new challenge that they would get there before the pending storm would break. Within the last few yards of the journey, Trader Bob heard small drops of rain hitting on his hat and when he looked up he felt the drops on his face. They left the main road and made their way up toward the mansion. By now it was about nine O'clock and he suspected that Byron would be with his people in the fields so he headed in that direction.

At the edge of the main tobacco field he could see the man standing there staring up at the dark sky and he witnessed the same thing that Byron saw. There in the sky was a large flock of humming birds flying backward across the fields. It was so amazing to see this unusual feat that everyone out there stood mesmerized by the sight. When the birds disappeared backwards over the horizon suddenly the clouds opened and all the rain that Byron thought was held up on back order got delivered. The torrential downpour was so hard that doing anything else in the fields that day was futile. Byron stood there with his arms outstretched and hopping on one foot then the other in pure excitement. He failed to see Trader Bob behind him, but at this moment he really didn't care who was there. As the rain continued to come down hard, Byron finally called to the workers and told them to go home and they went scrambling from the fields.

When Byron got to the edge of the field and saw Trader Bob he grabbed his hand and started pulling him toward the mansion. He was so happy at what he thought was his punishing methods yielding results that he wasn't the slightest bit concerned about why Bob had come back to see him so soon. They quick stepped to the porch and before going inside Byron hesitated turning around to look once again at the ferocious downpour. He slapped Trader Bob on the back and asked him if he had ever seen anything so magnificent. Bob was certainly aware of the drought even though it didn't affect him as much as the farmers so he was able to understand Byron's jubilation. However, he was more concerned with getting the proper signature on his ownership documents and quickly returning to his place. He allowed Byron to have his moments of happy expression and then he asked if they could go inside.

Once inside and Byron directed him to his parlor, Bob produced the papers and pointed out to Byron the impropriety of his signature that had gone unnoticed. Byron took the document looked at it and smiled.

"So I guess we don't really have a deal here do we?" Byron said facetiously.

"Will you be bringing my gal back?"

Trader Bob, who was a much more serious individual, especially when it came to his business, wasn't sure how to take Byron's comments so he looked at him for a minute before responding. When he was comfortable that Byron was being jocular he answered him.

"I know you'd like ta have her back, but tell me now why did ya sell her?"

Byron stopped smiling and thought seriously about the question.

"Oh I was more about trying to punish one of my slaves then anything agin her. Now she's gone it got my daughter all upset and my son he about to lose his mind. Only one happy around here is Charlotte and I know why."

"Well I'm truly sorry 'bout yo family, but I come here so we kin get this paper done right an I kin git on back home. If you jest sign yo whole legal name here then we be through."

"Now hold up a minute Bob you don't want to jump right back out there in all that rain do ya. Come on and have a little swalla with me until it lighten up some."

"No thank you. Now I dun tol ya b'fo Byron, I don mix ma binness with ma pleasures. Far as that rain go I bin through so much worse, this jest like a sprinkle. Now come on an sign the paper an let me go."

Byron reluctantly put the paper down on his desk scribbled out his whole signature in the right place then handed it back to Bob.

"Okay ya happy now?"

"Much obliged, much obliged Byron. The way they bin act'n at these auctions lately seem like they got more lawyas then buyers there an they all wanna see the papers. I don know what this Southland comin to. Some say there gonna be a war soon all over this slave thing."

"Yeah I bin hearing that for awhile now. Its all cause of some of them Yankees done come down here and don't know nothin about the way we do things. I tell ya if they wants a fight to stop our way a living, then I'm ready to give 'em one. You kin bet on that."

"Well Byron I don know 'bout gittin caught up in no war, it caint be good fer nobody, but I sure caint run my trade if'n one starts."

"Don't you worry none about that, ain't enuff of them who wanna come down here and do no serious fightin anyway, I don believe."

"Yeah, well I hope you right. Alright let me get on outta here and back on the road. Where's that man I come in here with, he mus be 'round somewhere?"

"I think he went back in the kitchen, let me go and find him for you an I'll send him right out."

Byron left the room and went to the kitchen where he found Bob's helper sitting down at the table talking to Aunt Tee with a big plate of food in front of him. Byron told him that Bob was ready to go and he was looking for him. The helper shoveled another heap of food in his mouth and got up from the table. He grabbed his hat and thanked Aunt Tee for her hospitality then quickly exited. Bob met him at the door and they both said goodbye to Byron as they headed out. It was still raining pretty hard, but Bob was anxious to get out of there, now that he had completed the business he had come for.

On the way back when they got close to the patrol station they could see a lot of activity. There were about twenty men walking around the outside with their rifles and shotguns at the ready. The dogs were straining at their leashes trying to get away. All of the focus was on the land behind the station. When Bob got close enough he hollered to one of the men and asked what was going on. The reply told him that some of the rebels from a plantation not too far away had made their way to this point and were running free just behind the station. Even in all the rain the men with their weather gear on were fanning out to cover the greatest amount of territory. As Bob was talking to the man, another one raised his gun up and fired at a figure that was running about fifty yards away. The shot missed and the runner ducked into the bush. The dogs were then unleashed and the chase started. Bob and his helper kept on going looking back occasionally to see if anybody got caught.

Within the hour Bob was back at his place and immediately went inside to finish getting his package in order for delivery. He stopped by the bunkhouse to check on his property and after consulting with the supervisor he left in charge it seemed that all was in order. Other than Linwood and Suliah he didn't think he had much to offer at this auction to bring him the kind of profit that he was accustomed to. The two men were estimated to be well into the thirty's and possibly early forties, but he purchased them on the recommendation of their previous owner who attested to their stellar work efforts. Physically they looked to be in relatively decent shape and were not scarred like some others that he had in the past. The woman was a bit younger and obviously had birthed some children, but she looked very sturdy and was told that she was an excellent cook and housekeeper.

When he sat down at his desk to price out his package he wondered if he could get the best deal by selling Linwood and Suliah as a package or would it be better to auction them off individually. His conclusion was that separate would get him the best profit. Then he considered the other three. If he had to, he thought that he might just throw in one or the other of the men when Linwood was up. He also considered pairing the two women for the best deal. For over an hour he wrestled with the way that he wanted to best present his chattel and was mindful of the likely set of buyers that would be there. At this auction he knew there would be some moneyed gentleman with aristocracy in their breeding so he was intent on getting the most out of his stock. His one big concern was that he would have to leave his items in the holding cells for some time until he would be able to call them to the block. Being very familiar with the security in the cells he was more afraid that Suliah might be assaulted before she even came up for the call than he was of not getting a good price for her. Keeping this in mind he decided to make some special arrangements for her the minute he arrived in town and had to deposit them there. His idea was to bribe the security chief with enough money to make it worth his while to protect his property. It was a good idea, but then he wondered about how trustworthy was this man even with a bribe.

The day came around and it was time to take his lot and move it to the showroom. Early that morning he got up and prepared himself for the journey then went down to the bunkhouse to have his helpers get them ready. It was still raining as it had been for the last two days. He couldn't be overly concerned with the rain because this auction was a major one and it didn't occur but so often. He told his helpers to make sure that his good wagon was made ready and that the cover was well secured over it. Knowing that the roads were going to be muddy and hard to ride on he also told them to make sure that the horses were well watered and the wheels inspected for safety. When all this was done the five slaves were loaded on and Bob with two of his men were ready to move out. One man rode beside Bob in the front seat while the other rode on horseback behind the wagon. As he suspected right from the start the road was in poor condition and the continuous rain wasn't going to make it easy to make the trip in any kind of reasonable time.

They set out with the light of day making it seem like it was much later because of the lack of sun. The clouds massing together and continuing to release their content made it a daunting trip. Bob maintained a steady pace with the horses and was being very careful to make sure that they were steered around any gullies in the road that could possibly cause them injury. Though it was a tough and uncomfortable ride the five slaves huddled together in the back of the wagon sat listening to the rain beating down on the canvass and looking at each other, but no one said a word. For Linwood and Suliah this would be a first for them and they were filled with apprehension about what was going to happen next. The other three had been through this before, but still each time it happened there was always some trepidation because of not knowing who was going to be running your life after the sale.

To get to Richmond from where Bob's place was would normally take about three hours, but today three hours had passed and they were just over half way there. He decided to rest the horses for a bit and let the slaves get out and stretch. In a large basket stored under the front seat he had his housekeeper pack a lunch sufficient for him and his men and even enough for a small amount to be given to the slaves. When they stopped he allowed his men to dig into the basket and get what they wanted, then he apportioned what was left to the stock. It was hard eating in the wet conditions, but they managed to fill themselves sufficiently for the rest of the journey. Back on the road Bob was intent on making up some time so he pushed the horses a little harder. The two steeds heeded the command and began moving at a faster pace. Though they were running in rhythm it was hard to keep in synch because of the condition of the road. Bob realized this, but there was nothing he could do so he allowed the horses to do whatever they had to, to keep the wagon moving forward.

According to Bob's timepiece it was now only three-forty but again the insufficient light of day made it seem like much later. He could see in the near distance lights coming from the outskirts of town. With a sigh of relief having made it, he slowed the pace of the horses just a bit. Then he turned around to see how his cargo was doing and satisfied himself that everything was as according to plan. Linwood had fallen asleep on his sister's shoulder and the other three were also leaning on each other but all were awake. With their eyes wide open each was looking out the back of the wagon to see if they could tell where they might be. They had already been told they were going to Richmond, but none of them had ever been there so they had no idea exactly where this Richmond place was. The rain had not let up so seeing anything that they might have recognized was almost impossible anyway.

A short time later they entered the border of Richmond city and Bob headed straight for the slave holding cells. The place was actually an old jail that had been converted just for the purpose of corralling slaves until the auction could be held. It was starting to get late and Bob wanted to secure his property as soon as possible and then get himself situated. He pulled up just outside the two-story building and went inside. As soon as he entered, the chief jailer met him and greeted him warmly since they had had many dealings on previous occasions. Bob returned the greeting and asked how space in the place was doing. The chief incarcerator replied that they were just about full, but there were two empty cells left that he could let him have. Bob then told him about his special item that he wanted to make sure nothing happened to and winked. The jailer got the message and casually extended his hand. Bob quickly complied and placed a bill in his hand then turned around to get his charges.

Once inside and all the charges were placed, Bob took a look around to see just how secure they would be and noticed that there were a few other jailers there hanging around in the back near the cells that his property would be housed. He reminded the chief about their agreement and was assured everything would be just as he left them. Bob then looked in the other cells that contained a good mix of men and women and satisfied himself that should these workers want to avail themselves of the perks of the position, there would be ample opportunity and supply to do so. He relied on the integrity of the chief to uphold their bargain and walked out. The nearest tavern and hotel was but a short walk away so he drove his wagon to the livery and arranged for overnight storage. The actual auction wasn't until ten o'clock tomorrow so he thought that he would enjoy the evening in the tavern with his two companions. When all the arrangements had been made he and his helpers entered the tavern where they ate and drank and enjoyed the company of the entertainers there for the rest of the night.

Back at the Candle Plantation for the last two days the rain had come down in torrents almost non-stop. Byron had gone out and down to the fields several times to savor the moments watching the earth being drenched. He examined some of his plants and easily noticed that their thirst was being quenched and the life in them that he thought was gone was thriving. Only a few of the slaves did he demand enter the fields to ensure that the crops were doing as well as he perceived. The rest were given other tasks to do like making repairs on whatever he decided needed attention whether it did or not. Even though the conditions for doing any real work outside were prohibitive, Byron was not one to allow them any idle time doing nothing. After the second day and things seemed to be going his way with the crops, when the rain continued through the night and he got up the next day and it was still going, he became a little less joyous. Looking out the window on the third day and seeing the road to the mansion be nothing but a pile of mud, he decided to make one more trip to the fields.

This time when he walked over the area he noticed that some of the plants were beginning to lose their footing and become uprooted. Though he was delighted that he had accomplished his goal of getting the defiant four to make it rain, he was now leery that they were taunting him by overdoing it. Not one to thank them for what he thought they already did he went in search to tell them it was okay to make it stop now. Thoroughly convinced that his punishment methods had worked, when he found them mending a fence high up in the hills of his newly acquired acreage, he called out to Daniel.

"Dan'l come on ova here boy I got somethin ta tell ya."

Daniel left his group and walked slowly over to Byron.

"This here rain ya got comin down I think you over doin it a bit. The crops done got a good drink and I think they be good for awhile so you all kin make it stop now."

Daniel looked up at the man smiled and said:

"The foolishness of a man twists his way, and his heart frets against the Lord. (Prov. 19:3)

I have told you before it is not I who commands the rain."

"There ya go with that god talk again. I don't care how ya do it, but make it stop by nightfall tonight or all y`all gonna feel my wrath agin. You hear me?"

Daniel didn't answer him, but stood there looking up at Byron without saying a word. Byron feeling that he made his point turned the horse and rode away. Daniel walked back to his group and communicated to them what had been said. They huddled for but a moment then continued working as if nothing had happened. The rainfall went on unabated and all those who were out in it were drenched. By late afternoon the land was completely saturated and where there had been dry land there was none to be found. The crops, tobacco, wheat, corn and the vegetables in the slave gardens were at the mercy of the downpour. Byron could see this and for the few days that he enjoyed watching it rain the time had come when his enjoyment ended. After commanding Daniel to make it stop he returned to the mansion to wait and see if his demands would be met.

Inside the house Aunt Tee and Clarence had mitigated their show of exuberance over the rainfall after the first day. They were joyful enough in the beginning just to show alignment with the master. But now that the rains had exceeded his requirement, they were inwardly celebrating the answer to her petition. Whenever they were with each other, but out of sight of the rest of the family, the smiles turned to giggles and laughter at how she was being avenged for the way that Byron had treated her. In the presence of the family the subservient disposition was as normal. Only Jethro seemed to pick up on this dichotomy in behavior, but he was still at odds with his father so he had no plans to advise him of his suspicions. Anna Lee was still living in the private world she created for herself and hardly came out of her room except to eat and attend her biological needs. Now that the rain had come, Charlotte was quietly beginning her plans to host the next major social event in the very near future.

Byron came in the house, but continued to look out the window as he did before the rain started, to see if there was any change in the sky. The last few days had elevated him to new heights of emotion, but now in the overcast darkness they were returning him to depths that he felt prior to them. The more he talked with Daniel the more he was convinced about the man's strange powers, but somehow the words that he said were starting to make him feel very uncomfortable. Byron was certainly not one who believed in the "god stuff" as he put it, but when he listened to Daniel speak each time there was a tingling inside him that he never felt outside of his presence. Turning away from the window he sat down in his favorite chair and reflected on all the recent things that had happened from the time that he sold Suliah and Jobba ran away.

His thoughts about Jobba ran more toward losing a valuable piece of property than any religious association he had previously made with Daniel. Since the time of his running there had been no word of any of the patrols seeing signs of his whereabouts. Even Sam who on occasion with one of the other overseers had crossed the river at night and made his own search in the mountains, had nothing positive to report. Byron was considering now whether this excessive rainfall had anything to do with these incidents. He was wondering if the rain didn't stop tonight and all of the crops started to wash away, what would he have gained by the rain coming. Torn between seconds of high hopes and minutes of despair he was tempted to turn to his special nectar, but he restrained himself by saying it was too early in the day.

It was a good thing too, because Charlotte came in right at the point he was debating the decision and sat down at his desk. She faced him and asked first if there was anything wrong. He quickly said no, but she was observant and pressed the issue.

"Now you know I know you better then that. I don't know why you in here with your head down when you're getting all the rain that you asked for and more. Whatever could be the matter now?"

Byron hearing these words tried to smile and acknowledge her wisdom, but it was difficult.

"Ya know darlin your absolutely right. I should be up dancin for joy at all this rain, but somehow when I go down there it just don't seem like its exactly what I asked for. Maybe it'll stop tonight then I kin feel better."

"It can't rain forever and I'm sure your precious crops will have all they need to keep them growing for a good while. Now Byron you said that when the rains came we could have another party. Well the rains are here so I've been thinking that now it's time. Jethro needs to see some new gals and now your daughter she's locking herself away from you and even me. Don't you think it's time?"

"When you talkin about doing this?"

"Oh I thought maybe the next weekend on Saturday. This Saturday we can all go into town and pickup everything we're gonna need and start dropping the word around. It will give us a full week to get ready. Right?"

Although Byron was listening he wasn't in agreement with what she was planning, but he couldn't think of a way to say no. He had already committed to her that as soon as there was some rain he would allow her to have her party. Now that the rains were here what could he offer as his excuse for another postponement. He mumbled his permission with the hope that something else might come up to prevent it actually happening. Upon hearing his consent Charlotte made some additional small talk, but was anxious to get out of the room and carry on her preparations. On her way out she ran into Jethro and was excited to tell him about the upcoming event. Jethro responded with a half-hearted great and continued on his way to the back porch where he had been going lately just to sit and watch the rain. Watching the downpour for him had become a kind of catharsis in seeing the display of such awesome power by nature. He remembered back to the time when he first accompanied his father to purchase slaves and the trip through the forest. It was at this time that he first really noticed nature's beauty through the vast expanse of the sky and the never-ending forest with the variety of sounds generated at night as they passed through.

He recalled asking his father then about God and why he stopped allowing the iterant preachers from coming to minister to the slaves. The answer he received then was confusing so he just filed it away and never referred to it again until now. As he gazed at the rain, he wondered once again why it was that one human being could actually own another one when they both were just human. The answer his father had given him just said that that's just the way things are, but he questioned the wisdom of the answer. Now that he and Byron had become practically estranged while living under the same roof, he wouldn't dare ask him to elaborate on his ideas.

The comfort Jethro felt in being alone and witnessing the ground being pummeled by the raindrops; prompted him to think that the earth that cried out for rain was now being assaulted by the same thing that they cried out for. Somehow he was able to see the irony in this and accepted that there was something, somewhere, someone with greater power that controlled the whole thing. He still thought about Suliah often but was now ready to concede that whatever or whoever controlled the whole thing was not someone he was interested in meeting if separating the two of them was within his control.

Blam! Blam! Blam! Blam! The sound of several gunshots could be heard across the river. Even those on the plantation side had no problem hearing them and distinguishing the intermittent shots of a normal hunt from those of the rapid fire of the flesh hunters. Most of the slaves had been allowed to return to their cabins because of the continued torrential downpour and Myanna was among them. When she heard the shots, her heart started racing. Fearing that Jobba might be with the mountain runaways yet still in those hills and not having moved on, her anxiety level soared to new heights. Disregarding the rain she pulled her makeshift poncho up over her head and ran down to the river's edge to see if she could see anything from this side. The shots reverberated throughout the hills, but there was nothing she could see that would tell her anything.

She walked up and down the shoreline for several minutes before realizing that this effort was futile and went back to the cabin.

On the other side, the hunters had spotted Jobba who was running with the band. It seems that those rebels who were seen running behind the patrol shack had crossed the road trying to join up with the mountaineers. In their attempt to link up with each other the mountain pack had strayed too close to the road and both sets of men were discovered. Running through the forest in the thick mud and the fallen limbs tangling your legs was extremely difficult The one saving grace for the slaves was that the conditions for them was the same as for the hunters. Managing to stay just a few yards in front of the pursuers most of them were able to duck the random shots fired in their direction. However, the rebels that had just entered the edge of the forest lost two of their members felled by shots that were not accurate but fortunate. The dogs at times looked like they were gaining ground, but the expertise developed by the runaways had developed to such a level that making the final catch, even for the dogs was not successful.

Jobba, who was at the rear of the mountaineer group, saw the two rebels go down and stopped to try and help them. When he did, the pack leader who was just ahead of him saw the action and grabbed Jobba pulling him away from the area. Bent over almost out of breath and running with great difficulty Jobba and the leader came to the bridge over the river and ran down under it. The dogs bent on pursuing the greater number in the pack continued the chase with the hunters right behind them. For the moment Jobba and the leader were safe under the bridge seated by the river. Both were huffing and puffing attempting to regain the rhythm of normal breathing.

"Jobba you okay?" the leader asked.

Jobba took a deep breath and answered.

"Yeah, I'se okay. You okay?"

"I'se okay too, but we caint stay here. We gotta move b'fo they turns 'round an come back."

"This de first time I bin down here close 'nuff to de plantation to swim 'cross dat river."

"You ain thinkin 'bout doin dat is ya?"

"Naw not now, but I knows if'n I haf ta dis is where I'm comin ta do it. I tol ya b'fo I got a wife down dere an one day I gwine back an gits her."

"Yeah you kin do dat long as ya keep livin out here. Now we betta git up an move."

"Where we runnin to dey got paterollers in both directions?"

"Foller me I knows where we kin go."

The leader got up and helped Jobba to his feet. Both men struck out running again under the bridge headed in the opposite direction of where they left the last group of hunters. Jobba was sure that they were running into the road where the patrol station was and he questioned the wisdom of the leader. The response he got reassured him of the leader's sanity when he was told that all the hunters would be concentrating on looking in the forest. They would never suspect that the prey would be sitting right behind their own house. They crossed the road and made their way to the woods behind the station. These woods were not as dense as the forest on the other side, but according to the leader they would be sufficient to rest in until nightfall and then cross back over. Both men drenched from the rain, sought shelter on this side and found a small cave carved into the hills. The leader, wily as a fox, led Jobba inside and immediately started looking for a secondary escape route. Jobba observed the cunning of this leader and marveled at his skills of avoidance. He was thoroughly content to follow him for the time that he would stay with the group. At the back of the cave he found a small opening just enough to crawl through, but it led to the outside. After seeing this, the leader told Jobba to look around for anything that would burn. Together they found some rocks, old branches and piles of dry leaves. Using the rocks as flint stones and the dry leaves as kindling the leader was able to start a small fire and they warmed themselves.

Getting warm by the heat of the fire was a welcome relief especially being in from the rain. The leader started taking off his shirt and advised Jobba to do the same to get out the wet clothing. They both took off shirts and pants and placed them on a cave ledge near the fire then sat down before it. When Jobba saw that the mark of Aunt Tee was still visible on the leader's chest he became curious and asked.

"You still got de mark?"

"Yes an I dono what good it be doin me 'cause it sho ain change nothin."

"Why ya don wash it off?"

"'cause I 'member what you tol me 'bout dat spell come ova you when you almos left here."

"Dat spell twern't 'cause I wash off de mark, it 'cause I didn go to de meetin."

"Well one way or de otha dere ain nobody out chere like you had, to save me if wash'n it off might cause de same thing. I ain ready ta take dat risk. B'sides, it may not be hep'n me, but it ain hurtin me neither."

"You dono how it's gwine ta hurt ya yet, you ain had it long 'nuff. My preacher say dat when de right time come an Jesus come back here ta git us, if'n you wearin the wrong mark, like you got, den its gonna be real bad for ya."

" Oh yeah, did dat preacher tell ya when he comin' back, 'cause I ain seen no signs of no Jesus anywhere 'round here is you?."

When the leader said that, Jobba backed off and ceased talking. He got up and went to find a bunch of dry leaves and clumped them together to make a mattress then dropped down to take a nap. The leader watched him for a minute or two then did the same thing. They both slept for some time in relative peace with the thoughts of what each other had said drifting through their minds. Jobba believed what Daniel had been preaching but the fact that there was no evidence of any imminent return of the one he believed in and the leader called it to his attention, was causing him some discomfort. The leader, because of what Jobba said about this Jesus coming back for them, was unsure now more than ever whether joining Aunt Tee and taking her mark was the right thing to do. So far it hadn't done a thing for him.

When they woke up and eased their way back to the front of the cave, though it was already dark and dreary when they came in, now they could tell that the hour was late. The leader stepped outside and looked around to make sure the way was clear and then told Jobba to follow him. With no one in sight they crossed back over the road and made their way into the forest where they were going to try and rejoin whoever was left of the pack. On the way they came across the two rebel bodies that had been hit. Lying there covered with fallen leaves and exposed to the heavy rain the bodies appeared like cattle downed by disease and no one wanted to deal with it. Both men stopped and stared at their fallen comrades for a moment then they picked the bodies up and carried them to the river. There they placed the bodies in the water and watched them float away with the current. It didn't take long before they were able to find the rest of the pack and reunite. The group had actually grown because only two of the rebels were shot out of the eight that had fled.

The hour was getting late, but during their tea and cordial get together after dinner all Charlotte could do was talk about her plans for the upcoming social event. She went on and on about whom she was going to invite and how exciting this one was going to be because they had not done it for a while. A special appeal was made to get Jethro pumped up and interested in helping put it together. Charlotte made a strong pitch to let him know that she was going to send out a special invitation to the new plantation owners that had purchased the land just the other side of town. It was her understanding from their last town visit that they had three daughters, two of which were around his age. Jethro listened politely to his mother, but didn't seem to get overly excited about the prospects. Anna Lee was being polite also and supported her mother's ambition by volunteering to do whatever she wanted her to. Byron's body was in the room, but his mind was certainly roaming around outside dodging the raindrops and wondering if his most recent threat to Daniel was going to succeed. He kept going over in his mind thinking how his threats and deeds of punishment had worked to such a degree that the rewards were overwhelmingly greater than the expectation. Although it was a good reward he thought it could be disastrous if it continued.

Aunt Tee and Clarence were lingering nearby, as they usually did, out of sight, but not out of hearing. Aunt Tee was so delighted at the rain that had been granted at the behest of her petition, that every time she saw Byron in the rooms or in a hallway she had to smile within herself when she looked at the expression on his face. Listening to Charlotte run on about her social gathering she knew was just making it more difficult for Byron. Though she couldn't bear witness to his demeanor in the room, she could just picture him trying to be attentive, but desperately wanting to be somewhere else. When the time came and the family decided that it was enough for the evening and were ready to retire, Clarence came in to retrieve the utensils while Aunt Tee remained in the hallway. As each family member exited she said goodnight, but gave a special one to Byron when he passed. He was a little surprised by his special greeting, but didn't pay it much mind as he went up to his room.

Before going to bed Byron looked out the window one more time in the hope that he would see something different than what he had seen for the last few nights. It was very dark and he could still hear the drops beating down on his roof so he knew that it had not abated. Disappointed that his recent command was not being obeyed he crawled into bed beside a jubilant Charlotte who was waiting for him. Sensing the glee in her tone when she asked him how he was doing, and suspecting what she had in mind next, he definitely was not up to it. He tried to redirect the conversation by telling her that he thought her plans for the party were just great and he thought it would be a nice affair. She was not to be deterred and was persistent in bringing the verbal exchange back to how he was feeling. Byron realized that it was going to be useless to try and keep up the misdirection so he responded to her desires and performed his husbandly duty.

The next morning when he woke up, the first thing he listened for was the sound of rain on the roof. He sat up and listened more attentively when he heard nothing. Wanting desperately to confirm his suspicion he jumped out of bed and ran to the window. Though it was still very early the skies had a definite blue hue to them and the number of lingering clouds didn't appear to be threatening. He rushed through his morning routine putting on his clothes and running down the stairs. Just as he was about to walk out the door he heard the rooster crowing and felt a rush of excitement he hadn't felt for days. When he got outside he looked up and saw that the sun was trying to make its appearance through the still slightly overcast sky. Satisfied that the rain had really stopped he turned around and went back inside. He went straight to the kitchen to get his coffee and saw Aunt Tee who already had it waiting for him.

"Good mornin' Aunt Tee" he said with a happy expression on his face.

"Good mornin'" she responded in kind.

It was as if they were playing some kind of cat and mouse game with their greetings, but only Aunt Tee knew what she had caused to happen and what should be the result. Byron oblivious to this was happy because he thought that his methods of punishment and demand were sufficient to gain the results he desired.

Byron grabbed his coffee and went and sat in the dining room waiting on his main breakfast. It wasn't long before Clarence entered with his tray and set it down before him.

"Good morning Clarence, how are you?" Byron said with the same jubilation that he offered Aunt Tee.

"Oh I'se fine massa Candle. I'se feelin pretty good taday."

That was the end of their brief conversation as Byron dug into his grits and eggs done exactly the way he liked them. He didn't spend a great deal of time in devouring his meal before he was up and out the door headed to the fields. He stopped by Sam's house to see if he had already left and met him coming out his door.

"Good monin' suh how ya doin?"

"I'm doin much betta now that this rain done stopped. Let's go and see how the crops are making out."

Byron and Sam headed down to the tobacco field first. Sam was on his horse and Byron walking. When he entered the field and surveyed the plants he was amazed at the growth and vitality they were showing in just these last few days. His smile broadened and he couldn't wait until Sam dismounted and joined him. Sam approached and Byron grabbed his arm and said: "Look like we gonna have a real good turn out this year anyhow."

"Yas suh sho look dat way."

Byron moved further down the row and surveyed some additional plants. Each had been given a new lease on life and it seemed like what just a few days ago was headed for a disastrous ending was now thriving. With his chest pushed out, Byron was so filled with himself that he felt invincible. To him he had not only made the defiant four do his bidding to make it start, but he also commanded the end to the matter. The second horn had sounded and the workers were moving into position to tend the crops. Byron stood there looking at them with his superior stance and waving his arms as if he was in command of a new army. When Daniel and his group walked by at the edge of this field headed to the next one, Byron waved at them and tipped his hat. It was not as a sign of thank you, but more to indicate that it was a good thing they obeyed his command. All of Daniel's crew saw the greeting, but chose to ignore it and kept on walking.

Byron walked out of that field and went to get his horse so he could go and inspect the others. Still pumped with the feeling of victory, he made his way around all of the fields and was satisfied with what he saw. The slaves couldn't help but notice the change in his demeanor and took it that he would be less severe with them because of it. It didn't take long for them to realize that this was not the case because instead of relaxing the rule about the longer work day or the one about no breaks, he allowed it to continue. The slaves couldn't understand this because they thought that once the rains came then he would be contented and more lenient. Though the work was hard and now that the land was drenched stepping in the mud was harder than it was when the ground was dry. They tried not to show it, but the divisive feelings between the factions was still festering and the extra burdens due to Byron and the weather was driving up the tension. Something was going to have to give; something had to happen.

The whole day was spent riding around the plantation like his overseers lording his master image over the laborers. He even took time to stop by where Daniel and his gang were to make sure that they saw him so he could lord his perceived conquest over them. Though he didn't get off his horse he sat at the edge of the field not too far from them and just stared in their direction while they worked. The gang all but ignored him as if he wasn't there which didn't seem to bother him at all because he just wanted them to know he was there. When the time came for Sam to sound the end of day horn, Byron held him up just a little while longer just to demonstrate his power and let everybody know that he was indeed the man in charge. Finally, after the horn sounded and the weary burden laden slaves walked slowly from the fields headed to their cabins, Byron remained at the head of the quarters way and watched them go home.

On the day of the auction Trader Bob was up early and having breakfast in the tavern while he waited for his helpers to join him. He looked all around to see if he recognized any of the auction patrons with the hope that he might strike up a conversation and advertise his wears. No one was familiar to him, but from the way that some of them were dressed it was obvious that they were not just passing through but were there for a specific purpose. The range of dress extended all the way from elegance and fine haberdashery to the casual farmer outfits. With Bob's keen eye for the moneyed sect he focused on memorizing the faces of those more aptly attired for his purpose. As he was scanning the room, his two helpers came in and sat down.

"Look like we got some good prospects here" Bob said.

"Yeah boss I think we gonna do good taday" replied one of the men.

"Y`all go `head an finish yo meal I'm gonna run on ova to the hold an see how ma property doin. Come an meet me there soon's you finish."

"Okay boss we be there soon."

Bob excused himself and got up from the table. As he walked toward the door he noticed that there was one middle-aged man who stood out from the crowd because he was exceptionally dressed. He was seated among a group of men who appeared to be men of distinction so Bob made it a point to go close to their table and nod to them so they could see who he was. The elegantly dressed man saw Bob's greeting and motioned for him to come to the table. Bob stopped in his tracks and redirected his movements.

"Good morning suh, how are you?" Bob asked.

"I'm doing rather well thank you. Aren't you the one they call Trader Bob?"

"Why yes suh, that would be me. What kin I do fer ya?"

"I understand that you are a trader in fine specimens and I was wondering whether you were going to be at the auction today?"

"Yes suh, I plan ta be there with the finest specimens you eva gonna see 'round these parts. I jest might have what you lookin' for."

"I hope so. I've come a long way and I'm planning on settling right here in this city. I need some good stock to help me set up and get going."

"Whateva you need I'm sure I got it. Are you lookin to get farm workers, you don look like you do no plantin."

"Oh no, no my good man I'm going to be doing some work with the government here and I need help mostly in setting up the house and driving me around and things like that."

"Yes suh, I understand. Well let me go on an get them ready for showin' an I'll see you there, okay?"

The elegant man nodded his head while the others looked on without saying anything and Bob walked out. During his short walk to the converted jailhouse, Bob was thinking to himself that if these men were part of the government here perhaps he could get in good with them. It could certainly be to his benefit if he had a connection on the inside that would help him with bending the new laws if he needed help. He was thinking that with the new anti sentiment against the slave trade that was growing in the state and up north, his business might be headed for a downturn without good connections. When he got to the hold there were several men standing around outside and he wondered if there was something going on that he should know about. As it turned out, they were there the same as he was coming to check on their interests. Since he didn't recognize any of them from previous gatherings he was surprised when he found out who they were.

Once inside he greeted the chief and asked to be led to his property. The chief tipped his hat and told Bob that everything was just as he left it and started walking him to the cells. On the way Bob saw that most of the others were still lying on the floor either sleeping or leaning up against the cell walls with their heads down. When he got to Linwood, Suliah and the rest of his chattel they looked at him in recognition, but no one moved. Bob asked whether they had been fed. The chief told him no, but he would get them something now if that's what he wanted. Bob got a little indignant thinking that this was something that should have been done already, and told the chief to feed them right away and get them cleaned up for showing. He then said he was going out for a short while and he expected them to be ready when he returned. The chief quickly acknowledged his demand and motioned to one of the other workers to comply.

Bob left the holding cell and went to the block where the auction would be held. He wanted to see just what kind of set up it was. Pleased with the way they had made a little stage that would give any bidders in the rear a good chance to view the merchandise, he moved on. He was satisfied that this part of the operation was in order so he went over to the auctioneer's office to talk with him about the time he wanted to get started. The time was confirmed at ten O'clock. He started walking back toward the tavern to catch up with his helpers and met them on the way. Bob advised them that their auction entries were not quite ready yet so they should walk around town for a while and then go back and get them. First they stopped at the livery to check on the horses then they went to the town hall to see if there were any announcements posted about changes to the slave laws. Bob was happy to see that nothing was posted so he trusted that all of his papers were in order and he could buy and sell above reproach.

Twenty minutes later they headed back to the cells. There was still about ten minutes before the auctioneer would call the buyers and sellers to the block so Bob examined his chattel to make sure that they were presentable the way he wanted. The clothing he provided, especially for the women was more like robes than dresses. As for the men thin loosely fitting shirts and burlap type genes made up their attire. He lined them up for the short walk to the block and was now waiting to hear the call. He took an extra glance at Suliah his top offering to make sure that the packaging was enticing and sure to bring the highest bid. Confident that he had assembled them in the order he thought would be most advantageous for quick sale, he was ready to go. Soon he heard a young man holler in the door that the auction was ready to start and all sellers were to come to the block.

The traders assembled and marched over to the block alongside their offerings and lined up in front of the auctioneer. Each seller then handed the auctioneer his information regarding how he wanted his property sold with special attention to minimum acceptable bids. The lineup for presentation was then given to the sellers and the order of sale was established. The auctioneer then got up on the stage and started his spiel. He began just like the tobacco auctioneers and got the crowd wound up expecting to see the greatest products that man could offer. By the time he was ready to present the first set of slaves he had every eye in the crowd looking to see what was coming. The crowd standing before the stage went four deep in rows and there were many standing around away from mingling in the rows, but definitely interested in the auction. As with all the auctions there were also plenty of men and some women who had no intention of bidding, but just came to ogle the women.

The first set stepped up to the stage consisting of a husband and wife who were being sold as a pair. The auctioneer ranted about how functional and strong they were and could be suited to either working in the fields or in the house. He instructed them both to turn around several times so that the bidders could see. Both were in their late twenties and of medium height. The first bidder asked the man to take off his shirt and turn around again so he could see his back. It was obvious he was looking to see whether there were any signs of whipping or other scars. The slave complied and the bidder satisfied that this could work for him started the bidding. Before the bids got to anywhere near the minimum level that had been set the auctioneer reminded the bidders that these were sturdy people with many years of work left in them and asked that the next bid at least meet the minimum.

When he said that the next bidder hollered out for the woman to open her dress and turn around. Without hesitation the woman unbuttoned the top of her dress and let it fall to the ground. She was rather plump all over with large but shapely breasts and showed no scars on her back or her front. The bidder satisfied at seeing this met the minimum bid and the real bidding began. Bids for this set went on for some time until finally it was settled that the original bidder came away with the pair. On and on it went with the presentation of individuals and sets for about an hour until it was time for Bob to move his chattel up to the stage. He had decided that he was not going to pair Linwood and Suliah as a package, but thought he could get more if they were offered individually. The first to be presented was one of his single men definitely suited for fieldwork. He was rather tall and muscular and probably in his early twenties. He was dark and regal looking like perhaps an African prince and the first bid made was over the minimum which brought a smile to Bob's face. He was sold quickly and then Bob's next offering was the man and the woman. They both were good looking and sturdy field workers who also brought above the minimum bids.

The bidding went on until finally it came down to Linwood and Suliah. Linwood was brought to the stage first and presented by the auctioneer as an excellent field worker who also had some leadership skills and could be made into a good headman. The final bid for Linwood well exceeded what Bob would have accepted and he felt like his day had already been made. But now his last offering was up and Bob noticed in the second row of the crowd that the well-dressed man he met in the tavern this morning was there. Bob hadn't really noticed him before although he thought the man had made one or two other purchases. When Suliah stepped forward and stood before the crowd there was an immediate hush for several minutes while the auctioneer gave them a chance to view her. Before he even said ten words about her the bidding began well over the minimum. It was now that the well dressed man stood out from the crowd in doubling the last bid made.

One bidder who was evidently nearing the limit of his spending and wanted to get the best view he could of the offering asked the auctioneer to make her disrobe. Suliah heard the request and hesitated, but when prompted strongly by the auctioneer she flung open the robe and held it open displaying her exceptionally beautiful naked body. A number of ooh's arose from the crowd as she unashamedly held the robe open. The well-dressed man increased his bid beyond the average means of most in the crowd and the bidding was closed. As Bob suspected would happen his top offering had been the prize of the day and he was anxious to close the deal by getting his money and then going out to celebrate. At the end of the auction and the buyers came to the auctioneer's office to close their deals Bob was curious about who this well-dressed man was and couldn't wait to hear the name placed on the sale documents.

Jonathan Adams was his name and he had just recently come over from England. It seemed that he was part of the royal line of kings and was a cousin of one of the candidates for governor in this state. He was expected to be one of the political pundits; and perhaps given an authoritative office once he established his residency requirement. Bob upon hearing this from the auctioneer in private made it his mission to try and get closer to this man and maybe strike up a friendship. He even considered lowering his price for Suliah, but that thought only lasted a minute. When the deal was done however, he did try to spend some time in talking with the man about her. Mr. Adams was cordial enough, but it became obvious, even to Trader Bob, that he was not interested in pursuing any type of long-term relationship with him. Bob sensing that he was approaching the point of becoming annoying backed off and offered his card saying that he could be reached through this auctioneer's office most of the time. Mr. Adams thanked him for the information, tipped his hat and left the office to claim his property.

After the auction ended the slaves were escorted back to the cells to wait until claimed by their new owners. For the others it was just another change in circumstance although each time they were sold it meant having to go through another readjustment period, but to Linwood and Suliah it was traumatic. This would be the first time that, not only were they going to be separated from their parents, but they would be pulled a distance apart from each other. Suliah was going to remain here in the city of Richmond, but Linwood would be traveling further south just outside the town of Hampton. As they sat on the cell bench holding each other tight neither wanted to release the hold on the other. The other woman in the group sat down beside her and said to Suliah she felt sorry for her, not because she was going to leave her only tie to her family, but because she was so pretty that the days ahead of her were going to be either extremely rough or she would be pampered so much it would turn her rotten. Either way she would have no choice in the matter. Suliah heard her words and reflected on what she said. Already she had demonstrated she was changing. She had definitely become aware of how her looks affected men and when she opened her robe at the auction and held it open with no feeling of remorse, she knew by the onlookers responses that she was something special.

It was hard saying goodbye, but Linwood managed to let Suliah know that one day no matter what he was going to find her and they would be together again. He also told her that they would go back to the Candle Plantation and get their parents. This was his promise to her. With tears in her eyes she listened to what he was saying and acknowledged his oath, but inside she knew that it might be only that. Later that afternoon, Mr. Adams came to get her and the other two men he had purchased. After clearing the release paperwork with the chief he told his associate to have the slaves brought to his home and gave him the address and he walked away. The chief's helper assembled the group and took them outside. There was a wagon waiting in which he loaded them and set out to make the delivery.

When they arrived at the final destination it was a large white house set back from the main road just outside the city limits. Though it was not big like the mansion that she had become accustomed to, it was large enough to have several rooms spread across the three-story building. The driver pulled up to the front door and knocked. A large dark skinned man came to the door nattily dressed in a butler's attire. He opened the door and addressed the driver in almost perfect english.

"Good day suh, may I help you?"

The driver was a little taken aback by the way the man spoke and hesitated a bit before he answered, but he did manage to regroup and get his words formed.

"This Mr. Adams house?"

"Yes it is what can I do for you?"

"Well I got these here niggers I'm `posed to bring here for him. You wanna take `em?

Mr. Adams dun bought `em taday at the auction."

The butler looked over the driver's shoulder and saw the group sitting in the back of the wagon. He told the driver to wait just a minute while he went and checked. The driver was a little offended at being told to wait outside by some black man, but he knew by the looks of this house that this was no ordinary darky. Moments later the butler returned and told the driver to bring them inside. The driver grunted and turned around to get his charges. One by one he led them up to the house and instructed them to go inside. Before leaving he asked the butler to get someone to sign for the delivery. When the butler told him to wait again he was very upset at being given orders by a dark servant. The butler went and got Jonathan's father who read the delivery document signed it and handed it back. The driver, who could barely read and write himself, looked at it closely.

Convinced that it was properly signed he went down from the porch looking back at the butler in wonderment.

Inside the butler told the new residents to follow him. He brought them into a large kitchen where there were four other slaves dressed as splendidly as the butler. There were two men and two women. He introduced each one of them and told the new arrivals what each one's job was. It quickly became apparent that he was the headman in this house and his word was law. Suliah was taken first to a room up on the second floor at the far end of the hall. She was told that one of the other women also occupied this room and she would be sharing it with her. She was then told that the other man and woman servants were married and they would be right next door. It was explained to her about the household and who lived in it. There was master Adams, his father and mother and two older sisters. It was also said but not made clear that master Adams was married, but his wife and two young children were still in the old country and it was not clear when they would be coming here. Although Suliah said nothing, in her mind she was thinking how bad could this be and she went right in to get herself settled.

In the mountains that same day the mountaineers were explaining to their new members about their way of life. They had found a new cave deep in the heart of these hills and it was large enough that it had not only one escape route, but there were three. They were now seated inside sitting in a circle with no fire. The leader was discussing with them that they might be able to use this place as a shelter for a while as long as they didn't do anything that could lead the patrols to them. He further explained to them that they could survive up here for some time because there was plenty of fish in the river and a lot of wild game running around. He told them they had learned to eat some of the berries that were all around here and leaves that served as vegetables. For water there was another stream with fresh running water just a little further up the hill.

He continued to point out that they had to be very careful when they moved by day because the hunters were still out looking for all of them. Now that the word had spread all around the county about the uprisings that some of these very same men had participated in and some of the owners were killed, the patrols were not going to give up too easily since they know that you're up here. They aren't too smart at finding us even with those stupid dogs he told them because they really don't know how to hunt. This brought some laughter to the group, but he was very serious when he said it. Finally he came to the memorial for those two brothers that had lost their lives trying to make it across the road. He told them what Jobba and he had done with the bodies and this seemed to be acceptable to the others. As his closing remarks for now, he told them it was time to get up and go fishing.

When they walked out of the cave the bright sunlight was a welcome sight given the kind of weather they had endured for the past few days. They separated into smaller groups and headed to different parts of the river. The leader had already told them although the river was filled with fish, every spot was different from another. Some places you might be able to catch something in just a few minutes, in others it might take all day. The more places they had men fishing the better the chances were that they could catch enough to feed the whole body. Just before separating, the leader reminded them one more time how important it was to keep their ears and eyes open so they wouldn't get caught or give the patrols anything they could use to trace them.

While walking in one of the groups Jobba struck up a conversation with one of the men who was involved in the uprising.

"I am Jobba an I used ta live down dere on dat plantation b'fo I run. Who you be?"

"I am given de name Buddy by de white man, but ma real name is Shaka, Shaka Kentea."

"Man, is you one o dem dat come here from Africa?"

"Yes, many suns ago I was taken from ma village with others of my family. Now we don know where we are an don know when we see each otha agin. I lived ova the long journey of hard times where many fell in de waters, but I make it here. No man is 'posed to live by de rules of this white man dat don even let us be free. Dat is why we fight."

"Buddy, I mean Shaka, I mean what chu want me ta call ya?"

"You kin call me Buddy, dat is what I become use to, but I will neva ferget ma real name."

"Well Buddy I wanna tell you I thinks a lot a y'all dat come here from dere. I had a dream a while ago 'bout dat land an I thinks 'bout it alla time. I dream I could speak dat talk y'all talk an I was in a village too. I dream I was huntin' one day when dey catch me an brought me ova here jest like you, but I know it was jest a dream. I run away 'cause dey ain got no right ta treat me like de animals an tie me up and whip me. One day we's all gonna be free if'n we kin get away from here."

"Jobba you are a good man an I think you will be free one day as you want."

They kept on walking and talking down to the section of the river that they were supposed to fish in. From where they were Jobba could see across the river the cabins where he knew his beloved Myanna was and he longed to just jump in the water and swim to her. It was hard for him to fight the feeling, but he knew that if he just showed up there, especially this time of day, one of the overseers would probably try to whip him or even worse. He put the thought out of his mind for now, but he was resigned to the idea and knew that the time would come soon when he would go to the narrowest part of the river and swim across.

It didn't take long for his group in this section to come up with a sufficient catch to feed all of the newly formed pack. Though the fishing instruments were crude and hastily improvised they served the purpose well and the fish seemed to jump on the crude lines. Wrapping the catch in bags made from dried leaves and vines they met up with the others and headed back to the cave. On the way they heard the loud barking of dogs that seemed not to be too far away. Ducking behind trees one of Jobba's group climbed up one to get a better look. From one of the higher limbs he saw that a large group of hunters were spreading out and covering a wide area of the forest. He quickly climbed down and informed the rest of the group about where they were and all of them scrambled to make it back to the cave for shelter.

Once inside they informed the leader about the hunters and he told them to go back out and make sure that they left no trail that would lead to the cave. The same man that climbed the tree volunteered to go erase any evidence that could be tracked to the cave. He was one who had been with the original group for some time and had become very savvy about forest living. His specialty had become creating new methods to mislead and misdirect the patrols that were chasing them, and he had become very skilled at it.

When he returned he reported that he no longer heard the dogs barking, but he couldn't be sure that the hunters had given up for the day. The leader then told the group to begin preparing for the night meal, but they were to wait until it got darker before starting the fire. One of the men who had just joined the group came up with the idea of building a cover for the cave front out of the branches and dried leaves they used to make the bags. This way they wouldn't have to worry about anyone seeing their fire at night. The leader lauded the new arrival for his thinking and encouraged all of the others to welcome any new ideas that would help them to survive.

The group was beginning to bond together and the camaraderie was growing more important to each one of them. There was one thing however that hadn't come up yet, but Jobba knew that at some point it was going to have to be discussed. He and the pack leader got along well as long as they didn't get into talking about their religious differences and for now that wasn't the topic of the day. None of the new members seemed to notice the markings on the pack members. It could be because they had seen all different kinds of markings on slaves that they had lived with, especially the ones who came directly from the motherland. Even on Buddy, he had special markings on his face and on his chest that were clearly visible and noticeable. No one asked him about it. The men set about finding the materials to make the covering and in a short time were able to put together a makeshift screen that would keep the light from outside getting in and the light of the fire from inside getting out.

Having completed this task, the leader directed that the fire be set and the cooking started. Almost like an organized army, the men had been assigned to certain duties and rotated in the assignments. Also like an army there were some who were better at cooking than others and there were some who were better at getting the items for cooking. It didn't come to matter much who did what, when and for how long because it was understood that they were all in this situation together and the survival of each depended on the cooperation of all. It was a group that was banded together for a cause, even though the outcome was uncertain for each man. Some, like Jobba considered it just a passing stage on the way to his desired target, some were waiting for that sign from Aunt Tee that they were sure was coming to set them free, some were still seeking the connection to the Underground Railroad conductor and some just weren't sure at all what they desired out of it. No matter at what stage they were in their private plans they knew that once they joined this group it was a matter of dedication to the cause, which was survival.

The cooking finished and dinner was ready. It was hardly the Richmond Tavern nor even the servings that most of them were used to when they were on the plantations, but it was enough to get them through each day. No one ever complained about the menu because more often than not it was about the same day after day, but each new rotational chef tried to make it more palatable by either adding to or subtracting from the dishes. Jobba always remembered how good a cook Myanna was and it made him long to be with her even more. The days were passing by and he knew that he had to make his move soon or it would be more difficult to do what he had in mind. He had come to really like the leader and learned a lot about how to survive in the forest. The things he learned he knew would help him when he struck out on his own, but just when that would be he couldn't decide. He believed he could make it to this city of Richmond they all talked about, but he wasn't even sure in which direction he should go. He asked the leader at one point, but he didn't know either. So far there was no one in the group that had any idea on how to get there and how long it might take.

After the meal was done and they were all satisfied for the night, they sat around the fire and talked. The leader usually started the group discussion by inviting new arrivals to tell their story. Most of the time it was basically the same story but the difference was that it would be told from the perspective of the new member. Some of the atrocities that were spoken about, on the surface were hard to believe, but when the scars were displayed and the anguish heard in the teller's voice then the veracity of the story became real. Jobba could identify with some of the brutal acts such as the whippings, but when he heard and saw evidence of other body mutilations, it was difficult for him to accept that one man could do this to another. He listened intently as the stories unfolded, but all the while he was thinking about the God he had been told about. If He was so merciful and filled with grace, then where was He when all of these things were being carried out?

When the last new member finished with his revelation, the leader asked the question addressing it to each one. What is it you want to do now and how do you think we can help? Almost as if the replies were coming from a prepared script, they answered that each wanted to gain freedom and they wanted help in getting it. They went on to say that if fighting was the only way to achieve that end, then they were ready to do that. Several of them who had been part of the uprising chimed in that they had already demonstrated their willingness to fight, but because they had no guns and no real access to any, then the odds of achieving the goal that way was futile. The leader listened to each man's testimony and assured him that when the time was right the fight would be done with adequate weapons to defeat the enemy. Meanwhile it was best for them to stay together here in the mountains until the sign was given for them to act. For those who were pursuing making contact with the railroad conductor, he advised that it was well known throughout the county about their existence and someone who could help with that will find them.

He went on to tell them about the sign that would be given and how it was to their advantage to be patient and continue to survive like they are doing now. The more he talked about this sign Jobba's patience was being strained. Although he had not gotten into his bid yet to have the newcomers attend the next ritual dance, Jobba suspected that this is what he was leading up to. It didn't take much longer in the leader's pitch before he brought his intended point to the forefront. He began to explain that there was a spiritual leader down there across the river that was possessed with powers given to her by a great god in a cave. This power was what protected those who had joined with her, and he referred to himself and the other older members, while they ran lose in these mountains. He then opened his shirt and showed the mark on his chest so that all could see and challenged the new people to take the mark if they wanted to be covered under this protection.

The eyes of the newcomers were glued on his chest display and many were interested, but there was one who had doubts. It was Buddy who spoke up introducing himself to the rest of the group as Shaka Kentea from the Gambia, Africa. The pride in his voice as he spoke made the others stop and pay attention to what he had to say.

"Not like you, I was not born slave. In my country I ran free for many suns until de day I was taken away. In chains I come with nothing but pain. On de way I pray to de ancestors to help me, but I git no answer. In de old country dey tell me Allah is de one to call on not some spirit hiding in a cave. In this new land I heard one called a preacher tell me 'bout another spirit. I don take no mark 'til I see de power work."

The leader was a little stunned by the resistance from the newcomer, but he maintained his composure and supplied the rebuttal.

"I knows you from Africa an you raised different b'fo ya got here, but now ya here an ya needs de protection dat's here not ova dere. Dat Allah dey tol ya 'bout ova dere, did he come wit chu?"

Shaka heard the response and didn't know how to answer at first, but he was not going to do something until he could see some evidence that it worked.

"I caint say he come too wit me, but de cave god you talk 'bout kin he go 'cross de deep waters like de big boats?"

"De cave god go everywhere an his speaka be right chere in de woman. You will meet her if'n ya wanna be protected. She gonna change you an give dis mark so's ya know ya covered. You see de power fo sure when ya take's de mark."

Shaka stopped talking and looked around at the others to see if anyone felt like he did. But when he saw no acknowledgement or agreement with his thinking he gave up and the leader had the last word. The others were more prone to agree with what he said and were ready to go to the ritual. Jobba sat there during the debate and said nothing waiting to see what the outcome would be. Although he certainly didn't agree with the leader on this matter, but neither did he acknowledge what Shaka was saying. He remembered in his dream while he was on the ship being brought to this country that the name Allah had been called upon by many of those who had been captured with him. At that time he didn't know who this Allah was, but now that he heard it from Shaka's lips he realized that this was the god that was served over there. When Shaka finished talking then Jobba also looked around to see if anyone else was not in agreement with the leader. He could no longer restrain himself, but had to make it clear to the newcomers what was at stake for them if they took the mark.

Before addressing the group, Jobba looked at the leader as if to get his permission to speak. There was no indication one-way or the other as to whether he should or he shouldn't so he began.

"I bin sittin' here listin ta what all y'all sayin'. I bin to de ritual dat the leader talkin' 'bout an I took de mark. But since dat time I bin through some terrible things dat I dono why de protection didn't work. I needs ta tell y'all 'bout anotha kinda spirit dat I bin tol 'bout by the preacher who is on dat same plantation down dere where I come from. Afta I took de mark, an my wife too, we try not ta go to one o dem meetin;san we got real sick. We got so sick dat if'n this preacher man not come when he did, I don think I be talkin'g with chu now. I tell you dis so ya knows dat de protection only work when ya don miss no meetin's, an I ain sho dat it work alla time anyway."

When Jobba said this, the leader started to interrupt him, but he saw that not only did he have the newcomer's attention, but even some of the originals were listening intently, so he let Jobba continue.

"De preacher man sayafta he brought us back from almos' dead dat de spirit in de cave an dat Aunt Tee dey is evil. He say dat dere is only one God who kin really help you when ya need it an He sent his son, call his name Jesus, to teach us how to behave an call on Him. He took us down in dat river an baptized us an say now we de chilren of de father. If'n ya go 'head an take dat mark like I did an den ya want ta change yo mind, ya may not be lucky like we was an gits brought back."

The leader was watching the expressions on the faces of the whole group and he saw that he was losing his new prospects so he jumped in.

"All y'all dat jest come here hearin' two sides ya needs ta talk wit some a us who bin goin down to rituals an hear 'bout what ya needs ta do. If'n ya listen to dis man an ya don do like I say, den ya ain gonna git de protection. Dis man though he be wit us is not under de protection of Aunt Tee an it won be long fo he be leavin' ta git caught by de paterollers. We cover him while he here, but know dis, he is not protected by Aunt Tee."

The challenge presented by the leader was causing a rift in the new group. When the leader finally said to them that in a week or so there would be another full moon and it would be time to make their choice, all of the newcomers except Shaka told the leader they would be ready to go with him. Shaka looked at Jobba and wanted to know more about this God that he was talking about. The leader reluctantly allowed him to continue.

As the fire burned brightly in the cave and the darkness outside permeated the land, Jobba reached deep down inside searching for the right words to convince not only the newcomers but also everybody there that there should be only one choice. His heart was filled with the desire to relay what he had been told with the same conviction as it had been taught to him. He delved into the inner recesses of his mind to recall all that Daniel had preached, but as he looked at the faces of the men who were now hanging on every word that he said he was coming up short. Before he started speaking again he closed his eyes and prayed silently for help at this moment. He recalled the words that Daniel had said one Sunday night by the river.

"Heavenly Fatha I comes ta you wit a humble heart lookin' fo yur hep. I knows you, but dese men dey don know ya. Give me de words ta say so's I kin make 'em believe dat dey shouldn't do dat thing dat dey's considerin' doin. Hep me bring dem ova ta you an git dem away from dat evil spirit. Lord, om askin' dat ya give me some words an den show dem yo power so's dey believe me. Amen!"

There was complete silence in the cave for several minutes and then Jobba started again talking to all the men, including the leader. The words issued forth from his mouth seemed not to be coming from him, but from another source.

"There is but one God in heaven and the earth. It is He who has created you in His own image and given you the freedom as to whom you will serve. He does not desire that you make idols your shrine for worship and He does not direct your choices. Of your own freewill you must choose for yourselves. But know this, thou shalt have no other gods before me neither shall you make any false images that thou will bow down to. The Lord God is a jealous God and Him only shall you serve. Make no mistake if you choose to accept the mark of the evil one, then you shall know the wrath of the one true God. Hear these words and be admonished."

Jobba finished speaking and the leader started to open his mouth and defend Aunt Tee's side when the walls of the cave started shaking violently. The fire rose up by itself to a new height and an image appeared within it. From the darkest reaches of the rear of the cave another image seemed to be manifesting. The cave walls began to glow like they were white hot and the men became truly frightened. It seemed like some kind of battle was starting and they were caught right in the middle. Many of them got up from the fire and ran toward the door, but before they moved far it happened.

Chapter 8 - Return and Prelude

Time and space is allotted to every man equally. A minute for one exists in duration the same amount of time as it does for another no matter where he is on the globe. One square foot or one square mile, whether it is measured in standard or metric terms, covers the same amount of space. If one is standing on a spot, then another cannot stand on that same spot until the first one vacates it. A man cannot touch fire and not be burned, neither can he stand naked in the rain and not get wet, nor can he jump in the air naturally and continue to ascend. These are the physical laws that were in place since the beginning of man's existence on the planet. Although there is still great controversy regarding how these laws came to develop and many theories abound from the Divine Intelligence to the evolutionary process, the one thing that all must agree upon is that they are here and must be obeyed. Even though man has devised many contrivances to attempt to circumvent the law, the bottom line remains that the law primarily still governs.

Just as the physical laws exist, so are there spiritual laws that co-exist. Man did not create either set, but he has defied obeying the second set since he was given freedom of choice at the very beginning. Many books have been written to define the physical laws, but there is only one written by many authors to interpret the spiritual laws. Down through the years the priests and the prophets have received the word and relayed the messages for all mankind to see, but because of freedom of choice more often than not, the elected choice is not the recommended one according to the spiritual law. In days of old, when slavery was in vogue even the Egyptians knew that it was not what should be. But because of the times in which they lived they continued to practice enslavement even though they knew it was wrong. From that time through the development of the slave trade business in the 17th and 18th centuries, man has consistently disobeyed the spiritual law that exhorts the treatment of each man as he would like to be treated himself.

The development of societies who obey the spiritual laws of an evil spirit are derived from the single angel who was once revered in the heavenly kingdom. Through the misinterpretation of the original spiritual laws and the deceptive practices of misleading those who would follow that teaching, the Aunt Tee's and Clarence's and the leader have persuaded many to acknowledge demon worship at the evil shrine and accept the mark of evil. Jobba in his attempt to redefine for some and admonish for others what they have done or are about to get into was trying to be like the preachers who knew and taught the right spiritual law. When he started in speaking the words that had been indwelled in him, it was more than the opposing spirit was ready to abide. It feared the warning led to the recovery of the fallen and the prevention of those who were headed for the same ditch. The battle for souls was underway, but it didn't physically involve any of them.

At the end of Jobba's speech in the cave and the fire rose up, the image that appeared in the blaze manifested itself into a raging demon that emerged and paralyzed all. The attempt to flee through the cave entrance was quelled and all those who had risen to run fell before the demon and cowered. At the same time from the rear of the cave another spirit was manifesting in the darkness and when it emerged it was like a ball of light floating in the air. The light floated toward the fire where the demon hovered about and the two engaged in a ferocious battle. The men were all on the floor watching, but unable to really see anything clearly because the light was so bright. They could feel the whole cave shaking and they trembled along with it. After several minutes of combat the men saw a large hole open up where the light had come from in the back of the cave and the demon that arose from the fire had been chained and was being tossed violently down into the bottomless pit. After it was thrown down, the hole closed as quickly as it opened and the light disappeared. Speechless and unable to move all the men sat on the ground and just looked at each other. It was sometime before they regained mobility and were able to get up. Both Jobba and the leader went over to where they approximated the hole was, but they weren't able to confirm that anything had happened anywhere around the spot. The leader got down on his knees and spread his hands around the area to see if the ground was even warm, but there was no sign of anything out of the ordinary.

The leader got up looked at Jobba and asked him whether he could explain what just happened. Jobba looked back at him and modestly said that he thought what had been displayed was the awesome power of his God. The leader not ready to accept that his demon had lost the battle walked away without responding and sat down among the men. He tried to justify what they saw by telling them that this was just a bad incident of them all seeing something that was not really there, a hallucination. The old timers accepted his explanation because he said it, but the newcomers, especially Shaka were less inclined to agree. The leader went on to say that in a short time when the moon was full that they would be shown the real power of the cave spirit and they would know that this was nothing. Jobba said nothing, but looked at the expressions on the men's faces and knew that his point had made.

They spent the rest of the night without any further incidents, but when the morning came the leader assembled the group. He told them that he had thought much about what they experienced last night and he came to the conclusion that to keep it from happening again, Jobba would have to leave the group. Since he was not under the protection of Aunt Tee, he was the cause. Anyone else who was not ready to attend the next ritual dance would have to go with him. It was not left up to any kind of democratic vote on his decision. His word ruled and the men accepted it. Half of the newcomers went along with the decision, but one other besides Shaka decided to go with Jobba whenever he left. Jobba told his supporters he was thankful for their decision not even so much that he wanted them to join with him, but that they were saving themselves from an evil that was going to eventually harm them. After hearing that, the leader insisted that Jobba go now and take with him those who wanted to follow.

Jobba walked out of the cave into the early morning sunlight and his two new traveling companions were right behind him. He knew he didn't have any idea what they should do next, but he felt confident just like he did after he first ran away that somehow a way would be made for him to survive. They started walking away from the cave and headed down toward the bridge where Jobba had observed the shortest distance between the plantation side and the forest side. It was a good walk to the spot and when they got there Jobba pointed out that this was a short swim to get to the other side. He asked if anyone couldn't swim? All replied they could and he moved on to the next question. He asked whether they wanted to go over there. Both men hesitated and Jobba saw the fear in their eyes. Shaka then asked him why they would want to return to a plantation when they had just fought to get away from one. Jobba took his time and explained the plan.

"Shaka you are a wise man an a survivor. I knows dat you don wanna get caught by de white man no mo. I don either, but ova dere I got a wife dat kin hep us get food an maybe some mo clothes. If'n we swim by night ova dere an I kin git ta her an let her know what we need den we kin git hep. We moves only at night an den we not be caught. I caint keep runnin' in dese woods like the leader waitin' fo some sign, I got to move on now. I think if'n we kin get to de place called Richmond we might kin fine a way to gits on dat train gwine up north an be free."

"Jobba I hear yo words, but can I truss yo plan?" Shaka said. "What'll happen ta us if we gits caught ova dere?"

"De overseers don live by where we gonna come up out de water. An dey ain got no reason ta be down dere at night. We ain gonna git caught if'n y`all foller me an do like I do."

Shaka was still reluctant, but when Jobba kept on telling him that they couldn't keep running around out here in these woods forever because sooner or later the patrols were going to get more men and surround the whole area. Shaka thought about this and it made sense to him, because he had seen first hand how quickly they could assemble a lot of men to hunt them down. He agreed to go and the third man went along. The question now was when were they going to do it. Jobba took the group to the same spot where he and the leader had stopped before and he told the men to rest here so he could figure out when to go. They sat there for a short while and then Jobba motioned to them that they should each go and find whatever they could to eat and then they were going to hide for the rest of the day until nightfall. At that time they would make the swim.

It was Friday and back on the Candle Plantation, Charlotte was walking around making her final preparations and listing what was needed when she went into town tomorrow. She had already enlisted the aid of Anna Lee and Jethro to accompany her, but Byron told her that he had other things to do and he wouldn't be going. Byron was still feeling the surge of triumph from his perceived victory over the four and he was basking in his glory. Most recently, even as of yesterday the crops were responding well to the drenching and it appeared that the remedy was working. His refusal to lighten the load on the slaves was however causing more of a problem than he realized and his ignorance regarding the situation created for him an unwarranted bliss.

In the fields this morning after the workers had reported and started their labors, there was a rift that had never happened before. One of the slaves from the believer faction refused to work with a slave from the other side. The tensions that had building up between them were finally coming to a head. Even in the cabins where some of them had been forced to share their living space it was becoming extremely more difficult to cohabit in the same space. Aunt Tee had contributed to the elevation by telling her group that they were responsible for convincing all the others to join her or be faced with the wrath of the cave spirit.

The overseer who was watching the action rode over and told them they had better stop and get to working or they would feel the lash of his whip. For the moment his admonition sufficed and they complied with his demand, but a short time later in another area a second breakout occurred and this time it was even more violent. The two men actually started fighting each other over something seemingly trivial to the overseer, but the contest was anything but trivial to the contenders. The overseer reached the battle and unfurled his whip lashing out at both the men. Before they ceased battling one of them turned his rage against the horse attempting to unseat the whip wielder but was unsuccessful. The overseer retaliated and increased his lashing on the man causing him to start bleeding from the wounds.

Another overseer in the area saw what was going on and galloped over to assist his colleague, but the rage of the two combatants had set off a general tension spiral. It was as if something had spread through the air affecting every worker. The laborers threw down their farm implements and besieged the two overseers before either could send out an alert to overseers in the other fields. The shear imbalance of the numbers was so overwhelming to the overseers that before they could replace using the whips with firing their rifles they were disarmed and running out of the fields fearing for their lives. Running for them was not a practice they were used to and within minutes they were caught by several of the more athletic workers and nearly beaten to the point of demise. The commotion got so that it carried to the mansion and Byron, who was sitting in his parlor, heard it and came to the back door. He could easily see what was going on so he ran to get his rifle and headed to the fields.

Most of the slaves had left the fields and were on their way down to the quarters when he fired the first blast in their direction. No one was hit, but the message sent was very clear and they stopped running. The two overseers were lying bloodied in the fields and were surrounded by the laborers who stayed there. Those who had run for some unknown reason left the overseer's rifles back on the field. When Byron fired a second shot into the air and waved his arms for them to return, they weren't sure what to do. Although they stopped running and turned around to face the master, no one started coming back in his direction. Byron, himself, wasn't sure what to do at this point. If he actually fired at one of them and hit him, then he would have one less worker to harvest his crops when the time came. On the other hand if he didn't do something to regain their fear of him, then he would have lost control. He decided to make an example out of one of them and he aimed very carefully so as to make sure that he hit him low enough not to cause any serious damage.

He took aim and fired at the one nearest him at the head of the quarters road hitting in the left leg. The man went down like a wounded animal holding his leg and Byron hollered at the others to pick him up and bring him to the house. At first nobody moved, but when Byron hollered again and raised his weapon, two of the slaves quickly moved and picked up their fallen brother and carried him to the mansion. By this time the overseers from the other fields including Sam who was with them, hearing the shots being fired were at the fracas site. They saw Byron moving toward the mansion following behind some slaves carrying one of their own. It was obvious that he had been injured, but whether it was from the shooting, they couldn't tell. When they looked around and saw that all the rest of the slaves were just standing around doing nothing they went over in force and commanded them to return to work. Reluctantly they complied with the order. The overseers spotted the two rifles still on the ground and retrieved them.

At the mansion, Byron commanded that the wounded slave be taken to the back porch where he was placed still bleeding on a mat. Aunt Tee was alerted and she came out to see what the matter was. It wasn't hard to see that the man had been shot from the gaping hole in his leg and the bone exposed. The shot had gone through the leg, but the bone was still intact. Aunt Tee hollered for Clarence to bring her some rags from the closet and when he did she tied off the leg to stop the bleeding. Byron was standing there not saying a word, but so were the two other slaves that brought him in. They were petrified not knowing what Byron was going to do next, but when he hollered at them to get back down to the fields they ran off the back porch at their top speed.

Aunt Tee continued doctoring the wounded, but she knew that her skills were not sufficient to do what this man needed. Even though the bleeding stopped she knew he needed the help of a real doctor. She told Byron that he had better send for the doctor. He grunted and hardly moved at first, but when she told him if he didn't this man may have to lose his leg. Byron certainly didn't want that because then he would be worthless, not only as a harvester but his resale value would be severely diminished. Byron went back inside and hollered upstairs for Jethro. When he came down Byron told him what was going on and to saddle up one of the horses and go get the doctor. Jethro looked out the back door at the wounded man then hopped off the porch and ran to the stable. Minutes later he had a horse saddled and was on his way down the road.

Byron left the porch and the wounded slave to Aunt Tee's care and he made his way back to the field. The two beaten overseers had been taken to Sam's house, where Sam was attending to them. Byron stepped in and asked them what the hell had happened out there. Still shaken but not extremely hurt, one man answered that he had never seen them acting so strangely as when the fight between two of them broke out. He went on to say it was as if something had possessed them and there was no way to control or stop them. Byron looked at him with a look of doubt and wondered if this man had lost his mind. Before Byron could say anything the second overseer chimed in and said that it wasn't something just with these two men, but all of them out there seemed possessed. He went on to say that he was through here and he would be leaving first thing in the morning. Both men had been pummeled pretty good but apparently there were no broken bones or internal damage.

Byron was at a loss for words temporarily, but he looked at Sam to try and get some kind of explanation about what was going on. Sam couldn't offer a reason any more than the overseer that first spoke. Then the two of them stood there looking at the other overseers. Byron finally made an appeal to the men telling him that it was getting close to the harvest season and he needed them to stay on at least until that was finished. Neither man was willing to do so, claiming what they had seen today was only going to get worse and they didn't want to be around when the full uprising happened. Byron gave them a disgusted look and told them fine now get off his land right now, not tomorrow. Both men struggled to their feet and stumbled out the door. Byron then turned to Sam and told him to get down to the patrol station and round him up two replacements for these men. Sam tried to remind him that with all the other trouble going on at other plantations and some slaves still running lose in the mountains, it might be hard to get any of them to take the job. Byron refused to hear what Sam was saying and told him to go down there and try. Sam sensing his argument was useless got on his horse and headed out.

About an hour later the local doctor arrived and came up on the back porch. He looked at the makeshift bandages and the blood spots and told Aunt Tee she did well to keep him alive. Then he removed the bandages and exposed the wound. Afterward he looked at Byron and asked him how this happened. Byron hesitated then told him the truth. The doctor was sympathetic with Byron and related to him that he had heard of many other rebellions and it seemed like there was an epidemic going around. The wounded slave was regaining consciousness and he tried to sit up when the doctor told him to lie back because what he was going to do next was going to hurt a little. The slave lay back down and the doctor started to cut around the wound to remove some bone fragments. It was obvious that he was in pain, but all the while the doctor was digging in the hole the slave just gritted his teeth and stared at Byron without saying anything.

When the doctor finished cleaning and patching up the wound he told Byron that he was lucky he had someone like Aunt Tee around to save this man's leg. Byron looked at her, but offered nothing. After he redressed the wound, the doctor packed up his gear and went into the house with Byron to settle his bill. By this time both Charlotte and Anna Lee had been made aware of what happened and Charlotte asked Byron if there was something going on with the slaves that she should know about. Byron just shrugged his shoulders and told her not to worry he had everything under control. Aunt Tee who was near enough to hear his comment smiled to herself and whispered: "you control nothing."

It was late afternoon by the time the doctor left and Byron went back down to the fields to see if order had been restored and the workers were doing what they were supposed to be. With two of his overseers gone now he had only five left to cover all of the fields. He felt confident though that Sam would come up with the two replacements he needed even though there were other pressing issues in the area. When he got to the main tobacco field the first thing he saw was the four huddled together as they usually did but at least they were working. He thought about going over and saying something to them about what happened but when they saw him and looked up at him, he changed his mind. For now it seemed that order had been restored and everything was functioning as per normal. He knew that the remaining overseers were going to have to be more vigilant to keep it this way so he called them over to him and instructed them to not be afraid to use the whip if they had to, but he didn't want any of them shot. They nodded in agreement and rode off.

Byron stayed out with the overseers until it was time to blow the horn. Sam had not returned yet and he wondered whether he was having trouble getting the replacements. Since it was Friday afternoon, until recently Sam had let the slaves off a little early but now that Byron was out there, the overseer who was filling in for Sam didn't know whether Byron wanted to let them off now or not. He took it upon himself to blow the horn, when Byron looked at his watch and then at the overseer. Byron started to ride over to the man, but the horn had already sounded and the workers were quitting. When Byron got next to the overseer first he asked him what he was doing blowing the horn so early, but when the overseer suspecting that Byron wasn't going along with his decision, replied that he was trying to avoid another incident, it made sense to Byron and he backed off. The day ended signaling the beginning of the war. A war that was still yet unrealized by the plantation master.

On the other side of the river Jobba and his two companions were preparing for their trip across the water. They had found sufficient food to carry them through the day and had not heard anything like dogs or man in pursuit. Shaka was still having reservations about going because he feared getting caught, so Jobba spent some extra time assuring him that it was going to be safe. He went over the plan in detail telling him that once they reached the other shore they would sneak up to the last cabin where he knew he had a friend. He went on to tell Shaka that under the cover of darkness no one of the overseers would be down in the area to see them. Though it was hard for them to keep track in the forest what day it was, Jobba seemed to recall that it was Friday and he remembered that Friday was a day when the slaves would get off early. Saturday was usually a half-day and they started in a little later. Jobba was not aware of the changes that had been made since he left.

When nightfall came and it was time to go, Jobba gathered the men together and told them to take nothing they couldn't do without. He went down to the edge of the river and dipped his foot in the water and quickly yanked it out. The water was very cold even though it was the beginning of summer. Jobba turned to the men and said this was going to be very challenging not only because the water was cold, but the current was strong and moving downstream. He went on to tell them that while they were out there they should be thinking all the time about how good it's going to be when they reach the other side and to focus their minds on that and that only and they will make it. He finished talking and took a deep breath then ran full speed into the water. Shaka was not immediately convinced this was doable until he saw Jobba swimming and making headway moving across the river. He then turned to the other man and the two of them ran into the water following Jobba.

To Shaka, saying the water was cold was a gross understatement as he paddled his arms with all his strength to keep from moving downstream with the current. About half way across Jobba turned to see how his companions were doing when he noticed that the other man was having some trouble maintaining his direction and was going more downstream than across. Shaka seemed to be making it okay. Jobba continued to stroke and as he neared the shore he looked around again and all he could see was Shaka a few yards behind him, there was no sign of the other man. When he reached the shore and staggered out of the water exhausted, he looked hard for the missing man, but in the darkness it was almost impossible to see. Shaka staggering and falling forward came upon the shore a few minutes later and collapsed on the beach. Both men lie there looking up at the sky as they tried to regain regular breathing and recover strength. Shaka then said that he too was worried about the other man because he saw him losing his struggle to maintain direction. They sat up and scoured the waters to try and spot him, but they saw only the ripples of the water as it continued to flow. There was nothing they could do so they paused a minute looking at each other in disbelief, but then moved on. Jobba told Shaka to keep low just like he was and he pointed to the cabin in the near distance.

They were almost crawling when they finally made it to the cabin. Just outside coming up from the rear, they stood up and moved around to the front door. Jobba knocked quietly at first, but when there was no answer he knocked again a little harder. No sound came from inside which made Jobba wonder if anything had happened and the preacher he longed to see was no longer there. Still outside he listened carefully to see if he could detect anything, he thought that perhaps the occupants might be praying and not disposed to interrupt their worship. But after a short while and not even low murmuring could be heard he chanced to open the door slowly. There was only a dim light from a single lantern turned down low illuminating the area so Jobba motioned to his companion to follow him stepping lightly. They moved across the room looking for any signs that someone was still living there and Jobba remembered that the four never did have many possessions. But from what he could recall it appeared that what they did have was still there just the same as before. He found his way to the table in the eating area and motioned for his companion to join him as they sat down to rest.

A few doors up, all during the day Myanna had a strange feeling that something was going to happen today. When the fight broke out and the mild uprising occurred, she resigned herself to thinking that the incident was what she had been feeling. But after that was over and the feeling still persisted she knew there was something more. When she came into the cabin that evening and went straight up to her level she became more concerned because the feeling was getting stronger and stronger and it bothered her. The relationship between her and the Harpers had become even more strained since Jobba left and also due to their being on different sides. Now it was at the point where they no longer ate together but each did their own cooking and she was forced to eat after they were finished. Since it was only she, eating late wasn't a bother, but she often wondered about the whereabouts of her man and her children.

Shaka and Jobba sat there for some time trying to figure out what to do next. Jobba knew that he had to get to his own cabin, but was afraid that if he walked up there now someone might see him and he couldn't be sure who it might be. Since it was Friday night, many of the slaves were prone to be up late and now that it was warm even standing around outside. Although he didn't see anybody when they came around to the front of the preacher's cabin, he was not yet comfortable enough to step outside and begin walking. He told Shaka what they had to do but he didn't have a plan yet and didn't want to expose both of them at the same time by going back outside again. On the other hand he didn't want to leave Shaka there by himself and have the preacher and his associates come in and find him not knowing whom he was. Shaka nodded in agreement and told Jobba that whatever he thought was best for them he would go along with.

While he was contemplating a plan he heard some shuffling outside the door. Not sure whether it was the preacher or not, Jobba jumped up and Shaka with him and hid in a dark corner of the room. The door opened and the entrants paused at the door before coming in sensing that something was not right. It was the preacher and the other three and they called out.

"I know that there is someone in here, I just ask are you for me or against me" Daniel said.

When Jobba heard his voice even though he could hardly recognize him, he sprang up from crouching in the corner and ran toward him. Grabbing the preacher around his shoulders he hugged him hard and greeted him.

"Daniel, Daniel it's me Jobba. It's good ta see ya" Jobba said excitedly as he leaned back to get a good look at him. Daniel hugged him back but showed no further emotion as he responded.

"Jobba it is good to see you also, but you should not have come at this time."

Jobba was surprised at the words and asked why because he had told the preacher a while ago about his plans. Now that he was acting on them, he thought that Daniel would be the one who would support him most, besides Myanna.

"Jobba you do not yet understand what is really happening in this place. It is good that you got away when you did, but coming back now may just cause a bigger problem."

Jobba had no idea what Daniel was talking about, but he went on to say he had to see Myanna before he went away to try and find this city called Richmond.

"Myanna is safe and she will be all the while, but hear my words Jobba. The evil that is present in this place is growing to such a degree that it can no longer be tolerated. The one who is called Aunt Tee has set in motion a plan to try and claim all souls who exist here, including the one who rules. It will not be so, but it will not be done without confrontation. You shall go now and see your beloved wife, but then return quickly also. Do not tarry there for your presence will be revealed."

Jobba heard his words and wondered about who was going to reveal him, but then he thought about Penniman. He wondered had it gotten to the point that his quasi friend would do that. At that point, Shaka stepped forward into the dim light and Jobba introduced him to Daniel and the others. Daniel acknowledged his presence and told Jobba that it was good that he has someone with him because two together would be good in case one fell into a ditch the other would be able to help him up. Again Jobba wasn't sure what he was trying to tell him, but he overlooked it and told Daniel that they needed food and clothing. Daniel told him to go and do what he had to do quickly and when he returned what he needed would be supplied. Daniel went on to further tell him that a way back across the river would be made for him. The next question for Jobba was whether Shaka should stay here or go with him and Daniel answered that it didn't matter because either way their presence would be known. Jobba decided to take Shaka with him.

Both men stepped into the night and paused before moving on looking around to see if anyone else was out. Sure enough there were a few slaves milling around in the quarters road so Jobba motioned to Shaka that they go around to the back of the cabins. Walking along the way behind the cabins Jobba carefully examined each one to make sure that he would be coming to the front at the right one. There was no one out there and in the dark it was easy to approach his cabin. When he got to the right one he motioned to Shaka that they were going to go around to the front and they both quietly did so.

At the front door, Jobba couldn't decide whether he should knock on his own door or just go right in. He decided to execute the latter thought. When he opened the door, Tralene and Penniman were sitting at the table, but the children were sleeping. Penniman saw him and the new man and jumped up from his chair. He wasn't sure how he should act or what he should say, but his first reaction was to get Jobba back out of the cabin before someone else knew he was there. His thought was that if the master found out Jobba was there and he didn't turn him in, then he would be the one to get punished.

"Jobba, what you do here? I think you be gone far away by now, if'n you ain dead. You caint stay massa might fine out you here. Who dis wit you?"

"Penniman I come to see ma wife not you an I ain worried 'bout no massa, not now. Dis here is ma friend an he gwine away wit me."

Myanna heard the commotion and thought she heard his voice. She came quickly down the stairs and when she saw him ran over. They hugged for a long time and then went upstairs. Shaka who was still standing in the doorway hesitated looking at Penniman, but then he followed Jobba. Upstairs the couple embraced again and kissed to the point where it was beginning to go further when Shaka coughed and cleared his throat. Jobba reluctantly pulled away and introduced him.

They all sat down at the table and Jobba started in telling her all about his adventures and what his plans were, when Shaka reminded him about what that preacher man said about time. Jobba agreed and tried to end the conversation by telling her that he was headed to Richmond and as soon as he made a connection with that Underground Railroad conductor, he would come back for her and they were going up north and be free. Myanna encouraged him, but was not quite ready to let him go so soon. She got up from the table went to him and put her arms around him one more time and kissed his neck. He held her arms and kissed them for he really didn't want to leave again either, but Shaka insisted that they go now before anyone comes. She released him and wished both well, even though inside she feared that she might never see him again.

They went back to Daniel's via the same route and when they got there he had two large bags waiting for them. Jobba saw the bags and inquired if they were for them and Daniel said yes. He went over looked inside them and was surprised to see that several changes of clothes for each and an ample supply of fruits and vegetables were in there. Jobba had a hard time figuring out where the preacher could have gotten these things so quickly, especially since he didn't even know they were coming, but having seen the man do all the things he did, Jobba kept silent. Daniel went on to tell the pair that they should leave now and that he would find someone waiting for them at the dock with a boat. The man there would ferry them back across the river, but they were not to speak to him or look directly at him. Jobba thought this a strange request, but with all that the preacher had done for him, he had no problem in complying with his directive. Before they left, Daniel added one more thing.

"Jobba, when you get back to the other side and begin the journey to your chosen destination, go to the place where the cave is and you will find a special tree nearby. This tree will be different from the others because it has not grown up straight, but leans to the side and stretches its branches over many others as a covering. In the upper branches of the tree, when the morning light comes you will look for a bird, a sparrow. It will not be an ordinary sparrow, but one of a different coloring. This bird will have an orange chest where it should be white. Spot the bird and do not lose sight of him, for he will lead you to your destination. When he rests you shall rest, when he flies follow him. Remember to keep your eyes on the sparrow and he will lead you, if you lose your focus you will become lost."

Jobba was now totally confused about all the things that Daniel said to him, but he took to heart the admonition about the sparrow. When the final words were finished and the preacher bid them farewell, Jobba and Shaka left the cabin and made their way down to the dock. There was no one else around, but they spotted the new boat and what seemed like a dwarf was waiting for them seated on the bench with the oars. As they got closer to the rower, Jobba remembered that they were not to look directly at him. This was difficult for the pair because there was something very strange about him. Both men got into the boat one in the front and one in the last row and the dwarf with his powerful arms showing began rowing. Jobba was doing all he could to resist the temptation to stare at this man and so was Shaka, but as they got further away from the shore the inclination to look lessened and they were more concerned about getting to the other side.

When they neared the far shore the dwarf turned the boat around and pointed to the edge. Realizing that he was not going to row the boat ashore Jobba and Shaka grabbed their bags and stepped into the shallow water. It was as cold as they remembered when they swam in it before, but the walk to the edge was just a few feet so it didn't bother them much. As soon as they were safely on the beach the dwarf started rowing again back toward the other side. Jobba and Shaka's curiosity had reached its maximum level and they could no longer resist the temptation. With their eyes straining to get a good look in the darkness they both peered at the figure, but by this time he was far enough away so all they saw was an outline of the man. In a matter of minutes the boat disappeared in the night and it was as if the water had not been disturbed. They then turned to find shelter for the night after both agreed that trying to find the cave now wouldn't be a good idea.

Charlotte was up unusually early this Saturday morning, even before the sun rose. She was bubbling with excitement like she had never been to town before. To her there was going to be something different about this trip because she was going to get the things needed to throw the shindig of the year. It had been some time since the last party the Candle's hosted and since she loved getting the attention from the sycophantic guests who attended she was intent on making this the best one ever. Byron still languished in the bed watching her dancing around the room and singing. He couldn't grasp the significance of this one party, but since he had agreed to it he indulged her and agreed to allow her do whatever she decided. He glanced out the window and saw that the sun was just beginning to rise and the horn for the Saturday call would not be sounding for a few more minutes, then turned over and tried to go back to sleep.

No more than ten minutes later, Byron heard the horn call and he sluggishly got out of bed, dressed and went downstairs. Charlotte by this time had already had breakfast and was roaming around the house surveying the rooms and making a last minute list of what she was going to get. Aunt Tee and Clarence, as usual, were in the kitchen preparing for the day and waiting for the rest of the family to come down and eat. When Byron arrived in the dining room, it was Clarence who greeted him first and asked about miss Charlotte being so full of life this morning. Byron replied that she was going out of her head and both men laughed out loud. Clarence quickly regained his composure however as he heard the footsteps of the house first lady coming near the room. He finished serving Byron's breakfast, poured his coffee and got out before she actually came in.

"Byron do you think we oughta invite those Arbristers, you know the last time he was here when he left he didn't even say goodbye and didn't look like he had a good time at all?"

Byron almost choked on his coffee as he tried to swallow, but composed himself long enough to respond.

"Oh I jest think he had a little too much of my punch, and it was gittin the best of him. Yeah, darlin you go on an ask him to come, I'd like ta see that ole boy again."

Although those were Byron's words to Charlotte, inside he was hoping that the invitation would get lost, because he really didn't want to confront Charlie Arbrister again since he asked for his money back.

Charlotte was still sitting in the dining room discussing the affair with Byron when both Anna Lee and Jethro came in at the same time; this was very unusual.

"Good mornin' daddy" Anna Lee said.

"Mornin' dad" Jethro offered unenthusiastically.

"Good mornin' to the both of you" he responded.

Charlotte jumped right in next even before Clarence had the chance to set their breakfast down before them.

"Now listen y'all I want to leave here within the hour so we can get in the stores before they get too busy, ya hear?"

"Yes mama we'll be ready" they both answered almost in unison.

Byron finished eating and asked Charlotte if there was anything else she needed from him. When she said no, he got up and went outside headed to the fields. Saturdays were usually a short day for the slaves under normal conditions, but after what had happened recently things would probably never be back to what was the old normal. Before, they would come out a half hour later and be finished by noon then have the rest of the day off, but now it would be up to Byron just what the hours and the conditions were going to be. He stopped by Sam's cabin first to follow-up on whether he was able to get some overseers to replace the ones that left. Sam was just coming out when he met him.

"Sam, how ya make out in gittin them new overseers?"

"Wellsuh, it twern't easy, seem like no one wanna come out chere. Wit all de ruckus goin on wit dem uprisin's an all, seem like they kin make mo money catchin' dem runaways den bein no overseers. But I did git three of 'em ta say they would come here taday an talk wit you 'bout the job. Should be here sometime dis aftanoon."

"So it's gonna be all about how much they can git, huh? Well when they get here we can work that out, cause I caint' let that mess happen again what happen before. Okay you did good, now let's git on out of here an get them workin like they supposed ta be."

About an hour later Charlotte was mustering her children and instructing Clarence to go and get the carriage ready. He made haste to go to the stable and harness the horse and ready the carriage, because he knew by now that she was excited and ready to roll. The horse and carriage were made ready and Clarence brought them around to the front of the house. Charlotte was already standing on the porch waiting for Anna Lee and Jethro. Clarence pulled up to the door and got down to help her get in. As she stepped off the porch, the door opened and out came the two siblings. Jethro, although he had agreed to go, by the expression on his face his heart was not in this trip. Anna Lee had absorbed some of her mother's enthusiasm and was now getting into the spirit of planning the party, so she was looking forward to the trip.

When all riders were seated and comfortable, Clarence snapped the reins and the horse set his hooves in motion. It was a beautiful day, just the kind that would make this a good travel day so they sat back and began to enjoy the journey. Inside Charlotte was going on and on about what they were supposed to look for and handed out a search assignment to each of her offspring. Jethro heard the instructions, but allowed them to pass right through his cranium while fervently agreeing with mother as they were handed out. Anna Lee duly took note of her assignment and even made suggestions about how they could do better what mother was planning.

Clarence was making unusually good time for this town trip. There were very few others on the road at this time in the morning on a Saturday, but when they passed the patrol station they saw an unusual amount of activity from men milling around in the area. Several were still mounted on their horses as if preparing to go on a hunt and others were coming and going from inside the office. Charlotte noticed the activity and asked Jethro what he thought it was all about. Jethro responded by telling her about all the uprisings and rebellions that had been going on in the area that Charlotte had paid no particular attention to hearing. Charlotte noted the curt response and reminded him about his manners, but she also was ready to pay more attention to the matter now that she saw all these armed men. For the rest of the trip she was less talkative, but definitely paid more attention to the surroundings as they passed them.

Her vigilance of the surroundings turned to excitement again as they entered town. When they got to the general store she and the kids got out then she instructed Clarence to go and attend to the horse at the livery as he usually did - then come back and wait for them behind the store. Before going in the store she took out her invitations and asked Jethro to take them to the mail delivery service. Jethro agreed and separated from them on his way. Anna Lee and Charlotte went inside the store and were greeted warmly by the proprietor. Right away she noticed that it was unusually crowded and commented to Anna Lee that she thought this was a good sign that people were coming out for the summer. As she walked around the counters to her planned first station, she saw someone she recognized and went over to say hello. It was someone who had attended her last affair and she was going to extend a verbal invitation in addition to the one she had just sent, but when she got close to the woman she greeted her, but the response was less than cordial.

The woman returned her greeting, but seemed less than desirous of extending any conversation. Charlotte was somewhat surprised at the attitude and tried to prolong the dialogue so she could find out what the matter was, but the woman was intent on getting away so she made an excuse about someone waiting outside for her and departed. Puzzled at the exchange, Charlotte went over to Anna Lee and asked her if she heard any of that. Anna Lee replied that she didn't because she was busy picking out the things she was supposed to get. Charlotte dismissed it with no second thought and went on about her shopping. It was not long before she encountered another neighbor who also had attended the last party and received almost the same treatment as the first party guest. Not wanting to be rude, but she had to know what was going on so she came right out and asked the woman if she had a problem with her. As the woman was making her excuses to get away she told Charlotte she needed to ask her husband. With that Charlotte allowed her to leave without trying to delay her any further.

Although her spirits were slightly dampened from the odd interactions, when she got into the swing of buying the things she wanted, her excitement returned. Jethro came in the store found them and the rest of the afternoon was spent in gathering all the things Charlotte had on her shopping list. By late afternoon they had bought all the planned things and then some things that were not on the list. The next step before heading home was to stop by the tobacco store and get Byron's favorite cigars. When they neared the carriage Charlotte noticed that two of the same three men that had tried to entice Suliah away before were there looking in the vehicle and talking to Clarence. They saw her coming and scampered. Charlotte arrived at the carriage and asked Clarence what they wanted. He responded that they recognized the carriage and were looking for that pretty gal that he brought there the last time. Charlotte didn't know whether she wanted to laugh at how Suliah was so remembered or get angry that these men had the nerve to approach the carriage again after she had warned them about who that "gal" belonged to.

The trip back was without incident although Charlotte again kept her eyes focused on everything that was going on around her. When they neared the patrol station she paid particular attention to what was going on there, but this time there were only a few men standing outside the office and things seemed to be okay. She sat back and relaxed. Jethro however saw something happening at the edge of the woods on the other side of the road. What he saw were several hunters spread out in a skirmish line with the dogs straining at their leashes and their guns raised to fire. Charlotte was looking in the other direction so she didn't notice it, so Jethro knowing that he had made her uncomfortable before when he reminded her of the rebellions, decided not to draw her attention to this action. They continued on and arrived safely back at the plantation where they unloaded all the packages and tended to their regular activities while Clarence took care of retiring the horse and storing the carriage.

Byron was interviewing the three men who came out for the overseer jobs. He was busy explaining to them the routine he required around the fields and pointing out how much territory they had to cover. Although all of them seemed to be interested to this point, the discussion of payment had not been broached yet. After he finished telling them the duties he expected them to perform he asked if they had any questions and that's when the interview stopped. The one man who acted like the spokesman for the other two asked how much Byron was paying and when he heard the answer, he turned away and started walking toward his horse followed by the other two. Byron realizing that the men were through listening and getting ready to leave was disappointed. He had offered them the same pay he gave the last men, but in these times of more lucrative employment as slave hunters, the earnest wage rate for overseers had risen. Before the men mounted up, he told them to wait a minute and let's talk.

The spokesman turned around and slowly walked back to Byron and said: "Okay om listnin"

"Now I caint pay y`all much more than I offered, just now, but after the harvest then I kin give you a little somethin' more. How's that?"

"How much mo, ya gonna give?"

I caint; tell you that now. I won't know `till I sell these here crops, but you kin see they lookin pretty good and should fetch a good price."

The spokesman looked around again at the field and then at the other men then he agreed they would take the job. He made Byron promise though that he would put that arrangement down on paper soon. Byron agreed and the men took off. They were going to start on Monday.

Byron watched the men go down the road and then went in the house. He saw all the packages sitting in the living room and wondered just how much she spent, but didn't ask. He walked over and started rummaging through some of the bags when Charlotte walked in and caught him.

"What you lookin' for, I got your cigars and put them in your parlor on the desk."

"I just want to see what all you bought. Look like ya got the whole store."

"You want to have a nice party don't you, well this is what we need."

Byron didn't say anymore, but then Charlotte started in telling him about the strange encounter she had with a couple of their previous party guests and she asked him why they would act like that. Byron shrugged off the question and told her that he thought they were being high browed and showing their jealousy because no one gave a party like she does. This brought a smile to her face and she dismissed further inquiry and then went on telling Byron about how she was going to do this party. He patiently listened to her, but inside he was not the least bit interested and couldn't wait until this whole thing was over.

That night after dinner and the family was sitting around drinking their tea and cordials, Jethro mentioned to Byron what he had seen on the way back from town. He told him that it looked like the hunters had some runaways cornered in the woods just above the bridge. Byron responded by saying that he hoped they caught them because that's awfully close to this place. Jethro also told him that he heard in town that the war those Yankees been talking about had already started somewhere down in the lower part of the state and it was likely to be coming up here soon. Byron said he didn't believe any of that because those Yankees are just talk and nothing else. Jethro disagreed with him and said he wasn't so sure about that, but Byron cut him off and that ended the conversation on that matter. The rest of the evening was spent listening to Charlotte go on about her party plans and everybody politely indulged her.

Aunt Tee and Clarence were in their usual positions just outside the living room during the after dinner function waiting until the family concluded it. While they waited, Clarence was telling her what he had seen and heard when he was in town today, especially about the hunters ready to capture some runaways in the woods. Aunt Tee answered him and said she hoped they got away because the word had been spread about the next ritual ceremony and she was expecting many new runaways to be coming. Then she reminded Clarence that they needed to plan how they were going to get away themselves from the party so they could conduct the ceremony. Clarence told her not to worry because he had it all figured out and would tell her his plan soon. She heard that and having all confidence in his schemes, she was through talking.

Down in the quarters that Sunday the whole village was talking about how Jobba had been there because Penniman told them he had sneaked back. His news didn't help the relationship between the two factions because everybody knew that if Jobba had gotten caught it would have been even harder than it was for everybody. The feelings on the Aunt Tee follower's side were that if he came back again Penniman should turn him in. Of course Myanna and her side were totally against any of that sentiment and vowed to protect him however they could should he come back. The sides were squarely divided on this issue as well as many others and the rift was still growing. It was getting to the point now that in the cabin the Harpers and Myanna hardly spoke to each other and it was becoming increasingly more difficult to coexist in the same abode. When there, Myanna stayed upstairs most of the time, except when she needed to eat or go out.

Although it was rough going for all of them, not only because of Byron, but now that the gauntlet had been clearly thrown down by the slaves, living and working on the same plantation could never be the same. It was just a matter of time before the fracas that erupted in the field last week was going to turn into a major brawl that there wouldn't be enough overseers in the county to quell. Somehow though, after the initial reaction to Jobba's return died down each family on both sides of the divide resorted to keeping to their constituent factions and left the others alone as they tried to enjoy their day of rest and have some fun.

Monday came around and the seed that Charlotte had planted about the upcoming party had taken root within the slave community because many of them were going to have to work it. Fieldwork was beginning to suffer as they looked forward to reaping the benefits of the aftermath of a Candle party. Usually after one of Charlotte's events most of the leftovers were distributed among the families and everyone loved that except Byron. He knew from past experience that whenever she hosted one that the week before and a day or two after, work was going to be less than productive, so he tolerated the slump, but was not happy about it. He tried to encourage them to keep up the pace first by threatening then cajoling then finally by telling them there would be no handouts if they didn't work hard. This worked.

The rest of the week went by without any major incidents and the workers because of Byron's threats to withhold their after party goodies, were performing up to par. When Friday came and those selected to work in the mansion the next day were given extra time off to get their serving clothes together and to get their instructions from Aunt Tee. Many of them were told to leave the fields and begin helping Aunt Tee and Clarence and the other house slaves to begin decorating the mansion. By the time Friday night came and those who were scheduled to work the party were still in the mansion preparing, it was a matter of who would be able to recover by early the next morning and do it again. Charlotte had instructed Aunt Tee that this time she wanted everything to be so elegant that anyone who had been to one before would know that this is the best one ever. She had created new decorations that Aunt Tee thought looked silly, but she could never say that. Anna Lee was busy providing her own creative touches wherever Charlotte would allow it and Jethro just hung around pretending to be helpful when all he did was walk from room to room observing everybody work.

Saturday morning came and Byron, as he usually did, made his special preparation of nectar. He called Aunt Tee over and was insistent again, that she instruct the servants to make sure every grown guest was given a sample to taste. All day things were moving along as planned and Charlotte was excited and happy at the results she saw. By late afternoon the house was ready and Charlotte told Anna Lee to go and pick out her best dress because she was going to be the bell of the ball. Charlotte even encouraged Jethro to spruce up because she had invited those girls from the new family she told him about. Jethro was still less than enthusiastic about the whole thing, but he tried to look interested. As the evening approached and Charlotte was expecting guests to start arriving, when none showed for sometime after the hour she had given on the invitations, she was beginning to worry. She recalled what was said in town at the general store and it was beginning to sink in and wondered if anybody was coming.

The first family to show up was the newcomers that had just purchased a plantation on the other side of town. This was the family with the three daughters and Charlotte was pleased to welcome them, but was embarrassed that they came at a time when nobody else was there. She greeted them and invited them inside while trying to make excuses for the lack of guests already there. The first greeting servant took their wraps and the next in the serving order offered Byron's punch to the mother and father. Charlotte then showed the family to the living room that was so flamboyantly decorated that the mother commented, tongue in cheek, on how lovely it was. She whispered to her husband out of Charlotte's hearing that she really thought it was gaudy looking. Charlotte showed them to comfortable seating and started in making conversation when she heard the sound of many other guests arriving.

Feeling somewhat relieved, Charlotte excused herself from the new family and went to greet the latest arrivals. At approximately the same time four other families came in and she greeted them all personally. It seems that they had a common excuse for being late. The word was that there was a lot going on in the woods just outside of this plantation. There were a number of slave hunters riding the roads and telling every white traveler to be vigilant for runaways roaming the area. Charlotte heard this and expressed the appropriate concern and told her guests that they would be safe here. Byron came in greeted the new guests and motioned to the beverage servant to give them drinks. After a while the rooms were filling up as more families arrived, each one giving an update on the activity going on in the roads nearby. Byron after hearing so many reports was beginning to wonder if he shouldn't go down and ask Sam to get some of his men together and scour the area to make sure none of them runaways was on his land. He gave it some thought, but decided that if there were a lot of patrols already out there then why bother Sam.

By eleven-thirty the party was in full swing and the musicians had everybody up dancing and generally enjoying themselves. The cuisine was as good as Aunt Tee had ever made and no one had any complaints about lack of sufficiency. Even Jethro was balling, for one of the daughters of the new plantation family, one near his own age, had caught his eye and he was devoting his time and attention to making sure she had a good time. Anna Lee had been introduced at the proper time, by Byron, and she made her timely appearance looking as lovely as she could. Over all Charlotte was pleased at another successful bash and without the presence of Suliah to detract from her daughter's spotlight, she just knew this would be the envy of all owners' wives.

In the kitchen however, there was a sub-plot brewing. The moon was out and it was full which meant that there was another party about to take place. The time had already been set for the ritual dance to take place and Clarence was going over the plan he devised with Aunt Tee. They both knew that just across the river many new runaways had found the mountaineers joined with them and were coming to the festival. At the right time, he had made provisions for all of Aunt Tee's followers working her party to escape from the house unseen. Under threats of revealing that Jobba had been back on the land to the master and put him on high alert, he made sure that the Daniel believers were going to cover for them. In her own sly way, Aunt Tee was having just as much fun as the Candle's guests, but for entirely opposing reasons. She went out of her way to ensure that Charlotte's guests had plenty to dine on and Clarence had the servers plying all the men and many women with enough nectar to insure that sobriety became just a word.

As Charlotte walked around trying to entertain all of her guests, she noticed that one young man had been spending a great deal of time with Anna Lee. In the past, it was Anna Lee who usually roamed around helping her mother entertain, but tonight her flirtations had been corralled by this potential suitor and had not gone from a mother's vision. Charlotte carefully, but dutifully began paying more attention to who this young man was and started inquiring about his credentials. Satisfied with the reports she was able to garner about his pedigree, she casually sauntered over to where they were and pretended she needed to talk with Anna Lee. Excusing herself, she invaded their conversation and waited to be introduced. Anna Lee took the bait and accommodated her by making the appropriate introduction. When the young man bowed kissed her hand and replied with the proper introductory response, Charlotte was sold on this being the right one for her daughter. As a consequence her mind was set off in a new direction of party planning, no matter how premature. Satisfied that she had done her motherly inquisition, she left the couple and continued making her rounds.

While this party was in full swing, on the other side of the river the leader was amassing his group to make the journey to Aunt Tee's party. Both boats that were normally tied up on the plantation side had been commandeered by Penniman and used to come and get the band. The group had grown beyond the capacity of a single boat as they did on previous occasions and Penniman was thrilled to see what was happening. At his command they boarded the crafts and set out to assemble once again at the last cabin on the row before the river and wait until time to make the trek up the mountain. Under the bright full moon the newcomers could see for many miles all around that the water was peaceful even though the trip across the river was both fearful and exciting. Pumped up from promises made by the leader regarding freedom and protection once they took the mark, the excitement for them mitigated their fears.

At the plantation dock they disembarked and headed for the cabin. Moving with great stealth for such a large group, they entered the cabin and were told the hour would be here soon when they would go to experience a great new change in their lives. Even though he was with them, there was one who had heard the words of Jobba before he left, and was now ambivalent about the decision he made to stay. The thoughts of receiving the mark and being subjected to evil as Jobba said, was now playing on his mind. After all he had just been through in running away from his former plantation, fleeing from the hunters, losing his brother on the way and not knowing what would become with the rest of his family, he wanted to be free and receive the new protection sure, but he wondered at what cost.

Back at the party, word had come up to Aunt Tee and Clarence that the mountaineers with the newcomers in tow had arrived at the cabin and all was set for tonight. She smiled her familiar broad smile and was anticipating that the party she would throw would be so much better than this one. She continued to monitor the food serving areas to make sure that the platters were full so the first lady of the house would have no need to look for her. Little did she realize that the house lady's condition was such that she wouldn't be looking for her anyway because she was nearing the point of seeking only to go to bed.

Byron too was enjoying the bash as he plied himself with his special brand of refreshment. He was glad to see that none of the guests who came were any of those whom he had pilfered land from in the past. Although many who were here were aware of his practices and on alert if he tried to conduct any business like that with them, they came because they had designs on doing to him as he had done to their friends. Many came so that they could see just how well Byron lived and perhaps get some information on how to bring about his demise and usurp the lands that he had conquered. Deception, misrepresentation and untruths abounded in the room and Byron was enjoying their company to the fullest. At one point he observed that one of Charlie Arbrister's near neighbors was there and he made his way over to him to inquire about Charlie's health.

"Hi, ain't you one of ole Charlie Arbrister's good friends? Seem like I dun seen you out at his place some time ago."

"Yeah, that's right I've seen you there before, while ago. Thanks for the invitation from your wife."

"Oh, we're glad you could come. Having a good time are ya?"

"Yes, quite good thank you."

"How's ole Charlie doin?"

"Well not too good actually. Seems like he got somethin that's bringing him down a bit, but I recon he'll be okay soon."

"That's too bad I'm sorry to hear that" Byron said while inside he was glad for the news that could keep Charlie away from his door.

The number of people in the house was elevating the heat level to new heights. Even though outside the night's warm air was not much of a relief, a few of the men decided to go out on the back porch and continue their libations. They excused themselves from the other guests and made their way to the back porch where they sat on the steps and on the wicker chairs. As they sat there looking out over Byron's fields and all the land behind them they were a bit envious that he acquired all this property. The view at night under the light of the full moon was exceedingly beautiful, but somehow presented a strange and ominous appearance. No matter in which direction they looked they could see symbols that resembled something strange and foreboding. There were trees that looked like giants, even the metal rooster on top of the stable looked threatening and the large rock formations around the stable looked like bad omens.

One man commented on the view and said this hooch Byron serves is the best I ever had, but it's making me see things. Almost at the same time one of the other men there said the same thing. It was almost as if a mass hypnotic spell was being cast over all of them. They started laughing aloud and slapping one another on the back in fun. The fun was pervasive and they were all participating when they heard the loud cry of what might have been coyote's, but it was so loud that it sounded like a bunch of them together and they knew that would be unusual. The cry alone was enough to make them stop laughing, but on top of that what they all saw next made them cringe.

Chapter 9 - New Horizons

As the calendar advanced and the days folded one into another since Jobba left, Myanna was able to free her mind during the day from the thought of him by throwing herself wholeheartedly into her labors. But at night the loneliness was overwhelming and beginning to take its toll on her. She was having great difficulty in keeping herself focused on the belief that he was coming back. Often when she finished her day's toil, she wouldn't go directly back to the cabin, but would stroll down to the river and just look longingly over to the other side. On most days all she could see was the shoreline and the vast forest in the mountains that stood behind it. She fantasized sometimes that whenever she saw what looked like the silhouette of a man, in her mind it became Jobba waving to her signaling he was alright. She would sit on the sand for hours looking up and down the shoreline then at the river hoping to see some sign that could comfort her.

When nightfall came like tonight, she would slowly walk back to the cabin and go upstairs to lay on the bed alone and cry. She would place her arm over the spot where Jobba should be, move it up and down as if to produce the body by some magic and hope that her spell would work. Each night found her going through the same routine, but as the days past the duration of the pattern lessened. Tonight, would normally be no different except that she knew it was a full moon night and therefore her cabin mates were going to be preparing for their trek to the mountains. While she was still lying on her bed, she heard them getting themselves ready downstairs. She overheard Penniman say that they had a bunch of new slaves that had come down from the mountains and they were anxious to get to the ceremony. On top of all the anguish she was going through, hearing that was the last thing she wanted to acknowledge.

She thought about going down to get herself something to eat, but then decided against it because they would be leaving soon and she would have the cabin all to herself - she would eat then. As the hour approached for them to go she could hear just outside the window the sounds of voices. She could also hear the sounds of many people moving as if a band of soldiers had assembled. It wasn't long before she heard her cabin door open and Penniman and Tralene going out. She got off the bed and looked out the window to see whether the group had grown any more than it did the last time she saw them. Shocked from her discovery, it appeared that it was almost twice the length of marchers than what she saw before. She crossed her arms to her shoulders and held herself tight, not wanting to believe that Aunt Tee was having that much success recruiting the area runaways.

It was almost midnight and because she had not eaten since noontime the hunger pangs were setting in so she made her way down to the cupboard and fixed a light dinner. Outside she could hear Penniman instructing the marchers about their procedures. She couldn't resist the temptation, so she got up and opened the door slightly, just enough to be able to look outside. She was right about the army concept. There they were all lined up like soldiers with their lanterns turned down low, but high enough to illuminate the road so they wouldn't stumble. Moments after Penniman finished his commands, the columns moved out at a steady pace, and they were on their way to the mountains.

The revelers on the porch at the mansion were almost petrified by what they saw coming up the road from the cabins. At first all they could see was the silhouette of something that looked like a large army of giant scarecrows lit up at the legs by fire and it truly frightened them. But as the marchers got closer, they could identify them not as scarecrows but as slaves coming out of the dark. There were so many of them that they might as well have been beasts, because the first thoughts that ran through the reveler's collective minds was that this was a rebellion, and their lives were in serious jeopardy. They quickly got off the porch and ran inside to alert Byron, who was still having an extremely good time. When they found him and told him their story, he first thought they were joking until one man grabbed his arm and started pulling him out to the back porch.

Byron hardly resisting the yanking was still laughing when they got to the back porch. By this time the marchers had already passed the mansion and were headed up the trail to the mountain. What could be seen was the back silhouette of their forms and the low glow from their lanterns. The man who was holding Byron pointed to the images and said that's what they saw and tried to explain what it was. Byron stopped laughing, yanked the man's arm from him and looked at him.

"You pull me out here for that? What's the matta with all y`all, caint ya see that its just a herd of some running deer going to the mountains."

"What I saw wasn't no deer" said one of the others. "Deer don't walk like that and they sure don't carry no lamps."

Byron just looked at all of them like they were crazy and told them to come on back in the house and enjoy the party. They went back in the house, but most of them had finished partying for the night. Once inside each started to make his excuses why he had to leave and the party was ending abruptly. Charlotte couldn't understand the turnaround and went to find Byron to ask him what happened. When she found him and put her question, he replied that they went outside and had a mass hallucination over some running deer that scared them. Charlotte still wasn't sure why that would be enough to frighten grown men away from a good party, but she accepted his explanation and almost ran to the front door to catch her guests leaving and say goodnight. Like wildfire the word had circulated throughout the crowd about what the men had seen, and since all the guests were already on high alert about runaway slaves in the area it wasn't hard to accept the rumor. The mass exodus out the door caught Charlotte by surprise. She thought that some of them were going to leave, but when everybody wanted the wrap they came in with, it became a challenge to accommodate the crowd quickly.

Finally, when the last guest had been taken care of and was ready to exit, Charlotte asked if they had a good time. There was a garbled response that was hardly audible, and the family scrambled quickly out the door. From the highest of highs when the party was in full swing to this new low was a first for Charlotte and she wasn't quite sure how to handle it. The high she was feeling from Byron's nectar had dissipated prematurely and the letdown was now the ruling emotion. She went to Byron again and told him she couldn't believe what just happened then went and sat in the living room staring at all her elaborate decorations. Anna Lee and Jethro came in to join her and they also wanted to know why everybody left so abruptly. The only one who was ready to accept the situation was Byron, because his high was still in full elevation and he was going to nurse it to the end. They all remained in the living room for some time after the guests left trying to come up with a reasonable explanation. There was none to be had that would suffice and they really needed Byron to supply a reason, but now he had left the party mentally, his eyes were closed as his head leaned back on the couch. Realizing they weren't going to solve the riddle tonight, Charlotte asked Jethro to help his father up to the bed. It was strange that no one called for Aunt Tee or Clarence, but they all went to bed while the remaining servants began cleaning up.

The march up to the cave had been swift and quiet. Even though they had been observed they had not been discovered. Inside Penniman and Aunt Tee were reveling at the number of new potential converts and were conducting the ritual with extra zeal. The drummer was playing with more verve than usual, and Aunt Tee was absolutely sure that the cave spirit was going to be pleased at this offering. However, when it was time for the beast to appear it emerged from the wall with an angry scowl and stood right before her.

"How dare you bring to me an infidel who is not ready to accept my mark?"

Aunt Tee was shaken and at a loss for words, but the beast seeing her surprise recognized that she didn't know one was amongst the worshipers.

"There in the last row, bring that one to me" and he pointed to the individual who in the boat was having second thoughts about not having gone with Jobba.

The robed one (Clarence) rushed to the front of the cave and secured the man who by now was shaking uncontrollably. He had to be dragged to the front because his legs wouldn't support him. When there he was thrown down before the beast and Aunt Tee.

"Why have you come here?' the beast asked.

"I dono" came the man's feeble answer and he cowered as low as he could.

"Do you seek my protection or do you not?" the beast continued.

The man, afraid for his life, thought that if he turned around now it would be the end of him responded in the affirmative pleading for the beast's pardon. After some hesitation, It was granted and the man was returned to his place. The rest of the ritual went on without any further interruptions and by the end all who had taken his mark were celebrating their victory. Aunt Tee most of all was riding high on a new emotional plane, being the one to have achieved such great numbers for the spirit.

Jobba and Shaka after their return from the plantation spent the night in the forest very near the river. Not being able to see any recognizable landmarks leading to the mountaineer cave, they were reluctant to traipse around in the woods for fear of stumbling upon the leader and his gang should they not be in the cave. But as soon as the morning came, they both awoke early and picked up the trail to the cave. Carefully making their way keeping on the alert for the mountaineers they arrived at the cave and immediately started looking for the tree that Daniel told them about. They walked around the cave and went up the hill just above the opening and searched diligently for the leaning cedar. It was not very near the cave like Jobba imagined, but it was some distance behind. Sure enough though when the pair found it, it was just as Daniel had described. It was a tall tree, but had grown almost horizontal to the ground and was leaning over like it was protecting a bunch of smaller and younger trees below it. Both men agreed this was an odd sight, but then they discovered the sparrow with the orange breast that was even more extraordinary. The bird was perched on one of the branches near the end of the tree which had it been standing up straight would have been at the very top. It sat there as if waiting for the arrival of the two and when they saw it, the bird took off.

Jobba started running while looking up at the bird with Shaka close behind him and ran right into another tree. He recoiled from the impact and fell flat on the ground with Shaka tumbling right on top of him. Neither man was injured, but as they got up laughing at being so focused on the bird as they were instructed, they forgot to watch where they were running. The bird seemed to have hovered in the air while they recovered and Jobba commented to Shaka that the bird must have been laughing too. The bird resumed its flight and this time Jobba and Shaka were careful to look for trails around the trees so as to avoid any other collisions with the immovable objects. They ran for what could have been an hour when both men were almost exhausted and ready to collapse trying to keep up with the sparrow. Suddenly, like the bird heard them gasping for breath, it landed on the top branch of another cedar where they could view it in plain sight.

Both men fell to the ground rolled over facing the sky and then just lie there. Jobba could see the bird clearly and it appeared that it was in no rush to move again, so he relaxed and enjoyed the break. Shaka, while still huffing and in between breaths, asked him what he thought of the bird and whether he thought this was a sign from his God. Jobba responded that he didn't know, but he was going to do whatever the preacher told him to do because he believed in him. For several minutes both men remained on the ground looking up at the bird and then it started walking along the branch as if to tell them it was time to start again. They turned over and got to their knees first and then finally struggled to their feet and were ready to go. For the rest of the morning, they ran after the bird until the sun was high in the sky and the sparrow led them to a clearing. Just beyond the clearing they could see a farmhouse and a few slaves out in the fields working.

Unsure whether they were led to this place by the bird to seek food and water they stopped when the bird perched on another tall tree to figure it out. They crept up to the edge of the clearing to get a better look at what the conditions were down in the fields. Looking particularly for any overseers they saw none and started to creep down the hill. When they were close enough to the workers, Jobba stood up and began waving his arms to attract some attention. He caught the eye of one of the men laboring in the dirt and the man stopped swinging his hoe and stood up. Jobba motioned to the man that he wanted him to come to him, but the man didn't move. Jobba moved a little closer to the man and waved his arms again for the man to come to him. Not sure whether there was some reason why the man would not move, Jobba looked around again very carefully, but he didn't see anything that looked like a master or an overseer. He started moving closer to the man when the man turned and started moving back toward the farmhouse. Jobba stopped in his tracks for fear that this may not be what it seems. Jobba started advancing again and the man moved toward the house again, the more Jobba tried to close the gap, the more the man opened it.

Not long after this little game went on, another worker saw Jobba and headed toward him along with a woman. The first man followed and walked toward Jobba with the other two. When they all came together Jobba told them who he and Shaka were and what they were trying to do. The second man and the woman greeted them and told them that they were free and were working this land that had been given to them by their former master who died. They explained too the reason why the first man wouldn't come to Jobba was because he's a deaf/mute and thought you might harm him. Jobba looked at the first man again and extended his hand to embrace him the man took his hand and displayed a sheepish smile. The second man and woman were husband and wife, and the first man was her brother. They invited Jobba and Shaka inside his house where there were three children that looked to be in the ten to fifteen age ranges. The older one was feeding the younger ones and when the couple came in he stopped and stared at Jobba and Shaka.

The father told him not to fear and that he should set plates for their new guests. Dutifully the son found some more plates and served Jobba and Shaka. They spent some time with the family after the meal, but told them that their journey they believed was a long one and they had to be going again. Before leaving, Jobba asked the man whether he knew where this Richmond place was, and the man told him that by horse it was almost a day's ride from there. So, from that Jobba gathered that he and Shaka would be spending at least the rest of this day and maybe tomorrow and the next day trying to get there. The father agreed and wished them a safe journey and cautioned about the hunters that were out in large forces all along the main roads. Jobba heeded his warning, thanked him for the food and water and they went back in the woods.

Retracing their steps, they tried to find the spot where they came out of the woods. Since they had moved quite a distance from the clearing, getting back to the exact spot was near impossible. Jobba looked around for some kind of landmark he could recognize, but there was none. For several minutes they walked back and forth along the tree line in the hope that something would trigger each memory. Before long they discovered the clearing, but at which side of it did, they come out still wasn't clear. Jobba decided to take a chance and follow his instincts so they both walked in on the far side of the clearing. Once they were a few feet into the forest they looked up at the top of the trees trying to locate the guide bird. There were many birds of all types seated on the branches or flying above them, but the special bird he looked for was not among them.

Fearing that they were lost, as Daniel warned, Jobba turned to Shaka and asked him if he saw the bird anywhere. Shaka replied in the negative and asked Jobba what he thought they should do now. Both men appeared bewildered and were about to just strike out in any direction when a loud cluster of birds were flapping their wings over a tall tree just beyond the spot where the men stood. They looked at them straining to see what the cause for the commotion was, but saw only the birds. As they started to walk in the direction of where the flapping birds were still making noise, just beyond that tree they spotted the orange-breasted sparrow sitting on a limb of a much shorter cedar. Relieved that they found their guide again Jobba and Shaka hurried to catch up with it.

When they got near the tree, the bird that appeared to have been sitting there waiting for them took off in a new direction. It seemed to Jobba that they were going in a direction they had just come from, and it puzzled him. But, not knowing where he was and even realizing they had gone off the trail they were originally following he kept faith that the bird was truly sent as their guide and continued on. For another hour the men pursued the bird keeping their eyes focused on it, but the strain of the pace and the position of the trees not making it easy for them to move around in them was taking its toll. The men, no longer moving with the capacity to keep up with bird stumbled and fell to the ground, just as before gasping for breath. On his way down, Jobba looked up to see whether the bird kept going, but to his amazement it had perched itself on a tree not too far ahead of them and sat patiently looking down at them. This rest period lasted for about fifteen minutes when the bird arose from the branch and began circling the area. The men struggled to their feet again and the journey restarted.

By now the day was near its end and both men were getting concerned whether they were anywhere near this Richmond town or not. Reflecting on what the man said at the house, Jobba believed they had traveled at least the distance he thought should be getting them close to their destination, but he had no way to substantiate the belief. He knew that their strength couldn't possibly continue to keep up with the bird that had no obstacles to deter him and he jokingly said to Shaka: "Oh that I had wings to fly, how happy would I be." Shaka heard him and the laugh shared by both gave them an added boost of strength even while their hearts were getting heavy. They continued running for some time then walking at a brisk pace and then finally moving at a much-retarded rate, until again the stress became too much and they sat down. By now the sun was almost fully descended and as the nightfall approached Jobba knew it was time to cease the chase for today. The bird must have sensed his desperation and found a perch for the night also.

Shaka spotted a small clearing in which he thought he saw some wild game that he believed he could catch for dinner. Both men called up the forest hunter skills they had learned from the mountaineers and dinner was caught. They found all the things needed to prepare the meal and after they ate, rested under the trees. Before closing his eyes, Jobba looked up at the stars as he did when he was in the cabin with his family, and he wondered whether Myanna was looking too. Then he thought about what had become of his children and it sent him into a melancholy mood that brought tears to his eyes as he challenged himself with the question: " Is what I'm doing what God wants and how do I know?"

In the province just outside of Richmond city Jonathan Adams was getting settled in and trying to make sure that he had the right compliment of servants to carry out the business he was intending to conduct. His political aspirations were such that he intended to become a very prominent figure in the state and eventually move up to government at the highest levels. It didn't hurt his ambitions that he had relatives in high places that were ready to advance his causes. When he purchased Suliah he had in mind she would be a great asset and would be helpful in achieving his goals. The house assignments that were handed out by the butler per his instructions included that she was to serve the guests at all parties and to generally be a handmaiden for the sisters and his mother.

Since the time she arrived in the house the demands made on Suliah were more than any of the other servants. Jonathan's sisters enjoyed making her run up and down the stairs when one trip would have been sufficient. He soon noticed this practice and confronted his sister's asking why the harsh treatment. It became obvious that the jealousy bug had bitten both of them. Although neither was an unattractive woman, when standing next to Suliah it would be hardly fair to make any comparisons, because of the inequity of nature's gifts. Jonathan made it very clear to them that he needed for her to be at her very best whenever his colleagues came to the house. This meant he didn't want her appearing overly tired or worn looking. The sister's got the message and reluctantly backed off, but not much, the unfair treatment. As for the other servants, Suliah was accepted as one of them and they embraced her with a full sincere welcome. Even Bernard, the head butler who was considerably older than her and a stickler for following the house regimen, was prone to forgive her little mishaps from time to time when she erred. Her roommate, who was close to her age, had no difficulty in getting close to her and they became more than just friends, but confidants.

It had been almost two weeks now since her arrival and Jonathan was preparing for his first major social gathering. Saturday was the selected day and Suliah remembering how it was at the Candle mansion when they threw a party was experiencing the same kind of excitement here that she felt there. On the day of the affair, she found herself running around like all of the other servants busy cleaning the house and putting up very moderate decorations. The decorations were very simple, nothing like what Charlotte envisioned as necessary, and when they were finished the house was adorned in an elegant, but modest state. Jonathan made it very clear to Bernard that the guests he was expecting were some high-ranking state government officials and they were not to be treated in any less a fashion then their offices would demand. Bernard who was accustomed to this type of affair from his previous owner assured his new master that everything would be in order. Jonathan purchased Bernard based on the recommendations of his former owner, sometime ago and he was very pleased in how he conducted himself. So when Bernard told him things would be in order, he left all of the arrangements to him.

Saturday morning came around and everyone in the house was up early taking care of last-minute preparations. Bernard had asked Suliah if she would make sure that the table was set up the way he had shown her and when the time came to serve the guests, she would be the last one to enter the dining room. She wasn't quite sure why he demanded this and when he winked at her, she knew that there was something more to his instruction then a casual command. She was further puzzled when the uniforms were handed out and some of the other women servants were more moderate than hers. Amanda, her roommate, instructed to accentuate certain parts of her anatomy had modified her uniform. She felt a little uneasy about walking in the dining room wearing it, but when she saw her roommate's looking almost the same, she relaxed a little. The other female servants who were not expected to serve in the dining room were more moderately attired. It was not until the party started and she observed whom the guests were that she understood why this was.

The guests began arriving around 6:30 and all of them were elegantly dressed with sartorial splendor. Two couples came in at about the same time and from then on the guests were mostly men. In all there were fourteen men and six women who in one way or another had some connection with the local and state government. Although the women didn't serve in any official capacity, there was no doubting that some of them were indeed the decision makers in the house. As for the men, the governor's deputy, the town mayor, the sheriff and his deputy, a state representative and a Senator were all present. Jonathan, after the butler had made his initial greeting and welcome, met his guests at the door and directed them into the living room where there was an ample supply of cocktails and hors-d'oeuvres strategically placed. Jonathan had been an officer in the English military before resigning his commission to come to America and was in the habit of seeing things done with great precision. He had passed this quality on to Bernard who executed his desires with all due respect.

Unlike the parties at the Candle mansion, the music here was rather subdued, but tasteful. As the guests mingled enjoying their cocktails it became readily apparent to all by the leading conversation of Jonathan that although this was supposedly a party, there was an agenda that was going to be followed. Around 7:30 when it was clear that all the invited guests were present, Jonathan instructed Bernard to ring the dinner bell and direct the guests to the dining room. It was done and with the guests seated in the order of their importance, according to Jonathan's reckoning, the meal serving was started. Bernard came in first with a serving cart that he parked at the head of the long table. Soon after, Amanda appeared and drew the first of many glances. She went to the serving cart and as she bent over to fill plates with the first course, exposing a good bit of her lower anatomy, the dinner immediately became more interesting.

Amanda completed serving the first course and stood by the door as Suliah made her entrance pushing another cart with the second course. All of the guests were impressed with the serving presentation made by Amanda, but the men were more dazzled by how she did it. When Suliah came in, it was as if the second act of a unique drama was unfolding. She began serving and placing plates in front of the guests when one of the men made a comment to Jonathan that his choice of help was superb, and he was to be commended on his excellent taste. Jonathan accepted the compliment with a gracious smile and hinted that the services of his help could be made available to serve in a post dinner fashion. For those men who were astute enough to recognize the double meaning in Jonathan's words, a gleam entered into their eyes, as they looked Suliah over more intently. The women at the table, who were also quite aware of his innuendo, looked intently at their husbands as if to provide a warning shot across their bows.

The cook had done a wonderful job in preparing the meal and everybody enjoyed it. At first the mealtime conversation was light ranging from the decor of the house to the latest in fashion trends among the women. But as the meal drew to a close and the guests finished eating, Jonathan launched into the real essence of the gathering. He started out by reminding them about what was taking place even right now in South Carolina regarding the issue of slavery. He was referring to the call for secession from the United States. From there he went on to speak about how slavery in general was going to be affected with this Mr. Lincoln becoming the new chief in the federal government. As he got deeper into his diatribe, the men especially joined in with him taking sides against the portents of freeing the slaves and a possible war coming. There was no denying that slavery was an issue that was going to separate the nation and he wanted to make sure that before it happened Virginia would be in a position to not just survive but to thrive.

"Mr. mayor you've been around here a long time and I'm sure you know how much of a profit the slave trade has brought into your fair city. Would you have that change?"Jonathan said.

"Yes, John I ----,"

"That's Jonathan."

"Yes of course I'm sorry Jonathan, but you're right about the money the city has taken in and no I don't want to see that change. However, if them Yankees are determined to come down and break it all up, are we gonna fight with them?"

"Well gentlemen I ask all of you, and I dare say that most of you have some slaves yourselves, what is it worth to you to maintain your way of life?"

The consensus around the table was that they would fight to keep it.

"There my good mayor, you see that like me most others who have a stake in the matter are willing to lay it all on the line if necessary. But gentlemen what I'm suggesting right now is not to launch a war, but to merely act like the South Carolinians and leave the federal government. That way we can continue to keep our way of life and set up a new government. I understand that there is a Mr. Davis who is willing to lead us along those lines. All I'm asking right now is that you let me get it started by appointing me your official spokesmen to the state legislature. Senator, do you agree with that?"

The state senator concurred with his assessment of the situation and strongly backed Jonathan. After hearing this from the senator, the other men at the table voiced their yeas on the subject and it was decided that on Monday a proclamation would be drawn up to allow Jonathan Adams to represent them. The senator pointed out however that it would have to be signed by a number of people in order for it to be valid. One of the other men, an influential political figure at the local level assured the senator that it would not be a problem. Jonathan sat back in his chair and smiled at having accomplished his goal. While the discussion was going on it didn't occur to any at the table that both Amanda and Suliah were still in the room and overheard everything that was said. Maybe it did occur to them, but they didn't see it as much of any significance. Not only did the two female servants hear the conversation, but standing just outside the dining room, was Bernard the head house servant.

After dinner and the formal conversation was over, the guests left the table and reassembled in the living room for more cocktails. By this time most of them, including the ladies were no longer the sober personalities that came to the house. In some cases, it reached the point where the genteel demeanor was abandoned and the masks were coming off, in others the observant wives were discovering this to be the case and strongly suggested that it was time to leave. The two couples that arrived first to the affair found Jonathan and complimented him on an excellent dinner party and bid goodnight. Shortly after, the other four women with their escorts left leaving just men. The refreshments continued to flow and the man who had been paying particular attention to Suliah all night asked Jonathan about his comment during dinner. He wanted him to elaborate on his after-dinner services statement. The mayor overheard the man and was also interested in the answer.

Jonathan responded by telling them if they would commit themselves to ensuring that he become the state representative, then he would ask the ladies to further entertain them. Without hesitation both men committed immediately and then asked what now? Jonathan looked over at Amanda who was standing by the doorway and motioned her over. When she came to him, he whispered something to her, and she left the room. Jonathan then went over to the mayor and told him to step outside and she would be waiting in the hallway to escort him to her room. The other man excited that he was going to get the other girl couldn't wait for the go-ahead signal. However, when Jonathan called for Suliah and whispered to her what he wanted, she recoiled and stepped away from him. The man saw what happened and his smile turned down. Jonathan apologized to the man told him to wait here, then grabbed Suliah's arm and pulled her into the hallway. There he told her in no uncertain terms that if she wanted to continue to be a part of his house, then she would comply with his wishes. He made sure that she understood if she didn't go along then she would be put back on the block again and sold to a cotton farmer down south. Suliah wasn't sure what the part about the cotton farmer meant, but she had heard from other slaves that in the Carolinas and Georgia and those other southern states, the slaves were treated a whole lot worse than they were here.

She started to cry, but he told her to stop it immediately if she knew what was good for her. Then he softened and told her it would not be so bad and she would get something extra in the morning. He continued with a stern rebuke and told her to stop it right now, Suliah was shaken and a bit frightened, but she composed herself and agreed to his demand. He then led her back into the room and put her hand in the man's hand and they both left the room. On the way to her room, she told the man she wanted to go in by herself for a moment and then she would come back and get him. When she opened the door to the room, the lamp was turned down low, but she could easily see on Amanda's side of the room that her bed was rocking, and she was bent over like a dog while the mayor savagely violated her. Suliah quickly turned around and ran to find Jonathan. He met her in the hallway and asked her what the matter was. When she told him what she wanted, at first, he was going to send her back to her room, but then he remembered there were extra rooms on the third floor one of which was already prepared for unexpected overnight guests. He told her to go up there and make sure it was okay, and he would tell the man to follow shortly. She agreed and turned away.

Moving slowly up the stairs she was trying to figure out a way to get out of what was expected of her. The thought of what Aunt Tee had told her some time ago came to her mind and she wondered if her protection was still with her. Once inside the room, she went over to the bed knelt down beside it and prayed to Aunt Tee's cave spirit. She knew she didn't have Aunt Tee's amulet, so she held the bracelet Jethro had given her hoping that it might have some power. All the while she was kneeling and hoping for some response from the cave spirit via Aunt Tee, miles away someone else was on her knees also. Even though great distances separated them, Bessie May never lost touch with her kindred spirit and whenever a situation arose that threatened one of her godchildren; she felt it. Bessie May called on the name of the Lord and asked His blessing and mercy on her child.

A chill ran down Suliah's spine and she shivered. At first she thought the cave spirit was responding to her call, but when she heard a voice whisper in her ear it was as if someone was in the room talking to her and she was sure it wasn't the cave spirit. The voice said to her:

No one can serve two masters;for either he will hate the one and love the other, or else he will be loyal to the one and despise the other.You cannot serve God and mammon. (Mt. 6:24)

When the voice finished, she got up still not sure what to do, but she knew that worshiping the cave spirit was the last thing she felt she wanted to do. As she started to walk toward the door and go downstairs and get the man, something in her heart compelled her to turn around and get back down on her knees. This time instead of calling on the cave spirit her heart guided her to call on the name of the Lord herself and she did. In her calling she confessed she didn't know what to do and asked for help. There was no response, but she felt comforted with a new feeling of empowerment that ran through her. Again, she got up and this time left the room. The man was still anxiously waiting in the hallway for her and she escorted him up to the room.

Once inside she shyly sat on the bed waiting for him. The man looked at her with such admiration that her beauty awed him. For a long time, he sat beside her just looking at her and she waited for him. Finally, he leaned over to kiss her and started to remove her clothing. She did not resist, but didn't make it easy for him either. He was able to remove her dress and undergarment revealing her magnificent charms but when he got to the last piece of clothing the excitement for him was overwhelming and he embarrassed himself. He was spent before he could initiate the final act. Suliah unsure what she should do just sat there and looked at him. Trying to recover from his embarrassment he told her to wait a few minutes and he would be ready. She didn't say anything, but lie back on the bed staring at the ceiling and he did the same beside her.

When the morning light shone through the window, both Suliah and the man were lying naked next to each other not having engaged in anything but a good night's sleep.

The man apologized to her and asked if he could see her again. Surprised at being asked and not told, Suliah didn't know what to say so she told him she would have to ask Jonathan. The man got up dressed and took a five dollar bill from his wallet and placed it in her hand as he left the room. She continued to sit there looking at the crisp five-dollar bill in her hand and wondered what was becoming of her. She was grateful that nothing happened, but wondered whether the fact that she had called on the name of the Lord had anything to do with it. Her conclusion was still uncertain in her mind, but the one thing she was certain about was Aunt Tee and the cave spirit's protection were gone from her.

At the Candle Plantation the morning after the party, Byron woke up with the feeling that his head was going to explode from the pounding. He tried several times to get up, but fell back on the bed groaning. Charlotte saw his attempts and although she wasn't feeling at her very best either managed to struggle out of bed and make her way to the wash basin. After she was done, she turned to Byron and asked him if he wanted her to bring him a cup of coffee. He thanked her over and over mumbling the last few times. Before she left the room, he did manage to raise himself up to sit on the side of the bed and look out the window. He called to her, as she was about to exit and told her he needed at least a piece of toast with the coffee. She nodded okay and went downstairs. As he sat there looking out the window, he could see by the position of the sun that it was well beyond the time that the rooster should have crowed. He thought to himself, perhaps he did, but he sure didn't hear it.

It was Sunday so down in the quarters the leisurely lifestyle for the day was well underway. However, for Myanna her anxious moments were still with her and getting a good night's sleep had lately become something foreign to her. She tossed and turned most of the time and when she did sleep the dreams that came to her were less than relaxing. Often, she thought of Jobba being caught by the patrols and something bad happening to him. If it wasn't about him then she dreamt about her children being tortured by some unscrupulous master. To top it all off her loneliness was becoming a burden not knowing whether her man was dead or alive. When she worked in the fields, she knew that some of the unattached men were looking at her, but she didn't pay much attention to it. Now as the days of his absence mounted up and her nights grew longer with longing, she wasn't so inattentive to their looks anymore. No one had actually approached her or made any advances, but she could sense that the time was coming when one would. What surprised her most though was that whenever Clarence had occasion to come down to the quarters for one reason or another he always managed to stop by the cabin and pretend to want to speak with Penniman. She became aware by overhearing their brief conversations that whenever he was there he always asked about her when he didn't see her downstairs.

She couldn't imagine herself having anything to do with him for two reasons. First, because he was one of them; and second, he was no replacement for Jobba. However, when he started leaving little things for her like extra food and trinkets over Penniman's objections she had to at least let him know that she was grateful. One day when she was down by the river after the workday ended, staring across to the other side looking for some sign of any activity that would raise her hopes her man was still alive, she felt someone standing behind her and turned around. To her surprise it was Clarence, and he had a gift of almost new bed linen that he commandeered from the mansion. She looked at it and told him she appreciated his thoughtfulness, but couldn't accept it. When he told her he couldn't take it back or he would get punished because no one knew it was gone, they both laughed. It was the first time she had laughed like that in a long time and she looked at him differently as she accepted his gift.

They sat down on the bank and talked for some time without the issue of their religious beliefs ever coming up. She had not talked to any other man on the farm for this long and felt a little strange in spending this kind of time with him. She told him she really missed Jobba and was looking forward to the day when he would come back and get her. Clarence apologized for what he was going to say next, but then he asked her if she was really sure that he had not been caught. When he said that she stopped talking and looked at him then thanked him again for the gift as she got up and started walking back to the cabin. Clarence realized that it was not yet his time, so he got up and followed a few steps behind her, but made sure she heard that he said he was coming back again to see her. She was at her door when he passed by and she paused to see him walking back to the mansion. Although she didn't want it, she found herself thinking about him.

That night in the mansion when the family was sitting around after dinner talking, Jethro mentioned to Byron that he heard more about the war being started. He went on to tell his father that he was thinking about going down to Richmond and finding out really what was going on. Byron asked him what his intentions were, if there was a war. When Jethro responded that he would join the army of the south; Byron almost fell out of his chair. He then asked his son was he out of his mind and then started to explain to him that he needed him to stay here with him should any war break out and help him run this place. For the first time since he was a young kid, Jethro heard his father ask him for something instead of telling him and he thought over his decision. Then after a brief pause, he came back and said that he felt he would be needed more to help defend the whole south, than just one plantation. Byron had to agree with his reasoning, but he still wanted him here with him. Charlotte wanted to intervene in the conversation, but she felt that this was a father-son issue, and it was not for her to weigh in, so she remained silent, as did Anna Lee. When the time came for the family to retire, it had been settled that Jethro would at least go to Richmond to see what was going on.

Sleeping on the damp ground was uncomfortable even with the leaves they gathered to make a simulated mattress, but when the morning came, both Jobba and Shaka felt rested and were ready to resume their journey. When they awoke the sun was still making its ascent in the sky and Jobba reasoned that it must be somewhere around 5 or 6 o'clock. His body fluids were very low caused by all the extra exertion from running yesterday and it cried out to be replenished. When he told Shaka he was thirsty, Shaka joined him in expressing his need for water and the search was on. As they looked for clues by examining the forest vegetation for a stream that could be feeding it, Shaka discovered some foliage that seemed to be thriving more than its surrounding neighbors. He motioned to Jobba to follow him and as they walked up the hill, they could hear the sounds of running water like a waterfall. When they reached the top and peered over the ridge there was the relief they sought. A waterfall issuing clear water cascaded down the mountain on its way to the river. Each man jumped for joy as they ran to the stream and jumped in it even before drinking.

Feeling refreshed from both bathing and drinking the water they stepped out of the stream and went back to the spot where they slept and looked for their guide bird. Once again it was nowhere in sight. They walked in circles widening with each rotation as they looked up at each tree trying to spot the sparrow. Wanting to move on and complete the journey the anxiety started to build up in Jobba and his frustration mounted. Neither man had any idea where they were. To complicate matters, being in the middle of a vast forest they didn't even know how to return to where they came from. Disappointed and angered with no sense of which direction they should go, they sat down and tried to figure out what to do next. Not long after they concluded that they were totally lost they heard the sounds of many birds chirping overhead and they looked up. At the front of the wedge was the orange-breasted sparrow leading the pack.

The birds circled the area once and then disbanded and flew off in different directions except for the sparrow that perched on a tree just above the pair. The men looked up at the bird and waited for some sign to restart their journey, but the bird just sat there. Jobba wasn't sure now what the bird was waiting for or even if it was going to continue to lead them. He stood up and waved his arms as if to get the sparrow's attention, but the bird ignored him and continued to sit. Shaka looked at Jobba flapping his arms and asked him if he was trying to fly up to the bird, Jobba laughed so hard that he doubled over. Moments later the sparrow left its perch and flew around for a minute before heading off in a new direction. Jobba and Shaka scrambled to get a good view and took off running after it. They hadn't run that long when Jobba noticed they were getting very near to a main road because he could hear the sound of horses and wagons moving along.

They kept running, but got so close to the forest edge that they could see the road and the wagon traffic that was traveling on it. Jobba was afraid that the bird was leading them too close to the road not to be discovered so he stopped just in front of Shaka. Not prepared for the sudden stop, Shaka ran right into him just like before and they both fell down. While lying on the ground Jobba looked out through the trees and could see a patrol group riding close behind one of the wagons. Shock ran through his body, and he didn't want to get up, but the bird was continuing to fly and he knew that if they were going to reach their destination he'd better keep going too. He got up and resumed running, but making sure that he kept well enough behind the tree line to not be discovered. About a half-hour later the bird perched on another tree that was very close to the forest edge. This time when Jobba peeked out through the trees he saw a sign on the road with some writing on it.

Although Jobba couldn't read Shaka had some reading skills and was able to determine that the sign was pointing to the town of Richmond.

Jobba wanted to get closer to the edge so he could get a better look at what was down the road, but he was afraid of running into some more patrols. Shaka was more courageous and told Jobba he would go out and look. He did so and for a few minutes stood right in the middle of the road peering at what was ahead. When he returned to Jobba he was excited when he told him that he could see the buildings of the town and it wasn't that far away. Jobba shared his excitement and both men ran back deeper into the forest happy that they knew exactly in what direction they had to go. It was good that they had this knowledge now because when they looked for the bird again, it was gone. Jobba said to Shaka that it didn't matter because in a short time they would arrive at where they wanted to be. Jobba had been running for so long the thought hadn't occurred to him about what he was going to do when he got in the town. Now as both men closed in on its borders, the issue surfaced.

Neither man had an idea about what it was that they were going to do once inside the town, but the joy of just getting there was enough to keep them going for a while. As they neared the outskirts of Richmond, they came across a few little farms that were just off the main road outside the forest. They decided to keep low in the trees until it started to get dark then they would approach one of them. For the rest of the day, they hunted food and observed the goings on in the farm that they set their sights on. It appeared that it was just a group of slaves working this farm and there were no overseers or any other white people anywhere around. When the time came and the sun was setting, the pair advanced toward the farm creeping very low as to keep out of sight before wanting to be discovered. Once they were inside the cornfield the stalks were high enough to conceal them while they got closer to the farmhouse. On the other side they came out just outside the house and could see two men and a woman sitting on the porch.

Again, they looked very closely for an overseer or a master, but saw neither. From the way that these slaves were just sitting casually on the porch Jobba wondered just what kind of master they had. He decided to get up and make himself known by walking directly up to the porch. Just as he got there the door opened and another man came out with a shotgun pointed at Jobba. He stopped short and raised his hands while hollering out who he and Shaka were and telling the group that he needed their help. The man with gun lowered it and came closer to Jobba and Shaka. He walked around both men perhaps looking to see if either had a weapon then told them to come up on the porch and sit. The family explained that they were free sharecroppers and didn't belong to nobody and this was their piece of the land. When Jobba and Shaka heard this, it reminded them of the first house they stopped in and were treated very well. The family invited them in and asked whether they were hungry.

Inside was another woman and five kids in all different age ranges the oldest being about twelve.

The family asked the pair just what they were going to do in the town and when neither had an answer they were told that their help could be used right here until harvest time came. Since they had no idea what it was, they were going to do, Jobba looked at Shaka and they agreed to work the farm until they could find out more about this Richmond town and what it had to offer. Around back of the house was a large barn in which Samson the eldest brother told Jobba and Shaka that they could make themselves a home there. The pair finished eating and then went to the barn to do as Samson suggested - make them a home. Besides the usual farm animals, two horses, a mule and a cow there was plenty of room inside and they ran straight to the hayloft and fell down in it rolling over and over delighted they had found someplace to stay.

Days went by and Jobba and Shaka, although they had not yet actually gone into the town, were learning a lot about it from their hosts and they were getting comfortable. The more they heard about the slave auctions and how some of the people in the town were against it, the more they wanted to know about this war they had heard about. Samson told them that he overheard some of the white people talking about the whole state leaving the United States and starting their own Confederate government. Jobba asked him what he thought of this Mr. Lincoln the new President. Samson responded that if he was going to set all of his brothers and sisters free, then he was all right with him. Jobba also asked him about the Underground Railroad he had heard about. Samson gave him a puzzled look and asked why he wanted to know. When Jobba told him about his wife still on a plantation up further north and how he wanted to go back and get her, Samson sympathized with him and started to tell him all he knew about the conductor who was in this area. Jobba's hopes were extremely heightened, and he couldn't wait to start planning how he was going to complete his overall plan.

All over the state in one county after another people were talking about what was happening since the Presidential election and what affect it was going to have on them. For most the thought had already crossed their minds, knowing that South Carolina had already seceded from the United States that Virginia should join with them in this new proposed confederacy. The word had quickly spread about Jonathan Adams the brash young man who was gaining immense popularity in Richmond as being a strong leader and worthy of the position of state Representative. His recommendation to secede was widely supported and when the skirmish broke out in the northern part of the state, more were in favor of war than were against it. The number of uprisings and rebellions were increasing as more and more slaves got wind of what was happening and the rumors about Lincoln freeing them immediately abounded.

Patrols on the highways and other main roads also increased. It got to the point where these hunters were not only searching the highways, but were going from farm to farm to challenge the legitimacy of those colored folk who claimed they were free. If they couldn't produce the proper papers, they were immediately declared runaways and hauled off to the over burgeoning jails in the city. When Samson was in town one day loading his wagon after purchasing some supplies at the general store, several of the hunters came up to him and demanded to see his papers. Most of the people around the store knew whom he was from having seen him come and go many times. But this time the challengers were not the local patrollers, but was a group hired by the mayor, from another county to help keep a lid on the rebellions. Samson produced his papers and waited for the lead man to approve it while one of his brothers waited in the wagon. The lead man finished with Samson then turned to his brother demanding to see the same from him. Unfortunately, his brother not suspecting anything like this to occur had not brought his papers with him. The lead man hollering, "I got one" yanked the brother called Zeke from the wagon and started to haul him off to the lock up, when Jonathan saw what was happening.

Jonathan was a supporter of slavery and wanted to maintain its existence, but was not one to unfairly dispose of those darkies, as he referred to them, who had been freed legitimately. He recognized Samson as a man he had seen often in the town and was aware that he had the recognition by many as a free man and came over to the lead patroller. The patroller didn't know who he was, but judging from the way he was dressed, it was clear that he was not part of the riffraff that frequented the streets, so the hunter asked him who he was. By this time the sheriff had heard the commotion and came running down the street when he saw that Jonathan was involved. He stepped between the men and stood in the face of the hunter demanding to know what he was doing with this man. The patrolman, not wanting to cross swords with the sheriff explained that he had found a runaway and was doing what he was hired to do. When Jonathan told the sheriff that the man was not a runaway and he would vouch for him, that was all the sheriff needed and he told Samson to take his stuff and get on his way.

The patroller was angered at his authority being overridden in front of the townsfolk who had gathered when the commotion started and vowed, he would get that nigger the next time he saw him. He walked away slowly along with his companions and went straight to the tavern. Samson overheard his declaration and wondered if this wasn't going to be the start of something he would have to keep alert for. When he got back to his farm, he told everybody there what had happened and that he would not be surprised if the patrols didn't start coming out there to look around. This put Jobba and Shaka on high alert and they wondered what would happen to them if they got caught.

Jonathan had gained a strong following among the townsfolk and was recognized by many in the state legislature. His ambition to gain a foothold in the highest levels of the government was coming to fruition and he was having much success in managing his affairs. An army recruiting station had been set up in the town and he was monitoring all who came to join. He was impressed when a young man by the name of Jethro came in one day and expressed his desire to want to join and listed among his reasons as being a staunch supporter of the southern way of life and did not want to see it change. Jonathan took an interest in the young man and told him that after he finished his training, he would like to have him come back here and talk with him about possibly getting involved in politics. Jethro was thrilled, although he really didn't know who this man was, but from the way that the rest of the officers and enlisted men in the station treated him, he knew that he must be somebody of tremendous importance. He accepted his invitation without the least hesitation and promised that once he completed his training he would come right back here.

The number of recruits volunteering to join the confederate army was growing at a rapid pace and even some former slaves came in to register. The slaves walking around the streets outside the station couldn't believe what they saw and the talk about what was happening ran rampant through the dark side of town. Word came quickly also that troops from up north, the Yankees, were already battling in the state and were moving down with great force. Though they didn't show it outwardly, for the most part the slaves were silently cheering the news and hoping that the move would speed up their path to freedom. In the houses in town those slave owners were becoming more and more uncomfortable with their charges as they continued to hear about slaves running away and even taking their anger out on their masters. It was very unsettling for many and some fearing that they might be harmed, even freed their charges and told to leave the house. Others, especially the farmers who could not afford to lose the help that was essential to their business success, put a tighter rein on them and made sure that they were well armed inside their farm houses.

After Jethro enlisted, he was given two days to go home and get his business in order before having to report back to the Richmond station. He got on his horse and headed home with due speed wanting to tell his father the great news he got from some higher up in the office. He was sure that Byron would be pleased that he had already made a good impression. At the time that Jethro first left to come here, Byron had not fully reconciled himself to the fact that he was actually going to do what he said, but the day he left it became all to real for him and he was saddened by the fact. Charlotte couldn't believe that her son was going off to war, but she was content in accepting that he was becoming a man, and this was what her young man wanted to do. She kissed him goodbye and told him that as soon as he finished helping to whip them Yankees and send them running back home, he should come back here and get married. Anna Lee too was surprised that her brother was so spirited about the war and anxious to get involved. She always knew that he had deep thoughts about a lot of things, but most of the time he never acted upon them. Now that he was moving on something he felt strongly about she was both proud, but confused by his sudden call to action.

Byron was standing outside on the porch when he saw Jethro galloping his horse up the main road toward the house. At first Byron thought it was one of the patrol guys, who had been coming by there a lot lately because of the runaways spotted in the area, but then as the man got closer, he could see that it was one of his horses and the rider was his son. His heart started to beat a little faster when he recognized that his relationship with his son was deeper than he wanted to admit. The closer Jethro got the more excited Byron became in anticipating all that his son would tell him about his latest adventures. He arrived at the house and in all his excitement jumped off the horse before he came to a full stop and started to fall but caught himself. As he staggered toward the porch rushing to greet his father, Byron laughed, and Jethro also laughed at what appeared to be a comedy of errors. Reaching his father's arms, he hugged him tightly and both went into the house laughing. Charlotte who was in the living room heard the laughter and came running out to see her son. Jethro separated from Byron and ran to his mother putting his arms around her and kissed her cheek. She was so glad to see him that she couldn't wait for him to tell her all about his trip.

It was still a little early for dinner, but Charlotte hollered out to Aunt Tee who was out on the back porch peeling potatoes that Jethro was home, and she would like to eat a little earlier. Aunt Tee heard her and came running in the house herself to see the young man and he embraced her too. She responded to Charlotte that she would start preparing a great dinner right now and then disappeared into the back of the house. Clarence who was also nearby, heard the commotion and came in to see what all the fuss was about. When he saw Jethro, he too was glad to see him, and they hugged. The family went into Byron's parlor and sat down when Jethro asked where his sister was. Charlotte cleared her throat first and then said proudly that Anna Lee was being courted by one of the newer plantation owners and she had gone to meet with the family and should be returning tomorrow. Byron sat back in his easy chair and laughed at the news saying he didn't think she could be interested in any of those boys, as she called them. They spent the rest of the afternoon listening to Jethro's tales about his trip and Byron telling him all that had been happening right here at home.

Dinnertime came and the family moved into the dining room where Jethro continued to spin his yarn about his adventures. He came to the part where he was telling them about this man he met called Jonathan

Adams. Byron interrupted and asked him whether this was the same man that was the state representative. Jethro responded that he thought he was one and the same, but he wasn't absolutely sure but he was definitely somebody important to the army.

"Well son, thats somebody ya needs to get to know real good. He can help you get yourself going even afta this war."

"Yeah I think so daddy. He even told me that when I finish my training I should come back to him and he said he would talk to me about some politics."

"He told you that for real?"

"Yeah daddy, that's what he said. Now I dono what he meant by politics, but I think its got something to do with his part in the government."

"You hear that Charlotte, my boy's gonna be one of them politicians and run this here state. What do ya think about that?"

"Byron now don't be jumpin' all ahead of things. You don't even know what this Mr. Adams was referring to. He must know that Jethro is still too young to get into all that mess, especially now that there's a war comin'.'"

"I dono about all that, but if the man got good eyes he cain see that this boy got potential an he's gonna make a pretty good soldier."

"Well thank you daddy, I'm gonna try to be the best that I can be and make you real proud."

"I'm already proud son. You're doing the right thing and I don't think this whole mess gonna last too long before them Yankees get all tired of being away from home an turn around and go there. From what I hear they're already losin that battle in the north part of this state."

They continued talking in the dining room well after the meal was finished and didn't even bother to retire to the living room for their usual after dinner cordials. For the first time in a long time Byron felt at ease with his son. He kept the conversation light and never got around to telling him how much the tension on the outside of the house had escalated to near rebellion among the slaves and he was doing all he could to keep the lid from blowing off the kettle. He wanted Jethro to go and do his duty without having to bear the extra burden of worrying about how the slaves could be threatening his family. Jethro told his father he had two more days to spend with him before he would be gone off for his training so he wanted to enjoy it with him for as long as he could.

Back at the Samson farm just outside the city Jobba and Shaka had really made a home for themselves and were enjoying the hospitality of the Sandlers. Whenever they had dinner together Jobba would make sure that he told them how he longed to go back and get his wife and go up north and get free. Samson and his brothers encouraged him by telling him that soon they would help him get in touch with the conductor who could get him passage on the train going up north. But they asked him how he was going to get his wife away from the plantation. Jobba had to laugh when asked because that part he hadn't figured out yet. Shaka also expressed his desire to get on this train whatever it was and get up north and be free. He then told his story about not being born on a plantation but being brought here by the big ship that carried him across the waters. The Sandlers were glad to hear his story and were very interested to hear about how things were in the motherland.

After they had talked for a good while Samson reminded them about his encounter with the patrolman in town the other day and how the man seemed to be driven to find Zeke. By now he was sure that the man had found out where he lived, and it wouldn't be long before one of them or all of them might be riding out here. Jobba asked Samson about what weapons he had, and Samson responded that all he had was that one shotgun and only a few shells. It wasn't easy for him to get ammunition because no one wanted to sell it to him. The way he got these few was through the town blacksmith who was a friend of his, but he couldn't make many for him without getting caught. Jobba told him that he would help him defend his house in whatever way he could, should that time come. Shaka also pledged his allegiance to the cause and said he would also help.

The next day it was almost as if Samson had had a premonition, when late in the afternoon the dust from many horses riding down the main road could be seen far in the distance. Samson, his brothers, the women and both Jobba and Shaka were busy tending to the fields when they first spotted the dust clouds. Samson yelled at the group saying there would be no reason for anyone to be riding that hard to come here unless it was those patrollers. Jobba and Shaka put their tools down immediately and took off for the barn. Samson went inside to get his gun, but his wife told him that she didn't want him to get shot because there were too many of them with more guns than he had. He listened to her and just waited until they arrived.

It wasn't long before the group of about six men rode up to the farmhouse and dismounted. The same man that had confronted Zeke in town called to him to come over to him. Zeke didn't move but asked him from where he was standing, what he wanted. The leader got real indignant and told Zeke if he didn't come over to him right now he was going to put a bullet in his leg. While the rest of the men surrounded the family, Zeke slowly walked over to the man.

"Now I dun tol you b'fo I wanna see yo papers sayin you is free. Now yo go an git 'em."

Zeke started to go inside the house to get his papers, when one of the other men came right up behind him and followed him in. Zeke found the papers and showed them to the man inside who took them and brought them out to the leader. The leader read the document and was disappointed to see that his former owner had emancipated the man. Not satisfied at getting his pleasure fulfilled he told Samson he wanted to look around this farm anyway to see if he ain't hiding some others here. Samson tried not to show any emotion when he told the man there wasn't anybody else here. The man ignored him and started walking around back toward the barn.

Jobba and Shaka were inside and had no idea that the men were coming around so when the barn door opened, they were sitting on the hayloft on the second level. The first man to come in was looking on the first level and Jobba spotted him. He was sitting in a position to be seen, but he knew now that if he moved the noise would clearly give him away. Shaka was seated beside him and both men froze. Three men were walking around the lower-level sticking forks in the bales of hay on the ground when one of them looked up. Both Jobba and Shaka jumped up and scrambled down the ladder on the barn's back side and ran out when the three men opened fire. The shots rang out and the other three who were still at the front of the house came running around back. Jobba and Shaka were able to exit the barn and were headed into the woods that were about fifty yards away. All the patrolmen came together, and the chase was on. In a hurry as they lifted their guns there was a barrage of bullets sent flying in the direction of the running men.

Running as fast as he could Jobba could feel the breath leaving his body as he stumbled and was going to the ground quickly. He didn't feel like he had been hit, there was no pain, and he didn't see any blood, but there was something definitely wrong. He looked around to see if Shaka had passed him and got to the woods, but he didn't see him. He started to close his eyes and accept his fate when as he was about to give up hope, a strange thing happened.

Chapter 10 - Escalation and Depression

From the rising of the sun to the going down of the same, each time the cycle repeated, the news of uprisings and rebellions spread all over the state. There were few farms or plantations that remained unaffected by the turmoil. Whether there were work gangs of thirty or more or just a few farm laborers, the spirit of wanting to be free permeated all counties in the state and the slaves relished the thought. When news was available about the Yankee incursion into their territory, no matter how hard slave owners tried to suppress it and keep their charges from hearing any, the news always seemed to reach them. Owners, especially those whose methods were so severe that their slaves were just waiting for ways to turn the tables, were now waking up each morning fearing that something bad was going to happen. Often it did. In many cases where slaves had not rebelled before, it was because they believed that there was nothing for them to fight for. But now that the possibility of being free was supported by force of arms coming from an army that had declared war on the very essence of the southern way of life with regard to them, it made sense to participate in advancing their own cause.

Not only were slaves rebelling against their owners, but were also running off the plantations and seizing town establishments. Gun shops were looted, general stores ransacked, and a general state of panic was present in many of the smaller towns where the militia and patrols had gone off to fight the war leaving the towns unprotected. The imminent threat of the union army making its way down the center of the state had called the less than wealthy volunteers and the sons of the wealthy to join with the confederate soldiers to try and prevent their advances. To the slaves this was a golden opportunity to leave the places where they had been chastised, brutalized, raped, emasculated and otherwise downgraded from the status of human being. Although the majority favored rebellion, there were also many who defended the masters out of fear that the rumors flying all about were just that, unsubstantiated truth.

When many of them assaulted their masters and took hold of as many possessions as they could carry in their flight, the roads became saturated with the runaways and the patrols had all they could handle trying to regain control. Shootings on the main roads were no longer a one-sided affair with the patrols consistently having the upper hand. Now as slaves gained access to weapons including muskets, rifles, pistols and ammunition for them, the patrols who had not volunteered for army duty and were left to try and maintain some form of dominant order found themselves fighting a war anyway. Slaves had generally taken to the roads, but for many of them traveling in the forest was a better way for them to fight. The forests had become rife with roving bands of fleeing servants whose destination was to get to the town of Manassas where they could join up with the Yankee army.

As more and more rebellions occurred and slaves took to traveling in the back woods, often they would come close to the farms of their free brothers who gave them temporary food and shelter and wished them well as they supported the cause. Such was the case at the Sandler farm which saw the fleeing Jobba and Shaka running for their lives from the hired predators that sought to originally claim Zeke as their prey. The predators were redirected when Zeke was able to confirm his free man status. Undeterred with their mission to find something or someone, the patrollers began searching the whole farm. Eventually they searched the barn and discovered Jobba and Shaka who immediately took flight headed into the woods.

Jobba, who thought he had been hit, started falling and when his eyes saw the ground rushing up at him in an effort to avert the impact of hitting his head, he turned at the last minute and was able to fall on his back. He was almost completely out of breath and was surprised at himself because not too long ago he had run for miles and not felt this kind of fatigue in such a short period. Then he remembered that at that time while running chasing that bird, his diet had been completely different. What he and Shaka ate in the forest then was mostly berries and some fish. Now that he had spent some time in the quasi opulence of the Sandler house and enjoyed the fat laden cuisine, he realized why he was out of breath. Even today not too long ago he had for breakfast, in addition to his heaping portion of bacon and eggs, he ate the fatback that had been placed alongside. Not having time to fully digest the meal before his body was commanded to perform at a high level it was reacting to the undigested load and stealing his breath with a vengeance.

The patroller's shots continued to fly over his head and his resignation to wait for the one that would claim his life was in effect. But then a strange happening interrupted his concession. At first he was slightly confused and while lying with his head still down, he became thoroughly confused. For now, the shots seemed to be coming from the opposite direction. When he heard several more seeming to come from that same direction, he recovered himself enough to raise his head up to look. What he saw got the better of him and he had to laugh even in the midst of this trial. The rebels who were roaming the woods just behind the Sandler farm had heard the patrol shots and approached the clearing to see what was happening. When they saw Jobba running and the patrols in hot pursuit, they responded by firing their own volley and hitting two of the pursuers. The hunters were so stunned by seeing a bunch of runaways coming out of the woods armed with as many guns as they had, they picked up their fallen comrades threw them on their horses and raced off down the road. Jobba got to his feet and continued with a hearty belly laugh for several minutes until it occurred to him that Shaka was nowhere around.

After this discovery, he stopped laughing and started calling out for his companion. The rebels who had fired the shots approached Jobba and asked him whom he was calling for. Jobba told them and they joined in. A short time later Shaka appeared coming out of the cornfield and he was as surprised to see Jobba still alive, as Jobba was to see him period. Shaka told him that he thought hiding in the cornfield was a better idea than running to the woods with no covering. When Jobba thought about what he said and realized he was absolutely right, he told his friend he hadn't given that idea any thought because his legs were doing all the thinking. Again, he laughed and this time the whole group joined in for a moment of peace in the midst of the storm.

The few days that Jethro had spent away from home totally on his own for the first time had given him an opportunity to see how people lived who didn't have the advantages he did. In Richmond he saw an assorted batch of men who ran the gamut from the slick gambler who spent most of his time in the tavern making a living in a sordid way to the high-class genteel statesman like Mr. Adams who showed him a different type of class from his father. His experiences helped him to appreciate his upbringing and now that he was back home, he couldn't remember when he had a better time since he was a little boy. Conscious that the time was growing short until when he had to leave to return to Richmond, he was making the best of what he had left. He gorged himself with Aunt Tee's cooking and even drank more than he should of Byron's nectar.

Now that it was time to go, he was having trouble saying goodbye to all of them and with the knowledge he could be gone for a long time he became a bit melancholy. Byron too was choking up as Jethro got on his horse and Charlotte along with Aunt Tee and Clarence had gone speechless. The silent moments were filled with emotion until Charlotte broke the spell and came to the horse to give Jethro one last goodbye kiss. He leaned down to kiss her and almost fell off the horse. For a minute, that lightened the tension. Recovering quickly, he sat back up and turned the horse away starting his journey. As he rode down the path leading to the main road the family waved goodbye and bid him a safe journey. For a long time they remained there watching until he was completely out of sight then they slowly returned to the mansion. He never did get to see Anna Lee who was detained at her suitor's place for reasons unknown at this time.

Jethro hadn't been riding more than fifteen minutes on the main road when he saw a bunch of patrollers coming in the opposite direction riding hard and moving fast. He pulled up to see whether they were running from something or in pursuit of someone, but when they passed him, he was able to discern neither. Once passed him they continued riding hard and he wondered what in the world could they be riding so fast to do?

The answer came to him in a flash as a column of soldiers in blue uniforms came galloping along. He was shocked to see union soldiers this close to his father's house and he wasn't sure whether to continue his trip or turn around and go back and help defend his land. Then he remembered the conversation he and Byron had on the night he said he was going to join and about fighting in the army would be for the greater good. Considering this, he prompted the horse to pick up the pace, for his desire to get to Richmond had intensified.

The rest of the time since that little incident, he spent riding without so much as seeing one other rider on the road. When he reached the city he saw there were a lot more confederate soldiers walking around the streets and he wondered if anything had happened here since he left. Arriving at the recruiting office the first thing he asked was if there had been any action here. The desk sergeant receiving him picked up on the earnest sincerity of his inquiry and interpreted it as a strong desire to get into some action.

"I like your spirit son what's the name?"

Almost out of breath from anxiously running inside to ask his question, Jethro responded: "I'm Jethro Candle from Fairfax County reporting for duty suh."

"Well come on in and sit down Jethro from Fairfax County. Let me find your paperwork here so I know where to send ya. We need more good boys like you to come on in and volunteer with the right spirit. Ah, here it is. Look like you gonna be going down right where the action is alright. You're going down to Fortress Monroe that's right in the Tidewater country where them Yankees done hold up. Our boys just took over that fort after a long battle so they can train you good there before them Yankees try to come back in. You go on over to the hotel where the quartermaster is set up an he gonna git you fitted up all nice and pretty with a real uniform. Then come on back here and you and the rest of those boys over there can start gettin ready to ride down there. Tell them otha boys waitin' 'round there they kin come back now too cause there's enough of y'all to get ta ridin."

Jethro took the papers from the sergeant and headed toward the hotel. He stepped inside and at first he saw several men dressed in gray uniforms standing and sitting in the lobby. Next, he noticed that most of them were in their mid to late twenty's. As he scanned the room for anyone who might be close to his age, he finally came across a young man sitting in the corner by himself who appeared to be. He started toward the youth but then saw the sign indicating that the quartermaster was on the second floor, so he turned and started up the stairs. Figuring that he would get that done and then try to strike up a conversation with the other young man, he bounded up the stairs two at a time. There were three others in line in front of him waiting to get fitted, but none of these was near his age either. He wondered if this is what the confederate army was made up of.

His turn came at the head of the line and the quartermaster told him to get up on a little platform so he could measure his feet first. Jethro complied and the quartermaster hollered out to a group of soldiers standing in another room: "Size 11 comin' in." The quartermaster then measured the rest of him, and he was given a slip of paper to take to the men in the other room. When he got in the room, he learned why the shoe size was given in advance. It seemed that boots were in sparse supply and extra time was needed to find the right size. As he walked through the line, he was handed a stack of clothes and told to go into another room and put them on. Excitement was starting to build up as he grasped the uniform. Feeling a sense of pride, he rushed to the room where several other men were trying on their new clothes. Jethro started fumbling impatient to get his on and some of the others laughed when they saw him put his pants on backwards. Rushing to correct his mistake he reddened embarrassed that he had been seen.

Once he was fully dressed properly and with his ill-fitting boots on he went and stood in front of the full-length mirror. He smiled a broad smile as he peered at himself standing there looking like a real soldier in the confederate gray coterie. He started to walk back in the main room when he felt the discomfort of his new boots. Unable to walk right he tried to get back to the quartermaster to let him know his problem but when he went to approach the counter; he was redirected by another soldier. He tried pleading his case to the soldier, but was told about the short supply and what he received was what he was going to get. Jethro took the boots off and made his way back downstairs to try and figure out what to do. He went over to where he saw the young man about his age and started talking to him. The other young man was glad he came over because he was sitting there frightened about what was going to become of him. He had not volunteered, but was told by his father, a staunch confederate, what his son should do. Jethro felt a little sympathy for the boy, but right now he had his own problem.

When he sat down in the chair next to him with his boots in his hand, he told his story. The other young man had no solution for him and told Jethro that his boots fit okay, but his jacket was way too big. Sitting not far away one of the older recruits heard their conversation and came over. He looked at both young men and with a kind of fatherly admonition told them this war wasn't about how good their uniforms fit, but they needed to get them foreigners off their land. Jethro who was still holding his boots in his hand looked up at the man and responded: "How am I gonna fight anybody an I caint even walk in these?" and he held up the boots. The older soldier took the boots looked for a minute at them then started twisting them and scrunching them up and bending them down. He did this for several minutes then handed them back to Jethro and told him to put them back on and walk up and down the aisle. Jethro put the boots on and did as he was instructed. He couldn't believe the difference. It was as if the man gave him a new pair. He walked a few steps and then started strutting feeling the new comfort of his boots. He thanked the man who then walked away and sat back down with his older group.

Jethro sat back down also and then remembered the instructions he had been given by the sergeant. He immediately jumped up and went to the hotel desk to ask that an announcement be made to get the men to go back down to the recruiting station. The desk clerk complied, made the announcement and the new recruits left for the station. In all there were about fifteen of them. At the station, the sergeant gave them further instructions about what was going to happen next. He told them they would be going down to Fortress Monroe, right outside of Hampton, where they would be given military training and issued weapons and a horse. Further, he went on to say that there was real fighting going on there and it was possible some of them might get a chance to see some action. Jethro, when he heard this had mixed emotions about the matter. On one side he felt that his desire was being fulfilled, while on the other he was for the first time thinking about the reality of war and its consequences.

Outside the station all the recruits got into a large extended wagon being pulled by a team of four horses. Jethro and his newfound friend about his age sat in the very front while the group of older men filled in the rear. Jethro, sitting opposite him, could see the fear in his friend's face and he tried to assure him that everything was going to be all right. The young man was obviously frightened, and no amount of talking was going to give him courage, but Jethro told him to try and relax because when they reached the fort he may not even have to fight. The young man heard Jethro's words and perked up for a second as he asked: "You think I might not have ta go fight?" Jethro, happy to see the man cheer up just a little, responded: "Well I don't really know, but they caint have everybody on the front line now can they? Who gonna take care a the supplyin'?" The young man listened intently to these words and relaxed a bit.

The wagon was fully loaded with men and supplies when the driver snapped the reins and the horse team moved forward. Little space was left in the wagon and the ride was bumpy and uncomfortable. Jethro had no idea how far Hampton was from Richmond, but listening to the older men he was able to gather that they were going to be riding for a few hours. He kept looking at his new friend trying to determine whether this young man was going to make it. After the earlier conversation it seemed that he was relaxed, but the longer they rode the more he seemed to be getting anxious again. There was nothing more Jethro could say to him that he hadn't already said so he decided to try and get a short nap himself. He pulled his hat down over his face and drifted off.

It wasn't long before he heard voices shouting. The wagon was approaching the gate to Fortress Monroe and the exchange between the driver and the tower guard was taking place. Once inside Jethro woke his friend up who had really gone into a deep sleep. As they pulled up to the main office and were told to get down, he could see that there were many well-dressed soldiers walking around with rifles and pistols and bayonets. He was impressed and ready to get with them. He looked over at one end of the fort and saw there was a group of younger looking men like himself and his buddy marching in a column being led by a sergeant shouting orders at them. This is the training, he thought to himself, that he was expecting. He got down from the wagon and responding to the driver's commands he lined up with the rest of them and waited for further instructions. A few minutes later a man came out with a neat fitting uniform with no stripes on it. Jethro assumed he must be an officer of some kind so he stood as tall and straight as he could. The answer to his question was given immediately as the well-dressed man identified himself as Captain Montague the commander of the fort. He told them that once they got assigned to their barracks, they were to fall in right back here to start training.

The captain went on to explain being here was not going to be a picnic because they were right in the heart of a battle zone and the sooner, they learned how to be soldiers, the better their chances of surviving would be. Jethro glanced over to see his friends face and again he saw the fear rise up. When the captain finished, the men were led to a long building down at the far end of the fort and inside were many rows of double bunk beds. The sergeant who had walked them over to the barracks told them to grab a bunk put their personal stuff down on it and then fall back in outside. His yell prompted the men to move quickly, and they each found a bed. Jethro and his friend located a bed right in the middle of the room and Jethro chose to take the top bunk. They tossed their personal things down and ran to form up outside. Once lined up, the sergeant told them the first thing they had to learn was how to move together as a group, so he gave them their first lesson on marching. As a test to see how they responded, he marched them over to the mess hall and then around the rest of the fort.

By the time nightfall came Jethro felt like he had marched far enough to be back home and his first experience with loading and firing a rifle was one he would never forget. He had eaten in the mess hall with some of the older experienced troopers and they had no mercy on initiating him into the army ways. His friend was persevering better than he thought he would and to his surprise he seemed to be enjoying the training. During the dinner meal he even responded well to the verbal abuse meted out by the veterans and was eager to do whatever they told him to. He was fine until some of the men started talking about battles, they had encountered and then he went silent. At bedtime, just after taps had sounded and the lamps were extinguished, he confided in Jethro that he was really scared to go outside the fort into battle. There was nothing Jethro thought he could say to help him, so he didn't even try.

On a small farm just outside the town of Hampton between the city and the fort the slave owner who had purchased Linwood and a few other men at the Richmond auction was having difficulty controlling them. Even though it was a small farm this master had been a ruthless slave driver and used the whip as his method of keeping order. Even Linwood who came there with the notion of being able to function as a quasi-overseer like he was becoming on the Candle Plantation had been lashed repeatedly. For some of the smallest infractions of the master's law the men were beaten. The few women, who were also listed as his possessions, had been subjected on a rotating basis to being raped and abused. Now that word had spread around the state about slaves on other farms rebelling and taking control, Linwood's master was afraid it was going to happen to him and armed himself and his one overseer heavily.

Each day saw the master and his overseer looking at the slaves more carefully and not hesitating in the least to issue punitive corrections, whether justified or not. At night, the master would lock his doors and bolt them while he slept with his pistol at his bedside. His family of a wife and two young children also were in fear of what they heard was happening around the area and even the word that Yankee soldiers had invaded their land. Linwood, who was a natural leader, had become the spokesmen for the workers and they were ready to move at his command on any rebellion that he thought could work. Linwood who was well aware of what was going on in the area was trying to keep from resorting to rebellion, but the more the master was fearful the more he treated his slaves like animals.

One day as the slaves were tilling the soil they looked up and in broad daylight a group of runaways were coming onto the land bearing guns and making their way toward the house. Linwood spotted them first and he stood up. The overseer saw them next and raised his rifle to fire. Before he could get off one shot, another slave in the field ran up behind him and knocked the rifle from his hand onto the ground. The overseer now paralyzed with fear started to bend down to pick it up when the swift kick from the attacking slave knocked him to the ground and pounced on him. By this time the runaways coming in off the main road had made their way to the fields and surrounded the working slaves. The leader of that pack asked the field workers if they wanted to go with them to join up with the union soldiers nearby. The field workers looked at Linwood for guidance and he said yes, so they went with him.

The master who had been watching from the porch of his house saw what was happening and ran inside. Linwood saw him run and discouraged the runaways from following him. The newly formed coalition then left the farm and headed toward Fortress Monroe to find the Yankees. Little did they know at this time that the confederates had taken the fort.

On the second day when Jethro was awakened at the crack of dawn by the sound of a bugle blowing reveille he was tempted to lie there and ignore the signal. However, when the sergeant came in hollering and screaming for the men to get out of the bed, the decision to continue lying there was immediately changed, and he jumped off the bunk. He hit the floor and hurt his ankle, but hearing the sergeant continue to rain down encouragement, in the fashion of a drill sergeant, he hurriedly put on his uniform and ran outside. He joined the other new recruits and was marched to breakfast. After the morning meal they were formed again and told that they were going outside the fort to sweep the area because some runaway slaves had been spotted. Jethro got excited at the news, and he was ready to go. He felt like this was going to be his first brush with some real action. He tried to locate his friend, but he didn't see him since breakfast ended. Although they sat together for the meal, when it was over his friend said he was going to relieve himself but that was the last time he saw him. Now that the column was getting ready to move out, Jethro's concern mounted when his friend was not in the formation.

The column of two's mounted side by side left the fort and started down the main road headed toward Hampton. Coming from the opposite direction was a sprawled out disorganized group of slaves who had more skills in farming than fighting. The runaways walked alongside the road keeping close enough to the trees so that when they saw anyone coming, they would run into the forest and duck out of sight. However, with the soldiers having extended vision through the use of binoculars the slaves were spotted a long time before they were close enough to the mounted troops to see them. The lieutenant, who was leading the columns, observed the rebels moving on the side of the road about a mile or so in front of them alerted his bugler to sound the alarm. The wily veterans in the group hollered at the young new recruits that their time had come. They soon took the lead and the column started galloping toward the slaves. The road dust that was kicked up could be seen for miles and it alerted the slaves that something was coming. Quickly they left the road and ran into the forest, but it was too late.

Linwood was running right in the middle of them and didn't know which way to turn. He watched the others run helter-skelter in all directions. It wasn't too long before the troops got to the spot where they entered the woods and the soldiers dismounted and started the chase. The sound of gunfire rang through the woods coming from both sides.

Some of the soldiers were surprised at receiving return fire from a group they thought would be an easy capture. When the soldiers realized that they were being fired back at, they scattered and took refuge behind the tall trees as the rebels kept running. Soon the soldiers saw the rebels getting away and they came out from their cover and resumed the chase. Every few steps they paused to fire a volley that went speeding toward their targets, but because of the dense forest not many hits registered. The rebels who turned long enough to get a round or two off had more success than the soldiers and with some random luck hit one of the soldiers. Embarrassed that he took a casualty without any slaves being felled the lieutenant halted the assault and called his men together.

When he assembled his troops, he started bending their ears because of their apparent ineptitude in the chase and warned them if they didn't perform better then he would have them all on report back at the fort. Then he went to the wounded trooper lying on the ground and saw that it was one of the new recruits that had just joined him. Jethro came over and to his surprise it was his friend who he thought had not even made the run. He was lying there with the most frightened look on his face that Jethro had seen him with yet. He was alive, but bleeding profusely. One of the other soldiers who had seen the hit told the lieutenant that the man froze and got too scared to even take cover when the command was given. The lieutenant ordered his wound be treated as best they could and they put him on his horse. Then one of the other men escorted him back to the fort.

Then the order was given to resume the chase at double the speed and the men had better come up with one of them dead or alive or they would hear it from him. Fearing the wrath of the lieutenant the soldiers redoubled their efforts and caught up with several of the runaways as they ran themselves into a dead end at the base of a steep mountain. Jethro was with the group that cornered the rebels and when he got close enough, he recognized one of his former slaves. It was Linwood. Standing about ten feet from him Jethro stopped and stood staring at him. Two other troopers came over and with their rifles raised they were about to shoot when Jethro raised his hands to stop. They lowered their weapons, but wondered why this newby would be halting the action. Jethro started to explain when shots rang out coming from the woods behind the trio and Jethro and one of the other soldiers fell to the ground. Not waiting for other soldiers to arrive the cornered slaves took off into the woods and escaped. Linwood started to run too, but paused hiding behind a tree just long enough to see what the fate of Jethro would be. Other soldiers came quickly and attended to the two downed troopers, but Linwood could see that his former master was badly hurt. When the lieutenant saw this with not one rebel lying on the ground anywhere, he went ballistic, called off the chase and headed back to the fort with his wounded.

The war was really beginning to escalate in several parts of the state and since Richmond was now declared the confederate capitol, activities involving Jonathan were on the rise. More and more clandestine meetings were held at the house and many high-level officials both in and out of the government were in attendance. Matters of secret information were discussed indiscriminately right in front of the servants as if they weren't there. Suliah, Amanda and Bernard took it all in like tape recorders left on permanent record. As they became privy to more information and plans for military action it was for them a matter of how to get the information to the soldiers in blue without getting caught. Jonathan's only slave that had access to the outside world was his driver and none of the other servants trusted him to receive the information they had. They believed he would even turn them in to the master.

At an important meeting one night Jonathan was discussing the issue of slaves leaving the city and joining up with the union army camped right outside their borders.

"Men, it has come to my attention that we have a problem growing right here under our noses. Our own darkies are running off the farms and plantations by night and joining up with those Yankees right outside our gates. What are we going to do about it?"

One of the ranking officials responded: "Jonathan unless we can provide enough of our boys to cover every farm and plantation in this area, there's no way we can keep them from running off. We just don't have the manpower to do that and fight the war too."

"Thank you senator for your astute insight now do you have anything positive to offer."

The snide remark directed by Jonathan at a high-level government official caught some of the others at the table by surprise, but it was well known by now that Jonathan was a man to be reckoned with so even the senator allowed the comment with no retort.

"What we need here is an action plan to either confront the enemy at our doorstep or get these owners to figure out how their charges are getting out at night and do something about it. Now do I hear any suggestions as to how that's going to be done gentlemen?"

The others at the table turned and looked all around at each other, but fearing that they would get the same treatment as the senator, nobody said anything.

"Come, come gentlemen you mean to tell me with the brain trust we have here none of you have any ideas about the matter?"

There was an extended silence for several minutes then one of the local officials stepped up and offered: "Jonathan what we could do is take all available manpower that is not committed to any war action, like those that are over there in the hotel acting as supply people and place them at night at the key points the slaves are using to leave the city. I know just them won't be enough, but we could deputize some of us to help out until we get the upper hand on the matter. What do you think?"

Jonathan listened to the man and paused before answering thinking over the proposal then responded.

"Okay now we're thinking. Let's figure out just how to make that proposal work."

The rest of the night was spent formulating a plan to bolster security on slave exits through town.

When the meeting was drawing to a close, the mayor who was in attendance asked Jonathan if he could enjoy the company of his gals like he did before. Jonathan who was not in a giving mood because of concerns about the war and the fact that he had already gained the status he needed the mayor's support for previously, politely told him: "Not tonight." Disappointed, the mayor looked longingly over at Suliah who was standing by the door, but he left quietly along with all the others. When they were all gone, Jonathan called for Bernard to fix him a toddy that he downed quickly and called for another. A few glasses later he called for Amanda and Suliah to come and sit with him in the parlor where he placed his burdens on them. After unloading his cares, he lowered his head back on the sofa and went to sleep.

Bernard made sure that Jonathan was fully asleep when he called for Amanda and Suliah to meet him in the kitchen. There he told them that it was up to them to get the information they had heard to the union army as quickly as they could. The problem now was to figure out how to do it. On occasion, Suliah would accompany Jonathan into the city, but there was no way to predict when the next time would be. Amanda almost never left the house so as a messenger she was not the right choice. The only time Bernard went to town was when he was going to order and pick-up supplies for the house and then he would be in the company of the driver who would observe him at all times. They sat at the table for almost an hour trying to come up with a plan and it was really getting late. Bernard was about to call it a night when the thought came to him. There was a slave who worked in the livery as a blacksmith who came by the house at least once a week to see if the master needed his services. Often, he would service the horses or bring a replacement for one. Bernard had gotten to know him fairly well so he believed that he could trust him to deliver the message. What made this a good idea was the fact that as a blacksmith he often rode out of town into the surrounding country to either break in a horse or to test a recently shoed one.

Bernard discussed the idea with the women and Suliah's question was what would happen to them if he got caught. Since Bernard was the only one who could read and write, he assured them that it would all be on him. Suliah agreed but she still wasn't comfortable about even him bearing the guilt alone. Amanda then asked Bernard if he had ever trusted this man with anything before. Bernard paused for a minute realizing that this was an excellent question, and the answer was that he hadn't. Then he said to them, we've been trying all night here and came up with nothing so unless there is another way, we have to trust this man. It was agreed then that the next time the blacksmith came Bernard would find a way to get him alone in the house and give him the written message he composed. With that agreement confirmed they said goodnight and retired.

In the morning when Jonathan awoke still fully clothed and lying on the couch, he was embarrassed when his mother came in and saw him. She asked him if he wasn't feeling well, and he responded with a grunt that he was fine and just needed to get himself washed up and ready for today's business. She knew that he was under a lot of pressure with all the new responsibilities he had assumed, but she worried that he was overdoing some things, like drinking. Though she would not address it with him she often told his father, but Jonathan had long ago made it clear that the parents were living in his house and not the other way around so what he did was what he wanted to do.

After getting cleaned up, Jonathan sought Sulia and asked her just what he talked to her and Amanda about last night. Sulia feigned surprise and acted as if she didn't know what he was talking about. He told her he remembered bringing both of them into the parlor and sitting them down, but then he didn't remember much after that. When she responded that he had just talked about the gathering and some of the ways of the people there, he laughed and assumed from the way she said it, that that's what he really did. He told her to go on about her chores and went in to eat breakfast. When Amanda came in to serve him, he looked closely at her and asked the same question. Amanda replied that she fell asleep almost the same time he did and didn't remember what he said. He accepted this and ate his meal.

Jonathan left the house early that day in a hurry to get down to the recruiting station to find out what the latest was on the war activities. When he got there the captain in command filled him in on the latest as far as he knew. Jonathan was made aware that battles were raging all around them and it wouldn't be long before this town would become a major target. Jonathan asked what was being done to fortify it and the captain responded that more troops were being dispatched from Fortress Monroe as soon as they were available. Jonathan then told him about the meeting he had last night and how a plan was developed to stop the local slaves from leaving and joining up with those Yankees. The captain was glad to hear it and thanked Jonathan for his efforts, but he responded that there were a number of slaves who had joined his forces so there may not be as many leaving as he thought. Jonathan thanked him for that information and said he had to get a better handle on what the numbers looked like. The captain told him he would look into getting it for him.

On the same day, it was fortuitous that the blacksmith came by the house and Bernard answered the door. Since Jonathan had already gone out this was the golden opportunity he was waiting for so he guided the man to the kitchen and told him to sit down because he had something real important to tell him. Before revealing his secret, Bernard asked the smithy what his feelings were about the war and the idea of slavery. At first the smithy looked at him curiously to see whether he was being set up, but when he saw the earnest look on Bernard's face, he knew right away that the chief butler and head slave was serious.

"I feels jest like you mus. Ain't nobody s'posed to own no otha man an tells him what ta do alla time. It ain't right now, an ain neva gonna be right. I hear tell dat it's all gonna change real soon cause dat Lincoln man dun got ta be the President an he sendin' his army down here ta do it."

"That's good Luther. I'm glad to hear you feel like that because I have a way for you to help the union army."

"What chu talkin' 'bout man I ain join'n no army - not dere army or dis army."

"No, no Luther you don't have to join the army, but you do have to get close to them. I have a way for you to help the army that's coming to change things like you said. I got some information here in this house that I'm going to give you to take to the officer in charge of the blue army. I know they're right outside the city somewhere between here and Chickahominy and you're the only one of us who can get it there.'

"You mean alls I hafta do is take 'em de message an dey knows what ta do?"

"That's right Luther just get the message to the soldier in charge and he'll know what to do. Will you do it?"

"When I gotta do it?"

"It's very important that it be done as soon as you can ride out there. They need to know this stuff right away. I don't know how long they'll be in that spot."

"You say it gonna hep them git us free?"

"Yes Luther it will help them win this war."

"Alright then I kin do it. I kin ride out dere taday by evenin' time. Hope dey ain left there 'cause I caint be ridin' all ova tryna fine 'em 'cause dem paterollers and now dis 'federate army be lookin' for runaways an dey might think om one of 'em."

"Yes Luther I understand, but I don't think they'll be gone this soon because I just heard my information last night. Let me go and get the paper now and give it to you."

Bernard went into his room and took the document from his locked trunk. Since he shared the room with Jonathan's driver, he had to be extra careful he didn't leave anything like that out in plain sight. He retrieved the papers and went back in the kitchen. Amanda had come in and was sitting there talking with the smithy when Bernard entered. The blacksmith was asking her whether she knew anything about what Bernard had told him trying to get some confirmation. Amanda didn't know how much Bernard had told the man, so she said she didn't know anything. Bernard interrupted the conversation and told him that he had better get going if he was going to deliver the message by this evening. Luther took the message and looked at the sealed envelope that was addressed to the Officer In Charge – US Army. He looked at it carefully pretending he was reading it, and Bernard looked at him wondering whether he really could. The answer was not given when the smithy turned and left. Bernard hollered out at him as he descended the stairs that he would tell the master he had been here.

At Fortress Monroe when the search patrol reported back in and brought the wounded to the makeshift hospital one man had expired on the way and the other two were hanging on. Jethro had been hit twice, once in the upper thigh and the other one in the lower back area. The other soldier had taken a shot in his upper torso near the heart and had lost a lot of blood. Both casualties were immediately given over to the surgical unit and the fort's doctor with his assorted team went to work. First on the surgical table was the soldier with the chest wound and the doctor plied his skills as best he could knowing the man had lost a great deal of blood. Chloroform was in short supply, so the doctor used what was available sparingly and placed a rolled towel in the man's mouth to bite on. He went in and got the musket ball successfully and stitched the wound, but the great loss of fluids made it almost impossible to predict any full recovery. His operating room assistants wheeled the patient out and into the first floor of one of the older barracks that had been converted into convalescing quarters. There were several others in the room lined up on bunks in a row on both sides and the men were moaning and groaning constantly. The conditions were less than sanitary that made it hard to recover from anything,but there was a war going on and the first priority was to patch the men up and get them back in the field.

Jethro was next to be wheeled in and placed on the table. Although he too had lost blood, it was fortunate for him that a trooper close to him tied off his wounds. The doctor looked at him and determined he would treat the leg first, so he gave Jethro a minimal dosage of the anesthesia and told him to hang on. Getting the bullet out of his leg wasn't difficult because the rifle bullet had lodged in the fat part of his thigh and missed all major arteries. He extracted it quickly and sewed up the wound, then told his assistants to turn the patient over. With Jethro lying on his stomach the doctor discovered that the other wound was more of a challenge. Where the bullet lodged was right around his spinal column right at the base and going in to extract it could cause some major damage and maybe paralyze this soldier for life. Trying not to let Jethro see the indecision on his face, the doctor turned away for a short time before turning back around and telling Jethro he was going to have a permanent war souvenir. Jethro in his dazed state wasn't clear on what he was saying, but when the doctor started sewing up the wound, he could still feel something in his back that he knew shouldn't be there.

Just before the assistants moved him off the table and on to the gurney, Jethro overheard the doctor say to one of them that they should keep a close eye on this man and watch out for infection setting in. The pain wasn't as severe as when he first got hit, but Jethro was afraid that having that bullet still in him was going to be a problem, and he was right. When they rolled him into the room with the other recovering patients, Jethro saw his frightened buddy lying on a bunk covered in bandages wrapped around his chest and his eyes were closed. He managed to ask one of the assistants if his friend was still alive and the reply was, just barely. Jethro asked if he could be placed near him and his wish was granted. Two bunks down from his friend Jethro lie on his bunk looking over at him to see if he really was still breathing. He could see that he was, but the motion was irregular and very shallow. Jethro watched him for a long time even ignoring his own pain to keep his head up. Finally, when maintaining his head in that position was becoming a strain and he was about to drop it, he noticed that even the shallow breaths had discontinued and he called loudly for an assistant.

The soldier nurse came over and told Jethro to keep it down but when directed by Jethro to the other soldier he went over and examined him. Moments later he pulled the sheet up over the man's face. Jethro couldn't believe it and stared at the ceiling for awhile, but finally he accepted it and went into a light sleep. The moaning and groaning from the other men continued and Jethro was having a hard time tuning out the sounds. He tried to turn over on his side, but found the pain trying to move was unbearable, so he continued on his stomach. It was a long time before anyone came to see about his friend, but when they finally arrived, they just rolled the man onto a gurney without any fanfare or ceremony and hauled him away. To Jethro it was a time when the stark reality of what war was all about started to set in and he realized that neither his friend nor he had even really been in the war. What he experienced was the result of something that could have happened even if there was no war. Contemplating the issue, he asked himself the question: "Was hunting down slaves and killing them for being slaves really a part of the war?"

When Jonathan came home that night after having a less than inspiring day communicating with the troops he went straight to his parlor and called for Bernard to fix him a toddy. The last piece of news he received from the captain before calling it a day was that confederate troops under Jackson's command had suffered a severe blow up in Berkeley County and the spirit of his troops was really low. This was not the kind of news he wanted to hear, and it sent his own spirit in a downward spiral. As he was sipping his refreshment, Suliah walked by the room on her way to the kitchen and he spotted her.

"Suliah, Suliah please come here."

She heard him call and turned around. When she entered the room, she could see the cup in his hand and knew that he was imbibing. Not sure what was going to happen next, she approached him cautiously.

"Yes massa?"

"Come sit down by me for awhile I want to talk with you."

She sat down and waited for him to start talking, but he just looked at her for several minutes.

"How do you like being here?"

"You mean if I could leave an go someplace else would I go?"

He was surprised by her response and started to laugh, but then he asked her the same question again.

"Well I don get no whippins like I hear some of the othas do an I got a good bed ta sleep in so I guess I likes it okay."

He continued staring at her and then added.

"You know you're a very pretty girl and that's going to take you a long way. Tonight after dinner I want you to come back here and sit with me some more so I can talk to you."

Suliah knew at that point what he was after because she had seen it so many times before now with the men that had come around her but there was nothing she could do so she hung her head and answered him.

"Okay massa I be here."

Suliah left the room and went to the kitchen where she ran into Amanda and told her what had happened. Amanda smiled at her and shook her head. Amanda had been the one that Jonathan used to entertain his important guests right from the start with his first affair, but he never showed any interest in her himself. She tried to pacify Suliah, knowing that she was scared of what was going to happen, by telling her that if she didn't do like he said then it could be a whole lot worse for her if she had to leave here. Suliah had heard this before even from Jonathan and with Amanda repeating it she knew it was true. The rest of the late afternoon until it was time to serve dinner, Suliah was walking around in kind of a daze trying to picture how it was going to be. Her first thoughts hearkened back to the time at the Candle farm when two of the sons of neighboring owners had tried to take her by force, but then she moved onto how nice it was with Jethro when he introduced her into womanhood. She wavered between thinking that Jonathan might be more like the time with Jethro, but then she thought about how ruthless he had treated her when he told her to entertain the house guest, so she was confused.

During dinner Jonathan who had had more than a few drinks was very lighthearted and was entertaining his parents and sisters by telling several off-key jokes. His mother didn't appreciate it, but hesitated to say anything to him because she recognized that something was troubling him and the drinking was his way of dealing with it. His father just looked at him occasionally, grunted every now and then and kept on eating. Both sisters thought he was amusing and laughed at his unfunny humor. By the time they all had finished eating and the dishes were being taken from the table Suliah tried to make a point of only removing those from other family members and staying away from him, but he called her over and made her take his. As she reached for them, he grabbed her arm and held it for a minute and looked at her. Everyone at the table knew what was happening, but what could they say.

After dinner the rest of the family scattered to other rooms in the house or went outside in the warm summer air and sat on the wicker lounge under the veranda. Jonathan went straight to his parlor and sat in his favorite chair waiting for Suliah to come to him. He sat there for a long time with no sign of Suliah coming in. His patience was growing thin, and he was getting angry, so he got up and went to look for her. He looked in the kitchen then he went to her room and then went out the back door and looked outside. She was nowhere in the house, and he started to get concerned so he went back to the room and asked Amanda where she was. Amanda replied that she hadn't seen her since dinner and didn't know where she could have gone. There was only one other place he could look, but he said to himself she couldn't possibly be in there. This was the converted barn in the back that housed some slaves he had purchased strictly to hire out as either farm workers or laborers in town. There were six of them, all men, in there and he couldn't imagine why she would even want to go in there because they were nothing like Bernard or any other house slave.

He got to the front door and opened it without knocking. It was now about 9:00 o'clock and dark outside, but they were sitting around with the lamp still lit, talking. When they saw Jonathan come in each man jumped to his feet expecting that he came there for them to do something. When he told them he didn't need them for anything, but was looking for one of the house girls they all responded that she wasn't there. Now he was really puzzled and didn't know where else to look so he went back in the house. By this time the rest of the family had gone to their rooms to retire so he not knowing what else to do and deciding she must be around somewhere went to do the same.

When he opened his door, he was completely surprised because there she was sitting on the side of his bed dressed in a loose fitting gown. All of his concerns disappeared as he took in the picture of beauty that sat on his bed. He walked over with his eyes steadily fixed on her and sat down beside her. Without saying anything he took her in his arms and kissed her hard. She didn't respond, but offered no resistance either. He kissed her again and gently pushed her down on the bed while trying to remove the gown. His efforts were not succeeding so he got up and told her to take it off. She complied with his command and slowly removed the gown revealing what his eyes had been picturing in his imagination all evening. When she was completely bare, he undressed and turned down the bed sheets then went and extinguished the flame in the lamp.

To Suliah this was the start of something she knew would change her life, but she resigned herself to believing that this was her destiny, so she went along. The experience was somewhere in between the plantation rogues and the gentleness of Jethro, but she convinced herself that if this was what he wanted, and it would guarantee her stay here then so be it. Jonathan was so pleased with the softness and suppleness of her body that he delighted in every curve. He spent most of the night trying to recover after each love episode so that he could anxiously get on to the next one. After the first encounter, even Suliah became responsive and was returning his efforts equally. By morning with both bodies completely exhausted from the exercise, the bright sun shone through the window, but neither body moved a muscle.

It took some effort but after enduring the direct sunlight on the bed for some time Jonathan managed to get out of bed. He got up and looked back at Suliah who was awake and looking at him and told her he wanted her to bring her things in here and start spending her nights with him. She just nodded her head. He got dressed and went downstairs to start his day. When he ran into Bernard, he told him that Suliah would be down in a little while and Bernard who suspected that she might be with him since she didn't report for her usual morning duty, said yes sir and continued on with his work.

For days Jethro lie in that bed trying to heal, but it seemed like each day was bringing him more misery than the day before. He was right in what he felt. Infection had started to set in and it was gaining strength from the inside. The tissue around the metal slug was rejecting the foreign matter and his body was reacting by external swelling and creating an internal environment that was conducive to infectious bacteria. The soldier nurses did not do as the doctor had instructed them and none paid much attention to the discoloration that was becoming markedly pronounced. On the third day when the doctor was making his rounds he came to Jethro and examined him. He was furious and lashed out at the attendants, but the damage was done and there was no way to reverse it. The doctor decided that there was nothing else he could do for this soldier here so he recommended that Jethro be moved immediately to the hospital in Richmond where he could receive the proper care for this type of malady.

In the captain's office the doctor reported that unless this man was taken immediately to the Richmond Hospital then the top officer in charge would lose another soldier under his command. The captain, who had already lost a considerable number of his troops, didn't need to have another one charged to him, especially if he could be saved so he gave the order to have a wagon made ready for the trip. Jethro was prepared for travel; a team of horses was hitched to the wagon and an escort of two soldiers besides the driver was assigned to the mission. They rode out in a hurry and even though Jethro was strapped down on a mattress in the wagon the bumpy ride was causing him excruciating pain and he suffered the whole way. After the hours it took to get there, Jethro was thoroughly relieved when they entered the city and removed him from the wagon. He was taken up to the ward where the confederate soldiers were being treated and was quickly attended to by the resident physicians. The team of doctors who looked at him shook their head in disbelief that this man had been allowed to deteriorate to this condition and they set in trying to relieve his pain and treat the infection.

Jonathan decided today when he arrived at the recruiting station that he was not going to get down even if the news greeting him was bad. He checked in with the captain and found out that there had been some moderate successes at Manassas and there was some new hope that things might be turning around. When Jonathan heard this his hopes got brighter, and he was beginning to enjoy the day almost as much as he had enjoyed the night. He looked around the station and saw that there were some mildly wounded men sitting around waiting for a reassignment and it dawned on him that it would be good for his image if he made an appearance over at the hospital to see the wounded there. He excused himself from the captain told him where he was going and that he would be coming back as soon as he finished over there. The captain thought it was a great idea and asked that Jonathan deliver his best wishes to the men for him. Jonathan said he would and left.

The hospital was a short ride from the recruiting station, so it only took him a few minutes to get there. He went inside and greeted the doctors first and asked where the soldiers were being housed. Most of the resident physicians knew who he was, and they were glad that he came by because now they thought he might be able to get them some extra supplies because they too were running low as a result of the war. Jonathan was escorted to the first of three wards where the soldiers were being treated and walked down the aisle shaking hands, talking briefly and saying words of encouragement to each trooper. When he entered the second ward and came to the third bed on the right, he stopped in his tracks and looked intently at the soldier lying on the bed. He couldn't believe his eyes at first and he wanted to make sure that his assessment of who he thought it was, was correct so he paused before approaching. When he was convinced that it was the same exuberant young man who had come to join the army so enthusiastically and was ready to get into action immediately, he quickened his pace to his bedside. Jethro's eyes were closed so he went to him softly and spoke.

"Soldier, I'm sorry I don't remember your name, but I recognize your face and I remember when you came in to join up. You were so excited to get started with the war I never thought you'd be the one I would see here."

Jethro opened his eyes looked up at him and recognized Jonathan also. A smile came across his face, even while he was experiencing pain and he raised his hand to shake Jonathans. Quickly, Jonathan took his and shook it vigorously.

"Suh, I'm glad ta see you. I never thought I'd be here either" he tried to laugh, but the pain prevented him from completing the effort.

"Now you get better soon son because what I told you about getting into politics with me I meant it. You come see me as soon as you get well."

When Jonathan finished talking and left the bedside, he went over to the doctor nearby and asked him about Jethro's condition. The doctor's reply caused Jonathan to have to sit down and he placed his head in his hands. Then he looked up and told the doctor that he didn't want this man to expire here, but to have him brought to his house and he would get the best of care for whatever time was left. The doctor told Jonathan that he would have to clear that with the military officers in charge of those types of things. Jonathan assured the doctor that it would not be a problem and he went on walking through the rest of that ward and the last one.

Later on, that day a wagon pulled up to the Adams residence escorted by a group of soldiers. When Bernard answered the door and saw them he thought it was very strange and asked the soldier in charge what this was all about. The trooper in charge explained the whole thing to him including Jonathan's instructions and Bernard immediately called for some of the other servants to help the soldiers take this man up to the third floor and make him comfortable. Bernard accompanied the group to the room and personally insured that everything was in order. He didn't want to have to answer to Jonathan if it wasn't because of the explicit directions that had been given to the escort about how this man should be treated. All the servants and the family in the house heard the commotion, but couldn't see who it was that was being brought in. Each one gathered that the man coming in had to be of some importance because of the way Bernard was giving him attention. They were extremely curious and anxious to find out who it was and how he could be related to Jonathan to receive such attention.

When the attendants came for him Jethro was surprised that he was being moved from the hospital because he had not been told about his condition. He thought that even with the increasing pain, he would eventually get better. When he was told whose house he was going to he couldn't believe his good fortune and wanted to heal quickly so he could get to know his mentor better. He wanted very badly to get a message to his father so he would know that he was getting close to a politician just like he wanted him to. Once inside the house he looked around his new room and saw that there were many little knick-knacks on the dresser and the wall that reminded him of his father's room, so he was starting to feel like he was home. When Bernard came to look in on him after a while he asked if he could write a letter and get it sent to his father. Bernard told him that he would be happy to write one for him since he was having trouble sitting up. Jethro thought the slave was kidding because he had never come across any of them who could read or write. When Bernard assured him that he could do it, Jethro was in no condition to refuse him. He knew that he would read it anyway when it was finished so what did he have to lose.

Bernard went and got some stationary then returned. Jethro jumped right in dictating his thoughts and was moving so fast that Bernard had to slow him down and remind him that he couldn't write as fast as he could talk. Jethro paused and gave him a sly smile, not sure that the man was even really doing what he said he could. When it was finished, Bernard handed it to Jethro and he read it with great surprise. He thanked Bernard several times and asked if he would make sure that it got sent. Bernard agreed and left the room.

Downstairs the whole house was buzzing about who had moved in. Bernard didn't know the man's name, but he told everybody that it was a soldier and Jonathan personally had told him to come here. Amanda and Suliah's curiosity soared to another level and they started making plans for sneaking up there and finding out who this man really was and what he looked like. The family was also curious, but no one made mention of making any attempts to visit the new resident. About an hour or so after his arrival Suliah had come up with the perfect plan. She was going to tell Bernard that she was going to go and take some extra pillows up to the new guest. Amanda would come up a little later under the pretense that she would be bringing some fresh water. It sounded like good strategy and both Amanda and Suliah agreed it would work so they ran it by the chief servant and he okayed it.

Suliah went to the linen closet and found two extra pillows. She made sure that the pillow covers were nice and white because she wanted to make a good impression. Then she started making her way upstairs. When she got to the second level she was careful to not be seen by the family so she quietly went to the end of the corridor where the final staircase was and eased her way up those stairs. She got to the bedroom door and knocked softly at first, but when there was no response she knocked a second time just a little harder. There was still no sound so she eased open the door and when she looked inside and saw the partially covered figure lying on the bed sleeping, she recognized who it was her mouth fell open and her heart skipped more than one beat.

Chapter 11 - Daring Time

Growing up on the Sutter Plantation Linwood and Suliah had as normal a childhood as could be had under the circumstances. Old man Sutter, as strict a disciplinarian as he was, loved his slave children and often would allow them to do things that on most plantations would warrant punishment. Until they reached the age of twelve none of them were put to work doing anything except some minor chores like feeding the chickens. Under the supervision of a nanny chosen from one of the older women who had exceeded her years for productive work in the fields, the children played and otherwise enjoyed themselves all day until their parents returned home. Suliah and Linwood even found extra favor from the big house because Bessie May had developed a special relationship with Jobba and even became the godmother for his children. That provided benefits for them that the other workers' children didn't get.

Timothy Sutter wasn't an especially religious man, but he believed that when his slaves were happy then they would perform their best and ultimately he would come out ahead because of their production. Even before he allowed itinerant preachers to come onto his land and minister to his charges, he used to listen to them singing and having worship services down by the river led by one of them who could neither read nor write. Mr. Sutter's driver who used to take the old man's wife to church on Sundays learned the scriptures by standing outside and listening to the preacher. He would then come back and be the worship leader by the riverside and regurgitate the message he heard almost word for word.

Sutter decided to let preachers come on the land because the driver had asked him to and he thought it would be good for his slaves. Jobba and Myanna were regular attendees at the services, and they made sure that Linwood and Suliah tagged along. So, it was both children were raised in the tradition of Christian worship until Mr. Sutter's boys started leaving the plantation and soon after his wife died. After that the preachers were disallowed from coming to the plantation and the whole climate of religious services changed. His tolerance of a lot of things that he used to allow disappeared also and the slaves suffered as a result. Because of the change Linwood and Suliah as they got older were not as exposed to the Word as if the preaching had continued. Jobba began to substitute things that he tried to recall being said, but often he had misunderstood the message and would confuse his reality with the truth.

By the time Suliah was thirteen and Linwood eleven, they had seen many things happen around the plantation including death. They saw slaves who were close to Jobba and Myanna pass away, and it was always especially traumatic for Suliah who had an unusual sensitivity to nature's cycles. It was hard for her to understand why death occurs and what happens to the ones who die when they die. Jobba tried often to explain to her what it was as he saw it. He even tried to remember some scripture he had heard that would help him make her understand, but he was not successful. Bessimay, her godmother who also had a deep sensitivity about the cycles of life along with her other gift of insight, was always able to comfort her whenever a death in the community occurred, but she was never able to get through to her how to handle accepting death as a part of life.

Suliah grew up suppressing her fears about death and she learned to disguise her feelings so she would fit in. Now that she was a young adult and functioning in a world that had sprung her into a maturity requirement that she really wasn't ready for, she was being confronted once again with the deepest emotional fear she had. Standing by the bedside looking at Jethro with bandages wrapped around him from his chest to his waist and another wrapping around his leg, all of the emotions she had started to feel for him when he first loved her began to surface. She moved closer to him and touched him lightly. He opened his eyes slowly and took a minute to focus, but when he saw that it was her, he immediately tried to turn over and sit up but couldn't.

She leaned forward to try and help him, but he was too heavy so he remained flat. Difficult and uncomfortable as it was, he used all his strength and rolled over on his back so he could face her and started to talk.

"I thought I'd never see you again. My father must have been outta his mind to let you go the way he did. For weeks I couldn't think of nothing else but you. I really missed you. The first time I ever saw your face I knew you were something special and I wanted to be with you. It didn't matter to me that you were a slave or that your color is different from mine. In your eyes I saw the sunshine and your smile captured me right from the start. These crazy laws they got keeping us from each other makes no sense to me and it never did. I don't know if I'm ever gonna be able to get up from this bed, but I wanted you ta know that whether it is right or wrong in the eyes of the law, I love you."

Suliah stood by the bed not knowing what to say to him after that and tears were welling up in her eyes as she tried. Seeing him in this condition was the last thing she ever could have imagined, and the right words just wouldn't form in her thoughts or her mouth. She just stood there staring in disbelief. He could see in her eyes that she was filled with emotion, so he took her hand and held it. Finally, she composed herself and was able to speak.

"I neva wanted to leave there or go way from you, but I guess dis is how it got to be. You was good ta me an I really liked you, but nothing eva could have been good for us tagether. I heard my daddy say a long time ago that the white man's laws won't eva be fair to slaves."

Jethro heard her words and the emotion rose in him too. He tried to respond, but was straining to keep talking. The infection had worsened and was draining him. Suliah could see that something was wrong and she squeezed his hand hard as if trying to squeeze him back to health. The color in his face was fading like the blood was leaving his body. She asked him what was wrong, but the more he tried to talk the less he was able to form words. Soon he gave up and emptiness came into his eyes as he looked on her for the last time and lay his head back completely and went silent. Suliah was still holding his hand and looking down on him when it started to go cold and stiffen before she pulled away and was frightened. All the fears she had learned to suppress these many years were now back in full force and the fact that the one lying before her was as close to any human passing that she had ever been, the emotion was too much for her and she feinted.

Amanda who had been waiting for Suliah to come down so she could exercise her option go up and see the new guest, was getting impatient and decided to scrap the plan and go anyway. She quietly ascended the stairway and made her way to the third floor just as Suliah did. When she got to the guestroom door she paused and listened to hear what might be going on. There was no sound coming from inside and she was curious thinking that maybe he had gone to another room. She opened the door and saw Suliah lying on the floor all sprawled out and ran over to her. Panic set in at first, but then she saw that Suliah was still breathing steadily so she got up and went over to the wash basin and dipped the washcloth in it. With the dampened cloth in her hand, she returned and placed it on Suliah's face. Suliah responded and slowly opened her eyes. She was still dazed and was surprised to look up at Amanda's face, but then it all started coming back to her and she started to scream. Amanda grabbed her and shook her asking what was wrong, and Suliah pointed to the bed.

Amanda turned and looked over at the still body of Jethro and she too got frightened. Quickly recomposing herself she picked her buddy up and helped her out the door and they both went downstairs to get Bernard. When Amanda rushed to tell him what she saw upstairs she was incoherent and stumbling trying to get the words out. Bernard grabbed hold of her and told her to calm down. In his strong grip she responded and managed to get the words out that something was wrong with the new man upstairs. Bernard fearing that he would be held accountable because the instructions to him when the man was brought into the house was that he was to be given the best of care, released Amanda and ran upstairs. At the guestroom door he didn't knock nor hesitate but opened it up and barged right in. He saw the man lying on the bed not moving and apparently not breathing either. Making his way quickly over to the bed he put his hand on Jethro's throat feeling for a pulse but found none. Then he put his hand in front of Jethro's nose but felt no air coming out.

There was nothing else he could do so he pulled the sheet up over Jethro's head and walked out of the room. Downstairs he told Jethro's father what the situation was, and the father told him to send word by one of the men in the bunkhouse down to the recruiting station and get Jonathan. It was done and the report back was that Jonathan was on his way. The rest of the family had been apprised and they all were concerned about how the man died since they couldn't see him clearly when he came in the house. The ladies were afraid that the man might have had some kind of sickness and that it could affect everyone in the house. Just as they were discussing it among themselves, the front door opened and in walked Jonathan. He walked right passed all of them who were standing around in the hallway, without saying a word and went up the stairs to the guestroom.

He entered and saw the sheet pulled up over Jethro's head. Aware that this was going to happen, he just wasn't prepared for it to happen this quickly since he didn't have a chance to prepare his family for the event. He slowly walked back downstairs and confronted the family and the house servants who were still congregating in the hall. When he started telling them the whole story about how he came to know this man and how much he came to like him, he didn't notice that Suliah was taking it harder than all of the others. It wasn't until, as he kept on talking about the things in this man that he admired even from the brief time he knew him, that Suliah's emotions got the better of her again and she fell to the floor passed out. Jonathan saw her go down and immediately stopped talking wondering what was wrong. He ran over to her and lifted up her head while he commanded that someone bring a glass of water quickly. The water was brought, and he put the glass to her lips, while his parents and sisters looked on with disgust because this was one of the same glasses that they drank out of. It never entered Jonathan's mind that this was what he was doing for his only concern at the moment was that his bed companion was on the floor. She drank the water, and her composure came back. Slowly she was able to stand on her feet while he held her. Jonathan dismissed everybody standing around telling them to go on back to whatever it was they were doing, and they disbursed.

Jonathan looked in her eyes and asked her what the matter was. She hung her head and tried to answer him, but her voice was so shaky that he couldn't understand her words. He walked her into his parlor and sat her down on his favorite chair and repeated the question. When she was finally able to answer him, she told him that on the plantation where she used to be the man upstairs was the son of the master and she knew him. Jonathan's mind immediately went to work, and he wondered how well did she know him that she should be this upset at his death. He pressed her for more information, but when she struggled in answering it didn't take long for him to figure out what the relationship had been. He couldn't really get upset because there was no way for him to know this and he imagined that as pretty as she is how could he blame the young man for his act. As for her part in the act he assessed her differently. He left Suliah sitting in the chair but told her not to come up to his room tonight.

Jonathan left the house and went back down to the recruiting station where he informed the captain that another one of his men had been lost. The captain relayed the word to the sergeant who was responsible for putting together the detail to go and let the next of kin know about their loved ones. It was too late in the day for the detail to form and go out to the Candle Plantation, but they sent word back to Jonathan that first thing in the morning the parents would be informed of their son's demise.

On the Sandler farm, while Jobba and Shaka had escaped the town's vigilante patrol with the help of some runaways who happened to have been in the area, they knew that they couldn't return to staying in the Sandler barn. The patrol was bound to regroup and come back with more men. Jobba thanked both the rebels and the Sandler's for all their help, but told them he now had to move on and find that train conductor so he could book passage for him and his wife. Samson gave him all the information he knew about the town blacksmith and how to make contact. He also told Jobba not to be spotted in town during the day or he would go right to jail or worse. Jobba acknowledged the warning and said he would go out only at night. Samson asked him where he would hide during the day and Jobba responded that he had no idea, but just as that bird led him here, something else would lead him and he walked away.

Jobba and Shaka left the farm and went back into the woods carrying a few supplies of food and water given to them by Samson. They were no strangers to running in the forest now and living off of nature's supplies, but having at least a day's worth of Samson's wife's cooking made both men feel deprived. Running now was different than before because they had a good idea of the direction they needed to go and how long it would take them to get inside the city. It was late afternoon when they left the farm and they decided to find a spot to camp out in and get an early start in the morning. The summer heat in this part of Virginia was not unbearable and when the sun went down the light breeze that wafted through the woods was pleasant. They found a clearing near the edge of the forest and as was their custom made bedding out of the dried leaves. Jobba checked the area for signs of snakes that he had seen before around here and then he closed his eyes and enjoyed a sound and peaceful sleep.

In the morning, even while the sun was just beginning to rise, Jobba woke up and awakened his travel companion. Feeling refreshed from a good night's uninterrupted sleep, both men voiced their need for water. Not wanting to drink the small container of water given to them, they struck out in search of a stream or a river. They started walking in the direction they had to go to get to the city and before long came across a shallow but clear stream that was a welcome sight. It was not deep enough to bathe in but both men stripped down and wallowed in the shallow water rolling over and over frolicking like a couple of young boys and taking in the coolness of the refreshing waters. After spending some time playing in the water they dried off and started their journey toward the city.

Moving in and out of walking close to the edge of the woods and traveling deep in the interior they looked when near the edge for any signs of patrols or confederate soldiers who might be looking for them. They did this for hours and when it came time to rest, they sat down close to the edge not too far from the main road. Just before they stopped to eat and rest Jobba spotted another farm just beyond a ridge and wondered whether they might take a chance and stop by there. As they ate their lunch Jobba asked Shaka what he thought about going to the farm and take the chance that they would meet with favor from the occupants. Shaka told Jobba that they have found much favor so far in their journey and he believed that his ancestors were looking out for both of them. Jobba wasn't quite sure when Shaka finished talking whether this meant he wanted to go or he didn't, so he had to ask him. Shaka laughed at him for not understanding what he was trying to tell him about the protection of his ancestors, but then he said clearly that he thought they should trust the spirits and go.

Lunch was done and each man rested for a bit then they got up and restarted the trek. Moving cautiously near the side of the main road they approached the farm. There was no easy entry like at the Sandler farm where they could get close by hiding in the corn fields until they were close enough to observe the farm occupants. All of the land around the farmhouse was flat and Jobba wondered what it was that they grew, but as they boldly moved toward the house the answer was given. On the far side of the house were wheat, corn and tobacco fields and Jobba reasoned that the land on this side was being given a chance to recover before being reseeded. He was impressed at this because it was something that he had always tried to tell old man Sutter about preserving the land for the future crops, but he never listened.

They realized that even though they were coming up in the front side of the house the reason why they didn't see anybody was probably because they were all out in the fields on the back side. Stepping more audaciously now they walked up to the house and circled around to the back and stopped. Looking out into the fields they saw several workers bent over tilling the ground. At first glance it looked like there was a mix of white and black workers, but he didn't see anything that looked like an overseer and the way the white workers were bent over just like the others, he definitely didn't think they were slave owners. Before going any further they stood alongside the house just out of sight to try and understand who who was out there but when each worker moved around it was as if they were sharing the load equally. Jobba got tired of waiting and motioned to Shaka that he was going to step out and be seen, but for him to remain behind just in case the situation got hostile. Shaka agreed and stayed behind

Jobba stepped away from the house and started walking toward the fields. The first worker that saw him was a white man who quickly alerted two others who were near him that a stranger was approaching. The other two were black men and they stood up with the farm implements still in their hands and hollered out to Jobba to stop right there and state his business. Jobba stopped and hollered back that he needed their help. The black man who was doing the talking hollered back, help for what? Jobba then asked to come closer because he didn't want to keep hollering like this. There was a great pause as the black man looked at the others then he said come closer.

"I's Jobba an I come from a long way off an I needs yo hep in gittin to de Richmond town. Kin ya hep me?"

"What kina help you lookin' for?" the black man asked.

"I needs ta know if'n om gwine in de right way an also if y`all kin give me a bite ta eat?"

The group spokesman again looked at the others and then called them over to him. They huddled for a few minutes before answering Jobba then they told him to come on in the house. Jobba acknowledged their invitation and then told them he had a traveling companion waiting next to the house and he would like to bring him down so they can see him. Again, the group paused before answering then agreed it was okay. Jobba turned around and motioned to Shaka who was watching from his stealth position beside the house to come down. Shaka complied and started walking toward the group. When he stood next to Jobba the whole group started moving toward the house with each side keeping an eye on the other.

Once inside Eli, the man who was doing the talking, motioned for Jobba and Shaka to sit down at the table and he went into another room and in a few minutes came back with a plate of food. Jobba's eyes lit up at seeing the full plate of greens, ham, and mashed potatoes. It was still early in the day and Jobba remembered his experience about trying to run from the patrols and running out of breath in a very short time so he asked Eli if there was any way he could put some of this good food in a bag that he could take with him. Eli looked at him wondering about his strange request, but answered that he had something he could put the food in that wouldn't let it spoil and he could carry that. Jobba thanked him sincerely and dug into the plate to eat a small portion.

While the two travelers were eating Eli kept talking asking them where they came from and why were they going to Richmond. Jobba hesitated a minute before answering looking at the white man standing in the corner wondering just what he was. Eli noticed him staring at the man and he said that he was a sharecropper just like they were, and he was helping to work this land for a Colonel Simpson who owned it all but allowed them to work it and live off of it while he was away. He continued that the colonel was away fighting in the war and when he came back, they would probably have to leave. Jobba went on talking and told the group where he and Shaka came from and that they were trying to get to Richmond to connect with the conductor of the Underground Railroad. Eli's eyes widened when he heard this, and he told Jobba about a colored church in the south side of Richmond that he needed to go to and meet the people. Someone there once they got to trust him could connect him with the contact he needed.

Again, Jobba thanked him and continued eating. When he and Shaka had dined sufficiently and Eli had wrapped up his take along bag, the pair got up and heeding the directions Eli gave them continued on their journey. Eli's instructions were not to go too deep in the forest, but stay near the main road just out of sight so they could keep their eye on a tall landmark that would keep the city in their sights. The landmark was a tall water tower that was right by the railroad tracks which is in the center of town. The pair set out in the heat of the noonday sun and immediately took to the woods not just for shelter from the sun, but to get the protective covering from any patrols passing by. They weaved their way in and out of the trees near the edge of the forest and after about an hour they could clearly see the top of the water tower. Seeing this encouraging sight Jobba said they might as well rest here since they were so close, they could make it before nightfall. Shaka agreed and the pair sat down under the shade of a mighty cedar and rested.

Almost as soon as he sat down and leaned against the tree Jobba nodded his head and went to sleep. Shaka lasted awake a little while longer, but then he too succumbed to the urge to nap and went to sleep. It became apparent when they woke up and the sun was almost down, that they were more tired from their trek then they realized. Jobba awoke first and called to his friend, and he responded with a look of surprise just as Jobba did when his eyes opened. Both men jumped to their feet and tried to make up the time they had lost by napping and started trotting along the forest edge. Now that it was starting to get dark moving through the trees was not as easy as it had been during the daylight hours. They persevered and soon came to the end of the woods and were near the outskirts of the city. Before they exposed themselves on the road that led into the heart of town each man looked around to get a good look and see if there were any confederate soldiers or patrols about.

Satisfied there were none they ran into town and hid behind the first building they came to. It was a three-story building with a store and two living units above it. They were on the backside and could look down to see the backs of several other buildings on that side but couldn't make out from that view just what they were. Jobba remembered that Eli said the church was in the south section of town but just where that was, he had no idea, so the problem now was to find out. He carefully walked around to the front and saw a lot of people walking around including many confederate soldiers. He quickly ducked back behind the building and told Shaka they needed to stay here until it was completely dark.

When it became dark enough, they ventured around to the front of the building again and this time the traffic in the streets was minimal. The few soldiers that were still present were busy entertaining themselves with the local women of the evening. Jobba seizing the opportunity beckoned to Shaka to move over to the other side of the road and see what was behind the buildings. They scampered across the road and made it to the other side undetected. Behind one of the larger buildings was an old, covered wagon that seemed to be the ideal place to hide for the night if it was empty. Slowly the pair creeped up to the vehicle and looked inside. Luckily it was empty except for some old tarpaulin and a few rain barrels. Jobba hopped in quickly and turned to help his companion in also. Once inside they peeked out to make sure they had not been seen and then hid under the tarp for the night.

It was Friday at 0800 hours and Lieutenant Mims and Sergeant Greenway were forming a detail to go out to the Candle Plantation to deliver the sad news. Normally a detail of four men would not be required to apprise a family of the demise of their loved one, but the lieutenant had received reports that there was hostile activity on the road and in the area of where they had to go, so he decided to take precautions. It had been told to him that there were slave rebels who were armed roaming the woods and also several union army soldiers in the area. He didn't anticipate he would encounter either and the duration of his mission was expected to be brief, so he told his men that they were going to go and deliver the message and come right back. Being responsible for addressing the family in these situations was a dreaded task that he hated but in this case, having to tell the family that their son didn't expire as the result of some hostile action defending their way of life in a military combat effort, made it even more challenging. He was having difficulty trying to formulate the words on how to tell the family their son died from gunshots by rebelling slaves. It would have been even more challenging if he knew that involved in the action was a former slave of the family.

The detail started out riding in a column of two's and they were making good headway when no more than a half hour into their journey they heard gunshots in the near distance. The shots seemed to be coming from the forest and as they neared the point where the sound was coming from, they saw several horses tied up. Cautiously the lieutenant led his men by the area not wanting to get involved with the action. He noticed that the insignia on the horses was that of the confederate army and he wondered where these men could have come from since he was not aware of any of his men being dispatched or being advised that men from Ft. Monroe were in the area. The only other place they would have come from would be Manassas, but he knew of no reason why they would be here. After seeing the insignia, he pondered whether he should stop assess the situation and see if his help was needed. While he was making his decision another volley of heavy gunfire sounded and he told his men to dismount and approach the woods with caution. Heeding the command, they dismounted and readied their weapons then went into the woods led by the lieutenant.

They were not too deep in the woods when they spotted confederate soldiers behind some trees about twenty yards in front of them firing at their targets about another fifteen to twenty yards ahead of them. Although the lieutenant couldn't clearly see the target himself, he waved his arms to attract the attention of one of the soldiers. The soldier saw him and raised his hand in acknowledgement and beckoned for the lieutenant to come over. Lieutenant Mims moved rapidly toward the soldier ducking low to keep cover. When he got there the soldier recognized the lieutenant's rank and threw up a hasty salute while explaining the situation. It seems that several union army soldiers had been trapped in another part of the woods, but managed to escape to this area and they were trying to hunt them down. The lieutenant told the man he was on another mission and asked whether they needed the help of him and his men. The soldier thanked him for the offer, but he thought that it would only be a matter of a short time before they would dispose of these infiltrators from the north. The lieutenant turned around and called his men to follow him out and they resumed their journey.

The Candle Plantation was still about an hour's ride from where they were at this point and the sun high overhead was beginning to take its toll. The lieutenant didn't want to stop again if he didn't have to, but he turned to his men and asked if they needed to break. Quickly the reply came that they should push on and get the mission accomplished. Hearing that he prompted his steed to pick up the pace and the others followed. Before long and according to the map, the Candle Plantation should be just up ahead. They came to the side path that would take them up to the mansion and they proceeded to move in that direction. Within minutes the group saw the mansion and commented on how stately the house was and knew that they were going to be dealing with someone of some wealth and possible power. In his mind the lieutenant was quickly rearranging his presentation to meet his new assessment of the situation.

When they got close to the mansion one of the servants came out to greet them while another one ran to alert Byron that some soldiers had come. A short time later Byron came riding up from the fields and welcomed the soldiers to his home.

"Welllooky here the cavalry done come to see me. Y`all come on in the house and set down awhile and you can tell me how ma boy's doin."

The soldiers dismounted and followed Byron into the house, but no one said a word until they were inside.

"Mr. Candle, that's why we're here, it is about your boy."

Byron never suspected that they were carrying sad news and just kept on talking about how he sent his son to help get them Yankees out of our land. The lieutenant hearing Byron rant about how his son was going to end the war was becoming a little uneasy about delivering his message, but he knew that it had to be done so he launched in.

"Mr. Candle please sit down there's something I have to tell you."

Byron picking up on the somber tone of the lieutenant allowed his smile to fall and sat down.

"Something wrong with my boy?" he asked.

"Yes sir, I regret to inform you that your son is dead as the result of an action taken place recently."

"Dead, dead you caint be tellin me my son is dead, he jest left here a few days ago how can he be dead?"

"Sir, please accept this letter signed by President Davis commending your son for his voluntary service and explaining all the details on his demise."

Byron's temper got the best of him and he told the lieutenant that he didn't want no letter he wanted his son back here. He was starting to get belligerent and moving around the room in an extremely agitated fashion when the lieutenant asked him to calm himself. Byron responded by telling him that he waltzed in here telling him that his son was dead and now he wants me to be calm - I don't believe how you got the nerve.

By now, the commotion could be heard throughout the house and first Charlotte came downstairs and Aunt Tee and Clarence came in from the rear of the house. Byron was still walking around the room in a heated rage when Charlotte asked him what was wrong. He quickly told her and when she heard the news, she stood for a moment without saying anything then fell to the floor unconscious.

"Now look at that, see what y`all done done" Byron said as he moved to attend to his wife.

"Sir, there's nothing more I can do here, but we need to know whether you want to have the body brought here to you?"

"Course I want his body here is you daff? But before ya go I want to know just how he got killed in such a short time?"

The lieutenant hesitated answering. He hoped that he would have gotten past having to reveal this, but when he looked at Byron's face he knew there was no getting around it so he began.

"Sir, last week there were reports down around Fortress Monroe that there were some rebel slaves running loose in the woods and were causing problems that could affect the operations of the fort. A detail was dispatched to round them up and bring them in or destroy them, but an armed military action broke out. Your son was included in this detail and unfortunately as a result of the action he was wounded and subsequently expired."

"Now wait a minute, you tryna tell me he got killed by some rebel niggers running loose in the forest?"

"Sir I'm sorry but that's exactly what I'm telling you."

Byron couldn't restrain himself any more and went berserk. He started throwing things around the room almost hitting Charlotte who had recovered and was sitting on the couch. The soldiers at the lieutenant's command took hold of Byron and restrained him sitting him down in his favorite chair. The lieutenant talked softly to him telling him he could understand how he felt, but there was nothing else that could be done now except to see his son receive a proper burial. Byron heard his words calmed down hung his head and cried. The lieutenant turned to Mrs. Candle and told her he would arrange to have their son's body brought in as soon as possible but right now he had to leave to get back to his post. Charlotte managed to say she understood, and she would deal with her husband. The soldiers left and Charlotte went and put her arms around her husband just as Anna Lee came in the room.

"What's all the ruckus about I could hear y'all all the way outside?"

Byron got excited again seeing her and jumped up from his chair.

"Yo brother dun got killed not from no war but by some worthless niggers runnin around in the woods."

"You mean he's dead?"

"Yeah, yeah that's what I mean he ain't coming back here no more."

Anna Lee took a minute to process what she heard and then went into shock stumbling over to the couch and fell on it. Charlotte went to attend her, but Byron left the room and went looking for his gun. Aunt Tee and Clarence were still in the room watching all the drama and inside she was smiling. With gun in hand, he stormed out of the house headed to the fields. Since it was midday, the workers were still busy toiling with their assigned tasks, and no one paid any attention to him coming. The overseers just assumed when they saw him carrying his gun that he was just exercising his right to do so, but when he got close and they saw the rage that shown easily on his face, even they wondered what he was about.

Sleeping in the wagon was uncomfortable, but it did afford the pair shelter for the night. Jobba awoke well before the sun was even beginning to rise and shook awake his partner. He peeked outside to see if anyone was around and slowly stepped down from the wagon. Since it was still very early in the morning not too many people were up, and the streets were almost deserted except for the few night owls who had been cavorting all night. Jobba motioned to Shaka that they should make their way to the center of the town and see if they could find something that would direct them to the south side. Carefully making their way behind the buildings to what they assumed must be at or close to the middle of the main street he eased around one of the taller buildings and went to the front. Stopping just before the end of the structure he looked out and saw the platform where the slave auctions were held and then he scanned his view taking in the converted jailhouse that now had been reconverted back to a jail since the start of the war.

He kept looking and came across a small black boy who was seated on a barrel in front of the general store. Wondering why this boy would be out so early in the morning apparently by himself, Jobba was tempted to go over and talk to him, but then he noticed that he appeared to be waiting for something. Jobba paused to see what it might be and sure enough a few minutes later a burly man came out of the store with a large bag of what looked to be some food. The man placed the bag on a small wooden wagon and said something to the boy then pointed to another building not too far away. The boy took hold of the rope and started pulling the wagon, straining to move the heavy bag, toward the building. Jobba decided this could be the chance they needed to catch up with the boy and ask him where the south side of town was and the church Eli talked about. Moving back behind the buildings both men moved along with the boy looking out between the buildings to see if they were keeping pace with him. Finally,the boy came to the front of the target destination and knocked on the door. Jobba moved to the front of his building and looked across the street to see a soldier come and open the door.

The soldier picked up the bag and carried it inside while the boy waited at the door. Soon the soldier returned and placed something in the boy's hand who then placed it in his pocket. As he started to turn to go back to the store, Jobba took a chance and exposed himself from behind the building and waved his arms ferociously to get the boy's attention. The boy spotted him and stopped his motion. Jobba beckoned the boy to come to him. At first the lad stood motionless then he looked around to see if anyone else was watching and walked slowly over to Jobba keeping his eyes focused directly on him.

When he was close enough to Jobba the boy stopped and stared and immediately Jobba asked his question with no introductions.

"Boy, we needs ta git to the south side of this here town an to the black church. Ya knows where it be?"

The boy hesitated before answering wondering whom these men were and if it was wise for him to say anything not knowing whether they were good or bad. Jobba seeing him hesitate told him that they were running and needed his help to stay safe. The boy looked both men up and down and decided they were telling the truth and pointed down the street to a sign on a building near the end of the main street. He told them that when they got to the sign then turn right and follow the road to the end and they would see the church. Jobba thanked the boy and ducked back behind the building while the boy picked up his rope and went on his way back to the store.

Jobba and Shaka were starting to make their way toward the building with the sign when almost as if a bell had sounded activity started happening in the street. People were waking up and beginning their daily activities. The sun was rising, and the light of day was turning on. Afraid of being exposed before they could get to the end of the street the pair ducked into an open door that led into one of the smaller buildings. It was dark in the hallway, but there was enough light to see that they were in the back of a tobacco store. Hugging the walls, they eased their way trying to get to the front and possibly sneak out the door and scamper across the street. The store was close enough to the end of the main street that if they could get out and run across the street, then they could scamper down the side street and possibly get to the church.

The plan seemed to be working as they got close to the front of the store. However, once there they found the door locked from the inside and there was no key around. Frustrated that they were caught in an apparent no win situation because they could hear someone coming down from upstairs, both men quickly hid behind two large barrels near the front door. The footsteps coming down sounded like someone who was large and heavy and the fear of getting caught rose rapidly in each man's mind as they cowered lower behind the cover. The man who was as they thought a big robust middle-aged man with a wide handlebar mustache and big arms, went to the door inserted his key and unlocked it. Once he unlocked the door, he reached for a sign on the counter barely missing seeing Jobba and placed it on the door. After he hung the sign, he turned and went back into the hallway that Jobba and Shaka had just left. When they saw this they jumped up and opened the door not caring about the noise they made and ran out.

Once outside they ran as fast as they could to the other side of the street and turned down the side street running for the church. Several people saw them running and it was unclear why no one paid any attention or made any moves to stop them, but they were able to get away from the main street and duck behind one of buildings on the side street. Behind the building was a large woodshed that they ran into to rest and look behind to see if they were being pursued. Fortunately, no one chased but when Shaka looked the other way, he could see that the church was quite a distance away. If they went back out now, the chances of them being seen by others now coming out of their houses, was very high. Jobba thought that if he and Shaka just walked out slowly and tried to blend into the scenery, because there were other blacks whether slave or free beginning to fill the streets also, they might be able to make it to the church for safety.

He stepped out, followed by Shaka and they started walking casually down the street headed toward the church. They had walked only a few steps when they heard someone shouting for them to come over. Jobba turned his head to see who it was and what they wanted, and he saw two soldiers standing near the corner. Both he and Shaka froze. The soldiers kept calling them and Jobba was thinking about running again, but when the soldiers raised their rifles, he decided that it was not a good idea and started walking to them. Both he and Shaka were just a few feet from the soldiers when another soldier who apparently outranked them gave an order for them to report to him. The soldiers facing the pair lowered their rifles and quick-stepped over to the ranking man. Jobba and Shaka didn't hesitate a minute but turned and also quick-stepped away from the spot. Walking briskly, they separated themselves far enough so that even if the soldiers came back they were out of range for their rifles.

They reached the church and went around behind to see if there was a back way in. There was a door, but it was locked, and the windows were also. Slowly they walked back around to the front and looked out to see if anyone else was around. When they saw that no one was there they tried the front door and found it open. Quickly they went inside and looked around. It was not a very big church but nicely arranged and neatly kept. They went up toward the pulpit and off to the side saw a door that led to the back. Jobba opened the door and went in. There were two rooms that apparently were used for office space. Since there was no one around the two men decided to sit down in one of the pews and wait. It was not very long before they heard the front door open, and someone was coming in. It was a man who was very tall in stature, even taller than Jobba, and he was dressed in black with a white collar at his neck in the manner of a preacher. He was startled when he saw the pair sitting up in the first row and he stopped short from coming any further.

"What are you doing here?" he asked.

"I'se Jobba an dis be Shaka an we comes here ta git yo hep."

"Are you runaways?"

When the preacher asked that and the way he said it Jobba wasn't so sure that they were in safe company but he answered anyway.

"Yes we dun come from a far off an we's lookin for dat Underground Railroad station."

"Shhh," the preacher said as he moved forward closer to the men. He grabbed Jobba's arm and started leading him through the door into his office.

"I don't know where you heard about us, but we don't talk about that in the open around here. Where are you staying at?"

"We ain't got nowheres ta stay. We bin movin from one place to de otha since we got near dis town. I needs ta fine out soon how ta git on dat train so's I kin go back an git ma wife who still be on de plantation."

"Well booking passage on the train is not that simple and it's going to take some time to set it up. Why don't you come with me back in the sanctuary and let me pray for you while I petition God for some instructions on how to help you. Shaka wasn't so sure about this and Jobba too was a bit skeptical because he didn't feel that this man, even if he did have on the garb of a preaching man, was genuine. However, they really didn't have any choice, so they followed him out into the sanctuary. There the preacher knelt before the cross on the pulpit and motioned for the pair to kneel down with him and started to pray:

"Precious Lord our heavenly father, eternal and all wise God, I come to you seeking your guidance for these men who have come here for help. I thank you for having given this church the knowledge and wisdom to meet their needs, but Lord, I need you to guide me on how to protect them while we wait for your plan. Lead us O Lord according to your tender mercies and let not the evil that pursues these men overtake them. Lord it is by your hand that all deliverance comes and if it be your will then let me be the instrument of your choosing to lead these men to the freedom they seek. I ask this blessing in the name of Jesus and in His name I pray. Amen!

Jobba felt something, a stirring, a tingling, a shiver moving in his body as the preacher prayed and he got a little uncomfortable at feeling this way because he had not felt like this since the days down at the river listening to Daniel. He got up with the preacher and Shaka and they moved to sit down on the pew and talked. The preacher explained to him that they had a hidden room underneath the pulpit, and they could spend the night there while he tried to get in contact with the railroad conductor and book passage for him. Both men agreed wholeheartedly and Jobba was getting excited thinking that his journey had been successful, and his dreams were beginning to come true. Shaka, on the other hand, although feeling the excitement that Jobba felt just because Jobba was feeling it, was not quite as confident in this man and he had his doubts about this arrangement.

Jobba asked if they could see the room and the preacher agreed. He got up and walked over to the pulpit stepped up on it and stood behind the lectern. With a hard push he swung the sacred desk to the side exposing a trap door beneath it. Then he pulled on a handle that had been cut into the wooden panel and lifted it up. Jobba and Shaka moved over and stepped to the pulpit also. Once they were in position, they could see a wooden ladder leading to a small but well-fortified room with two beds and a lamp in it. Jobba wanted to go down and take a closer look, but Shaka cautioned him when he said that there was no way out of there except for coming up through this opening. Jobba heard this and was reminded of one of the things he learned while running in the woods and hiding in the caves behind the Candle Plantation. Always look for a second way out. He paused and gave it some serious thought for about a minute then he said to Shaka,"if this is how I'm gonna go, then I'm glad it will be in this place and nowhere else." At first, Shaka didn't understand the meaning of his reply, but when he gave it some thought he realized that Jobba was talking about the church and nodded his head in approval.

For the rest of the afternoon, Jobba and Shaka hung around the church helping the preacher with odd chores like cleaning and painting areas of the structure that needed attention. Several church members came in and out all during the day and the preacher didn't hesitate to introduce the pair as possible new congregants. There were even some white men who stopped by to see if the preacher needed any help, and this alarmed Jobba because he didn't believe he would ever hear a white man volunteer to help a black man. He was still suspicious when the preacher introduced him, and Shaka and he kept looking at the last white man to enter as though he had seen him before. It was not until the man left that it occurred to him, he had indeed seen this man before. It registered in his mind that this was one of the men who was in the patrol that had come onto Samson Sandler's farm and tried to take his brother Zeke away and subsequently tried to shoot down he and Shaka. At that point he knew it would be just a matter of time before that man would remember who he was and come back for them. Quickly he told the preacher the situation and said that both he and Shaka had to get out of there right now. The preacher couldn't believe his story because he told Jobba that this man was a real helper to this congregation, and it was not likely that he would be part of any patrol hunting down slaves. Jobba responded that he was sure it was the same man, and he asked the preacher if any of his members had gone missing over the last few weeks. The preacher paused before answering and thought about the question. When he finally answered the surprise on his face told Jobba what he needed to know. The preacher affirmed there were some of his congregants who recently had disappeared, and no one could account for their whereabouts.

Jobba just shook his head and told the preacher that this man was not a friend to him or the church, but would systematically kill each one of them one by one as he was given the opportunity. The preacher acknowledged Jobba's warning and told him that he would go on high alert and advise his people to do the same. He also said that they would start watching every move the man made when he came to the church. Jobba said that was good but as for him and Shaka they had to leave now and hide somewhere until he could tell them about the ticket on the train. The preacher agreed and told Jobba where they could go for some temporary shelter that would be safe. The place was the home of the preacher's brother who lived just outside of town off the main road but deep enough in the woods to be able to see anyone coming. Now the question was how they were going to get there. If they started walking in broad daylight, then it was possible that the same man or one of the soldiers might be patrolling and capture them.

Jobba asked if any of the preacher's members were nearby and maybe had a wagon they could hide in while he took them to the house. The preacher answered that the blacksmith who ran the local livery was one of his people and he has a wagon but whether he could get away to perform the task now was a big question. Jobba asked how far away the livery was thinking that if it was close enough then he could run there before getting spotted, but when the preacher told him that it was in the middle of town Jobba withdrew his suggestion. The preacher realized that if the message was going to get to the blacksmith, then he had to be the one to deliver it. He told the duo that they had better hide in the secret room while he went, just in case that man remembered who they were and decided to come back for them now. He went back to the lectern and opened the secret room overhead door and Jobba and Shaka reluctantly climbed down into the dark room.

In the room they were reluctant to light the lamp for fear of the lamp giving off the smell of something burning and anyone not familiar with the room might think that the building was on fire. Shaka said to Jobba that he felt very uncomfortable about being in this room with no way out and he felt like the animals on the farm when they were caught in a trap. Jobba agreed with him but answered that he hoped it would only be for a short time until the preacher came back and let them out. They kept talking for what seemed like hours and the anxiety level for both was beginning to rise. Not only was the heat in the small room rising from their own bodies, but the air was also becoming a factor in their survival. With fresh oxygen becoming scarce and taking each breath more difficult, both men stopped talking and inwardly wondered if they were going to get out of here alive. Jobba stood up and started to walk around to try and relieve the stress while Shaka remained reclined on the bed not wanting to build up any excess need for more oxygen. Panic was really starting to set in for both men, when they heard a sound above them like the door was opening. The sudden exposure to the light was shocking to the eye and it took a little while for them to adjust but the pair were so glad to breathe deeply the fresh air in the sanctuary that the recent ordeal melted away with the relief.

The preacher told them that he had successfully made arrangements with the blacksmith to come by within the next half hour and drive the men out to his brother's house. Thoroughly relieved at hearing the news Jobba and Shaka went and sat in the preacher's office out of sight and waited for their ride to come. The preacher went on about his normal activities and was in the middle of one of his chores when the door opened and the man who they suspected of being a patroller came in with two other white men. He greeted the preacher politely as he normally did and casually asked about the two men that he met before. He was asking if he could speak to them again. The preacher now very aware that what Jobba told him must indeed be really true, told the patroller that the men had gone away, and he wasn't sure where they might have gone. The man looked at him suspiciously and for the first time since they had known each other the preacher saw something in the man's eyes that he had never observed before. It was a sign of hatred that had been covered up with the ruse of friendship. The patroller saw the door beside the pulpit but assumed that it led to the outside and was unaware that there were any more rooms in the building. They turned around and started to leave but stopped and told the preacher that if those men should come back, he would like to talk to them.

Jobba and Shaka who were just on the other side of the wall and could hear all that was being said got ready to scramble out of the window should the patrollers come through the door. Happy that it didn't become necessary, they settled back in the chairs and confident that those men wouldn't be coming back since they had already been here, they relaxed. The preacher came through the door shortly after the men left and confirmed to Jobba all that he had been told and apologized for not being able to see through this man's guise in the first place. Further the preacher told Jobba and Shaka that they should stay at his brother's house until Sunday and then come back to hear him preach. He said that it was funny what happened should occur at this time, because the sermon he is going to deliver on Sunday has to do with Lies and Deception. They all had a good laugh that set the tension level at near zero and they enjoyed the moment.

While they were still in the back enjoying their brief respite from the day's troubles, the sound of a wagon pulling up was heard and the preacher got up to see if it was in fact the blacksmith. He opened the church door and invited the smithy in to meet his passengers. The introductions were made quickly because the smithy explained that due to the heavy activity of the army's involvement in the war and the escalated presence of the military in town, he had to make this a short and hurried trip and get back to his livery. Jobba and Shaka got in the back of the open wagon and hid under the many blankets strewn around. It was a short ride from the church to the preacher's brother's house and they made it without incident from the army patrolling the area. It was not unusual for the blacksmith to be seen going and coming from the town to the outer lying area and stopping him every time got to be a nuisance, so the army stopped doing it. They arrived at the house and since the preacher's brother was not expecting anyone the blacksmith had to take some extra time that he really didn't want to expend, to explain the preacher's wishes. The brother was busy at work with his crops so when the wagon arrived, he was surprised to get the visit, but when the smithy told him the reason for the call, he was glad to be able to help the cause.

He invited Jobba and Shaka in the house and introduced them to his family. There was his wife and three kids and also a male cousin and his wife and two kids who shared the house. In addition, there were three other men who didn't live with them but came as day workers to help with the farming chores. When Jobba looked at the house he was reminded of his place at the Candle Plantation in that it had a large lower level and a fairly large loft that must have had at least the same amount of space. He saw that there were several beds on the first level so he wondered if he and Shaka might be sharing the upper level for the few days they would be there. The answer for him came quickly when the brother pointed to the barn in the back and told them that they could put up there for the night. In Jobba's mind this seemed like it was a repeat of the scene at the Sandler's, and he silently hoped that the outcome would not be the same.

Jobba and Shaka went to the barn and made sleeping places for themselves while the brother, his family and his workers returned to the fields to complete their day's tasks.

Jobba came back from the barn and walked down to the fields and offered to help, but he was told that his help was not needed just yet. After the work for the day was completed and the day workers departed, the family came in the house and prepared to eat dinner. One of the children was sent to the barn to fetch the visiting guests and Jobba and Shaka came in and sat at the table. The table was just large enough to accommodate all of the adults, so the children were given their plates and told to sit at a small table in the back of the house near the sleeping area.

All through the meal Jobba was very uncomfortable because the preacher's brother's wife kept staring at him. He tried to ignore it by making light conversation with the brother and telling him about the journey he and Shaka had made coming from a far off. The more he tried to ignore it the more it seemed that she was enamored of his adventurous tales. Shaka must have noticed it too because he tried to engage her in some conversation that would make her redirect her attention, but the diverging strategy only lasted a short time before she returned her attention to Jobba. It was hard to tell whether the brother was aware of the situation for he said nothing to indicate his displeasure nor did he do anything to chastise his wife. When they all had finished eating Jobba was glad to excuse himself and get up from the table. He had no sooner stepped outside the door headed back to the barn when the brother came out and started talking to him and Shaka.

"I'se sure y'all notice dat ma wife seem like she got dem rovin eyes, but she don mean nothin by it. Sometime she think she gots ta do that wheneva strangers come about 'cause she say I don pay 'nuff 'tention ta her. Y'all don pay her no mind an jest go on 'bout yo bidness whiles ya here an we be fine."

Jobba heard more in the man's explanation then what the words were saying and he wondered if he shouldn't be more attentive to what was really going on in the family's internal affairs. When the brother finished and went back in the house, Jobba looked at Shaka and asked him what he thought that was all about. Shaka replied that he thought their welcome here might not be as gracious as they pretended, and the stay should not be extended any longer than absolutely necessary to take care of the business they needed done. Jobba wholeheartedly agreed adding that the barn may be the safest place for them away from the house tonight. He didn't know how wrong he was.

It was starting to get dark, and the duo prepared to bed down in the hastily made straw mattress and horse saddle pillows. There were two horses in the stalls, but the men paid no attention to the fact that the smell was not exactly conducive to getting a good night's sleep. Not long after dark and Jobba was just getting into the rhythm of a good sleep when he felt the presence of another body snuggling up against him. He immediately woke up and turned over to see the brother's wife lying down beside him. All she had on was a thin night gown that was already half open at the top exposing all that she had to offer there, which was more than an ample supply. He looked over to where Shaka was to see if he was still awake and then back at the woman who was smiling at him.

It had been sometime since he had enjoyed the company of his wife and his manly desires were being aroused even as he realized the brevity of this situation. He couldn't resist staring at the inviting cleavage and then she started to peal down the gown the rest of the way for him to get an even better look. Jobba was caught between wanting to do the right thing and the temptation of lust for this woman. He knew he should get up from there and run out, but when she grabbed him and kissed him hard on the lips the latter part of his dilemma was starting to prevail, and he was about to succumb to the temptation of lust. He was responding to her kiss and ready to take the next step when he heard the horses become agitated and the barn door open. He jumped up immediately pulled his pants up and ran to the other end of the barn and looked out from behind a stall. Thinking that it was the brother who had come looking for his wife, Jobba was all ready to flee the barn and escape into the night, even if he didn't know where he would go. However, it was not the brother but the cousin's wife who came to get her and wrapped her up in a robe she had brought with her and led her outside and back to the house. Jobba slowly came back to his makeshift bed and wondered if there was something wrong with this woman, but then he focused on himself and wondered if there was something wrong with him that he would have given in, and then he thought about Myanna and whether she might be being tempted the same way.

The morning came and one of the children entered the barn looking for the duo to come to breakfast. Jobba and Shaka responded, went, and sat down at the table. Jobba looked at the wife and then at the brother and then at the cousin's wife and it was as if nothing had happened. He waited for the man to say something and when he did all he talked about was what was on the schedule for today's tasks. Jobba looked again at the cousin's wife, and she almost lost it trying to contain a laugh, so she covered her face with her hand and pretended to cough. Jobba looked at the wife more closely and the blank expression on her face told him more about her than he saw when he first met her. The brother went on talking about what he had to do today, and he also mentioned to Jobba that he was expecting his brother, the preacher to come by today and let him know about what's going on in town. Jobba contributed to the light conversation by saying that he too was interested in hearing that. The breakfast ended and the group broke up and everybody went to do what they normally did on a Saturday morning.

It was just after the noon day hour when the preacher came and went into the house. The family had finished their half day work in the fields, and they were just settling in to relax and enjoy the rest of the afternoon, when the preacher told them that there was some stepped up activity around town looking for several runaways that had come in from down the Hampton way looking to join up with the Yankee soldiers in this area. Jobba asked him what kind of activity and the preacher said that it was not safe for any blacks to be seen on the main roads again unless they had a white man or a valid pass with them. Jobba then asked him whether he had heard anything about him getting his ticket on the train. The preacher hesitated answering and looked around the room to assess whether Jobba had mentioned anything about this to the family. Seeing a blank expression on their faces he assumed that nothing had been said and he told Jobba that he would talk to him outside about the matter. Jobba was a little suspicious as to why this would be such a private issue and he started to ask, when the preacher motioned to him to wait.

Jobba anxious to hear what the preacher would have to say got up and started to walk outside while the preacher went in the back of the house to talk with his brother. Moments later he too came outside and talked with Jobba and Shaka. He told them that he didn't want his brother to know about his involvement with the Underground Railroad because, in case they hadn't noticed his wife was slightly less than wholesome mentally and was prone to tell anybody everything she heard. He continued that he was expecting the conductor or a contact to be at the service on Sunday and then he would know how to make the proper arrangements after that. Jobba was happy to hear this news and he was content to wait, but he asked the preacher if he thought it would be alright for him to go back into town tonight because he needed to retrieve something he had left in a wagon where they hid out a couple of nights ago. The preacher asked him how important was it that he had to go back and get it and risk getting caught. Jobba assured him it was very important, so the preacher said try it.

Jobba talked with the preacher's brother and told him his plight and asked if he could borrow a horse for his midnight ride. The brother was accommodating and told him to be sure that he was careful after hearing what the preacher had just told him about the stepped-up activities. When Jobba told Shaka about his mission and what he had left behind Shaka said he wanted to go with him, but Jobba at first told him no, but then he rethought his answer when he reflected on all they had been through together. He remembered what had been said to him about two being better than one and falling into a ditch so he invited his companion to go even though they would have only one horse.

They waited until it was very dark before setting out then the two men mounted up and headed to the city. The road at night didn't seem to be heavily patrolled so they believed that when they were getting close to the city limits, they would be able to tie the horse up to a post at the edge of town and then sneak back into where the wagon was that they slept in two nights ago. It seemed strange to Shaka that based on what the preacher said that the entrance to town would seem so abandoned and they approached very slowly. The two men were able to cross the line marking the city limits and got even as far as a hitching post where they were going to tie up the horse. They didn't see it coming nor did they hear any sound of someone approaching, but before they could turn around and run to any secure area, destiny took over and the outcome of their fate was determined.

Chapter 12 - Desperation

These were dark days at the Candle place ever since a few days ago in a fit of rage Byron, after hearing the news about his son, ran into the fields and shot to death one of his workers and wounded another. Had it not been for Sam the overseer who intervened while Byron was trying to reload, the carnage might have been much worse. Sam wrestled the gun away from Byron and shouted at him that he was destroying his own property. Appealing to his sense of money and the loss of it, Sam was convinced that this message would get through to the enraged man and he was right. Byron looked at the fallen slave and then at the other worker holding himself, but still standing. He sank to the ground and sat rocking back and forth with his arms folded over his legs. Sam went to him and asked him what the matter was Byron didn't answer, but kept rocking. Getting no answer, Sam helped the master to his feet and started walking him back to the house where Charlotte after hearing the gunshots was waiting on the porch.

When she saw Sam practically carrying her husband she wondered if he had been the recipient of any of the shots. Sam got to the porch and sat Byron down on the steps and told Charlotte what had happened then asked what was wrong. Charlotte explained to him about Jethro and Sam in sympathy said that he could understand his rage, but killing the ones who would have to help bring in the harvest was not smart. Charlotte looked at him for a minute trying to assess whether he was being sarcastic or genuinely sincere with his remarks. She then told Sam to help Byron into the house so she could put him to bed. Sam lifted Byron up and walked him in the house and up the stairs to his room where he placed him on the bed. Charlotte thanked him for his service and told him he could leave now. Sam took one final look at the master of the house in this pitiful condition and shook his head then left.

Aunt Tee who was tuned in to all that was going on especially in light of Byron committing murder, was secretly praising her demon for stirring up the turmoil and discordance on the land. She was provoking the spirit to boost the tension so that she could claim the balance of the souls who had not given in to her invitations to join with her. Byron was just the beginning of what she was hoping would be the start of the final battle for supremacy on the plantation where her demons would cast out the Daniel people and rein over the land. Disposing of Byron or allowing him to continue but not in his right mind, would be the spark she needed to convince the skeptical believers that she truly had the power to rule.

Clarence reveled also at what looked like the conquering of the resistant. However, he was caught in a private dilemma. Since he had been going to see Myanna and becoming more enamored of her whenever he got close; he couldn't bring himself to harm her or to even place her in harm's way. Myanna had not yet begun to return his overtures, but he knew that with every visit and the small gifts that he would bring her, it was just a matter of time. The fact that she still held to her views regarding Daniel and his preaching didn't deter him. For as strongly as she believed in her God so he did in his demon, and he was convinced that his would prevail.

The time was coming when he would put her in a position where she had to either refute his advances openly or give him some sign that he was winning her affections. Tonight, he determined that the time had come, and it was the right time. He was going to the cabin and demand that Penniman and Tralene leave and take the kids out for a while and enjoy the summer breeze down by the river. Since he was the second in command under Aunt Tee, he knew that Penniman was prone to obey. In the mansion, the normal after dinner cordial hour had been dispensed with since the death of Jethro and Byron had become very withdrawn making an evening of chit chat undesirable. Now after dinner the family would disperse each to his desired area of comfort and do whatever it took to get through the rest of the day. This situation presented plenty of opportunity for Clarence to get away and head down to the quarters. This time, intent on carrying out his plan, he gathered his most precious gift yet and headed out.

In the quarters Myanna had just finished her late dinner alone after the Harpers had vacated the table and she was feeling tired. The children were outside playing and Penniman and Tralene were in the back lying down. Myanna ascended the stairs headed to her bed to lie down when she felt a sudden urge to look out the window. It had been sometime since she did this and the strong urge bothered her. She started reflecting on the times when she and Jobba would do this together and even the times when the children would view the stars with them, and it was such a warm feeling. However, this time the feeling wasn't warm, but an eerie one drawing her to look deeply into the night stars. It was a beautiful night, and the jet-black sky was speckled with thousands of stars twinkling, each trying to outshine the other. As she looked up and focused her gaze on one, it seemed that it was indeed much brighter than the rest and it became as a giant silken canvass.

She continued staring and gradually images started to appear on the canvass in a quadrant. In the first square she could see the form of an older woman lying on a bed reaching out to her with some desperation. At first, she couldn't make out who it was, but as she fixed her gaze it became clear that the woman was Bessie May, and she was trying to speak to her. Although no words came out of her mouth, by the motions she displayed Myanna could tell she was dying and was attempting to impart her last wishes or warnings to her. Myanna's heart was pounding, and she was trying to dismiss the sight as just her imagination, but her eyes were locked on the canvass as if frozen in the position. Bessimay was trying to speak but she was also pointing to the second square. In that square Myanna saw the image of Suliah sitting by herself in the corner of a room with her head in her hands and crying. Myanna wanted to reach out to her and comfort her, but she realized this was impossible and she looked back at Bessie May who then pointed to the third square in which Linwood appeared. He was dressed in a soldier's uniform and sitting in an encampment with other black military men leaning over a man who was severely wounded. She couldn't tell if he was also wounded, but from the expression on his face she could see that he was scared.

Finally, with her last ditch effort Bessimay pointed to the remaining square and held it there for a while then her arm dropped and the image faded from the screen. Myanna felt in her heart that Bessimay had made her last connection with all of them and then transitioned to the next phase of existence. She closed her eyes for a moment and breathed deeply to try and regain her composure, but when she opened them and viewed the last square what composure she had regained was suddenly lost. In that square, she saw her beloved Jobba and Shaka surrounded by confederate soldiers. They began tightening the circle with their guns pointed directly at the duo's heads. This was more than Myanna could take and she staggered over to her bed where she collapsed.

The connection that Bessie May made with her last ounce of strength was seen not only by Myanna but at some point, in the night both Suliah and Linwood saw it also and they knew their father was in trouble but there was nothing they could do about it.

"Alright niggers stop right there and put your hands over your heads" one of the soldiers said.

Jobba hung his head and the thought briefly ran through his mind to strike out running, but the enemy was all around him and there was no chance he could get away. The soldiers approached them and roped the two men together with their arms tied behind their backs and marched them off to the reconverted jail in the center of town. Once inside Jobba and Shaka were thrown into a cell with several other slaves who were in various states of existence. Some were sick and smelly near the point of death and others were hanging on. Jobba and Shaka moved carefully among them trying to find a spot where they could sit down away from the sick ones. There wasn't much room in the overly crowded cell so finding space for their desire was difficult.

They managed to find a small gap in the group and eased down to the floor with their backs against each other. A guard passed by and laughingly said to the group that they wouldn't have to endure this long because in the morning they were all going to be hung. When Jobba heard this, he got up from the floor and pushed his way back to the front of the jail and confronted the jailer.

"Why's we gonna be hung suh?"

"Cause you on the wrong side an you was runnin' niggah."

"Suh, we wasn runnin we's jest comin ta town."

"Yeah, yeah I know you was comin ta do some shoppin, but ya picked the wrong time ta do it" he said as he walked away laughing heartily.

Jobba slid down the bars to the floor and with his head looking out between them he felt his whole being becoming like a wet rag. His feeling of desperation drew him back to when he was on the Sutter Plantation, and he had those dreams where he was on the slave ship being brought to this country. He felt some strength coming back because he remembered that in his dream he called out to God and somehow, he was able to get loose from the bowels of the ship and get free. Struggling to get up again he stumbled over some of the men making his way back to Shaka. When he reached his companion, he told him about his dream and what he did to survive. Shaka looked at him strangely not believing that it could work but since Jobba was so insistent on trying, Shaka had to join with him.

Jobba took his companion's hand and led him to a corner of the cell where he knelt down and started to pray. Shaka watched him at first then knelt beside him not completely understanding which god he was trying to contact. For him it was the ancestors that he should have been seeking to get in touch with.

"God in heaven I knows you up dere an I believes ya kin hep me an dis man here. We bin tryna git to de man dat runs dat railroad so's we kin go 'way from here an be free. But now we's here in dis jail an I dono how we gonna git out. If'n ya heps us git outta here den we gonna be de best men we knows how ta be an we gonna thank ya mighty grateful. I 'member when I'se back on de plantation dat preacher Daniel say he works ta serve you an if we wanna be really free den we needs ta serve ya too. Well I won mind servin' ya an I think dis man here will do de same if'n we gits out. So God, om lookin' for ya ta show us how. Daniel say when we asks fer somethin', we needs ta ask in de name of dat Jesus an it gonna be done, so God om askin' in his name an hopin' ya hear me prayin'. Dat's all for now, but we ain got long ta stay here 'fore dey gonna hang us, so we need ya now. Amen!"

Shaka joined him in saying Amen because Joba said it and the pair leaned back against the wall. The moans of the sick ones and the agitated circle walking of others, was getting on Jobba's nerves and he felt like he was going to be sick himself. Between the foul stench and the thought of being hanged the next day his stomach was tied up in knots and his muscles were extremely tense. Shaka looked at him in his agony and then he said to his friend:

"Jobba, you believe in your God?"

"Ya heard me prayin' ta him didn't ya, so why ya ask me dat?"

"'Cause if'n ya really believes dat he kin do what ya ask him, den why ya lookin like ya don't believe. You all bent ova like ya already dead."

When Jobba heard his friend's words he realized that the wisdom coming out of his mouth sounded so much like Daniel he wondered if the preacher had not possessed him. He turned and looked at Shaka to see if there was any change that had come over the man, but he was still the same. Jobba pulled himself together and reflected on something else he had heard from Daniel,

But without faith it is impossible to please Him, for he who comes to God must believe that He is, and that He is a rewarder of those who diligently seek Him. (Heb. 11:6)

As he thought about these instructions from Daniel and internalized them the strength he lost returned and his nerves settled down. He lowered his head to his chest and tried to sleep. Shaka sat beside him and marveled at the change wondering if some unseen spirit had suddenly eased his discomfort. To Shaka, this thing called the religion of the Jesus believers must be very powerful and he was becoming convinced. He said to himself, if a way for them to get out of here happens then he would be thoroughly persuaded to believe himself.

Feeling more relaxed but unsettled, Jobba wafted in and out of an anything but peaceful sleep. Shaka had managed to drift into a rather peaceful slumber as if he trusted more in Jobba's god then Jobba seemingly did. Along about the hour just before sunrise a loud commotion was heard outside the jailhouse. At first it sounded like men shouting and then several gunshots were heard ringing rapidly about the jail's exterior. Suddenly the front door flew open, and the guards inside jumped to their feet in an attempt to defend themselves. Coming through the door was an element of the Union Army that was the advance scouts for an attack on the city of Richmond. Before the guards could get off shots of their own, the soldiers fired hitting two of them closest to the entrance. There were three others at the rear of the building who, seeing the Yankee contingent, fled out the back door and were confronted by bluecoat soldiers positioned there.

Stepping over the fallen guards and retrieving keys, the soldiers hastily opened the cell doors and exclaimed to the prisoners they could go free, but they needed to run now. The stampede out of the cells caused some of those who were less able to run to fall. Jobba and Shaka who were at the rear of their cell picked those up and dragged them to the front and then outside where they deposited them on a bench. They didn't stop to see what the fate of the fallen would be, but they ran straight to the place where they had tied up the preacher's brother's horse hoping that it would still be there. When they found the horse still tied to the hitching post just as they left it, Shaka was thoroughly convinced that Jobba's god could work magic. They climbed on the horse and galloped out of the area headed back to the preacher's house. Jobba knew they couldn't stay there, but he had to return the horse as he promised.

Clarence was making his way down to the quarters smiling and greeting all of the cabin residents regardless of who they served as he passed them. The way was filled with children and adults playing and sitting outside enjoying the warmth of the summer, but he knew that even though things seemed to be pleasant and peaceful the tensions between the two religious factions was at its peak. Aunt Tee at the last cave ritual had informed her followers that the time was near when the cave spirit would demand that all the inhabitants of this plantation, including the master and his family, would either become his or suffer his wrath. Clarence, tonight was not only going to make his pitch as a suitor, but also as a proselyte for Aunt Tee. As he approached the Harper abode, he quickened his steps bolstered by the anticipation of a successful evening. In front of the door, he noticed that the Harper children were already outside, so he envisioned that half of his mission had already been accomplished. He knocked and the response was slow, but Penniman came and answered. Quickly Clarence told Penniman of his recruiting plan and that he needed to be alone with his target. Penniman, understanding the need, reluctantly agreed to give up the place and went to the back and got Tralene and they walked out.

Alone in the cabin Clarence made his way quietly up the stairs and when he got to the top, he noticed that the lamp was very low, and he could hardly make out where Myanna was. He scanned the room and in the dim light he saw that she was lying on the bed in a kind of awkward position. As he walked over to her he noticed that she was breathing but in an irregular pattern. Suspecting that something might be wrong, when he reached the bed, he reached out and shook her. She responded groggily and strained to focus her eyes on who was attending her. Clarence looked around the room to see if there was any water available, but seeing none he got up and went down to get some. By the time he made his way back Myanna was sitting up, but still appearing somewhat shaken. Clarence offered her water which she drank and then asked her what was wrong.

She hesitated for an unusually long period after hearing the question looking at the floor then she finally raised her head and looked at him.

"I jest had a bad vision an it scared me."

"What did ya see?"

"I caint tell ya all I see'd but it was 'bout Jobba an my chil'ren."

"You don't believe he still 'live does ya?"

"I dono now 'cause dat vision seem like he was almos' gone but I didn' see no end to it."

"Well if'n ya saw mos of it, den ya gotta believe he gone. Now I dun come here ta hep ya git ova dem feelin's for dat man 'cause he ain comin' back here no mo. Here I got somthin' cheer ya up."

He reached in his pocket and took out a necklace he had crafted from costume jewelry thrown away by the ladies of the mansion. It was indeed a beautiful piece and after he had polished it to a high brilliance it sparkled when he presented it. Myanna looked at it in his hand and started not to accept it.

"Mr. Clarence I knows ya bin tryna be good ta me, an I thanks ya, but I caint take dat from ya."

"Woman, yo man is dead an I might be all's ya got lef' here. Take it an be happy. I made it jest fer you so's ya gonna hurt me if'n ya don accept it."

Myanna held out a little longer, but the more she looked at it, the appeal was getting stronger, and her resistance was getting weaker. She took it and started to put it around her neck when he got on the bed and kneeled behind her to help. While behind her and fastening the piece he placed his arms around her shoulders and kissed her neck. At first, she was surprised, but when she didn't get up, he did it again and then gently pulled her down on the bed. Once he had her fully reclined, he kissed her full on the lips. Myanna, who had wanted to be with her man for so long, was reacting to the loneliness, the longing and almost succumbed to the moment. Somehow though she managed to recover and resisted him pushing him away. Clarence declaring that he was not to be denied started to force the act, but Myanna was able to push him aside long enough for her to slide out from under him and get up

"Mr. Clarence, I thanks ya for the gift, but I caint do dat now, I jest dono' fer sho 'bout Jobba."

Clarence got up from the bed disappointed at his attempt being rejected, but gathered himself and then moved on to his next mission.

"Ya knows de time is comin' soon when you an dat Daniel man an all a y'all got ta join up wit Aunt Tee an me an takes de mark of de cave spirit or its gonna go bad fer ya. I kin make it easy but ya got ta do it soon. Why don' ya come to de next moon dance an change back ova? When ya change ova den she kin tell ya if yo man be dead or live."

When he said that Myanna started thinking about the vision she saw earlier and was getting depressed again. She thanked him one more time for the gift, but asked him to leave because she wasn't feeling good. He agreed, but before he left he made her promise that she would consider the offer and said he would be coming back again soon. She agreed, to get him out of the cabin and once he left she went back to looking out the window hoping to see the star that might give her the answer she sought.

Huddled in the corner of her room with her knees pulled up tight against her chest, Suliah cried bitterly into her folded arms. Amanda was up on the third floor entertaining one of Jonathan's political cronies and she feared that she was going to be called on next since there were still other guests in the house. Lately as the war intensified and Jonathan was getting more active in the politics behind the war decisions, he was having more frequent gatherings to appease his guests and gain political advantage. Since Jethro's death and Jonathan's discovery of the relationship between him and Suliah, Jonathan treated her badly. Now in his eyes she was no longer considered the trophy that he had claimed at the auction, but was just another slave to be used as he saw fit. She was given harder tasks than the rest and when she performed them poorly because of lack of training and skill he would chastise her severely. It had gotten to the point now where no matter what she tried to do she was afraid of him.

Even her friend and roommate Amanda had turned against her when she saw that Suliah was no longer the master's favorite. Sleeping at night became difficult and when she did the nightmares, she dreamed were haunting. Even tonight as she contemplated finding a way to end it all because she could see no end to her suffering, something was drawing her to look out her window. She felt the urge but fought it as hard as she could thinking that what her nightmares had foretold might be intensified out there. The more she resisted it, the stronger the urge got, and she finally gave in and got up. She walked over to the window and looked out at the night filled with many stars. The same scene appeared before her that had been seen by her mother and Linwood and when she looked at the square showing the state of Bessimay she froze in disbelief. Her fear of death and the emotions tied to it were even more disconcerting than when she witnessed Jethro's passing. Somehow, she managed to look at the rest of the quadrant and when she came to the last one and saw the image of her father and his predicament the combination of all the images drove her to scream at the top of her lungs before she went into shock and sank to the floor. She sat there leaning against the wall rocking furiously back and forth.

Bernard who was closest to her in his room heard the screams and came running followed shortly by Jonathan. They both entered her room and saw her rocking. Jonathan just looked at her like she had lost her mind and told Bernard to take care of her and he left. Bernard bent down and wrapped his arms around her to try and comfort her, but she would not be comforted. He picked her up walked her over to the bed and placed her on it. Her eyes had taken on a vacant stare and when he talked to her, she was unresponsive. Figuring that he needed to get her some water, he left the room. When he returned with the water the room was empty. Afraid that she was going to do something to harm herself he turned around immediately and looked first in the hallway and then in the kitchen. Since Jonathan still had a couple of gentlemen guests waiting for their turn to experience his special hospitality, Bernard knew that she wouldn't have gone into the front part of the house.

He left the kitchen and started toward the back door that he found to be partially open. Thinking she may have gone out he quickly rushed through the door and looked around. He didn't see her anywhere in the back so he decided to walk around to the front believing that in her state of mind she may just have started to walk into the city. He looked down the road as far as he could see, but there was no sign of her. As he turned around to go back into the house, he happened to look up to the small balcony on the third floor. By the light of the moon that shone brightly he saw a silhouette of something standing on the balcony. He moved forward to get a better look and as he got closer, he recognized that it was her standing there with her hands on the railing looking down at the ground with the same blank stare.

Bernard moved forward until he was almost right under her waving his arms vigorously not wanting to shout because of Jonathan's remaining guests inside. He was trying desperately to get her attention, but to no avail. Even while he was waving, she moved her head from side and then started to climb onto the railing. He knew that there was no way that he could get up there in time to pull her back so he just kept waving his arms hoping that she might come to her senses.

Suliah's mind was reliving the death of Jethro and Bessimay and now what she believed would be her father and then finally all of the death's she had witnessed throughout her young life came together. The fall from grace within the eyes of Jonathan and his malicious treatment of her caused her to envision a bleak future without any hope for a happy ending. This state of mind created in her a darkness that didn't come from the night, but from a richer shade of blackness that absorbed all of the bright colors of the world into a hodgepodge. The thickness of the darkness clouded her mind so much so that she couldn't remember what the presence of light looked like. This blackness was not of the night, but of a spiritual darkness that possesses one who is ready to leap into the bottomless pit and fall into oblivion.

Bernard was close enough now to get a good look at the expression on her face and it was as if she was being guided not by anything that she had control over, but by something else that was driving her. He continued to wave his arms furiously and then jumping up and down until they were getting sore from the effort. Suliah had completed her climb on the railing and was now standing on it still staring down at the ground. He didn't know whether she saw him or was looking past or through him, but his efforts to snap her out of the trance with his motions wasn't working. He didn't know what else to do so he stopped waving and just looked on. What he saw next he couldn't bring himself to accept, right there before his eyes - she jumped.

Just a few miles north of Fortress Monroe a Union Army detachment was encamped in an area that had been set up right after the most recent battle. The unit had taken heavy casualties and it seemed like the South was going to prevail in the war. Linwood had been exposed to his first close combat and it was taking its toll on him. He had lost some friends that he was just getting to know and it made him very uneasy that this could happen to them in such a short time. Tonight, as he lay just outside his tent staring up at the stars, the same vision that occurred to his mother and Suliah was shown to him also. He saw the state of Bessie May as well as that of his father and felt a strong yearning to do something, but realized that even if he was there by the side of either, what could he do? For Bessie May, a tear welled up in his eyes that he fought back to keep from allowing any of the other men outside to witness. For his father he wished with all his inner being that somehow his fate might be the same as when they were rolling down the hill in a wagon headed toward certain death when whatever powers might be, intervened and saved all of them. Since he had left the tutelage of Daniel, Linwood had backed off in believing what Daniel preached and was now moving backward in his faith and slipping into darkness.

As he lay there trying to keep from falling into a deep state of depression the voice of the lieutenant shouted out for the men to get their gear together because they were about to move out. Linwood could hardly believe what he was hearing because it was still dark and before now, they had never done any fighting after sunset. The lieutenant hollered again for the men to get themselves up and get moving. The urgency in his voice made Linwood believe that there was something right in the immediate area that needed their attention. Once the men were assembled, the lieutenant told them that not too far away a small group of Union soldiers had been cornered in a valley and one of their men had managed to escape and get word to him. He said they were moving out now under cover of darkness so they could get close enough to launch a counterattack at first light and surprise the enemy.

At first this action sounded exciting to Linwood, moving out in the darkness and chasing the enemy through the forest and he was getting all pumped up to go on the mission, but then he thought about the last battle he saw firsthand and the vision of all the carnage came to his mind. The excitement quickly disappeared and was replaced by a spirit of foreboding. The men grabbed their gear and mounted the horses waiting for the command to begin. As the lieutenant rode up and down the ranks getting a count of the number of able men, he had to launch his attack he shook his head remembering just a few days ago that number was almost double. He was an experienced career soldier and when he thought about the number of men under his command that had just recently entered into service, he was very uncomfortable about taking this group into the type of skirmish that he envisioned for this mission. In his eyes he saw a mixture of some wily career veterans but for the most part they were young men who only knew they were here because they wanted to preserve the union. In others, he saw the group of black men separated from them who were here because they had the real mission and that was to gain their freedom.

After surveying his troop strength and gathering the last of the information available from the soldier who was at the battle site, he ordered his men to move out and the mission began. To Linwood who was lined up at the rear of the two columns along with the other black soldiers, riding in the dead of night was a first and he felt a mixture of fear and excitement. They left the safety of the encampment and in short order were on the main road headed toward the valley. Suspecting they might encounter some confederate troops hiding in the woods just off the main road the commander cautioned his men to keep alert and not allow the darkness to lull them into a false sense of security. The columns moved along at a moderate pace and before long they came to an area just outside of a small town. The lieutenant gave the order to halt then he called forward one of his more experienced troopers and told him to pick another man and move ahead to scout out the area of the town borders. He wanted to know whether the town was under a friendly flag or was it still covered by the grays. The corporal received the order and went back and selected another soldier who he had seen handle himself well during the last outing. The selected soldier eagerly responded to the invitation and the two men rode out ahead of the pack.

The lieutenant told the men to dismount and break for a short while until the scouts returned with their report. He was careful to instruct the men not to smoke or light up anything that could cause a light to be seen. He further reminded them of their training about how far light could be seen in the darkness and how the light was more powerful and greater than the darkness. Linwood heard the words of the officer and it kind of reminded him of the teachings of Daniel as he sat on the side of the road with the other men wondering what lay ahead of them. It wasn't long before the scouts returned and reported that there was no indication as to whether the town was in the hands of one side or the other. Since it was late, most of the townspeople had retired for the night and those that were still walking the streets were not the ones that could give a straight or reliable answer.

After hearing the report, it was decided the columns would continue on the main road right through the heart of the town and move quickly and quietly. As they neared the first building at the edge of the town, a light came on in one of the floors and the lieutenant raised his hand to stop the column's movement. However, almost as quickly as the light came on it was extinguished, and he decided to move on. The whole column moved through the town in a matter of minutes and the dust that was left behind quickly settled covering their tracks. Being at the rear

Linwood looked behind to see if everything was as clear as when they passed through, but he noticed that even though there was no one up then, he saw many people coming out of the buildings. He wondered if he should alert the lieutenant or just let it be. It didn't seem that anyone was pursuing or was preparing to follow them, so Linwood decided to forget about what he saw.

It wasn't long before a loud sound was heard and when the lieutenant looked back at the town a great light shot into the sky illuminating the area around it for several seconds. Moments later another one was heard and then seen, and he knew that they were signal flares set off by someone in the town who had seen them pass through. He couldn't be sure whether this was sent to assemble troops that would come out of town or from someplace else. He didn't have long to ponder because within minutes he heard the rumble of many horses coming from the direction in front of him. He ordered his men to dismount and take cover in the woods just off the road and they waited for the approaching horsemen to arrive. They didn't have long to wait before a well-fortified cavalry of gray coats, more troops than he had, passed by them on the way toward the town. Fortunately, they road by not even noticing the union horses tied to trees just off the road. The enemy was moving fast, but the lieutenant noticed that they had a small canon attached to a wagon that should they have been spotted, could have easily taken out his small band without much resistance.

He ordered his men to mount up again quickly and they rode hard to get out of the area for he knew that it wouldn't be long before the gray coats realized they had overshot their objective and would turn around to give chase. The men continued to ride hard and when the soldier who provided the original location report told the lieutenant they were almost at the valley where the battle took place, the officer ordered the men to slow down so that he could listen and assess what the possible situation might be. As they moved closer and were able to see the valley, the commander heard nothing that sounded like warfare, but he was cautious because it was night and both sides were more than likely hunkered down somewhere waiting for the sunrise. He then ordered his men to enter the valley and set up an encampment a few yards down the embankment. Strategically placing his lookouts, he ordered the men to bed down and get some rest because at first light they were going to search and engage whatever enemy was still in the valley and rescue their fellow union soldiers.

The men responded to the order and made preparation for the night. Meanwhile he called again on his trusted veteran and ordered him to go further down into the valley and reconnoiter the area. He was instructed that if he spotted the enemy he was to come right back and report; if he saw the men, they were there to rescue he was to make contact and let them know that help was in the area. The veteran acknowledged his orders and set out down the hill. The lieutenant then made his rounds inspecting the area that the men had set up ensuring that should they be discovered before he was ready to make his own attack they wouldn't be caught in an indefensible position. Satisfied with his perimeter defenses he made his own area to rest and bid the men goodnight but stayed up himself waiting for his veteran to report back.

Inching through the trees in the valley not being able to see clearly accept by the light of the moon, the veteran was cautious to try and make as little noise as possible. However, the dead branches and dried leaves strewn all over the ground made it difficult to move without making any noise and since sound like light were betrayers in the dead of night, he moved only a few steps at a time before pausing and listening. The farther down the hill he moved until nearing the base of the valley he could see nothing but trees and more forest. Finally, when he was about to conclude his search he paused for the last time between steps, he thought he heard some movement in the not far distance. He dropped low to the ground and strained his eyes trying to detect what was causing the movement. What he thought he saw at first was the silhouette of a body that was crouched behind a tree, but portions were still exposed. There was no way for him to make out initially whether it was friend or foe, so he held his position.

For several minutes the two figures scoped each other's positions, neither daring to expose himself any further than had already been seen. After a while they both realized that they couldn't stay like this the whole night so the wily veteran picked up a rock and threw it in a direction on the other side of his opponent and just behind him, the man reacted to the sound behind him and moved just far enough away from the tree so that the wily veteran could see the portion of his uniform that he needed to see to identify him as a friend. When the man realized that he had been duped and tried to regain his cover, the wily veteran moved out from his cover and got close enough to the man to let him know who he was. Still with very little light to substantiate his identity the man allowed the wily veteran to get close enough to him to see not only his uniform but his face. When the veteran told him that there were more troops just up the hill and they had come to rescue them, he was told there were only three of them left of the ones trapped here. The rest had either been killed or taken prisoner and his other two men were up in the trees just to the right.

The veteran asked if he could see his men and was told no, but he knew they were there. Next, he asked the man who he now could identify as a sergeant whether he wanted to try and call them down and come back to the encampment with him or whether he wanted to wait here until light? The sergeant replied that if they continued to make noise, even talking, the greater the chances where the enemy was going to hear them and know exactly where to come. The veteran acknowledged the advice and nodded his head then with hand signals indicated that he was going back to his commander and report. The sergeant nodded his head in agreement and the veteran left. Quietly making his way back up the hill, the veteran looked around the area to see if he could tell where the enemy might be dug in, but there were no signs. When he got back to the lieutenant, he reported what he found, and they spent the better portion of the rest of the night making plans on how they were going to get their fellow soldiers out and destroy the enemy if they were discovered.

Once he saw Suliah leap in the air and begin to descend toward the ground, Bernard instinctively moved under her with his arms extended to the max preparing to try and catch her. She fell on him with her full weight and they both dropped to the ground. He fell backward hitting his head on the ground, but aside from feeling a dizzying headache he appeared to be okay. With Suliah still lying on top of him, he wasn't sure whether she had suffered any more than he did but when he saw her breathing steadily, he rolled her off of him and to the side. She just lay there staring up at the sky with the wide-eyed vacant stare and he felt that she must be under some kind of spell. He started to pick her up when he felt the sharp pain in his back and realized that he was more hurt than just the throbbing in his head. Next, he tried rolling her to a standing position where he could walk her back into the house and get her to her bed. This time he was successful and gingerly he was able to complete his task. Once inside the room, he saw Amanda lying on her bed partially clothed and looking completely exhausted not even bothering trying to cover herself up when he entered. He didn't know whether to feel sorrier for her, knowing what she had just been through, or for the one he was still holding, but right now he had to get Suliah to the bed and hope that she was going to stay there for the night.

After he placed Suliah under her sheets, he attended to Amanda and did the same for her. When he got back in his own room, the feeling he had regarding the treatment of his people, especially his sisters, was getting to weigh too heavily on him and he wondered when it was going to all end. The messages he had been sending to the Union troops just outside the city by way of the blacksmith, giving them secret information, he wondered if they were doing any good because in all the reports, he was getting back via the same contact seemed to be telling him the South was winning. He hung his head and listened as he heard the last of the gentlemen preparing to leave thank Jonathan for his outstanding service to the cause and his generous hospitality. They all commented on his excellent selection of hostesses and told him that as soon as this war was over, they were going to see that he was sent to Washington as their high representative. The only one who was disappointed was the mayor who at every one of these gatherings was still making efforts to get to Suliah. For some reason Jonathan was withholding her from him, perhaps waiting until he had a greater need from the political pundit.

When the morning came, Suliah awoke before the others and looked over at Amanda. Amanda knew that she wouldn't be called on to do anything for a while for that was Jonathan's way of repaying her for her service. But Suliah knew that she didn't have the same protection and soon Bernard would be knocking on the door telling her she had to get up and begin her chores starting with serving breakfast. She couldn't remember much about what happened last night, but when she looked at her arms and legs, she saw large bruises on both and started to recall some of what went on. Her recall of the images of Bessimay and her father once again started her down the road of melancholy and despair was returning when the dreaded knock was heard on the door and the voice of Bernard sounded. This time right after the knock, he didn't hesitate, but barged in the room and looked at her. By this time, she was sitting up and looking out the window not even acknowledging his entrance but when he spoke to her, she answered.

He was glad to hear that she had returned to her seemingly right mind and when he asked her how she felt she said with some reservation, that she was okay. He only half believed her, but he reminded her that the day was starting, and the master and the family would be getting up soon and they expected their breakfast be ready when they came down. She nodded her head and started to get up when she felt some dizziness and fell back on the bed. When Bernard saw this, he asked her again if she was alright. She sat there for a few minutes more and then managed to get to her feet successfully this time and said she was okay a second time. Bernard observed for a little longer and saw that she was moving okay then he left to begin rounding up the other workers and get them started.

Suliah got herself ready and before going in the kitchen to help with the breakfast preparation, she stepped outside to get some fresh air. The beginning of a new day had always been refreshing for her, especially in the summer when the morning air was the freshest as the sun made its way to the sky top. She took several deep breaths which seemed to give her new life, but when she looked at her surroundings, at the bunkhouse behind the house where the slaves for rent lived, and then at the horses who were tied up in the stable and then at the house where she had to return to begin a day of forced labor, she wondered who had the greater misery in life and the refreshing feeling diminished. She turned and made her way slowly back into the house again contemplating the thoughts she held yesterday about ending it all, but this time she put them out of her mind as she met Bernard coming out of the house to dump the trash and he smiled at her. It was the smile on his face that seemed to say to her, that life was worth living even in the worst of situations and she was encouraged for the day.

About an hour later Jonathan came down looking tired and very unenthused about what he was supposed to do today. The rest of the family had already been down and had breakfast and disappeared to do whatever it was they had in mind for the day. Of late it was rare that they even saw Jonathan much less had opportunity to have a conversation with him. He was so tied up in the war efforts and making a name for himself in the political world that his family was the least thing on his mind. Even his personal family that was still abroad didn't' seem to occupy much space in his thinking because he never even mentioned them. As he sat at the table and Suliah came in to serve him when she got to the table he looked at her very hard as if to see whether she was in her right mind. When she set his plate and poured his coffee, he was satisfied that she appeared to be back to normal, but he was still anxious to know what happened to her last night.

He contemplated asking her about it for a moment, then dismissed the thought and concentrated on figuring out how he was going to accomplish the task ahead of him. Although in the back of his mind he was really concerned about her, for each time he saw her he could never dismiss the times that he had spent lying next to her and enjoying her favors. Whenever he looked at her, even though he took a stern approach to treating her like she deserved, inside his mixed emotions couldn't bring him to make a decision on how he really felt. He wouldn't even admit it to himself that the attraction that she held over him was more than he wanted to concede. Her innate beauty marked by her graceful moves even though she tried desperately to do nothing to excite him would always cause him to react in a way that he would regret later. Around her he acted like a schoolboy with a crush on a girl who was out of his reach but in this case, he had the power to make the situation bend to whatever his whim dictated.

She served his meal and then started to leave the room when he couldn't contain himself any longer and he had to ask.

"Suliah" he called to her, as she was about to exit the room.

"What was wrong with you last night? I came in and saw you sitting on the floor crying and acting like someone was after you."

She immediately stopped and turned around to respond to this question.

"Massa Jonathan I bin feelin real low here lately an I jest dono how ta handle it. I bin thinkin `bout lotta things an dey's all comin down on me tagether."

"What do you mean? Is it because of the way I treat you?"

"No massa, you has de right ta do what ya will wit me, but lately I dun seen a lot a things in my dreams dat seem ta be comin true."

"What do you mean by things coming true?"

"Massa I seed a vision last night of ma ole godmotha dyin on her bed, an den I seed my fatha gittin caught by some of yo soldiers an gittin killed. It was makin me real unhappy."

"You know that was just a dream don't you and dreams can't hurt you."

The more Jonathan talked to her and sensed her feelings the more he was weakening about how he was resisting her. He was being drawn into her world without even realizing that he was. Finally, before he allowed her to exit he told her that he wanted her to come up to his room tonight and he would talk to her further about her dreams. Upon hearing his directive, she wasn't sure how she felt about his decision, but in a sense, she was relieved that she was going to be sharing his bed again, even if for only one night.

Suliah left the room and Jonathan returned to thinking about his challenge for the day. After last night's gathering it had come to his attention that the Union Army was paused just outside the city limits to launch a major attack. He was invited to meet with President Davis along with several other prominent leaders of the high-level political circle and discuss possible solutions to not only resisting any oncoming immediate assaults, but visions of how they were going to grow their political schemes after the war was over. Jonathan's ambitions had grown so much since he arrived in this country and saw how the division of the country was being elevated over the people's concerns about whether to keep slavery as a viable function or to abandon it. When he talked to the people closest to him and they told him about the high profitability of the industry, he was highly inclined to maintain the status quo. However, when he talked with some of the soldiers at the operations base in the center of the city and they informed him about the military capabilities of the army from the North and how the factories up there could produce more weapons at a faster rate than they could in the South, the outlook wasn't as rosy as it was when he heard only one side.

The challenge for him today was to decide which side he identified more with and present his views to the president. If he sided with those who endorsed slavery and would fight to the very end to sustain it, then he knew that he would be in the good graces of the president, but if he presented the other side and showed a concession kind of scenario that would attempt to reconcile the differences between the North and the South and seek some kind of mutual concessions, he felt like he would be betraying a trust that had been given to him by his cronies who had been courting him for months now as their un-elected leader. Unsure of just which way he was going to enter at the meeting, he was having trouble digesting his food for his stomach was on edge and he saw his political future riding on the very presentation that he would make today.

When Bernard came in the dining room and informed him that the carriage was ready for his ride to the statehouse, Jonathan was still trying to digest the last portion of his meal and finish his coffee, but he put everything down and got up from the table. He entered the foyer and Bernard helped him with the donning of his impressive semi-formal attire that was suited for the occasion. Jonathan looked at Bernard, directly in his eyes and hesitated for a moment before going out, but thanked him for helping and Bernard saw in his eyes an expression that he had never seen before. Jonathan who was always so confident about what he was about showed the first signs of fear that Bernard had ever seen. To Bernard he wondered if this show of fear by his master might not be indicative of something being exhibited by the many masters all around the city and the country.

Jonathan arrived at the statehouse and was announced as one of the prominent citizens and he made his way into the chambers where the meeting was to be held. Inside the chamber many partisans had assembled and the crux of the agenda for the meeting was what they were going to do about the rebel uprisings right outside their own town and the advancing of the Union forces to positions on their doorstep. Jonathan took his assigned seat right near the front of the chamber where the president and his immediate cabinet were seated. He hadn't been seated long before President Davis banged his gavel and brought the meeting to order. As expected, the first order of business was a discussion about the rebel uprisings. More specifically he addressed the jailbreak that had occurred right under their noses by rebels who were bold enough to come into the town and free all of the slaves that had been captured and slated for execution by hanging.

Jonathan had heard about the jailhouse rescue and was aware that it was indeed a bold move, but he never would have suspected that the woman who had and would be sharing his bed again was the daughter of one who was among those who were slated for execution and now part of the escapees. He listened to testimony from all of the guards who were present during the outbreak and then from the town officers like the mayor and his constituents about what was being done to correct the situation. Nothing he heard convinced him that the town was again under the control of the locals and the meager confederate troops that were available to defend the city were not nearly enough to keep order should an attack actually be launched against the city. When it came time for Jonathan to speak, he stood up and addressed the chamber.

"My fellow citizens the time has come when we must face a peril that none of us has envisioned during the course of this war. Thus far we have experienced some successes in skirmishes both north and south of here, but it has not come near our doorstep until now. We have witnessed the moving of the Union Army on our soil and penetrating our territory with swiftness that we have not been able to withstand. It is time for us to consider the merits of our stance on the slavery issue and consider what the outcome could be should we persist in our views. Right now, we know that there are many blue-coated troops paused right outside our city waiting for the command to enter and attack. If the issue is really about whether we want to prolong our way of life and continue to treat these people who were brought here primarily against their will to perform the tasks of toiling without the benefit of any concessions on our part on our farms and plantations or is it about our so-called manifest destiny that under the eyes of God we claim to be superior and willing to fight to enforce that belief."

When Jonathan finished speaking the whole chamber fell silent including the president who had heard of Jonathan's prowess among the locals in his area, but he never thought he would hear this kind of talk coming out the mouth of this man. Unable to fathom what the bottom line of Jonathan's speech was all about, President Davis boldly asked him to clarify what his position was and what he was recommending be done to thwart the oncoming invasion of the city. When Jonathan stood up again his last words were even more confusing than his first tirade.

"Mr. President, we have a situation here that begs the question of whether we want to survive as a separate country without the benefit of an already established government that has the wherewithal to sustain its military might and the economic power to continue to support its troops or do, we want to fight against the odds of possible victory being turned away and suffer the consequences of becoming an occupied city under the control of our enemies. As you requested, Mr. President the bottom line for me is to call in all of our available troops in the area and go out and attack them before they come and attack us. Even though I believe that there is a greater force at work here then we realize, we must act on our principles and fight to preserve our way of life, no matter what the outcome as dictated by that force may be."

When President Davis heard Jonathan's final statement, he was convinced that the man's heart was in the right place and supportive of the confederate efforts. The floor was opened to any final comments and then a vote was to be made on how to handle the situation. In the end the vote was made, and it came down to calling all available troops in the area to come into the city of Richmond to defend the capitol. The meeting was adjourned, and the order was given to instruct the commander of the local troops to get word out to soldiers in the surrounding area to prepare to come to the city. Jonathan heard the outcome of the vote, and he heeded the order, but he was still unconvinced that the right thing had been done. Since he had seen, even from the time he first came to this country, the trials and tribulations suffered by the slaves, even the ones he owned, something was getting inside of him that he wasn't comfortable with. It seemed that the pangs of consciousness regarding what was right or wrong in the eyes of the greater power he referred to was beginning to play out in his heart and he couldn't quite understand where it might be coming from.

He left the statehouse and returned to his home where he was greeted by Bernard and the rest of his servants, but he looked at them now in a different light and he had a hard time trying to assess what it was that was coming over him. He acknowledged their greetings and then went into his study where he sat down at his desk and began to write a letter to his family back in England. In the letter he tried to describe what it was that he was experiencing and how he felt about his new situation. The words he put down on the paper were more of an expression of his guilt then any explanation of what he thought should be the case of how slavery should be handled in this country. He told his wife how he had not thought about her for some time, but now he knew that deep in his heart he wanted her to come here to be with him and he would make arrangements for her to get here. He had placed his thoughts in the letter, but as soon as he left the parlor and saw Suliah again the letter became just a thought, and it never left the room.

First light came and the lieutenant, even though he had not gotten much sleep, arose and assembled his men by various hand motions. He pointed to an area at the base of the valley in which he suspected that the enemy might be entrenched. From what his scout had already told him he knew that he could move down to get those three men still entrapped on this side of whatever skirmish line there might be, but he now thought that this might be a good opportunity to engage the enemy in a surprise attack and claim a greater victory than just a rescue mission. Once the men were up and ready for combat, he motioned for them to move down the hill in battle formation and be ready to engage the enemy. They moved swiftly and descended the hill with great skill and came upon a clearing in which they saw the first signs of the confederate soldiers casually walking around without the least concern that those few remaining bluecoats they assaulted yesterday could do anything to them. The lieutenant again using hand signals motioned for his men to assume positions that would surround the enemy. They were beginning their attack when a shot rang out from the enemy camp. A lookout perched in the trees had spotted the lieutenant's assault and the confrontation began.

The confederate troops quickly moved from their casual stance to one more fitting of a regular army. Under the direction of their commander, they placed themselves in positions that were defensible. The Union army lieutenant was trying to assess their troop strength, but it was not easily discernable because several of the confederate soldiers had assumed positions during the night beyond the base of the valley area. From what he could see the numbers were about equal, but the element of surprise had been lost. However, when shots came in from another area of the valley, the lieutenant knew that he was outnumbered, and his idea of a quick victory didn't seem as doable as he first thought. He motioned for his men to continue to descend the hill and get into a better position to confront the enemy, but when he realized how spread out the confederate troops where he called for a regrouping of his men.

His plan now was to hit the enemy right in the center of their flanks and break them apart and then work outward to achieve his objective. He motioned for his men to get up and run toward the center of the opponents with fixed bayonets and engage them in hand-to-hand combat and hope he would prevail. The daylight at this time presented an excellent opportunity for both sides to clearly see their enemy. Coming down from the top of the hill gave a limited advantage to the lieutenant, but in light of the superior number of enemy forces, he couldn't be sure that his strategy was going to work. He led the charge boldly and was right in front when the two forces clashed.

Linwood lagged behind in the second wave that was to descend the hill but when he saw his comrades in the first wave begin to fall when they entered the fracas he was reminded of the last battle where he saw his friends hit the ground for the last time. Fear rose up in his body and the adrenalin that rushed through his system was not enough to allay the trepidation that he was feeling. When the lieutenant gave the order for the second wave to begin its descent down the hill, Linwood hesitated. He looked around to see if anyone else was holding back like he was, but when he saw that he was the only one lagging behind he mustered up his courage and ran to try and catch up with his fellow soldiers. Running with his weapon in his hand directly at the opposing forces he wasn't sure whether he was more afraid of getting stuck with their bayonets or being shot by some errant bullet that wasn't even aimed at him.

As he drew closer to the heart of the battle, he saw that several of his fellow soldiers had managed to slay the enemy and used them as stepping blocks to move on to the next objective. Emboldened by their successes his courage mounted, as he got closer to engaging his first one on one encounter. The man in the gray coat opposite him looking back with the same expression of vicious intent he was giving raised his weapon with the long knife sticking out the end and lunged at him. Linwood remembered his brief, but effective training and side stepped the thrust then countered with his own lunge that met its mark. He felt the bayonet plunge into the chest of his opponent and the effort to push the shaft in farther was not as easy as he thought it was going to be. To complete the kill, he had to use a great deal of strength to make sure that the plunge was effective. In trying to withdraw his blade he found that that was not an easy task either, as he had seen in his training. Getting the bayonet out was indeed difficult. With the weapon still engaged in the man, he struggled to disengage it. This was even tougher than he thought because the man was holding the weapon trying to prevent it from going any further into his body. Finally, as the enemy's resistance wore down from loss of blood, Linwood was able to extract his bayonet and join his comrades in moving on to the next objective.

The hand-to-hand combat was in full engagement with one side seeming to be gaining the upper hand on the other and then the balance of power would shift just as one side thought they were successful. Linwood, after his first encounter was feeling more invincible as he moved on to the next, but when he came to an area where he was confronted by more than one man, the odds of being able to subdue both of them seemed not to be in his favor and he turned and ran from that situation. However, there wasn't much room to escape to and with the two men pursuing him he ran himself into a corner that presented him no alternative but to turn and fight. Realizing this was his only option he turned and raised his weapon as the two men moved forward. As the first one lunged at him he was able to sidestep and deflect that charge, but when the second came right after him it appeared that he wouldn't miss his objective. Linwood saw the charge coming and before he could recover from sidestepping the first charge, the second man was upon him. He could see the fury in the eyes of his enemy and the closer he got the more it seemed like the gray coat was growing larger and taller with each step.

The length of the bayonet that was facing him seemed also to become longer as it came closer to entering his body. He tried to sidestep this thrust, but now after being so successful with his first encounters, it seemed as if his legs were frozen to the ground and wouldn't move. He raised his own weapon to parry the thrust but miscalculated the distance from which the thrust was coming. In his mind, it seemed that this was it for him and his last effort to move aside was not achieving the goal. He backed completely up against the wall of the mountain and prepared himself for the inevitable. The thoughts that ran through his mind at this moment were not that of what was going to happen to him, but strangely he thought about his sister and where was she. Just as what he thought was going to be his final moment was ready to happen, the guardians of his fate stepped in.

Chapter 13 -The Return

The summer ended with a dazzling display of artistry created by the master painter. The mountains were covered like a canvass displaying a rich array of warm colors. The warmth of the colors was deceiving in that the weeks to follow would be anything but warm. Except for the evergreen pines, the trees featured leaves of gold and bronze, red, brown and yellow along with an assortment of hues in between. With the changing of the season came harvest time and on the Candle Plantation the focus was on getting the crops ready to go to market.

Byron usually got excited around this time of year because in times past it always signaled a period in which he would reap the benefits of a bountiful return on his investment. This year was different. Although the crops had been severely threatened early in the season by monsoon like rains, they managed to come through that rough period. The final yield for his wheat, barley, corn, and tobacco plants was now expected to bring at least a comparable return as in former years. What made the current time so different was the change in the family structure. For years it had always been Jethro tagging along after his father in the fields watching the slaves cultivate and bring in the harvest. Even Anna Lee on occasion would also venture out and cause her father to draw his focus away from the work to pay attention to her.

Now that Jethro had been lost by way of collateral damages from the war and Anna Lee, who had postponed her nuptials for as long as her fiancé' was going to abide, had gotten married and joined her husband on their own place, the excitement was dull. Byron was just going through the motions with no enthusiasm or zeal for a good outcome of the harvest and Charlotte was spending more time in her sewing room creating things that she would never use. As for the workers, the slaves were heavily involved in trying to keep a lid on the boiling pot of tension as the climate of a war inside the war continued to grow on the land.

Each day seemed to present a new challenge for the family as well as the slave population. When the time came for the product to be taken to market, two of the larger wagons that were used for hauling broke down and required repairs which Byron didn't have the necessary parts on hand. He had to send out for replacement parts that took two days and held up his getting a jump on the best prices being offered. It seemed that incidents like this were becoming more frequent and Byron felt like there was something that he couldn't understand causing it. Aunt Tee and Clarence secretly reveled at the misery growing in the family and were patiently waiting for the time when the pair would seek the go-ahead command from the cave demon to launch a full attack on all who would not join their evil cause.

If the breakdown of equipment and other minor delays wasn't enough to pique the ire of Byron, then the fact that his neighbors rejected him when he reached out to them for help was the final straw. The roads to the market had become treacherous as a result of the war and slave rebels still running free in the woods surrounding them. Byron needed help in escorting his harvest and he was not about to arm his slaves to do so, even if he had enough weapons to do it. The fear that should they be given arms; they would turn against him was real and he like many other slave owners was very suspicious of the attitudes of their charges during this time of them hearing more and more about successful rebellions. He had appealed to other landowners asking that they provide some of their overseers to ride with him, but most of them, remembering how he had swindled them out of their property, refused. The ones that didn't come right out and refuse him to his face because he didn't actually offend them, were reluctant to help because of their respect for the others. Even the patrollers refused to help, not because of anything that he did to them, but they were extremely busy in trying to hold the rebels in check while keeping the union forces from totally dominating the roads.

His dilemma now was how to get the product to market and then return home safely with his profits. The wagons had been repaired and the crops loaded so now he had to decide just what to do. Charlotte was very concerned, not just because he was going to be taking a chance in riding with just his few overseers on roads that she knew were going to be unsafe, but since he was taking all the overseers with him, she was going to be left in the mansion alone subject to the whim of an overwhelming number of slaves. More and more she tried to ingratiate herself to Aunt Tee and Clarence who she felt had enough control over them to protect her should an insurrection occur. As Byron was preparing to embark on his two-day journey at minimum, she was desperately trying to get him to leave at least one of the overseers with her, but he told her he needed all the men he had to get his crops to market. Disappointed at his response, she felt alone but had to agree with his reasoning.

It was early Monday morning when Byron set out with three wagons loaded with his yield headed for the market. Normally it would be a day trip in one direction and then he would stay overnight after selling his products before returning home. But now he wasn't so sure just how long it was going to take, given the unstable conditions of the roads. Along with him and his overseers he took two of his most trusted slaves and hoped they would join with him should an encounter with either union forces or rebels should occur. He really couldn't be sure of them because this type of situation had never occurred before and they were never tested, but somehow he believed that if the time presented itself their allegiance would be with him.

As they rode along, and the sun was beginning to reach its highest point Byron noticed that the roads were unusually quiet. He had not seen another horseman or wagon in either direction and it was beginning to concern him. Even when they passed by the patrol shack where there was usually at least one horse tied up outside, it was completely vacant. He turned to his overseers and told them how uncomfortable he was feeling at this point, and he cautioned them to keep alert. It wasn't long before his fears were to be realized for coming in the opposite direction, he could hear the sounds of many horses galloping toward him. All he could see from where he stood was a lot of dust, but he knew that from the sounds the horses were riding hard, and this couldn't be an indication of anything good.

There was not much he could do with the three wagons sitting in the middle of the road so he instructed his overseers to all come up to the front and prepare to defend his property should it become necessary. As the approaching riders got closer, he could see that there were two long columns of union soldiers who seemed to be racing toward something or running desperately away from something else. He got down and prepared to defend his ground but when the soldiers got close to his party, they didn't even slow down but rode quickly right by them. He felt a great sigh of relief, but he was still wondering about whether the soldiers were going to or coming from something that made them ride at the speed they were going. As he got back on the wagon and his men followed, they looked around the area one more time to see if there wasn't something that might give them a clue about what was going on.

By the time they reached the outskirts of Richmond they caught up with several other wagons apparently going to the city for the same purpose that he was. Although he didn't recognize any of the other plantation masters, he observed their crops and got a good feeling about his offerings. It appeared that his crops had feared much better than most and he was sure he was going to turn a handsome profit. At the edge of the city there was a line of confederate soldiers stopping every wagon coming into town. When he inquired what they were looking for, he was told that recently a band of rebel slaves accompanied by some union soldiers had entered into the town and freed all of the prisoners they had locked up in the jail. He was also told that some of the rebels had hid in covered wagons and managed to get by the guards on duty. Byron wanted to ask whether they had been recaptured, but looking at the embarrassing expression on the soldier's face when he was talking, Byron thought better of asking him for more detail on the subject.

He moved his wagon along just ahead of another who was right behind him and made his way to the field house where the crops would be judged and sold As he looked around the town, he got a feeling that things were not normal for the people moved around cautiously. He noticed that most of the men were carrying firearms and when he passed by the jail in the center of town the doors were hanging off the hinges. Apparently, there was no effort made to repair the jail after the raid he was told about, and he wondered just what was going on here. This was supposed to be the confederate capitol so how could some rebels get inside and make an assault on the jail. He began to wonder just how secure this city was and whether this was any indication on how the war in general was going.

They reached the field house and Byron drove his wagon around to the back where they were to unload his merchandise and sort it out according to type. He noticed there too that it seemed to have a heightened sense of tension. The slaves who were there to do the unloading were moving at a snail's pace and no one said a word to them. It seemed as if no one wanted to say anything that would set off a confrontation. Byron was getting slightly aggravated at having his cargo be unloaded so slowly and even his own slaves adopted the attitude of the others. When he hollered at them to pick up the pace, suddenly the others stopped, and his-own slaves joined the stoppage. They looked at him with such fire in their eyes it scared him. He hadn't seen such defiance in any darkies he had ever come across and he looked around at some of the other white men to see if he had help should he advance the confrontation. The other white men eased back and moved inside the field house leaving Byron to deal with the situation with only his overseers at his side. Byron couldn't believe what he was seeing, and he started to take his pistol out of its holster when he heard the click of another pistol behind him. He turned around slowly to see who it was and saw a confederate soldier telling him to release his weapon. Curious as to why the soldier was seemingly taking the side of the darkies, he asked the soldier why. The answer was these few slaves were all that was left who were willing to work at all and he didn't want them being killed without good reason.

It seemed that most of the slaves who had been living in and around the town had runaway over the last few weeks and made their way to the safety of union forces nearby. The jailbreak that freed those who had been captured just served to emphasize the fragile state of the security in the town. Byron eased his hand off his gun turned back around and faced the slaves who were standing there with a half-smile looking at him with an air of defiance but continued to unload the cargo. Frustrated but willing to concede he was in a compromising position he allowed them to move at their own pace and it reminded him of his defiant four back home. When they finished unloading, Byron went inside and began dealing with the buyers. After haggling over the price of his goods for some time Byron, as was his usual strategy, bargained with such aggressive passion that he achieved his goal. The final outcome he considered a victory.

Leaving the marketplace he and his overseers went to the local hotel and registered for the night. He told his slaves they were to bed down in the wagon until morning and he would see that they got something to eat. Once inside the hotel he looked around and saw that soldiers mostly occupied it. After having seen what he did at the marketplace he was a little surprised to see so many of them lounging around in the hotel when he thought they should have been out protecting the town. He casually went over to one of them and asked why they were in the hotel, and he was told that these were new recruits waiting for assignment. This made sense to Byron, but when he asked the next question which was how long they had been waiting and received an answer that said almost a week, he was really confused. Why would it take a week for the men to get assigned to help fight the war? Later that evening he talked to an officer at dinner and found out that because all the facilities used for training were heavily involved in defending themselves against heavy attacks there was no way they could take on any new soldiers and train them.

When Byron heard this and thought about how he had lost his son he became very depressed. He thought the confederate army was faring poorly and wondered if they were going to prevail at all in the war effort. He took his men left the restaurant and went to the tavern where they proceeded to avail themselves of the liquid refreshment as well as the other entertainment available. When they returned to the hotel a short time later the scene had changed. No longer were the soldiers by themselves but ladies of the evening had come out and in varying states of dress occupied the soldier's attentions. Byron, even in his inebriated state couldn't stomach this image of how these boys were whooping it up and disgracing the uniform when his son was dead. He was about to go upstairs and go to bed when he heard someone come through the door shouting that a contingent of union soldiers were headed toward the town. He paused just long enough to see what the reaction of the lounging soldiers was going to be and when none of them seemed to be the least bit concerned, he shook his head and continued upstairs to go to bed.

The man who made the announcement in the hotel was a civilian who had just come from down the Fortress Monroe way and witnessed the hard riding of the troops heading in this direction. When he hollered out the alert and got no response from the soldiers he quickly left and sought refuge elsewhere. It seemed none of the men believed his story and ignored his warning. Meanwhile the advancing troops were nearing the city and preparing to launch a major attack. This was the same outfit that Linwood was part of, and he was riding among them feeling grateful for the miraculous set of events that had recently spared his life.

When he was cornered in the valley and facing what he thought to be certain death from a gray coat that was standing just a few feet in front of him paused to impale him with his bayonet, a miracle happened. Linwood was already prepared to accept his fate when somehow his weapon, that he thought was empty, discharged, and the shot lodged in the forehead of the enemy causing him to bury his bayonet in the ground at Linwood's feet. When Linwood opened his eyes and saw his dead enemy leaning on his rifle with the bayonet fixed firmly in the ground, he had a hard time at first understanding just what happened. Then he thought about the incident with his family and the wagon rolling down the hill and the same thought he had wished for his father after he saw the images in the quadrant, he believed now applied to him. Since neither he nor Suliah or Myanna saw the outcome of his father's escape because Bessie May had expired before it happened, they didn't know he was safe.

As the two union army columns continued to charge on toward the city, Linwood was again feeling invincible even though a short time ago when he sat beside his wounded comrades, he had sunk to a level of despair that he had never felt before. His own recent escape from the jaws of death had prompted him to return to the belief that when this was all over there would be something waiting for him that was much better than all this. He wasn't sure just what it could be, but when he reflected on some of the teachings that he had heard while listening to Daniel he now believed that the other side of all this promised to be a new beginning in which he and Suliah would be reunited with their father and mother and they would see a glorious future.

The time came when the soldiers were ready to enter the town and some of them paused to see if there were any confederate soldiers anywhere in sight. As they paused, they saw something that really got their attention. It was the appearance of an image that they were not ready for. It was the sign of an evil spirit that was hovering over the whole area. The spirit was telling them to put down their weapons or it would be the last thing they would do. Linwood saw it himself and said to the men this was nothing more than a way for them to be misled by this lying spirit that had been sent to discourage them from achieving a victory. The lieutenant who was leading the charge hesitated to listen to Linwood first because he was black and secondly because he was a new recruit, but when he heard the conviction in Linwood's voice he took notice and heeded his advice. He ordered the men to keep advancing on the objective.

The perimeter of the town was protected by the fortifications of the confederate army and there were many men hidden behind the barriers that covered the town's entrance. As the union troops got closer to the entrance, they could see the fortification. The lieutenant ordered them to halt until he could assess the situation. The men complied with the order and spread out. Linwood meanwhile moved up to the front of the column and again spoke to the lieutenant.

"Suh, I think we might do good if'n we was ta go round to de otha side an `tack `em from dere."

"Why are you saying that son?" the lieutenant asked him.

"`Cause somethin' keep a tellin me dat ova dere is where dey is weak."

"What do you mean something, what something?"

"I caint tell yasuh, but I knows I got dis strong feelin' dat dat's what we supposed ta do."

The more the lieutenant listened to Linwood the more he was convinced that something really was leading him, and he responded to his advice and ordered the men to change directions and ride around to the other side of the town's entrance.

When they got to the new position, he could see that the fortification they saw at the other place was vastly superior to what he was seeing here. He knew then that Linwood was right, and he ordered the men to charge hard into the town and secure it.

Jobba and Shaka reached the pastor's brother's house in the dead of night and started knocking on the door. It was sometime before someone answered and the angry voice that responded sounded threatening. Jobba hollered through the door saying who it was, and the door opened slowly. When the man looked and saw that it really was Jobba he opened the door all the way and told them to come in. By this time the rest of the household had heard all the noise and they were up wanting to see who it was. When they all saw that it was Jobba and Shaka they were pleased to see them again. The lamps were lit and the group sat around the table talking about what had happened since the two men left there and Jobba responded by telling them that he and Shaka had been captured and were going to be hung, but somehow managed to escape.

Just like before the man's wife was there staring at Jobba again and he became uneasy. Shaka then asked the man if they could again spend the night in the barn and they would leave early in the morning. It was agreed then the man took Jobba aside and whispered to him that the Underground Railroad contact he was seeking was going to be coming by here tomorrow so if he really wanted to book his passage he should wait and meet the man. Jobba's eyes opened wide when he heard this and he eagerly agreed they would stay. Jobba and Shaka then got up and made their way out to the barn and bedded down for the rest of the short night.

In the morning just about sunrise Jobba awoke with a strange feeling running through his body. He couldn't quite make sense out of it, but it seemed as if something was going on in his life that he couldn't understand. He thought about all the things he and Shaka had gone through over the last few weeks and how they had suffered a number of trials that should have been fatal for them, but somehow they managed to get through. He thought about how dark his life seemed to be at times and when he felt there was no clear solution to his problems something good would happen and he would be set back on the right track. The feeling he had now though was different than anything he had felt before and it was niggling him in a way that he was very uncomfortable with. He got up and went in search for the horse trough so he could wash up, but he couldn't find it. Then he remembered from when they stayed there before that it was right behind the house, not the barn. He stepped out from the barn and headed in that direction when he heard the sounds of horses coming up the road.

Since it was early in the morning, he couldn't believe that someone would be coming to visit. He ducked back into the barn, but peeked out to see if he could get a good look at whom it was. When the riders got closer, Jobba could see that it was two men both dressed in black like the preacher, but neither was he. He didn't expose himself, but he went back and shook Shaka telling him to get up because two men had just come to the house, and he didn't know what was going on. Shaka got up and both men eased their way out of the barn and went up to the side of the house where they could look in through a window and listen from the outside to what was going on.

When the men knocked on the door the voice inside responded like it did last night angry and threatening. The men responded by telling him who they were and immediately the tone of the voice inside changed, and the door quickly opened. The men went inside and Jobba and Shaka paused to listened from below the window. They heard that these were the contacts from the Underground Railroad that the preacher's brother spoke about last night. He said that the reason they had ridden out so early was because there was something going on in the town that they should be aware of. Jobba strained to hear what it was, because the man who was talking had lowered his voice as if to whisper. Unable to make out what was being said, Jobba motioned to Shaka it was time to make their entrance and introduce themselves.

Shaka agreed and they walked around to the front and knocked on the door. Suspecting who it might be the man opened the door and invited them in. Jobba entered and looked at the two men then at his host and waited for him to take charge. The preacher's brother introduced Jobba and Shaka and said this was the town blacksmith and his helper. Not only was he the blacksmith but also the main contact for booking passage on the railroad that could lead them up north and to freedom. Jobba grabbed the blacksmith's hand and started shaking it vigorously like he wasn't going to let go and told him how glad he was to meet him. The blacksmith responded by saying he was glad to meet him too, but there wasn't much time for him if he wanted to make his move up north. He advised the next run would be leaving tomorrow night. Jobba's expression changed dramatically as he told the man he couldn't go by himself because he had a wife back on a plantation that he had to go back and get. The blacksmith said that if he missed this train there wouldn't be another one until at least another week and the times were getting tougher now because of all that was happening with the war and the rebellions.

Jobba was a little disappointed, but he repeated that he wasn't going anywhere unless his beloved Myanna went too. The conductor sympathized with him, but said this train didn't wait for nobody it ran when it had to run, no earlier and no later. The preacher's brother told the men to sit down, and he would go and make breakfast for everybody. The two men however, thanked him for the offer but said they had to get back into town before the townspeople awoke so they would be at the livery before anyone knew they were gone. The preacher's brother said he understood and bid them farewell as they left. Jobba told the conductor that now he knew how to book his passage he was going to leave today and go back and get his wife. He hoped he could get back here in time to catch the next run. The blacksmith replied he looked forward to seeing him again and when he got back just let the preacher know he was ready. Jobba heartily agreed and the two men left.

After the blacksmith left Jobba and Shaka sat down to breakfast with the family. Jobba thanked them for all they had done for him and Shaka and especially for their hospitality. He then went on to say that he had to be leaving to get back to his plantation and get his wife. The preacher's brother cautioned him about traveling during the day and reminded him that not only was the war at Richmond's doorstep, but both sides in the battle would be stalking the woods capturing anything and everything that was not their own. Jobba acknowledged the warning but emphasized that he wanted no part of the battle, and his only goal was to get back home and see his wife.

Later that day after Jobba and Shaka rested awhile longer in the barn they felt energized and since the sun was starting its descent, they stopped by the house one more time to say goodbye. The preacher's wife answered the door this time and with the same longing look she had been staring at Jobba before, invited him in, but he quickly declined. He looked passed her and saw his host and repeated his thanks while saying that they were leaving now, and they hoped to return soon. Everybody inside wished them well in their journey and the host once again provided some traveling supplies. Jobba was so grateful for the food that he promised that when he returned the next time, he would have something to repay the family for their generosity. He accepted the food bag, and they were on their way.

After a short walk they were in the forest again but moving in the opposite direction from before. Having no special bird to guide them this time the travelers had to rely strictly on their memory. Jobba knew now that if he followed the main road staying just inside the woods, they would be successful in getting home, but he was concerned that if he stayed too near the road they would be spotted. It became a matter of how close was close enough but not too close. The two men started out at a brisk pace and before long they had made their way quite a distance from the city. When they ventured out to the road to check their bearings, they could see the peak of the water tower and it seemed like a feint image from what they remembered. What surprised Jobba as they traveled was that there were very few people traveling the main road. There were no troops, no regular travelers nobody was using the road at this time of day and that was strange. The number of times they ventured out to the road to reestablish their direction became more frequent as they boldly headed north. As nightfall set in the pair were getting tired and decided to find a place that they could hide for the night and get an early start in the morning before sunrise. Negotiating the forest had become an art for them and finding suitable shelter was easy. When they located what seemed like a good place to camp, they settled in and prepared to lodge for the night.

It was not long after they had settled in, that Shaka heard noises coming from the direction of the main road. It sounded like several horses moving slowly up the road. Afraid they were close enough to the road to be seen, Jobba crept up to the edge of the road and peered out from behind a tree to see who was coming. In the dusk he could make out that it looked like a long line of soldiers moving toward the city. From where he was, he couldn't tell which color uniforms they were wearing, but to him it really didn't matter because he didn't want to have anything to do with either side. As the soldiers got closer and were about to pass them, he could see some of the men riding in front and it looked like they were wearing blue coats and hats. Inside he felt a little better, but he wasn't sure why because from what he had heard when he was in the jail, the south was winning the war and the soldiers from the north were about to be defeated.

The soldiers moved passed them and both men returned to their camp and bedded down for the night. Before he closed his eyes Jobba stared up at the stars as he had been doing more often recently and wondered if his Myanna might be doing the same thing. The more he gazed the more he thought about her and the times when they used to share stargazing moments together. He also thought about his children and wondered just what hand fate had dealt them. While he was in this mood, again the feeling he felt while in the barn came back and now it was beginning to bother him because it was getting stronger. It seemed to be telling him all was not right back at the plantation, and it had something to do with his beloved Myanna.

He closed his eyes and almost immediately fell into a deep sleep. As he slept, he felt himself being transported through the air just like he had dreamed some time ago while still on the Sutter Plantation. He was moving ever so lightly on a cloud that seemed to be moving him higher and higher until he could see the whole world below him as if it was a small ball. Surrounding the world, he saw many points of light, but below them was nothing but darkness. The points of light were moving systematically as if they were trying to punch holes in the darkness, but the darkness was preventing them from getting through. Then he heard a voice calling to him that sounded like the thunder after a heavy lightning strike. At first, he was frightened because the voice was loud and penetrating to his hearing, but when the voice told him not to be afraid but to listen closely, he calmed down.

The voice continued and told him that he was about to be shown many things, which are going to happen in his life that would appear to be his end, but it would not be. In the times just ahead, forces of evil surrounding the place where he is going were coming into a cosmic battle of the times and he would be caught right in the middle. His beloved wife, who thinks he is dead, is now being confronted by a very strong force and is persuading her to act in a way that she does not want to. The lights, which you see hovering over the planet are angels assigned to protect the faithful, but they are being withstood because of the current ruler of the world who is the evil one. It will be just a matter of time before his reign will be terminated and the world will be restored under the leadership of a new ruler and that reign will be forever. But until that time comes, you along with your newfound friend will undergo many more trials and tribulations, which will throw you into a darkness that you have never experienced before, but you shall not fear.

From the time that you were born until now, you have been allowed to see through spiritual eyes in dreams shown to you about the injustice of man to man. Your spirit guide, the man called Daniel, has tried to show you what the truth is about these conditions, but you failed to understand his teachings. Let me now try to make you understand that in this world you will have troubles because that is the way life for all mankind has come to develop with the gift of freewill. Troubles will abound always and how you deal with them is the key to whether you are successful or whether you succumb to the pressures of living. No one who is a true believer needs to be afraid to experience life and its vicissitudes, for he who believes and calls on the name of Jesus will ever stumble or fall without being able to get up.

As you continue your journey on the morrow you shall know the bird that brought you here is still available to take you home if you so desire. Look closely in the treetops when you awake for the sign of the bird and he will direct your path for the way home. Remember that the darkest hour of the night is just before dawn and when you look to the heavens know that there is always someone looking back at you. The voice finished speaking and from his perch on the cloud Jobba couldn't see who or what it was that was talking to him, but he felt a sense of security like he had never felt in his life. The voice was reassuring and comforting and the rest of his slumber for the night was so peaceful he could not understand but it was wonderful.

Byron woke up the next morning with a mild headache and got mad at himself for allowing this to happen. The first thing he did was to pull out the dresser drawer and make sure the money bags containing his profits were still there. Satisfied he was still in control and in possession of his loot he prepared to get himself ready to go downstairs collect his slaves and head home. He looked out the window to see what was going on in the town then he remembered the scene in the hotel last night and wondered what ever became of that warning given by the man who stormed in. Nothing seemed to be out of the ordinary, so he figured it was just a hoax like the soldiers suspected and put the thought out of his mind. He finished getting ready walked down the hall and knocked on the door of his overseers' room telling them to meet him downstairs because he wanted to leave right away. They affirmed his order and started getting ready.

Downstairs he looked around and was surprised to see the lobby almost empty. There were no soldiers and no other guests only a few of the hotel staff and a couple of slaves cleaning up. He went to the desk to settle his account and asked just what happened to all the soldiers who were there last night. The desk clerk told him that very early this morning a high-ranking officer came in chewed them all out and told them to get their gear and follow him out. Where he took them nobody knew. Byron felt a little pride in hearing this because now he felt like there was still some pride in his confederate army and maybe hope for victory. He settled his bill and told the clerk to direct his people to the restaurant where he would be waiting for them. In the restaurant he saw a few more guests, but the crowd that was there when he first checked in was gone. He thought maybe because it was early no one else was up yet and then he saw the look on some of the other guest's faces and he wondered why they were so sullen. He took a seat behind a table that had a few of them and he listened to their conversation.

The tone of the conversation was somber and the gist of it was that the south was losing the war on all fronts and it was just a matter of time before the union army would be entering this city and taking it over. The group was apparently some political officials, and they were trying to come up with a way to prepare a surrender that would allow them to maintain their positions in whatever new government might be established. Byron overheard one of the men being called Jonathan and it seemed like he was the leader of the group. As the conversation went on, he also heard a reference to someone called Suliah and it sounded like she had become his consort. Byron's curiosity peaked and he was about to position himself so he could get a look at the gentlemen's face and hear better, but as he was about to move his chair, the overseers came to the table and sat down. He was trapped between them.

His men greeted him with a good morning salutation and he motioned to them to speak softly, but when he did one of the group at the table behind noticed it and suspected he had been eavesdropping so they got up and walked out. Byron admonished his men for spoiling what he thought was going to be some interesting news about the war and perhaps a slave that he once owned. He specifically told Sam who knew her that the name Suliah had been mentioned and he wondered if it could possibly be the same one. Sam said that since it was such an unusual name it was likely that it was her. Byron agreed and wished he could have heard more. As the group was leaving, Byron saw the face of the man called Jonathan clearly and it appeared to him to look just like that, which his son had described as being the political big wig he met before he died. Byron's curiosity was really getting the best of him now and he started to get up and stop the man before he left and ask him if he knew his son. However, before he could do so his food order came, and he changed his mind.

The men finished breakfast and headed to the livery to get the wagons and the slaves and get started heading home. When they arrived, they saw the wagons and the horses, but there was no sign of the slaves. Byron inquired about them to the blacksmith and was told the same night they arrived they were met by a group of other slaves who were running out of town, and they went with them. Upon hearing this Byron went into a rage and threatened to hit the smithy for letting them escape, but when he realized that the blacksmith had a large hammer in his hand, he regained his composure quickly. Frustrated and not wanting to go through a long process of getting the local law involved which he knew would be very time consuming, he decided to accept his loss and move on. He thought; besides he had done very well with his crop sale and when he got home he would just replace the ones he lost. He told his overseers to tie their horses to the wagons and they would have to drive the wagons home. It was done and they were soon on the road again.

The trip back was uneventful and to Byron's surprise there was very little going on. On the main road there was hardly any travelers and the few that he passed seemed to be so caught up in getting to where it was, they were going, there was hardly any exchange of greeting between them. The three or four confederate soldiers he saw riding slowly seemed to be so wary that he thought about stopping them to inquire how the war effort was going, but when he looked more closely at their faces it didn't seem like a good idea. As they got close to home and passed by the patrol shack, where there was only one horse outside on the way out, now there were several there that meant that there were many men inside. To Byron this was a good sign because it seemed like everything was back to normal there.

They reached the side road to the mansion and turned off. Not far from the house as they got closer Byron could hear what sounded like a lot of shouting and confusion. He prompted his horse to pick up the pace so he could get closer and see what was going on. Just a few yards from the house he could see several of his slaves fighting with each other using sticks and stones and whatever else was available. They were battling with serious intent, and some were bloodied struggling to keep standing. Byron pulled his pistol out and fired several shots in the air which sent them scurrying in all directions. He didn't pursue them but fearing that something might be wrong in the house he galloped the horse right up to the front and dismounted. He threw open the door and ran inside. As soon as he entered, there in his parlor he saw Aunt Tee sitting in his favorite chair staring back at him.

He was stunned at first to see her sitting in his chair, but when he went to approach her to let her know his displeasure, he felt a sudden sharp pain run down his back and stopped immediately. She continued to stare at him with an impish grin and the look in her eyes was challenging as if daring him to come any further. Byron felt helpless for the moment, so he turned ran out then bolted up the stairs headed to his bedroom to find Charlotte. He bounded the stairs two at a time and pushed open the bedroom door to find her sitting at her sewing table, but she wasn't sewing just sitting there. He ran over to her and turned her around in the chair. She looked at him with a kind of blank stare, but when he shook her violently she started to babble.

"Spirits,..ghosts..,monsters...new..master….bad…spirits..,monsters, ghosts......new master" she kept on babbling over and over.

Byron shook her again and again trying to get her to make sense. Finally, he picked her up and walked over to the bed where he placed her down and went over to the water basin. He dipped the washcloth in the water and quick stepped back to the bed where he placed the cold wet cloth on her face and rubbed it around. She shook her head at the touch of the cold cloth, but just moved her head around and around without saying anything further. Byron sensing that he wasn't going to get anything more out of her now left the room and went back downstairs to confront Aunt Tee again.

This time he was determined to get close enough to lay his hands on her and get some answers. But as soon as he entered the room he heard her say: "Stop there or you'll feel de wrath of my power. You is no longa de massa of dis house an de cave spirits gonna rule ova here soon."

He heard the words and couldn't believe what she was saying so he advanced closer to her. But when he reached out to touch her, he felt such a pain in his arm he retreated and gave up trying. He then turned around and walked to the room that she shared with Clarence hoping he would make some sense out of what was going on. Not hesitating to knock he pushed open the door and barged in to find the place empty. Quickly he turned around and went out the back door to see if maybe he was on the porch. Not there either, Byron looked across to the stable hoping to see him there but no sign. Getting more and more frustrated at his inability to make sense of what had happened on his land since he left, he stormed down to Sam's place to get him and then go down to the quarters.

At Sam's cabin, he found the other overseers there too sitting around having a drink after their long afternoon ride. Byron stormed in and hollered at them because they didn't seem to notice that anything was amiss. They were too far behind Byron in the wagons to see or even hear the fracas that he did so they had no idea what had happened. When Sam looked at him curiously and then asked what he was talking about. Byron spewed the words out of his mouth so rushed that he sounded unintelligible. Sam tried to get him to slow down and say it again, but Byron was so mad he just grabbed Sam and motioned to the others to follow him out the door.

They responded to his command and the group bolted out the door headed to the quarters. When they got close to Penniman's cabin Byron was able to convey to Sam that he was trying to find Clarence his head house slave to find out what had gotten into Charlotte. Sam understood and followed close behind Byron to the cabin. At the door, Bryon didn't knock but barged in to find Penniman and Tralene sitting at their table talking. When the door flew open Penniman got up to see who was coming in like that and he even dared to confront Byron. Byron was shocked by this new behavior, and he was about to go over to Penniman and strike him when he heard a noise upstairs. He turned his attention away from Penniman and headed to the stairs.

Quickly he ascended the stairs and when he got to the top, he experienced another surprise. There in the bed were Clarence and Myanna going at it in the middle of the day hot and heavy. He was stunned because he had no idea that this had been going on. There was no way for him to know that Clarence had been pursuing and wearing down Jobba's wife until she could hold out no longer and gave in to her loneliness. Byron didn't know what to do or say now so he went back downstairs and talked to Penniman who had calmed down from his first reaction and humbled himself again. Byron asked how long this had been going on and Penniman filled him in. Determined to get some answers out of Clarence, Byron recomposed himself and went back up the stairs. This time he made a lot of noise ascending the stairs and when he got to the top Clarence was getting dressed ready to come down. Byron told him he wanted to talk to him right now and Clarence responded.

They left the cabin and went outside where Byron asked Clarence in a heated rage just what had happened here and what was wrong with Charlotte. Clarence started talking to Byron in a very calm voice trying to sooth his rage and he told him that things were changing on the land. Byron still didn't understand what he was talking about and kept pushing him to get to the point. Clarence continued to take his time knowing that Byron was near his boiling point. Finally, Clarence feeling that Byron was about to blow said: "In two day time at night when de moon be full you gonna see things here you see once before but remember not. You gonna know everything den."

Byron was so mad now because Clarence was making no sense that he hit him and knocked him to the ground. Clarence just sat there and looked up with the same kind of grin that Aunt Tee displayed. Byron was frustrated and furious, but he left Clarence sitting there and went back to the house to see about Charlotte. Sam and the overseers followed him fearing that he was going to hurt somebody. When he got inside the house, he went to the parlor first but Aunt Tee was not there. He then went up to the bedroom and found Charlotte sleeping peacefully, so he left her alone. This mumbo jumbo that Clarence had been talking about with the full moon and all that stuff was getting the best of Byron. He went back in the parlor with his posse behind him pulled out his favorite nectar and poured everybody a large glass.

In the morning when Jobba awoke he felt refreshed and feeling a new energy surge. He remembered his dream and cleared his eyes so that he could focus and search the treetops. Scanning a full 360 degrees he didn't see anything that looked like the bird that had led them there, so he started thinking that it was just a dream. He lowered his head and looked at Shaka who was still sleeping. He was trying to decide whether to wake him or let him slumber a little longer when he heard a commotion above his head. As he looked up to where he thought the sounds were coming from, he saw a large wedge of birds zeroing in on a particular tree and fluttering above the highest branch. On that branch where Jobba had just looked seconds before, now sat the strange looking bird that appeared to be the same one as before. He couldn't believe it, but now sensed that the dream was more than just a dream. Without delaying further, he woke Shaka up and explained the dream to him and then pointed to the treetop where the bird sat as if waiting for them to get ready to move out.

They got up and searched for a stream or a pond or something where they could get cleaned up. As they were looking around Jobba heard the birds flapping their wings again and the strange bird was flying around in a circle prompting the pair to follow. At first, they were uncertain about what to do but when the bird started to fly out of the circle Jobba knew that it was time to follow. Forgetting about washing up the men took out after the bird and began the journey. Just as before the bird flew at a pace that was demanding for the men, but they managed to keep up for the better part of the day. Again, as before, when it seemed that they couldn't walk another step at the pace, the bird seemed to sense their fatigue and found a treetop to settle on. Jobba fell to the ground first and rolled over on his back to keep a vigilant watch for the bird. Shaka joined him on the ground just moments later and the two men exhausted lie there breathing heavily. While they were still prone Jobba heard something that sounded like running water and he strained himself to get up and check on it. He stumbled toward what looked like a cliff but when he pushed his way through the trees, he saw the most beautiful waterfall that he had ever seen. With every ounce of strength, he could muster he made his way to the bottom of the falls and plunged into the chilly waters. Shaka was right behind him, and the two men frolicked there like a couple of kids.

They spent an inordinate amount of time both bathing and drinking the water when the sound of the birds again attracted their attention. It was time to move out. Leaving the water refreshed and feeling energized they resumed their trek, this time at an even faster pace than before as if to make up for lost time. Jobba couldn't imagine what was driving the bird, but he got a strong feeling there was a sense of urgency in its flight. They were moving now more at a jogging pace rather than walking. The flight of the guide had abandoned their route staying close to the main road but had taken a path carrying them deep into the forest. Jobba felt uncomfortable because he thought if they lost sight of the bird then they would be totally lost. However, the way the bird was moving it was always in plain sight.

For the whole day the men followed the bird resting at intervals when they couldn't go on any further. As the sun started to set, the hunger pangs set in and they both realized they hadn't eaten since early that morning. The rations given to them by the preacher's brother had long since been consumed and now they were confronted with having to resort to their hunting skills to feed themselves. With the experience they gained living off the land before for some time it gave them an advantage and they soon found dinner. After they ate Jobba questioned how far could they be from the plantation, because it seemed to him they had been traveling longer than they did the first time they came this way. He searched the area with his eyes trying to see if there was anything he recognized, but now in the twilight all the trees blended together in one mass green scene and nothing was distinguishable. He was hoping that he might return to the same dream that he found comfort in before. Although the night air was chilly they found warmth in the dried leaves piled together.

The next day both men woke early feeling cold, but they were anxious to resume their journey. Jobba looked around to see if there was anything that he recognized because it felt to him like they had been traveling as long now as it did when they first came out here. He didn't see a thing that was distinguishable, so he waited for the bird to move. When the bird lifted off and circled the air twice, the pair knew it was time to go. They moved out again at a fast pace and it wasn't long before they came to an area that Jobba seemed to spot things he knew he had seen before. He wasn't absolutely sure, but it seemed now that signs were coming up that pointed to the cave where they had departed company with the mountain rebels. Sure enough as they moved about a hundred yards further the entrance to the cave was visible. Suddenly Jobba looked up and their guide bird was flying around in circles again, but this time it was not a signal type of circle but one that seemed to indicate some distress. Jobba wondered if the bird was sick after this long journey and flying at such a fast pace. It wasn't long before a group of other birds came flying in and encircled their guide as if forming a protective circle. They formed a wedge and together they flew off into the distance. Jobba was amazed how it appeared that they were rescuing one of their own and as it had guided him and Shaka, it was being guided to safety. He realized now that the bird had completed its mission and gotten the men to the point where they could now function on their own and complete theirs. He pondered how such timing was possible, inside he really knew the answer but still hesitated to embrace it.

After the wedge of birds disappeared beyond the horizon Jobba and Shaka pressed on toward the cave and went inside. They searched for signs that the mountain men might still be living there, but what they saw was only an indication that the cave had been abandoned some time ago. The remains were rotten scraps of food that gave off an awful odor and they wasted no time in quickly exiting the hole to seek fresh air. Once outside, Jobba remembered that the cave was not too far from the edge of the woods and from there he could see the patrol shack. When he told Shaka what he was planning to do, Shaka reminded him that from there if they got too close to the road they could be seen and possibly caught. He was afraid of getting caught now that they had come so far and reminded Jobba that he was now very close to home and his wife. Jobba agreed, but his curiosity was getting the best of him and he just had to go and see what was going on.

They moved cautiously through the woods listening for any sounds that would indicate they were not alone out there. When they got to the edge of the woods they paused and hid behind some trees just off the road and scanned the area. Seeing nothing they came from behind the trees and moved up to the road. From there Jobba could see that they had come past the shack, but it was clearly visible. What he saw was different than what he remembered. Where it used to be just the horses of the patrol men now there were several horses that from the insignia indicated that these were confederate soldiers' horses. He saw this and moved quickly back into the protection of the trees before they could be spotted. The presence of additional horses meant that there were more men available to search the woods and this possibility was not in their favor.

He looked around and tried to get his bearings so that they could move toward the bridge and the point where they could cross the river again as they did before. As he moved out, he noticed that Shaka was moving more slowly than usual and he slowed down to see what the matter was.

"Is you okay?" Jobba said.

"Jest lemme sitchere a minute an I be fine" Shaka responded.

Jobba sensing that something was wrong went over to his friend and placed his hand on his forehead. The man was burning up and Jobba knew that fever was building up. He said to Shaka.

"You stay here an rest. I's gwin fine sum 'erbs like ma Bessie May usta give us when we sick. It make ya all betta, soon."

Shaka nodded his head and lie down on the cold ground. Jobba moved out in search of the herb, but then he remembered that when Bessimay used to give it to his family she always served it in some hot water, but he knew that this was impossible because even if he made a fire they had nothing to mix it in. Then he thought that if he just found the herb eating it raw might be just as good especially when there was nothing else. He moved around in a wide circle and after looking desperately at every tree base and the surrounding bushes he finally came across what he thought looked like the root he needed. He picked up the root and smelled it. It smelled like the real thing and when he looked closely at it, it appeared to have the same look, so he picked a little more and brought it back to his friend.

At first when Shaka looked at the ugly plant, he refused to eat any of it. When Jobba told him that he had fever in his body, and it was building up and that if he was going to continue with him, he needed to get well quick. He went on and said tonight they had to swim across that river in the dark and he was going to need his strength. Jobba to encourage his friend took hold of one of the plants and shook off some of the portions that looked less nutritious and ate the leaves. Shaka watched for a few minutes to see his reaction then reluctantly shook off some more and placed a couple of the leaves in his mouth. He was surprised to find it had a taste like mint and he chewed some of the leaves and took a few more from Jobba's hand. When he had consumed a good portion of the plant, he reclined again. Jobba went and gathered several handfuls of dried leaves and covered him with them then said he was going in search of the bridge. He promised he would return soon. Shaka nodded yes and closed his eyes.

Jobba looked closely again at his friend for a minute and felt that he was going to be alright, so he went out in search of the bridge. He didn't travel far before he saw some markings on a tree that he knew he definitely seen before because these were markings used by the rebels to let him know where they would be. Jobba followed the markings and it led him down to the river where they used to have a boat tied up to ferry the rebels back and forth to the rituals. When he got there, he didn't find any boat, but he could now see the plantation across the river and even the dock on the other side where the plantation boats were. He felt such a strong emotion right then, seeing the place where his Myanna was, that had it not been for his friend lying back there waiting for his return he would have jumped in the water and started swimming across the widest part of the river right now. He gave it some serious thought for a few minutes, but then came to his senses and moved along the river knowing that it would not be long before he came to the spot where the river was its narrowest and the place where they could swim the easiest.

Now that he was at the bridge and the place where he wanted to be, he looked around for someplace where he and his friend might rest and keep warm before they set out on their perilous swim. He found the place where they had been before and even some of the materials they used before were still there. He gathered sticks, leaves, and branches and tied them together with vines making a makeshift but sturdy hut that would keep them protected from the cold. When he completed building the shelter under the bridge and felt confident that it would be there when he returned, he set out to go back and get his friend. Since he had come some distance to where he left Shaka, Jobba was a little confused about the direction. He looked back at the way he came to where he was now and thought that going back that way was going far from his friend. When he considered it and concluded that if he went in another direction, he should be able to come to his friend he felt confident in his decision and started out.

After he had walked for a while and didn't see any signs of where he left Shaka, his confidence level was slowly diminishing and he was no longer sure about his decision. But now he had gone past knowing how to even get back to the place where he was which really confused him. Getting frustrated and feeling a sense of desperation for two reasons he stopped in his tracks. First, he felt like he had let his friend down because he had not been wise as his friend used to say of him and secondly, he felt that a real wise man would have left a trail to follow. While he paused thinking about what to do next and pondering giving up, a strong feeling came over him and what sounded like the wind whispered in his ear that he should proceed going in the direction straight ahead of him and he would find his friend. The wind lasted but a few seconds, but the message was clear, and he stepped out in the direction given. The trees just ahead of him seemed like they were thicker and closer together than all the others, but as he navigated around them, it wasn't long before he came to the spot where he saw Shaka lying under the leaves.

When he spotted Shaka, he ran the last few steps to him and stopped at his feet to make sure that he was still breathing. Shaka looked like he was just sleeping comfortably, so Jobba gently shook him to make sure. Shaka responded and opened his eyes looking up at Jobba with a slightly dazed look. It took a moment for him to gather himself, but when he spoke Shaka said that he felt like he had been in a deep sleep, and he felt much better. Jobba knelt down and felt his forehead again. This time his head was still warm, but not burning up like it was before and Jobba felt reassured that the herbs had done their job and the fever was gone. He helped Shaka to his feet and told him that he had found the spot where they could cross the river and he had built them a shelter where they could rest awhile. Shaka, feeling somewhat refreshed held out his hand motioning for Jobba to lead the way.

Jobba started out walking slowly looking behind him every few steps to see if Shaka was keeping pace and when he saw that he was he picked up the pace. Going back to the hut under the bridge wasn't difficult this time because Jobba was following a new sense of direction that was coming from within. He followed his instincts, and it was only a short time before they were at the bridge and Jobba helped his friend down the slight embankment. Even though the sun was at its zenith the air was still chilly and Jobba wondered whether Shaka would be able to survive the swim. Quickly he hustled him into the makeshift shelter and told him to lie down and rest as much as he could. Once again, he was going to venture out to the edge of the woods and see if anything was happening with the patrols and the soldiers. Shaka went in and found the place where Jobba had already prepared a kind of mattress for him that would give him some warmth and comfort. He turned to his friend before he left and thanked him repeatedly by bowing and placing his hands together almost in a praying fashion in front of him. Jobba acknowledged his gratitude and motioned for him to just go in and lie down while he went to spy out the road.

When Jobba reached the edge of the woods this time and saw the patrol shack, there wasn't a single horse tied up outside. This brought much concern to his mind for he wondered if they weren't in the shack then could they be roaming somewhere around in the woods. He moved back from the road and hastily made his way back to the hut listening all the while to try and hear any activity beside him in the forest. It was early in the afternoon so there were many sounds in the woods from the larger animals preying on the smaller ones to the smaller ones running to avoid being their meal for the day. Jobba with his woodland experience could now easily distinguish between what was man and what sounds belonged to the animals, so he was confident when he heard nothing that sounded like that of men. He got back to the hut and found Shaka sleeping peacefully again, but when he touched him to wake him this time his body felt warmer than when they started out earlier.

Jobba didn't think to bring any of the medicinal roots he found before and he felt badly that he didn't. When Shaka woke up he was sluggish and his speech was a bit slurred, but he told Jobba he felt okay and he would be ready. Jobba looked at him suspiciously but there was nothing more he could do so he left him alone to lie down again and he sat down to take a nap too. The hours passed by slowly because every few minutes Jobba kept waking up to see what the position of the sun was and each time it seemed like it hadn't moved at all. His excitement was beginning to build, and his anxiety level was rising as he anticipated getting home and sleeping in a real bed again. His concern for Shaka however, dampened his spirits and he was worried about his friend getting in the cold water. He let Shaka continue to sleep as long as possible and when the time finally came that they should make the attempt he asked Shaka whether he felt ready. Shaka not wanting to disappoint his companion said he was, but inside he was not feeling his best.

The sun had set and the darkness covered the water when Jobba led the way down to the river. He stepped in first and quickly withdrew his foot for the water was very cold and the current was already moving swiftly. After he recoiled a couple of times, he said to himself that this is how it had to be for there was no other way to get across and come up on the other side without being seen. This time he took a few steps backward and then ran full speed into the water and started his strokes. Shaka had watched him and was not encouraged seeing his antics, but when Jobba finally made his plunge and started to swim, he knew that he had to be next. He did the same as Jobba and took a few steps backwards then ran full steam into the water. The shock of the cold water on Shaka caused his body to tremble and he felt a mighty drain on his strength. He started his strokes as best he could, fighting hard to maintain his direction, but the current was too strong and he was losing the battle. Although Jobba was a few yards ahead of him he tried every so often to look behind him to view Shaka but with the current pulling at him and the dark of the deep, it was nearly impossible.

As he swam Jobba recalled that it seemed like this was a repeat of the time when he last made this swim and lost one of his friends. He hoped within himself that this would not be the same case, but when he finally reached the other side and crawled out of the water, he turned himself on the shore still lying on the beach and looked desperately for his friend. After severely straining his eyes, he was finally able to see Shaka making his last-ditch strokes trying to right his direction, but then it seemed like Shaka just gave up and the current carried him downstream into oblivion. Jobba's heart fell, and he wanted to get back in the water to help his friend, but he knew this would be foolish. His head sank into the sand, and he lie there motionless for what seemed like an eternity before he was able to recover himself and get up. Just like before he crawled as far as he could to reach the first cabin and then got up but still crouching as he made his way around to the back of the house.

There was a small light burning in the rear of the cabin and he sneaked up to the back window to see if he could perhaps spot Daniel or one of his associates. He looked through the window and saw the lamp burning at a low level, but there was no one else around. He then moved around to the front and viewed the quarters to see if anyone was walking around even then, but there were no signs of any activity. He knew that he had been away for some time, but as he remembered usually there would be at least a few slaves out in the quarters even this late at night doing nothing but socializing. He moved past Daniel's place and eased his way up toward his own. When he was getting closer, he noticed that there was a lot of light coming from the cabin across from Daniel's and he wondered if there was something going on inside.

He changed his direction for the moment and retreated back to take a look. Moving around to the back he looked through the window and inside he saw a large group of slaves bowing to an idol that had been placed in the center of the room. Jobba looked around the room to see if he recognized anybody, but none of the faces he could make out were familiar. Then as he was still watching another figure came in the room from the front of the cabin carrying what looked like a small child. Jobba edged forward to get a better look when he stumbled and fell over a broken chair that had been discarded behind the house. The noise he made he was afraid was going to attract attention and send somebody outside to check on it, but the group inside was chanting so loudly that it appeared no one heard him.

Jobba got back up and peered again in the window and this time got a better look at what the man was carrying. Not only did he recognize what was being carried, but he also recognized who the man was doing the toting. It was Penniman and he was carrying a dead goat that had been prepared with wrappings to look like a child. He came forward to the center of the group and placed the goat at the foot of the idol while the chanting grew even louder. Suddenly everybody in the group stood up and moved forward toward the center and touched the idol and the goat then they stood up. The blood from the goat was now smeared on the idol and they resumed their kneeling positions chanting furiously. The whole scene was getting to Jobba, and he wondered where all these new people had come from. He also wondered just where Daniel was and whether he knew that all this was going on right across the way from him.

He started to go back to Daniel's place and knock on the door to let him know. But when he thought more about it, he hadn't been there in so long how could he know if Daniel was even still on the plantation. Moving around from the back to the front and into the quarters again now he knew where at least half of the people were, but then he asked himself where then were the other half, the believers. Since the quarters looked deserted, he became bolder in his movements as he started again toward his cabin. When he got near the front door, he decided then for his own safety that he would also go around to the back to see if there was anything that had changed. At the back of the cabin, he looked through the window and saw the children sleeping in their beds, but no Tralene. He knew where Penniman was so he had to assume that Tralene was one of those people with her back to the window and he couldn't see her face. He crouched down again and eased his way to the front and slowly opened the door so as not to wake the kids.

There was a low light coming from upstairs so he assumed that Myanna might still be up and he started getting excited again as he eased his way up the stairs. On the way up he could see that some changes had been made to what he could see from the bottom of the stairs. At the top of the stairs where there used to be a tapestry that had been woven by Myanna over many months when they lived at the Sutter Plantation. In that tapestry she had carefully inserted the images of Jobba, Suliah and Linwood. Now where it used to hang was a commercial picture that had obviously come from the mansion. It seemed strange that she would take down something of her own and replace it with that, but he didn't give it another thought as he continued to ease his way up the stairs.

At the top of the stairs, he first looked over to where the kids used to sleep to try and remember how it was when the family was together, but when he turned to look in the other direction he heard low noises like sighing coming from where his bed was. In the low light he eased a bit closer to get a clearer view and the shock of what he saw almost catapulted him back down the stairs. His eyes refused to focus clearly on what was in front of him and the shock sent a surge of adrenaline throughout his body. It was there in front of him, but his whole body was refusing to accept the image as truth. As he stared at the movements his whole being was tested and he could no longer restrain himself, so he acted.

Chapter 14 - Prophecy Fulfilled

From the beginning of man's existence on this world, forces of good and evil have opposed each other vying for total domination. Unseen not visible to the human eye they have influenced man's behavior and manifested in various ways throughout history. For one man to possess another in an ownership condition is not natural and does not follow the natural order of man's creation. Yet the unnatural condition of slavery in defiance of the natural order has survived through the ages and has never ceased to exist. From one country to another, in one society or the other the inhumanity of man to man reflects the manifestation of the evil forces and the promulgation of eternal darkness.

Wars have been fought to preserve the right to continue the unnatural condition and lives have been lost to abolish it. Whether it happened in days of old on the continent of Africa or in more recent times on the North American continent, the unnatural condition did not spring from normal evolution, but from the influence of the force wielded by the current ruler of this world. For Jonathan, preserving the unnatural condition wasn't a matter of him defying the natural order so much as it was seeking to bolster his selfish aggrandizement using the condition as his steppingstone. The institution of slavery and the fact that he arrived in the country at a time when it was a lucrative business, was ideally suited for his aspirations. Unfortunately, for him the opposing force representing the good portion of the good versus evil equation marred the achievement of his political goals.

As a child growing up in the old country and hearing from his father about how he had been to Africa and witnessed the dominance of the white man over the blacks and how he enjoyed the status that it gave him, Jonathan had absorbed these stories as the natural order of life and accepted it as what should be everywhere. When his uncles arrived before him in the new land, called America, and reported back how they were living wonderful lives from trading in human traffic and how they had risen politically as a result, this only served to corroborate his father's assessment of what is the natural order. From that time on, he obsessed over wanting to be like them and rise even higher. Coming to America he had no idea what would befall him when he stepped on the shores holding onto the beliefs that he had.

From the time he arrived and began setting up his house and his affairs and making the right contacts to launch his political career, he observed how the artists in the business such as trader Bob made their fortunes. He also utilized his family contacts to get introduced in the right political circles and with his natural charisma he was well on his way in an unusually short time. His rise to stardom was moving along extremely well until the war broke out and he found himself caught in the middle of what now appeared to be a losing effort and the battle was right at his doorstep. Compounding his dilemma was the fact that he had taken to a slave girl who had first captured his attention for reasons that were ignoble. His planned exploitation of her to advance his political career was now enslaving him to her beauty. The more he had tried to ignore it and use her for his political gain, the more he found that whenever she was in his company or nearby, what he may have understood in growing up as the natural order, he found to be very unnatural. His conflicted emotions were causing him to question what he had received from his father and uncles and what he was now experiencing firsthand on his own.

After the period when he banished her from his bedroom over a jealous reaction to something he couldn't understand, he found himself experiencing things happening to him that he wanted to blame her for also. He tried to restrain his feelings by blaming her for all that happened to him, but the more he did the more he found himself attracted to her and finally gave in to the absurdity of his thinking. When she returned to his bed, he became so enamored of her that he confided in her more than he should have even knowing that she still longed to be free. Whenever she heard him talk of something secret, she would pass it on to Bernard who would give it to the blacksmith who would finally carry it to the union army in the area. As the news of the war became increasingly more depressing for him, he would imbibe in a toddy or two and tell her things far beyond her level of understanding knowing that she didn't comprehend but the way she looked at him comforted him. When he finished talking, the final act of devotion was always soothing for him as he fell asleep.

Suliah after an extended period of time in her new status felt some physical discomfort, especially in the morning, and she reacted angrily to comments from her former roommate about her gaining weight. It wasn't until she really became sick daily in the morning, and she couldn't walk by a mirror without looking at her new appearance that she conceded to what the other women were telling her. The new life that was germinating inside her was confusing and she didn't know how to respond. She hesitated to tell Jonathan because from all that she had been hearing from him lately, he really didn't need to hear about this now, so she went on daily just letting things develop as they would. Amanda and the others continued to chide her because of her preferred position, and she was becoming depressed again. Her only consolation was Bernard, who told her that one day she would see a time when she would be the lady of the house, even if it's not this one.

Jonathan had just arrived at the command headquarters for the city that morning when he heard some officers talking furiously in a side room about the advancing union troops that were just beyond the town borders. They were carrying on about their inability to stop the enemy at a previous holding line and were trying to decide what to do. He broke into their conversation and demanded to know who was in charge.

"Who's in command here?" he screamed.

"I am sir" the response came from a major who was standing near the doorway.

"What the devil is all this talk about them Yankees coming into our town?"

"Well sir, there's a large contingent of union soldiers just a few miles from here and they've breeched our first line of defense."

"Well what are you doing about it?"

"We have enough troops here to defend the city on all fronts but one side and that's what we're talking about now. Unless we get more help from up north which is going to take some time, or convince these townsfolk to join with us, then we're going to have trouble here."

Jonathan couldn't believe what he was hearing, the army having to rely on a bunch of civilians to win the battle, but he saw the anxiety in the major's eyes and he told him he would take on the task of appealing to the citizens for help. The major welcomed his involvement already knowing about Jonathan's influence in persuading people to respond to his requests. He felt assured that help would be forthcoming soon. Jonathan left the headquarters and went straight to the mayor's office.

At the office he barged in the front door and headed straight to the back room where he found the mayor already in and sitting around his conference table with a group of the leading townspeople. Without hesitation he interrupted their meeting and spoke loudly.

"Mayor Bradley, are you aware of what's going on right down the road from here?"

"Come right in Jonathan" he responded trying to keep a pleasant tone in his voice even though he was internally offended at the rude interruption.

"Yes, we've heard the news and were discussing it when you arrived. It seems that those Yankees are a bit more ready to fight than what we thought."

"Ready – ready, are you joking. They're right at our doorstep and you're talking about their readiness. Did that major over there at the headquarters tell you about his predicament Tom?"

"What predicament, other than he's about to have a big fight?"

"His predicament about needing more troops which he can't get right away."

"What do you mean by that?"

"I just left there and he's asking the townspeople to get involved and sure up his defenses until the additional soldiers can get here."

"What, he wants us to become soldiers?"

"That's about it, Tom. If we want to keep this town safe and preserve our interests than we'd better get out of here and start rounding up every able-bodied man who has a gun and get him over to the headquarters and report to the major."

Mayor Bradley looked at the others around the table in a state of shock at first, but when Jonathan kept repeating that it was their only choice if they wanted to save themselves and their families, they reluctantly agreed. All of them got up from the table and moved out to recruit the needed help. Jonathan left also and went back to the headquarters to report his success. In a matter of a few hours, about 50 men armed with an assortment of weapons ranging from muskets to derringers, showed up at the command headquarters. The major thanked Johnathan first then welcomed them and immediately began explaining what the mission was. Eager to get started several of the men wanted to go right to the defense position right away but the major cautioned them and said that he wanted to give them just a brief bit of training before they deployed. He went through some basic defense strategies and tactics. When he was confident that each man understood what his role was, he instructed them to gather in front and board the wagons that he had ordered brought up.

It was about noonday now and the ride to the defense position that was in the southernmost part of the city took only a few minutes. When they arrived, the major ordered the men to get out and take up positions behind a barrier that had been hastily constructed within the last few hours. The barrier extended from one side of the main road to the other and didn't allow for any other entrance, but through this route. As they settled in and signaled to the major that they were ready for action, the major ordered one of his regular scouts to go out down the road and spy on the whereabouts of the enemy. The young trooper heeded the command and struck out riding hard from the protected area. He was not gone more than fifteen minutes when he came back riding harder than he did when he left.

"Major, major they're coming hard right behind me," he shouted as he crossed the line.

The major heeded his warning and shouted the command for all the men on the barrier to check the status of their weapons and get ready to fire.

"Don't start shooting until they're close enough for you to actually hit 'em. Let's not waste shots, we need to make every one count for something," he shouted.

He hadn't finished shouting the rest of his orders when suddenly a few yards in front of the barrier a cannon ball hit the ground and tore up the turf in a wide area throwing dirt and debris in all directions. The major hollered at the men to duck and keep their heads down until the enemy troops started advancing. Moments later another round landed even closer to the barrier and this time some of the shrapnel struck the barrier injuring one or two of the men posted. The major was amazed that the cannon balls were hitting his defenses from such a distance, because he couldn't even see from where the canon was firing. When the next round hit, the answer to his question became clearer as he was able to see through his field glasses that the canon was firing from a wagon that after a round was fired moved a little closer each time. The last round was so accurate that it tore a hole in the center of the barrier big enough for a horse to get through.

The major quickly ordered that the hole be repaired and stuffed with anything that was available to patch the breech. Men went scurrying in all directions as they raided the surrounding stores and houses taking whatever they thought could be helpful. The breech was sealed, and the men resumed their positions. Another volley was fired, this time the round overshot the mark and landed well behind the barrier tearing up the main road with a big hole right in the center. The major knew then that the foot soldier assault must be near, and he warned the men to get ready. Within minutes he could see with the glasses that the Calvary was advancing first at a gallop and behind them moving quickly were the foot soldiers.

He barked his final orders telling the men just about how far away the enemy was and how long he thought it would take for them to get here. On the line some of the men when they heard the major's assessment of how soon the battle would begin, they got up from their positions and started running to the rear. The major shouting obscenities, calling them cowards and threatening to shoot them himself was thoroughly disappointed with what he had and admonished the remaining men to make up for the cowardice of their neighbors. He also told them that when they were successful after this confrontation, he would make sure that they had a chance to address their neighbors. There was no time to dwell on their actions as he commanded the brave men left to keep focused on the situation in front of them and be ready to fire when he gave the order.

The first wave of horses was right upon them when the major hollered fire and shots rang out. Some of the horses fell just before the barrier. However, a number of the mounted troops were able to hurdle the barrier and landed behind it. The regular troops who were positioned behind the new recruits as a reserve were able to dispatch this first wave and the men on the barrier shouted a victory shout. It was short lived however, because no sooner had they done away with the first wave then a second wave of horses was upon them, and they were struggling to deal with them. The second round was not as successful as the first and they didn't make it to the barrier before being shot down. Right behind them though was the main force of foot soldiers running with a broad front of men bearing down on the barrier with guns blazing and the steel of their bayonets could be seen without the aid of field glasses.

Quickly the onslaught of the foot soldiers was upon the barrier and before the men had time to reload, they were over run. Hand to hand combat ensued and the trained union army easily overpowered the townspeople and advanced to the confederate soldiers in reserve. Even there the match was one sided and the union army claimed the victory. Now that they had entered the south end of the city, they started looting the stores and houses as they moved along. The major seeing that this was a lost effort had ordered what was left of the barrier resistance to fall back and move toward the center of the city with the union soldiers in hot pursuit. The confederate reserves and the townspeople were able to escape because the union soldiers stopped to avail themselves of the booty that was left in the shops.

The union army commander ordered his men to cease looting and continue the mission, but his orders were falling on deaf ears because of all the goodies that were being exposed by the fleeing confederates. Frustrated at his orders being ignored, the commander ordered the canon to be fired straight up in the air just in front of their position. When this was done and the round landed just ahead of the men making a loud noise, it got their attention, and the commander was able to regain his authority. He then placed three sentries at the front of the line to look out for any returning confederate soldiers then called for an assembly in the middle of the road and addressed his troops. After he had chastised them severely, he happened to spot Linwood who was seated near the rear and he called him up. Linwood fearing that he was going to be singled out for looting also, was very surprised when he heard the commander praise him for having the courage to tell him about his feelings regarding this port of entry to the city. He told the men that Linwood was responsible for them having such an easy victory to this point. As the men cheered, Linwood wasn't sure how to feel since he had never been recognized like this before.

At the end of the verbal reprimand and praise session the troops were told to stand to their feet and resume the task at hand. They reassembled in formation and started moving toward the center of the city. As they moved along, several shots rang down from snipers hidden on the rooftops and in the alleyways between buildings. The union soldiers kept moving and as they neared the town center the resistance got stronger. Finally, the ultimate confrontation took place when they got to it. This was the all-out battle. No longer could they move forward and now they were surrounded by confederate troops who had circled around them. Linwood's group was right in the heart of the battle and his thinking by now that he was a seasoned veteran still had the jitters as the whistling of rifle fire moved over and around his head.

At one point, when he raised up to fire from behind a wagon that had been turned over for cover, he felt his hat quickly lift off his head and when he looked around at it on the ground, he saw the hole in its center. At that point he realized, that had he stood up a moment sooner, the hole would not have been in his hat. He fell back down to the ground and just sat there trying to compose himself. He then heard the commander ordering then to get up and advance on the enemy just ahead. At first, he contemplated lagging behind when the others moved out, but then he reflected on the high praise he had just been given and he stood up and moved out with the others.

He ran toward the enemy with his rifle raised and his bayonet poised to strike. When he reached the objective, he was confronted by two of the confederate regulars and it took all that he had to remember his training as the man-on-man battle began. Linwood using his athletic abilities was able to down both men and to his surprise he had made way for his fellow soldiers who witnessed the action to move into the command headquarters behind him. The battle inside the headquarters lasted for over an hour, but the final outcome was inevitable. The confederate soldiers who were able abandoned the building and fled out of the city through the north side. As they were running, they began to set fire to as many buildings as they were able, and Richmond became a city on fire.

The union army under the direction of the commander extinguished, as many fires as they were able, but they also allowed many of the buildings to just burn out on their own. The sun was setting and the men very tired but feeling good about their victories were able to rest. They took over the local hotel and for the first time in months they enjoyed the luxury of sleeping in real beds. Linwood was especially confident now with himself, feeling that he had become truly a man of valor as the commander had said of him.

In the morning, the commander roused the troops up bright and early and told them a new mission was about to start based on some information that had come to him during the night. He was alerted that one of the top confederate government officials was living in a house just outside the city and they were to go there and arrest him. This mission wasn't going to require the whole unit so a certain number of select troopers were give. the task. Linwood was among the chosen few. As they prepared to undertake the task for the day, Linwood wondered who this high-level official might be because a strange feeling came over him. He gathered his gear and joined the others as they climbed into three wagons that had been confiscated from the enemy. With 12 men assigned to each wagon the convoy set out with the captain, a lieutenant and a sergeant leading the way riding on horseback.

As they rode out of the city, they passed what was left of the munitions factory that had been the main supplier of the confederate troops both in the area and throughout the state. The confederates themselves had destroyed the plant on their way out and the charred remains still reeked with the smell of gunpowder. Linwood looked at the massive structure and thought to himself, with the capacity to make arms from this big a plant how could the grays be losing the war. It really didn't matter now because the city belonged to them and as the rest of their contingent swept through it from house to house capturing the military stragglers and freeing those slaves who had been left behind, it was clearly evident who was in charge. Once they reached the outskirts of the city, the commander alerted the men to be vigilant for any last desperate stands by confederate troops who may have dug themselves in waiting for them to come out.

There were no incidents and the wagons arrived at Jonathan's house about mid-morning. Assured by his information that this was the right place, the commander positioned the wagons directly in front of the house and ordered the men to disembark. He took a few men with him to the door, but the rest he told to circle the house and make sure that there would be no escape through any rear exits. The men positioned themselves around the house and took up attack stances waiting for further orders. The knock on the door was not with any sense of urgency nor did the commander try to be boisterous with his stand. The door opened and the head servant, Bernard looked at the military presence both in front of him and beyond the commander and was not unnerved, but in his mild-mannered personality asked the major what he wanted. The major responded telling him that they were looking for the owner of the house.

Bernard hesitated hoping that Jonathan heard what was going on and would have a chance to get out the back way. Even though he valued his freedom opportunity as much as any of the other slaves both in the house and in the back shack, he didn't want to see any undue harm come to the master that had treated him fairly ever since he came to him. Jonathan did indeed hear what was happening, but realizing that the time had come when his part in the war was finished, he came to the door and confronted the captain.

"I am the owner sir, how may I help you?" he said.

"Are you Jonathan Adams, the people's representative for this district?"

"Yes I am."

"Then I have orders to arrest you and take you into custody for high crimes against the sovereign government of the United States of America."

Jonathan heard the charges and just looked at the commander for a moment before he responded.

"You have come to my house to arrest me, and it is within your power to do so, but you have not ended the idea that the people of the south still cling to. We, my good man, shall yet prevail in this matter and the outcome will be entirely different in a very short time."

Jonathan truly believed, even though he was aware that Richmond had been overrun, that somehow something would happen to turn things around and help would come from some source to make them win. While he kept this in his heart, he was not quite ready to give up his home, so he asked the officer to let him have one more moment with his charges before he was taken away. Jonathan called all of his house slaves together in the hallway and addressed them. Even his own immediate family came down to hear what was going on.

"As you can now see, my efforts in winning the war to preserve our way of life has been fought and it seems we are at a great disadvantage trying to keep you in servitude. This being the case, I am going to provide you with the one thing that you all have been seeking. To me your plight was never about how much better I am than you, but more about how much loftier I wanted to be than your people. So here and now with my last statement in your presence, I am going to set all of you free to pursue your own way in this land and make the best of whatever you can and wherever you will. I will now set my hand to this paper and decree that you are no longer indentured to me or to any other master by my free will and via the testimony on this document."

Jonathan completed writing on the paper, then handed it over to the officer and instructed him to see that it was made official by whatever new government would be set up in this city and in this state. The captain took the paper and ordered his men to take custody of Jonathan. As he started to leave, he turned around one last time and saw Suliah standing in the doorway of his study. With the full evidence on display of her entry into the middle stages of her second trimester, he said to her: "When that child is born, and it will be a boy, tell my son all about me and that under other conditions how much I could have loved his mother. He finished talking and walked out the door. Suliah was filled with so many mixed emotions she couldn't decide whether to cry at his plight or rejoice at her long sought-after new freedom. When the soldiers came to escort Jonathan down the stairs, one of them looked in the hallway to make sure there was nothing else that needed their attention and spotted Suliah. He completely stopped what he was doing and stared at her trying to make sure the woman he was looking at was really who he thought she was. The soldier was Linwood and the shock at seeing his sister for the first time in many months caused him to disregard his officer's orders.

When the officer noticed that his command wasn't being carried out, he stopped descending the stairs and turned to see what was causing the delay. Linwood was still standing inside the doorway not moving, but looking intently at Suliah. Suliah thought she recognized him too, but in his uniform with the hat pulled low and covering a good portion of his face she really wasn't sure. The officer came back up the stairs spun Linwood around and looked directly in his face.

"Soldier I gave you an order why aren't you carrying it out?"

"Suh, dat's ma sister right dere an I ain seen her in a long long time."

The captain looked at the pretty young woman standing in the doorway with the big swollen belly and surmised what the situation must have been.

"Okay soldier you've got ten minutes to talk to your sister then you get back outside and join us. We're leaving here right away. You there come up and take his place and put this man in custody" the officer said to one of the other soldiers.

Linwood then took off his hat and moved further into the hallway getting closer to Suliah. When he was close enough for her to see that it really was her brother she quickly stepped forward and threw her arms around him in a tight embrace.

"Linwood, Linwood is it really you. I didn't know if'n you was dead or not an I gave up even thinkin more `bout you."

"Yeah, sister its me an ya kin see om jest as alive as b'fo but much older inside `cause I dun bin thru some hard times. Its good ta see ya. I didn't know what happen ta you either afta we got sol ta different massas. How ya git like dat is ya married?" he said jokingly.

Suliah hung her head briefly appearing ashamed, then responded:

"No I ain married, but de massa took a real likin ta me an dis is what happen."

The expression on her face told Linwood that his joke was not very funny and he immediately apologized for it.

"Om sorry sister, ya know I don mean nuthin by dat. I knows how dey treats our womens an das why I join up wit dis army so's we kin make all de stuff like dat jest stop. I gotta go now, but when om finished wit dis soldier thing om gonna come back here an git you, den we gwine back home ta daddy's house, ya hear me. Das a promise."

"Yeah brother I hear ya, an I be lookin fer it ta happen. I donno how much longa I be here since de massa gone, but if'n I can, I be right here. You keep yaself safe now an don git killed or nuthin."

Linwood grabbed Suliah and kissed her cheek while he hugged her tightly, then turned and quick stepped out the hallway and down the stairs to join his waiting company. The officer looked at him for a moment to see if he was okay then gave the command to move out and the unit headed back to the city.

Inside the house the shock of the master being taken away was still resonating with everybody there as they stood in the hallway wondering what to do next. Byron's father attempted to take charge and ordered them to go back and continue doing their chores, but at this point the house servants who had never listened to him before unless anything he said was backed up by Jonathan, just looked at him. When he saw that his commands were not about to be heeded, he shrugged his shoulders lowered his head and made his way up to his room followed by his wife and daughters. Even before he was completely gone, the servants started laughing and rejoicing at their new freedom, even though not one of them had any idea about what they were going to do next.

Bernard, who even when Jonathan was there was the next in command of the house motioned for all of them to follow him into the kitchen where he sat down and started talking about the future.

"The master is gone and we are free now what are you going to do?"

The question sounded to them like something out of the mouth of a master and they couldn't image how to respond. It was not as if any of them had envisioned something like this happening any time soon, so they were totally unprepared. All of them were aware of what was happening with the war, but none knew just how close the final freedom act would be coming to them. After several moments of silence, Suliah was the one to speak up.

"I donno `bout y`all, but om gonna wait here for ma brother ta come an git me, den we goin back home."

"Suliah, you don't know how long that's going to be" Bernard said. It might be sometime before they let him out of that army. We can't stay here without no money comin' in and I don't think whoever's left in the city is going to help us none. I'm gonna pack my things first thing in the morning and I'm going up north where I know they got jobs we can do. Why don't you come with me? A pretty gal like you, once you drop that baby ain't going to have no problem finding work."

"No, I can't go, I tol ma brother I'd be here."

"Who's gonna take care of you and the baby while you're waiting?"

"I donno but I ain goin nowhere. Besides, massa Jonathan's father he still be here, an he gotta eat too. I eat, what he leave."

"He ain't sure himself how he's going to eat, much less have something to leave for you. You better think about coming with me before morning, because after that you're gonna be on your own."

Suliah thought really hard about what he was saying for a while and she looked at the others to see if they were having any reactions to his words. Except for Amanda who was getting ready to speak, the others just continued to sit around baffled at just what it was they were going to do.

"Suliah, you kin stay here if'n ya wanna, but I knows where om goin. Massa Jonathan dun taught me how ta make money fer ma self. I bin savin some from all dose men he had commin ta me. Each time dey lef, each one gave me a little piece a money an I bin keepin it hid 'til now I got plenny. Even so I bet now if I go down ta dat hotel in the city an I talk's ta that man I know who run the place I'se sho he gonna hep me. He like me the mos when he come here, an he also give de mos money. So if'n I goes dere an work's fer him, I know om gonna be okay. Das what om gonna do."

Suliah heard what Amanda was saying and she felt kind of sorry for her because she knew very well what she had been through since she came to the house. In the beginning, Amanda resisted having to do what Jonathan forced her to, but after a while Suliah could see that it no longer bothered her. In fact, it seemed that she was even beginning to enjoy her role in the house, especially when she was able to sleep late the next morning. However, Suliah had no idea that Amanda was making money doing what she did. It never occurred to her that this could be a way of sustaining herself. It didn't matter to her anyway, because in her condition, even if she considered doing it, that method was now out of the question for her.

The whole group spent the rest of the afternoon sitting around the table talking and laughing and contemplating their futures. It was not until sometime late in the afternoon, that daddy Adams came downstairs again and demanded that he know what they were going to do. Apparently, Bernard was right about his assessment. Senior Mr. Adams wasn't sure himself how he was going to continue to run the house. All the money making had been done by Jonathan and some of the schemes that he was into, didn't involve anybody else in the house but him. The sources of income that he had other than the rental of the slaves who resided in the shack out in the back of the house, were tied up in political dealings. Now that the city was no longer in the hands of his political cronies, Mr. Adams knew that it was going to be hard to even get Jonathan's former contacts, if they were not already in custody themselves, to advance him any kind of loan.

Mr. Adams demands were aimed more at Bernard than any of the others because he was well aware that as Bernard went so would the others go. Bernard listened to his ranting and raving casually, almost ignoring them and when he did finally respond he was very direct but courteous.

"Mr. Adams, I served your son well for years and he was good to me. But now that I am a free man, my allegiance is not to you, your wife or any of those selfish girls you call daughters up there. When the morning light comes, I will be leaving this place and finding the first thing I can headed up north and that's the last you will see of me unless by some stroke of fate our paths may cross in the future up there."

Senior Adams was stunned by the reply, and he fell back against the wall and then had to sit down. The stark realization that without his son running things in the house and all of the rest of his help might be gone, he was on the brink of having a nervous breakdown episode. Not knowing what else to do, he did as he had seen his son do so many times when he was under stress. He made his way to the parlor and found Jonathan's favorite liquid refreshment and he availed himself of a large portion of the same. One by one the others were gravitating toward the decision that Bernard had made, and they were now asking him all about what he knew of the possibilities of them getting work up north and how were they going to get there. Bernard launched into telling them all about the Underground Railroad and how it was used to get slaves up north by night. But now that freedom was here he thought the train may not need to run by night, but all during the day and he was going to find out just how to catch it. When he found out then he would tell all of them. They spent the rest of the afternoon and well into the night talking and planning how they were going to leave this place and find freedom up north.

As the war was winding down in Richmond, another war was just beginning not too far away. The combatants in this war, however, were more than soldiers made of flesh and blood; they were supernatural spirits rising above the normal plane. What had been brewing for a long time was now about to come to the brew master's head. Both sides declared their allegiance to the doctrine they supported, and neither was ready to concede any mitigation of their declaration. Tensions had been high for a good while, but now the level was elevated to a height that no one could deny could go any higher without some kind of resolution. The battle would not determine who was right or wrong, but who would be left.

Jobba had come home after months of running through the woods, hiding out in strange houses and barns and caves and almost experiencing death at several junctions. He never lost sight of what his mission was, and he always had that deeply seated in his heart and kept his focus. His love for Myanna drove him on with a sense of purpose that the task must be accomplished. Finding a way to get both of them to freedom never left his mind. Now that he had arrived back home, he was anxious to deliver his good news. But his first greeting was surprising, and it alerted him to how things had changed. The things he observed in a house of evil just across from his mentor Daniel puzzled him, but it never could have prepared him for the thing he was about to see next.

After creeping up the quarters slowly but confident he wouldn't be seen because it appeared that all of the foes were in the house of evil, he got to the front door of his cabin. He opened the door and stepped lightly toward the stairs so as not to awaken Penniman's children who were sleeping. Easing his way up the stairs he could hear muffled sounds of hard breathing and he thought that it might be Myanna having a bad dream. When he reached the top of the stairs in the light of the lamp turned down real low, he could see the movements of two figures on the bed where he used to sleep. At first his eyes had great difficulty in processing what he thought he was seeing, but when he moved a step closer there was no denying it. Where he used to be was another man, what was his was now someone else's and what he had been struggling to fight for now seemed no longer valuable.

When his mind finally clearly processed the realization of what was going on, the rage that built up inside of him was uncontrollable. With a leap of great force, he covered the few feet between him and the bed and was on Clarence like the winds in a hurricane toppling mighty cedars. Grabbing him by the neck with one hand and wrapping his arm around his waist with the other arm, he lifted him off the bed and threw him across the room. Myanna screamed at the shock and Jobba just stared at her nakedness for a minute then turned his attention again to Clarence who was still on the floor near the stairway. Jobba moved quickly over to him, picked him up again and threw him headlong down the stairs. From the position that Clarence ended up in, Jobba looked down and believed that he had ended the matter. He returned to Myanna who was still in shock, but recovered enough to stand up and come over to where he was with open arms crying bitterly.

"I thought chu was daid Jobba, I thought chu was daid" she cried. I got so lonely, so lonely what chu want me ta do?"

Jobba stood looking at her with a strange unforgiving coldness in his eyes. When she went to embrace him, he pushed her away and just stared at her.

"I bin runnin fo ma life an gittin shot at an beaten an locked up in jail tryna fine dat conductor on de railroad so's we kin git on de train an go free, an I comes back here an what I find. You layin up in de bed wit dis man who don even 'spect me."

"Jobba, he said ya was daid an he kept on tellin me dat 'til I believe him. I got so alone, I needed somebody. I love you Jobba, you know I love you." Myanna said through her sobbing pleas.

Jobba was still raging inside and refused to believe her story and before he even realized it the back of his hand had been raised high in the air. In an instant it came crushing down on her face with the might of a mule's kick and she went tumbling back across the room. The rage still burning in his eyes and his mind rehashing the scene he just saw wouldn't permit him to hear nothing more of what she tried to say through her swelling mouth. He stared at her for another minute as she lay bawling on the bed, then turned and went down the stairs to dispose of his kill. To his surprise when he got to the stairs and looked down, Clarence was no longer there. Jobba jumped down the stairs two at a time and ran quickly to the door and slung it open. As he looked up the quarters he could see not far in the distance, someone hobbling badly, but moving toward the mansion. He had to assume that it was Clarence, so he cut off his pursuit because he didn't want to go anywhere near the big house. Although he had no idea how things had changed there, he was afraid to be discovered before he was ready.

Jobba, still enraged from his most recent find, turned and walked down to Daniel's cabin hoping this time to find him there. When he arrived, he again knocked lightly on the door at first, but when there was no response, he pushed it open. Inside he found nothing, not even a sign that the four were still occupying the cabin. He was completely at a loss now as to what to do next, so he went to the table and sat down putting his head on it and wept. Within a short time, span, the door opened and Jobba lifted up his head to see his mentor and the associates coming in with lamps in their hands. Thoroughly relieved to see them he got up to greet Daniel but was motioned to remain seated as Daniel spoke.

"Greetings my son peace be unto you. You have returned at a critical time and the next few days shall be like none you have ever seen before. There will be times when you shall wish to end it all, but now is not the time for you. Your journey has been long and arduous, and you have much to be thankful for, yet you have much to forgive. Come lie down here and be refreshed for the time ahead will be challenging for you."

Jobba listened to the words of the pastor and heeded his warning. Before he got up, he asked him why he couldn't find him before. Daniel responded that they had been down to the river praying the final prayer of faith before the outbreak of the war. Jobba again was puzzled by his words, but he knew that something was brewing for he had witnessed the other side preparing for battle when he first arrived. Daniel then directed him to the bed in the back of the cabin and he closed his eyes and slept until morning.

When the morning came although he knew it was a weekday, he didn't hear any horns sounding nor did he hear any movement from outside the house signaling anyone getting up to go to the fields. It was really strange not hearing any movement at all, so he got up and went to the front door and opened it. Even Daniel and his associates had not risen. He looked outside and the quarters were deserted, as if someone or something had come during the night and taken everybody away. Not sure what to do, he hesitated to awaken Daniel before he was ready to get up, so he sat back down on his bed thinking about what was going on.

Outside the cabin what was going on was that the two factions had separated themselves into barricaded houses. The believers, although now few in number had taken the upper few cabins while the greater number of Aunt Tee followers that included fallen believers, were occupying the lower few cabins across from Daniel. Daniel's was the only cabin that was in their midst. At the mansion, Byron was thoroughly at the mercy of Aunt Tee who was now preparing for tonight's big ritual offering during which she had been told was the night of the beginning. The moon was anticipated to be full and the brisk fall air was expected to be just right for what was to happen.

Byron moped around the house trying to attend to Charlotte who was still in a semi-conscious state continuing to babble about things she had seen while he was away. She constantly talked about evil spirits running through the house and a new master being born. There was absolutely no work being performed on the farm and the overseers were baffled about why Byron had not come out to discipline the slaves for not reporting to the fields. However, after a few days of seeing no activity and no effort on the part of the master to take charge, the day worker overseers stopped showing up and Sam was the only one left on the property. Even Sam, Byron's most trusted underling was baffled about what was happening, but hesitated to confront his employer on the matter so he just enjoyed his time off.

As Jobba continued to sit on the bed wondering about things, he heard the sounds of movement coming from upstairs where Daniel and the others were. It sounded as if they were preparing to come down. Jobba was so looking forward to hearing again from his leader about what was going on, but when he did descend the stairs, he said nothing to Jobba but a morning greeting. Disappointed, Jobba started to ask him again about what was happening or going to happen, hoping to get more detail this time, but when he looked into Daniel's eyes and saw the look of extreme calm somehow it was passed on to him and whatever was going to happen next didn't seem so urgent to know any more.

They all sat down at the table and one of the associates prepared breakfast. Daniel said a short blessing and while they ate there was silence until near the end when Daniel got up and told Jobba to follow him. Jobba responded along with the rest, and they went out the door headed to the river walking right through the territory that was now supposedly the enemy's. Jobba noticed that the cabin opposite Daniel's had several onlookers surveying the movements of Daniel, but none ventured out to detain him. At the riverfront Daniel knelt down and invited Jobba to do the same. He launched into a long prayer joined in support by the others. The gist of the prayer, as much of it as Jobba could understand was asking for strength and courage in the upcoming battle and wisdom and guidance on how to protect his sheep. The parts that Jobba couldn't understand seemed to be spoken in a language that he had never heard before, even in his dreams while on the mother continent.

After the prayer session, Daniel got up and led the group back to the house where they sat around talking about Jobba's recent journey. They spent the whole day just talking and as Daniel said, waiting for the enemy. Jobba didn't understand this completely, but he was content just being with his mentor again and whatever Daniel said was fine with him. As the hour grew late and the sun began to set, it started to get dark unusually early and what had been a rather remarkably sunny fall day was now overcast as storm clouds moved in. Jobba went to the door and looked out and up at the sky. Daniel saw his concern and told him that the time was near when those same clouds would offer no light on the morrow. Again Jobba thought he was talking in riddles, but he asked for no explanation.

At the other end of the plantation, Aunt Tee and Clarence, who had been nursed by her back to a reasonable condition of health after his confrontation with Jobba, were preparing for their ritual. Clarence had gotten the sacrifice and Aunt Tee was getting it ready. Byron, as usual was still mopping around the house while Charlotte sat at her sewing table staring out the window but sewing nothing. Byron at this point spent most of his time nursing his special nectar until the period in the day that he was drunk was getting earlier and earlier. Aunt Tee paid him no mind, as did the rest of the house servants who were enjoying their newfound freedom as if the outside war had already saved them. As nightfall approached Aunt Tee was becoming more excited and she went down to the portion of the cabins that contained her followers and encouraged them to be jubilant about the upcoming ceremony because tonight would be the most liberating night for them when they would take over the plantation completely.

The now overcast sky was deceptive in that the setting of the sun was not complete but was hidden from its observable descent. However, it didn't take an astrologer to know that the hour was fast approaching when the sun's work was done, and the moon would take over in its full and magnificent illumination. Inside the mansion Aunt Tee was ready as well as Clarence. Inside the Tee follower cabins the excitement was high and the wait in anticipation was getting to a fever pitch even before the official ceremony began. For the believers, it was an approaching night that filled them with trepidation as they tried to prepare for what they had been told would be a night to remember. They had been instructed by Daniel that after the infidel's left their cabins tonight and went to the mountains, they were to assemble down by the riverside and bring their lanterns filled with oil for it would be a long night.

Jobba's mind was filled with all kinds of thoughts in anticipation of what was about to come. He couldn't believe that in the middle of all this and after all that he had been through he felt some solace in just being in the company of Daniel and his companions. Whatever was about to come, it would not be more than he thought the foursome could handle. The others who were still in their cabins had no idea of the magnitude of what was to come, but from the words of Daniel they knew that it would not be any ordinary experience. The time that they had spent in the company of the man they had come to know not only as their pastor, but also as a friend who would not leave them in distress no matter what the challenge would be. The time was fast approaching when the battle between good and evil would be made manifest on the plantation and the choices would finally have to be made as to whom you would serve. Whether it was going to be serving the evil demon from the cave or whether they would choose to follow Jesus was something that had to be decided tonight, for there would be no opportunity for choice come the morning.

In the cave, there were small animals moving around looking for something to eat, but when a loud noise shouted at them, they all scurried to exit the mountain hole with all due haste. The noise was coming from the cave demon who was calling out spiritually to his cohorts to begin preparing to join him in the final conquest of souls on the night. When the moon was full and the ritual was begun it would be time for them to claim all those that they had been preparing to claim. Aunt Tee who was their true servant in the flesh would become indwelled with a portion of one who was called the Magdalene of the world or the host of evil incarnate. There was no need for additional animals to be present and hence the clearing of the cave was done.

The hour had come, and nightfall was upon the whole plantation. Lamps were lit and slowly the infidels moved out of their cabins and assembled in the center of the quarters' road. Jobba went upstairs in Daniel's cabin to get a better view of their grouping. He couldn't understand how so many of them had come to the plantation. When he left before, he knew that the numbers were growing from what he had heard from Penniman about the rebels in the mountains coming down to get protected by Aunt Tee. But there was no way he could have prepared for what he was seeing now. Even after hearing Penniman, he couldn't imagine that the size would be this big. In front of him lining up in columns of two's were over a hundred slaves carrying lanterns getting ready to march to the hills. He looked up at the sky and the full moon shadowed by a million stars seemed to be giving them extra illumination so that the way for them was made extremely clear. When they started to move out led by their subordinate leader Clarence, Jobba had a mind to run down the stairs and finish the job on him that he started, but some resistance in him that he couldn't overcome told him to stay put and justice would be done in due time.

The columns moved out walking at a brisk pace fed by the excitement and the anxiety of each one looking forward to receiving what they had been told would be their final salvation and overall protection from any further servitude in slavery. Even the little ones who had prior to this been banned from the ceremonies were now trailing along behind their parents as they were led. On previous ritual nights, when they marched the chanting didn't begin until they reached the mouth of the cave, but now since they no longer feared any repercussions from the master, they started singing first at a low level, but as they moved closer to the mountain the louder the chanting rose. By the time they had reached the mansion and were ready to pass it, Sam who heard all the noise came out of his cabin to see the long line of slaves moving along. Frightened by the sight he immediately went back inside barred his door and grabbed his shotgun.

The trail to the mouth of the cave was so worn by now that even a blind man could walk it without being led. Inside the cave the fire had already been started and as the group approached the entrance, they could see that Aunt Tee had already prepared the altar for the sacrifice and was ready for them. Moving in by two's they formed the circle around the fire and the chanting and swaying became as it was so many times before a frenzy of rhythmic gyrations. When the last of the group had made his way into the cave, Clarence dressed in his finest robe strolled around the followers once and then made his way toward the fire and threw the incense into it. As was the custom, the fire responded by shooting up in a blaze and turning a bright red in color with the flames reaching high toward the ceiling of the cave. The strong burning and the smell of an indescribable odor would have been offensive to the normal senses, but those who were participating absorbed the smell as a sweet aroma and breathed in every ounce of air that it produced.

As the chanting grew louder and the swaying became more intense, at the mouth of the cave a new entry was being brought in. Suddenly the whole circle ceased to sway, and all eyes turned to the entrance to see who was coming in. Clarence waved his staff, and the new entry was brought to the front of the cave at the foot of the altar. The guards bearing the new entry forced the unwilling patron to kneel before the altar. The hood over the victim was removed and all eyes saw that it was Byron. As he was still in a kneeling position the sacrifice was made and the blood of the goat was sprinkled on his forehead. Byron was in a trance from the time he came in and even now he appeared not to be aware of what was happening to him, but when the last drop of blood reached his stomach, he stood up and hollered at the top of his lungs declaring his allegiance to the demon. Aunt Tee pleased at her newest conquest implored the demon to emerge once again from the wall and almost immediately she was accommodated.

The demon spirit from the wall appeared and a mighty shout went up from all the followers. Quickly they went from standing and swaying to bowing and rocking in a kneeling position worshipping the demon.

"Hail spirit of de wall, hail de mighty one, the supreme-being," they shouted.

"You have done well my devoted worshippers and tonight you shall be rewarded for your faith. Tonight, you shall witness the power of the dark side and you shall know that the freedom you have been seeking shall be yours. As a gift to you, I give you in spirit the one whom you have called master for many years, now he is yours to do as you will with, but his soul belongs to me."

The crowd sent up another mighty shout and some of the men started forward to grab Byron, but the spirit stopped them.

"My house shall not be defiled by your reckless actions. As long as he is in my presence here and has sworn his allegiance to me as he has just done, he shall not be harmed. But for his treatment of you while he was in power, when you leave this place, do with him as you will."

The men retreated back to their positions in the circle and Byron still in a trancelike state didn't seem to understand the predicament he was in, but continued to look up at the demon in admiration. Around the cave suddenly six more demons emerged from the wall and surrounded the group, and the patrons began chanting and swaying again. The feverish pitch of the excitement seemed like it couldn't rise any higher but the chanting and singing moved along as if there would be no end. Even the children had joined in with their parents and felt the spirit moving them in such a manner that some of them fell to the ground writhing in the midst of all the emotions. For hours the chanting continued until it was well after midnight and then the head demon commanded that the hour had come for which they all had been prepared. It was now time to go down the mountain and confront those who would not accept his invitation to join with him and take my mark. It was now time to give them one final opportunity to convert or be destroyed by a mighty force that would consume all of them where they stood.

Just as they entered, the group lined up in columns of two's and they descended down the mountain rocking back and forth as they walked. The difference in how they came up the mountain and how they were descending was that Aunt Tee was no longer leading the pack but an image that glowed like a fire breathing red dragon was leading the way and Aunt Tee and Clarence followed close behind. As they moved down the mountain the light of the moon seemed to have gotten brighter and the chanting grew to the highest fever pitch that they had reached yet. Each step that brought them closer to the mansion sent shivers up and down the spine of all who were in the throng. At the doorstep of the mansion, Charlotte was standing on the porch with her eyes open, but really not seeing what was happening to her husband. Though she sensed he was there in the crowd, she couldn't really acknowledge it was he, due to her continued state of a mind in a mist.

In the believer district of the cabins, shortly after the infidels had vacated their houses and left for the mountains, Jobba came out along with Daniel and the others. Under Daniel's direction they moved quietly toward the river each one carrying a lamp with an extra can of oil in the other hand. Their children were also with them, and the throng walked silently. There was no fanfare, and the mood was somber. They did not line up like soldiers in columns of two's but held hands and walked three and four abreast feeling the warmth of the person walking beside them. Even Daniel was silent as they moved and only a few from the group said anything. Jobba was feeling an assortment of emotions coming from within. Uppermost on his mind was the welfare of Myanna. He didn't know whether she had gone over to the other side as a result of his actions recently, or had she converted even before he came home. He couldn't help but wonder about this and the thought of her being one of them wouldn't leave him alone.

When they reached the riverside, Daniel told them to form ranks and face the road that they had just come down. The group did as they were instructed, and the number of their ranks came out to four rows of ten including the children. He further advised that at no time should they fear the outcome of the battle that they were about to witness because the battle was not theirs but was the Lord's. He said for them to stand still and see the salvation of the Lord. When they finished forming the lines, they could see in the near distance the lights of the lamps of the enemy as the columns moved toward them led by the fire of the dragon going before them. Those that were seated in the first line of the believer ranks, even though they had been admonished to dismiss any fear, felt themselves welling up with a tension they couldn't let go of. They knew that at their backs was the deep river with water as cold as it could be this time of the year, and in front of them was certain extinction unless they yielded to the demon. As they saw the enemy coming closer and closer it was hard just to sit there and see that imminent death could be approaching.

At a distance of approximately 20 yards, Daniel went down on his knees one more time and raised his hands high in the night sky and prayed fervently. At the conclusion of his prayer what looked like stars descended to the earth and with ten thousand points of light formed a wall right in front of the believers. Disregarding the wall closer and closer the foes moved toward the believer's ranks and within a few yards the mouth of the dragon opened, and a final offer was made. Out of his mouth prior to the words came fire and smoke lighting up the area.

"You have been warned, yet you do not obey. You have been given opportunity, but you do not take advantage now witness the power of the dark side and if you do not come across the line that has been drawn in the sand, then you shall surely die."

As if by some unseen hand, when the dragon finished speaking a line of fire was drawn deep in the sand which ran quickly across just in front of the first rank of the believers.

"Heed now my final offer and become brothers and sisters with those who had been among you, but have seen the benefits of my powers and joined with me."

At that point Aunt Tee and Clarence stepped forward and in their own words appealed to the crowd. Aunt Tee, not knowing what had happened in Richmond, offered them freedom like they have always wanted. Clarence chimed in with his offer of salvation in becoming part of the mighty and the powerful. When they finished speaking, not one of the believers moved or even said a word as they continued to sit there behind the wall of lights. The dragon got angry at being ignored and out of his mouth came the most fearsome display of fire shooting out toward the believers with such force that the sand in front of them burned. So hot was the fire that portions of the sand turned to glass and reflected the evil image back to all those who were in front of the wall. The image of the dragon then commanded the infidels to storm the believers and kill without mercy all those who were seated. They were further instructed to destroy Daniel and his associates with the vilest blows they could muster, for he knew that Daniel would be a most formidable foe.

As the first order of infidels charged the wall of lights, when they touched it each one immediately burned up and was disintegrated.   Not to be stopped the next orders advanced and continued until one by one they all contacted the wall and disappeared until only a few were left who became hesitant after witnessing their brethren fall in the combat. The dragon was not to be deterred, nor would he allow those that were left to disobey his commands. He admonished them to continue to pursue, but when they hesitated he along with the other six demons moved closer to the wall. Before they touched the wall, a final command was given to Aunt Tee and Clarence who had lagged behind the rest of their troops. Aunt Tee along with Clarence moved by the power of the demon ran full speed toward the wall and were able to penetrate it stepping forward to the other side. However, just as they were about to lay hands on Daniel and his men, they too burst into flames and were disintegrated.

The only ones left were the few who had hesitated and the dragon with his six demons. The final order was given to those few, but instead of moving forward toward the wall they turned and ran headed back toward the mountain. In a rage, fire flew out of the dragon's mouth and consumed them as they ran. Then the dragon turned back toward the wall and confronted Daniel.

"It is written that I am the ruler of this world and I have been given the power to consume as I will, therefore you shall not defeat me."

Having said this the dragon and his six demon followers lunged toward the wall and burst through coming within footsteps of reaching Daniel and the believers. But just as with Aunt Tee and Clarence before they could lay hands on even one of the believers much less Daniel, they were consumed by their own fire and disappeared. Jobba seeing all of this started to run through the wall from his side for he wanted to see if Myanna was still in their cabin, or had she been part of the ones who now were not. Just before he got to the wall Daniel grabbed him and told him not to touch it, lest he become like all those who had made contact before. Jobba stopped short and turned to Daniel and asked what about Myanna.

Daniel told him that she was not among those who disappeared, but was in the mansion lying on a bed near death. She had become so distraught after he rejected her that she went there and consumed a potion that Aunt Tee gave her to end her misery. Clarence, spiteful over Jobba's treatment of him no longer desired her and stood by as she drank it. Daniel continued, telling him that he had the power to save her by the laying on of his hands, but first he must truly forgive her in his heart and truly believe that she would be made well. Further, Daniel reminded him that a long time ago he was told that the matter would be taken care of, and he didn't understand. Now that he has seen the matter that was referred to, which was the evil pervading this land, when he goes to Myanna and heals her the prophecy will truly and completely be taken care of. Finally, he concluded by saying that nothing could be done until morning when the wall of lights would be removed, and the land would be healed. Until then Myanna would be kept in suspended animation and her spirit would not leave her until Jobba made his decision to forgive or not. Jobba heard his words and was glad to hear she was not gone, but the rage that still burned inside him over what he saw her doing, was making it difficult to forgive anything.

The rest of the night was spent behind the wall and even though the night air got very cold, no one complained about feeling anything but warm over the sensation of knowing that their very lives had been spared. Even the children who were huddled among their families complained not for their parents did comfort them. After the battle ended, the night fell into total darkness. The starlight went out and the moon lost its glow. Jobba looked around and exclaimed that this was the darkest night he had ever seen.

With a light breeze moving gently across their faces in the morning, the believers were awakened to the clearness of a cloudless blue sky. It was first light and no one among them had ever felt more refreshed after having spent the night outside then they did now. Jobba anxious to get up to the mansion and see about Myanna approached Daniel who was already up and in prayer giving thanks for the victory. He paused long enough to allow Daniel to complete his sacrifice of praise then blurted out what he wanted to do. Once he received the go-ahead nod, Jobba quickly crossed the line that was still evident in the sand and as he jogged up to the mansion, he saw the outline of those infidels that had disobeyed the dragon's command and tried to run away. He dared not run across the images, but he sidestepped and jogged around them, but didn't miss a step in his stride.

At the door of the mansion, he stopped to see if any of the infidels had not made the trip down to the river last night and might still be lurking in the house. He eased open the door and stopped to listen first before moving on. He heard absolutely nothing. The sound of silence in a place where there always used to be some kind of activity going on at all hours of the day or night seemed eerily strange for him to hear this now. He looked in the parlor and saw no one. Then he moved to the kitchen and saw no one there either. Finally, he moved to the room where he knew Aunt Tee and Clarence used to be and opened the door. When he looked inside there a presence met him at the door, but it was not as if it greeted him with any ill intent, but it felt to him as if it was a spirit leaving the room for the last time. He turned then and made his way up to the second floor where Byron and Charlotte had their room. Pausing long enough to look quickly in there he saw Charlotte, but she was once again at her sewing table staring out the window at absolutely nothing.

His last stop was to go up to the third floor where Suliah had been kept for a short time before she was sold away. There when he opened the door, he saw Myanna wrapped in the tapestry she had made with the images of Jobba, Suliah and Linwood woven into the fabric. In each hand she clutched a reminder of her family. In her right hand was the necklace that Jobba had given to Suliah, and she returned it to him before she was sold away. In her left hand was the teddy bear that belonged to Linwood. When Jobba saw this tears began to well up in his eyes and he was struck with such emotion that he knew deep within that the love he felt for this woman could never really leave him.

As he moved closer to the bed, he could see that she was still breathing, albeit very slowly and with shallow motions. At the side of the bed he took the reminders from her hands and removed the tapestry and laid them on the rocking chair. Then he knelt down beside her and began to ask for help from the Divine Source.

"Lawd, I knows ya bin good ta me an ya kept me ova de mighty long way dat I come thru. Right now though, I donno jest what ta do or even say ta dis woman who bin wit me fo a long time. I needs ya hep an I needs ta know what ya want me ta do here. I knows I don't know how ta pray like dat man Daniel ya dun sent here, but om aksin Lawd if'n ya don mind ta reach down an touch dis woman so dat ya brings her back ta me all healed an feelin good. We dun bin thru a whole lot tagether an I donno how I got ova soma de things dat I did, but I believe dat ya had yo hand tied up in dem sumhow an ya hep me den I know. But now Lawd I needs fer ya to hep dis woman an make her strong agin. If'n ya brings her back om gonna tell her dat I forgives her an dat I still loves her jest like b'fo. I donno what else ta say Lawd so om gwine shut up an let ya do what chu do."

Jobba placed his hands on her hands and waited patiently for a response. She was still warm and breathing with shallow breaths, but he didn't see any change in her. He sat there motionless for some time and when he finally thought that either there was no god or that the God that he thought he knew wasn't paying any attention to him he started to get up. Just about the time when he was rising, a bright light shown through the window and the beam filled the room with such warmth that it almost seemed like summer again. Jobba picked up the things on the chair and sat down as these words seemed to form in the very air in front of him and his hearing was flooded with sound.

Jobba before you were formed in your mother's womb, I knew you. Before you came into this world, I had already planned a way for you to become what you are about to become. The trials and tribulations that I allowed you to go through were in preparation for the glorious future that you now enter into. The time has come when you shall know that all that you have experienced even to the point of death, was not to be ended until you had fallen to your lowest point and the thing that you loved the most taken away from you.

I am not the god of evil nor am I the god of disappointment, but I am the God of mercy and forgiving. Just as you had to learn how to forgive so must you also teach those who will come after you that mercy suits their cases at all times. As for the woman that lies before you, she shall be made whole and together you shall become as one once again. The time that yet lies ahead for both of you will be times when you will need each other as you have never needed before. It is my plan for you that you will in your heritage become the grandparents of one who shall serve me in a great capacity for even now that seed has been formed in the womb of your offspring. She shall become the mother to one who will aspire to great things and do great deeds that benefit not only your own people but also all mankind. It will be within his providence. that he shall become the leader of a people not strong, but of good faith and loyalty to me. Hear these words that I'm telling you for they shall strengthen you and keep you in perfect peace for the rest of your days.

What you have known as the condition of slavery is not one of servitude of one man to another, but of a discipline of lawlessness not of my teachings but of man's own ill-fated decisions. It was never intended that one man should rule over another in a manner that would create hostility for either. At the very beginning freewill was given to man as a matter of being able to have dominion over the world to replenish it and tend to its fruit, but in his brutish manner right from the start when his offspring became murderous and destroyed the brother that was created along with him his destiny was preset and his way was made difficult. The laws that man created to rule over other men did not come from me, nor did they have any basis in the laws that I gave to be followed. When I instructed Moses to provide the law for living it was not with the intention that these laws should be modified neither to suit man's desires nor to have man distort them to prolong his quest for power. The laws were given to aid man in living lives that would be productive in maintaining the earth and all of its fullness that was already provided. Until the time came when man defiled the very earth itself, all that had been provided for him was in a garden replete with all that he would ever need to exist.

The evil that befalls man now was also present at the onset of life when I created mankind. But the evil was restrained until loosed by the disobedience of the woman that I gave man as a companion for life. It was not the fault of the woman that she should succumb to the evil, but it was the failure of the man that he did not instruct her about what would be the outcome of her choice. Life is filled with choices even as I gave man choices on how to live.

You have known slavery all of your life, but you have not known what it means to be free within your mind until now. Freedom does not mean only the liberty from being restrained from pursuing your own way, but it means that you have the ability to choose those things in life that will make you strong or weak in your faith. To choose to believe in things that are not true are also a matter of free will, but the consequences of that choice lead to the destruction of anyone who makes the wrong choice. To choose evil over the good, leads to a path of self-destruction and makes the way of life harder than it needs to be.

When I sent my son to walk among you in the flesh, it was with the design that He should experience life just as you do. It was for Him to know how it feels to have free will and to observe the consequences when my will is disobeyed. He did not succumb to the temptations that were presented to Him, yet even He could not understand how it was that man was so easily disposed to ignore all of my warnings through the many prophets that I sent among you. Within man there has always been a predisposition to do evil and reject the good even as man sees the evil be the destroyer of all that is good. None who walk in the paths of righteousness have ever defaulted on the promises that have been given to him regarding long life, health and prosperity. But those who choose to follow in the footsteps of the evil one is destined to become all that the evil one promises in a lie.

From the time that you began to dream, and the dreams appeared to be real to you, they were merely a glimpse of what was and yet what was to become of you. You were given the chance to see in hindsight what was a condition that you would be confronted with in the present and the future. Dreams are my way of speaking to your mind with the intention that you should know what could be the very future that you experience. Around the time that you had your first dream, the condition of slavery that you were in was to show you that it had indeed happened within your own family in times before your father's father. Slavery as justified by man, even using my holy writ to accomplish and prolong the evil tasks, will never end as long as some men believe in superiority justified by things that are not written in my word. You have been shown how real power does not come from following any spirits who dwell in caves or in mountains or in any other place that does not bear witness to me and my son..

I am the Lord thy God and besides me there is no other. All that you see and all that you have witnessed I have allowed so that you could see my salvation and become a true witness for me. I am a Spirit, and you are my hands and feet, but in order to serve me you must first have a testimony. In order to have a testimony you must first have been tested. Therefore, for all those who would be my witnesses, they must be tested and tried in the fields of trial and tribulation and must learn to trust in me without doubt and believe with all their hearts that they shall receive as they ask with humbled hearts and minds free of distortion. As you have seen anyone can aspire to become a leader, but to lead and not to have a foundation in my word is to lead and not have the guidance that is needed to lead with success. Leadership is given by my will and all who aspire to be a leader must first learn to serve as the lowliest in the order. Even kings of old had to learn that basic lesson in order to be successful.

There is no one who can lead who does not know how to follow. None can be successful until he learns how to obey the principles that I set forth for success.

All of these things that I am telling you now should not leave your mind and you shall put them into practice when you leave here. A new day is dawning in your land and the government that you know shall be changed to set all men free. But again, I say, that the new freedom you will gain comes not as free as you think. The fight for freedom from servitude to man is being accomplished through this war of the flesh, but it does not free him from serving other gods created in his own mind. To be truly free man must acknowledge the Son that I sent into your world to teach you how to be free in mind, body and spirit. The way to that freedom is a narrow path, but at the end of the path is the final salvation that will lead to eternal life in the kingdom to come.

The darkness that you have seen is an example of man's failure to recognize the light. For the light was sent into this world and dominates the darkness but when man will not recognize it, to him it is always dark.

"And this is the condemnation that the light has come into the world and men loved darkness rather than light, because their deeds were evil. For everyone practicing evil hates the light and does not come to the light lest his deeds should be exposed. But he who does the truth comes to the light, that his deeds may be clearly seen, that they have been done in God."(John 3:19-21).

Hear now these words that I have given you and be blessed in your new life with the one that you have healed by your faith. As she rises take her now and do not live in fear ever again of any man becoming your master. Live to the glory of God and be blessed by the power of the Holy Spirit that dwells within you now and forever more.

When the words were finished Jobba awakened from his trance like state and the beam of light disappeared. He looked over at the bed and Myanna was beginning to stir. He got up and walked over to her as she opened her eyes.

"Welcome back" he said.

"Jobba is that you, is you really here wit me?"

"Yes, om here an I ain eva gwine leave ya agin. Why you do dat. Why ya try ta kill yoself?"

"Jobba when ya say ya don want me no mo, dere ain nuthin I needs ta be here for. I donno where my chilren are. I don even knows if dey be alive or daid. Witout you nuthin else gonna matta."

"When I saw ya wit dat man, I jest can't hep maself. an I let ma hand go befo I thinks 'bout what I'se doin. But when I heard dat you might be one of dem, then I knows dat I caint go long wit dat an I hadda git ya back. I talk ta de preacher an he tol what ya did, den I knew dat ya mus still love me so I come ta git ya. He tol me if'n I lay ma hands on ya, an believe wit all I got dat ya gonna git betta, den he say das what gonna happen. Sure 'nuff dats 'xactly what happen an here ya is. Ya still looks tired, but I guess when ya be where you bin, ya mus git tired. Om jest glad ta see yo eyes open, an ya talkin good, an ya wanna git back wit me, so's I jest gonna let ya sleep some mo an I gwine outside an see what the end's gonna be."

When Jobba finished talking, Myanna squeezed his hands and closed her eyes. This time it was not the sleep of eternity, but a natural sleep that would strengthen her and allow her to refresh so that when her eyes opened again she would know a new life that was about to begin. Jobba covered her up kissed her on the cheek and look lovingly at the one who had shared his life for so long and had witnessed so much of the darkness that he had experienced early in their union. He was now convinced that in the trials and tribulations that he had gone through there was something that was driving him and now he realized that that something was wrapped in the vision that was before his eyes right now. He turned and started toward the door, but when he saw the two things that were left of what he knew of his children he had to pick them up and hold them one more time.

As Jobba walked slowly out of the mansion, his mind filled with the images of the atrocities that he and his family had suffered over the past several years. It was not as if he felt there was no hope for the future, not as if he had succumbed to the temptation of believing that all in this world was lost, but it was a feeling of triumph even in the midst of adversity. The tears that welled up in his eyes were about to exceed their boundary and overflow the soft tissue that restrained them. The emotions that had been pent up for so long were now able to run free and he just fell to the ground clutching to his chest the two things that he held on to remember his children with. He longed desperately for some sign that God would finally answer his persistent and fervent prayers and let him see them one more time.

While his head was still bowed to the ground and tears still flowing, an unseen hand touched his shoulder and prompted him to look up. There in the distance he could barely make out two figures coming up the road seated in an old wagon drawn by a single old horse. He rubbed his eyes hard as he strained to regain the clarity that he demanded from them. The images, even while yet still far off, were distinctly that of a man and a woman moving slowly up the road and closer to him. He got up from the ground and stood looking intently at the couple. In his heart he felt a surge of anxiety and a glimmer of hope rose to a higher level.

The closer the couple came, and the images were no longer feint, the more he realized that this was his prayer being answered. Finally, when they were within hearing range, he hollered out the names Suliah and Linwood and both recognizing their father's voice prompted the horse to step up the pace. When they got close enough, Linwood jumped down from the wagon and helped her down and they immediately started running to him. Time for the moment no longer existed as the reunion took place. He threw his arms around both of them with a renewed strength and as they embraced all the months of tears and sorrow seemed to melt away. For several minutes they basked in this new feeling of elation, looking at one another as if seeing each for the first time. His attempts at forming words to express his gratitude for the blessing were feeble and his mouth just couldn't perform the task.

As he continued to hold on to his children, he finally was able to compose himself long enough to again fall to the ground. This time he went down in a position to genuflect and thank God. Though the times ahead were not assured, he knew that the times behind him would never be repeated in the same manner. The trials and tribulations that had already come only strengthened him and reinforced his spiritual foundation in the knowledge that all men struggle when it is hard to see. But for those who truly believe and trust in Him, what may appear for a time to be blindness due to darkness, remember that through your spiritual eyes you can see, and you will know that "Darkness Is Not Eternal".

(Seek And You Shall Find)

<u>Darkness Is Not Eternal</u>

The End

About the Author

Sidney L. Jackson is the founder of El Cid's Books, a website (Elcidsbooks.com) offering published books using his pseudonym El Cid. He is an accomplished novelist and short story writer who brings to the reader wholesome stories that will both entertain and enlighten him or her about the spiritual value of Biblical knowledge. As the reader is engaged in the various adventures and challenging situations which mirror real life, Sidney provides within the novel relevant scriptures that deal with the predicaments.

Born 1942, New York City in the section of the metropolis known as Harlem, Sidney was exposed, at an early age, to many of the situations that he writes about. He spent his later childhood and young adult years growing up in the city of Newark, NJ where his interests in music and sociology was spawned. Gravitating toward the field of jazz he attended Arts High School, which has become known for producing jazz greats such as Sarah Vaughan, Wayne Shorter and Woody Shaw in addition to several movie and TV sitcom stars.

After high school, he matriculated at Hampton University where he received the Bachelor of Science degree in Music Education. While studying at this university, during the years of the early Civil Rights movements, he became aware of the disparity between what many religious patrons preached and what they practiced. This led to his interest in Biblical studies and the relevance of scripture to life's journey. With this in mind, he furthered his education at Seton Hall University and Rutgers University studying at the post graduate level guidance andcounseling and business modeling.

Driven to write about the need for Biblical faith in certain situations using his experience both in the military as a Viet Nam soldier and living in the inner city during some turbulent times, he has penned short stories and completed three novels. Contact information and more about the author may be found on his website (http://www.elcidsbooks.com). The mailing address is: El Cids Books, P.O. Box 2948, Plainfield, NJ 07062, U.S.A.